Paperback ISBN: 979-8-9902554-2-5

E-book ISBN: 979-8-9902554-3-2

Hardback ISBN- 979-8-9902554-4-9

Paperback Book Cover by B.M. Light

E-book and Hardback Cover by Chastity H.

THE WOLF WITHIN

B.M.LIGHT

Dedication

For those of us who need to find our own inner alpha to handle the curveballs life throws our way.

Chapter One
DAKOTA

For as long as I can remember, I have always been fascinated with wolves. How the pack hierarchy was formed. How the alphas would protect their pack in different ways. Either by leading the strongest into a skirmish with another pack to broaden their territory or by trailing behind them when moving to another area altogether so they can be sure that the youngest and oldest of the pack can make the journey.

The thing that I found both sweet and heartbreaking is that once a wolf finds their mate, it would stay with that one wolf for the rest of its life and most times be alone if the mate was killed in some way. I didn't truly understand my fascination with wolves until the first semester of college, and little did I know that things I once thought were fantasy, just stories that were told over campfires to scare little kids into behaving, would soon become reality.

While sitting at my medium-sized oak desk looking at my schedule for my first semester of college that starts in the morning, and for the first time in my twenty years on this Earth, I begin to feel anxious for the upcoming school year and I don't know why. I look out the large window in front of me that faces the street and let out a calming breath as I push a piece of my light brown hair behind my ear. For some reason, I can't shake the feeling that this year is going to be different, and I don't like that. I look back at my schedule again, and I know they're classes that I can manage with no issues, so why am I nervous about this year? I sigh as I go to toss my schedule into my backpack, so I will have it with me tomorrow when my phone begins to ring. I don't even have to look at the caller ID to know it's my best friend, Quilla Rose.

"Hi, Quilla."

"Hey, Dakota. You okay?" Quilla asks.

"Yeah." I sigh. "Just looking at my schedule again for tomorrow and trying not to freak out about it."

"Don't worry about it. You're the smartest person I know. I mean, come on, you ace all your classes and you barely study. So, I wouldn't sweat your class load one bit."

I start to feel a sense of calmness flood my veins. It happens almost every time I talk to Quilla. I take a cleansing breath before I speak again.

"You're right, Quilla. But I still can't shake the feeling that something big is coming, and I don't like that."

Movement outside my window catches my eye and I see a huge twenty-six-foot U-Haul truck with a giant sea turtle design on the sides, pull up to the house across the street that sold about a week ago when the last tenants retired and moved to Florida two months earlier. The truck backs up into the driveway, and I quietly sit and watch to see who gets out of the cab. The driver gets out first, and I notice he's about six-foot-five, with black hair and a muscular build. Even with his build, I say he's in his fifties. I try to get a better look at his features, but for some reason, I can't look at his face. Even from this far away, my eyes can only focus on his strong cheekbones but not directly in his eyes.

"Dakota, you still there?" Quilla asks, breaking the silence.

"Yeah, I'm here. The new neighbor just pulled up." I say my voice tight with confusion.

Then I watch as the passenger gets out. It's a blonde guy, and while he's not as tall as the other man, he's still about six-foot-three and has the same muscular build to his frame. Just as I'm about to tell Quilla about this other guy, something makes my breath catch in my throat, and I swear I hear someone whisper,

"Mate?"

At first, the word didn't register, but it sounded like more of a question than a statement, but then I remember I am alone in my room and the light, female voice didn't sound like Quilla.

"Quilla, did you hear that?" I ask, my voice shaking with fear.

"Hear what, Chica?"

"So you didn't just hear someone whisper the word 'Mate'?" I ask not caring if the word sounds weird, yet right coming from my lips.

"No, I didn't. You sure you're okay?"

"I've gotta be going nuts then." I reply with a dry laugh.

"I'll be over in ten minutes, okay, Dakota?" Quilla says, picking up on my fear even over the phone.

"Okay. I'll see ya soon."

I stand up from my desk chair enough to reach for the blinds so I can close them, but not fast enough before the blonde dude and I lock eyes for a moment and something deep inside me wants to go out to meet him. To be near him. But I push it down and shut the blinds, the rustling of the plastic material filling the space of my room.

Kai

Once my dad, Tobias, parks the U-Haul in the driveway of our new home, I get out and take a deep breath of the fresh, new air around me to let all the different scents fill my nose.

"Ah yes, the Elder was right. I feel this was an excellent place to expand the pack to." Dad says as he exhales in appreciation of the space around him.

"I agree with you, Father." I begin, "K and I are pleased with how it smells here. It's different, but at the same time we feel it can become home." I say, and K, my inner wolf rumbles in agreement.

Before I can shut the passenger door of the U-Haul, there is another scent that tickles my nose, and I feel K perk up,, letting me know he wants to follow the smell and see where it leads to. I allow his traits to come forward, making my hazel human eyes sharper in this form and my nose even more sensitive so I can find the scent that's floating through the air. It seems to be coming from the second-story window of the house across the street. I can see a girl staring back at me, and I lock onto her eyes, and they are the most beautiful blue eyes I have ever seen. It's like looking into an endless sparkling ocean.

"*Mate.*" K grumbles possessively.

"How do you know this is our mate, K? It could be coming from the house behind that one." I say speaking to my inner wolf.

"I just know." K says without further explanation.

"Okay. Maybe she goes to the same college that we enrolled in.

"What's wrong, son? I notice you've been quiet. Do you not like the new area?"

"Oh, no, it's not that. I just wanted to take my time categorizing all the different scents here. That's all."

"Okay. Just making sure. Come, let's unload the truck." Dad says.

I follow him to the back as he unlocks the padlock from the latch. While I wait for him to open the sliding door, I take a quick look at the house again, and we lock eyes once more before she swiftly closes the blinds on me.

"Why would she close them?" I ask as I absentmindedly scratch the left side of my chest.

Tobias

I notice out of the corner of my eye that my son is staring over at the house across the street, and my heart soars when I notice him scratching the left side of his chest. The same place where my own mating mark resides on my skin and travels up my neck to just below my jaw.

I take in the scent of Kai, and it's barely noticeable, but there is a change to it. The musk of his wolf is slightly stronger than it was before we arrived here. In my five hundred years on this earth, I have only seen a handful of times where the mate bond is so strong they don't even have to meet face to face for the bond to form.

Pure happiness fills my soul when that thought crosses my mind. It seems that the Great Luna has blessed my one and only son today. Hell, it took me three hundred years to find my mate and not a mere twenty-two years like Kai is now.

"She must be a strong-willed alpha like Kai," I think to myself, and Tobi, my inner wolf, agrees with a snort.

"Come on, son. Look alive! We have a house to make into a home." I exclaim, trying to distract him for the time being.
We are in a new territory, and we must tread carefully for now.

Chapter Two

DAKOTA

Quilla arrives at my house in exactly ten minutes, as she promised, and I walk downstairs to meet her. As she parks her red 2016 Nissan Sentra, I peer out the little side window connected to the front door and wait for her to get out of her car. Some impractical part of me is afraid that if I open the door, I will see that blonde guy again and I will throw caution to the wind and go over, which again is not like me at all. I don't care about dating guys. The ones I've met throughout high school are nice and all, but they didn't attract me.

Quilla finally gets out of her car, and I swiftly open the door for her to dash inside. We pass my father, Nathan, who is working out of the den/office to the left of the living room. I can hear he's on the phone with one of his clients, Mr. Chamberlain from California, verifying his bank accounts. Dad usually doesn't work with people outside of North Dakota, but he told me one day that Mr. Chamberlain was friends with his accounting classmate's son from college, so Dad was always willing to help where he could. Especially since his classmate passed away three years ago in a freak accident, and Dad was adamant that Mr. Chamberlain's and Mr. Larson's work was a good thing for the world, so he was happy to help.

I get his attention enough while pointing to Quilla and then up to the ceiling, letting him know we will be upstairs in my room. Dad gives me a wink to let me know he understood my gesture, and his brown eyes shine with happiness at Quilla's company.

If only you knew why she was here. I think to myself.

I start walking towards my room with Quilla following behind me, and I open my bedroom door with a nervous sigh. I head to the middle of my room where I begin pacing in circles. As Quilla follows me inside, she gently shuts the door behind her and leans against it, just watching me pace the floor a few moments before speaking.

"So, what's up, Dakota?" Quilla asks, cocking her head to the side, making her long, auburn hair that she curled into soft beachy waves fall into her eyes. She pushes her hair behind her ear as she crosses the room and sits cross-legged on my bed to wait for my reply.

I pace for a few more strides before I finally turn to her and I let loose a defeated sigh. "Okay. This is gonna sound weird." I begin. "But like I said over the phone, I could have sworn I heard something, or someone say 'Mate'. I have no idea where that came from."

From the sad look that crosses her face, it's almost like Quilla can feel my fear for this voice as if it were a tangible thing in the air. She pushes her glasses up higher on her nose and pats the empty space on the bed next to her. I quietly go over to her and sit next to her on my bed while she rubs soothing circles on my back, instantly setting me at ease.

"I don't know how you do this, but I am so grateful for you, Quilla." I say with a sigh of relief.

"I don't know either. But I know I have always been able to calm you and a few other people. I'd love to know what it is about me that calms people." Quilla laughs as she runs her hands over my shoulder-length light brown hair.

I find myself leaning into her touch and letting whatever she does that calms me flood my body. After a few minutes, we hear a knock on my door, and I reluctantly get up to answer it. My mom, Lori, is standing in the doorway, her medium brown hair is up in her trademark messy bun, and her deep blue eyes shine with love.

"Hey Mom, Quilla and I needed some girl time for a while."

"Oh, I understand. I was going to ask if Quilla wanted to stay for dinner?"

"I'd love to, Mrs. Shade, but I need to get things ready for my classes tomorrow." Quilla replies.

"Oh, okay. It was nice seeing you again, Quilla. Dakota is so lucky to have you as a friend," Mom says with a smile.

"I couldn't agree more, Mom." I say.

"Well, Dakota, dinner will be ready in about five minutes." Mom says as she closes the door behind her.

"So are you going to tell your parents about what you heard?" Quilla asks a few moments later.

"Are you the crazy one now?" I ask in shock. "I can't tell them about that. They will send me to the closest looney bin and throw away the key."

"I seriously don't think they would do that, Dakota." Quilla says while shaking her head. "But trust your gut. If you feel it's something they should know, then tell them." She gives me a firm hug, and I return the gesture.

She pulls back and gives me a kiss on the cheek. "I gotta go, Chica. But you call me if you need anyone to talk to. Okay?"

"You got it. Love ya." I say with a smile.

I take another cleansing breath as I walk with Quilla downstairs and to the front door. I make sure she gets in her car before I join my mother in the dining room and wait for my father to set the stew that I can smell cooking from the kitchen on the table.

Nathan

Once I see Dakota sit at the dining table with her mother, I bring out the vegetable stew with extra meat in it and set it on the table. I give my wife a sound kiss on the lips as I pass behind her, and I smile against Lori's lips when I hear Dakota's groan at our affection for one another. I pull away from Lori, and I see her own smile is just as bright as mine. Just this simple touch sets our souls on fire. Just as it should be.

I fill Lori's plate with the stew and set it in front of her, and I do the same with Dakota, but something about her makes me freeze as I set the plate down. A piece of my dark brown hair falls in front of my brown eyes just in time to hide the flicker of something more in them.

"What is that smell?" I ask.

"I don't know." My inner wolf, Nate, answers. His voice gravelly in my mind. *"She does smell different than she did this morning. Almost musky like a wolf, but not all the way."*

"We've been around half-Were's before, but this is different. It's so diluted. Just there enough for us to pick it up."

"But she's not a Were. We've known that for a while, Nathan." Nate says.

"Lori, did you change laundry detergent?" I ask out loud.

Lori cocks her head to the side in such an animalist fashion that I almost think she's a wolf too.

"No, why?" Lori asks.

She tries to hide the note of fear in her voice when she sees that my eyes are a lighter shade of brown. The telling sign that Nate is close to the surface. She motions for me to sit next to her while she fills my plate and sets it in front of me. At the gentle touch of her leg against mine from under the table, I feel Nate begin to calm down at the closeness of our mate.

"If you didn't change detergent, Lori, then did you get a new perfume, Dakota?" I ask now that Nate has pulled back.

"No, Dad. Why are you being so weird?" Dakota asks with annoyance. "Maybe Quilla had a new perfume on."

"Maybe that's it. I mean, it smells good." I taste the lie for what it is. I just hope Dakota doesn't pick up on it like Lori did just now as I feel her body stiffen at my side.

"What is it, Nathan?" Lori asks using our mental mate bond.

"I don't know. But Nate and I agree that Dakota smells different."

Even though Lori is one hundred percent human, she is still every bit my true mate. And with that comes the mating bond, which includes being able to feel, see, and talk to one another through a mental connection. Just like right now, I can feel Lori's fear like it's my own.

"Let's see if you still smell it on her after she gets her shower for bed," Lori offers.

"Okay. Maybe she's right and Quilla had some kind of new perfume on."

"You mean to question my ability to detect a scent, Nathan?" Nate growls.

"As of this second, yes. It's just the human part of me that doesn't want to believe it, Nate. I do trust your ability to scent something different in our daughter. We just need to figure out what that is." I explain.

I feel Nate fade back into his forest deep in my soul with an irritated huff, but satisfied with my answer. So we continue our dinner with Dakota talking about the upcoming school year and how she feels about it being her first semester in college, while she was none the wiser of the silent conversation around her just moments before.

Once dinner is finished, Lori offers to clean up the kitchen and talks Dakota into helping her while I go to get my shower first in an effort to clear the scents from my nose. After the ladies finish their own showers, Lori slides into bed with me, resting her head on my bare chest, and I encircle my arms around her, trying to calm us both down for a moment. Dakota comes into the room about ten minutes later, and I motion her to my side of the bed so I can give her a hug and a kiss goodnight first. I softly take in her scent, and while my stomach drops at what I smell, something lifts off my chest at the same time.

"Good night, Honey." I say.

"Night Dad. Love you."

She then goes over to Lori's side and gives her mother a hug and a kiss as well.

"Have a good night's rest, Sweetheart. You'll do fine in school, don't worry one bit. Love you."

"Thanks, Mom. Love you too. Night."

Dakota walks out of our room and closes the door behind her. Lori waits until the latch snicks shut before she turns to me, the expectant look in her eyes is like a vice to my heart.

I shake my head, and she rests her cheek against my chest. "The smell is gone. Dakota is still our normal human daughter."

Chapter Three

Kai

I wake up the next morning just before my alarm blares at me that it's six am and time to get up for school. I roll over to switch my alarm clock off and I take a moment to rub the sleep from my eyes. Then I sit up in bed, tossing my gray comforter to the side, before stretching the sleep from my lithe and muscular body. The room is just chilly enough to cause a ripple of goosebumps to roll across my bare chest and back.

As I stand up, I absentmindedly scratch the left side of my chest. I don't think too much of it until I pass by my mirror. I look at my rumpled blonde hair and my sleepy hazel eyes, but what I also see staring back at me fills me with confusion. A light gray marking swirls and curves along my pec and up the side of my neck, showing that I am an alpha in my own right. I then feel K perk up in the back of my mind at the sight reflecting in the mirror.

"The Mate Marking." He says with pride.

I don't get the chance to respond to him before my mother, Coraline, opens my bedroom door with a slight knock. She's wearing one of her favorite blue Victorian-style dresses, and her blonde hair is styled perfectly straight on her shoulders. When her eyes meet mine in the mirror, I see her attention slide to my chest, at the sight of my new marking. I watch as her features flash between fear, happiness, to pure love.

"Tobias! Come here, now!" She yells over her shoulder then looks back at me with pride.

Dad then comes rushing into my room with all the grace of the powerful alpha he is.

"What is the matt-" He pauses mid-sentence when he notices the change in me. His normally slicked-back black hair is hanging into his eyes.

This is not the look that many get to see of the great alpha to the largest Werewolf pack in Montana.

"I know what this is, but the question is, why do I have it? I haven't even met my mate face-to-face yet. How can this happen?"

I hate the hint of fear that I can't keep from my voice. I feel K scoff at me, and I don't blame him. I shouldn't be scared of this, but some small part of me is.

"Kai, I've told you of the rare occasions that mates do not have to meet face to face for the mating bond to snap into place. They only have to pick up on each other's scent for the wolf within you both to mark the other." Dad tells me.

"I know you did, Dad. But just as you stated, it's rare and usually happens with older Were's, not with a pup like me." I tell him.

"Are you not happy that not even twenty-four hours have passed since we moved here that you found your mate?" Mom asks with disappointment coloring her words.

"Oh, Mother." I say gently and take her hands in mine. "I'm sorry, I didn't mean it that way. Yes, I am very happy this happened. I just don't understand why the Great Luna has blessed me like this at such a young age."

Dad walks up to me and smacks me on my bare shoulder and smiles at me.

"I'll be honest, son. I noticed you scratching your chest yesterday while we were unloading the U-Haul. But I wanted to wait to see if you noticed anything and came to me about it."

I feel the atmosphere change a bit, and I know that Dad is tapping into his Alpha power, and I am forced to look just barely to the right of his eye, but not fully away, since I am again pretty much his equal.

"But, I am a little disappointed that you didn't notice and talk to me sooner."

"I'm sorry, Alpha." I reply, flicking my eyes down for just a moment in a sign of submission. The only form of submission that another alpha will show. I do not have to bare my neck like betas or lower members of the pack.

"You will learn, son. But I will warn you." Dad pauses so I can look at him in his brown eyes, which shine brighter for a moment, and I feel K rise in response to the sternness in his tone.

"You must be extremely cautious today at school. Remember, there are other Were's here, and even though you are an alpha yourself, you are still new to this territory. If these Were's know anything about mate markings, they will know that the light color that you now don means that while you have found your mate, you both are still unbonded. Do you know what that means for you and your mate?"

I take a breath, letting my own power fill the room between the three of us. "Yes, Alpha. This means that both my mate and I are targets. However, I will have the bigger target on my back due to me being new to this area, and the other members here may think I came in and stole their potential mate."

With these words, K and I are instantly in agreement on several things. One, no one is going to lay a hand or paw on our mate. Second, we hate the feeling of being prey, and third, we can't wait to meet her. Dad then comes over to me and pats me on the back while Mom gives me a tight hug and a kiss on the cheek.

"Good. I have taught you the laws of the wolf well, Kai. Good luck, son. May the Great Luna protect you and your mate," Dad says.

"You should get dressed now. You don't want to be late for class." Mom says as she releases her hold on me.

As my parents walk out of my room, I hear a car door shu,t and when I look out my window, I just miss the girl across the street leaving in her gray Nissan Altima. I shake off the disappointed feeling of missing her and I force myself to get dressed.

When I make my way downstairs and turn left into the living room, Dad throws something my way and I catch it with ease. When I open my hand, I see a set of keys, and I look back at my father with confusion on my face.

"You needed a way to get to school. I mean you shouldn't phase and run there." Dad says with a smile. "It's parked in the driveway." He motions with his thumb over his shoulder.

I fly out the front door and I see sitting on the kickstand a black and blue Yamaha R-Series motorcycle. I had a motorcycle back in Montana, but it was fifty years old with rusting holes all over it, so there was no way it would be street-legal. I look back toward the front door, and I see Dad walk out of the house to join me.

"I thought I'd get this for you as a token of good luck for this school year."

"Thank you, Father." I say with a smile and give him a quick hug.

"Now get going before you're late. But be careful and alert, son."

I give him a firm nod as I slip my helmet on. I fire up the bike, and the way the wind whips around my body is much like when I run in my wolf form. I feel free and content. I just hope that I can feel that way in the coming days.

CHAPTER FOUR
DAKOTA

My alarm screams at me to get up, and I groan at the sound. I roll over to shut the alarm off and let another groan escape before I force myself from the comfort of my bed and I take a quick cool shower to help myself wake up.

I make my way downstairs fifteen minutes later and when I walk into the kitchen, I see that Dad's famous chocolate chip pancakes are stacked on a plate and waiting for me on the counter. I make quick work of them and I double-check to make sure I have all the notebooks, pens, and paper I need for classes as well as my schedule before I walk out the door.

Just as I open the front door, I remember the strange voice and the guy across the street. I'm terrified that if I look at the house and see him, I will hear the phantom voice again, so I keep my head down as I walk to my 2018 gray Nissan Altima, drop into the driver's seat, and head to school.

Once I get to campus, I meet up with Quilla in the parking lot. She's standing next to her Nissan Sentra with her face already in a History textbook.

"Good morning, Dakota." She says without looking up from the page.

"You seriously have a textbook out already? The semester hasn't even started yet." I ask with raised brows.

"It's never too early to be ahead of the game."

I roll my eyes and give her a sly smile. "Quilla Rose, the Queen of planning ahead."

She gives me an embarrassed smile and pushes her glasses up higher on her nose. Then we hear the doors open to the gym for the morning introductions for all the new students starting the semester today, and I pluck the book from her hand.

"Alright, enough planning, let's go to this introduction meeting."

We walk in and we follow the rows of freshmen that line the back walls. The dean of the college, Mr. Coleman, who is a slender man with dark brown hair and touches of gray near his temples, stands in the middle of the gym with a microphone in hand.

"Good morning, students! Welcome back to another semester for some of you, and I want to wish a warm welcome to all our freshmen! Let me introduce them to you."

As he reads off the names of freshmen, they take their seats on the bleachers on the other side of the gym. Quilla is ahead of me in the lineup since we are divided into alphabetical order, so when she gets called for introduction, she saves me a seat until my name is called.

"Up next is Dakota Shade! Give her a warm welcome!" Mr. Coleman announces.

I wave at the large student body and make my way next to Quilla. There are two faces that I am shocked to see from my high school: Jeffrey Carmichael and creepy lackey, Caleb Jackson. I roll my eyes and ignore them both, but I can feel their eyes lingering on my back.

Once I take my seat by Quilla, I partially drown out the rest of the announcements because it's the same thing that happened at high school. What the plan is for the school year, when all the dances will be that I will *never* get asked out to, and then when graduation will be for the seniors. When Mr. Coleman announces a last-minute addition for the new students a few minutes later, something in me can't help but look up.

"Students, I would like to announce a late addition to the freshman group. Everyone, please meet Kai Huntington!"

As I stare down from my perch in the bleacher, it's like my ears go underwater. I almost hear nothing else but the man standing in the center of the gym floor. My gaze meets the most beautiful set of hazel eyes I have ever seen. I realize it's my new neighbor, and then the roar of the gym comes back to me.

"Mate! It's our mate!"

I hear this light female voice again, only this time, it's not a whisper. It's as loud as the voices filling the gym, and I cannot act like I didn't hear anything. Then my left shoulder blade starts to itch out of nowhere, but I force myself to ignore it.

"Earth to Dakota!"

I look over at Quilla, who is waving her hand in my face, and I realize that she's been trying to get my attention since my mini-private meltdown.

"Are you okay?" Quilla asks as she places a hand on my shoulder.

I instantly feel calmer when she does this, and I take a breath before I look at her again. I notice my reflection in her glasses, and I almost think that my eyes are lighter than they normally are, but I pass that off as just the lighting in the gym and also from my panic attack.

I remember that Quilla is waiting for an answer, so I nod my head as I say, "Yeah. I'm good."

I look back at the center of the gym but the new guy is no longer standing there and for some reason that I do not want to understand right now, the thought that I cannot find him hurts me to the very depths of my soul.

Kai

I arrive at school in the middle of the introduction meeting that was discussed in the pamphlet, and I'm hoping that I can just slip in unnoticed, but Mr. Coleman waves me down just as a student finishes telling everyone when the dances and graduation will be. I internally groan but I make my way over to him.

"Hello, Mr. Huntington. Come, let's introduce you to the students here."

"So much for blending in." I growl.

But the only good thing that comes from being the center of attention is I get to see the owner of those beautiful ocean-blue eyes in the flesh.

"Mate." K growls.

In the next instant, I feel something change in the air around me, and I look around to find several pairs of glowing eyes staring back at me.

"Oh yeah. Totally blending in here." I say.

I let my own alpha power fill the room to let them know that I am no normal wolf walking among them. I notice that either our mate is amazing at blending in, or she didn't feel the shift in the atmosphere.

"I am not worried. Let them come. We are next in line to be Alpha, and I am not shy to show them our strength." K says with pride.

"While that is true, K, we cannot be so cocky. We don't know how old these wolves are. Plus, just because we are next in line as Alpha, any of these wolves may already be in that position." I tell him. *"If it were not for our mate, I'd be right with you in showing them exactly who we are. But we also have to think of her now as well, and what our actions may cause."*

"This is why the Great Luna made us the way we are. You are able to reason through my animalistic thinking." K says.

"That's right. Now let's get out of here before we make a scene."

Dakota

As we start to leave the gym, Quilla and I are stopped by Jeffrey and Caleb. I don't know why, but these two have always rubbed me the wrong way throughout high school ,and it's the same here, but only worse now.

"Where are you going, Darling? It's so nice to see you again." Jeffrey croons while running his hand through his black hair, his amber-colored eyes shining with a primal hunger.

"Don't call me 'darling', fleabag." I spit.

"Oh, come on, you like it, I know you do." He says as he reaches out to try to caress my cheek.

I pull back from him, earning a disgusted scowl. "You know what? I'm not wasting my time with you. Get. Out. Of. My. Way." I say, punctuating each word with venom filling my tone.

Jeffrey's eyes flare with something close to shock and fear, but at my demand, he actually moves to the side as if by an invisible force. I walk past him with my head held high, and I know Quilla is right on my heels, grabbing the back of my shirt to keep us together. She looks over her shoulder to see if the creepy duo is doing anything, but at Jeffrey's sly smile she spins back around and we walk through the gym doors.

Jeffrey

I smile as I watch Dakota walk through the doors with that friend of hers on her heels. I turn to my beta once she is out of sight.

"Follow Dakota. Something in her has changed. I can smell it, and I want her as my mate. I can tell she will be a powerful alpha, even if she is only a half-breed."

Caleb's brown eyes flash at me as his wolf hears my demand. He only nods as he pulls his hoodie up over his short brown hair and follows my order with no questions asked. I will have Dakota as my mate, either by her own free will or by force.

Dakota

Once we make it out of the gym, I walk over to a nearby oak tree, suddenly feeling tired and my knees rubbery, like I've run a marathon. I lean against the tree; the bark scratching through my shirt against my hot skin.

"What was that about, Chica?" Quilla asks, still looking back toward the gym door to make sure we aren't being followed yet.

"I have no idea." I say, my voice still wavering from the events of the morning. "I was just tired of Jeffrey and I wanted him out of the way." I lean my head back against the bark and take a deep breath.

"All I know is when you told him to move, he freaking *moved*. I can tell he didn't want to either."

"Well, that's not all." I begin, lifting my head to look at her. "I heard that voice again."

Quilla looks at me with shock, and she takes a step closer to me.

"This time though, it was a lot clearer." I look around the parking lot trying to find something else to focus on, but failing. "Maybe I should tell my parents what's been going on."

"Yes, you should. Also, you should trust me."

I hear this light female voice again, and I decide then and there that I am tired of running from this. So, I decide to try to talk back to this 'voice'.

"Who are you?"

"You know who I am, Dakota. You just need to let me in again. Think back to when you were younger, and it will all make sense."

Her words ring a bell somewhere deep inside, but the alarm that screams from Quilla's phone to remind us that classes are about to start keeps me from delving deeper in that thought.

"I think you should talk to your parents, Dakota." Quilla says, unaware of the mental conversation that just took place.

Chapter Five

KAI

On my way to my first class of the morning, I turn the corner in the hallway and I run smack into another student. I am instantly hit with the musky smell of a Werewolf and from the power rolling from him, I can tell he's a Beta.

"Watch where you're walking, Beta." I growl as I let a pulse of my power flow around him.

His eyes go wide, and he instantly bends his neck to the side in a form of submission to me.

"What's your name?"

"It's Caleb, sir." He says while doing his best to hide the growl in his tone.

I see him take a small scent of me and his eyes widen again for a moment before he takes a step back.

"Well, Caleb, you need to watch where you're going next time. Another Alpha may not be as lenient as I am." I warn.

"Yes, Alpha. I apologize."

The male in front of me has no choice but to respond this way from the warning I just put over him since his own Alpha is not present.

"Now get out of my way."

He moves without question, and I head to my class without any further issues or unwanted visitors.

Caleb

I take a breath as I round the corner from this new alpha. "Oh, this is gonna be interesting." I smirk.

"Alpha. I have learned something that may be of interest to you."

"Go on." Jeffrey instantly replies.

"That new wolf from this morning, he has the same smell as Dakota."

"He what?!" Jeffrey yells through the connection. *"Are you certain, Caleb?"*

"Yes, Alpha. I am certain Kai has the same scent as your mate." I tell him.

"I want you to keep Kai away from Dakota. When you find her alone, I want you to bring her to me." Jeffrey demands.

"As you say, so it shall be, Alpha."

Dakota

The school day continues with no other issues or voices in my head. Quilla and I have a peaceful lunch in the comfort of her car before I head to my last class of the day, and it's the only one that I don't share with Quilla, Chemistry. It's on the fourth floor of the Science building that sits off to the edge of the school grounds near a line of tall pine trees of the neighboring forest.

I end up arriving sooner than the professor or other students, so I sit on the oak bench in the hallway and pull my phone out of the back pocket of my jeans before sitting down. I take one earbud out of my purple charging case and stuff it in my left ear so I can listen to my playlist on Spotify to pass the time.

Just as I am about to push play on my phone, I pause for a moment. I almost swear I hear something coming from the stairwell to my left. I pull out my earbud so I can listen better, and it almost sounds like claws on the metal stairway. I brush it off as maybe a small animal got inside and is trying to find its way out, but when I go to put my earbud back in, the sound gets louder and now I hear what I am almost certain is like a dog, no, *dogs*, panting.

Something tells me that I need to stand up to be prepared to run, but what comes lunging out of the stairwell is a sight I would never be prepared for.

Three huge, and I mean fucking huge, wolves.

Compared to my five-foot-five frame, they each would come to the middle of my stomach. All three of them, their fur in various shades of brown and gray, lunge from the stairwell, and their heads whip in my direction. I take a single step back, but their snarls and low growls make me freeze for a moment.

Out of the corner of my eye, I see a glass door to my right, and I know this is the only way I can get some distance between me and these animals. I push my fear deep down in my chest and as I take a step to the side, I am rewarded with a warning growl from the brown wolf with bits of black running through its fur, making it look scraggly, and it takes a step toward me.

I keep slowly backing up until my hand makes contact with the crash bar. I try to keep my fear from building, but these wolves continue to approach, following me like I'm their prey. I can't keep my terror at bay, and in that moment I know I have to get away from them before they scent it in the air and it makes them feral.

Without taking my eyes off the three animals in front of me, I quickly push against the crash bar to make a break for it, knowing there is a fire escape on the roof. If I can only make it to that I can then call for help. I run the length of the roof, and I am almost to the fire escape, but when I hear a vicious snarl that is *way* too close for comfort, I find myself turning my head. And of course when I do that I end up tripping on a pipe, falling flat on my face and about two feet away from my lifeline.

I force myself to roll over on my back so I can at least face my imminent death head-on. I watch as all three wolves inch towards me, their jaws open, showing me their sharp teeth dripping in saliva, their tongues lulling to the side.

Suddenly, I hear another vicious snarl, but it's not from any of the ones in front of me. All four of us look up, and I watch as this beautiful brown and blonde marble-colored wolf jumps from the balcony above me and lands in between me and the three wolves. I hear this one snarl again and the others back up, but not enough.

I want to move, but I can't get my legs to work. This wolf is somehow buying me time, but I can't fucking move. He barks at me once, and I just look at him like the stupid human girl that I am. I swear I see this wolf roll its eyes at me and then in one swift motion it changes forms right before my eyes. The wolf turns into a naked man, and he runs for me, scooping me up in his arms, and literally jumps off the damn roof and lands feet-first into a bush. I'm shocked for a split second, but then I remember I am in the arms of a man.

A butt-naked man who just jumped off a fucking building and is not screaming in pain. Who was also just a damn *wolf* and changed in front of my eyes.

I lean back a bit in his arms, shock making me a statue, and the strange thing is, I find myself looking at him. His hazel eyes filled with worry, his soft blonde hair falling into his face, and I can only imagine what it would feel like to run my fingers through it. I can't help when my eyes travel the expanse of his broad shoulders and chest. When my eyes land on the gray swirling tattoo that travels down his neck and onto his chest, something in me wants to trace it with my finger. He smiles when he sees me looking at his tattoo, and something in me warms at the thought of that smile. When I get that thought that I want to run my tongue over those gray lines, I freeze for a moment.

"Where the hell did that thought come from?"

I then quickly pry myself from his arms once my brain catches up to the insane situation before me, and I back up a few small steps.

"Are you okay? They didn't hurt you, did they?" He says as he reaches his hand out to stroke my arm.

I pull my arm back, and for some reason, that movement hurts me. Not physically, but emotionally. As the reality of what just happened hits me, how he jumped off a building, landed so hard he dented the *fucking ground,* and didn't break both of his legs, he's clearly not normal. Plus, being comfortable with his naked body in front of a strange woman, if that doesn't scream weirdo, I don't know what does.

"Don't touch me. Don't ever touch me again."

I go to stand up, and the look on his face somehow matches the feeling that is now blooming in my chest.

Denial and rejection.

Again, the statement that seems to be my mantra today fills my mind, and it is really getting on my damn nerves.

I have this feeling, and I don't know why.

Kai

I am sitting in my last class of the day, English 101. Halfway through the lesson, I start to hear something odd. So, I call on K and allow his wolf hearing to take over, and I pick up on what sounds like claws echoing in the metal stairway. At first, I don't let it bother me, but when I pick up on their scents, it's familiar to the beta I ran into earlier in the hall, but what makes my chest tighten to the point of pain is I pick up on *her* scent as well.

"Our mate's in trouble!" K growls. *"We must get to her before they do."*

I get up out of my chair, and I feel the professor's eyes snap to me at my sudden movement. I look back over my shoulder as I keep walking.

"Sorry, I don't feel so well."

Which isn't a total lie, but to others it may sound like a piss-poor excuse, but right now I don't care.

The professor waves me off all the same, and I walk out into the hall and look around. I know there is a floor under me, so I look to the right, and I see a glass door that leads to the roof, and I dash for it, swinging the door open behind me. Once outside, I am immediately greeted with the sounds of snarling wolves below me, and I pick up on the smell of our mate's fear, and it breaks my heart. I run to the edge of the balcony, and I let a vicious snarl rip from my throat as I phase mid-air and land in between the three wolves and our mate.

"Mate, please run. I'll hold them here." K says mentally and gives a short bark.

When we are met with silence, I take a moment to look over my shoulde,r and I just see her staring at us.

"Please, run." K tries again.

No response.

"It's no use, K. She can't hear us, and these mangy mutts won't back the hell up." I growl again at them, but they only back up a few steps.

I roll my eyes and then say to K, *"Oh, screw it, phase back."*

In one swift movement, K pulls back from my mind, and I'm changing back into my human form. Closing the distance between me and our mate, I scoop her up against my chest before leaping over the side of the building. We fall three floors down, and I land on the ground so hard that I create a small divot around me.

At first, I just hold her, taking in her sweet honeysuckle and strawberry scent that warms me to my very soul. I pull back enough from her, and when she's looking over my chest, I know she sees my mating mark, and it warms me even further. She then pries herself from my arms, and I reluctantly let her go.

"Are you okay? They didn't hurt you, did they?" I say as I try to touch her arm again, but she pulls back. Her movement feels like someone just smacked me on the face, and fear grips my heart for an entirely different reason.

She goes to stand up, and the look on her face matches what is burning in my chest.

"Don't touch me. Don't ever touch me again."

With those words, she may as well have stabbed me in the heart with a silver blade; the pain is just as real. I can tell the words hurt her just as much, but she still walks away. So I am left alone, naked, and my soul hurting like a fresh wound.

"She rejected us." K whines.

"Yes, she did." I force myself to say. *"Where does that leave us now?"*

"I have no idea. I think we should tell our Alpha."

"You think that's actually a good plan?" I scoff. *"I can't take any more rejection or the look of disapproval on his face right now. Let's just go home."*

I phase quickly and follow the scent home, quickly dashing up to my room and kicking the door shut behind me.

Chapter Six

DAKOTA

When I get home, I am still shaking from the events of the day with silent tears rolling down my cheeks. I roughly wipe the tears away with the back of my hand as I slam the door and throw my backpack onto the floor with a loud thud. I slide down the length of the door, my legs no longer able to hold my body, just as Mom comes around the corner. Her face morphs from curiosity to fear at my arrival. She helps me to my feet, leads me into the dining room, and sits me on one of the chairs while resting her palm on my forehead to make sure I'm not running a fever.

"You're not running a fever, Honey. Are you okay? You look pale as a ghost."

This time I can't hold back the tears as they spill down my face. "No, Mom. I'm not okay. Something crazy happened at school today." I sob. "I've been hearing this voice in my head since yesterday. Then these freakishly huge wolves came out of the stairwell at school and tried to attack me, but another wolf jumped from the balcony above me, and when the other wolves wouldn't back up, he changed into a man, then he picked me up and jumped off the fourth floor of the Science building and he didn't break anything. And then-" I rush through the explanation, but the memory of my actions toward that man, the emotions and pain that followed, makes me stop, and I just let everything flow from my soul.

Mom pulls me into her side, and she rubs my back in a soothing motion, trying to get me to calm down. After a few moments I am able to gather myself enough to where I have the dry heaves, but I'm not a blubbering fool now. As I pull away from her, I hear a car door slam outside, and we look through the window to see Quilla's Sentra parked in the driveway. She opens the door, walks right in, and sits down beside me in the dining room without a word, and I am instantly set at ease when Quilla rests her hand on my shoulders.

"How did you know to come over, Quilla?" Mom asks.

"I don't know. I had a feeling that Dakota needed me."

"I'm going to call your father. I'll be right back," Mom says as she leaves the room long enough to grab her cell phone.

"What happened?" Quilla asks.

"It's so unbelievable, Quilla, I'm almost wondering if I imagined it all."

"Hey Nathan, we need you home...now." Mom tells my dad on the phone. "Everything's okay, at least I think so. No one is hurt at least. Dakota just needs your help. Okay, Sweetheart. See you soon."

She comes back into the dining room and she sits beside me, taking my hand in her own. "I know you did not imagine what you saw today, Dakota. Wait until your father gets home. I think he will be able to help you."

Fifteen minutes later, Dad walks through the door, and he rushes into the dining room. Mom stands from her seat next to me so Dad can sit in her place. He pauses, taking a deep breath and releasing it through his nose before he takes my hand in his and gives it a comforting squeeze.

"Please, Dakota. Tell me what happened today at school." Dad asks gently.

So, I tell him, this time it's not the hysterical version I spouted to Mom.

"Did you notice anything about him that you may have left out?" Dad pauses. "I need you to think, Dakota, please. It is very important."

I think for a moment, and there are actually two things I didn't tell them about.

"He, uh, he had this tattoo on the left side of his neck and chest. It looked like some kind of tribal scroll thing."

Dad takes another breath and squeezes the bridge of his nose with his index finger and thumb. He releases a heavy sigh as he leans his head back on the chair for a moment before lifting it again to look at me.

"Did his tattoo look similar to this?" Dad asks as he unbuttons his navy shirt, revealing his own tattoo that is inked into his chest and travels up to the middle of his neck.

I knew that Mom and Dad had matching tattoos for as long as I can remember, and I always figured that it was something they did when they were younger and they thought it would be a cool thing to show their love for one another.

"Yeah, but it wasn't black like yours and Mom's. It was a light gray color." I say as the image of his tattoo enters my mind, and even with the high emotions rolling through me, I almost want to smile at the thought.

But then the next thing that enters my mind wipes that smile right from my lips.

"There's more." I begin, and Dad looks at me with apprehension. "After I tore myself from his arms, he tried to touch me again." I pause, forcing myself to swallow the pain that blooms in my chest at the memory. "And I told him not to touch me again." I whisper.

I watch as Dad's face floods with pain and sorrow that almost matches my own, and I feel a few more silent tears fall from my face.

"You told him not to touch you again?" Dad asks, his voice tight and gentle.

"Yeah," I whisper. "Why does it hurt so much, Dad?" I sob.

"Oh, Sweetheart." Dad croons.

Just as he's about to pull me into his chest for a comforting embrace, I feel something strange wash over me. I can only explain it as a pulse of raw power. Dad must also feel this because he stiffens, and I see his eyes go from his normal brown to an eerie light glossy color. A moment passes before he stands up and starts to make his way to the door, then I hear the light female voice again.

"That is Jeffrey at the door. We cannot let our father answer it. Our father is a Beta, and he will have no choice but to let Jeffrey in if he commands it." The voice rushes to explain.

"And what are we gonna do?"

"Do you trust me?"

I see my father getting closer to the door, and I know I cannot let him answer that door.

"I trust you."

I take a breath, and I feel something flow within me, and when I take a step forward, I somehow know to push this new power onto my dad.

"Dad. Stop."

I feel this crack in the air at my command, and Dad stops dead in his tracks and looks back at me over his shoulder. His glowing eyes are wide with a mix of confusion and wonder. Mom and Quilla exchange looks as I walk out of the dining room and towards the front door.

"Step away from the door, please." I say, but I can pick up that my vocal tone is not fully my own. Whatever is inside me is also talking at the same time.

Dad then steps aside, as if moved by an invisible force.

I place a hand on his shoulder, and he relaxes under my touch. "I'm sorry, but I am the only one that can do this." I say with my own voice again. "Please go into the kitchen and protect Mom and Quilla for me."

He nods, taking the two women and leading them into the kitchen, but Dad stays at the threshold like a sentry, watching my back. I take a breath and before the uninvited guest can even knock, I whip open the door and I am greeted with Jeffrey's annoying presence.

"Hello, my Darling."

"I told you, I am *not* your darling." I spit.

"Oh, but you see, I beg to differ." He croons as he tries to caress my face with his hand.

I pull back from his touch, and his face shifts from calm and what one would think of as loving to bright-red anger at my rejection. He raises his hand as if to backhand me across the face, but I catch it before he can even move it towards me. There is another crack of power in the air, but it's even more powerful than I used on my father. Jeffrey is forced to his knees, and from the corner of my eye, I even see Dad, Mom, and Quilla back up from this strange power I possess.

Jeffrey tries to back away from me, but I grab him by the back of the neck, digging my fingernails into his flesh. He freezes under my hand as I lean in close to his face.

"Don't you *ever* raise a hand to me again." I growl, actually growl. But this voice coming from me is not fully my own again, but I let it say what I feel it needs to. "No mate would raise an ill-minded hand to something so precious. Listen to me well, Jeffrey, for I will only say this once. I will never be your mate. I will sooner cut off my own tail than to be a mate to the likes of you. Do I make myself clear?"

The power still filling the room is so thick and heavy that I know I am the only one who can breathe without issue.

"Yes, crystal," Jeffrey answers, averting his eyes to the right in a sign of submission.

"Good. Now leave my territory and do not set foot back onto it. You and yours are not welcome." I snap while letting go of his neck, my nails leaving bloody half-circles on his skin.

He backs away from me, and only when he is off the porch does he turn around and walk away without a word. I slowly close the door and lock it before I collapse to one knee as I feel the power around me slowly fade. Dad rushes to my side, putting his hand on my back to steady me. I lift my head to look at him, and he takes a step back in shock.

"What's wrong?" I ask, fear filling my voice.

Dad gives me a soft smile as he picks up a small mirror that Mom had sitting on the little table near the front door. When I look at my reflection, I am in no way prepared for what I see looking back at me.

Chapter Seven
DAKOTA

"Why the hell are my eyes glowing?! What was all that power shit I just did? Why did you stop walking when I told you, Dad?" I shoot off question after question to my father in rapid succession.

I close my eyes when I hear my mother and Quilla come out of the kitchen. I don't want them to see me like this. Quilla comes right over to me, not caring one bit about my outburst and she rubs soothing circles on my upper back. I am instantly at ease and when I open my eyes again, they are back to normal.

"Quilla, you're a Tamer?" Dad asks in shock.

"I'm a what? Sorry Mr. Shade, but I don't follow."

Dad takes a deep breath and looks between me and Quilla. "Okay. I need both of you girls back in the dining room." He then turns to Mom and takes her hand gently in his own. "Lori, Baby, can you please make some coffee? I'm gonna need it." He groans near the end.

Mom nods and heads off to the kitchen while we follow Dad into the dining room and sit in our usual spots. Dad is at the head of the table with the door in his line of sight, and I am to the left of him with Quilla to my right.

Mom brings out a carafe of coffee and sits Dad's mug, which is already filled with the steaming liquid, in front of him. She takes her seat to the right of him and wraps her hands around his forearm. He takes a sip of coffee and lets out a sigh after he swallows.

"Okay, Dakota. I don't know how to make this any easier for you." He pauses and then chuckles, "But with the power that was coming from you, I think you will handle it."

He takes my hand and gives it a gentle squeeze,. "Tell me what, Dad?" I ask with apprehension.

"You, my beautiful, strong daughter, are a Werewolf."

"He's right. I am your inner wolf."

"So you were the one that gave me that power?" I ask.

"Yes."

"Where have you been all this time?"

She sighs, and I can feel whatever she's about to tell me fills her with sorrow. *"When you were little, I tried to show myself to you. But something happened, and then you blocked me out. Since you are a half-Were I cannot force myself to exist with you. You have to be the one to allow it."*

"I'm sorry." I whisper.

"You can let me in now, that is if you trust me."

"I trust you. What is your name?" I ask.

"You already know my name, Dakota. You just have to remember." She chuckles.

I sit for a few minutes thinking about what she means by this. I think about her voice more, and I get this quick image of a light blondish-brown wolf, and then a name hits me.

"Kota."

With that name slipping from my lips, something in the air changes, breaking that barrier that's been separating me and Kota for twenty long years.

"Finally," Kota sighs. *"Hello there, old friend."*

I realize I closed my eyes at some point, and when I open them again, I find myself in a bright, lush green forest, and in front of me is a huge blondish-brown wolf, her thick bushy tail held high in greeting. She takes a step forward, resting her head on my stomach, and I place my hand right between her ears at the top of her skull.

"I can actually touch you." I say in shock.

"Yes, this is the place I spend my time when I am not in control." Kota explains.

"It's beautiful here."

I feel something touch me on my shoulder, and when I look toward the sensation, I am ripped from Kota's forest. I end up back in the real world, and the hand that touched me was Dad trying to get my attention.

"You and your wolf connected, didn't you?"

I open my mouth to respond to him, but I notice things are vastly different than they were five minutes ago. My sight is so much better than it was before. I can look out the window and see a bird perched in a tree two streets over. The smells of the world are stronger too. I loved the smell of coffee, but now, I can smell the rich, earthy scent and the sweetness of the cream and sugar sitting on the table. I notice that Mom, Quilla, and even Dad have their own unique scent, but I can't quite place what they are, other than Dad. I pick up on the same musky smell that is coming from me now. Then I realize that he is still waiting for my reply.

"Yes, we did. Sorry, it's a lot to take in."

"I'm sure it is, Honey." Dad chuckles.

"Everything is so different. I can smell you, smell the wolf on you. So you're a Werewolf too?" I ask.

"Yes, I am."

"So I guess that makes sense now." I say suddenly.

"What makes sense, Dakota?" Mom asks.

"A few years ago I noticed a wolf walk up to you one night when you were out back," I tell my mother. "I looked away for a few minutes, and then when I looked back, I saw you standing there with Dad."

"Seriously? And this is the first time I've heard about this?" Dad asks in shock.

"I figured I was seeing things. I mean, come on, that is not something you go to your parents and ask about." I say in defense.

"Okay. We'll talk about that later. Right now we need to go back over what happened today and please start from the beginning again. When did you start hearing Kota?" Dad asks.

"It was yesterday morning. When the new neighbors moved in next door. I noticed the son, and I heard Kota whisper, 'Mate'. I didn't understand it at first, but when he was at the introduction meeting this morning and we kind of met face to face, Kota came to the front and spoke like I am speaking now. She said 'mate' again and my shoulder started to itch. And that's when Jeffrey tried to pull his first stunt in the gym, and I did the same thing to him as I did with you, I forced him aside." I pause and I take a breath when I picture the last event at school in my mind again.

"Then I was waiting for my last class, and I heard claws scraping in the metal stairwell, and I was ambushed by three wolves. I tried to run away from them on the balcony, but I fell, and that is when the other wolf jumped down to block them from me. When the other three wouldn't back up enough, he changed and was a human. He picked me up and jumped off the building and onto the ground below. I was freaking out, and I fought to get away from him. I, uh, tried not to look at his body, you know why." I say as my cheeks heat from embarrassment at the memory. "I noticed the marking on his chest, and he seemed proud that I noticed that." Pain fills my chest again, but I make myself finish the story. "When he tried to touch me, I told him not to. It's weird though, because my own words hurt me. Hurt something deep down, and I ran to my car and came home. And you know the rest."

As the afternoon turns into evening and I slowly come to terms with what all happened today, Mom fixes a light dinner for all of us so we can talk more while we eat. Then something that Dad said earlier hits me, and I look between my parents again for a moment before I voice my thoughts.

"So the tattoos you two have aren't really tattoos, are they?"

"No, Honey. They aren't. They're our mate markings." Mom explains.

"So... I should have the same one as Kai then?" I ask.

Dad takes a deep breath then drains his coffee cup. "Um, yeah. You should actually."

I want to look, but for some reason the thought of Dad seeing this strange marking makes me shudder.

"I want to see if I have one, but I don't want you to look at it. Why?" I ask him.

"Mate markings are usually private. Only Mates, their children, Alpha's, and pack healers see them without permission. So that's why I was able to show you mine without issue." Dad explains. "But if you don't want me to see, you can have your mother check. Usually, it's fine if another female of the same pack sees it."

My eyes slide to my mother, and she gets up with a smile on her face. She walks around to the back of my chair and tugs the collar of my shirt down, exposing my shoulder blade, and she chuckles lightly.

"It's there, Honey. You have, I'm sure, the same mark as he does." Mom says gently.

I am ecstatic at her words, but yet I am terrified in the same breath. I look back to my father. "What do I do now?"

Dad takes a breath. "First, we need to get you and your mate back on speaking terms. With you explaining what you told him, I'm sure he's thinking you rejected him. I know I would if your mother did that to me."

My heart constricts in my chest at his words, "So this is why I feel like my heart is being squeezed? From my words to him?"

"Yes, Sweetheart. Words mean a lot in my world. You will learn it soon enough. Have you tried to talk to him through your mate bond?" Dad asks.

"That's a thing?" I ask, looking between them both.

"Yes, it is." Dad says as he looks at the clock.

I follow his gaze to the clock over the doorway of the dining room, and I realize how much time has flown by. It's already ten o'clock at night, but Dad's next words make my stomach twist.

"It's too late to try it now. It will be harder for you to connect if he's sleeping. Hopefully, he'll be at school tomorrow." Dad says, but then his tone goes from gentle to something harder. One I've never heard from him before. "But Dakota, I need you to understand something for me. This is very important. Your mate, you said his name was Kai?" Dad asks, and I nod. "Okay. Kai is a new wolf here, and he has already found his mate. It usually takes *years* to find our mates, and you have found yours at twenty. So he is already a target for an attack from other wolves."

When Dad says this, I hurt in a different way. I do not want to see this still strange man to me, hurt in any way. Dad reaches out and takes my hand in his and gives it a gentle squeeze.

"I know this is a lot to take in, Dakota. And I am so sorry I failed you, but I didn't know you picked up this gene from me. We always thought you were a normal human like your mother."

I look him in the eye as I say, "Please tell me what I need to know. Let's make up for lost time." I say, wanting to take control of this situation the best I can.

Dad smiles and nods his head, but the light fades from his face once more as he says, "Another major thing first. Just like Kai is the target for attack, so are you, Dakota. You need to get on the same wavelength as Kota. She will be able to help you keep an eye out for attacks."

I nod as I actually feel Kota perk up at her new role for me, and somehow I can tell she's looking around the house.

"That is so weird. I can actually feel her looking around."

"You'll get used to it after a while. I hardly ever feel Nate unless he's trying to come to the surface." Dad says.

"Nate?" I ask, never hearing that name before.

"Oh, my wolf. You will meet soon enough. We need to focus on one thing at a time. I don't know if you are or not since you're a half-Were, but silver is a weakness of ours. It can hurt and even kill us," Dad explains somberly.

"Seriously?" I reply in shock.

"Yeah. I mean, how many times, for example, have you seen me cut myself while cooking?"

"None. Except for one time."

"Right. When I ordered a new cooking knife online, it was supposed to be stainless steel, but it was somehow coated in silver alloy, and I cut myself badly on the blade."

"Yeah, I remember that one."

"So, you just need to watch your back. And especially now since you rejected Jeffrey's inquiry about being his mate and used your alpha power to get him to leave. He will be after you as well now." Dad says.

"So that's what that power was?" I ask, feeling stupid for not knowing. "But why could I make you listen to me too? Aren't you the alpha here, for us?"

"I was, I guess, for a time before you came to be what you are. With the last pack I was a part of, I was what is called a Beta. The Alpha's right-hand wolf. If an alpha can't be somewhere, then he or she will send the Beta in their place, because most of the time Beta's are stronger than normal pack members and can assert dominance if needed."

Hearing Dad talk this way is making my head spin. One part of me is completely confused, but the other part, I guess the side coming from Kota, somewhat understands it.

"Okay. I've had enough for tonight." I look to my right and I see that Quilla has been quiet this whole time, just taking everything in. "Quilla, I'm sorry I've kept you here all this time. You just wanna crash here tonight?"

"Oh, it's no problem at all, and sure I don't mind crashing here. Plus, I still need to talk to your dad about what he called me earlier. But that can wait until tomorrow."

"Go on, you two. Go get some rest. You both need it." Mom says, and we both head out of the dining room to go upstairs.

Nathan

After the girls go upstairs, I stay in my chair and rest my head in my hands while blowing out a defeated sigh through my nose. Lori scoots in next to me and rubs the curve of my tense shoulders, helping me relax just a little.

"I've always wanted Dakota to be like me, but I never thought it would come out like this, or that she would be a half-Were alpha and she would find her mate at only twenty." I say, then chuckle, "I feel like I've aged another hundred years."

"Hey, I did not marry a two-hundred-year-old Were. I'm too young looking for that old of a mate." Lori jokes, making a much-needed smile bloom across my face. "We will get through this situation. We always have, and we always will." She says sternly.

"Lori she's powerful. Jeffrey was strong, but Dakota, she took him down like a normal member of the pack." I say in shock, thinking back to the confrontation.

"I know. I even felt her power, and I usually don't feel things like that."

"I can only imagine who her mate is to help make her this powerful. I just hope he doesn't reject her because of my own failure of not teaching her the wolf laws." I say as I look away from Lori with shame burning in my chest.

"If we had half a thought that Dakota would one day be like this, you would have told her. We kept this from her to protect her. We both know that."

I hear the truth in Lori's words. I look back at her, and she has the soft smile on her face that I fell in love with so many years ago. "You're right, my Love. Thank you for keeping this old Were in line." I force a sad smile to my lips.

"Now, let's go to bed. Why don't you make sure the house is secure for us, *my* alpha."

At her words, I feel Nate perk up, and he growls in my mind.

"*Protect.*"

"You always know how to pull me out of my own head and insecurities, don't you, Sweetheart?" I ask.

"If I haven't figured out what makes my mate tick, then I am horrible at this kind of thing, aren't I?" Lori teases.

I growl at her, and the way her eyes widen tells me that Nate is close to the surface. She always looks like that when my eyes glow brightly for her. So, I proceed to make sure the house is safe and locked up for the protection of my little pack.

Chapter Eight
DAKOTA

I wake up about fifteen minutes before my alarm goes off, and stare at the dark ceiling. My bedroom is still lightless, the sun not even above the horizon yet. With only the sound of Quilla's slumbering breath filling the air, I replay everything that happened yesterday.

I am a Werewolf. Something that is told in stories. Something that shouldn't be real, but it is. I am a walking oddity.

"You say that like it's a bad thing." Kota snorts in what could sound like her version of a chuckle.

"It's just hard to believe that's all."

After a few minutes of feeling Kota in the back of my mind, I think back to the night I watched the wolf walk up to Mom. Now that I know the wolf to be Dad, I think about him and Kai changing their forms.

"Can we change forms like Dad and Kai?" I ask.

"In theory, we should be able to, yes. But you have to trust me and let me in the front of your mind," Kota replies.

I take a deep breath, and I glance over at Quilla.

I start to wonder if she will hear me, Kota chimes in. *"If we do this right, she won't hear a thing."*

I nod my head in response to her. *"So, what do I do?"*

"Just let me to the front of your mind and I will do the rest."

I nod and try my best to push any fear and uncertainty I have to the back of my mind. I can just make out Kota's forest around me, but something is keeping her from completely taking over, and I feel my confusion mix with her own. Kota pushes harder, and when I think I begin to feel something changing, we hear the metallic ring of a pan being dropped in the kitchen followed by Mom's curse and then her airy laughter. I jump in reaction to the sound, and I somehow feel Kota get flung backward into her forest. I immediately reach out to her to make sure she's okay.

"I am so sorry, Kota!" I run over and kneel in front of her, running my hand over her large head, her fur coarse under my fingers.

"I'm okay. At least I was able to get to the front of your mind. With practice, I know we'll get there."

"At least one of us has confidence." I say.

"Hey, we will get there. We just need to work on it." Kota tells me with determination in her tone. *"Now, let's get ready for class so we can meet up with our mate."*

At her words, warmth fills my chest. My mate. I just hope that he will understand where I am coming from so we can start over, and that my words to him yesterday didn't irrevocably break us apart before we even began.

After Quilla and I eat a quick breakfast, we arrive at the school twenty minutes before the start of our classes, just sitting in her car and nervously waiting with the hopes that we can catch Kai when he pulls in. As the minutes tick by, I start to get nervous that he won't show; that he dropped out because of what I unknowingly did. Another ten minutes pass, and Quilla's alarm blares in the silence between us letting us know class is about to start.

But still no sign of Kai.

Panic starts to set in, and the feeling that I now understand as rejection hits me deep in the chest again. Quilla puts her hand on my upper arm, and the feeling lifts, but only slightly.

"Hey, why don't you go to his house and talk to him? Besides, that might be the best thing for you two right now, with the leader of fleabags and all walking around." Quilla says as she spots Jeffrey and Caleb walk into the brick building in front of us.

"I can't miss class on the second day." I whine, but I already know I am one hundred percent willing to high-tail it out of here if I can see Kai.

"Yes, you can and you will," Quilla says as she bends backward into her backseat to grab her backpack and opens the driver's side door. "Take my car. I'll call an Uber later. Go get your man." She gives me a wink as she gets out.

"You are the best, you know that, Quilla?" I ask as I slide across her console and settle into the driver's seat.

"I'll bring your homework over later. I better hear that you two kissed and made up." She smiles.

I wait long enough to make sure that Quilla gets inside the school, and I rush out of the parking lot to head to Kai's place.

I pull up in front of his house, parking out on the curb about fifteen minutes later, and I take a cleansing breath as I get out of the car, shutting the door behind me with a metallic creak. I walk up to the spacious porch to ring the doorbell, and a few moments pass before the door finally opens. A tall, dark-haired man fills the doorway, and I immediately feel small and terrified. From what I have come to know in the short fifteen hours since feeling my own alpha power, I know this man can easily overpower mine by just breathing. The power is just rolling from him like smoke off a block of dry ice. I can only imagine what it would feel like to have that power forced on you under a command, and I shudder at the thought.

Once I get past the shock of his strength, I finally take in the man himself. He's in gray dress slacks with a matching vest and a silky black long-sleeve button-up shirt with the top three buttons undone, showing off the black tattoo. No, his own mating mark that travels from the base of his jaw and disappears under his shirt. His black hair is slicked back and pushed to the left side of his head, his face showing the barest hint of smile lines, but his brown eyes are hard and assessing.

"Kota, I need your help here. What should I do?"

"Keep your eyes to the right of his. You are an alpha too, so you don't need to bare your neck to him." Kota coaches.

"How can I help you, Miss?"

His voice is gentle, but it's not to be mistaken for weakness.

I keep my eyes focused on his right ear, and I let Kota help me with my words.

"Hello, Alpha. My name is Dakota, and I am here to speak with Kai. Is he home?"

"Thank you, Kota." She's able to keep the waver from my voice, and I feel her pleasure flow through me at my acknowledgement of her help.

"Ah, I understand. Please come in."

He steps aside and gestures for me to enter his home. I walk into the foyer, and just when I am out of the way of the door, I feel a pulse of his power wash over me, and I am helplessly frozen in place. I hear Kota whimper in her forest at the intensity of his power. I take a breath and will my heart to slow and try to push a comforting feeling to Kota.

"It's okay. He's probably just making sure we won't do anything stupid in his house." I tell Kota, and I send my own pulse of alpha power over her, and I feel her anxiety evaporate instantly. *"I won't let anyone hurt us. I don't care who they are."*

At that declaration to Kota, I feel the man's power change and the hold he had on us instantly fades before he walks into the living room on the left of the house and I follow without a word.

"Make yourself at home, Miss Dakota. My name is Tobias Huntington, by the way. What is the reason for this request of my son?" Tobias asks.

"I need to talk to him about what happened yesterday. There is reason for me to think that he is my mate, and things got a little hectic. I want to explain myself to him."

"I understand. Please sit, let me talk to my son," Tobias says as he gestures to a fine deep brown leather sofa and then walks out of the living room, leaving me alone in the empty house.

"Holy shit. The power *rolling off that dude."* I exclaim, and I can't keep the fear buried anymore now that he's out of the room.

"Yes, he is indeed powerful. I can feel he has a very *large pack behind him."* Kota says.

"Yeah, and little ole me, who can't even fucking shift, is the mate to his son? What kind of damn joke is this?"

"I cannot lie, I am intimidated too."

Feeling Kota's fear is one thing, but hearing her actually voice that she's scared too, makes me feel overwhelmed again. What kind of messed up mojo in the universe put me and this powerhouse together?

Before I can tumble too far into my panic, I can sense Tobias coming back in my direction, and I instinctually know that I should be standing before he enters the room, as an alpha-to-alpha thing.

"Picking up on things already." Kota croons with approval in her voice.

I again keep my eyes averted to the right of Tobias' and wait for him to speak, to lead me where Kai is.

"I'm sorry, but my son does not want to see you." He says with sadness in his voice.

I look away from the Alpha in front of me as the burn in my chest at his words threatens to steal my breath. It's like a hot poker was stabbed right through my heart. Part of me wants to walk out the door before the tears start to flood my cheeks, but something keeps me from moving.

Maybe it's the alpha in me that I have yet to fully explore, I don't know. But one thing I do know is, I am not leaving this house until I talk to Kai. I don't give two shits if it's through his door.

I look back at Tobias. Right in his dark brown eyes, and I take a step forward, squaring my shoulders.

"What are you doing?!" Kota yells.

"I apologize for the disrespect, Alpha, but that won't sit well with me."

Shock flickers across the Alpha's face. I get the feeling this is something that most do not get the privilege to see and live to face another day. But he actually doesn't push his power back at me as punishment, so I continue my plea.

"Please, show me to Kai's room. Let me explain myself to him through the door at least. He has no idea of what I have been through over the last sixteen hours. Then after I have said my peace, if he still doesn't let me in, then I will leave. No questions asked." I force the last part out because I am hoping beyond hope that he will understand, that he will let me in, but I have to leave that option on the table.

Tobias never takes his eyes off me, and I do not back down. This may be stupid, but I find that same power that I pushed on Jeffrey last night and let it pulse over Tobias. After a moment, he actually smiles and gives an amused chuckle as he leads me back to Kai's door without a word.

"That was very bold, and very stupid, Dakota."

"But it got us here, didn't it?" I say.

Kota growls at me in response, and I can tell she is a little bit deeper in her forest. I don't feel her as much in the back of my mind, but she is still present.

Tobias gestures to Kai's door and then gives me a sorrowful smile as he leaves me alone in the hallway. I lift my hand, knocking twice against the door, and wait. I don't hear anything on the other side, so I decide to just talk to him from here.

"Kai, it's Dakota Shade. Please let me explain what happened the other day. I did not mean what I said. That I didn't want you to touch me. I was scared, confused, and I just wanted to run and hide." I plead while touching the door as if touching the wood will help me connect with him. "Kai, I did not know I was a werewolf until last night, so I was not aware of my words and what they would make you feel like. I mean, they hurt me, and I didn't understand them at the time. Please, let me in so we can start over."

I let my words hang in the air for a few minutes, but I don't hear movement from his room. I rest my head against his door, the tears silently flowing from my eyes as the sting of his silence echoes through me.

"Okay, I understand. But just know that Jeffrey came by the house last night; he wanted to make me his mate. I rejected his request, Kai, and that made him royally pissed off. So please lie low, mate of mine." I take a breath, wiping away the tears. "I can't stand the thought of you hurting because of me." I choke out then I walk away from his door with my heart torn to ribbons.

I take five steps before I hear a door rip open behind me and a pair of strong arms wrap around my waist pulling me close to his chest, my head resting on the soft fabric of his black shirt. I break down at his touch, sobbing loudly into his shirt as he pulls us into his room and settles down into his oversized LoveSac until I stop crying.

Chapter Nine

KAI

I didn't sleep well last night after Dakota's rejection. So, when I told my parents at four o'clock this morning that I was not going to school today, they only nodded their understanding and left me alone in my room. They both know this is a horrific thing to go through, and at such a young age too. I will be alone and mateless for the rest of my days. Wolves only get one mate, the equal part to their soul; and if it's rejected, there is no other.

Throughout the morning I feel Dad's alpha power rolling through the house, with bits of Mom's power just underneath, and I am finally lulled into a somewhat restful slumber.

A few hours later I wake up to Dad's power flooding the house, but it's different. It's the power he uses when he's testing out another wolf, to see how they will react to him, and to remind them who is really in control. Then I feel another power; it's foreign yet familiar all the same. It's strong, but unsure of itself. I try to ignore the power struggle coming from the living room, figuring Dad has it on lock and I don't need to concern myself with this other wolf in our home. So, I turn over and try to doze back off.

A few minutes later, I hear a knock on the door, and when I open my eyes, I can feel Dad standing on the other side. I force myself out of bed to answer it, and I immediately pick up on Dakota's honeysuckle and strawberry scent coming from the living room.

So that's who I've been feeling. Her power.

K instantly wants to push past Dad and run to her, but I force him to hold his ground, and he growls in response.

"Son, she wants to speak with you."

I don't even think about my response. "Tell her I don't want to see her." I say, the words leaving a bitter taste in my mouth.

As I shut the door on my father without another word, I lean against the wooden surface trying to fight my roiling stomach. I hear Dad finally walk away, so I walk over to the corner of my room and sit in the over-ly-sized blue LoveSac since there is no way I am going back to sleep with her still in the house.

"You want to tell me why we are sitting here and not going to our mate?" K growls, letting his anger at my reaction bleed through our bond.

"Come on, K. She rejected us. I am not going to allow us to be the groveling type and run back to her when she's ready to talk." I tell him, even though I am fighting with every fiber of my being not to run to her. I vibrate with the need to be close to her.

I continue to feel the tug-o-war of power in the living room, but something changes for an instant. Then I feel Dad's amusement bloom through the unique pack-alpha bond we share, and I have to force my curiosity to the back of my mind, and not reach out to see what made him show me that emotion. A few moments later, I hear another knock on the door, and I don't even have to get up to know Dakota is on the other side. Her scent floats under my door and right to my nose, to my heart. K growls again, but I sink deeper into the LoveSac, standing my ground to him. I listen to her muffled voice plead her case through the door, and it rips my heart into little broken pieces that I know only she would be able to mend. I am about to shout at her to leave, but when she speaks next, my whole body freezes.

"Okay, I understand. But just know that Jeffrey came by the house last night; he wanted to make me his mate. I rejected his request, Kai, and that made him royally pissed off. So please lie low, mate of mine." She pauses. *"I can't stand the thought of you hurting because of me."*

Her words are the straw that broke the proverbial camel's back. I can no longer sit here and let her be terrified, broken, and alone anymore. I hear her take a few steps, and I rush to my door.

"Ah, screw it, I will be anything she needs me to be. The hell with my pride, I will be a groveling fool for her."

I feel K's lupine smile at my words as I rip open the door, barely remembering not to tear it from its hinges, and pull my mate close to my chest as she sobs into my shirt. I slowly take her with me into my room and settle down into my LoveSac and I just hold her. I thread my fingers through her soft, light brown hair while I run my hand soothingly down her back.

After a few minutes of just holding her, Dakota lifts her head, and I see my beautiful ocean blue eyes, red from crying, and I hate that I am part cause of those tears.

"I am so sorry for pushing you away." She hiccups. "Like I said, I didn't understand what my words meant until Jeffrey came by the house last night and I finally connected to my inner wolf. Then, my dad explained everything to me. I was going to talk to you sooner, but it was too late last night and–" She rambles on but I cut her off.

"It's never too late to come to me. I don't care what time it is." I push my alpha power toward her to make that point, and her eyes snap back to mine for a moment before she looks away.

"What's wrong, Love?" I ask gently.

She doesn't answer me or look up, so I gently hook my index finger under her chin and make her look at me. Her eyes bounce back and forth between mine, and I let all the love I can show for her shine in my hazel eyes.

"I don't understand how I was matched with someone of your caliber. I mean, come on, I don't know much at all, but I know your father is a very powerful Alpha and so are you. So how do I, a half-breed Werewolf who can't even change forms, even begin to compare?" Dakota says. "I mean, what kind of sick joke is this?"

She turns her head from me again, like she's afraid of seeing the disappointment on my face at her words. This hurts deep within my soul in a way I can't explain. It hurts to think that she doesn't feel worthy of my love for her when she is perfect in every sense of the word.

I tighten my hold on her as I lean in closer to her ear, and I watch as the gooseflesh blooms across the delicate skin of her kissable neck. "I don't see it as a joke at all, Dakota. And for the matter of you beginning to compare," I say as I take her chin in my hand again to make her look at me. "You are just as powerful as I am. I felt you when you first came in. You submitted to my father like you were supposed to. But when he told you that I didn't want to see you, I felt your power change. You looked my father in the eye, didn't you?" I ask.

Dakota sits dumbfounded for a moment, then recognition flashes across her face, before an embarrassed smile blooms across her lips.

"Oh yeah, I did." She chuckles. "Kota, my wolf, yelled at me for looking your father in the eye."

I smile at her, and I push a strand of her hair out of her eye. "See? My little Alpha."

Dakota

At Kai's words, I start to feel better about everything that's been happening. And the love that I already hear in his voice makes me warm and fuzzy inside. I lean back a bit to get a better look at him. He's lounging back in the corner of the LoveSac, and his arms are around my waist in a mindful embrace. Just high enough on my back to keep me upright, but nowhere near my ass to make it creepy. I find myself resting my hands on his chest, fiddling with the fabric of his shirt. My eyes then notice the tattoo, no, the mate marking on his neck, the rest of it disappearing under his shirt.

Kai must pick up on this because he smiles at me. "Do you want to see it again?" He asks, his voice low and with a bit of a growl rumbling in his chest.

I tear my eyes away from the marking, and when I look up, I see that his hazel eyes are glowing, which must mean that his wolf is closer to the surface. At his stare, I can't help the blush that floods my cheeks.

"Yes," I whisper, but it sounds like more of a question.

"Oh, come now." Kai challenges, "You are not *that* timid. Show me that Alpha power you used on my father."

I hear the challenge in his voice, and both Kota and I want to rise to that challenge.

"You ready?"

I close my eyes as I take a breath to steady myself.

"Yes, I'm ready."

I feel Kota's power flow through me, and I hear Kai's growl in response. I can somehow tell it's not an angry or a warning growl, it's one of approval. I open my eyes, and Kai's is glowing brightly in response to my power. I notice my reflection in his and my own eyes are also shining a bright blue, just like when I used my power yesterday against Jeffrey.

"That's right, my beautiful mate. Show me your power." Kai growls, and this spurs me on. "Now I ask you one more time, do you want to see our marking?"

"Show me." I command.

I can feel our powers almost mixing in the air, and Kai grins. He leans forward enough to tug his shirt over his head and tosses it aside on his beige-carpeted floor. I take my time studying every angle of his form, since the last time I was running for my life from a wolf attack and didn't get the chance to. He has a broad, muscular chest, strong, well-built arms with veins protruding from his elbows, and traveling down his defined forearms. His washboard abs are next in my line of sight. My eyes begin to travel lower, to the strong V of his stomach that disappears below his royal blue shorts, and I swallow embarrassingly hard before I make my eyes travel back up the expanse of his body.

"That's better, my little Alpha."

I grin at his praise, and my eyes settle on the mating mark again. How it swirls over the entire left side of his pec and up the side of his neck. I reach out to touch it, but I pause for a moment. Kai nods his head, beckoning me forward. So, I close the small distance between us, and I run my finger along the gray swirls and lines. At my touch, Kai releases a contented sigh as he closes his eyes, leaning his head back against the wall with a soft thud while opening his body to me and giving me free rein to touch it as I please.

Kai

I can feel my heart pounding so hard I think it's about to beat out of my chest. Then, as Dakota continues to trace my marking, I can't help the growl that begins to rumble low in my chest. I hear her chuckle at the sound, but I don't care. I could stay here all day and just let her touch me like this. Each touch is magical and makes every nerve ending come alive with pleasure. And it's not a sexual pleasure at all. It's just the fact of being touched and acknowledged by my mate that has me melting under each brush of her fingers.

I can only imagine what more would feel like.

After she's had her fill of caressing my marking, she removes her hand, and I relax a little.

"Was it that bad?" She chuckles but knows it was far from that.

"That was exhilarating." I heave a contented sigh.

Then I remember something Dad told me, and I can't stop the growl, and I know my eyes are shining brightly when Dakota stiffens in anticipation, not of fear.

"Turn around." I command and push my power over her enough to let her know that even though my tone is laced with a possessive growl, my words are meant to be a gentle request. She turns without complaint. "You should have a mark matching mine, right here."

I place my hand on her left shoulder blade, and she shudders under my touch, and in that moment I know she knows what is hidden from me and what it means. I have to force my shaking hand to still. To not rip this shirt down the middle and see what is mine hiding underneath. Dakota is still new to this whole thing, and I want to make this entrance to the Werewolf world as easy as I can make it.

"May I lower your shirt and look at our marking, Mate?"

She turns her head over her shoulder to look back at me, her eyes still shining that bright sky blue, and she gives me a warm smile.

"Thank you for asking, Kai, and not going all possessive alpha on me." She chuckles, somehow knowing that's *exactly* what I wanted to do. "Yes, you may look and touch as you wish."

I gently pull the fabric down and on her beautiful delicate back, I see the mirror image of my own mark. A growl rumbles in my chest, and she shivers as it resonates through her. When I begin tracing my middle finger down the lines and swirls of her mark, her head falls forward and to the side, allowing me complete access to her. She lets out a soft moan at my touch, and it sends fire through my veins and ends right between my legs, making a visible tent in my blue shorts. A fire that I cannot act on right now because of Werewolf Law, but the human male side of me just wants to throw caution to the wind and make this woman in front of me, *mine* in every sense of the word. K is the only one that is thinking clearly right now, and he is the one to hold me back this time.

"You want to tell me why we aren't making our mate happy right now?" I throw a variation of his words right back at him.

"Think with your big *brain, Kai."* K chuckles, knowing that I am just fucking with him right now as a distraction. *"You know we cannot have any sexual relations until after we officially make her our mate. And that takes time."*

Dakota

"Oh my God. If this is what I made him feel like when I traced his mark, I'm surprised he didn't explode. It feels like he's touching my soul. I don't want him to stop. I know words will never be able to explain the feeling. I wish I could show him what I feel." I say to Kota.

She doesn't respond, and I think she's letting me have this moment alone with Kai. Because right now I am on fire from his touch, and the heat is pooling between my legs and I know Kai is the only man that will be able to cause this sensation and be the one to relieve it. Kota is able to somehow keep me from acting on this desire flooding my body. She somehow knows that we need to keep a check on our emotions, even if she doesn't fully understand why.

I begin to hear birds chirping, and I find myself in her forest and when I see the trees appear I'm shocked to find Kota curled up with the form of another wolf, but the form is hazy to me like it has its own fog around it. I can just make out the coloring though—a chocolate and light blonde marble coat—and I realize that this must be Kai's wolf.

Kota looks up at me, and she gives me a lupine smile as she stands. This other wolf follows her, and as they get closer, the wolf becomes clearer, and I somehow know what his name is and I can hear a muffled voice following him.

"Your name is K, isn't it?" I ask.

K nods, and he comes forward, his cold nose brushing my hand, and the muffled voice that follows him becomes as clear as my own voice, and I tear myself from Kota's forest so quickly that it makes my head spin.

CHAPTER TEN
DAKOTA

"*She is so beautiful. I am so lucky to have found someone like her.*"

I slip out from under Kai's hand and I turn to look at him, trying to keep my fear from showing on my face, but even I can smell it drifting in the air.

"What's wrong?" Kai asks, his voice taking on a concerned tone. "Did I do something to upset you?"

"I, uh, I think... I heard your voice." I pause, and for some reason, I whisper, "In my head."

"Is that a bad thing?" He chuckles.

I then remember Dad telling me about how mates can talk to each other through their bond. Kai runs his hand up my back in a gentle caress, and I remember that he is waiting for an answer to his question.

"No. It's not a bad thing. I just wasn't prepared to hear it, that's all."

I feel something flow from him and envelop my mind and body. I can even feel the sensation in my bones. At first, I can't place the feeling, but as I concentrate on it, I understand it.

It's pure love and understanding.

I look into his hazel eyes and study him for a moment. I somehow let him into my mind, and I can *feel* him. Feel his strength, both physical and his own alpha power. He is so sure of himself and what he would be able to do if the need calls for it. To protect me and others weaker than he is. And me? I am so full of confusion and self-doubt that I feel myself almost drowning in insecurities.

"Talk to me, Love. Please share your thoughts with me. I can tell you're trying to keep me out." Kai says through our bond.

He's right, I'm trying to imagine a wall between us so he can't feel what a complete mess I am. But at his gentle prod against my mental wall, I can't help but crumble.

"I don't know the first thing about being a Werewolf, a mate, or an alpha. And here I am being thrown into all three at once. How am I supposed to be what you need when I don't even know what that is?"

Kai

I hear Dakota in my mind for the first time, but I can't celebrate it when I can feel her fear and self-doubt like it's my own. Fear of having her world turned upside down. Fear of finding out she is not a normal human anymore. Fear that she will never be enough for me, and feeling embarrassed for not knowing things that are second nature to other werewolves. I pull her into my chest, and I try to pour my love, understanding, and comfort over her. After a few minutes, I feel her relax in my arms.

"Dakota, please listen well and take to heart what I am about to say. You are in no sense of the word inadequate. You are powerful, strong, and beautiful. And for what you don't know about werewolf law, you have several teachers. Me for one. My parents will be happy to help you, and I'm sure your father will be more than willing to help too. All you have to do is ask." I pull her back enough to look into her beautiful face, and I place a light kiss on her cheek. "I understand that you knew nothing about my world before you met me, but believe me, Love, finding your mate is no accident. My father moved us from Montana, where he had a very large pack under his command, but when the elder told him to move us, or mainly me, to North Dakota, I didn't understand why at first. But I moved to North Dakota so that I could find *my Dakota.*"

She's quiet for a few minutes, so I whisper to her through the bond, *"Please, say something, Love."*

"You're gonna have a lot to teach me and maybe even remind me that I do belong by your side." She pauses, her hands tightening on my forearms like I'm her lifeline. *"I can't even shift forms, Kai."*

I can feel the sense of failure pouring from her side of the bond. *"I can explain to you what needs to happen to be able to phase, as we call it, but ultimately, it needs to be you and Kota on the same wavelength. You have to trust her without a doubt, and without an ounce of fear. But that will all come in due time, Mate of mine."*

I pull out of her mind and I say, "We will take it one day at a time, no matter how long that is. But maybe we can start teaching you tomorrow during the full moon."

"The full moon? Does that make it easier to shi– I mean phase?" Dakota corrects herself to use the correct term.

"See, you're learning already, Babe." I smile at her correction. "Yes, it does make it easier. The moon calls to us and brings our wolves closer to the surface. During the full moon is when Werewolves are at their strongest, so maybe that will trigger your change."

Then we hear a knock on the door, and Mom pops her head in after I'm sure Dad told her everything, and I can feel he's sneaking around too.

"I feel you, Dad. Stop being a weirdo." I chuckle.

"I have to make sure you're being a gentleman. I was your age once, Kai. I know the thoughts that roam in the head of a male."

"And how long ago were you my age, Dad? Like four hundred and fifty years ago? Things have changed." I try to call on his bullshit, but I know he's still spot on from the hardness that is finally starting to fade from my shorts.

I just hear Dad's chuff in response.

"Hello Kai, I was just checking in on you two. Tobias told me you and your mate were talking in here." Mom looks at Dakota, who is still tangled in my arms. "My name is Coraline, Sweetheart. It's so nice to meet you."

Dakota turns in my arms to face my mother, but I never let go of her waist. Part of me feels like if I do she will disappear.

"It's an honor to meet you, Ma'am." Dakota says with a smile.

"We are perfect, Mom. Just getting to know one another."

I see Dakota's marking peeking out from her shirt, and I can't help myself when I run my thumb over her marking. She shivers in response, and I feel her enter my mind with ease.

"Oh, you're bad. So, so bad, Fido."

I laugh out loud, and Mom looks at us with confusion while Dad pushes into my room and looks wildly between us.

"You heard her thoughts, son?"

I gather myself, and I look at my father. "Yes, Alpha." I chuckle. "I heard her thoughts. Loud and clear."

Dakota sits next to me, her face going three shades of red, and I pull her back into my chest and whisper in her ear, "Don't worry, Love. That comment will forever be between you and me."

I go in to nuzzle her neck, but all laughter fades from me when she pulls back from my embrace again with a look of fear on her face, and my body freezes at her movement.

CHAPTER ELEVEN
DAKOTA

I feel Kai's nose press into my neck and my brain goes from, 'This is hot' to, 'Oh shit his parents are watching us' and I pull back from his embrace. The silence that fills the room after I move away from him is so loud that it makes my ears ring. When I see Kai's face and the hurt that fills his eyes, I realize with clarity what I did...again.

"Oh God, no. Please, Kai, don't give me that look." I plead, but then I let my alpha power flow through the room. "Please hear me out. I did not reject you. I will *never* reject you. I just didn't want you to kiss me in front of your parents. That's all."

I feel Kai relax at my promise, and I know he can feel the truth in my words.

"How about we have some lunch, you two?" Coraline offers.

"That sounds like a good idea, Darling," Tobias croons. "Kai, please get dressed and meet us in the dining room. Dakota, you can come with us."

I give Kai a small smile before I stand up and follow the two alpha's out of my mate's bedroom. Once we reach the bottom step, Coraline branches off to the kitchen while Tobias beckons for me to follow him into the dining room. It's a naturally lit room with a large bay window in the center of the wall that faces the street. The table is a warm cherry color and long enough to hold eight chairs comfortably. Tobias sits at the head of the table much like my father does, within easy sight of the main door. I leave the chair to his right free for Coraline, so I take the second chair to the left, where I know Kai will sit next to his father.

Coraline comes in a few minutes later with Kai on her heels, which he is now dressed in a gray t-shirt and a pair of black jeans. He sits a bowl of salad down in the middle of the table while Coraline sets a platter of steak and eggs in front of Tobias.

"You are very strong for a half-werewolf, do you know that, Dakota?" Tobias says as he fills his and Coraline's plate.

I turn to look at him, but again I can only get my eyes to look just to the right of his. "So I've been told. I still have to say I don't fully understand what that means. How did I get so strong?" I ask while Kai mirrors his father's motions, filling his plate and then mine, but I don't think much of it. "From what my father told me, he was a Beta from his last pack." I pause as something in the flow of Tobias' power tells me he wants me to challenge him. I find myself grinning as I say. "So how can a half-breed like me make myself as strong as you?"

I make my power pulse somehow, and I look Tobias right in the eye and hold his stare until Kota finally makes me break it. I hear both Kai and Coraline gasp at my little stunt, and my mate's arms tighten around my shoulders in preparation for retaliation from his father.

"You're going to get us killed if you keep doing that." Kota scolds.

"If it was any other alpha maybe, but I can tell Tobias likes it, he thinks it's funny." I say as I proudly take a bite of my steak.

"I like her, Kai. She's feisty." Tobias laughs.

"You mean you are okay with her looking you in the eye?" Kai asks with disbelief coloring his voice.

"I know she means it as no challenge. But not many can meet your old man's eye, even with challenging intent." Tobias replies.

After lunch is over and Coraline insists she and Tobias will take care of the dishes, Kai and I go back up to his room and collapse into the LoveSac again. I snuggle into his side while my hand rests on the left side of his chest. After a few minutes, Kai takes a breath, and he pulls me back enough to look me in the eye.

"Can you tell me again what happened yesterday with this Jeffrey guy?"

I nod as I slide my hand up his shirt in the hopes that this little bit of skin-to-skin contact will help me stay calm enough to recount the event and for Kai to stay calm enough to listen.

We don't realize how much time has passed as I'm telling my story until we hear a knock on the bedroom door and Coraline pops her head in.

"I am sorry to cut this chat short, but I think it's time you take your mate home, Kai. Have you two noticed the time?" Coraline asks.

Kai and I both look out his window, and we see that it's already getting dark out.

"Wow, time flies when you are making up with your mate." I say with a smile.

Saying terms like alpha, mate, beta, and pack are still foreign on my tongue, but I have to get used to them soon since they are going to be a big part of my life now.

"Yes, it does, Babe. Let me walk you over." Kai says as he stands then offers me his hand to help me to my feet.

"Oh, Dakota, before you go, do you think your parents, or at least your father, will join us tomorrow for the full moon? Maybe we can help you phase for the first time." Tobias asks.

"I'm sure Dad will love that. Thank you." I say.

Kai takes my hand and leads me from his room and downstairs into the living room. He then actually walks me across the street just as a Civic pulls up to my house. I see Quilla jump out of what I now understand is her Uber, and she walks over to me.

"You are just leaving his house?" Quilla whispers as she is passing Kai, so I know he hears every word.

I roll my eyes at my friend as she stands by my side, and a sly smile plays at the corner of my lips. "This afternoon was *amazing.*" I croon.

"Careful, Love, or I'll take you back over and make sure your night is just as *amazing.*" Kai says as he leans in to kiss the tip of my nose.

Quilla lets out a little squeak as she dashes into the house.

"You better get inside before I make that fake promise a reality."

Heat blooms in my stomach, and I nod as I walk in behind Quilla. I look back over my shoulder, and Kai is still waiting in the driveway for me to close the door.

"Possessive much?" I deadpan.

"Yes. Please go in so I know you are safe." Kai prods gently.

I give him a smile and a small wave goodbye as I close the door behind me. When I enter the house, the smell of Mom cooking spaghetti in the kitchen fills my nose as I run over to the dining room to peek out through the window. I silently watch Kai walk across the street to his house, and just as he is about to open his front door, I enter his mind.

"Dream of me tonight."

"Always, from here on out, my Love."

I smile as he walks inside, and I let the curtain close as Quilla walks in the dining room.

"So how'd it go? What *didn't* you two do?" Quilla asks while wiggling her eyebrows.

"All we *did* was talk, Quilla. Nothing more." I say.

Then I see Dad pull into the driveway, and he walks into the foyer, and his eyes lock on Quilla and me.

"Oh good. You're both here. Quilla, I want to talk to you about what I think you are and what you mean to every wolf you may meet." Dad says.

"What do you mean, 'what Quilla is'? Is she a Were too?" I ask as I follow Dad to the dining room table, that seems to be our regular meeting and info-dumping place.

"No, she's not. But she's an important part of a pack. Something I don't think we've seen in about a hundred and twenty years." Dad says.

"What am I, Mr. Shade?" Quilla asks.

I smell her fear begin to gather in the air, so I go over and place a hand on her shoulder and give it a light squeeze.

"Hey, at least you're not a Were and have to worry about another form inside of you." I try to lighten the mood.

Quilla smiles a bit and looks back at my father. "Okay, lay it on me, Mr. Shade."

"You, Quilla, are what we call a Tamer. At first, I didn't put two and two together but over the years since you have been friends with Dakota, I have noticed traits of a Tamer in you, but since I didn't know that

Dakota had inactive Were blood in her, I didn't think anything of it." Dad says.

"What is a *Tamer* and why do you think I am one of them?" Quilla asks.

Dad smiles and takes her hand in his. I watch as he and Quilla sit there for a moment. Quilla absentmindedly runs her thumb over the back of Dad's hand, and he releases a contented sigh.

"I've forgotten how good a Tamer feels. Even with a wolf having a mate, it's still different." Dad sighs. "A Tamer, as the name implies, helps to 'tame' the wolf within with a simple touch." He explains. "This is especially helpful for wolves who have not found a mate or have lost one. It keeps the wolf from spiraling into darkness and out of control, or Feral as we call it; and makes us strong again, when we are on the same wavelength with our inner wolf. Over the years I have noticed that when Dakota has been stressed over something and her mother or I couldn't help her, you have been the one that could calm her."

Dad gives us a few minutes to process this information, and Quilla is the first to break the silence.

"At least now I know what it is about me that helps to calm you down, Dakota." She says while staring at her hands.

I give her another light squeeze on her shoulder and offer her a warm smile. "Hey, no matter what, you are still my best friend. Nothing has changed between us."

She lifts her head, looking at me, and gives me a small smile. "You're right. We just finally understand what we are to one another."

"I do have more I need to tell you girls." Dad interrupts.

I hear the seriousness in his tone, and it makes me step closer to Quilla. As if my body can protect her from his words.

"Like I said, Tamers are rare. So, we need to protect you just as much as Dakota right now," Dad tells Quilla.

"Why, who would mean her harm?" I ask.

Dad looks at me, and I see his eyes widen in shock as his head starts to bend to the right, almost exposing his neck to me. I finally realize that my alpha power is flowing from me, demanding to know how I can keep Quilla safe.

"Sorry, I don't quite know how to turn that off yet." I say as I will my power to fade from the air.

"It's okay, Dakota. You will learn soon." Dad says as he shakes off the effect of my power. "I think we are going to have to protect her from Jeffrey. If he's as old as I think he is, then I may know the reason he's going after Dakota."

"Wait, how old are you, Dad?" I ask.

"Do you want to know the answer to that, Sweetheart?" Dad asks with a crooked smile.

I think for a moment, and then I know I have to face this possibility sooner or later. So might as well be with family first. "Yes, I do."

"Okay. I am one hundred and three years old."

I look at him when I hear this. My father doesn't look a day over forty-five. Mom comes out of the kitchen, wipes her hands on a dish towel, and walks over to my father.

"I know Dakota. I was just as shocked as you are when I found out how old your father was. He was eighty-two when we met." Mom smiles as she kisses him soundly on the lips.

Last week that would have grossed me out, to see my parents show affection like this. But now that I know the feeling of being a mate, I understand the blessing that it is. My father had to wait eighty-two years before he found Mom, and with me and Kai, we only had to wait twenty. This makes me wonder how old Jeffrey is, and even though I dread the answer, I force my throat to voice the question.

"Dad, how old do you think Jeffrey is?"

He sighs before saying, "I think he's at least three hundred-and-forty."

"Shit. That old huh? Then why is he on a college campus?" I ask, but as soon as the question leaves my lips I already know the answer, and it twists my gut.

"He's trying to find a mate to bond with. Be it a Were or human, he doesn't care."

"Exactly, just as long as they are eighteen per Werewolf law and human law that's all he cares about," Dad growls.

Then I feel Quilla's fear fill the air around her, and I kneel in front of her to get her attention. "Quilla?" I begin, but she cuts me off.

"So that's why I'm in danger. If he finds out I'm a Tamer, he can use me to calm his wolf and make him strong enough to be able to hurt Kai and Dakota." She says her eyes are filled with fearful tears.

"Hey." I begin, pushing my alpha power over her, willing her to look me in the eye. She must feel the command because she lifts her eyes, and I see my own reflecting back at me, glowing a bright blue. "Listen to me, Quilla. No one is going to get near you. You will not be a toy for this sick, twisted, wanna-be alpha. I don't know if I can do this, but you are *my* Tamer, and *no one* is going to take you from me."

I push my power over her again, and she closes her eyes as if taking in the promise I made to her through that invisible power flowing through her soul.

"Okay, Chica. I believe you," Quilla says as she gives me a shaky, yet genuine smile.

"Dakota, can you and Kai talk through your mate bond yet?" Dad asks.

"Yes, we can."

"You may be able to do the same with Quilla. Especially since you are an alpha and should be able to make new connections to those you view as part of your pack," Dad says.

"Really?" I ask in shock, then disappointment that I again failed at being a good alpha flares in my gut, but I immediately feel Kai's drowsy presence in the back of my mind and that feeling fades in an instant.

"That's my Little Alpha. I don't know what you are talking about that would make you feel that way, but stop it. Again, you are learning everything in such a short amount of time that others learn over years. Just take it one minute at a time, Love."

"Thank you, Kai. I'm sorry if I woke you." I respond.

"Don't be sorry. I will always be here when you need me." Kai says.

I swear I feel his hand caress my cheek, and I can't help the sigh that follows. I hear Dad clear his throat, and my eyes snap open as my cheeks turn two shades of red, and I hear Kai's laughter in my mind.

"Yeah, I'll absolutely take that as a yes that you can talk to him." Dad grins.

"Oh, Nathan, give her a break. It's a weird thing to get used to." Mom scolds him.

"You're still not fully used to it, Lori," Dad says with a cocky smile that I almost never see on his face, and his eyes shine bright for a moment.

"Nate! Don't you dare, wolf." Mom squeals while smacking at her ass.

"Oh God, Dad. Come on!" I can't help it this time. Mate or not, I do not want to see my father or his wolf grope my mother.

He laughs and puts his hands up in surrender. "Okay, okay. We'll behave." He says with a wink, and he must say something to my mother because her face turns as red as mine was when Kai was touching me.

"Hey, focus!" I snap my fingers, and my power pulses for a moment. All play instantly leaves Dad's face, and he straightens in his chair.

"I'm sorry, Alpha." He says as he bends his neck to me.

"Now, how can I make a connection with Quilla?" I ask.

CHAPTER TWELVE
DAKOTA

"Do you remember how you connected with Kai?" Dad asks.

"Yeah, Kota found K, Kai's wolf, and brought him to me. But how can I do that with Quilla? She's not a wolf." I ask.

"It is a little different, but not much." Dad says. "If Kota found Kai's wolf, then she should be able to find something in Quilla to gr,ab onto."

I nod and I feel that Kota is ready to try and help me connect with Quilla.

"Are you ready for this?" I ask her. "If you aren't, just tell me. I know this was a lot to hear tonight." I pause for a moment. "It's okay if you want to wait."

"Why? Will this help us to talk to each other through this connection?" Quilla directs the question to Dad.

"This will allow you two to be able to talk to one another without having to use your phone. So in case something happens and you need to be able to get a hold of the other, you can with no issues." Dad explains.

Quilla looks at me, and I can tell for the first time in our friendship I am the one she is looking to for comfort. I take a note from Kai and what he did with me before we connected, and I push what I think is my full alpha power over her. To show her that she is safe with me and that I love her just like I did yesterday before everything went to the loony bin. I can tell she feels every ounce of what is flowing around the room, and she smiles her first genuine smile since she came over this evening.

"Okay. Let's do this."

I nod once, and I take Quilla's hand in mine, and when I close my eyes, I call on Kota so she can be closer to the surface, to be able to search for whatever she needs to find in Quilla to connect us. When I open my eyes again, I know they are glowing eerie blue.

"Ready?" I ask.

Quilla nods, her voice filling with confidence again. "Ready."

"Okay, girls, now both of you close your eyes and relax." Dad instructs.

"Kota, do you know what you're looking for?" I ask.

"No, but I didn't know what I was looking for when I found K. So I'm just going to try to hunt for something in Quilla that we can connect to." Kota says.

After a few minutes, no connection forms between me and Quilla. I am almost about to call it a night when I get an idea. I remember that before I was taken to Kota's forest, I was thinking that I wanted to be able to let Kai know what his touch felt like to me. So, I wonder if Quilla and I think of the same thing, if that will help us make the connection.

"Hey Dad, do you think that if Quilla and I think about the same thing we can start the connection that way?" I ask. "That was something similar to what happened this afternoon with Kai. I wanted to be able to talk to him more privately and be able to share my feelings with him, and the thing that connected us was our wolves. So, if Quilla and I think about the same thing together, do you think Kota can find that and make the connection?"

"I don't see why it couldn't work." Dad says.

"You want to try that Quilla?" I ask.

"Yeah, what did you have in mind?"

I take a moment to think about something in our lives that both of us wouldn't have an issue thinking about, and then it hits me.

"How about we think about the time we first met in grade school?" I ask, smiling ear to ear.

Quilla's smile matches mine as she takes my hands in hers and says, "That's perfect."

Then we both close our eyes.

I think back to my first few days in the first grade. Honestly, now that I think of it, I always tried to lead whatever group I was in. I would try to divide up the tasks between everyone in the group and tell them what I thought would be the best way to get it done. My classmates would always complain and tell me that I was way too bossy, and they didn't like working or playing with me. But one little girl with braided pigtails in a frilly pink jean jumper would always tag along with no complaints. She didn't talk much, so I never got her name at first.

During recess the following week, I was playing near the swing set, and I noticed my classmates wanted to swing as well. I was trying to get everyone to line up in terms of age, youngest to oldest, so everyone would have a turn on the swings and be happy. I realize I was leading the 'pack' again now that I understand what I was doing back then.

The kids, though, did not understand, and they were tired of my bossiness. The oldest of the boys and girls started to throw rocks, sticks, and dirt at me. Then another boy rushed up and shoved me to the ground, kicking dirt into my face. I can feel tears begin to sting my eyes as I wonder why they don't want me as a leader. Why don't they like order?

Then after a few moments, I hear the boy that shoved me to the ground cry out in pain. I open my eyes to find him clutching his shin with tears rolling down his cheeks, staring at someone in front of me. I look up and I notice a plaid green and yellow dress, braided pigtails, and glasses glinting in the sunlight. It's the little quiet girl that is the only one that seems to want to be around me. She's the one that just kicked that other kid's leg.

She then starts to throw rocks at the other kids as she yells, "Stop being mean to her!"

I am shocked that someone actually stood up for me, and it was this little quiet girl who showed she cared. The other kids finally give up, and the girl helps me to my feet, dusting the dirt and sticks from my back. I turn around to face this girl, and she has a slight smile playing on her lips, like she knew she did a bad thing, but yet she's glad to have helped a friend.

"What's your name?" I finally ask.

"Quilla Rose."

"I remember that day so well." I think to my present self and push the thought toward Kota at the same time. *"That was the first day that I found a true friend."*

"Yeah. It was a good day."

My eyes fly open as I hear the chuckle of what I swear was Quilla's voice in my head at my words. My friend still has her eyes closed, so I decided to try and find that voice again.

"Quilla? Open your eyes."

Her eyes fly open and lock onto mine as fear and shock flow over her features.

"Quilla, do you hear this? If you do, all you need to do is think of me and then what you want to say." I explain.

"Yes, I hear you."

When I hear Quilla's timid voice in my mind, I jump up from my chair with a bright smile and pull her into a tight hug before pushing her back at arm's length to look her over again, making sure she's okay.

"This is amazing. It's weird to feel you in my head when I talk to you, but it's still cool." Quilla says.

"Just imagine what we can do on tests now!" I exclaim. *"Question ten, is the answer C?"* I say through our new bond.

Quilla laughs out loud while shaking her head. "You are so bad, Chica."

"What? You can't blame me for tryin'."

I feel the sensation of happiness flow from my father from my accomplishments, and it warms my heart to know that I was finally able to do something right in this new world.

Later that night over a dinner consisting of grilled steak, mashed potatoes, and green beans, I tell my parents and Quilla how Kai and I made up and made our mental bond.

"Oh, and I'm guessing the full moon is tomorrow?" I ask as I take a sip of water.

"Yes, it is." Dad sighs while rubbing at his forearm. "I can already feel the pull of it. Makes my skin so tight and itchy."

"Well, Kai's father, Tobias—"

"Wait. Kai's father is Tobias. *The* Tobias Huntington?" Dad asks in shock.

"Yeah... why?" I ask casually.

"It's just Tobias is the alpha to one of the largest packs in the States, aside from Texas, of course."

"Oh yeah, I know. He is no joke. Even my little, inexperienced mind can feel the power coming from him." I take a bite of my steak and say as I chew, "But I can still look him in the eye."

I hear Dad's fork clatter onto his dish, his brown eyes widening to saucers while glowing brightly in shock.

"What did you just say?" Dad asks slowly as if he's afraid to hear the answer.

I know what he's referring to, so I decide to play dumb. "I said, I know his alpha power is no joke."

"Not that, you *know* what I'm talking about." Dad snaps.

For an instant, I feel his power roll across the table, and it actually makes me and Kota want to back up from him. Whether I like it or not, his power is telling me that at this instant he is the alpha of this house and I am to answer his question without sass.

"That I can look him in the eye." I say, but it's more of a shy question.

"You're telling me that you looked an alpha, no, *The* alpha of Montana, in the eye and he didn't declaw you?!" Dad shouts.

"No. He actually found it funny." I say. "He told me that it's even hard for those who want to challenge him to look him in the eye."

"Oh Great Luna, save me." Dad groans. "My daughter in what, only forty-eight hours found out she is one, a half-Were, two, she's an alpha, three she's mated to the son of one of the strongest alphas known and four she can look said alpha in the eye and walk away? Do I have all that right, Lori?" Dad asks in rapid succession with worry hitching his voice near the end.

"Yeah, you're right, Sweetheart," Mom says with a smile, then while rubbing his back, she adds, "You always told her to go for the best or nothing."

Dad stares daggers at her and growls, "You're not helping, Lori."

Mom rolls her eyes and looks back at me. "Anyway, Dakota. What did Tobias say about tomorrow?"

"Oh damn, and she calls him by his first name." Dad whines and drops his head in his hands.

I laugh at Dad's reaction and I look to Mom when I answer her, "He wants you *and* Dad to come over tomorrow to join him under the full moon." I say, then I feel my smile fade as I add, "He wants to see if the full moon will help me phase. I can't do that yet."

Dad's head snaps up at my admission, and his stressed features change in an instant to pure concern and hurt at my words.

"You still can't phase, Dakota?"

I shake my head and I take a breath as I push my own alpha power over the table to fill the room.

"No, I can't. So when you think I don't know *exactly* what and how important *Alpha* Tobias is, I do. I kept thinking this was some big, colossal joke. A huge slap in the face that I, a half-breed, was the mate to the son of the most powerful alpha in the world. So believe me, when I first met Tobias, I gave him all the respect he deserved, because I knew deep down he could make my life a living hell if he wanted to. But when he told me that Kai didn't want to see me, I somehow knew he was testing me. My determination. I think he *knew* what I would be capable of, and he was trying to help me grab onto it." I say.

Dad stands up from his chair and kneels before me, pulling Mom with him, both acting as a united front.

"Spoken like the true alpha you are, my sweet, beautiful daughter. Your mother and I would be honored to spend time tomorrow under the full moon with you and yours."

This time when Dad fully bares his neck to me, I don't stop him. I somehow know this needs to be done between us. I try to pull back my alpha power so he and Mom can stand and take their seats again.

After a few minutes of quiet, all of us taking in what just happened, I can't take the solemn silence anymore.

"So, how about the weather we're having, huh?"

At first, everyone is looking at me like I lost my marbles, then Quilla is the first to laugh, followed by Mom, then finally Dad while shaking his head and clapping me on the shoulder.

"You always know how to control the room, Honey."

"Yeah, turns out it's in my blood." I say, waving my hand.

I watch as the seriousness fades from the air and it's replaced by the laughter of my family.

CHAPTER THIRTEEN
DAKOTA

The next morning I wake up before my alarm goes off, and I can tell something is different than it was last night. Like Dad explained it, it feels like my skin is so tight that if I move too quickly, I may burst open at the seams. I can also feel that Kota is just under the surface. Like she's so close to the front of my mind and pushing up against mental glass.

I roll out of bed and walk into the hall bathroom to get my shower, but when I look in the mirror, I freeze at what I see looking back at me. My eyes are already glowing a bright eerie blue, and I instantly reach out for Kai. I can tell he's already awake as well, so I push myself further in his mind.

"Good morning, Love."

"Morning." I reply, and I can tell my voice wavers a bit from worry.

"Can you show me what you're seeing? Just imagine what you want to show me, and I should be able to see it as well." Kai coaches.

I picture my reflection, and I push that image toward him, and I am rewarded with a growl that warms my whole body. But the voice that answers me isn't Kai, and I turn my head to find my father looking at my reflection in the mirror.

"So the pull of the moon does affect you now."

I take in my father's appearance, and I notice his eyes are also glowing a bright golden brown, and I turn around to face him head on.

"How did I not ever notice this growing up?" I ask.

"Your mother and I did a lot of planning." He sighs. "I would make sure I got up before you did, or when you got home from school you either had Quilla over or your mother would keep you distracted," Dad explains. "Remember one time I started wearing sunglasses and told you I had a bad headache and the glasses helped with the light?"

"I do remember that. I also remember that one night you were leaving for a 'last-minute work meeting.'" I say with air quotations. "I remember begging you to take me, and you had this look come over your face that said you wanted to, but you didn't. You said you couldn't take me." I say with sorrow filling my voice. "Why didn't you tell me sooner, Dad?"

He sighs, "I wanted to. Believe me. There were so many times I wanted to tell you everything, but." He pauses as he brushes the hair out of my face with a loving, fatherly touch. "But I wouldn't have been able to handle it if I scared you for what I am." Dad whispers.

His words seem to unlock something buried deep inside me. A long-forgotten memory.

The image of me at about four years old comes to mind. I'm playing on my bedroom floor with a few of my little Polly Pocket dolls. I remember seeing this medium, golden blonde, gangly puppy sitting next to me, and she wanted to play with me too. At first, I liked this puppy; she was fun and rambunctious, but then Dad opens my door to get me for dinner, and something about him spooks this pup, and she snarls at him then disappears into thin air.

I don't see the little puppy until later that night when I'm in bed and trying to go to sleep. She's playfully wagging her tail trying to get my attention.

"Do you want to play with me?" The puppy asks.

"No! Go away! You were mean to my daddy! You're a bad doggie." I say as my little hand smacks her on her little black nose.

She whines as she evaporates into smoke before me, and that was the last time I ever saw that puppy until recently.

"Dakota. Dakota!" Dad shouts. "Are you okay?"

As Dad's words bring me back to the present, I feel silent tears streaming down my face. "Oh my God. It's my fault we can't phase. It's all my fault." I sob, and I don't block my mind from Kai in time before I feel his terror mingle with my own.

Kai

I feel Dakota's terror and heartache like it's my own before I feel her mental walls lock into place. I fly out of my room, down the stairs, and out the front door, not even bothering to change from the shorts and shirt I slept in the night before. I do have the sense to at least knock on her front door and impatiently wait for it to open. A woman that looks and smells like her mother answers the door and lets me in where I meet up with her father in the middle of the living room.

"What is wrong with my mate?" I try to desperately keep the growl and my power under control. "It felt like she was heartbroken?" I ask in confusion since I have no idea why I would feel this from her.

The man in front of me must finally realize who I am and feel my alpha power that I am slowly losing my mental grip on, and he bares his neck to me in submission while kneeling on one knee before me.

I take a calming breath and reel my power back. "Please spare me the pleasantries right now, Beta. Tell me what is wrong with my mate."

He stands as he says, "We were just talking about how she never saw the signs of the full moon on me, and she asked me why I never showed her what I was sooner. When I told her I didn't want her to be scared of me, she went blank and then she came back and was saying it's her fault that she and Kota can't phase. Then she ran into her room."

"Please, take me to her." I ask.

He nods and leads me to her door without a word.

"Thank you–?" I ask, drawing out the question in a way to have him tell me his name.

"It's Nathan. Nathan and Nate Shade." He says as again he bares his neck to me.

"Thank you for bringing me to Dakota, Nathan. Now, if you please, I would like some privacy with my mate."

He nods as he joins his own mate at the base of the stairs.

I turn my head back to Dakota's door and I softly knock on the white-painted wood. "Dakota, Baby, please let me in. I want to help you."

After a few heartbeats, I hear in my mind, *"I'm sorry I worried you, Kai, but please, I need you to let me talk to Kota alone for a while."*

"Please let me in to help you with this." I beg.

"I'm sorry, but this is something that Kota and I have to deal with. But thank you for coming and being willing to help me, Kai." She says, and she pushes her love and appreciation through the bond, and I feel a little bit more relaxed at her emotions.

"Okay. I understand. I will be right downstairs if you need me."

"Okay, Babe." Dakota chuckles.

Dakota

I leave Kai's mind as I lie down on my bed and close my eyes. I think about Kota and her forest, and before I know it, I hear the birds singing a pleasant song around me and the gentle bubbling of a brook nearby. I open my eyes and see the familiar blondish-brown wolf lying in the grass and taking in the bright, warm sun against her fur. I slowly approach her and sit down a few feet from her, but I keep my head down while fiddling with a piece of lush, green grass.

"Kota." I whisper.

I see her turn her head toward me out of the corner of my eye, her ears flicking to the side and forward again to listen to me, but I keep my focus on the blade of grass between my fingers.

"Dakota, please look at me," Kota urges.

I don't move at first, but when I feel her cold, wet nose tap my cheek, I can't help but look over at her. Look into blue eyes that are so much like my own, it feels like I'm looking into a mirror.

"I'm sorry." I say as tears begin to fall. "It's all my fault. I shut you out. I didn't understand what you were to me back then. I am so, so sorry."

"Please don't cry, Dakota." Kota says as she licks the salty tears from my cheeks. *"It's just as much my fault too. I should have never snarled at our father like I did. But I didn't understand his wolf at that time. And it scared me at first."*

I look Kota in the eye and I pull her into me, putting my forehead against hers and running my fingers through her coarse fur.

"Do you forgive me for pushing you away?" I ask.

"Only if you forgive me for scaring you." Kota counters.

I playfully push Kota away with a laugh. "Don't play alpha with me, missy. You and I are equals."

We look at one another again, and at the same time, we say into the other's mind.

"I forgive you."

Kota lets out a little yip as she bends down onto her front paws with her butt and tail high in the air, looking every bit a puppy at play. I laugh at her and try to chase her, but she dashes off with a sharp and playful bark. I try to run after her into the forest, but she's too nimble and fast for me to keep up.

I turn for a moment, and I lose track of her, and for an instant, I feel like I've lost her all over again. I hear a twig snap behind me, and as I turn around, I see Kota bound out of the tree line and tackle me to the forest floor, pinning me down with her paws on my shoulders.

"Got ya." She chuffs.

"Sneaky brat. Get off me." I mumble.

Kota lifts her snout to bare her teeth and bites at the air just before my nose. I would be scared if I didn't see the amused lupine glint in her eyes. She then backs off my body, and I sit up to look at her.

"So, we good?"

"Yes. Now let's get back to our mate." Kota croons as she shakes out her coat.

I stand to my feet, but I don't make a move to follow her. She turns her head while cocking it to the side in a silent question.

"Do you think we will be able to phase tonight?"

"I don't know. We will have to see," Kota says. *"But I don't think it will be from us not being connected. This is the closest I have ever been to you."*

"Yeah, I know. I feel the same way." I say as I kneel down to her and give her a loving embrace before I let myself fade from her forest and come back to my bedroom.

CHAPTER FOURTEEN

DAKOTA

I finally emerge from my room, and when I descend the stairs, I see Mom and Dad sitting on the couch, and Kai is standing in front of the window. Dad is the first to notice me, and he rises to greet me as I hit the bottom step.

"Dakota, are you okay?"

"Yes, I'm fine now. I'm sorry I scared you. All of you."

Kai walks over from his place by the window, and when he approaches me, Dad quietly moves to the side. Kai then wraps his arms gently around my waist, pulling me close to his chest. I rest my head against him while he rubs soothing circles down my back.

"I'm glad you're okay now, Baby," Kai whispers.

I pull back enough to look into Kai's bright hazel eyes and give him a soft smile. "Yeah, I'm okay now. I figured out why Kota and I never bonded when I was younger. Since I'm half-Were, I had to allow her to co-exist with me, and that never happened. One day when you came in to get me for dinner, Dad, Kota saw or smelled your inner wolf, and she got scared and snarled at it." I take a breath as I continue to explain what happened. "I told her later that night that she was a bad puppy." I say in a young version of my voice near the end.

Kai snorts at my voice, and I smack him on the chest. "Hey, it was a memory from when I was like four. So bite me."

"I'd be glad to, but would you want your parents to see that?"

I hear Kai's sultry voice in my mind, and warmth flows through my body, filling me in all the right places.

"Careful, Love. You don't want your father to pick up on the subtle change in your scent, do you?"

I freeze because I am an arm's length away from Dad and I can pick up on that subtle change in Kai's scent. It's muskier, but not his wolf's scent. I take an involuntary step away from Kai, and I hear his dark chuckle in my mind.

"I love the color red on you, Baby."

"I thought wolves couldn't see the color red?" I shoot back.

"That's only domesticated dogs. But I could be blind and I'd still know the color red on you."

"I'm sorry for scaring Kota when you both were younger." Dad says, interrupting my mental conversation/tease session with Kai.

"It's not your fault, Dad. Don't blame yourself."

"Are you okay to go to school today, Dakota?" Mom asks.

"Yeah, I'm good. Kota and I made up, and we are on good terms now. I even feel her more than I did this morning."

"Then you will need sunglasses today too, Love," Kai says.

I remember my own glowing eyes as I see Dad's and Kai's shining brightly in my direction.

"Can't we just say we have contacts in?"

"That would fool the humans, maybe, but the other Were's, not so much." Kai says.

"So? They can smell us anyways, can't they?" I ask.

"Well, yes. But blending in is still better than broadcasting it to the entire campus."

Then, I feel a power roll through the house, and I know it's Tobias before he knocks on the door, and I feel a wicked smile form on my lips.

Catching my devious smile, I feel Kai slip into my mind. "*What is going on in that mind of yours, Love?*"

"*Nothing, oh wolf of mine.*" I croon.

Kai turns to open the door to let his father in, and I see his assessing gaze instantly go from Kai to me with just a flicker of fear in his shining brown eyes.

"Kai, is your mate alright? Your mother said you went rushing out of the house while I was on the phone." Tobias asks.

Out of the corner of my eye, I see Dad and Mom instantly kneel down on one knee before Tobias, both baring their necks to him in submission. Tobias simply nods at them and gestures with his right hand for them to rise.

"I'm fine now, Tobias. I'm sorry to have worried you too. But thank you for asking about me, I appreciate it." I say, keeping my eyes to the right of the alpha in front of me.

I can feel Dad's eyes burning into the back of my head, and I can feel his apprehension in the air like it's a tangible thing.

"I'm glad to hear that. Please try not to scare your mate like that again," Tobias requests.

I grin as I look Tobias in the eye. I hear my father's sharp intake of breath as I say, "Duly noted, Tobias. If I need to have a mental breakdown, I'll be sure to let you know beforehand."

"Dakota!" Dad scolds. "I sincerely apologize for her brash behavior, Alpha Huntington. I never–" Dad begins, but Tobias' booming laugh fills the living room, leaving Dad looking shocked and confused.

"No need to apologize for anything, Beta. Your daughter is something else. But I know deep down she does know her place in our little pack." Tobias says.

"Not a lot of people have the guts to even try to look me in the eye, so I like the change of pace your daughter brings to my life now." His tone changes to the alpha I am sure he is well known for as he says, "But know this, Beta, your daughter is stronger than you think. She just has to come into her power on her own."

"Thank you, Alpha Tobias. I appreciate that coming from someone of your power." I say with true appreciation and nod my head a bit in his direction.

I feel Kai come up behind me, pulling my back against his chest, and I get the image of our mate markings matching up perfectly underneath our clothes, and it sends a shiver through my body.

"See, I told you that you and I were meant to be together. Dad even knows you'll be a great alpha one day." Kai whispers, his breath tickling the curve of my ear.

I lean my head back on his shoulder, and I take in his scent for the first time. Pine needles and mint. If I thought his voice made me all warm inside, then this scent swirling around me makes me want to melt into him and take in every ounce of him into my soul.

"Are you still going to join us tonight, Dakota? And I do apologize, Beta, I never got your or your mate's name," Tobias asks.

"It's alright, Alpha. My name is Nathan, and this is my mate and wife, Lori," Dad says.

"It's my honor to meet you, Nathan and Lori." Tobias looks at Dad, studying him for a moment, and I can tell Dad does not like his intense stare, but he forces himself to weather the scrutiny.

"I know, my husband and mate is such a looker for a hundred and three, isn't he?" Mom jokes while picking up on Dad's uncomfortable stance.

"Ah, now I see where Dakota gets her spark from." Tobias croons with a lupine smile.

This is the first time that I am watching my parents in a different light. Not just as my mother and father, not as husband and wife, like my human mind wants to think of them as, but as mates. When Dad is starting to lose his confidence in himself on something, then Mom is there to boost him up. The same goes when he feels Mom is being threatened; he rises to protect his mate no matter what. Even if it's against someone who could kill them both, he will fight until his last breath for her.

It's still a good thing that Kai is holding me because I am weak in the knees for an entirely different reason. It's awe for a love so pure that makes me want to sink to my knees and watch the two mates before me.

At Tobias' words about my mother, I watch as my father's eyes darken, even while shining so brightly with the pull of the moon that is still hiding in the sky. If I didn't know Tobias, even I would have perceived his words as a threat.

"Calm yourself, Nathan. I mean no harm to you and yours. I was just making an observation, is all. My apologies if that came off as a threat." Tobias says as he lifts his right arm over his chest, resting his fist over his heart, and bows his head a bit.

"I even picked up on the implication there, Tobias." I snicker.

"Well, my sincerest apologies and to you as well, Lori, mate of Nathan."

"Apology accepted, Alpha." Mom nods.

"I was just trying to place where I would have heard about you, Nathan. Your scent still has something familiar buried deep inside."

I watch as something flickers across Dad and Mom's faces, and she stands next to him, wrapping her arms around his. "That is, respectively, a story for another time, Alpha." Dad says with a hint of sadness in his voice.

"I understand. Just know the offer still stands if you and yours would like to join us tonight." Tobias says. "Son, be sure you are alert today." He adds, facing Kai a moment later.

Kai nods as his father walks out the door, gently closing it behind him. After he leaves, I see Dad deflate a bit, and Mom chuckles as she pats his chest lovingly.

"Alright, you two," She says, pointing to me and Kai, "have class to get to, and you, mister, need to get to work." She says while giving Dad a gentle kiss.

"Your mother's right; we need to get moving before we all are late." Dad says as his eyes shine bright again. "Kai, I would be happy to join you and your alpha's tonight."

"Sounds like a plan, Nathan." Kai grins.

"Kai, is there anything special I should bring over tonight?" Mom asks.

"No, my mother is making a huge potluck for us. We celebrate every full moon with a small party of sorts." Kai says. "Maybe bring a cake if you want to, but it's not necessary."

"Okay. I'll make my famous triple chocolate cake." Mom grins.

Kai nods to her as he takes my hand and we begin to walk for the door, but Mom's voice stops us.

"Uh, Dakota, Kai? You need to get dressed. You both are still in the clothes you slept in."

Shock colors both our faces that we didn't notice.

"I'll pick you up in fifteen minutes?" Kai asks.

I nod and quickly dash up to the bathroom and get ready. And as promised, fifteen minutes later, Kai is waiting next to my Altima, backpack slung over his shoulder, as I walk out my front door.

"Let me drive you, Love," Kai says as he extends his hand for my keys.

"Alright. Thank you." I toss him the car keys, and he opens my door.

I sink into the passenger seat, and Kai takes my backpack from me as he closes my door. He opens the rear driver's side door and puts both backpacks into the back seat before dropping in behind the wheel to take us to school.

The closer we get to the college, I try to keep the worry about what may happen today buried deep in my chest. The one thing that keeps me grounded is knowing I am not going through this alone. I have my mate with me to protect me if I need it.

Chapter Fifteen

LORI

After Dakota walks through the door to go to school with Kai, I turn to Nathan, and I can tell he's still uptight about what Tobias said to me even though he apologized. So, I go over to him and I coax him into pulling my back into his chest. Marking to marking. He instantly relaxes now that we are alone, and he has me in his arms.

"I am in no danger, Nathan. You need to believe it also, Nate." I say, calling to the wolf that is just barely under the surface today.

"I know. I just can't help it, Lori. I *need* to protect you. To keep you safe from anyone that may want to harm you. It's been too long since we've been around other wolves, and I'm terrified again." Nathan says.

I turn in his arms, placing my hands on his chest, tracing the part of his marking that pokes up from the collar of his shirt and runs up his neck.

"It's not gonna be like that again, Nathan. I can tell Tobias is safe. And he is a fair alpha."

I stand on my tiptoes to give my mate a sound kiss on the lips, and I am rewarded with a low growl, deep in his chest, that rattles through my fingers that are still resting against the fabric of his shirt.

"I suggest you stop that if I am to be to work on time." Nathan croons.

"Stop what?" I ask teasingly.

"Lori. Sweetheart, don't tempt an emotionally charged wolf."

I lean in to kiss him again, knowing this will help him get out of his current headspace. I run my hands up his chest and encircle them around his neck as he runs his own hands up my back and strokes where my own mating mark hides under my shirt on my left shoulder blade. His gentle touch sends an electrical heatwave right to my core.

"That will never get old." I gasp.

"Let's see what else never gets old, Mate of ours."

I can tell that Nate is talking to me now. The growl in his voice is a dead giveaway.

I pull away from Nathan's arms as I lead him back to the bedroom. His body trailing after mine in pure hunter mode, and I would feel like prey if the look in Nathan's eyes didn't show every ounce of love this man could muster.

"Oh yes, I forgot with you being *so* old and all, I have to remind you of *certain* things." I tease.

"Let me show you just how age is just a number, Sweetheart."

At Nathan's words, he picks me up and in several quick strides he opens the bedroom door and tosses me on the bed while stripping his shirt, revealing his lean muscular form.

I lean back on my elbows, beckoning him towards me with my index finger, and he gives me a full lupine grin as he slowly crawls up the bed until his body is hovering over mine. He slips his hand under my shirt, trailing his fingers over my side until he is able to lift the shirt from my body, exposing my white, lacy bra. He then leans in closer to me and begins trailing tender kisses down my neck. I bend my head to the side to allow him more access, and Nathan continues his exploration over my throat until his teeth scrape over the sensitive spot where my neck curves into my shoulder, and I gasp at the sensation.

"More." I pant.

While pulling me with him, Nathan sits up enough where he deftly unclasps my bra with one hand, exposing my breasts to him. I watch as his eyes fill with desire, admiration, and love as he bends his head into me, taking my right nipple into his mouth. My head tips back as I feel his tongue swirl and tease the peeked flesh, and it sends a wave of desire to my already hot and aching center. Nathan gently sets me back onto the bed, and I thread my fingers through his hair as he takes the time to explore my other breast.

While never taking his mouth from my skin, I feel Nathan's hand slide down my belly and lower. While I want nothing more than to feel his fingers curl inside me, something deep down demands for more. Not just these teasing touches. When I go to pull at his pants, Nathan growls against my breast.

"So eager." He croons deeply and lazily.

He pulls away for a moment; the loss of his touch, his heat, is like losing a piece of myself, and only he can give it back to me again.

The next thing I know, we have nothing but air between us, and I can almost feel the length of him teasing my core. I try to arch my back to close the distance, but he holds back for what seems like a lifetime before his lips crash into mine.

"Thank the Great Luna that Dakota is out of the house because you are going to be screaming my name, Sweetheart."

Just as Nathan says this, he fills me in one powerful thrust, and that little part of myself that he seemed to take a moment ago, drops back into place deep within my soul as the shape of him fills me with an intoxicating stretch. He then pulls his hips back, leaving just the tip, and then fills me again, and I claw at his back as I wholeheartedly scream his name.

"Oh, Nathan!"

"That's right, Sweetheart. Let me love you like a mate should."

We love like this for a while longer, until it's just barely enough time for Nathan to get ready for work, but he's not ready to let go of me just yet. So he pulls me along with him, and we take a shower together.

After we force ourselves out of the shower and Nathan is just about ready to walk out the door, he pulls me into his arms again and gives me a gentle kiss on the cheek.

"Thank you, Lori. You knew what would make me and Nate get out of our heads."

"Again, Nathan, if I didn't know what made you two tick, then I am failing as a mate. I just needed to make sure you knew that I was safe and that I am safe with you." I gently caress the side of his face. "I don't like the thought of you fighting again, but I know that's something you would have done for me if you thought I was in danger."

His eyes go distant for a moment, but I pull him from that memory with a gentle touch on his shoulder. "Go to work for me, Nathan. Focus on something else for a while. Then let's have a good time tonight under the full moon with Dakota and her new mate. It will make you feel better to be with a pack again."

"You are my pack, Lori."

"You know what I mean, Nathan." I say flatly.

He sighs, knowing what I'm talking about, and nods his head. "Yeah, being within a pack setting will be a good thing."

Nathan gives me a kiss on the cheek and walks out without another word. I go into the kitchen after he leaves, and I make sure I have all the ingredients for my famous cake so I can have it ready before night falls.

Chapter Sixteen

DAKOTA

Once we arrive on campus, and park beside Quilla's empty Sentra, I watch as Kai grabs for his backpack from the backseat, unzips the front pouch, and pulls two pairs of blue lensed aviator sunglasses. When he slips one set onto his face, the lens completely blocks his eyes from my sight.

"Remind me why we need sunglasses again?" I ask in mock ignorance.

Kai pulls his glasses down the bridge of his nose, his left eyebrow arching up in question.

"Oh yeah. The glowing eyes are a dead giveaway that we aren't human, huh?"

"Yeah, just a little bit, Babe." Kai chuckles while handing me the other pair of sunglasses before he exits the car.

I watch through the windshield as he walks around the vehicle and opens the back passenger door to grab our backpacks, slinging them both over one shoulder before opening my door to help me to my feet. Just as he shuts my door, I hear the large, red metal door of the school open behind us, and I see Quilla walking out to join us in the parking lot.

She looks at me, and she takes a step back with a small squeak. "Wow, your eyes are bright today, Dakota."

"So you wouldn't believe me if I said they were contacts?" I ask.

"Yeah... no. Sorry. Not taking that bait, Chica."

"Ha! Told ya, Babe." Kai says while sliding his own glasses back into place.

"Oh, bite me, wolf-boy." I say, and he gives me a devilish smile.

"Wow, Kai. Your eyes are even brighter than Dakota's." Quilla says in shock.

"Hence the glasses. In my high school back home with human students, I just say I have a migraine and they didn't question me. So hopefully it will be the same here." Kai says.

"Oh, I wanted to let you guys know that I have not seen a certain fleabag yet this morning." Quilla says.

"Really? That's kinda shocking." I reply.

"No, not really." Kai begins as we walk toward the school. "You may not be able to pick up on it, Dakota, but my alpha status is just rolling off me. I can't help it today because of the full moon coming and K being so close to the surface. So, any less dominant wolf will have a hard time being around me."

"So, the leader of fleabag's stayed home because he knew you would be at your best?" I ask.

"That's correct." Kai says, pushing a wave of pride at me for coming to that conclusion. "Which is a good thing, because if he did try anything, I don't think I could stop myself from ripping him apart even if I wanted to." Kai ends on a growl.

At hearing this growl in his voice, I somehow know this is also K talking too. I step in front of Kai, making him break his stride, and I place my hand on his chest, right where I know our mating mark hides under his shirt. I feel him relax at my touch, calming him a bit.

"We will get through today. You will not do anything to threaten your safety." I say, and I feel my power pulse in tandem with my words, and even through the glasses, I see Kai's eyes flare brighter for a moment.

"Yes, Love." Kai growls in his own voice again. "You better get to class."

"Yeah, Dakota, let's go," Quilla says as she pulls me by my hand.

"Fine. I'll see you later, Kai." I say as I slip on my own dark shades.

He gives us a small wave as we go in different directions. I keep my glasses on as Quilla and I walk into our first class of the morning and take our seats in the middle of the classroom, just as the professor closes the door to begin her lecture.

"Miss Shade, could you remove the sunglasses, please?" The professor asks as she walks back over to her desk.

I think of the excuse that Kai said earlier and try to use it myself. "I'm sorry, Professor Brown, but I have a migraine this morning, and the glasses help with the fluorescent lighting."

"Okay, Miss Shade," Professor Brown says.

A moment later I hear someone whisper behind me, "I hear her eyes are glowing like some freak."

I would have missed Caleb's words if it wasn't for my heightened hearing. But he probably said it loud enough for me to hear anyway, to get under my skin.

And it works.

"Kota, do you think you can pull back for just a few seconds? I want to put this asshole in his place."

"Yes. But be quick. I won't be able to hold back for long." Kota says.

"That's fine. I just need twenty seconds."

I turn around in my chair and face Caleb, the cocky smile playing on his lips at the thought he's calling my bluff aggravating me even more. I notice he's not wearing glasses today, and his eyes seem normal. If it wasn't for my new, heightened eyesight, I never would have noticed the brown contacts resting in his obnoxious eyes.

"You read too many comics, Caleb. Glowing eyes, really?" I snap.

"Show me then, *Dakota.*" He spits my name as if he's mocking me, knowing full well that my own eyes glow behind my dark shades and trying to catch me in the lie.

"He's a cocky bastard. Make him regret challenging us, Dakota." Kota growls.

I feel her pull back, and I take that moment to lower my glasses enough that I can see my reflection first, and my eyes shift from the bright wolf blue to my normal color before I completely take them down. I look up to Caleb, and I watch with satisfaction as he freezes in his seat. His face morphs from cocky triumph to pure shock and fear.

"Are my eyes glowing, *Caleb*?" I demand.

He recovers a moment later and with a cocky smile and he raises his hands up in surrender as he says, "No, Dakota. They are not."

"Now, why don't you sit back and shut the fuck up."

I feel my alpha power roll from me in waves across the classroom, and a few students subtly lower their heads toward their desks and bare their necks to me. It's enough for me to pick up on, but oblivious to the humans around them. I quickly slip my glasses back on as I feel Kota start to slip toward the front of my mind again. I lean forward in my seat, elbows on the desk in front of me, and act like I am massaging my temple with my index and middle finger, as if yelling at Caleb made my migraine worse.

"If your headache is that bad, Miss Shade, perhaps you should go home and rest." Professor Brown offers.

I look up at her through my glasses, and I then feel Quilla enter my mind.

"Yeah, let's go, Dakota. I don't want to be here with Caleb anymore. What if Jeffrey finally showed up too?"

I feel Quilla's fear as if it's my own, and I think back to what Kai said earlier if Jeffrey did anything stupid.

"Okay. Thank you. Quilla, will you drive me home?" I ask, giving her an out.

"Sure. Let's go." She says while giving Caleb a sideways glance.

As we pass the professor, she barely bends her neck and lowers her head to me as a sign of submission that I am slowly getting used to as an alpha.

"Now, that shocked me." Kota says.

"No way. She's a–?" I begin to ask but don't want to think about just how many more werewolves are hiding among us on campus, with five being in just this one class, including me and Caleb.

Once we make it into the safety of the silent hall, I turn to Quilla. "Wow. I think there are more Werewolves than we thought in this school."

"Really?" Quilla says, then rubs her chin as she thinks for a moment. "Well, that would make sense now that we know what Jeffrey's plan was."

"Come on, let's get out of here." I say.

"Hey, how did you get your eyes to stop glowing when you looked at Caleb?"

"I had Kota pull back from my mind enough to let them go back to normal. But she could only do it for a few seconds."

She nods in understanding as we reach the main door and walk outside, the bright sunshine warming our backs.

"So, you gonna tell Wolf-boy to join us?" Quilla asks.

"Yeah. I was gonna reach out to him once we got in the car. I worried that Jeffrey is here since Caleb is too."

I open the passenger side door to my car and sink into the leather seat while she gets in on the driver's side, and then I reach out to Kai.

"Miss me already, Love?"

His voice is a caress to my heart, and I can't help but smile at the feeling of him in my mind.

"Always, Babe." I begin as I imagine myself rubbing his shoulders to relax the growing uneasiness I feel flowing from him because he's stuck inside a classroom when I can tell all he wants to do is run with his pack.

"Hey, I wanted to let you know that Caleb is here." I feel his attention snap solely to me, and I continue, *"We just had a bit of a showdown in the classroom. Quilla and I left class and are in my car. You want to join us?"*

"Stay put. I'll be right there." Kai growls. *"Besides, I'm getting tired of the mindless drivel here in class anyway."*

I feel him pull away from my mind, and I turn to Quilla.

"He's gonna be right out." I say, and we wait for Kai to come out so we can go home and wait for the full moon to grace the skies tonight.

CHAPTER SEVENTEEN

DAKOTA

As Kai exits the school, he jogs over to my car and opens the passenger door so he can look at me. His eyes roam over my body, and I swallow hard under his heated gaze.

"Are you okay? Did that mutt hurt you?" Kai asks.

"I'm fine, Kai. No one touched me." I say as I pull his hand into mine.

"Let's get you two home before someone does end up getting hurt." Quilla pipes up from the driver's seat.

"Yeah. Good idea." I say.

Kai shuts my door, and he helps Quilla out of the driver's seat and takes her to her own vehicle, making sure she's safe inside before he comes back over to mine and drops into the seat behind the wheel. I notice Kai is still quiet on the way home, and I catch him glancing at me out of the corner of his eye. So, I take his hand and give him a gentle smile.

"What's wrong?"

"It's nothing." Kai says, shaking his head.

"Hey. Tell me. Maybe it's something I can help with."

"I'm just pissed that another wolf tried to challenge you and I wasn't there to kick his ass into submission."

"So you're just itching to find a reason for a fight, huh?" I chuckle.

"Yeah, I guess. And I'm trying to make myself believe that you are alright and not push the boundaries." Kai says as he grips the steering wheel tighter, his knuckles turning white and the leather groaning under his hand.

"What boundaries, Kai?"

He sighs and glances over at me for a few heartbeats before he looks back toward the road.

"You really want to know what's going through my mind right now?" Kai asks, and he glances back at me, his eyes shining so bright I know K is just a whisper away. "What I say may scare you."

I think for a moment, but no matter what he may tell me, I don't think I'll be scared. All I want to know is how I can help him understand that I am safe and no harm has been done to me today by Caleb.

"Tell me. What's going through your mind right now?"

"I want to put my scent on you. I want others to know you are *mine*, and if they hurt you or challenge you in any way, then they are fucking with the wrong wolf's mate, and I will tear them apart *very* slowly." Kai growls.

I take a moment to let his words sink in and I find that I am not the least bit scared of what he just told me.

"That didn't scare me, Kai. I kinda like the thought that you'd protect me that way, if that makes sense." I say while nervously chuckling.

When we pull up to my house a few minutes later, Kai throws the gearshift into park, but I place my hand over his to keep him from moving. "What would you need to do to put your scent on me? Now that sounds interesting." I add while giving him a sultry smile.

He turns to me and he leans in over the center console, his face dangerously close to my neck.

"All I have to do is either let my breath caress your skin, or I could kiss you here." Kai whispers next to my ear, being mindful to keep his breath off my skin for now.

Heat erupts in my veins while my heart hammers in my chest due to his proximity, and I know for a fact he can hear it.

"Which one lasts longer?" I force my throat to form the words.

"They both last about two weeks, but kissing you makes it fun for the both of us." Kai croons.

He lifts the hand off the gearshift, bringing it to the nape of my neck, pressing his fingers into my skin enough for me to understand the silent request not to move.

"Why can't you just make me your mate now?" I ask, trying to keep my head on straight.

Kai sighs while he strokes my neck with the pad of his thumb.

"Per Werewolf law, mates need to still get to know one another before the bonding will take place. It's usually about three months before the ceremony. And that means we cannot have sex until that ceremony, or it's said the bond will have turmoil and hardships for the rest of their lives. After the bond is consummated, that is when the mates will always carry the scent of the other." Kai explains. "But that doesn't mean I can't drive you crazy."

Kai lifts his other hand, and he gently kneads my right breast, teasing my nipple through my shirt with his thumb in soft, tantalizing circles. I can't stop the breathless moan that escapes my throat at his touch or the intense heat that pools in my core.

"So what'll it be, Love?" He asks, his nose nuzzling the soft spot between my neck and shoulder. "Just my breath or a soft, loving kiss for now?"

"I want you to–"

We both jump when we hear someone knocking on the driver's window, and I'm mortified to find that it's Mom. Kai and I jump back from one another, but my ears catch his low growl at being interrupted.

"Why don't you two help with the groceries?" Mom's muffled voice reaches my still red-hot ears.

"Coming." I say, my voice squeaking from embarrassment.

"*Not yet.*" Kai chuckles darkly.

I feel my face go three shades of red, and his chuckle turns into full laughter as we get out of the car.

"Care to share with everyone, Dakota?" Quilla asks as she joins my mother at the trunk of her car.

"No!" I say a little too loudly.

Quilla looks at me dumbfounded, but Mom just looks between me and Kai. I can tell she knows about the tension between us, but she continues walking in the house without another word.

"You all are home early." Mom says instead.

I relax a bit, thankful that she's not pushing to know what my reaction was all about.

"Yeah. Caleb was being an asshole."

I bring in my own load of groceries while Quilla and Kai follow suit with the rest.

"What happened?" Mom asks.

"He wanted me to take off my glasses in the middle of class. So I did."

"What about your eyes?"

"I had Kota pull back enough, so they weren't glowing. That shut him right up." I say with a grin.

"But we were worried that Jeffrey would be there, so we just decided to come on home where it's safe." Quilla adds.

"Yeah, that sounds like it was the best thing to do." Mom says.

Kai and Quilla then unload the items from the bags and place them on the counter while Mom and I put everything away. The task, no matter how small, helps to ease some of the tension, both from this morning at school and from what happened between Kai and me in the car a few minutes ago.

"If you ladies don't need anything else I am going to go over and help my mother with dinner." Kai says as I place the last grocery item in the cabinet.

"We are good, Kai." Mom says. "I'm just going to bake a cake for tonight, and then we will be over."

"Dakota, do you need anything?" Kai asks.

"No. I'm fine. Go help your mom." I say.

He nods and gives me a quick kiss on the cheek, then walks out the door, letting it snick shut gently behind him.

"So what else happened? I know more than that worried you all enough to come home." Mom asks.

"Damn, you're good." I grumble.

"No, I've been married to a Werewolf for the last twenty-one years, and I know they can be territorial of their mates." Mom says.

"Yes. I was worried that Kai would get into a fight if Jeffrey was there. Kai already said if he did something stupid he wouldn't hold back from ripping him apart."

"Yup. Your father is the same way. If he or Nate thought I was in any danger, your father would have a hard time staying in control." Mom says.

"Whatever happened to Dad? Why is he no longer a Beta or with other wolves?" I gently ask.

"That is something your father needs to tell you. It's mainly his story." Mom replies with a tinge of sorrow in her tone.

Mom then shakes her head as if forcing old memories from her mind, and plasters a bright smile on her face. "Who wants to help me with the cake?"

Chapter Eighteen

DAKOTA

"Hey Dakota, why don't we look for some board games for me and your mom to play while you all are out doing your wolfie thing?" Quilla asks as we are waiting on the cake to finish baking in the oven.

"Did you seriously just say, *wolfie thing?*" I ask with a chuckle.

Quilla smiles as she makes her way over to the shelves by the TV where we keep the board games. She picks up *Monopoly* and *The Game of LIFE* while waving them toward Mom.

"Which one would you like, Mrs. Shade?"

"I like *The Game of LIFE,* or there's a deck of cards there too. We can play Gin Rummy or something," Mom says.

Quilla nods and puts both games in her backpack, that she recently emptied of schoolwork, so she could carry them over to the Huntington's. I hear the front door open a few minutes later, as Dad walks in from work. Even though he has his own office at the local bank, people still come in to have their balances verified, and I can see him visibly relax the moment he walks through the door, ditching his glasses and pulling the tie off his neck.

I look at the clock and I see it's one-thirty in the afternoon, and I laugh humorlessly as Dad sits on the couch beside me.

"I don't know how you did it, Dad; I didn't even last an hour at school this morning." I say.

"Oh, I didn't come out of my office until I left, and I kept my glasses on the whole time. Plus, it does help that I'm not around other wolves." Dad says. "So, I make myself work until one, then I'm out." He adds flatly.

I tell Dad about my morning, and while he's upset that it happened to me, he's proud that I was able to handle the situation the way I did.

Later that evening, about two hours before dusk, we head across the street to join Kai and his parents for what he calls a full moon feast. Mom decided to make little finger sandwiches of roast beef and turkey with white cheese to go along with the meal. Dad takes the plate of sandwiches while Mom carries the triple chocolate cake over, and Quilla has her backpack filled with board games thrown over one shoulder.

I reach out to Kai through our bond as we walk up the driveway, and I feel his loving presence instantly fill my mind. *"Hey Babe, we are in the driveway, can you get the door for us?"*

"Sure thing, Love."

When we approach the first concrete step on the large porch, Kai opens the front door and steps to the side to let us all walk in. Quilla sticks next to me since this is the first time she's been in Kai's house, and I can tell she must also feel Tobias and Coraline's power filling the space.

"Welcome, everyone." Coraline says cheerfully from the kitchen.

She meets Dad at the threshold of the kitchen, and she takes the tray of sandwiches from him and motions for Mom to join her with the cake. Tobias then greets us in the foyer, and Dad instantly bares his neck to the alpha. I watch as Tobias smiles and places a gentle hand on my father's shoulder.

"Nathan, please relax. You are among friends and family tonight."

"I'm sorry. It's just the power coming from you three is a little overwhelming." Dad says with a nervous smile toward Tobias and Kai before his eyes flick toward the kitchen where Coraline is.

"I think you may have forgotten your own strength, Nathan." Tobias says coolly.

I pick up on something in Tobias' words. It's not a threat, but a gentle challenge if Dad wants to take the bait.

"Well, I am starving. Let's eat." I say while taking some of the heat off Dad for now.

Tobias nods, and he wordlessly leads us into the dining room, where I see Mom and Coraline setting the table filled with steaks, lobster, macaroni and cheese, broccoli with a bed of rice, the little finger sandwiches, and Mom's chocolate cake.

"The food looks amazing, ladies." Tobias croons while walking in behind his mate and gently kissing her on the cheek.

"This is all for us and the pack, Alpha." Coraline smiles.

Tobias takes his place at the farthest end of the table where he is in view of the door. Coraline is to his left, then Kai to his right. I take my place on Kai's right side, then Dad takes his place on Coraline's left, followed by Mom. Quilla takes the seat next to me, and Tobias motions for us all to sit while he stays on his feet. He fills his plate first with the items he wants, then he serves Coraline, placing the food she points to onto her plate. Tobias then motions with his hand to Kai, and he fills his own plate, then turns to me.

"What would you like, Love?" Kai asks.

"I can fill my own; it's okay." I say as I go to grab the spoon he used for the macaroni from his hand, but he pulls it back a fraction.

"Dakota, it's customary when eating a formal dinner with alpha's that they serve the pack. And since Kai is your mate, the responsibility belongs to him." Dad says. "I'm sorry; I should have told you beforehand."

"Oh, it's okay, Dad." I turn back to Kai as he was patiently waiting for me to learn this new pack rule. "Thank you for waiting, Kai. I'll have the steak, mac and cheese, and broccoli."

Kai quickly fills my plate for me, and then he hands the spoon to Dad, and he follows suit as well, while also filling Quilla's plate for her too.

Once we all have been served, I noticed the way we all filled our plates was the same way that wolves in the wild would feast. The alpha's first, then their pups, then the rest of the pack going down in rank.

"Forgive me if this is a little forward, Nathan, but why are you no longer an active Beta?" Tobias asks after a few moments of silence.

Nathan

I find myself wishing people would stop asking about my past. And just as I am about to tell Tobias to respectfully shut it, I feel Lori in the back of my mind and I stop the retort that's on my tongue.

"Go on, Nathan. Dakota actually asked that this morning too." She rests her hand on my forearm to help ground me.

I let my love for her flood across our bond as I take a cleansing breath.

"I used to be the Beta to the alpha of the South Dakota pack. And when I met Lori and found she was my mate, I took her to meet the pack one day. Of course, she was scared to meet a house full of Werewolves, but she wanted to be part of my world. But let's just say the alpha was not happy with Lori being human, and he told me that if I chose a human for a mate, I would be banished from the pack." I begin, but my throat closes from the memory that floods my mind, and I'm grateful for Lori to pick up where I am forced to stop.

"Needless to say, he chose me over that twisted pack. That was actually the first night I saw him phase, and it was to protect me from the ones who he thought of as his brothers and sisters. Yes, I was terrified, but I knew that if an alpha told a pack member to dump his mate, then that alpha was a piece of shit. And I said that to his face too." Lori adds, and Tobias chuckles at her choice of words.

"I also found that night, as Nathan told Dakota, words mean a lot to this world, so I had a few choice words for that alpha and we left." Lori says.

Once I am able to find my voice again, I tell the rest of the abbreviated story. "Then we moved here to North Dakota, and I'll be honest, I was depressed for a while. Felt like a lone wolf, but when we found out that Lori quickly got pregnant with Dakota, I was brought back to life. I felt like I had my own little pack again." I say, then for the first time tonight, something perks up inside me at the feel of Tobias' power floating in the air. Like he said, it's the long-forgotten power I had as a Beta.

"*You want to see where this goes, Nate?*" I ask.

"*You never have to ask me. I know your thoughts, Nathan, and I will follow you no matter what.*" Nate replies with pride.

I take a note out of Dakota's book and I look the most powerful alpha of Montana in the eye as I say, "So, now you understand a little bit more of why I am so protective of my mate."

Tobias just looks at me with an amused smile, and I let my own power flow over him; to show him I am a strong beta. Granted, not as powerful as he is, but it's nothing to laugh at. Before Tobias can respond, Dakota gets up from her chair with tears in her eyes and comes over to hug me and her mother.

"I am so sorry to hear that, Dad. It sounds horrible."

I open my mind, and I create my own bond with her since I am finally feeling like my old self again.

"I would do it all over again, no questions asked, to make sure I had your mother and you in my life."

"Woah, since when can we do this?" Dakota asks.

"Since I stopped being terrified of my past and actually found someone that would accept my little pack for what it is. I am a Beta by blood, so I can make connections to anyone that I claim as part of the pack."

We continue our meal with mild chatter throughout the evening. When we are all finished, Tobias, Kai, and I clean up the table and the kitchen before we all head out back onto the large stone patio just as the sun is setting and the pull of the moon gets to an all-time high.

Tobias looks at his mate, who gives him a nod at some unspoken question; then over to me with a bright smile on his face, and I feel apprehension bloom in my chest on what his next words will be.

"Nathan, I have been thinking of expanding my pack here to this area as well since we now have a reason to be here for Kai and Dakota." Tobias begins and I hold his stare, not out of challenge, but out of a mix of fear and longing to be part of a pack again.

"So, I ask you, Nathan Shade, former Beta to Alpha Baldric of South Dakota, would you accept my offer to be *my* Beta to the new North Dakota pack?"

I am frozen to the spot at his request. To be an official Beta again makes my blood sing, but to be a Beta to *this* powerful of an alpha is something of my dreams.

I feel like only seconds have passed before I feel Lori walk over to me and wrap her hand around my left arm and her worry for me floods through the bond and I know it's been a few minutes of awkward silence.

"Darling, he's waiting for your answer." Lori prods.

Her words snap me out of my shock, and I look over Tobias, and Coraline. My new potential alphas if I accept.

"You better accept, Nathan. If you don't, I won't let you live it down." Nate growls.

I chuckle internally at him, and I look down to Lori and I see love shining through her tear-filled eyes, knowing just how much this means to me, to us.

"I accept your offer, Tobias Huntington, Alpha of Montana and now to the North Dakota pack, to be your Beta. My mate and I would be honored to be a part of your pack." I say with pride filling my chest, and my power rises to meet Tobias'.

He then steps forward and takes me into a quick welcoming embrace as I feel him open the mental bond that he and I will now share as pack to alpha. And while I can still feel Lori and Dakota in my mind, I sense every wolf that is bonded to Tobias too, and I feel hot, euphoric tears burn in my eyes. I try to hide them from the alpha, but I know it's no use to hide my feelings from him, now that he can feel everything about me through this new bond.

"Beta, cry if you must! This is a joyous occasion!" Tobias' booming voice surrounds us all. "Come! Let us bask in the light of this full moon as a whole pack!"

Tobias takes his place at the end of the patio and looks over all of us, and we each offer our subtle submission to the alpha by just averting our eyes. It warms me further to know that I no longer have to bear my neck in hopes that it would be enough to keep me and my mate safe.

"Nathan." I feel Tobias enter my mind and while his words are intense, I only pause to listen to his request.

"Yes, Alpha?"

"When we all phase and if Dakota still cannot, wait for my ears to flatten for a moment before you step over to guard my son."

Chapter Nineteen

DAKOTA

As I watch Tobias walk to the center of the patio, I can feel the pull of the moon on my skin. I hold on to the hope that I will finally be able to phase with the help of its light.

"It's time! Let us bask in the moonlight together," Tobias urges.

He turns around, and in a motion that is as fluid as water, he phases into his wolf form. Stepping out of his discarded clothing, I see a massive, pure black wolf with bright brown eyes looking back at us. Coraline is the next one to phase, and she is just as fluid as her mate. Her pure white coat is iridescent under the moonlight, her ice-blue eyes in striking contrast against the purity of her fur.

When she steps up to Tobias, she nuzzles her snout under his chin, and their tails wrap around one another. The lightness and darkness of their coats complement one another beautifully.

They look like a yin and yang symbol. I think to myself.

Kai is the next one to phase. This is the first time that I have seen him in his wolf form since the attack the other day. His brown coat has areas of swirling blonde strips that go down the middle of his chest, wrap around his back, and continue down to his tail.

"You are beautiful, Babe." I whisper in his mind.

"Thank you, Love." Kai replies as he walks over to me and rests his large head against my stomach. I run my hands over his coarse fur, and I am rewarded with a contented sigh.

We look up, and I watch as Dad gives Mom a sound kiss on the lips and he effortlessly phases into the same dark gray wolf that I saw as a child. Tobias gives Kai a short bark, and he walks over to sit beside my dad. I realize I now have four wolves staring me down.

"It's your turn, Love." Kai encourages.

"Oh yeah, sorry." I chuckle nervously.

I close my eyes, and I try to focus on Kota. To let her come to the front of my mind. I can see her trying to take over my form, but it's like something is still blocking her.

"It doesn't make sense. I can feel you. I feel the pull of the moon. I don't feel any fear or apprehension from you. So why the hell can we not phase?" Kota growls.

I open my eyes while running my hands through my hair in frustration, and let out an aggravated growl.

"Damn it! I still can't phase, even under a fucking full moon!" I look over to Tobias and I see his ears go flat to his head for a moment before they perk back up, almost like my shouts hurt his ears, and Dad casually steps in front of Kai.

"What is wrong with me?!" I sob into my hands.

I hear Mom take a sharp breath, and when I look up, I find Tobias stalking me like prey. His head low, and eyes pinned on mine. I hear Kai growl against my father, but I cannot pry my eyes from the alpha in front of me, and for the first time since meeting Tobias, I feel pure fear flood my veins.

"Tobias?" I ask, my voice shaking.

At the sound of my voice, he gathers his legs under his massive form and he leaps toward me. Teeth barred, and a terrifying snarl ripping from his throat. I try to scramble out of his way, but my legs won't listen to me. I hear snarls to my left. From Kai, who I realize is trying to get past my father, but Dad is able to somehow keep him pinned to the spot with ease. Tobias makes me focus solely on him when his huge paws roughly pin my shoulders to the ground, making the concrete pavers of the patio dig into my skin.

I feel the full brunt of his alpha power flood my body, my mind, and my soul, clean through into Kota's forest, and I hear her pleading whines echo in my head.

"Phase wolf."

That single command pierces through my body, and I can feel Kota desperately try to obey the command. Clawing at my mind to make us phase. My screams of terror fill the real world as Kota's own pleading barks and whines fill my mind as our body refuses to listen to the command of our alpha.

"You dare defy your alpha's command, wolf?" Tobias' voice growls in my mind.

"No!" Kota and I scream in unison.

"No! Alpha!" I beg with my own sobbing voice, "Please, I can't."

I can smell my own terror filling my nose and it threatens to bring up the wonderful meal I had just a short thirty minutes ago.

"Father!" A voice bellows through the chaos. I realize that it's Kai yelling at his father.

Tobias pauses his assault, his teeth so close to my ear that I feel his hot breath against my skin. Kai finally gets past my father and is racing toward me.

"Alpha, this is enough!" Kai growls as he closes the distance and pushes his father away from me with a low, threatening growl. "Was that necessary?"

With Kai being this close, I can tell he's somehow phased enough to be able to talk so we all can hear the conversation, even if it is gravelly and with a bit of a lisp from K's long, sharp canine teeth.

Tobias also phases his own throat enough to speak, and his words are gentle, yet pure alpha. "I had to try, son. I'm sorry if it was to your disliking, but I simply thought that if she was made to believe she was in danger, she would phase out of the need to protect herself."

Kai growls again in response to his father's words, and I see him stand over my still prone body, tail held high in what even I would take as a challenge.

"Are you okay, Dakota?" Mom asks as she kneels down beside me.

"No," I say sharply. "That scared the absolute shit out of me." I say.

I notice that Kai is still staring his father down, daring him to move, but somehow I do understand where Tobias was coming from. I reach out through the bond and I feel Kai's mind is a jumbled mess of him and K fighting for control. I keep hearing over and over phrases of, *"Our mate was in danger"*, and *"Protect her."*

"Kai, Babe, please stand down." I say.

"He attacked you." I hear K's snarling voice in my mind, and I can't feel Kai at all.

"K, please listen to me." I begin while pushing my own alpha power toward him. *"Tobias was trying to help me. Yes, it scared the hell out of me.*

Yes, I thought he was going to hurt me and Kota if we didn't obey, but it was all to see if I could phase out of the need for survival." I say as I feel Kai start to take control a bit more over K. "*Now come here and make sure that I am okay. That will help you and Kai feel better. That and I don't want you to stand against your father.*"

I can tell that Kai is in full control again, and I feel him relax a bit in my mind.

"*Thank you, Love. I'm sorry, K was in total control there.*"

Kai finally backs away from his father with a sorrowful whine at his actions toward the alpha and closes the distance between us. He lies down with his large head in my lap while I stroke the soft spot of fur between his eyes and lets out a content groan at my touch.

Dad is now sitting beside Tobias, his tail flicking lazily against the ground like nothing at all happened twenty seconds ago, but I pin my father with a glare.

"I understand why you did that, Tobias, and deep down I do appreciate the help, but Dad, really? Your first act as Beta was to keep Kai back from this."

"*I'm sorry, Dakota, but we had to try,*" Dad replies.

"Yeah, Nathan! I'm mad at you too!" Mom says with her hands on her hips.

I watch as Dad trots up to her and tries to jump up on her like a common house pet.

"Bad boy!"

Mom scolds while smacking at Dad's nose. Even with everything that just went on, I find myself laughing at their antics. He looks a little ashamed, but I think that was mostly from Mom's actions towards him. I notice her face turning beat red and I can only imagine what images

Dad put there. I shudder at the thought when Dad trots over to me and Kai. He lowers his head and bares his neck in apology, then he jumps back and goes into a playful downward position where his tail is high in the air while his front paws are splayed out, and his tongue hangs out the side of his mouth.

"You're such a dork, Dad." I snort.

I turn my attention to Kai, and I can feel he wants to spend his time with me and not take advantage of the full moon the way I think he should. Running through the nearby forest with his pack.

"Kai, please, go run with your parents and my dad. I'll be fine. I'll be with Mom and Quilla playing board games in the house until you all come back."

Tobias gives a playful bark, and Dad runs over to him and Coraline, gently nipping at one another. Kai's tail raises in response to the energy pouring from the three wolves.

"Go, I'll be here waiting on you."

"We'll be back soon. I love you, Dakota." Kai says lovingly, and he bounds off into the woods with his parents and his newly acquired beta.

"Are you sure you're okay?" Mom asks.

"Yeah. I'm still shaken up, but I'm good." I say. "So what game are we playing first?"

Chapter Twenty

NATHAN

As I run through the forest, the wind rippling through my dark gray fur, the ground beating against my powerful paws, I feel alive for the first time in twenty-one years. I'm back in a pack setting again. Granted, it's a small one here in North Dakota with only seven members, but it's a pack that I can help lead and protect with Tobias and Coraline. He must feel my joy flowing through my bond with him because Tobias playfully bites at my right flank, and I respond with a playful bark.

"Catch me if you can, Alpha!" I tease.

I lengthen my stride, eating up more of the forest floor to cover more ground, and I can feel Tobias close on my heels in his eagerness from the chase. We leave Coraline and Kai behind as we race across the hills and valleys of my hometown.

Kai

I watch as Nathan and my father run into the forest, and I feel that K wants to run with the pack, but I still have flashes of Dakota in my mind, and I want nothing more than to be with her and to soothe her.

"Kai, I know what you're thinking. But you should run with your father and the new Beta," Mom says as she walks up to me, her piercing blue eyes staring back at me from her bright, white face while her ears are perked forward. *"Your father did what was necessary to try to help your mate. You must believe that, son."*

"I know, Mother." I sigh, *"I just hated to hear, feel, and smell her fear. I have never seen her that terrified, and I never want to see it again."*

"I can tell you, son, when you become alpha one day, there will be many times in your long life when you feel her fear like it's a tangible thing in the air, but you have to be her rock and help her get through the things that terrify her. And in doing so, she will be that for you as well." Mom says. *"Remember, son, it's all about balance between mates."*

I hear her words and I know them to be true, and I realize that, like Dakota, I have a lot to learn about what it means to be a strong and supportive mate myself. And like Mom said, we have to find a balance between us.

"Kai! Come on, son! Join us."

Dad and Nathan are standing atop a nearby hill, tongues lolling out the sides of their mouths, panting from their run. Mom gives me a nudge to my shoulder with her nose, urging me to join them. I give her a wolfish grin and I dash up the hill toward the two wolves with my mother trailing behind me. Dad lets out a loud yip and takes off with Nathan close to him, and I chase them both down.

After we had our fill of running for three hours, we make our way back to the house. Or should I say, Dad, Nathan, and I make it a race. Nathan is in the lead with Dad in second place, but I am gaining on my old man. I go to nip at his left ankle when he jumps out of my way at the last minute and I stumble a few steps. Tumbling head over tail, I end up colliding with Nathan as he enters the yard, and we are a tangle of paw and tails as we come skidding to a stop near the edge of the patio. Dad and Mom come trotting in like the cool, collected alpha's they are, and I can feel Dad's amusement flow from his side of the bond.

"Smooth son. Very smooth entrance." He mocks.

"Screw you, old man. You made me trip." I playfully throw back, and he snorts in response.

We hear the backdoor slide open, and I lift my head to see Dakota, her mother, and Quilla walk out of the house while trying to hide their cackling laughter.

"Oh my gosh, Babe. Are you okay?" Dakota laughs.

"Yeah, that looked like it hurt, Honey." Lori adds to her mate.

I roll my eyes as I untangle myself from Nathan, and we both shake out our coats. As Dakota sits on the top step of the patio, I trot over to her outstretched hand, and she rubs in between my eyes with her thumb while her hand caresses the rest of my skull.

"Did you have fun?" She asks in a baby voice, and I again roll my eyes at her.

I jump up, placing my paw on her shoulders, and I give her a slobbery lick on the cheek, and her squeals of laughter fill my ears as she pushes me away.

"That was so gross, Babe." Dakota laughs as she wipes her cheek.

I give her a wolfish grin and spin around to flick the soft fur of my tail into her face.

"Kai!"

She laughs my name, and it warms my heart so much I can't even put words to what I feel for this woman.

"*I love the way I can make you laugh. Even after the events of the night.*"

"Isn't that what mates are supposed to do? Be there to lift the other one up when they're feeling down?"

"*Absolutely, Love.*" I say, and I let all the admiration I can muster flow over to her, and I see her almost lean into that invisible feeling.

Lori then comes back out to the patio with our discarded clothing, the unspoken notice that if we want to phase back, we can. Nathan is the first to go and grab his clothing in his mouth and goes around the corner of the house to phase and dress. Dakota goes over to her mother to take my jeans and t-shirt from her and walks back over to me.

Nathan then comes back around the corner, human and wearing only his jeans while running his fingers through his dark brown hair.

"Oh man, that was the best full moon I've had in a while," Nathan exclaims.

"I'm glad, Sweetheart. You deserve it." Lori says.

Nathan pulls his mate close to him, his eyes glowing brightly as he looks into her face. I try to keep my eyes from noticing the way his hand is gripping her ass, but with her hips being right in my line of sight, it's kinda hard to miss. He then gives her a sound, heated kiss, and I hear Dakota groan and make a gagging motion with her index finger.

"Oh God. Mom, Dad! Go get a damn room!"

"Sorry, Dakota. I'll tone it down." Nathan says.

I give Dakota a low growl, and her attention drifts back over to me.

"May I have my clothes back now?"

She taps her index finger to her chin, like she's thinking if she wants to give me my clothes back.

"Do a trick for me, Fido," Dakota teases.

"I have no issues with being naked in front of everyone, Dakota." I growl.

As the shock flashes across her features, I leap up, snatching my clothes out of her hand, and trot around to the same area that Nathan changed in.

"You did that to distract me, Kai!" Dakota yells.

I phase and as I tug my jeans up over my hips and zip them up, I decide to forego my shirt as well and I love the way Dakota's eyes instantly take in my form, knowing she's looking at the marking that flows down my neck and across my chest.

"It worked, didn't it?" I ask with a smile as I tug her into my body.

The high after running with the pack is making it hard not to touch Dakota in the same way that Nathan did for his mate. I am again filled with the need to mark her, to let every single wolf know she is mine, but K helps hold me back, even if it's only a little bit. I go for the subtle movements that only she and I will share. So I pull her close where my thigh is pressed into her hot center, and I feel her freeze under my hand.

"Kai."

I can feel that her plea is a mix of warning just as much as it is a plea of encouragement. I then run my hand up her back and over the hidden marking under her shirt. I begin to rub my thumb over the area as her head falls against my bare chest at my touch.

"One day, Love, I will make you whole." I say as I push my thigh closer to her core, igniting her sensitive bundle of nerves. She grabs onto my arms as she fights not to make a sound.

"Hey! Get your paws off my daughter or get a room!" Nathan shouts, but I pick up on the hint of the lightness in his voice.

"Oh my god, Dad!" Dakota groans finally finding her voice, before burying her head back into my chest.

I feel the heat of her desire and mortification mix together at her father's words. *"We could go somewhere more private, if you want, Babe."*

"What about the laws saying we can't have sex?"

"There's more than one way I can get you off that is still within the boundaries, Love." I croon.

I begin to push images of her writhing body on my bed, but I feel Dad's pulse of power and the images fade in a puff of mental smoke between us before I can show her how I was touching her and I almost chuckle at her low growl in my father's direction.

"I think it's best that we all turn in for the night and take a much-needed rest." Dad says as he walks around the corner of the house with him and Mom fully clothed now. "Kai, Dakota, and Quilla have class in the morning, and I'm sure that Nathan has work.

"And you, mister, are playing a dangerous boundary game."

I feel Dad enter my mind along with a pulse of his power that makes all flirtation fade from my blood.

"I will not *let you taint this bloodline for a second time. It's too special of a blessing to fuck it up."*

"Yes, Alpha." I say, knowing what he is referring to. *"But I do know how far I can push it. Believe me, K is keeping mini me in line."* I hear my father's grumble in mind as he shuts down the connection.

I pull back from Dakota, and I give her a light kiss on the cheek. "Dad's right. It's late, and you should go get some rest." I run my thumb across her cheekbone. "Remember, I am just a thought away."

"Okay," Dakota whispers.

"I'll walk you over to your place."

I pick up my shirt as I walk her and her family back through the house and out the front door. We cross the street, and Nathan is the first to walk inside with Lori close behind. They give us a few moments alone on the porch and with Dad's warning fresh in my mind, I reign in the hormones and just relish in her being close to me, her hands resting softly on my chest, and being able to breathe the same air she does.

"We will have other full moons to spend together that will be less... nerve-wracking." I chuckle.

"As long as you're there, I'll be happy." Dakota says as she fiddles with the collar of my shirt.

"Always, Babe. I love you, Dakota Shade, and I can't wait to spend the rest of my life with you, and mind you, it will be a *very* long life."

"I'm counting on it." Dakota says with a bright smile.

I give her a playful kiss on the nose as I open the door and watch her walk inside. When she gently shuts and locks the door behind her, I walk back across the street with the moon's light shining down on my back, and I soak up the rays before I walk in my own house to rest as my alpha requested.

Chapter Twenty-One

KAI

After a restful night, filled with dreams of running with my pack under the full moon, I get up before my alarm goes off the next morning. I take Dakota and Quilla to school in Dakota's car, being sure to give my mate a quick kiss on the cheek before she heads off in the opposite direction. I pass Caleb on the way to my first class of the morning, and I know he's watching my every step. I keep my head held high, completely ignoring him.

Later that afternoon, as I'm heading to my last class of the day, English 101, I notice Caleb talking to two other males. I pick up on the same scent that links them all to Jeffrey, and these are also the same mutts that tried to attack Dakota. I fight against the growl that threatens to bubble up in my chest as I walk past them, but I am able to pick up on their conversation.

"Do you think that a true mate would hurt one another?" Caleb asks.

"Hell yeah. Especially if she had a mouth on her and talked back. I'd slap that bitch into submission." One male laughs.

His words send shivers of irritation and anger down my spine. With talk like that, the bastard doesn't deserve a mate.

"What do you think, Kai? Would you hurt *your* mate?" Caleb croons with a smirk.

"I think you all are fucking nut jobs if you think that is even a question to ask someone with a mate." I growl as I let a pulse of my alpha power flow over the three wolves in front of me. "I would sooner rip the beating heart from my chest than hurt my mate."

"Thought so. Nice talk." Caleb chuckles darkly as the three of them walk off laughing at each other.

I shake my head, and I walk into class, trying to forget those three assholes behind me.

That night as I am lying in bed, I feel Dakota tap against my mental shields. The side of my mouth lifts up as I let her into my mind.

"Hello, Love."

"Hi, you okay? You've been kinda quiet today." Dakota asks, and I feel her worry for me flow through the bond.

"Yes. I'm sorry, Babe. It was just a rough day." I reply.

"Anything I can help with?"

"No. I just heard our favorite mutt talking to his underlings if a mate would hurt the other, and it pissed me off on their responses." I say as I show her what happened in the hall in a mental video of sorts.

"Woah. That's cool. How'd you do that?"

"*It's similar to the images I can show you, but you just remember the scene for what it was and project that through the bond.*" I explain.

"*Oh, that's cool.*" Dakota pauses. "*I'm sorry you had to experience that. I know a mate could never hurt the other. If rejection hurts like a knife, I can only imagine what it would feel like to actually inflict harm on a mate.*" Her voice is full of sorrow at the thought.

"*I would* never *lay a hand on you in that way. Even if it was an order of an alpha, I would fight with everything that I am to disobey that order.*" I declare.

"*I believe you, Kai. And I would do the same thing.*"

I feel her love flowing through our bond, and I let it fill my heart and soul.

"*It's getting late, Love, you should get some sleep.*"

"*Alight you bossy butt. As long as you get some sleep too.*" Her airy laugh fills my mind, and I smile.

"*Deal. I'll see you in the morning.*"

I feel her pull back from my mind, and I set my alarm before I turn over to look out the window, and when I see the light click off in her bedroom, I let my eyes fall with images of Dakota in my mind.

The next morning as I head to class, I again pass Caleb in the hall. He clumsily shoulder-checks me, making me drop the book and pencil I was carrying in the crook of my arm.

"My apologies. I slipped." He grins.

"I don't know what you have up your sleeve, but I suggest you fucking stop while you're ahead." I snap.

"Caleb! Leave the wolf alone."

We look up, and I see Jeffrey strolling towards us, hands in his pockets, and I notice his eyes look a bit on the glassy side, but I don't think too much of it.

"Sorry, Alpha," Caleb says as he bares his neck to his alpha. He hands me my pencil; the eraser pointing towards me. "Here's your pencil back."

I snatch it without a word and I walk into my History class, plopping down into the desk chair while placing the pencil in the little slot in the faux wood of the table. The professor then stands from his desk and hands out a stack of papers to the students in the front rows.

"Pop quiz today, everyone!" The professor says, with a chorus of groans filling the room. "Please take a test off the top and pass it back to the end of your rows. You have the entire class period to complete it. Good luck."

I take my test from the top of the stack before passing it over my shoulder to the student behind me, pick up my pencil to write my name at the top of the page, and get to work. As I go down the list of questions, I easily fill in the answers thanks to my Werewolf memory, but to keep up appearances of the test being hard, I begin to chew on my pencil as if I'm thinking about the answer when in reality it's a way to keep me from flying through the questions.

After a few minutes, I feel someone staring at me. I lift my head to find Caleb and Jeffrey filling the little window in the heavy wooden door of the classroom, just staring at me. We lock eyes, and I see Caleb's lips form a wicked smile, and they both walk off a heartbeat later.

Crazy mutt. I think to myself, and I hear K snort in agreement.

I am still the first one to finish the test, and I am free to go after I turn in my paper. I head to the cafeteria in the next building, and I reach out to Dakota to let her know where I am and to meet me when she's out of class.

"Hey, Kai," Dakota says about twenty minutes later as she and Quilla walk up to the table I grabbed for us.

"Hey Baby," I rise and I give her a light kiss on the lips.

"That algebra test was hard." Quilla groans.

"Well, my good Tamer friend, you won't let me *help* you."

"That is cheating, *Dakota*." Quilla says.

Dakota laughs as she wraps her hands around my arm when I begin to lead them to the line of students forming near the kitchen.

"How'd your test go, Kai?"

"Oh, you know with *Werewolf* memory, I aced it." I whisper so I'm not overheard.

"You know what, you two can bite me. I have to study my ass off, and I think I barely passed." Quilla groans.

"Again, you have an ace in your sleeve, Quilla." Dakota says in a singsong voice.

"Didn't we have this conversation before, Dakota Shade?"

"Um, I don't know. The memory seems kinda foggy." Dakota says as she puts a finger thoughtfully to her lips.

"Okay, Dakota, be nice." I laugh.

A few minutes later, after we get in line, K gets the sense that someone is staring at us. I turn to look over my shoulder and I see Jeffrey leaning against the wall near the main entrance to the cafeteria with a smug look on his face. I can't take my eyes off him, and I know they must be glowing because his flashes a moment before he dips his head enough for others not to see, while still keeping his eyes locked in my direction.

"What's wrong, Babe?" Dakota asks, picking up on my sudden lack of conversation. *"And keep your eyes down; they aren't exactly human right now."* She adds in my mind.

"I don't know. I felt Jeffrey staring at me, and I can't break eye contact." I say roughly.

Dakota looks his way, and I feel her pulse of power flow around us. Jeffrey finally relents, and I deflate like a balloon.

"Since that's taken care of, you wanna go outside and eat?" Dakota asks.

"Actually, yeah. That's a good idea. I don't want to be in the same room as him right now." I let loose a frustrated sigh.

We all fill our lunch trays and we head outside, making our way to Dakota's car to eat in peace. I turn over the engine to run the AC so we can eat in comfort as well.

"Okay. Tell me what happened this morning. I know something did since you just had a staring contest with another alpha." Dakota says as she takes a bite of her meatloaf.

I tell her the events of this morning, and as I tell her, I feel tension begin to build in my shoulders, and I lean my head back on the headrest to try to calm myself.

"Do you want to go home? I can tell you're on edge."

"No, I'll be okay. Besides, I don't want him to think I ran just because we had a stare-down." I say, the alpha in me doesn't like the idea of showing weakness and fear by running from a potential fight.

"But it won't be running if you can stop a fight. You would be protecting me and others in this school." Dakota says, and I also hear the alpha in her analyzing the situation. "There is no shame in retreating and looking at things from a different angle."

I mull over her words, and they make sense. I let out a frustrated sigh and I look over at her. "Okay. You're right. Let's go home."

"Do you want me to get your homework from your classes?" Quilla asks.

"No. I know what's coming up from the syllabus. But thank you anyway, Quilla." I say.

Dakota and I wait long enough for Quilla to take our trays back into the cafeteria, Dakota making sure to keep her mental connection open while Quilla is inside. When she comes back and hops into the rear passenger seat, I drive us home and try to forget the events of the day.

I pull Dakota's car into her driveway, and I go around to open both doors for the ladies so they can exit the car. I let Dakota open the door to her house, only because she has the keys, and I visibly relax as we all walk in.

"Feeling better already?" Dakota asks.

"Yes, I am."

Lori greets us as we settle into the living room, and she doesn't press for an explanation on why we are home, which I am glad of. I don't want to have to recall the scene and get angry all over again.

As the evening goes on, Dakota, Quilla, Lori and I all watch movies in companionable silence. When Nathan gets home from work, he fixes dinner for everyone, and thankfully he's the one to make conversation about landing a new client with a huge account for the bank he works at.

Once we finish dinner, Dakota and I take the couch again while Quilla puts in another movie. I'm lying on my back with my head resting in Dakota's lap, while she runs her fingers lazily through my blonde hair.

"Thank you." I begin. "For keeping me calm today with Jeffrey. I just realized I didn't thank you for what you did today." I say as I look up at her.

"What happened?" Nathan asks, overhearing our conversation.

Shit. I think to myself.

So, I finally tell him and Lori what happened, and I can tell he's just as proud of his daughter for her reasoning as I am.

"I just don't trust those fleabags. You never know what's going through their heads. I mean, yesterday they were egging you on about hurting your own mate. That's nothing to sneeze at." Dakota says.

"I don't trust them either." I say as I get up off her lap and rise from the couch. "I'll be right back." I say as I point to where the bathroom is down the hall.

As I go to close the door behind me, I feel a violent, bone-rattling shiver roll over every cell in my body. I realize the shiver is the same one I feel right before I phase, only it's usually far less painful. I stand against the doorframe and try to figure out what the hell caused that when I feel the shiver wrack my body again, almost like some outside influence is trying to force me to phase and my body wants to fight against it. The blinding pain that follows the next shiver forces me to my knees, and I can't block Dakota off fast enough before she feels my pain and terror over our bond.

CHAPTER TWENTY-TWO
DAKOTA

I feel Kai's pain through the bond like it's my own. I spring from the couch, making my way to the hall bathroom only to find him curled up in the fetal position on the beige tile floor, writhing and screaming in pain as his muscles and skin ripple under his shirt.

"Kai! What's wrong?" I yell, fear flooding my veins.

With one final cry, he phases before me, ripping his shirt and jeans as his wolf body fills the floor. Mom, Dad, and Quilla fill the hallway behind me as Kai seems to settle after what I realize is a forced phase.

"What happened?" Mom asks.

"I... I don't know." I stammer. "He was fine. He just went to use the bathroom, and I felt his pain burst through his end of the bond. When I got here, he was trying not to phase, but it was like he couldn't stop it." I look at my father with tears in my eyes. "Dad, what happened to him?"

"I don't know, Sweetheart."

Kai slowly stands up, shaking his fur out as he gets his bearings again, and I feel him enter my mind.

"Babe, please go get my father. He may know what happened to me."

"I don't want to leave you." I sob.

"I'll watch him."

I look back and I see Quilla staring at Kai, like she's only seeing him and his potential issue. It's in that moment, I trust that she knows something that we may not.

"Okay, I'll get Tobias. I'll be right back." I say as I jump to my feet and rush out the front door.

Quilla

After Dakota rushes out of the house, Nathan, Lori, Kai and I don't move a muscle. An unspoken fear that the slightest movement would set Kai off again. But then, something deep inside me wants to touch Kai. To find out what this ailment is and cure him. At first, I try to ignore this desire, but I remembered Nathan's words to me a few days ago. That I am a Tamer. And while I am able to calm the wolf inside, I feel that I can be more if needed. So, I turn towards Kai, his hazel eyes tracking me.

"Can I touch you?" I ask.

He tilts his head to the side in what I assume is a silent question to my request.

"I don't know. Call it Tamer intuition." I say with a small smile.

He nods his huge wolf head and I lean in, threading my fingers through his coarse fur on his cheeks, as I close my eyes and let my still unexplored ability as a Tamer flow through me.

As I concentrate on Kai, I start to feel K as well, and I can almost see him approach me in a foggy mist in my mind, so I start to search both of their bodies. I can almost see translucent images of their bones, muscles, tendons, and blood vessels. Nothing jumps out at me at first, until I feel a pull to look at their blood closer. As I do, I get this fuzzy image of what looks like a flower. This delicate violet flower reminds me of those women on the Las Vegas strip with those overly large feather hats. But the name of this flower is just out of my grasp. I push deeper within myself to figure out what this flower is. I have to in order to help my friends.

Even though they don't say a word, I feel Dakota, Tobias, and Coraline walk back into the house and wait for me to tell them what's going on. Just as I am about to give up and let them know I am just as clueless as before Dakota left, the name of this flower hits me, and I somehow know, deep in my gut, that this is not good.

"What's wrong with him, Quilla?" Tobias asks urgently.

I open my eyes and look over my shoulder at the alpha, and I can pick up on the fear he's trying to keep a check on, but I can still feel it. I can feel everyone's fear, including my own, and it's overwhelming. I take a breath, steeling myself, knowing I cannot run from this. I have to keep it together if we have any chance of helping Kai in time.

"Wolfsbane." I say. "He's been drugged with Wolfsbane. That's what forced the phase."

"I thought Wolfsbane had healing properties?" Nathan asks.

"I thought so too." Coraline says.

"No, I think there are several ways to make it where it would have different effects." I say, somehow knowing more about this plant than the wolves in front of me. I continue with the information that is now flowing through my mind. "If it's simmered low and slow over a few hours, it will have healing abilities. But if it's made quickly, in under an hour, it will make the wolf phase, but nothing else will happen. However, if it's made in under thirty minutes." I pause and I glance over at the two alphas, Nathan, Lori, and finally Dakota and Kai, and I force my lips to voice the scenario that I pray will not happen, "Then the wolf will lose control and attack anything in its path."

"Understood, Quilla. I would like to have you and my pack doctor back in Montana meet over Zoom to discuss the best antidote. Would you kindly follow me?" Tobias asks.

"Yes. Anything I can do to help, I want to do it." I look at Dakota and then take in Kai's wolf form. "I *will* figure out a way to fix this."

"Thanks, Quilla. I believe in you." Dakota says with a shaky smile.

I give her a quick hug as I look at Tobias, and he leads me over to his home, where I meet with the pack doctor.

CHAPTER TWENTY-THREE

QUILLA

I walk over with Tobias to meet his pack doctor over a Zoom meeting. I can tell he is trying to keep his composure, but I still see the single, soft wrinkle forming near his left eye. I reach out my hand and set it on his elbow, letting whatever this Tamer ability I have flow over him, and I watch as the worry and stress instantly fade from his shoulders.

"Thank you, Quilla. I appreciated that." Tobias says as we walk up on the porch and he opens the front door.

I walk in behind him, and he makes sure to close and lock the door before heading deeper into the house. We walk down a long hallway and turn left into a large office. The massive, solid oak desk fills the middle of the room, with a large window to the left of the desk while it rests against a solid wall to the right. Behind the desk is a line of shelves built into the wall that are filled with books of all different colors and sizes.

Tobias sits in the overly large, deep brown leather desk chair, typing on the keyboard of his sleek, white all-in-one HP desktop computer. I hear the beep of a program being loaded in and then a male voice pours from the speakers, his voice low, and I pick up a bit of an Irish lilt in his tone. I find his voice is soothing, but yet all business.

"Hello Alpha. How is Kai's condition?"

"It's grave, I'm afraid, Atticus. Seems that it was Wolfsbane that made him phase, but we don't know how it was prepared when he unknowingly ingested it."

"Then we are on a time clock. What can I do to help you?" Atticus asks.

"We have a Tamer here, Miss Quilla Rose, and I think you two would be of great importance to his situation." Tobias says as he motions for me to step in behind him.

I walk around the desk, but I stay to his left side. I feel it would be wrong to be at the back of an alpha. I have no idea where that thought came from, but I trust my instinct. I turn my attention to the male on the computer. His red hair is tied up in a man-bun, his bangs hanging a bit low into his emerald green eyes. He's wearing a heathered gray vest with a black button-up shirt underneath.

"Quilla, this is my pack doctor, Atticus Remington. Granted, Quilla is still new to all this, but I can already tell she's going to be a wonderful asset to the pack."

Atticus nods his head in my direction and gives me a warm smile. "Hello, Miss Rose. It's a pleasure to meet a Tamer such as yourself."

"Now, I will let you two talk and figure out the best way to help my son." Tobias' voice goes from friendly to serious in a blink of an eye.

Tobias rolls the desk chair back, standing to his full six-foot-five height, and holds the chair out for me. I take my seat, the whoosh of air as the leather morphs to the shape and pressure of my body filling the room while Tobias pushes me into the desk.

"We will figure this out, Tobias. I promise," Atticus says.

"I know you will. That's why I suggested you two work together on this."

He walks out without another word, and I am left with this man staring back at me through the computer screen, his green eyes shining through the locks of his red hair.

"Okay, Miss Rose." Atticus begins, but I stop him.

"Please, it's Quilla. My mother is Miss Rose. Plus, we are part of the same pack, aren't we?" I ask, pausing on the word *pack* as it still feels strange on my tongue.

Atticus chuckles and nods his head. "Yes, I suppose you're right. So, Quilla, do you know anything about Wolfsbane? What it looks like, or where it grows?"

"Not where it grows." I say, shaking my head. "I only know what it looks like from looking into Kai. I still don't really know how I did that, to be honest." I say while pushing a piece of my own auburn hair shyly behind my ear. "I was able to see a faint outline of what it looked like, though."

"Alright. At least you know what to look for. If Kai was drugged with it, then I am hoping there is a patch of the plant somewhere near your location." Atticus says as I hear his fingers fly across the keyboard hidden from sight.

"Why do we need to see where it grows?" I ask. "Don't we need something else for an antidote?"

His eyes shift back over to mine, and he holds my gaze through the screen; the barest hint of a smile pulls at the corner of his mouth.

"Tell me, *Tamer. W*hen you found out that it was Wolfsbane, did you have any other inclinations about the plant?"

At first, I don't understand why he's asking me this. How would I? I've never seen this plant before, but then it hits me. I *do* know the different properties of this plant. I smile at him, a silent thank you for making me think as a Tamer.

"We are going to make a Wolfsbane healing tea, aren't we?" I ask.

"Aye."

I look at him, confused on what he just said, and he shakes his head with a grimace.

"Sorry, hard habit to break for this century." Atticus begins, "I said yes in a *very* outdated way. My apologies."

"It's okay. So, what do I need to do to help Kai?" I ask, while trying not to wonder how old this guy is if he's using terms like *aye*.

"I found a small cluster about twenty minutes from the Alpha's residence. But only you can pick them, Quilla. Wolfsbane in the raw floral form is deadly to werewolves if handled improperly. If we were to pick it, we would need to have several layers of gloves on, and even then it would make us look like someone hit the bottle too hard." Atticus explains. "Eyes would be glassy like they are completely inebriated."

"Got it. So keep it away from anything that can turn furry."

His lips form a close-mouthed smile at my words, and I feel a slight blush creep up my cheeks. I quickly shake my head once to clear my mind. One, there is no time to gawk at the handsome doctor, plus if he's as old as I think, he must have a mate by now.

"You should pick about twenty stems. Then after you do that, you need to have a private kitchen to bring the flowers to a boil. Again, this needs to be away from any other Were's until the first ten minutes pass. Then it would be safe for a Were to be around and breathe in."

"Okay, um, how can I get in contact with you to make sure I'm making it right?" I ask. "I'll have to cook them at my place, I guess. That's the only spot that wouldn't have any wolves around."

"What's your email address? I'll add it to my contact list, and then when you get to a safe spot we can pick back up from here."

"It's cheesy, *quillaannerose@gmail.com.*"

"It's better than what Tobias made for me, *atticusremi_healer@msn .com.*" He chuckles.

"Awe, I think it fits you."

Shut up, Quilla. Stop your flirting before his mate hears you. I internally scold myself.

"I'll email you the location of the flower patch now, and just let me know as soon as you get back to your home." Atticus says.

"Got it." I say in both understanding his request as well as getting his email.

He seems to understand the statement because he nods, says his goodbye, and disconnects from the Zoom meeting. I pull up the tagged location on my phone as I walk out of Tobias' office and right into the solid form of his body.

"Oh, I'm so sorry!"

"Where do you need to go?"

"Atticus said no other Were's can come with me. It's dangerous to you all if you touch the stems."

"I will take you to the patch. It may be guarded, and we cannot risk you getting hurt, Quilla." Tobias says. "If you put the bundle in the trunk and clean your hands well, I will be fine."

I nod, and I follow Tobias out the door, where he drives me to the location of the flower patch.

We arrive twenty minutes later, just as Atticus promised, and I look through the passenger window to the small field, no larger than my backyard, full of purple flowers with their lush green leaves and stems swaying in the breeze.

"Stay here a moment. I need to make sure that no one is around before you get out," Tobias says as he opens the door and walks around a bit while being mindful to stay downwind of the breeze.

After he is satisfied that everything is safe, I get out, rush over to the flowers, and begin to cut off the whole stem as close to the ground as I can as Atticus mentioned in his email. Placing the stems in a grocery bag that I grabbed from Tobias' house, I make my way back to his car, and he backs away as he pops the trunk for me. I place the bundle in the corner of the truck, trying to keep it as far away from the cab as I can, and I shut the lid. I then take the two bottles of water Tobias grabbed and the Dawn dish detergent to wash and rinse my hands well before getting into the car with the alpha.

"Okay, we need to go to my place now. Atticus and I will talk over Zoom again to make the antidote."

"Alright, Quilla. You have done very well so far." Tobias says.

"We still have a long way to go, but we will get there."

He takes me to my house, and I grab the bag of flowers from the trunk, then walk inside to begin making the antidote, praying that I'm not too late.

Chapter Twenty-Four

DAKOTA

I'm sitting on the tile floor of the bathroom beside Kai; the silence in the small room is deafening. Kai was drugged. And said drug could make him feral. My mind goes back to what Kai told me Caleb was provoking him about the other day.

Would a mate hurt the other?

My blood turns from cold fear to red-hot anger. I tried to overlook them taunting Kai, but to cause him harm? I want to tear their fucking throats out. I feel a cold, wet nose press against my right hand, and I look down to see Kai staring back at me. His hazel eyes searching mine while trying to hold his own fear in check.

"Babe, what are you thinking?" Kai asks. *"Please, talk to me."*

"I'm thinking several things at once, Kai. I don't know where to start."

"Tell me everything. Just go down the line, Love."

"I want to track Jeffrey and Caleb down, and I want to tear them apart. They hurt what is mine, *and I want them to pay."* I growl into his mind, *"But I'm mostly scared for you, and what will happen, Kai."* I say as I cover my face in my hands and let the hot tears flow over my cheeks.

"*Hey.*" Kai croons down the bond.

I look up at him, meeting his eyes, and I see nothing but pure confidence in them.

"*We will get through this. We don't know what type of Wolfsbane they drugged me with. Maybe I'll just stay a wolf for a while and phase back. I'm sure everything will be fine. And if they expect me to hurt my mate, they have another thing coming. I would never hurt you for as long as I can live. Remember what I told you, Love? We live a long time.*"

"*I'm not scared of that Kai, I know you wouldn't hurt me.*" I say as I run my hand over the fur on the top of his head. "*But I know you. If you hurt an innocent person, you'd never forgive yourself.*"

"*Then* if *it comes down to that,*" Kai begins, his voice gravelly in my mind, "*Stop me.*"

I look at Kai, and I can feel the unspoken challenge in his words, and that damn little seed of self-doubt tries to bloom in my chest before I can stop it. Kai seems to sense this in me, and he stands on all four feet, and he takes one step towards me, this time the challenge evident in his stance.

Kai

"*Remember Love, I come from a strong line of alphas and therefore, my mate must be just as strong. Please, Dakota, do* not *doubt your strength if the unthinkable happens.*" I plead to my mate.

Dakota nods her head at me, finally feeling the challenge I just placed in the air between us.

"I will not doubt my own power if *the time comes. I will get you back if you go off the deep end."*

I feel her alpha power flow over me, and I try to lean into her strength. Try to believe she will be able to tame the beast I may very well become if Quilla isn't fast enough with the antidote. I can feel my mood already turning sour, and it's not just from the fact of being stuck. I don't like all these eyes on me, it makes me feel cornered and I want to fight my way out. I have to keep reminding myself that I am around pack, and they mean me no harm. So, Dakota has got to believe that she's on the same level as I am if she has any chance of taming us if we go feral. I don't even want to think about how Dad may need to get involved. I have no other choice but to put this challenge in the air between us.

"Everything will be fine, though, Babe." I say again. *"But it never hurts to have a safety net."*

We all finally pick ourselves up off the bathroom floor and we make our way to the living room. Dakota takes her seat on the couch again, and I jump up next to her, resting my head in her lap while tucking my legs up under my stomach and letting my tail hang over the side of the cushion. I watch Lori and Nathan sit on the loveseat across from us, and I notice her lips are in a tight line. Like she wants to say something, but she's holding it back. I lift my head, cocking it to the right in a silent question toward her, then I hear Dakota's soft chuckle and I turn my head in her direction waiting for her to explain.

"Oh sorry. Mom doesn't like dog hair on the couch."

"Remind your mother that I am not some common house pet." I growl as I pin my ears back against my skull.

Dakota smiles and lets a light laugh bubble up from her, and it starts to piss me off, but I try to force the feeling from my mind. It's normal for humans to have an issue with animal hair on couches.

"What did he say, Dakota?" Lori asks, her cheeks red with embarrassment.

"He said to remind you that he is not a common house pet."

Lori follows suit with Dakota's laughter, and I can't help the anger that flares this time.

"I'm glad I could be the evening entertainment." I snap at Dakota, and her laughter dies automatically. *"You try being stuck like this."*

I jump down from Lori's precious couch and I make my way to the back door as I hear Dad come in from the front door after he dropped Quilla off to talk to Atticus. As I go to lift my right hand to turn the knob on Dakota's back door, I remember I have paws, so no opposable thumbs. I feel a low growl bubble in my throat at the door and at my trapped body. Dad walks over to me, and I slide my gaze to him, and I lift my lip in a silent snarl.

"One word, Dad. Just one fucking word from you." I growl in warning, filling both his mind and echoing off the walls of the house.

Dad grins, and he leans in and coos, "Does someone need to go outside?"

"Oh, go to hell and let me out this damn door."

"Easy, son. I'll open the door for you."

He finally opens it, and I push my nose through the crack, and I dash out into Dakota's backyard.

CHAPTER TWENTY-FIVE
DAKOTA

I hear the growling from Kai and Tobias' mocking childlike voice say, *"Does someone need to go outside?"* echo from the kitchen. After Kai darts into the backyard, Tobias leaves the door open enough so Kai can push his nose in the crack if he wants to come back inside.

"That was actually kinda mean, Tobias," I say when he sits down next to his mate and me on the couch.

"I know, but I have always tried to teach my son to take things in stride, to find the light in each dark situation, and sometimes that's from making a lighthearted joke."

"One day he will understand your ways, Darling." Coraline says, "Even if he views them as a bit brutish and demeaning at times. All males need to know how to be humble in humiliating situations."

"Yes, that is true, Luna. That is why he is going to have a very *humbling* experience tomorrow when he goes to school with you, Dakota." Tobias grins.

"Um...what?" I snap in confusion.

"While Kai may think he's not going to be leaving this house until he phases back, he's going to be sorely mistaken. By him not hiding away until he's phased back is showing Jeffrey that Kai has won this battle." Tobias says. "I have the paperwork being made right now to show that K is a service animal in training and you, Dakota, are his handler."

I burst out laughing at the alpha to the point where my eyes are tearing up, but his stoic expression and his relaxed body tells me he's one hundred percent serious about this. My laughter dies, and I sit up straight on the couch to look at him head-on.

"Tobias, have you lost your ever-loving *old* mind?! Kai will never in a million years go for that!" I exclaim. "Have you gone senile in your old age?"

"No, I have not, *young* one." Tobias says, flaring his alpha power over me. Not in challenge to my words, but to let me know he's thought this through. "But I will not be the one to talk him into it; you will." He adds with a wicked smile.

"Oh, you are a sly, wicked man, Tobias," I say. "Are you sure he's up to date on his shots? You know, I don't want to get rabies when he bites me after I tell him the news."

Tobias' booming laughter fills the room along with Mom, Dad and even Coraline's chuckles mingling in the air.

"My son is lucky to have you, Dakota." Tobias says as his chuckles fade and his stern voice echoes in the living room, "Just make sure he understands what he has to lose."

Kai has been out back for a few hours now, and it's just about to hit nine o'clock at night. So, I go outside to see if he wants to come inside to sleep or stay outside. Plus, I still have to tell him about Tobias' little plan.

Heaven help me.

Walking out the back door and I see Kai sleeping next to a wooden doghouse that has been in the backyard for as long as I can remember. The warped gray siding and the fading blue roof show how it hasn't been taken care of or housed an occupant. As I step closer, Kai's left ear twitches at my approaching footsteps, and he opens the same eye on that side.

"You know, now I finally understand why we never had a dog while I was growing up." I say as I touch the splintered blue roof with my index finger. "Dad and the dog would never have gotten along."

I sit down next to Kai, but I can feel his mood is still sour from what was said earlier. So, I lean my back against the rough gray siding and I let my hand rest on the grass. A silent invitation for him to touch me when he's ready. After a moment he slithers on his belly, closing the few-inch gap between us and pressing his warm, wet nose under my hand, and I slide my fingers to the top of his head in between his soft ears.

"I'm sorry for picking on you earlier. It was unfair, and I didn't realize how much it hurt you." I say softly.

"It's okay." Kai begins as he lifts his head to look at me. *"I'm just sore from the whole situation. I mean, come on, it's humiliating to be stuck like this. Me, an alpha, stuck in one form all because of a stupid fucking plant."*

"Well, it's about to get worse, Babe." I cringe.

"Why?"

I feel Kai's apprehension and anger flare from his end of the bond, but I remember Tobias' words that he has to take any situation and find the light in the hardship.

"Well... your dad has a plan." I begin, "He's getting paperwork togeth-er for you."

"Oh, thank the Great Luna. So, I'm gonna be able to make up classes once this shit gets sorted out."

"Well..." I cringe again.

"What do you mean well?" Kai asks, mocking my words.

"What I mean is, you are still going to school. As a service dog in training."

Kai jumps to his feet, walking away a few paces from me while snorting a wolven laugh. His own laughter rolls in my head through the bond.

"You have got to be kidding me?" Kai asks as he turns back around to face me, and at my own straight face all laughter fades from him and red-hot anger takes its place

"No! Not in a million years! No fucking way! This is a recipe for disaster, and you know it!"

"Kai," I begin calmly as I let a pulse of my power flow over him in an effort to stop his spiral. "Believe me, I tried to tell your father he was crazy for suggesting it. But listen to me for a minute." I say as I pat the ground next to me. Kai gives me a sideways glance, but he listens and sits down, keeping his tail tucked in tight into his left hind leg. "Do you want Jeffrey to think he's won?"

After a moment of silence, Kai says, *"No, I don't"*

"Every time that Caleb and Jeffrey have done something to get under our skin, we have been able to throw it back in their face. So we can't stop now. Show them that you are the bigger man, the bigger *alpha,* and walk into that university tomorrow with your head and tail held high."

"You seriously think we can pull it off?"

I place a hand to my chest in mock offense. "You have no faith in me, Mate? Oh, I'm hurt."

Kai growls in response, *"Stop with the dramatics. You know this will be hard for me, right?"*

"Yes, Kai. I do. But remember, I will be right with you. And if I feel you are about to lose it, then I'll crack the whip."

I send him an image of said whip, but in a much *different* situation that involves him in my bed with the three tasseled strips of leather in my hand, and the growl that follows is not laced with any anger whatsoever.

Just make sure he understands what he has to lose.

Tobias' words fill my mind, and I know what he was talking about now. Kai has to understand that if he is not able to keep things in check; if he is not able to think outside the box and allow this, albeit demeaning, situation to happen, he may very well lose me in one way or another.

"Okay. I guess I don't have much of a choice, do I?"

"Good. Now let's go back inside and go to bed."

I rise to my feet, dusting the dirt and dried grass from my pants, and I lead Kai back into the house. Once I shut the door behind me, we both hear Tobias' voice fill the living room, apparently telling my parents some kind of story that we just caught the end of. I watch as Kai shakes out his coat and begins walking into the living room, his head and tail held high.

"Dakota told me about the plan for tomorrow." I hear Kai tell his father through the bond. Apparently, it can be split between pack members. I tuck that little trick into my checklist of things I need to know as an up-and-coming alpha. *"While I still don't like the idea of me, walking into that school, I do understand. And Jeffrey will not get one over on me. So, I will go and be this, service dog that you spoke of."*

"That's my boy. That was spoken like a true alpha, Kai," Tobias praises.

"It is getting late. You two should try to get some sleep." Mom says.

I look at the clock and I notice it's almost ten-thirty. "Mom's right; we need to get to bed." I say as I look over at Kai. "Why don't you stay the night with me, Kai?"

He looks at me, his right ear twitching as if thinking over my request. *"Are you sure?"*

"Kai. Please stay with me. It would make both of us feel better."

"Alright," Kai says as he walks over to his parents to tell them good night.

As Tobias leads his mate to the door, I notice Coraline catch my eye, and I follow the two alphas through the door and onto the front porch.

"If you need us, please don't hesitate to reach out." Tobias says.

"I will, Tobias." I tell him. I look at Coraline, and I take the alpha's left hand in mine. "I will take care of him. He will not be alone tonight. I promise that Quilla and I will get your son back."

"Thank you for being what he needs tonight." Coraline says, her voice tight with emotion, and although she's trying to keep off her face, I can still see the motherly worry swirling in her blue eyes.

"Try to sleep well, Coraline. You too, Tobias." I say, nodding my head to the two quiet alphas as they step down off the porch, and I watch them walk over to their house.

I walk back into the living room, and Dad passes me before I can shut the door. "I am going to do a quick perimeter check. Make sure no one is lurking in the forest behind the house."

"Thank you, Dad." I say with a small smile.

He shuts the door behind me as I walk into the kitchen, where Kai is drinking out of a large turkey roaster that Mom put on the floor.

"Just another reason that we never had a dog while you were growing up, Dakota. I would always forget to put water down." Mom gives a soft, sad smile.

"We are horrible." I lightly chuckle.

"Thankfully, he was able to make that mental connection to me because I'm connected to your father." Mom laughs this time. "Or at least I think that's how it worked. I made my head hurt for a minute when Kai explained it."

"Believe me, I know the feeling. But I'm glad he was able to figure that out." I say, then turn my attention to Kai. "You ready to go to bed, Babe?"

"Yeah, you need to get some sleep." Kai says. *"Thank you for the water, Mrs. Shade."* I hear Kai tell Mom.

We make our way upstairs, and I pause at the top of the steps. I remember I still need a bath, but yet I don't want to leave Kai alone. Not right now.

"Hey Babe, you wanna lay in the bathroom while I get a quick shower, or you wanna go in my room and get comfy in bed?"

"You won't be afraid I'll take a peek at ya while in the shower?"

"I mean, as long as that doesn't push the boundary, I may be down for that." I say with a sly smirk. "Give ya a little striptease."

Kai shakes his head, and I see a bit of amusement shine in his eyes. *"No, I'll be okay. You only get to have so many more private showers before we are bonded. So, I think it wise to make them count, Love."*

I get the image of him and me in the shower, my body pressed against the tiled surface, his human body towering over mine, his lips close to my neck, but then the scene fades when we hear the front door slam shut as Dad comes back from checking around the house.

"Go and get your shower, Dakota. I'll be waiting for you."

After grabbing my pajamas from my dresser, I quickly take my shower. When I walk into my room a few minutes later, Kai is on my bed, curled up in the corner of the mattress that is the closest to the door. Before I can greet my mate again, I feel Tobias' presence fill my mind for a moment, and the image of a computer flashes in my mind. I make my way over to my desk in front of the large window that faces Kai's house, and I boot up my laptop. I chuckle as I pull up the email that was sent over a few minutes ago and I click print on the attached document. I feel Kai's eyes lingering on my back as I turn to grab the piece of paper off the printer, so I sit beside him on the bed to show him his papers.

"Your dad just sent me your papers for tomorrow."

"Are you kidding me?"

I show him the paperwork that has the logo for the American Service Dog Society at the top and below lists the key information I will need to 'prove' his status.

Handler: Dakota Shade

Canine's Name: K

Breed: Husky Mix

Service Training For: Emotional Support, Anxiety attacks.

Kai gives a wolfish laugh as he reads the paper.

"Husky mix? Seriously?"

"Hey, at least you're laughing about it." I smile. "I think it's cool they put K's name on here and didn't make up a random dog name."

He gives me another grin and rolls over, stretching out over the right side of the bed with a huff. I notice that his body takes up just about the same space that I feel his human form would. I lean over the side of the mattress to put the paper in my backpack before I turn my attention back to Kai.

"Your coat is beautiful, you know that?" I ask as I trace my left index finger over his head and across his side where a swirl of blonde fur runs down and curls around the softness of his belly.

"Why would you say that? I am supposed to be this fearful creature." Kai says with mock evil in his voice.

I laugh at his joke, and I run my hand down his side again while going toward his belly, but being mindful of how low I go. He is still all *male* wolf here. So, I run my hand down his spine, and when I get to the base of his tail, I make a tunnel with my thumb and middle finger so I can slip over his tail.

"Only you, my loving mate, can make me a puddle beneath your feet. I love you rubbing me like this. And being mindful *of where you rub."* Kai sighs into my head. *"It almost makes being stuck like this manageable."*

My face goes three shades of red knowing exactly what he's talking about.

He sits up to look me in the eye as he croons, *"See, I told you I could still see your red cheeks as a wolf."*

"Oh, shut up." I say as I playfully push him back down on the mattress.

I get up to turn my light off and with the light from the streetlamp shining through the window, I can see Kai sitting back up on his belly, his back legs stretched out and his front paws crossed over the other at his wrists, tail swishing contently against the comforter. His bushy, pointed ears are at full attention and pointing in my direction, and his hazel eyes shine brightly in the low light. I know then and there that most people would be running for the hills at something this regal and powerful lying on their bed, but knowing who this is, knowing it's my soul mate, I am in awe at the creature before me.

"You are beautiful, regal, powerful, and *mine.*" I growl the last word.

"*Absolutely, mate.*" Kai agrees, his voice deep and radiating power. "*Just as you are* mine.*"

I slip into bed, grabbing his head in my hands, and I give him a kiss between the eyes, and I hold his stare with only a sliver of air between our foreheads.

"We will get through this. I am not going to lose you this easily."

I lie down on my side, pulling the covers back to invite him under them with me. He curls up beside me where his nose almost touches my own, and we drift off to sleep, praying that things go smoothly tomorrow.

CHAPTER TWENTY-SIX
DAKOTA

I am pulled from my deep slumber all too soon when my alarm clock starts blaring at me. I go to reach for Kai's furry shoulder, but I don't feel him next to me. I sit up onto my elbows while smacking the alarm to silence it and look for Kai. I spot him at the foot of the bed, wide awake and curled up in a tight circle, his head on his paws with his tail just under his feet.

"Good morning. How long have you been awake?" I ask while rubbing the sleep from my own eyes.

"About two and a half hours. I couldn't sleep anymore."

"You should have woken me up instead of being alone." I say as I sit up in bed with the covers still over my legs.

"I didn't want to wake you at four in the morning. Besides, I've never seen you sleep before." Kai chuckles. *"You're cute when you sleep. You have the most adorable snore."*

"I do not snore."

"Whatever you say, Babe." Kai says as he jumps off my bed, stretching his lithe body across my floor and then shaking his coat out.

I shake my head as I roll out of bed myself. Going over to the closet, I grab a pair of jean shorts and a pink t-shirt, then make my way to the bathroom to get ready for school. Once we make our way downstairs, Dad has breakfast consisting of scrambled eggs, bacon, sausage, and strip steak cooking on the griddle and Mom is already perched on a barstool at the island with a cup of coffee in her hand and a half-eaten plate before her. When Dad sees the two of us enter the kitchen, he makes my plate and a bowl for Kai.

"Thank you, Dad. Breakfast looks amazing." I say.

"Thank you, Beta, for the meal." Kai says as he steps up to the bowl of food and water Dad put down on the floor.

I've noticed that when Kai talks to other people, he includes me in the conversations, and I reach out to him through bond to privately ask him why.

"Hey, Babe. I noticed that when you spoke to Mom last night and now Dad this morning, you included me in your conversation. Why are you doing that?"

"Because I'm trying to make it seem as normal as possible. If I were human, you would hear me talk to them."

I nod, letting him know I understand. I feel my own anger flare again at what Jeffrey and Caleb did to him, but I try to bottle up the anger and not let it get the best of me.

After we finish breakfast, we have ten minutes before we have to leave for class, and as I go to grab my backpack from the floor beside me, I see Kai glance sheepishly toward the back door.

"What's wrong, Kai?" I ask.

I hear his stomach growl, but I know it can't be from hunger. As the thought hits me, I give him a small smile and I walk over to the back door.

"I'm sorry that I didn't think of it sooner. Still gotta use the facilities, huh?" I open the back door and point with my head as I say, "Go on. Just meet me out front when you're done."

"*Thank you for the privacy.*"

"Hey, I wouldn't walk in on you while you're human. You may be in a different body, but it's still *you,* Kai."

"*Thank you, Love. I'll see you out front.*" He says as he dashes outside, and I close the door behind him.

I make my way to the front door and sitting on the little table nestled in the corner is a blue and black Service Dog vest with an eight-foot leash attached that Tobias must have brought over before we came down this morning along with a baggie of beef jerky in one of those waist pouches that trainers wear for rewarding dogs for doing a good job. With a shake of my head, I grab the vest and the pouch, wave goodbye to my parents, and walk out the front door while trying to keep a smile on my face and not think about what could happen today.

I open my rear driver's door and I throw my backpack in the backseat before heading to the other side to put the vest and pouch on the front passenger floorboard while I wait for Kai to finish out back. I glance over the roof of my car and I see Kai easily jump the six-foot fence and trot over to the driver's side of the car out of habit of him being the one to take us to school.

I meet him by the driver's door, opening it as I say, "In ya go, but I'm drivin' us to school today."

He takes a bounding leap over my seat and the center console, landing gracefully in the passenger seat while sitting tall and regal. He glances down, and he slowly takes in the vest and pouch that is resting on the floorboard, and the sound of my door closing is the only thing that breaks his stare.

"Why is there a vest on the floorboard? And why do I smell jerky?"

"Because it's what all the service dogs are wearing, Kai. It's *all the rage.* Plus, I figured you'd want a snack at some point today." I don't have the heart to tell him the real reason why I have that pouch, not yet at least.

I can see the anger starting to bubble in his eyes, and I can feel a twinge of it starting to flow from his side of the bond, and I know I need to get his attitude on this situation under control.

"Kai. Stop. I know this is hard on you, but you have got to try to work with what you've been given, and just deal with it." I say, letting my alpha power flow over him. I see him take a breath, and the anger fades on the exhale. "Just be lucky it wasn't pink, okay?"

"Thanks, Dakota. Thank you for making me put things into a different perspective. You're right, I need to deal with this with a level head."

"Okay, so now that we got that straightened out, let's go to school."

When we arrive at the university, I pull into a parking spot that is as close to the door as I can in case I need to get Kai out quickly.

"Stay here. Let me come around and help you into your vest." I say as I get out of the car.

I open his door, grabbing the vest from the floorboard, and as I turn it over in my hands to inspect it, it seems fairly easy to put on. I unbuckle the large strap that will fasten around his belly and, while keeping the built-in collar together, I adjust the size so I can slip it over his large head without choking him. He pins his ears back for a moment to make it easier for me to slide it down his neck, and the strap settles on the base of his throat.

"Okay, can you jump out so I can fasten it under your stomach?"

I back up a step so Kai can jump down and stand beside the car. Reaching down, again being mindful of *things* and I grab the strap to fasten it to the buckle that is on the side of the vest. I then grab for the leash and clip it into the eyelet that's attached to the reinforced nylon that runs the length of his back.

"A leash, really"

"Kai." I scold.

He pins his ears back and lets out a snort of disgust but doesn't say anymore. I grab the pouch to buckle it around my hips before I open the rear passenger door to grab my backpack and take a moment to steel myself before we walk in. It's at this time I realize that I don't see Quilla's car here at all. At first, part of me wants to reach out to her, to make sure she's okay, but I have the feeling that I would know if something bad happened to her. So, I just hold on to hope that she's getting closer to figuring out a way to help Kai. I turn back to my mate, who's been sitting on the pavement, patiently waiting for me to walk with him.

"You ready?"

"About as ready as I'll ever be," He says, but then I feel amusement flow from his end of the bond. *"I will say, I am excited to see the looks on those assholes' faces when I walk in those doors."*

"There's my alpha talking." I smile. "Let's do this. Just keep your head held high, Babe. And remember I'll keep you in line." I say as I let a pulse of my alpha power flow over him.

He stands beside me, and I wrap my hands around the nylon handle running down his back and walk into the school.

Chapter Twenty-Seven
DAKOTA

When we walk toward the school, I notice that Kai is walking fairly well on a leash, and I feel pride swell in my chest for him, but I realize I don't block my thoughts from him in time. He whips his head back in my direction and gives me a bit of a snarl before turning back around.

"Hey, it's just that you are supposed to be this *evil,* and *mean* creature, I didn't think you'd be good on a leash, okay?"

Kai gives me a low growl in response but keeps walking. As we enter the building, I can see and feel all eyes on us, but they continue on their way without a word. I keep a light steady flow of my alpha power flowing over Kai to keep him calm, and it seems to work for now. As we enter my first class, I am stopped by the professor when I walk by his desk.

"Miss Shade, you know there are no animals allowed in the class-rooms."

My stomach falls to my knees at his words.

This isn't going to work.

I take a breath and with a shaky hand, I pull out the paperwork that I stuffed in my backpack last night and show it to the professor.

"I signed up to be a service dog trainer last week, and K is my first animal I'm training." I explain.

The professor looks at the paperwork and then to Kai, who is now sitting close to my side and nudging my hand to help me steady my nerves.

"Nice touch, Babe." I tell him. He is supposed to help with anxiety and all. I unzip my pouch and pull out a piece of jerky and offer it to Kai before saying, "Good boy, K"

I can feel Kai's confusion and then a slight flare of anger through the bond. *"Do I look like a fucking dog that needs a treat for when I do a good job?"*

"Right now, yes. Now shut it and take the jerky."

Kai reluctantly takes the offered piece of jerky from my hand, and the professor notices his actions before handing the paperwork back to me.

"Alright, but keep him quiet and under the desk."

"Yes, sir."

I walk to my normal seat in the center of the room and I motion for Kai to lie under the desk.

"We might actually pull this service dog thing off." He chuckles.

I give him a small smile and listen to the professor give his lecture.

When my first class ends three hours later, my classmates want to pet Kai on their way out since he's been such a 'good boy' during the lecture. I know that a normal service animal should not be touched, so I politely decline their advances and walk out into the hall with Kai close to my hip.

"Thanks, Babe, for keeping people away from me."

"I knew you wouldn't like that, Kai. So, no thanks is needed." I give him a small smile as I continue to walk down the hallway to my next class.

As we turn the corner and head down the six steps to a lower floor, we pass Jeffrey and Caleb leaning casually next to the bathroom doors. I feel Kai's body tense up at the sight of the alpha and his beta, and I send a strong pulse of my power toward Kai to keep him in line, and I know I just barely stopped the growl from bubbling from his throat.

"I'm not going to be able to do this. I want to fucking rip them apart, Dakota." Kai growls in my head, and I can feel his anger color his thoughts.

"You will not *break. Do you hear me?"* I say as I push my power over him yet again, and it seems to break his thought process completely this time.

"Now, the next class I have is with Caleb. So you need to try to keep it together."

While I don't hear a growl, I know he despises it all the same.

So we head to my next class a bit before Professor Brown arrives, and we are already the talk of this class too. I hear the hushed whispers as I take my seat next to the window while Kai settles under the desk. I again politely decline anyone who asks to touch him, and most understand, other than the one asshole that gives me a dirty look, but I just pointedly ignore him.

Professor Brown comes in and then, a heartbeat later, Caleb follows with a dark chuckle rumbling from his chest. Before I can stop him, Kai crawls out from under my desk and sits beside me, his eyes locked on Caleb as he takes his usual seat in the corner of the room. When Professor Brown starts her lesson, I try to leave Kai alone in the hopes that Caleb would make the smart move and avert his gaze, but twenty minutes go by and they are still in a stare down. I can see the muscles in Kai's shoulder start to twitch, and I can feel through the bond that he's trying like hell not to attack this asshole for his obvious disrespect for an alpha. I also know for a fact that Kai will not be the one to break eye contact first, so I am going to have to make Caleb avert his gaze.

"Kai, stay here at my desk."

"What are you going to do?" Kai asks as his right ear flicks toward my body, the only acknowledgment of my words to him.

"I'm gonna put a little wanna-be beta in his place because I know you will not be the first to break eye contact, which I don't blame you."

"Nope, and I'm trying real fucking hard not to growl at his blatant disrespect to someone higher than he is." Kai says as his muscles start to tremble further down his leg in agitation.

I raise my hand to get Professor Brown's attention, and she stops mid-sentence and looks toward me, signaling me to speak.

"I'm sorry to interrupt, but can you please tell Caleb to *stop* staring at my service dog?" I say as I shoot him a sharp glare.

He has the audacity to laugh. It's so loud that it rattles off the windows to my right, and I see Kai's muzzle lift in a silent snarl. I release a burst of my alpha power, like an invisible whip between us, and he settles down a bit.

"You call that *thing* a dog?" Caleb points to Kai and chuckles, "*Honey*, you need your eyes checked." He says in a chastising tone.

Kai rises to his feet at the mocking tone toward me, and I hear his low growl start to bubble in his throat.

"K! Quiet!" I snap again, pushing my command onto him.

My arms and legs begin to feel heavy, like they are lined with lead, and I'm assuming it's from using my alpha power in a way that I am not used to yet. But I find it within myself to keep that tether on my mate while also shoving my power, as swift as a snake lashing out to strike at Caleb. As the invisible force hits him, he sits back in his seat, his cocky smile weakening for a moment before he tries to set it back in full force.

I stand from my desk, striding over to Caleb's little corner, while keeping my back to the humans so they won't see the inhuman exchange about to happen.

I take a breath as I gather what strength I have left, and when I lift my gaze to Caleb's, his brown eyes flash in response to my own glowing brightly in return. I lower my voice to the point where he's the only one to hear me.

"You and your wanna-be alpha brought this on yourself. Drugging him with Wolfsbane," I chuckle darkly, as my right knee starts to shake from the power rolling off me that I can't seem to stop. I know I have to end this soon before I lose what ground I was able to gain "But know this, *Caleb,* we will always come back bigger and stronger than you two. So, I suggest you keep your mouth shut and eyes averted because one little falter in my hold on him and he will rip your Fucking. Throat. Out."

I spin on my heel, leaving him shocked and speechless as I head back to my seat. Kai slowly goes back under my desk with a soft whine, knowing I'm at my breaking point.

"Are we good now?" Professor Brown asks.

Just as I am about to answer her, Caleb suddenly jumps from his desk, causing Kai to rise to his feet again, but Caleb rushes out the door without looking back.

"I guess I did something to piss him off." I say innocently to Kai.

"Oh well, too damn bad." Kai growls in response.

We get through this class without further distractions, but the two hours that pass does nothing to help build my strength back, so I decide to just call it a day and go home early.

"I'm sorry, Dakota. I forced you to use too much power today."

We are alone in the hallway, so I just talk to him normally, plus I'm too tired to use the bond that way to be honest.

"It's okay. I understand where you were coming from, Kai. I just need to learn to get stronger." I sigh, "And what's a better way to do that than using my power?"

"Not like the way you needed to today, Babe. Let's go home so you can rest."

I feel his worry, love, and strength bloom from his side of the bond, and I try to lean into those feelings, willing his strength into me.

I open the main door that leads to the parking lot, and as I take one step onto the asphalt, I hear a sharp, vicious warning growl rip from Kai's throat. His body gets lower to the ground, readying himself for an attack as his hackles rise to make him look even bigger and deadlier than he already is. I lift my head and I see Jeffrey leaning calmly against the side panel of my car, arms folded over his chest and his legs crossed at the ankle. He looks up at me, completely ignoring Kai like he's a teacup poodle and not a huge two-hundred-and-twenty-pound Werewolf that could rip him to shreds without a second thought.

"You have no sense of personal space, do you?" I snap over Kai's snarls and exposed, sharp canines.

"Awe, how was *doggy's* first day?" Jeffrey asks, ignoring my question.

Kai lunges for him at his mocking comment, only stopping short by the leash that I have attached to his harness and the fact that I do have the unnatural strength to hold him back. But I don't pull him back to my side. I let him do what he needs. To show that he's not afraid to attack in broad daylight, and I'm not impartial in letting go.

"Jeffrey, I will give you one chance. Move, or I will let Kai rip you to shreds here and now. Hell, I might even get in on the action." I say with surprising calm. "You hurt what is *mine*, my mate, and I do *not* take kindly to that."

Jeffrey laughs heartlessly and takes a step toward me, completely side-stepping Kai again and locking eyes with me. I stiffen my spine and somehow find my power again, willing it to create an invisible wall between us. Granted, it's a fragile wall with my waning strength, but it's enough to make him take a single step back from me.

"You still say this mutt is your mate?"

He acknowledges Kai, but at his disapproving scowl, it makes my blood boil.

"He's not even a true alpha yet. Come with me. With a true alpha of power and I can show you just how strong you can become, Darling."

Jeffrey leans in to try to caress my cheek, and I can see in his eyes it's a way to get Kai's scent off me and replace it with his. The thought sends sickening shivers through my bones, but before I can even think to take a step back, Kai barks viciously, drool foaming around his lower canines, and jumps up trying to bite at Jeffrey's hand to get it away from me.

"Oh my, someone needs obedience training, doesn't he?" Jeffrey croons mockingly. "Looks like you better get to work, Darling."

"Don't call me darling, flea-bag."

Jeffrey steps back a few paces, but he gives me a shit-eating grin before he says, "You win for now. But will you have the strength left to bring him back from the brink? Let's see just how much you *love* him."

Chapter Twenty-Eight

DAKOTA

I watch Jeffrey walk away. His cocky swagger, his hands in his pockets without a care in the world as he enters the red brick building of the school. I still hear Kai growling, low and threateningly, to my right, eyes still fixed on the large metal door that Jeffrey walked through, waiting for him to come back out. I kneel down to him, setting my hand gently on his shoulder, and I try to gather my alpha power to calm him, but I feel myself sputter on the power. I can barely feel Kota in my mind, and I can tell she's just as tired as I am but equally as furious.

"Kai." I say gently to get his attention.

His left ear twitches, and after a moment, that seems to break him from his trance.

"Are you okay, Love?"

"Yeah. I'm okay. Let's get out of here." I whisper.

I stand up and walk over to the passenger side of my car, and Kai follows without an issue. When I open the door, he jumps up into the seat and sits down, curling his tail over his feet.

"Here, let's get this off you. You don't need it now."

I slip my hand under his belly to unclasp the metal buckle of his vest, then as I pull the neck strap over his head, I drop the vest onto the floorboard with a clink of metal upon metal filling the silence between us. He shakes his coat out and gives me a quiet nod as I shut the door.

Kai

After Dakota removes my vest, I try to block my mind from her because I can feel my anger continuing to build over the encounter with Jeffrey. All I want to do is hunt him down and rip him to fucking shreds. For one, even attempting to touch Dakota, to put his scent on her instead of mine. For even putting that seed of doubt in her mind of whether she will be strong enough to bring me back from the brink. Then yes, for having the audacity to not look the least bit terrified of me. That is going to be his downfall. Because once I'm pissed off and challenged, I don't stop until I come out on top. My body trembles from the need to spill his blood. To make him pay.

When that thought crosses my mind, I shake my coat out again, trying to clear the thoughts from my mind before Dakota drops into the driver's seat beside me. We both ride in silence, so I try to lie down on the front seat with my ass pressed firmly against the door while I rest my head on my front paws near the center console. My eyes want to close on me, but when I feel fingers start to rub my left ear, my eyes snap open and I catch Dakota still looking forward at the road, but her fingers are gently rubbing my ear and it helps ease the tension and anger still bubbling under the surface. I can tell she's exhausted. Even when I open my mind to her, I barely feel her, and it makes my heart constrict to the point of pain. I can only hope that I can hold on to my slowly ebbing sanity long enough for her to recover.

Dakota

I pull into the driveway and I see that Mom and Dad are home, which I am thankful for. Part of me wants to be around those that I feel are pack for some reason that I don't understand.

"Come on, Babe. Let's go inside." I say as I gently stroke his head, his ears folding under my hand.

I open my door, and Kai stands, leaps across the console to gracefully land on the driveway, and turns back to watch me close the door. I give him a small, weak smile as I walk into the house.

As soon as I open the door, I am met with the curious eyes of Mom and Dad. With one look at my tired face, Dad is immediately on his feet and helping me to the couch.

"What happened?"

"It's just Caleb and Jeffrey being their typical asshole selves." I say.

"They both had their fair share of trying to piss us off today." Kai growls.

Ever since the tiff with Jeffrey, Kai has been closed off, and when he does speak, it's with a hard, snappy tone. I start to worry about him and hope that Quilla is almost ready with that antidote. I want to reach out to her, but again I think it's best to leave her alone.

"Dakota, you look exhausted; please lie down for a while," Dad says gently.

I nod and I go to lie down on the couch while Mom moves to the loveseat with Dad. Kai comes over to the couch and lies on the floor, where my head is above him on the couch. So, I turn over on my stomach and put my hand on his back while digging my fingers deep into his rough coat, his muscles jumping at my touch. I don't know if it's just my hand moving his fur or something deeper, something darker, that makes his muscles shiver under my hand. Like he may not want me to touch him right now. I still can't feel him in the back of my mind like I normally do, and when I try to find my slowly renewing strength to push into his mind, I find there is a solid line of something similar to trees blocking me. Part of this hurts me, but yet I understand. Hell, I'm pissed over what all happened today, so I can only imagine what is going through his head. And with that, I don't try to push into his mind, and I let my eyes fall, willing sleep to take me.

A few minutes later, I feel Kai move under my hand, shifting to lie on his side. I try to remember where I should put my hand to be mindful of his body, and I let myself drift again, feeling his ribcage rise and fall with each breath. I feel him move again, this time back onto his belly, my hand sliding to my original position on his back. I crack open one eye to look around, and I notice that Mom and Dad have also fallen asleep on the loveseat. Dad sitting up with his head resting against the back of the loveseat, and Mom's head is cradled in his lap while his hand rests on her left shoulder.

I reach out to Kai again, and this time I can find just a sliver of an opening in his shield, so I pry my way in.

"You okay?"

"No. I don't want to be cooped up in the house. I'm sorry, but can you let me out in the backyard?" His voice is his own, but I can still feel it's tense, and he's trying to keep his tone civil toward me.

"Sure. I'll leave the door cracked so if you want to come back in, you can."

"Thank you."

I stand up and make my way to the back door as Kai follows behind me. His head is hung low, and he's looking at me through half-lidded eyes. This is the first time that I feel like I have a real beast behind me, but I tamp down my fear, hoping it's just from him being pinned up.

"I'm gonna try to get some rest, and you should too if you can." I say.

Kai walks past me, but I feel like he's walking *away* from me.

"Kai?" I say, and he stops with his right front paw still in the air, as if his name from my lips made him freeze. I don't know what I want to say at this moment, so I opt for what I still know. "I love you."

"I love you too." He whispers, voice so low that even in my mind I barely hear it. *"Please get some rest, Love."*

With that, he continues to walk into my backyard and toward the broken-down doghouse. It's almost like that dilapidated structure matches his soul right now.

Kai

I lie down next to the doghouse, the sun beating down on my back, but it doesn't warm me. It's like this form is now becoming a shell, the internal turmoil the only thing that I can feel. I will my eyes to close and I focus on K's forest. It takes me a few minutes, but when I open my eyes,

I am in my own human body again, and as I take in the familiar forest around me, my heart freezes in my chest.

Instead of calm blue skies with wispy white clouds and chirping birds, the sky is dark with low storm clouds filling the tree line, and it's deathly quiet. Not one chirping song of a bird can be heard. Not even the stream nearby makes a sound.

"K!?" I yell, my heart pounding painfully against my chest. "Where are you?!"

I begin to walk the forest, but I find that I want to get lost easily. This is not the same forest that I grew up with. It might as well be a foreign country.

"K, where are you?" I scream again, twisting my head all around to try to find my wolf.

Then I hear a loud, long, deep howl, and I am frozen to the spot. The sound sends shivers down my spine as I recognize what that howl means.

It's a hunting howl, and for the first time, I feel like prey. I hear a branch snap behind me and I spin around, crouching low to the ground as I see K stalk from the forest. His eyes are wide and feral, his lip curled up in a silent snarl.

"Hello, Kai." K croons, voice low and with a growl lacing his words.

"K, this is not you. Come on, you need to fight this drug." I plead.

K snarls and takes a step toward me, and I am forced to take a step back at his sudden outburst. *"No! I feel so much more powerful than I have* ever *felt."* K exclaims. *"You need to* embrace *this power you feel flowing through our veins. I know you feel it."*

He's right. I do feel the power. It's like I could make anyone bow to me. I could fight an entire pack and I would come out on top. But at what cost? I know it's cliche to think about in a time like this, but the saying that Uncle Ben told Peter Parker about *great power, comes great responsibility* flows in my mind. With strength like this, there is bound to be backlash at some point. That thought is what keeps my human self from succumbing to the effects totally.

"K, you know this is not us. Deep down I *know* you realize this. Please fight this. Fight for our mate."

He ignores my pleas, and he stalks me now, but this time I see him coming, and I force myself to stand my ground. We are equals, and I do not back down from my own wolf.

"*You said it yourself; you want blood. I heard you. And frankly, so do I.*"

He gathers his hind legs under him and, with a toothy grin, he leaps at me, shoving my back and shoulders into the dried grass.

"*Now sit back, shut the fuck up and let me in control!*"

I feel him take over the body back in the real world, and I feel something snap between us so fast that I cannot stop it from leaking over to Dakota.

CHAPTER TWENTY-NINE
DAKOTA

I am jarred awake from something on Kai's end of the bond. The best way I can explain it is that something was severed between me and Kai. I glance up at the digital clock on the TV stand, the white, blocky font showing I've been asleep for an hour. From the partially open back door, I hear the most terrifyingly vicious snarl come from the backyard.

At this sound, Mom, Dad, and I jump from our seats and rush across the house. I'm the first one to grab onto the doorknob, wrenching the door open in time to catch Kai running off through the yard towards the line of trees beyond the fence.

"Kai!" I scream, but then I can feel something different when I go to reach for the mind of the body in front of me, for the pure wolf in front of me. This is K in full force. I can't feel Kai at all, and that makes my blood run ice cold.

"K! Please come back!"

He whips his head around to me as the sound of my voice hits his ears, lets a warning snarl rip from his throat, and then easily jumps over the fence and runs deeper into the forest. I feel Dad and Mom come up behind me, but as I lose sight of the chocolaty-blonde color of his coat, I shove past my parents and race over to Tobias' house. I fly up the stairs of the concrete porch and I shove open the door, not caring if I somehow broke the lock or not.

"Tobias!" I scream. "Forgive the rude entry, but Kai and K have gone mad!"

Tobias comes rushing out of a back room, and Coraline enters from the kitchen a moment later.

"Damn it." Tobias curses. "I felt something different from him, but I didn't know what it was at first."

He pulls out his phone, and whoever is on the other line answers on the first ring.

"I need that antidote *now*. He has gone mad."

"I'll be there. We finally found the right concoction that would be strong enough." I hear Quilla's voice filter through the alpha's phone.

Tobias hangs up without another word and turns to look at me for a moment as I feel tears prick the corners of my eyes.

I can still save him.

"While we have the antidote, Dakota, it has to be you to find him and keep him still long enough to make him drink the liquid." Tobias says as he walks out the front door that I just burst through. The same one that I now realize I ripped the lock from the frame. "K will only see me as nothing but a challenge. I'm hoping that seeing his mate will calm him." Tobias continues.

"So you're saying that K may actually attack me, even being his mate?" I ask with dread, remembering Caleb and now Jeffrey's taunts.

The bastards knew *exactly* what they were doing. I just hope the hour's nap I had was good enough to bring back the power I need to subdue K.

"I'm not going to lie to you, Dakota." Tobias says as he walks over to his GMC Denali and opens the passenger door for me. "It's a possibility that he will attack. This is a pure battle of willpower. Are you stronger than the wolf, or will he be the stronger one?"

Just before Tobias closes the passenger door, I feel a sharp pain in my right temple and I get flashes of a crowded downtown street near a flower shop, people running away, screaming, but no one is hurt yet, thankfully.

"We gotta move, *now!*" I shout.

Tobias rushes into the driver's seat as I show him the images flashing through my mind. He peels out of the driveway and, with his quick reflexes, we make our way through the mid-afternoon traffic without incident. I take a moment and reach out to Quilla so I can let her know where I need her to meet us.

"Quilla, I need you in the shopping center downtown, near the flower shop."

"I am on it. I'm sorry I didn't get it done in time. We needed to make sure it would handle the worst version of the Wolfsbane, and it took a few trial runs."

"You can help stop this, Quilla. That's what I want now."

I pull back from her mind when I hear Tobias take a breath and look in the rearview mirror. I look over my shoulder and I see my father's Nissan Rogue trailing us. I glance at Tobias, and he gives me a quick nod before focusing back on the road.

"I called your father in case you needed help. While Nathan is dominant, he's not as dominant as I am. So, if needed, your father can be the muscle for you." He pauses, and he looks at me with such sorrow in his eyes that I dread his next words.

"If I need to step in, it will be because he's gone too far off the deep end that I will have no choice but to kill him."

My mind is running a mile a minute due to this info dump from Tobias. I hate the thought of my father fighting K to keep me safe. But I hate the thought that if I cannot talk K down, if I cannot get through his Wolfsbane-induced bloodlust, Tobias will step in to kill him even more. I refuse to let that image take root in my head.

"I understand, Alpha. I will do everything in my power to keep that from happening." I say, feeling the need to let him know that I understand how much it will hurt the most powerful alpha of the states to possibly have to take one of his own, his son, down like that.

Fifteen minutes later, we finally arrived at the plaza downtown. I open my door to the sounds of people screaming while running away in all directions. I hear the snarls, growls, and sharp barks of K mingling through the chaos around me. Dad walks up behind me, and I can feel his power, his strength, flow over me, and I somehow grab onto that sensation as I take a calming breath. I know I cannot let any fear bubble to the surface, or K will attack before I even have a chance to do anything.

I look back at Dad, and his eyes are a bright honey brown, letting me know that Nate is only a breath away and is ready to make my father's form change to protect me. I give him a firm nod and we begin to make our way into the still scrambling crowd while Tobias stays back to help guide the people to safety and makes sure no one distracts me while I pull the feral wolf back from the brink of his own possible destruction.

Kai

I run across the landscape of K's forest, which has become my prison. The dark sky is still looming overhead, and it's so eerily quiet that I can hear my footfalls and my heavy breathing echo off each and every tree. I come up to the river that runs through the tree line and fall on my hands and knees to peer through the water, which gives me a one-way view of what's going on outside. I can see K lunge at people—men, women, and children. I thank the Great Luna that he hasn't bitten anyone, but still, this isn't us. We don't hurt anyone that hasn't tried to hurt us first.

"K! You have to stop this!"

I try to push my hand through the water in the same way I have done for years to be able to get to the front of our mind, to take control of our wolven body, but instead of my hand dipping under the water, I am met with something similar to solid glass. Only my fingers break the surface, but not enough to make any kind of connection to my wolf.

"K! Listen to me. Stop this!" I scream as I roll my hand into a fist, beating against the clear wall between us.

I can hear the screams of the people around us becoming less and less and for a moment I think we have ventured into a less crowded area, but the person that comes into our line of sight is one that I wish would have stayed far, far away from us.

"K, you need to stop this."

I hear her voice. So calm, and gentle. With the index finger of my right hand, I run it over the image of her before me, the water rippling off her form at my touch. Then I hear K snarl viciously at her appearance, at her words. I beat my open palm against the glass once, twice, three times.

Water drenches my hair, face, and clothes as I bellow into the water, *"Stop snarling at our mate, you stupid wolf!"*

"K, please stop this and come back to me, mate of mine." Dakota gently says while reaching out her hand to the wolf before her.

I hear K snarl again at her and I somehow hear him say as he takes a step toward her, *"No, I want blood."*

"Dakota, please mate, get out of here! I don't want to see you get hurt!"

I push the thought to Dakota, but this is when I realize that since K somehow partially severed our connection, I can't reach Dakota at all and that thought makes my heart sink to my stomach like a rock.

"The K I know would not kill senselessly," Dakota says coolly but with a hint of a sharpness to her tone.

"You will not stop me from spilling blood!" K roars.

Dakota gives a bit of a pained smile, but she takes a step forward, and even through the fractured bond, I feel her alpha power trickle through the water-logged glass below me, so I am sure that K is feeling her full power.

"STAND DOWN, K!"

I barely hear K's whine reverberate through the water before he growls back at her, the sound sending chills down my spine. It's a warning growl before he attacks.

"You want blood so badly, K?" Dakota asks K, and what she does next has my heart freezing in my chest, and I don't dare take a breath. I watch as my mate drops to her knees, making herself an easy target for K to attack. "If you want to spill blood as badly as you say, then take mine. But will you truly hurt your mate, K?"

She looks the wolf directly in the eye, and I can hear the challenge in her tone, and I know K feels it settle on his shoulders. The silent question of what drives him more at this moment. Taking blood, no matter whose it is, or not hurting his mate? I can feel Dakota's alpha power again, stronger this time, but I can tell it wants to sputter, and at that moment, I know she's still not recovered from this morning.

"Now I will tell you once more, K, or I will get physical if you force me to. *Stand down!*"

I see K drop to his belly for a heartbeat and feel a smile start to bloom on my lips. We then hear the sound of a car door slamming, which makes K jump and snarl again at Quilla, who is exiting her Sentra with a clear water bottle.

"Ah, damn it, you hardhead." Dakota groans.

Even though I know deep down she can't hear me, I can't just sit here and not try to reach out to her. So, I put my hand flat against the phantom glass in the water, hot tears rolling down my face, and plead, *"Please, Dakota, I can't stand to see you get hurt because of this. I can tell you're at your limit, Mate. Please, let our father kill us."*

Dakota

I am at my limit and with K now snarling at Quilla's arrival, I know I am just about screwed six ways from Sunday. I *have* to do something. I refuse to let it come down to Tobias needing to kill K and Kai because I failed them. I had K on his belly in submission once, and I need to get that to happen again. I look to my father and I see him holding Quilla behind him to keep her safe, but it's that familiar power flowing off him that draws my attention again. Kota perks up at this feeling, wanting to pull that power toward her.

"You think we can tap into Dad's power as a beta to help us?" I ask quickly.

"Yes. I think so. I think, with us being at the level of alpha, we can pull power from parts of the pack."

"Do it. Whatever we need. Do it before we lose him again." I snap, but I know she doesn't take my tone personally.

I feel her reach out to Dad's wolf, to his power, and it fuels me again. I watch as K fights against what's left of the command I put on him, watch as he takes another step toward me, drool now dripping from his jaws. Suddenly, on the next street over, I hear a car backfiring, and that makes me flinch and look over my shoulder for a split second. The next thing I know is I hear a bone rattling snarl erupt in front of me, and I watch as K leaps at me with a feral gleam in his eyes. I crouch down to make myself smaller, but I am, frozen to the spot. I can't get my feet to move. It's like being back on that roof at the university again, fear paralyzing me where I am at the mercy of my attacker.

I see a dark form dart from my peripheral vision and meet K's attack from the side, knocking him off his trajectory and rolling with him across the pavement and onto the sidewalk. I close my eyes and wait for the scream of death that I'm sure K will make when Tobias rips his throat out.

I failed him, failed all of my new pack even before I started to learn what it was to be a mate and alpha.

A heartbeat later, when I only hear swift, angry snarls, I open my eyes and look to my left. I realize the other wolf is my dad. His dark gray coat contrasts with K's chocolate and blonde fur. Both are still snarling, lips curled up to show their canines. Dad's front paw is pressed into the curve of K's shoulder trying to keep him pinned to the sidewalk. The side eye glare that Dad is giving K dares him to move. I then notice that Dad is only slightly taller than K, but K makes up for the height difference in bulk.

I let loose a breath as K acts like he is going to submit to my father, and I am about to walk over to try to get K back under my control again but in the blink of an eye, K is launching up toward my father's throat. Dad jumps back enough, but K still pulls out a tuft of fur with his teeth as Dad moves out of the bite zone. Before Dad can get his feet back on the ground, K jumps into him again, and this time his teeth graze Dad's shoulder. I watch as the bright red, coppery liquid flows across Dad's dark fur. I hear a satisfied growl bloom from K, and his words from earlier flood my mind; *I want to spill blood,* and this makes my own blood boil. He hurt my father, my pack and I have to stop this.

I steel myself as I then reach out for Tobias' strength without thinking, and I am filled with power that amplifies my own. I take a breath as I march down the sidewalk, letting my refueled power roll from me. I imagine mental chains snaking up from the ground to latch onto K's legs, and he lets out another low warning growl, and I let my own rip right back at him. I watch as his eyes go wide, and I reach out with my hand, grabbing him by the scruff, and I dig my fingers deep into his coat until I feel my nails dig into his skin.

"Shut the hell up!" I command. "Don't you move a muscle."

My voice is not my own as I speak these commands. I feel Kota so close to the front of my mind, it's almost like we are each looking through an eye. When K's huge head looks up at me, I see my own eyes glowing a bright blue in the reflection of his own. I feel K calm down under my hand, but I don't wait for him to get a second wind. I look at my father out of the side of my eye, and I can tell he's waiting for my next command.

"Dad, open the hatch to your SUV."

He complies without a word, shifting smoothly, the blood running down his arm and chest. Quilla quickly hands him his pants, and he steps into them as he keeps walking while glancing back to make sure Quilla stays close. Once he opens the hatch, I look back to K and I gather my power again, directing to it him, and he whines under my scrutiny.

"Walk." I command.

I keep my hand buried into the scruff of his neck while he stands and slowly walks over to Dad's SUV. When we reach the bumper, K pauses, and I realize I didn't give him permission to get in the SUV.

"Smart wolf." I say. "Jump up and lie down." I add with a sharpness in my tone.

He easily leaps up into the hatch, turns back to face me then lies down with his head between his paws. I look to my dad again and I give him a nod to allow Quilla to move from his protection. I need to get this done and over with because I am starting to fade again. I can feel it.

"Quilla, please come here."

She rushes from behind my father and up to the space beside me.

"This is the healing version of Wolfsbane. This *will* remove the harmful, maddening version that is in his veins now."

I nod and turn my gaze back to K, who is still lying down, but his eyes are starting to dart around wildly as if trying to find a way out of my grasp. I find the last ounce of power and force one more command on him before I am spiritually bled dry.

"Drink."

Quilla then pours this tea into a small plastic bowl, and I watch as K laps at the liquid. Once he's finished, I wait with bated breath to see if it works.

No one moves a muscle, but I can feel where everyone is. Dad and Quilla are off to my left. Tobias is a few feet behind us, enough to be out of K's sight, but I'm sure close enough to keep an eye on what's going on. I see K close his eyes as he takes a deep breath while letting a small growl rumble in his chest. I push Quilla behind me while Dad takes a step closer to me, the blood from his shoulder slowly ebbing as it clots.

I push my hand deeper into K's fur, a silent warning not to do anything stupid, and we wait for a heartbeat, then another. I feel something fall into place within K, but I am not sure if what I'm feeling is a good thing or not.

"Come on, K. Please come back to me." I beg.

I feel waves of calmness flow from K, and the voice that I hear fill my mind makes me fall to my knees, my forehead resting against the warm metal of the vehicle.

"Dakota, you are amazing, Love. Thank you for saving us."

I hear Kai's voice, which is equally as tired as I am, echo in my head. Even though he is still in his wolf form, I can tell he is looking at me with a clear mind.

"Thank goodness." I say as I stand up on wobbly knees and climb into the hatch with him. "I told you I'd get you back." I say softly as I finally let go of that fraying cord of my power and allow myself to fall into the exhaustion that is now dragging me under whether I want to go or not.

I am conscious long enough to see Kai phase effortlessly to catch my collapsing body, but he too falls with me, the both of us landing as a worn-out tangle of legs and arms as darkness takes both of us.

Chapter Thirty
TOBIAS

I hear Dakota's words and I watch as she collapses in the back of Nathan's SUV. Kai fluidly phasing to catch his mate before she falls out onto the ground. He moves just enough to keep himself in the vehicle before he too collapses.

"Nathan! What happened?" I ask as I walk closer to the group before me.

"The antidote worked, Alpha," Nathan responds.

I feel as if a boulder lifts from my shoulders, and I immediately reach out to my mate.

"Our son lives, my Luna."

"Oh, thank goodness." Her voice breaks in my mind, and it matches my heart right now too.

As I approach the SUV, I see that Quilla's hands are on my son's bare shoulders, her eyes are closed and her brows scrunched in concentration. I realize then that she is searching his body for any lingering remnants of the drug, so I keep quiet and let the Tamer before me work. I make a mental note to get her to talk to Atticus more, maybe even meet in person sometime soon. I know that would be a help to both the Tamer and my old friend since I am not around him much after moving here.

"I did it. I made the herbal tea strong enough to heal Kai." Quilla turns back to look at me, and I see pure happiness and accomplishment shining in her green eyes. "I, no, Atticus and I were able to help with this. We *all* were able to save him." She adds as she looks at Dakota's sleeping form.

"Yes, you did. We can all celebrate a little later. Right now, let's go home and rest." I say.

I gently close the hatch to Nathan's SUV, and I walk over to my own, taking a moment to gather myself as I replay the scene again in my head. How fearless Dakota was. She trusted herself, and when she felt her power weakening, she knew to pull her power from the pack just like a true alpha does. I am thankful to Nathan for stepping in when he did.

When K leaped for Dakota, I was ready to intervene at that moment, to put a stop to the madness. I am beyond grateful that Nathan took that moment to step in before I acted. Then, I felt Dakota pull from my power to help her save her mate. I am so proud that she was able to be the stronger wolf today.

"Alpha, where do you want to let these two rest?" Nathan asks as we start to make our way home.

"Let's take them to my house. You and yours are more than welcome to stay. I have a guest room you may use. But I think for the recovery, it would be best to have both of them under the roof of their alphas."

"I agree." Nathan says.

We pull into my driveway fifteen minutes later, and Nathan backs into the space next to my vehicle and pops the hatch. Kai and Dakota are still tangled together, holding one another in their blissful slumber.

"I'll get Dakota, you get Kai." Nathan says as he meets me at the rear of the vehicle now fully clothed, but the dried blood is still evident on his arm, middle, and ring fingers.

"While you both do that, I am going to warm up some more tea. Atticus said that they both should drink some to help get their strength back." Quilla says while putting her phone into her back pocket after reading the apparent text message from the doctor. He's usually so distant from technology, even more so than I am, so to see him texting the Tamer is a nice change of pace.

I nod at Quilla as I lift my son's naked body to carry him inside and up to his room. I dress him in a pair of shorts so Nathan can be a little more comfortable when he lays his daughter down next to Kai in his bed. As mates, it's best to keep them together so they can help the other heal. When Nathan gently sets Dakota down, Kai instantly reaches for her hand, like he knows where she is at all times.

I feel a smile tug at the corner of my mouth because even I can tell where my mate is at all times. Even that time I was injured in the war, I knew where Coraline was. She gave me the reason to coax my body to continue healing that day.

I pull the comforter up over their forms, and I nod my head to my Beta to follow me toward the door. "Now, let's leave them to rest."

I pull the door closed, leaving it cracked enough so we can all hear them in the living room. As we make our way downstairs, I see Coraline opening the door for Lori to enter. I give her a warm smile as she walks over to Nathan, and he pulls her to his chest.

"Is she; are they both alright?" Lori asks with tears in her eyes.

"Yes, Sweetheart. They are both fine. Just resting." Nathan croons.

As Lori rests her head on her mate's chest, she notices the dried blood on his arm, and her head whips back up to meet his eyes.

"Oh, Nathan, you're hurt."

"It's alright. I'm already healed. K just got a lucky shot, but it's nothing, Sweetheart." Nathan says, and he gently strokes his mate's cheek.

I step over to Nathan and softly clap him on the uninjured shoulder. "You did well today, Beta. Thank you for stepping in when you were greatly needed."

I send him the image of what I was about to do, and I see his eyes widen just a tad, and he gives me a sharp nod.

"I'm glad I was able to step in when it meant the most."

"Nathan." Coraline begins as she steps into my side, and I lightly drape my arm over her shoulder. "If you like, you and your mate can take that guest room. It has a bathroom in it if you would like to get cleaned up and tend to your wound if needed."

"Thank you, Alpha." Nathan says, then he turns to his mate and gives her a playful smile. "Would you like to come along and tend to your old mate?"

Lori laughs and gives him a light smack on the same shoulder that is freshly healed, and he gives a pained look that is Oscar-worthy, and that only makes her laugh harder. I find myself smiling at them as well. At the pure love in both of them, and I need to see that right now because the images that I was so close to having to bring to life still haunt me.

Once we hear the guest bedroom door close, Coraline turns to me with a knowing look on her face, and I know I can't keep quiet even if I want to.

I sigh as I say, "We were so close to planning his funeral today, Coraline." My voice wobbling near the end. My mate being the only one to ever see me at my breaking point.

"Let's give thanks that our son's mate and her father were there and were strong enough to keep that from happening." She rubs soothing circles down my back, and I lean into her touch while trying to mend my frazzled nerves.

"She was amazing, though, Coraline. She knew to pull from the pack for more power. She even pulled from me, and it's been so long since I felt another wolf stronger than I am." I say with a smile. "And Nathan stepping in when K tried to attack Dakota. He did it without even thinking about his own safety."

"This just again shows you that you have a good eye when it comes to picking wolves for your pack, Darling," Coraline croons. "Come on. Why don't you help me with dinner so that we can eat once everyone recovers."

Nathan

As we walk into the bathroom, I put the toilet lid down as Lori starts to run water in the sink. I run my fingers through my hair, my shoulder only pulling a little bit from the new skin and muscle still forming.

"Take your shirt off for me, Nathan." Lori says, her voice tight with worry that I know she's trying to hide but doing a horrible job of it right now.

I comply as I grab at the back of my shirt, pulling it over my head. Lori wrings out the white washcloth, and she stands between my legs as she stares at the dried blood.

"I'm okay, Lori."

"I know. I know." Lori says, her bottom lip trembling a moment before she pulls it between her teeth.

"Hey, you better stop that adorable lip-biting if you know what's good for you. I don't think you want the alphas to hear you scream my name just yet." I say, to try to get her out of her head.

And it works.

"Oh, my God! Nathan!"

Her cheeks flush two shades of red, and I smile at her as I place my hands on her hips, hoping my touch will help her relax a bit.

"Tell me what's going through your mind." I ask gently.

She takes the washcloth and wipes the dried blood from my shoulder, her eyes tracking her own movement.

"I'm just remembering the last time I cleaned this type of wound on you."

"This was a different circumstance, Lori. I was protecting our daughter, not my mate." I watch as Lori washes out the washcloth and comes back over to me, picking up my arm to wipe next. "I tell you though, Dakota is amazing."

"What happened?"

I can tell Lori didn't want to ask it, but she needs to know as Dakota's mother. So, I tell her the whole thing.

"Even with her being thrown into everything, she has natural instincts. She just needs to trust herself more." I say. "I am so proud of her,

Lori. I know she will be a great alpha at Kai's side one day." I add with pride filling my voice.

"Well, it helps when she comes from an amazing beta like her father." Lori says lovingly as she finishes cleaning the blood from my body.

"Well, she's stubborn and strong like her mother." I chuckle.

"Then Kai is going to have his work cut out for him, huh?" Lori smiles.

"Yeah, he is. You think I should give him a few pointers?"

Lori thinks a moment before I see a mischievous smile form on her lips. "Nah. That'll ruin the surprise for him."

"You are horrible, you know that?"

"Oh well. What can I say? It's fun to keep you on your toes, so why shouldn't Dakota enjoy that same thing with Kai?" Lori says, then wiggles her eyebrows. "Maybe *I'll* give Dakota some pointers."

I pull my mate close to my leg, her warm center hovering right above my kneecap, and her eyes blow wide, and her teeth click shut.

"Remember what I said, Mate? I don't think you'd like our new alphas to hear while I have *my* fun with you." I croon.

I just barely press my knee into her jean-clad core, and she stiffens as she closes her eyes.

"Okay, Okay," She pants. "I won't give Dakota pointers."

I chuckle as I release my hold of her, and she backs up out of my reach. She lets the water drain out of the sink, and she washes the cloth out before tossing it into the hamper on the back wall. She then opens the door and walks to the threshold before looking back over her shoulder at me.

I see the twinkle in her eye as she adds, "Unless she asks me for pointers."

Then Lori makes a break for the living room, and I let a playful growl bubble in my chest that chases her down the hall.

"Just wait, you little tease. I will make you pay for that."

"Oh, such scary words for someone who can't chase his mate."

"What do you—"

For the first time in my life, I regret teaching my mate how to touch the other through the bond. Because right now I am *strangled* and trying to not react. She literally has me by the balls, and she's right, I can't chase her.

"You win for now, *Mate."*

Her laughter fills my mind, and I can feel her love and joy at our banter. She finally releases me, and I join her in the living room with the alphas and wait for Kai and Dakota to wake up.

CHAPTER THIRTY-ONE

KAI

I don't know how long I've been out, but I start to edge into consciousness to the familiar scents of my bedroom. The cool mint of my body wash mixed with the musk of Dad's cologne. I feel Dad's power rippling through my room, and it takes me a moment to force my eyes to open. The evening sun shining right through my window makes me blink a few times to get my eyes to adjust.

When the room around me finally comes into focus, I see another form lying next to me, and I realize it's Dakota. In my bed. If I wasn't so tired, I'd have a field day with this, but exhaustion still makes my limbs feel like they are filled with lead. Even just lifting my arm to brush a stray piece of hair off her lip takes effort.

Then I feel Dad enter the room, his power flowing over me, and I let out a tired sigh at the feeling. Allowing it to caress me and renew my strength.

"I felt you were awake, so I thought I'd come up to check on you." Dad says as he pulls the desk chair closer to the bed so he can look at me and Dakota at the same time. *"So, how are you feeling?"*

"I feel so drained, Dad. That was the *worst thing to feel. I could see* everything, *and I couldn't do a damn thing to stop it. K was able to cut me off and wouldn't listen to me at all."*

"I knew something happened to you before Dakota rushed over, but I just wasn't sure what. No wolf of mine has ever been drugged with Wolfsbane like that." Dad says.

I look back to Dakota, and I feel tears prick at the corners of my eyes.

"I was terrified for her when I saw her walk into the plaza." I say, my voice shaking at the memory. *"I kept begging her to run and to let you kill us. I didn't want to watch her get hurt because of me, of us."*

I hear the raw brokenness in my voice, but right now I am just too tired to care. Dad stands from the chair, walks around my bed, and sits behind the crook of my knees. He then places a comforting hand on my bare shoulder, and I lean into his touch.

"I know, son." Dad then gives me a warm smile as he says, *"Your mate was brave and strong today. I told her what she would be possibly facing, what I may have to do if K attacked her."* I look back at my father in shock as he continues. *"I couldn't let her go in blind, son. Dakota needed to know what was at stake if she couldn't make K submit enough where she had some control over him."*

A memory flashes through my mind of K leaping at her and another wolf getting in the way. As the memory becomes clearer, my eyes snap to my father, and I know they are wide with fear.

"Please tell me that Nathan is okay."

"Yes. The Beta is fine and already healed." Dad smiles for a moment, then his lips form a firm line. *"I was about to jump in when I saw K take that dive for Dakota, but I think Nathan knew what could happen, and he stepped in before I could."*

"I owe him my life then."

"I agree, son. You owe him and your mate." Dad ruffles my hair just like he used to when I was a boy as he stands to his full height, looking back at me and Dakota's still sleeping form beside me. *"Rest a while longer, son. Quilla is making more of her Wolfsbane healing tea for you and Dakota. It will be ready when you two get up in a bit."*

"Thank you, Alpha. For being there for my mate when I couldn't and helping her through this."

"She was mostly able to do this herself." Dad says.

"I know. Granted, it was muted because of my frayed connection to K, but yeah, I felt it too." I say in awe at the memory.

Dad nods as he quietly walks out of my room and after he leaves, I make sure Dakota is still asleep before I close my eyes to check on K. The gentle breeze coming from the forest warms my skin and even though my eyes are still closed, I can tell it's brighter here than it was. When I open my eyes, I see that the sun is shining, and the sky is a bright robin's egg blue with white, wispy clouds hovering above me. I move closer to a clearing, and I hear birds start to sing a relaxing melody in the treetops.

As I break through the treeline, I see my counterpart sprawled out on his side; the sun shining down on his chocolatey blonde fur. His eyes are closed, but his ear twitches, letting me know he still hears me coming.

"Enjoying the sun, K?" I ask.

"Yes. I am."

I hear him trying to be his normal snarky self, but I can still pick up on his exhaustion and a touch of sorrow in his voice. I close the distance between us and I quietly sit down in the grass next to him. I lean back on my left arm while I use my right one to rub his side, much in the same way that Dakota did the other day.

"I'm sorry, Kai."

"For what?"

"Did you hit your head while I trapped you in here?" K snaps.

"No. I didn't. But K, it's not your fault or mine. We were drugged."

"We, I almost killed our mate, Kai! How can you look at me?" K shouts and gets up to walk a few steps away from me.

"K, come back here, please." I ask, and my wolf reluctantly lies back down beside me. "I can still look at you because I know that wasn't the real you, K." I lay down on my side to look my wolf in the eye. It takes him a few beats, but he finally meets my matching gaze. It's like looking in a mirror since we share the same eyes. "I know you would rather be killed than hurt our mate. I feel the same way."

"Will Dakota and Kota even look at me the same way again? Will they look at me and feel fear? I don't think I can handle that, Kai."

"Hey, the girls will not be afraid of you. I promise my friend. It was all the Wolfsbane. So there is nothing to forgive."

"I still need to apologize to both girls and the Beta. I still feel like I have his blood in my mouth. No matter how much water I drink, or if I go hunting here, I can taste him on my damn tongue."

"Maybe the tea that Quilla made will be able to help you too when I drink more of it." I offer. "But you are still you, K. I still want you here. And I still love my other half."

I push my love and the feeling of being one with him toward him, and I hear him sigh in contentment.

"I think I will be better once I have made my apologies. Even though I was drugged *as you say, I still knew what I was doing, but I didn't care at the time."*

"Fair enough, friend. Let me rest a bit longer and then drink some of Quilla's tea before you come forward. Deal?" I ask, holding out my hand to my wolf.

He sits up on his hind legs, and he lifts his right paw to me, and I shake it twice.

"Deal."

I will myself to leave K's forest, now satisfied that he can also rest a bit more peacefully too, and he's not beating himself up over something he could not control. I take in Dakota's sleeping form once more, and I let myself fall into a restful slumber as well.

CHAPTER THIRTY-TWO
DAKOTA

I feel someone playing with a lock of hair, and that sensation starts to push away the deep, blissful darkness that has surrounded me for I don't know how long. I will my eyes to open and the feel of my body hits me like a Mack truck. I feel so heavy, and I'm sore all over. Through the darkness, I pick up on a scent that reminds me of Kai.

Pine needles and cool mint.

I snuggle closer into that scent. So close that I swear I feel the bare skin of his chest against my cheek. I hear him chuckle, and his deft fingers continue to play with my hair, tucking it behind my ear over and over again. My eyes finally fly open at his touch, and when I lift my head from the crook of his arm, I meet his lively, hazel eyes.

"I'm sorry, Love. I didn't mean to wake you." Kai whispers. He's leaning on his left side, his head resting on his fist to look down at me. "I just couldn't keep from touching you any longer."

"You're back." I say with shock coloring my voice. "Oh, thank the Great Luna." I say with tears welling up in my eyes.

With his right arm, Kai tightens his hold on me while he uses the pad of his thumb on his left hand to gently dry the salty wetness from my cheeks.

"You are truly amazing, Baby. Do you know that?"

I look away from him as his compliment makes me blush, but he hooks his index finger under my chin, making me look back into his eyes. I can tell he's still tired from his own ordeal, but I see all the love and happiness for me shining in his hazel eyes.

"How did you get so brave, Love? I keep replaying what you did yesterday in my mind."

"Yesterday? What time is it?" I ask quickly.

"It's six o'clock in the morning. You slept the whole night, Love."

I think about his words, and I don't know if what I did would be considered being brave or stupidly desperate.

"All I could think about was getting K under control. Kota was the one that figured out we could pull the power we needed." I say as I trace the swirls of the gray-colored marking on his chest.

"I am so glad she did." Kai sighs as I touch him.

He turns over to lie on his back, gently pulling me into his chest while he slowly rubs my shoulder where my mate marking hides under my shirt.

"I have never been so terrified in my life." Kai whispers.

I hear his fear for what happened flood his soft voice. Snuggling closer into him, I trace his marking again while he continues to do the same. Like we each are caressing the other's soul to make this conversation as easy as it can be.

"I was trying to tell you to run. To get somewhere safe, but since K cut the bond between me and him, it cut the connection we had too." Kai takes a deep breath, and I can hear the crack in his voice as he continues to talk. "When I watched you get down on your knees to be at K's level, I lost it. I was pleading with you to get away from us. To let Dad kill us if it would keep you safe."

I take my left arm, draping it over his stomach, and pull him closer to me. At my touch he breaks down, tears flowing freely down his face, and I join him. Each of us breaking and consoling the other as images of what we both went through yesterday flood our minds like a silent 1920s movie.

After we both let our fears flow from our hearts and down our cheeks, Kai is the first to break the silence. "Thank you is such an inadequate word for what you did for me and K. You saved my life, Dakota. How can I ever show you how much that means to me?" Kai asks.

"All you need to do is love me. To be here with me. And when I doubt myself, remind me of just how strong I can be." I say as I pull myself up on my elbow to look him in the eye, pushing his hair back from his face. "Besides, what kind of mate would I be if I can't match your power?" I tease.

Kai grins and with his powerful body he flips me onto my back so fast I can't help the squeak that slips out. His hands are braced on either side of my head, his hips pressed firmly against mine where I feel the bulge of him pressed right against my hot core.

"We are equals, Babe. But if you ever need reminding-" Kai croons as he leans in closer, his eyes glowing brightly and a lazy grin playing at the corner of his mouth.

I arch my back instinctually, pushing our throbbing and pulsing centers together, and he growls at me.

"Remind me, Kai."

My pleading moan fills his room. Kai obliges as leans down onto his forearms to keep himself just barely above my body, and when his lips meet mine, it's like fireworks explode in my mind. We kiss for what seems like just moments in time, but then he's sweeping his lips down my jawline, my neck, and across my collarbone. Something inside me cracks, and I want him closer. I want his body crushing mine. I blindly reach up, somehow knowing where every part of his body is in comparison to mine, and I wrap my hand around his strong, muscular neck and pull him down on me.

His lips travel back up my neck, and I bend my head to allow him more access as I thread my hand through his hair. He growls at my movements, and it rockets right to my hot and needy core. His lips meet mine and gladly open up for him, his tongue darting in and I moan into his mouth.

"You are so fucking beautiful, Dakota. I can't wait to make you *mine*," Kai growls as he grinds his cotton-covered bulge into me.

I feel bold in this moment with his words echoing in my ears, and I don't think about it when I roll Kai onto his back and straddle his hips.

When I look into his eyes, they shine brighter than I have ever seen them, and I know it's from the sight of me sitting on him like this. I have half a thought to rip the clothes away that's keeping me from finally seating myself on the hardness of him.

So, instead, I lean down and place a tender kiss on his chest, right over his mark, and I trail my lips up over his neck like he did with me, over his jaw and ending on his lips. I take his bottom lip between my teeth, and I'm rewarded with a possessive growl, and he slips his hand at the base of my neck, gathering a fistful of hair to keep my head still as he devours my mouth.

We are all lips, tongues, and teeth as we continue our make-out session. I moan into his mouth again as he starts to knead my breast with his strong hand. I go to grab his other hand, suddenly wanting it lower, but this seems to snap him back to reality, and he reluctantly pulls away. I growl at the absence of him against my body.

"Babe. I think we need to stop. Believe me, I don't want to. But we need to stop while we still can," Kai says while trying to catch his breath.

Then it's like my sex-crazed mind catches up to what we just did. I take in Kai's plump, well-kissed lips, the red marks that are sadly, already fading from his neck and chest and I sit up to straddle his stomach because I know if I go lower, it will ignite us again and he's right, we don't need to push the boundaries any more than we have.

"I'm sorry. I don't know what came over me."

Suddenly Kai's door swings open, and our heads whip over to the noise. I see Quilla standing in the doorway with a tray holding two steaming cups of what I can smell as herbal tea. Her eyes widen, and she lets out an embarrassed yelp at the sight of me still sitting on top of Kai. I try to roll off him, but he grips my hips, and I see a sly smirk form on his lips.

"Omigod! I'm so sorry!" Quilla blurts out in a rush, slamming the door behind her.

I snap my head back to Kai, amusement still dancing in his eyes. "That was mean for both me and Quilla, you asshole!" I scold as I playfully smack him on his chest.

"What can I say? I love seeing you flustered." He croons as he finally lets me go so I can roll off him.

As I stand up, I see there is a clean pink t-shirt and a pair of black leggings sitting on his long dresser by the door. Kai notices my gaze, and he comes up behind me, pulling my back against his chest.

"Go get a shower, Love," He leans in closer to whisper in my ear. "Remember, you only get so many more *alone*." He sends me a quick image of me pressed up against the tile and his hand between my legs, making me a writhing mess under his touch.

"Damn it, Kai. Stop that." I gasp as I lean my head back on his shoulder. "Stop teasing me."

"I will for now."

He releases me, and I snatch my clothes and rush into the bathroom.

CHAPTER THIRTY-THREE
DAKOTA

I close the bathroom door behind me, and as I step into the shower and squeeze a dollop of shampoo into my hand, I take a moment to look in on Kota. I find her lying on her side next to a gently flowing river while letting the sun's rays warm her blondish-brown coat.

"Hey Kota. How are you doing?"

"Still a little tired, but slowly feeling better. I think being near Kai helped some."

"Yeah, I think so too."

"I'm so glad you didn't question me as I pulled the extra power we needed from Tobias. When I watched our father get hurt by K, I knew something needed to be done, and quickly, before the alpha had to step in."

"Thank you for knowing what to do, and helping me save them. I say we make a damn good team." I chuckle, trying to lighten the mood.

"Yeah, we do. I'm glad that you're my human, Dakota. We are going to be a force to be reckoned with one day. I know it." She says with a wolfish grin.

"That's what I like to hear. Now, let me finish my shower and maybe we can get more of Quilla's tea. I think that's what she was going to have us drink when she caught me and Kai—" I trail off as the memory of what we did not ten minutes ago floods my mind.

"Yeah… I don't want to think about that. 'Cause it was hot." Kota snorts.

"Hey, go after your own species!" I laugh.

Her ears quickly fold back on her head, and she looks away from me for a moment. *"He won't talk to me. I'm sure he blames himself for what he did, but it wasn't his fault."* She says somberly.

My smile fades as I say, "Give him time. I'm sure he'll come around."

Kota nods, and I slip out of her forest so I can finish my shower and get dressed. I open the door, letting the steam roll past me and into the hall, as I catch Kai coming out of another room. He is shirtless again, but he has a white shirt draped over the crook of his arm, and he has black sweatshorts on. He grins at me as he's towel drying his hair, and I have the sudden urge to run my fingers through the damp locks again. I push that thought to the back of my mind as he gives me a lazy smile. He pulls me into his chest again, and I take in his post-shower scent of pine needles and a mountain stream.

"You ready to go down and see our parents?" Kai whispers in my ear.

"Can't we just be by ourselves a little bit longer?" I ask through the bond.

"No, Love." Kai chuckles. "We need to be with our pack. It helps with the recovery process. Plus, K needs to talk to a few people." He adds with a touch of sadness in his voice.

I look at him, and I remember what Kota said about K not talking to her yet.

"I understand. I hope that after he says his peace it will make him feel better." I offer.

Kai smiles as he tosses his towel into the dirty laundry basket and tugs his shirt over his head.

"Come on, Love. Let's join our pack," Kai says as he takes my hand and we walk down the stairs. Once we hit the bottom step and turn left into the living room, we have three heads turn in our direction, pausing mid-conversation at our entrance.

My eyes lock with Quilla, who is sitting next to my father on the couch. Her cheeks turn an embarrassed shade of pink, and I know she's thinking about walking in on me and Kai. Dad looks from her to me, and his eyes narrow on Kai. He picks up on Dad's stare at him, and he lets go of my hand.

"Go talk to them, Love," Kai whispers in my mind.

I smile at him as I make my way over to the couch. "Hey." I say with a small smile.

Quilla smiles back at me, and Dad sets his arm on my shoulder, pulling me in for a sideways hug.

"Hey, Sweety." Dad says as he moves over to make room for me to sit down.

"Where's Mom?" I ask.

"She's in the kitchen with Coraline fixing breakfast."

I look across the house and in the little cutout that backs to the living room; I see my mother and the regal alpha smiling as they continue to cook in the kitchen.

"Coraline, Lori!" Tobias shouts from the loveseat where Kai is sitting beside his father. "The kids are awake."

Mom comes rushing out of the kitchen, and she is instantly pulling me into her chest and stroking my hair while Coraline gently hugs Kai.

She pushes him back at arm's length to look him over and then pulls him back into her again.

Mom sobs, "Oh thank God. You're okay."

"Yeah. I'm alright, Mom. Just still tired."

She releases her grip on me and goes to sit down on Dad's lap while I take the spot next to him again.

"Oh!" Quilla exclaims for the first time since I entered the living room. "I'll go get you two some more tea."

"*Yeah, since she was shell-shocked at what she walked into.*" Kai taunts as he sits back down on the loveseat when his mother goes back into the kitchen.

"*You make it sound so much worse than it was.*" I chuckle.

"Care to tell the class what you two are talking about?" Dad asks while staring daggers at Kai.

"No!" I shout.

I try to cover my face with my hands, but I feel Kai's phantom touch on my cheek, and I look up at him as I say. "It's nothing. We were just talking when we woke up."

Kai can't hide his smile before he leans his head back against the loveseat. Tobias then gives him a pointed stare that I would not want directed at me.

"Son?" Tobias starts.

The way that Kai is staring at his father must mean that he is talking to him through their bond. Tobias then bursts out laughing, and I feel confusion and mortification flood my face.

"Okay. I have to admit that was mean but funny."

"Kai?!" I yell.

"What? When the alpha asks, you answer." Kai shrugs.

"Traitor." I scoff.

Quilla comes back with the two mugs, handing one to Kai, and when she sits on the couch again, she hands the other to me. I take a slow inhale of the tea, and it warms my chest.

"Thank you, Quilla."

Dad takes my hand in his own, and Mom follows, placing hers on top of his. He looks at me, and I see amazement, and love, and how proud he is of me swirl in his brown eyes. I put the mug down on the coffee table, already feeling stronger after a few sips.

"My little girl isn't so little anymore, are you?" Dad asks with a soft smile.

"What makes you say that?"

"You were so brave, smart, and *powerful* yesterday. You were thrown into all this, and you became the alpha you needed to be to save Kai. So, I know you will be an amazing leader one day. I know you had doubts when this all started, but Sweety, don't let those doubts fill your mind anymore."

I smile at my father's words, and I remember what Kai said to me this morning. For the first time, I'm truly starting to believe that I can be the mate, the alpha, who can stand by Kai's side with my head held high and lead our own pack one day.

"Thank you, Dad. Kai said something similar too. And I'm beginning to believe it." I say.

"Dakota."

Then, I feel a pulse of power come from Tobias to get my attention.

I let go of my parent's hands as I stand and take a few steps over to the alpha. When he rises to his feet, he pulls Coraline with him. I know confusion is written on my face, but I keep quiet and wait to see what happens next. Tobias gives me a small warm smile, and then they do something I never thought I would witness. Both alphas to the largest wolf pack in the States, kneel on one knee before me. Tobias crosses his right arm over his chest, resting his fist over his heart, and both alpha's bear their necks to me in complete submission.

The two strongest alpha's kneeling before me like *they* are lower members of the pack and I am *their* alpha.

I stay quiet. Mostly because I'm speechless at their actions, but also because it feels right to be silent. I can see Kai out of my peripheral vision, and he has his hands covering his mouth like he is just as shocked as I am.

"Dakota, you have proven yourself to be an extremely strong alpha when the time calls for it. You were able to save my son, your mate, from a gruesome death at my hand if he could not be subdued. And for that, I am truly grateful for the tremendous power you possess," Tobias says from the floor.

"Yes. Thank you, Dakota, for bringing my son back home. I will be forever grateful for your bravery," Coraline says as she looks up at me, but I notice she does not look me directly in the eye. She's looking at my right ear.

With tears in my eyes, I give them both a gentle smile, and I gesture with my right hand for them to stand as I say, "Thank you both for your kind words. It means the world coming from you two."

The two alphas stand, and while they take their place back on the loveseat, I go back over to the couch with Dad, Mom, and Quilla and pick up my mug to take another long drink from it.

"I have to say, Quilla, this tea is amazing." I say as I pull her into my side. "I think we both fell into our newfound roles pretty well, don't you? You, my friend, are an amazing Tamer."

"Yeah, we have." Quilla says with a bright smile. "And I will do anything to help with my new family. My new...pack."

"And Quilla?" I begin as I put my mug back down on the coffee table. "Thank you for figuring out this herbal tea that helped K. I owe *you* everything too."

"I agree with Dakota," Tobias says as he also walks over to us and kneels before Quilla. "Thank you, Quilla, for being another big part in saving my son."

"Well, I couldn't have done it without Atticus." Quilla blushes.

"Ohhh," I say in a sing-song voice through the bond, *"Do you have a crush on the doctor?"*

"No." Quila answers quickly, *"Besides, he's hella old. He says 'aye' for goodness sake. So he's got to have a mate."*

I pin her with a stare that tells her I am silently calling her out on her bullshit cop-out, but I don't push the issue.

Kai

I feel K poke the back of my mind, reminding me that he wants to say his peace.

"I know, my friend. I'll get their attention."

I take another long drink of Quilla's tea and clear my throat a bit after I sit the mug on the table beside the loveseat. Dad's eyes slide over to mine, and I let myself enter his mind again.

"K feels the need to say something to Nathan and Dakota."

"I understand. Go ahead."

"May I say something?" I look over at Nathan and Dakota, and they nod their heads, urging me to keep talking.

"K would like to talk to you, Nathan." I say, flicking my hand in his direction, and my eyes flit over to Dakota, "And to our mate as well as her wolf."

Nathan nods his head and motions for Lori to sit by their daughter. He then sits on the arm of the sofa, letting his long legs stretch out in front of him while crossing them casually at the ankles.

Showing he's not a threat, which I let K see in the forest.

"I'm ready." K says.

I let him feel my smile as he takes over our body.

CHAPTER THIRTY-FOUR

KAI

I find myself in his peaceful and serene forest, and I go where I usually do when we phase. Right next to the river. I can't help but to reach my hand out toward the water, and instead of the invisible glass wall, my hand easily slips into the river, well up past my wrist. And I know for a fact that I can get back to the real world whenever I want to. So, I let my wolf do what he feels he needs to make things right in his eyes.

K

I shake my coat out while I feel Kai settle into my forest. The phase feels good, and I can feel Kai in my mind, unlike what happened yester-day in my bloodlust-filled rage. I look toward Nathan and then to our mate; both are quietly waiting for me to begin.

"Kai, can you come forward enough to let me talk?"

"Sure thing."

I feel my vocal cords change from those that would normally only be used for growls, howling, and barking, to a mix of something that allows me to use Kai's rough voice as my own.

"I wanted to speak to my father's Beta as well as our mate personally about what happened yesterday." I begin.

I can feel the love from Dakota pour from her. Like she's silently telling me what happened doesn't matter, but it still does. *I* did that. And I need to apologize.

"Beta, I want to sincerely apologize for attacking you like I did. I lured you into thinking I submitted to you. I used your lack of being around a pack to my advantage, and in doing so, I made another pack member bleed with my fangs. You have every right to exact your ounce of flesh, Beta." I say as I look him in the eye, letting the offer settle between us.

I can feel all eyes dart between us, especially Dakota's, but I try to ignore them and focus on the male in front of me.

"You're right, K. I do have the right to take my ounce of flesh from you." Nathan says as he takes a step forward, and I steel myself for his attack.

"Dad!?" Dakota exclaims.

She begins to get up, but we all feel Tobias' pulse of power flow across the room, and Dakota, while she does sit back down, I can feel her worry about what her father will do to me.

He closes the distance and stands directly in front of me for a moment. When Nathan gets down on one knee, he looks me directly in the eye before he snaps his right hand out, latching on to the back of my neck and I feel his fingers dig into the muscles and tendons, much like Dakota did to break through my drug-induced haze.

I hear Dakota's quiet gasp, but I can't make myself look at her. I can only stare at the Beta in front of me. His eyes are shining a bright honey brown, and I know his wolf is going to make the decision. His nails lengthen to just barely nick at my skin through my rough coat.

"You are correct. We have the right to spill blood from you just as you spilled from us." He pauses, his eyes scanning my face thoughtfully. "We choose not to take our ounce of flesh." Nathan's gravelly voice fills the room.

"Oh, thank God." I hear Dakota whisper.

"Since you were drugged and not acting with a clear mind, we do not take that you attacked us and spilled our blood personally." Nathan says.

He removes his hand, smoothing my fur back into place, and heads back over to the arm of the sofa.

"Thank you, Beta." I say simply.

I know his words to be true, and that lifts a huge burden that has been weighing on my shoulders. But as I turn to Dakota and her tear-filled eyes, the other burden I have takes its place.

"Dakota, do you think you can have Kota listen in to our conversation?" I ask as I look into her light blue eyes.

She nods as she closes her own eyes, and a moment passes between us and when she opens them again, they are glowing an eerie blue, and I can feel Kota in the back of my mind.

"Hello, you two." I begin as I pad forward and sit in front of our mate.

"You don't have to do this, K." I can hear Kota's voice coming from Dakota's mouth, and I drop my eyes at her words.

"Yes, my mate. I do."

"Then look me in the eye like the alpha you are."

At my mate's words, I look up at her. I swear I can see her beautiful wolven face flash in my mind. Her pointed blonde ears pitched forward, her eyes pinning me to the spot and taking in everything about me. I give a wolfish smile as I take in her mental image.

"Kota, I want to apologize to you and to your human counterpart as well. I was out to spill your blood just as much as I was out for the Beta's. And I would have if he had not stepped in when he did. So, for that threat alone, mate, you and Dakota have the right to your own ounce of flesh." I say.

I can feel Kota slip away from my mind a bit, I'm sure talking to Dakota. I try not to let her absence get to me. Then after a few minutes, I feel Kota fill my mind again

"No K, we will not take our ounce of flesh either. It is not necessary since you were not of sound mind, Mate of mine." She makes Dakota reach out her hand to me, and I close the distance between us. She pulls me in towards her face, letting our noses touch, much like we do in our forests when we can connect for the short periods of time when Kai and Dakota are asleep.

"You have *nothing* to be sorry for. Please take that to heart, Mate. I love you." Kota says, and I then hear a mix of her light growl mixed with Dakota's soothing voice as she says, "We both love you and Kai. Never in your right mind would you cause us harm. Now stop being a hardhead like your human counterpart and forgive *yourself*."

I give her a firm nod. "Yes, Mate."

I step back from her, and while picking up Kai's discarded shorts and shirt, I trot into the powder room to phase so he can spend time with his family.

"You feel better now?" Kai asks as he looks at our reflection in the mirror.

"Yes, I do. Thank you for letting me say my peace."

"Anytime, buddy."

Kai

I walk out of the bathroom, taking my place next to my dad on the loveseat again while giving Dakota a quick wink as I sit down. She quickly picks up her mug from the coffee table and takes another sip of the still-warm tea to cover the blush that begins to creep up her neck. I gently enter her mind, and I can feel she's starting to get tired again, and I'm sure it was from the stress of not knowing if her father would really harm us a minute ago or not.

"Hey, Babe?" I ask, and her eyes glide over to me in answer. *"Come sit by me, please. You're starting to look a little tired."*

"You know me so well, don't you?" She asks playfully.

"What kind of mate would I be if I didn't know the deepest desire of my girl?"

I stare at her as I push a mental image of us in bed, much like we were this morning. My larger body hovering over hers, but this time she's completely naked before me. I trace my lips over her jaw, her neck, and collarbone. Then I dip lower, my lips just barely brushing against the supple skin of her perfectly soft breast.

I can feel Dakota's desire flood my mind from her end of the bond, and I see the tiny flutter in her neck from her pulse skyrocketing. She desperately tries to keep the mug close to her lips so it can help keep her poker face in place, but that gorgeous tint of pink starts to edge up her neck and I find myself fighting to keep the smile off my face.

"One day soon, Love, I can make these images come to life for you."

She smiles, and she finally gets up and walks over to me with her mug of tea and sits beside me on the couch. Thankfully, Dad takes this time to go back into his office for a few minutes.

"You are such a tease." She chuckles.

"Oh, I have only just begun, Baby."

I show her how I plan on teasing her clit with the pad of my thumb, pushing her to that blissful edge, but pulling back at the last second to keep her from falling over. The pink on her neck spreads to the base of her jaw, and she stares back at me, almost dropping the ceramic mug. I lift my hand to hers to help steady it and I drag my thumb over the back of her hand. Her eyes flit down to our fingers, tracking my thumb, and I know by the way her eyes widen, she's thinking about what I just showed her.

As she puts the mug back on the coffee table, she squirms her legs a bit to release some pent-up energy I created, and I have to pick up my own mug to hide my smile.

"I love the color pink on you just as much as I do the color red, Love."

"You are horrible, you know that?"

"But you like it."

Then Dad comes back into the living room, but he, thankfully, takes Nathan with him into the dining room to prepare the table for breakfast. Out of the corner of my eye, I see Quilla look from us to the kitchen and back again, and after a moment she stands awkwardly while gesturing toward the kitchen again.

"I'm going to see if your parents need my help with anything." She says as dashes out of the living room, leaving me and Dakota alone on the couch.

I brush a piece of her light brown hair behind her ear, and she leans into my hand. "Come here, Love. Rest a bit, for real this time." I say with a smile.

I lie back on the couch, pulling her down where her stomach is flush against me, and her chest rests against mine. I tenderly run the fingers of my right hand through her hair while my left hand strokes her back. She wraps her hand around my bicep, and her thumb idly traces the vein that runs down the middle of the muscle, and I can't help the quiet growl that bubbles in my throat at her touch.

"You okay there?" Dakota chuckles.

"Always when you are touching me, Babe."

Dakota

After drinking a full cup of Quilla's herbal tea, I am starting to feel the healing effects flow through me. I feel so relaxed and even a bit stronger already. As I keep tracing the little vein that runs through Kai's bicep, I slowly ease into his mind to check on him and how he's feeling. I can feel his strength slowly returning, and that makes my chest fill with happiness.

"You know you can always ask me how I'm feeling rather than sneaking around in my head to see what's going on, Love."

I snap my head up to look into his handsome face. He has that playful smirk on his lips, the same one that makes me want to kiss him anytime I see it.

"Would you have told me the truth if I asked?"

His eyes dart off to the side for a heartbeat before looking at me again, and I shake my head as I rest my head back on his chest.

"Yeah, I figured so, hence the sneaky poking."

"You're right, Dakota. I should let you know how I am feeling. As mates, we should be able to tell each other anything. So yes, Love, I am feeling stronger since I have had some of Quilla's tea and with you being in my arms." Kai says.

I smile as I start to feel my eyes drift closed, and I allow myself to relax deeper into Kai's strong body as sleep starts to take the both of us.

Forty-five minutes later, Coraline's voice wakes both of us up when she announces that breakfast is ready. Kai helps me up, and he leads me over to the dining room, and we all eat among idle chatter.

After we are finished with our meal, Tobias and Kai offer to clean up the dishes and the kitchen. I watch as the two men work together like a well-oiled machine. Tobias filling the sink with soapy water and Kai picking up our plates from the table and putting them in the sink so Tobias can wash them as Kai dries and puts them away.

As I continue to watch them and the idle clatter of glass and silverware filters through the house, I find myself starting to think about our good ole duo. This sick, twisted asshole will apparently stop at nothing to prove that I am with the wrong guy. I catch Kai's eye, and he gives me a bright smile as I try not to think about what or when Jeffrey's next sadistic plan will be.

CHAPTER THIRTY-FIVE

KAI

The weekend goes by all too quickly, and I wake up about fifteen minutes before my alarm goes off on Monday morning. I look down to my right and I see Dakota snuggled into my side with her head on my chest and her right hand over the mate marking on my left pec. I love watching her sleep, and I feel the corner of my mouth tilt up in a half smile as she lets out a small snore.

As the clock ticks closer to going off, I begin to think about facing Jeffrey and Caleb at school today. They're hoping the Wolfsbane was enough to get me killed so he can swoop in and force Dakota to be his mate. That thought makes my veins fill with fire. Images of his hands on her body, his disgusting mouth on hers, and him being the one to take her virtue instead of me. It all makes me sick to my stomach. But then, when they see me walk into that university with her on my arm, I'm terrified of the backlash that I'm sure will come my way and that Dakota will get caught in the crossfire.

"Hey, Babe," Dakota says sleepily as she lazily runs her index finger down my marking, tracing the gray swirling pattern. "Are you okay?"

"Yeah. I'm okay. I'm sorry, I didn't mean to wake you."

"I felt... anger, disgust, and then apprehension about going to class today from your end of the bond. Anything you want to talk about?"

I scrub at my face as I say, "I'm afraid of how far they are willing to go to get me out of the picture." I say,

Dakota sits up while still keeping her hand on my chest, and she gives me a warm, confident smile. "Hey, they will *never* beat us. We've been able to beat them at their own game too many times now. But if they want a true fight, then we'll bring it to them." She adds as she playfully pokes at my chest.

"Do I need to put a leash on you, Love?" I try to joke to lighten the mood.

She rolls her eyes as she says, "Oh my God, you're never gonna let me live that down, are you?"

I give her a crooked smile, and she flicks the tip of my nose.

"I will say though, I am tired of dealing with those two. Can't you call like an alpha meeting or something?" She asks while tracing her finger over my collarbone, which makes gooseflesh bubble on my skin.

"Actually, yes. I can challenge him."

At Dakota's silence, I sigh as I cover my eyes with the crook of my elbow because I don't think I can stomach seeing her face with what I am about to say.

"Please don't take this the wrong way, Dakota." I begin, "But I can challenge him... for the rights to you. I can call a Meeting of Alpha's and declare that we have a fight to the death to determine which one of us is the strongest and therefore who is your rightful mate." Since she's not speaking, I'm just going to lay it all out on the table. "And at his death, his pack can become ours, unless they think of me as an unfit leader, and then they all can challenge me as well. And I'll have to take on every wolf that thinks that they could do better than me until the pack finally accepts the winner."

I keep my arm over my eyes as I wait for Dakota to speak.

Dakota

At first, I'm a little peeved at being thought of as a piece of property for a male to own, but part of my human mind might actually understand the reasoning behind my mate's words. I feel Kota come to the front of my mind to help me understand what Kai just dumped into my lap all before six a.m. from the wolf standpoint.

"Think about it, Dakota. If another female came up and said she wanted Kai as a mate and you lost the fight, but you lived, you would always pine after him and neither of you would ever have peace."

"Thank you, Kota. I was thinking that, but I'm glad you confirmed it."

Kai is still lying on his back with his arm covering his face, and I can't imagine a life where I don't have him next to me, where I am in another man's bed. That thought makes my skin crawl, so I shake the thought from my mind and I reach out to take Kai's hand while interlacing our fingers.

"I understand, Kai." I say simply.

Kai's head snaps up as his arm falls across his sculpted chest. "You do?"

"Yes, I do. And if it comes down to his pack wanting to challenge you as their alpha, just know that I will help you fight back in any way I can.

I may not be able to phase, but I would also be their alpha at that point too, and I will fight by your side no matter what."

Kai lifts his right hand to cup the base of my neck and pulls me down to him to kiss me lovingly on the lips. At first, the kiss is tender and slow, but I can never get enough of this man before me. So, I open my mouth to invite him deeper, to take more of me. I feel him smile against my lips, and his tongue darts in to claim me an instant later. I run my hands through his blonde hair, and as he growls with contentment and I eagerly swallow his sound.

Then, just like last night, he effortlessly flips me onto my bac,k and a breathy laugh escapes me as his body hovers over mine, his arms caging my head against his bed. He looks at me, his eyes dancing back and forth between mine, and that sly smile blooms on his lips again. I pull his mouth down to mine again for what seems like only a moment before he's pulling away again.

"You are such an amazing woman, mate, and alpha, Dakota. You complete me in ways I never knew I was missing. And the way you fell into this role of mate and alpha was so graceful. To have you walk this path by my side and have no complaints is amazing." He gently brushes a lock of my light brown hair out of my face. "You step up to any challenge that's thrown your way with a 'come and try me' attitude, and I fucking love that about you. I love you so much, Baby." He says as he kisses me again as if to seal the words between us.

When Kai breaks the kiss, his words repeat in my mind, and I don't realize I'm crying until he swipes at my cheeks with the pad of his thumb. I wrap my arms around his neck again, but this time I just want to have his body on mine. This is not driven by a deep sexual desire that's been torturing us the last few days. This is just the desire to have his weight on me to help keep me grounded.

"I love you too, Kai. I feel the same way with you." I say as his face settles into the crook of my neck and I feel his steady breath caress my skin.

"You are such an understanding man. You are constantly reminding me that what I think are my shortcomings are actually my greatest strength. And I push myself harder because I know that you and our little pack are counting on me to be an alpha that is worthy of them."

Kai sits up in bed while pulling me with him, and we sit up with our legs tangled together. Then, he's wordlessly pulling me into his chest, and I can feel every ounce of his love flood my mind, body, and soul. It warms me from the tips of my ears clean down to my toes, and I soak it all in like he's my only source of water in an endless desert.

When the alarm finally blares at us at six a.m., we look over at the sound and Kai reaches across the bed to turn off the clock and I get a good look at the lean muscles in his arms and back.

"You ready to tackle this day, Love?"

"Abso-fuckin'-lutley." I grin.

We both get ready for school, and as we are coming down the steps, I see Tobias, Coraline, Mom, and Dad waiting on us. I realize that they must have stayed overnight, and a part of me is glad that I had my parents with me under the same roof. We all have a quick breakfast of chocolate chip pancakes, steak, and eggs with hash browns, all courtesy of Dad's cooking.

"One day, Nathan, you and I are going to have to have a cook-off. I don't mean to brag, but I have been in the kitchen providing for my pack a lot longer than you have, so I'm sure I have more tricks up my sleeve."

Tobias challenges, but I see the glint in his eyes saying this is all in good humor, but I know my dad better than the alpha.

"Oh okay. You wanna put your money where your mouth is, Tobias?"

I carefully chew my pancake at Dad's reaction to Tobias' prodding. I find myself smiling at them because Dad is finally showing the alpha's his true colors and how I get my own personality from both of my parents.

Tobias chuckles and extends a hand to my father. "Most definitely, Nathan. May the best cook win. I'll let you know when I plan on wiping the floor with you."

We all can't help but laugh now. I catch Tobias' eyes for a moment, and he gives me a private wink before he goes back to talking with my dad. I shake my head and give a small smile. This guy totally knows his pack and how to make them feel better and how to give them something else to focus on even if it's only for a little while.

"Thank you, Alpha. I know Kai and I needed this banter this morning. Did he tell you what he told me about the possibility of challenging Jeffrey for me?"

"Not in so many words, but I could tell something was going on in his head." Tobias replies.

After breakfast, Mom and Coraline pick up the dishes this time and go to clean the kitchen while my father gets ready for work. Kai and I get up from the table, and Kai picks up both of our backpacks that we find by the front door, slinging them both over one shoulder. As we get ready to leave, Tobias stops us at the door, clapping a hand on his son's shoulder.

"May the Great Luna protect you both today."

I nod to him, and I'm not surprised that he already knows that Kai and I are walking into a metaphorical lion's den this morning once Jeffrey sees that Kai is alive and well and still with me.

"Thank you, Alpha." Kai answers as he takes my hand and leads me through the door that Tobias is holding open for us.

We arrive at the university thirty minutes later, and we notice there is a commotion coming from the gym, so we walk over to see what all the fuss is about. As we close the distance, we start to hear music. The solid bass of the drum reverberates through my chest, and the sound of the acoustic guitar playing is a sweet melody to my ears. Even more so now with my hearing being heightened thanks to Kota.

Kai reaches his arm out to open the door when we hear a car door slam behind us. I turn to see Quilla cross the length of three parking spots to join us by the entrance.

"Hey, you two." She says breathlessly. "How are you both feeling today?"

"We are feeling amazing. Thank you again, Quilla. You are the best!"

Kai smiles and says, "You will be a wonderful Tamer once you trust yourself more, Quilla."

Quilla blushes at Kai's words, and he opens the door to lead us inside the gym. As we follow just a breath behind him, we take in the little, early morning concert that some of the musical students are putting on. Just as Quilla and I step forward to get a better view, I hear a low, warning growl come from Kai, and I look back at him over my shoulder. He's looking off to the right, near the back of the gym, and low and behold we see Jeffrey staring Kai down with a look of pure anger written all over his face while Caleb cowers behind his alpha's shoulder, his face is a mix of being terrified and pissed off. Jeffrey stiffly turns on his heel, storming off through the back of the gym with his beta close to his back.

"Well, let's see if shit hits the fan later." Kai growls as he lets out a breath to calm himself.

Jeffrey

After seeing *him* still alive, I storm out of the gym, and I can feel my beta nervously following me. Once the metallic sound of the door shutting hits my ears, I spin around, grabbing Caleb by the throat with my left hand, and I pin him to the wall with such force that the bricks crack a bit from the impact of his body.

"Tell me why he's still ALIVE?" I snarl so loud that the birds in the trees above us take flight.

Smart birds.

"Alpha, I thought for sure the Wolfsbane that we forced Emma's sire to create would be enough to drive him to the point of hysterical bloodlust and his alpha would be forced to kill him." Caleb forces out through his mildly crushed windpipe.

"I should have known better than to trust you and that fucking half-breed's human sire. You have failed me twice now, Caleb. First, the roof incident where you were supposed to bring Dakota to me, and now this."

I look into his fear-filled brown eyes and I give him a dark smile before releasing my grip on his throat and walking away. I see him massaging his neck as I turn back around to pin him with a glare while at the same time letting a dark pulse of my power roll over him. He freezes, his hand mid-stroke on his neck, and awaits his next order.

"I will give you one more chance, Caleb. But this time, you are going to go after Dakota again. We need to show her what happens when she sticks around with the wrong alpha. That *kid* can't be around her all the time, and we are going to use that to our advantage." I say.

"What do you want me to do to her, Alpha?" Caleb croaks out.

I give him a grin that makes his skin pale, and it sends a thrill through my blood. "You are going to attack her with silver."

"How the fuck do you expect me to do that without killing myself in the process?" Caleb snaps, finally getting his voice back.

"I don't give a shit how you do it. Scratch her. Bite her for all I care! I know you're smart, Caleb. You'll figure out a way to keep the silver from touching you." I put a finger to my chin in a sudden thought and I smile as I turn to walk away, "And let's give Emma's human sire one last chance to make himself useful before I end up killing him and his bitch of a Werewolf mate who dared to create Emma with tainted human blood while in my pack."

I turn to walk away from Caleb because the more I think about that *pup* inside the gym, the more I want to go back in and rip him apart for thinking he can take Dakota away from me. I had my eyes on her for years now, ever since I met her in her first semester of high school. So, I have been waiting for her for six years now, which is nothing compared to how long I have been waiting just to feel any potential mate connection with another female. I will have her before the end of all this. I just have to convince her who the stronger alpha is and who she will flourish under.

And with the power she showed me that day at her house when she took me to my knees, I know she will be a powerful alpha once she is shown her true potential. And what amazing pups she will be able to bear for me. I am almost giddy with excitement of how she'll provide what this pack sorely needs, whether she wants to or not. She will help populate my pack with only the strongest pups, and if not, then I will kill off the weak ones, and I will keep filling her with pup after pup until her last breath.

Dakota

Kai and Quilla and I notice Jeffrey and Caleb leaving the parking lot in his car just as the concert ends.

"Well, at least we don't have to deal with them today." I say while I'm trying to shake the feeling that something bigger will happen again.

Kai pins me with a look, and before he can even say anything, I put up a hand to keep him from talking.

"I know, I know. Them running off like that is a bad sign."

Chapter Thirty-Six
QUILLA

Kai drops me off at my house later that afternoon once classes are done for the day. I wave goodbye to them as I walk into my house and I stand by the window to watch Dakota's car drive off once Kai knows I'm safe inside.

I find myself longing for a connection to someone like that. A man who will be there for me just like Kai is there for Dakota. To keep her safe, and to tell her she's doing an amazing job, to challenge her to be a better person. I've had my fair share of dates with guys, but it never goes any further than the second date. I don't know why, it's like something in my heart just knows he's not *the one* that people talk about. However, when a certain red-headed, green-eyed doctor pops into my head, I feel my face and ears heat.

I have got to stop thinking about Atticus, and how hot he is.

As I walk through the house, I shake my head to clear my raging thoughts, and after searching the living room and kitchen, I find the house to be empty.

My parents must still be at work.

Deciding I need to keep my mind busy, I make my way up to my bedroom on the second floor and head to my crisp white, faux wood desk. I pull out the pink and white ergonomic computer chair and sink down into the soft foam seat. Before I sit my backpack down beside the desk, I pull out a notebook and my Algebra textbook to get a head start on the homework that was given out today.

About halfway through my second assignment, my phone dings with a text message. Looking at the name that pops up, I find myself smiling and eagerly opening the message.

Atticus has been messaging me since Kai's Wolfsbane incident with different pictures of plants to see what kind of information I can glean from them. This time the image is of a green stick-like plant with little knots all over the stalk. As I study the image, I get the feeling that it will help with fevers, and I find myself grinning as I message him back with the name of this plant.

Me:

This is Guduchi. It helps with fevers.

Atticus:

That's correct Quilla

Then, a moment later, my phone lights up with another message from him.

Atticus:

Thank you

As I look at the message, I get the feeling that he's upset about something. He usually praises me more than this when I get something right, using emojis and everything, but this time it's short and to the point. I try to ignore it, but when his 'thank you' came in, those two words on the screen seemed to carry a heaviness that I cannot ignore. I pull my laptop from one of the drawers of my desk, and once the system boots up, I send him a Zoom request, and he answers on the third ring.

When the feed loads, I can tell from the angle that he's on his phone, and I can instantly see the look on his face is both tired and worried.

"What's wrong?" I ask. "Are you okay?"

"It's—" He pauses. "I'm fine, Quilla." Atticus says, his Irish voice soft and equally tired.

"Who's sick or injured?" I demand since he's not going to tell me outright.

He lets out a defeated sigh and looks over the phone to whoever is in front of him and then back to me.

"One of our border patrols got into a leg trap, and the damn bloody thing was coated in silver." Atticus says, growling near the end.

"That's terrible. Is he going to be alright?"

"I don't know. He was trapped in it for half a day before another patrol found him. No matter what I do, I can't get his bloody fever to break." He rakes his hand through his coppery red hair with such agitation that his man-bun comes undone and hangs loose around his neck. "That's why I sent that picture of the Guduchi plant to you. I wanted to make sure it could be used for his fever." Atticus says while looking back at his patient over the phone again.

He wanted my opinion on something because he was second-guessing himself.

Once that thought hits me, I find myself wanting to tell him that he's crazy for doubting himself. Just when I'm about to tell him that, I pause when he looks at me again. I can see something else swirling in his emerald eyes, but I can't put my finger on exactly what it is. It's almost like panic, but something tells me it's deeper than that. One thing I do know is he needs to get his head back on straight. So, I do what I do best. I calm the wolf on the other side of the screen.

"Atticus Remington," I say, and his eyes widen in shock. "I don't ever want to hear you second guess yourself again."

His eyes search mine through the screen, and I swear I can almost feel his doubt and a twinge of darkness flow through the screen between us. I mentally grab onto those feelings and I somehow push them away from him.

"You are an amazing doctor. If you weren't, I don't think Tobias would have had you talk to me last week about Kai. Now *you* tell me what you can do for this wolf to heal him." I say with a firmness I usually don't use in my voice.

A smile lifts the right side of his mouth as he processes my words. He props his phone up on a table, and he pulls his hair back up into his normal neat man-bun. When he looks back at me through the screen, he's wearing a full smile that brightens his whole face.

"Thank you for making me see past the doubt I was starting to feel, Rosie."

I flick my eyes down from my PC screen, blushing at the nickname he used. When I look back up at him, he smiles again and gives me a lively wink before snatching a piece of paper to write down what I'm assuming are herbs that would be best for fevers and pain. He rattles off a few names of herbs that I have never heard of, but one pops in my mind and I know it will help with the swelling around the injury site.

"Make sure you add echinacea to the list." I smile.

Atticus looks at me, and he chuckles as he adds the herb to the list. "You're gonna give me a run for my money if you ever come here, Rosie."

"Well, I don't know if I'd go that far. But it helps when I have a good teacher like you."

He looks at me again and nods his head. I suddenly realize that we are just staring at one another, and again I get the feeling that his mate is going to be coming in at any moment. I mean the marking on the left side of his neck. The one that looks like branches of a tree, the mark that I can't keep my eyes off of. The same mark that I feel the need to run my fingers over has to mean that he belongs to another. Doesn't it?

I shake my head, suddenly so confused by my thoughts about this man filling the screen before me. I hope he doesn't notice that my cheeks are flushed.

"I'll, uh, let you go so you can go take care of your patient." I say quickly.

"I'll let you know how he's doing after this next treatment." Atticus says and disconnects the call before I tell him that's not necessary.

After closing my laptop, I pick up my phone so I can close out of Atticus' text thread, and just as I go to set my phone down on the desk I get another notification.

Samsung Health: Cycle Tracking

> *Your Fertile Period Starts Today*

That must be the problem. I'm just hormonal. I'll look at any guy that I think is hot and want to ogle them right now. So it isn't just Atticus. Right?

I hear the front door open, and my parents' voices filter up through the hallway. I look at the clock above my desk and I realize I was on the Zoom call for about an hour. I shut my notebook before placing it in my backpack and I go downstairs to help Mom fix dinner, all the while trying to ignore my phone for any updates.

Tobias

Atticus told me through our mental bond earlier that there was a major injury within the pack. As I enter through the backdoor after grilling some steak for lunch for Coraline, something tells me to talk to my doctor over Zoom instead of our bond. And over the years I have come to trust this intuition.

"I will be right back, Luna, I need to talk to Atticus about an incident in the pack. I will update you once I know more." I tell her as I set her plate down in front of her and give her shoulder a gentle squeeze.

"Shall I wait for you to come back?" She asks while pointing to her still sizzling steak and a side salad.

"No, Luna. Please eat. I'll be back." I tell her as I walk to my office and softly shut the door behind me.

After the second ring echoes through the speakers of my computer, Atticus' face comes into focus from the camera on his phone, and I lift an eyebrow at the smile playing on his lips.

"Hello, Atticus. I take it the smile means the patient is doing well?" I ask.

Atticus runs his hand over the left side of his neck and gives a slight chuckle as he nods. I immediately notice a few gray smudges branching out over his skin. I don't think too much about it as Atticus tells me about the severity of the wound my patrolman received.

After hearing how bad the injury was, I can't help but ask the question that's lingering on my mind. "If he was injured that badly, then why are you smiling? That's not the typical bedside manner that I'm used to seeing from you."

He's usually so stoic, firm, and professional. No smile in sight, even if it's amazing news. I've only seen this man smile a few times in his life, and that is when he helps a female bring a new life into the world.

"Aye, it's not my typical behavior. But I was talking to Quilla for a while, and she—I don't know, Tobias—she helped me see things in a different light, and now I know that what I did for this wolf will help him get back on his feet." Atticus says while massaging his right shoulder.

My eyes snap to the left side of his neck again when I notice the gray smudge is gone. I know he didn't wipe his neck with anything, and he's not dirty in any other way. I make sure to keep my face neutral, but I may have to start looking into things in a bit more detail for our good doctor.

"Well, I'm glad Quilla was able to give you the insight you needed, Atticus. Is there anything else I should know?" I press.

"Nay. Everything is good here now."

"Alright. Keep me updated if anything changes. Keep up the good work, Atticus."

I find the connection between us and send a pulse of my power toward him. He closes his eyes and takes a deep breath, and I can feel the darkness that lingers in his soul vanish at my power.

I hope that whoever he met at the mansion today, figures out she's his mate. I don't think I'll be able to stay here much longer before he spirals out of control. He's been without my presence too long, and I fear I'm walking a thin line here.

I am sure to keep my thoughts to myself, and when Atticus nods and disconnects the call. I let go of my own calming breath and join my mate, who is still at the dining table with one bite of steak left, so she can still eat with me.

CHAPTER THIRTY-SEVEN
DAKOTA

It's been two weeks since Kai's Wolfbane incident, and Jeffrey and Caleb have not made an attempt to attack us. Part of me hopes they finally grew a brain cell and stopped trying to come after us, but I know better. They are making us wait to get us on edge so when they do finally make their move, we will be caught off guard. And I don't like that one bit.

So, to try to get our minds off of our flea-bag duo, Quilla, Kai, and I are all sitting at the dining room table doing the last bit of homework this morning so we can have a free weekend to ourselves. I notice that Quilla's phone has been getting more text messages than usual, and my eyes drift over to Kai.

"What?"

"Can you see who's been texting Quilla?" I ask.

"You want me to spy on your friend?" Kai asks incredulously.

"Hell ya. I need to know who she's talking to so I know he's a good guy."

Kai shakes his head and gives me a half smile. *"While it's spoken like a true alpha by wanting to keep your pack member safe, I'll have to decline on being your* inside *man."*

I grumble internally at him, and he winks at me.

"It's probably a guy she met at school. Give her the time to have a normal life with a human. Luna knows she's going to have enough weird shit with us wolves in her life."

"Okay. I guess you're right."

After about two hours of work, Kai and I close our books, and Quilla follows with a loud groan.

"Finally! If I do one more algebra equation, I think I'll explode, and you'll have to scrape me off your ceiling, Dakota."

"Oh, come on, it's not that bad." I say.

I pick up my textbooks and notebooks that match each subject and I toss them into my backpack before Kai puts them by the front door so we can grab them on the way out on Monday morning. I turn back to Quilla, who is again looking at another text message, and I suddenly get an idea.

"Hey Quilla, how about we go shopping for a while? It's been so long since we've had a girls day out on the town."

"Oh, that sounds so fun! Hell yes!" Quilla exclaims.

I turn to see Kai leaning against the door frame that separates the living room from the dining room while his arms are folded over his broad chest.

"A girl's day? Sounds boring." He teases with a hint of mischief in his hazel eyes.

"Yeah, a girls day, and no guys allowed. That even goes for Werewolf mates too." I tease.

Kai smiles at me as he pushes off the wall to make his way over to me. He cups his hand around the back of my neck and tenderly places a kiss on the crown of my head.

"Go on, Love. You and Quilla go have fun. Besides, I may go over to my place and see if my father wants to spar for a bit. K and I have been itching for a mock fight for the last few days."

"Okay. And go easy on your dad; I don't want him breaking a hip or something and we have to step up and take his pack over." I say while dragging my finger across his chest and over the marking that swirls up his neck.

"I'll be sure to tell him you are worried about his old hips." Kai grins.

I grab Quilla's hand and I drag her upstairs to change into something that's more fitting for an evening out on the town instead of our yoga pants and baggy t-shirts we were wearing.

I opt for a light blue babydoll blouse with a pair of black skinny jeans while Quilla takes a green short-sleeved shirt and a pair of my denim jeans. That's both a good and a bad thing about being the same size as your best friend—you can raid the others closet.

Once we are dressed and ready to go, we make our way back downstairs to pick up our purses, and I grab my keys off the little rack by the fridge. I wave to my mother, who is now curled up on the couch watching a game show on TV with a cup of coffee in her hand. She waves back to me and Quilla as Kai walks us out to my car before heading over to his place to spend time with his father.

On the drive into town, Quilla gets another text message, and I see a smile start to play on her lips. I try to remember Kai's words and not prod into her life. So, ignoring the fact that her nose is buried in her phone, I continue driving to the shopping center downtown.

"Okay, where do you want to go first?" I ask as I parallel park on the street a few minutes later.

Quilla pockets her phone, and she looks around before spotting the first store she wants to walk into.

"Oh! Let's go to that new clothing store that opened up last month. I've been dying to go there. I hear it has custom-made things as well as designer clothing."

"Okay," I say with a smile as I check in my side view mirror to make sure no cars are coming down the road before I open my door and meet Quilla on the sidewalk.

When we enter the store, a sharp beep trills overhead as I open the door, followed by a quaint, soothing melody echoing from the speakers hidden in the ceiling, giving the space a calm and quiet atmosphere. And with all that happened over the last two weeks, I need some calmness around me.

After looking around for a few minutes, I pick out a couple of flowy dresses in blush pink and a beautiful lush green to add to my basket. Quilla finds a beige dress that has yellow roses in all stages of bloom printed across the fabric with a cute brown lacy bow stitched in at the hip.

"That is adorable, Quilla." I say joyfully.

I turn to make my way to the checkout counter when I see the locally made shop section. I walk over and I see a t-shirt that has a silhouette of a wolf howling at a full moon. I show it to Quilla, and she laughs while shaking her head at me.

"That is too funny, Dakota."

"Hey, I figured if I can't." I pause to look around the shop before continuing, "*Phase,* I can still rock the wolf this way."

Quilla looks at me, and the laughter fades from her eyes, and she sets a hand on my shoulder.

"You'll get there one day, Chica. I know you will. You just need time, that's all."

"Yeah, well, I don't know how much more time I need, Quilla." I say, "I mean, come on, you've seen what I can do. How *powerful* I am. What else is there?"

"You are strong, Dakota. But maybe you're just trying too hard. You and Kota are so desperate to *change* that it just won't happen." Quilla offers.

"Maybe you're right." I say as we go to the checkout counter.

When we leave, I look down the street, and I notice an F.Y.E store, and I poke Quilla in the arm.

"Hey, you wanna go to that store next? Look at the latest releases and see what unique things they have in there?"

"Sure!"

We walk down the sidewalk a bit, and once again Quilla gets a text message. I internally groan and walk ahead of her a few steps to open the glass and metal framed door for us.

We go through each and every aisle looking at the different anime figures, squishmallows, and everything else they have until we've spent about forty-five minutes in the store. When we finally check out, the only things we have in our basket are the latest album of Taylor Swift and the Greatest Hits mashup from Justin Timberlake.

Once we finally emerge from the F.Y.E. store, I hear Quilla's stomach growl and I chuckle. "Let's take these things to the car and then we'll go eat."

She nods, and we walk to my car to deposit our bags into the trunk, and then we go to the little eatery down the block on the corner. After we order some sandwiches and wait for our drinks to come out, Quilla gets one final text, and I can't keep my mouth shut anymore. I have to know who's texting her.

"Okay, Chica. Who has been texting you all day?" I ask, waving my hand toward her phone.

I see her cheeks flush a bright pink, and she shyly tucks her phone away.

"Oh no. Don't get all shy on me now. I mean, I don't care who he is. As long as he's good to you, that's all I care about. So, do I know him?"

She thinks about this for a moment, and she shakes her head. "No, you don't."

"Ohhh. Okay. So who's the lucky guy? What's his name?" I ask while wiggling my eyebrows.

Our sandwiches come before she can answer, and once the waitress walks away, I look to Quilla again.

"It's Atticus, okay?" Quilla says while popping a fry in her mouth.

"Seriously?!" I whisper shout. "When did you start talking to him this much?" I pause. "You like him, don't you?" I add quickly.

"Since he helped me with the Wolfsbane tea for Kai and you. He's been helping me get better at... being what I am, so he's been sending me pictures of herbs to see what I can gather from them." Quilla explains. "And no, I don't. I can't." She whispers.

"Awe, that's sweet of him. I'll have to remember to thank him once I meet him." I say as I take a sip of my Coke.

"Plus, I kinda helped him the other day with one of his patients." Quilla says.

She tells me about how she helped Atticus figure out the best way to heal that poor patrolman, and I find myself smiling at her. I am proud of her for being what Atticus needed at that moment.

"You are amazing, Quilla. Don't you ever forget that." I reach over the table to squeeze her hand.

I've known since I met Kai that she feels like the odd one out. And even now, I can feel her loneliness. Like she'll never find someone that completes her like I did with Kai.

"And I promise, the man that is out there for you will become the luckiest man alive to be able to breathe the same air as you. It will come, Quilla. Maybe not in the way you are expecting, but it will happen one day." I give her a smile, and she flashes her own in return while she wipes the beginning of tears from her eyes.

"You always know what to say to make me cry." She says with a slight wobble to her voice.

"I know what makes my sister from another mister tick." I wink.

After we finish our meal, it's four-thirty in the afternoon, so we make our way back to my car with our arms wrapped around each other and feeling a little lighter than we did this morning. Atticus texts Quilla again, and she shows me the image and tells me what the herb is and what it does while she messages Atticus at the same time. Just as we are about to approach my car, I feel Kota perk up, and without another thought, I allow her to the front of my mind to be able to make my eyes and nose sharper. His scent hits me before I see who it is. The person standing across the street staring us down is the last person I want to see.

Caleb.

CHAPTER THIRTY-EIGHT
DAKOTA

"**Q**uilla, don't look back. Just keep walking to the car." I say my voice surprisingly calm.

Quilla begins to look at me, but I just place a firm hand on my friend's shoulder and keep her moving forward.

"Don't look. Caleb is across the street, and he's staring at us down so hard that I'm surprised we don't have holes in us yet."

She nods and keeps her eyes forward while I keep the mutt in my peripheral vision. We almost make it to the passenger door of my car when I see Caleb phase in broad daylight. His mangy-looking black and gray form darts across the street so he can effectively cut me and Quilla off from getting to my car.

"Caleb, you don't want to do this." I warn.

He lets a vicious snarl rip from his throat, drool dripping in long, thick strands down his muzzle. I push Quilla away from me, putting her back into the building next to us in an attempt to keep him focused on me. I take a split second to listen to sounds around me, and I notice that it's quiet. The streets are empty.

Of course, they wouldn't be. It's close to quitting time. People are either just getting off work or are already home.

As I'm trying to figure out what to do, I notice Caleb's eyes flick toward the right. Towards Quilla. A heartbeat later, the muscles in his legs coil, and he lunges at her, his mouth wide open for the attack. I jump in front of him while pushing Quilla out of the way, and when his jaws clamp down on my left shoulder, I have to bite my lip to keep from screaming out. His long, sharp bottom canines pierce my skin right above my collarbone while his top canines dig into my back near my shoulder blade.

I reach up with my right hand, grabbing him by the scruff to pull him off of me and throw him a few feet down the sidewalk. I barely register the blood starting to pour from my wounds as his feet hit the concrete, and he's lunging at me again. I can tell from his eyes that he's going for my throat this time, and I lift my right arm up in time to protect myself. His teeth sink deeply into my forearm, and the all-consuming white-hot pain that envelopes my shoulder and arm is enough to take my breath away, and I can't hold my screams this time.

I gather what strength I have left and I swing my arm backward, ramming his wolven head into the brick building beside me. He lets go of my arm with a yelp of pain, then crumples to the ground before me. After a heartbeat, he shakes his head from what I'm sure is a hell of a headache before running away from me.

I force myself to stay on my feet until I see him cross the street and disappear into the neighboring forest before my body finally collapses on itself. I keep my arm folded tight against my chest while trying to hold my shoulder to staunch the flow of blood, but nothing works and blood freely drips onto the sidewalk.

All I know is pain.

Pain from each and every tooth feels like white-hot pokers in my skin, making each breath a struggle.

"Dakota!" Quilla screams as she runs over to me. "Oh, my God. We gotta get you home."

She helps me stand, and I sway on my feet before she tightens her hold on me. I can feel myself getting weaker from blood loss and from whatever the hell was on his teeth that makes the wounds burn and ache with each movement. Quilla quickly opens the passenger side door and helps me sit sideways in the seat. I feel blood flowing between my fingers, and a cold sweat has broken out on my brow. I look up at Quilla, her olive green eyes shining bright with fear but wanting to know what I need for her to do.

"How do you feel, Dakota? Tell me exactly what hurts."

"I don't know. This burns so much. What the fuck was on his teeth?" I hiss as another wave of hot pain flows through my body.

"I wish I knew. Let's get you home," Quilla says as she helps me sit forward in the seat, and the movement pulls another wave of pain through me, and I groan in response.

"Take me to Kai's place..." I pant. "He's with his dad."

Once Quilla closes my door, she hops into the driver's seat and races to Kai's house. While she drives, I close my eyes and look in at Kota to see if she's okay. I am instantly taken to her forest, and I see her near her little lake, lying on her side whimpering in pain. I stagger towards her, and when I am about three feet from her, I fall to my knees, crawling the rest of the way to her side.

"Hey, it's okay. Kai will know what to do. And so will Quilla. We just got to figure out what the asshole bit us with."

Kota just nods as she lets out another whimper. I lean in to kiss the top of her fury head before I start to hear Quilla's soft voice echo through the forest. I open my eyes, and I just barely catch the question she asked.

"You think you should tell Kai what happened?"

Quilla hits a bump in the road, and I moan when it jars my shoulder and arm. "Okay." I grunt and I reach out to Kai.

Kai

I'm in the backyard with my father, both of us in our wolven forms. His black coat picks up on any remaining light of the evening and reflects it back at me. We have been doing mock drills consisting of going for the other's throat, belly and trying to take out the back legs to cripple our opponent. I'm just about to move in a way that will make him think I'm going for his back leg, but my target is the side of his throat as he parries my attack, but that is cut short when my whole body buckles from intense pain in my left shoulder and right foreleg. I know my body is uninjured, so I immediately reach out to Dakota.

"What happened, Dakota?" I plead.

Dad rushes over to me, his claws digging into the grass and dirt while waiting for me to elaborate on what happened.

"It's Dakota. She's hurt. Badly. *I'm trying to get her to talk to me."* I tell him.

He nods and bounds off into the house so he can phase and grab our clothes. I pick myself up off the ground, shaking out my fur, since I know the pain I feel is not my own, and I reach for Dakota again now that I feel her a little bit more in my mind.

"Please, Love, tell me what happened?" I phase and quickly dress while I wait for her to respond.

"Caleb. He attacked us." She says, and her voice is even breathless in my mind. *"He was going for Quilla. I had to protect her."* She hisses as we both feel another wave of pain wash over her. *"Damn it, it hurts so much, Kai."*

"It's going to be okay, Baby. As soon as you get here, we'll get you fixed up." I send the feeling of my hand caressing her cheek, and I can feel her relax for a moment before the pain forces itself front and center again.

I rush out the front door as I hear an engine approaching the house, and I see Quilla pull Dakota's car into the driveway behind Dad's Yukon. I rush over to the passenger side door, forcing it open, just stopping short of ripping it from the hinges. When I put my hand on her bleeding shoulder, my body instantly goes weak, and my hand starts to burn while nausea hits me like a freight train. I snap my hand back as another smell hits me through the coppery, iron scent of the fresh blood pouring from her, and my heart drops to my stomach.

Quilla slams the driver's side door and rushes to my side. I try to keep my tone civil, but all I want to do is phase and track that fucker down for attacking my Tamer and my mate and slowly rip him to shreds.

"Quilla, get her inside now." I force myself to back away from Dakota, because right now, no matter how much I want to be near her, to help her through this, I can't.

"What's wrong with her, Kai?" Quilla asks as she notices me reluctantly backing away from her.

"She has silver in the wounds." I say as I kneel down on rubbery legs and wipe the blood from my still-burning and now angry red hand onto the grass.

Dakota

At hearing Kai's words, I remember what Dad told me when we first figured out I was a Were.

Silver can seriously injure or even kill a Were.

I look to Kai with pleading eyes. "Please go get my mom."

"Dakota, I am not—" Kai begins, but I cut him off.

"Kai, please get her. You can't be around me Babe, or you'll get hurt, sick, or whatever silver does to you." I try to move my shoulder, but I'm rewarded with another wave of fire. "Please, don't fight me on this." I beg.

Kai looks at me for a second before he takes off across the street toward my house. I hear footsteps crunching in the grass to my left, and I see Tobias standing in the middle of his yard.

"Quilla, take her to the laundry room. We have a drain in the middle of the floor so you can flush her wounds out in there."

Quilla nods as she helps me out of the car. When I stand, I begin to sway on my feet as my head starts to spin, and she helps me steady myself before I take my agonizingly slow steps toward Tobias' house. I stumble my way up the stairs leading to the porch, but Quilla is able to keep me on my feet the whole time.

Tobias holds the door open for us as we step into the foyer, but he stays behind the solid wooden door, like that will somehow protect him from the silver that I now know is coursing through my veins.

When Quilla finally leads me to the laundry room, it feels like we walked miles instead of a few feet. My body is beginning to shake from the blood loss, which makes the pain renew with vicious clarity. Quilla looks around for a chair so I can sit, but the space is empty except for a metal fold-out ironing board in the middle of the room. I look at the wall that's closest to me and I point my head towards it.

"Quilla, lean me against the wall until you find a chair." I tell her as I grip my left shoulder a bit harder to try to slow the blood still dripping down my arm.

I lean my head back on the cool wall and I close my eyes, willing my knees to hold me until Quilla comes back with a chair.

After a few seconds, she brings in a wooden chair from the dining table and sits it in the middle of the room, right over the little square metal drain on the floor. She gently takes my right arm in her hand, not bothered one bit about the blood coating my body, and leads me over to the chair. As I sit down, I lean my head against the back of the chair while trying to breathe through the pain of being moved, but something is different about the pain; it's deeper in my skin. I almost feel like my skin is getting tighter, and I feel the same thing from each tooth mark. I look at my forearm and I realize the new sensation is from me beginning to heal over the silver lodged under my skin.

Lori

I am just starting to pick up the living room after I've had my fill of coffee, snacks, and The Game Show Network when the front door flies open and I see a terror-filled Kai burst through the door. I drop the ceramic mug without a second thought and rush to meet him in the foyer.

"Kai, what's wrong?" I demand.

"It's Dakota. She's badly hurt with silver. I need you and Quilla to help save her."

I take a step towards him, and he leads me over to his house, where I see Dakota's car parked in the driveway. Blood coats the interior, and a trail of the irony substance covers the grass in spots and continues into the house. I wouldn't even need to have Kai show me where she is, I could just follow the trail of her blood. And knowing that my baby is hurt, brings out the momma bear in me, and I want to find who did this and beat them to a pulp.

I enter the laundry room, and I take a split second to look at my daughter. Her baby blue blouse is blotched in red, her skin is pale, and she's bent over, her head hanging loosely while her elbows rest on her knees, and I notice that her shoulders are starting to tremble. Kai stays a step behind me, and I know with heartbreaking clarity that he is forcing himself to stay away from the silver, but I can see the turmoil in his eyes all the same. He wants to be there for her, but the survival instinct is too strong to go near her. I give him a firm nod before I step into the laundry room.

"Hey, Honey. I'm here. We are going to get you all fixed up. Don't you worry."

"Mom," Dakota pleads. She doesn't pick her head up, but I can hear her voice is tight with unshed tears. "Please hurry, I think I'm trying to heal over the silver."

"Okay."

I look to my right, where I see Coraline standing in the other doorway that leads into the kitchen.

"Coraline, do you have any syringes or anything to flush her wounds out with?"

"Yes, I do." Coraline responds stiffly.

I look over at Quilla, who is gently rubbing Dakota's good shoulder. "Quilla, please go with Coraline and make sure you get some saltwater to fill them with."

As Quilla leaves with Coraline, I turn to my daughter as I hear a moan flow from her lips that is so pain filled and tired that it breaks my heart.

"Let me help you out of that shirt. Can you put your arm up a little bit?"

She hisses as gingerly lifts her arms, but I am able to get the shirt off her, leaving her in only her gray sports bra. I automatically move a little closer to her back so Tobias doesn't see her mate marking. And right now, so Kai doesn't see it either. Because one of the puncture wounds is so incredibly close to her marking, I fear if he sees it he will go into a frenzy and track down who did this to her and rip them apart.

Quilla finally comes back with the syringes, salt water with little dried flowers floating on top, a small knife, and a lighter.

"Are you ready, Dakota?" Quilla asks as she places the items on the counter across from us.

"Not really." Dakota groans, "But I want this burning to stop."

"Okay, your mom and I are gonna help you, but we need to open the wounds again before we can flush the silver out." Quilla says as she pulls the lighter out, quickly sparking the flint to sterilize the blade with the heat of the flame.

CHAPTER THIRTY-NINE

KAI

I stare at my mate. My bloody, broken mate and I shake with the need to be by her side, to console her, to let her know that she's gonna be okay. But in reality, I don't know if that's true. I am shocked that she hasn't blacked out yet. I know if the roles were reversed, I would be out cold by now and in grave danger to my life.

As Quilla and Lori step around her to begin the extraction process, Dakota lifts her head to me, her eyes are glowing a bright blue and I can see her fear, how tired she's getting all swirling in her eyes, and I know she can see the pure agony in my own for her.

"Hey, I'm gonna be okay now." She says, her voice sounding so weak in my head. *"I get the feeling that silver might not affect me the way it should for a full Were."*

"It is affecting you differently. By this time, you should have been un-conscious. But it's killing me that I can't be near you, to comfort you when you're in pain."

"Okay, Dakota. Here we go." Quilla warns.

Dakota wraps her hand around the wooden arm of the chair, the same one that I remember watching Dad carve when I was younger in his workshop back in Montana. She takes a breath, trying to prepare for the new wave of pain that will follow as Quilla brings the knife down against her once flawless skin. Skin that I love tracing my fingers over, the skin which is now red with her blood and swollen in places where those fucking tooth wounds marr her flesh.

I also know that Lori tried to keep me from seeing just how close that one canine came to shredding through her mate marking. The only reason that my feet are still planted on the floor is because I can't leave her until I know she can get through this. After that point, all fucking bets are off the table. The only two things that will keep me from walking out this door are a direct order from my father, which truth be told, I would probably fight like hell against, or a request from my mate to stay by her side as she heals.

I can tell Dakota tries not to tense her shoulders up as Quilla begins to dig the knife into her skin, but the scream that rips from her throat feels like I just got stabbed in the heart. Jeffrey and Caleb really knew how to hurt me this time, and it pisses me off to no end.

As Quilla continues to reopen the wounds, Dakota's grip gets tighter and tighter on the arm of the chair until it finally relents and splinters in her hands.
And as the wood splinters, so does my resolve.

Before I can comprehend what I'm doing, I hear a soft growl from K in my mind, but the growl is filled with understanding. I take three long strides into the laundry room; the scent of silver hitting my nose instantly, even over the stench of the iron and fear hanging in the air. My knees automatically go to rubber, and nausea roils in my stomach, threatening to claw its way up my throat. I coax my lead-filled limbs to grab Dakota's hand as I am finally forced to my knees; the silver in her body saps my strength like a tree in a sudden drought, but I don't care right now. She needs me, and I will be there for her, no matter what.

Dakota

I feel the knife connect with my skin, and at first, the cool metal is like a block of dry ice to a raging fire. It feels so good until the bite of the blade follows, and it reignites the flames ten times over. As I scream and grip the arm of the chair with my hand, it doesn't register that I just completely destroyed the arm until I feel my hand being caressed with trembling fingers. The splinters slowly being pulled from my skin.

I open my eyes, and I see Kai kneeling on the floor before me. His skin sporting a tint of a greenish hue while carefully pulling each splinter from my hand.

"Kai, please, Babe, back up. I don't need you hurt either."

"I'm fine, Love." Kai forces out, "But I can't stand by and watch you go through this alone anymore."

I see movement out of the corner of my eye, and I glance over to find Coraline standing against the tall, solid form of Tobias. Both of them silently watching me and Kai. I glance back down to the now missing arm on the chair, and I glance back at Coraline with a small, regretful smile.

"I'm... sorry...about the chair." I grind out as I feel Quilla finally pull a long piece of silver from my shoulder. I let out a closed-mouthed scream while trying my best to keep still.

"It's okay, Sweetheart. Tobias can fix it later." Coraline says in forced sweetness. I can tell this is hurting her and her mate just as much as it hurts the man before me.

I focus back on Kai, and I can feel just how weak the silver is making him, and that is when I know for a fact that silver does affect me in a completely different way than it does him. I can feel he's fighting to move his body, even just his fingers, to caress my hand. It's like they are filled with lead, and it takes effort just to move them. I try to move my own fingers, and they move without issue. Granted, it makes the muscles in my back twitch with agony, but they are not weighed down by some invisible force.

Part of me wants to make him get back, to protect himself, but I know one, he's not able to move and two, deep down, I don't know if I want him to leave my side. Just from holding his hand in my own, I feel calmer, more grounded, and can handle the pain of Mom and Quilla pulling the pieces of silver from my wounds a little bit better.

Just as that thought hits me, Quilla pulls one from the top of my shoulder, and I suck in a sharp breath as I squeeze Kai's hand tighter.

"I'm gonna...end up breaking your hand, Babe." I pant into his mind.

"And if you do, I have another one for you to use while that one heals." Kai replies simply.

I give him a small smile, but it quickly turns into a grimace when I feel Mom begin to flush out my freshly open wounds with the mixture of salt water and what smells like dried Wolfsbane flowers.

"I'm sorry, Honey, but we need to make sure the wounds are clean."

I nod my head as Quilla starts to work on yet another wound on my back.

"Can you lean forward just a bit for me, Dakota?" Quilla asks.

I begin to lean forward as she requested, and a wave of dizziness and exhaustion hits me so hard that I begin to fall forward. Kai pushes himself up higher on his knees to catch me by hooking his right arm under my armpit. As his arm touches my back, I hear his sharp intake of breath, and even through our bond, I feel the intense burn that flares across his skin from the lingering silver in my wounds.

I try to push him away from me with my right arm, but I miss his shoulder completely. I fall into his chest while my right arm collides with his left side. When my arm bushes against his shirt, blood coats the fabric, seeping through and soaking his skin. Kai groans as the burning also flares from that point of contact. Mom finally catches me and pulls me upright in the chair again and away from Kai. He tries to get back to his knees, but he falls back with another grunt of pain before he can pull his shirt over his head to get the blood-soaked fabric off his side.

Once he gets his shirt off, I see that on his forearm as well as his side are angry, red, third-degree burns on his perfect skin, and dark, red blood oozes from the wounds. All this was caused by just a quick touch of my silver-laced blood.

"Kai... I'm sorry." I say.

His hazel eyes snap to mine, and he shakes his head once. "Don't you dare be sorry, Love." He says through gritted teeth. "This is in no way your fault."

"We need to wipe the burn down to get the silver off your skin." Quilla says as she kneels beside Kai with a white washcloth in her hand while trying to wipe at his skin, but he pulls back from her with an apologetic half grin on his face.

"I can do it. Please, continue to take care of my mate, Quilla."

As Quilla turns back to me, I peer around her waist and I catch glimpses of Kai wiping at his skin and wincing as the cloth makes contact with the irritated flesh. At the sight of my mate on the floor dabbing at his own burns, I start to feel something else through all this pain, and it's red-hot anger. Not only did they try to go after my Tamer, but they hurt me, and now they've hurt my mate yet again. Just as I start to shake with rage at the situation, Quilla pulls yet another piece of silver in the shape of a long canine tooth from my shoulder, which quickly replaces the anger with my painful moans.

Kai

I try to fight against the burn on my skin as I drag the washcloth down the silver-induced wound. My limbs quickly become weaker with each second, and the darkness that's rapidly gathering at the corner of my vision threatens to take me under, but K and I somehow fight back with everything we have. We cannot leave Dakota alone to deal with this.

Quilla stands at my mate's side and looks at Lori, trying to figure out a way to keep Dakota in the chair. I can feel her exhaustion mingle with my own through the bond, and it breaks my already fractured heart.

"Quilla, can you help me turn Dakota around in the chair so she can lean on the back?" Lori asks.

Quilla nods, and both women move Dakota around so she is sitting backward on the chair and she's able to lean her head against the backrest. I'm sure it's not comfortable at all, but right now safety is first, and she's safer in that position.

Once I finally get the burn on my arm under control to where it's a dull ache, I go to work on my side where it still feels like fire is licking against my skin. I lift my arm, and I see another washcloth drop to the floor beside me to replace the bloody one currently in my hand. I look up to see my mother staring at me. Her blue eyes are glassy with unshed tears.

"Thank you, Mother." I whisper into her mind.

She simply nods back at me, pure anguish written all over her face. I know that she can feel my sorrow, anger, fear, and pain through our own unique bond as mother to child. I begin to feel her warmth, calmness, and love flow over me, and I greedily take it in. As I do, it does help ease the darkness at the edge of my vision enough for me to wipe Dakota's blood off my side. I still won't be able to heal completely until I get away from all the silver in the room, but that will come soon enough.

I glance over to my strong and beautiful mate and watch as her mother and our Tamer continue to tend to her wounds. I notice that Dakota is opening and closing her hand, trying to stay still as they pull the remaining few slivers of silver from her shoulder. So, I force myself up on my rubbery legs and I walk closer to the chair. I planned to slowly sit on the floor, but as I get closer to the silver still in her right arm, my legs give out completely and I fall to the floor, thankfully on my good side. Dakota opens her eyes enough to look at me, and the moan that escapes her lips is more for my own pain than hers.

"Talk to me, Love." I ask as I lift my trembling hand to hers.

Her grip tightens on my hand as her eyes open more to take me in.

"I'm so tired." She begins, and I hear her voice whisper in my mind. *"I don't know if it's from the blood loss, the pain, or if the silver is finally starting to get to me."*

"I'm sorry, Love, but you may also be picking up on how I feel too, and that's making you feel worse." I say with regret in my voice.

"Maybe. I feel bad saying this, but now that you're here, I don't want you to go." She says while gripping my hand tighter.

"I go where you go, Love. I will not leave your side, no matter what. I would rather die in your arms than stay away when you need me the most."

She looks at me, shock filling her face at my words. Before she's able to say anything in response, she takes a quick, sharp breath through her teeth as Quilla pulls the last piece of silver from her back. As Lori takes up flushing out the remaining wounds on Dakota's back, Quilla makes quick work on her forearm, all the while being mindful of me and keeping as much of the silver away as she can.

I start to relax a bit when color begins to come back to Dakota's skin and her breathing starts to even out. I bring her hand closer to my lips and I press a gentle kiss to her knuckles.

"Thank the Great Luna that we have an amazing Tamer and that your mother is very brave too. And you, Love. You are so strong. I am so lucky to call you mine."

Dakota

As Kai's words echo in my mind, I can feel my strength slowly returning. I can't help it when I go to search Kai's mind to make sure he's getting better too. I am rewarded with a chuckle when he feels me poking again.

"Didn't we already have this discussion, Dakota? You can ask me how I am doing instead of sneaking around."

"I just needed to feel it for myself that you were okay."

"Mhm...Sure." Kai softly croons in my mind, and it makes me smile for the first time since the attack.

"Would you have told me the truth?" I shoot back.

At his silence, I give him a sharp look and shake his hand once to let him know that I called him on his bullshit. His weak smile in return tells me that I hit the nail on the head.

Mom and Quilla then start to bandage my shoulder and forearm, and again I catch little dried flowers in the dressings as they tape them to my wounds. Once my injuries are all covered, the women behind me start to clean up the laundry room, giving me as well as Kai time to recover a bit before being moved from our respective spots.

Quilla disposes of the silver while Mom uses a long hose attachment on the little sink in the corner of the room to flush the blood-slicked floor down the drain. During all this, I just hold Kai's hand and be what we need for each other. An anchor to help the other through the lingering pain and fear.

Once the laundry is cleaned and the silver disposed of, I am given a clean t-shirt and pair of shorts to change into, which my mate reluctantly looks away to give me the privacy I need. Then after I'm dressed, Quilla and Mom stand on either side of me so they can try to help me to my feet. I let go of Kai and place my right hand on the back of the chair to help push my lower body off the seat while swinging my right leg around the chair. Once I am standing next to Quilla with Kai in front of me, I pause for a moment so I can make sure my legs will handle my weight. I begin to take a step when my knee buckles, and thankfully Quilla and Kai catch me before I can fall flat on my face.

"Easy, Love. Take it slow."

I nod at him, and they both eventually help me to the living room and sit me down on the loveseat, where Kai quickly takes his place by my side. Quilla then rushes off into the kitchen and after a few minutes, she brings out two mugs of steaming hot herbal tea.

"You're really falling into this Tamer role, Chica." I smile while taking a sip from my mug.

"Well, I have to. You two are going to run me ragged. So, I have to be good at this."

As I take another sip of tea, the front door suddenly bursts open and my father rushes into the living room, panic written all over his face then relief follows when he sees me sitting on the couch with Kai's head on my right shoulder and our hands intertwined on his thigh.

"I came as soon as your mother told me. Are you alright, Honey?" Dad asks.

"Yes, I'm fine now, Dad." I say as I smile at him.

Dad pulls Mom into his side, and they both go in behind the loveseat to gently caress my neck since Kai's head is on my good shoulder. I lean into both of their hands and relish in the power that I feel coming from my father. I prove to him through our bond how I feel, and he places a gentle kiss on the crown of my head.

Tobias then steps forward, his face in a relieved yet stern scowl as he looks me over, and I can instantly tell this is not just Tobias standing before me. This is Alpha Huntington out in full force. His son being drugged was one thing, but for another to be attacked so viciously and with silver, I can see in his eyes that he is out for blood.

"Dakota, how are you feeling now?" His deep voice rumbles through the room.

I look at his right ear when I answer him. "I am better now, Alpha. Thank you."

"Can you explain what happened this afternoon? Please give as much detail as you can."

I feel Kai tense up beside me, and I turn my head to look at him. *"Easy, Babe."* I croon softly.

"You have no idea how badly I want to go hunt that fucker down and slowly rip him apart for trying to attack Quilla and then hurting you."

"Well, your father looks like he wants to join you on that endeavor." I say as I flick my eyes over toward the stiff-backed man before me. *"Can I get in on that too? You're right, this started because he tried to attack Quilla; he tried again to hurt what is* mine." I growl near the end.

"You sound more and more like an alpha every day, Love." Kai chuckles.

"I have the best teacher." I say as I gently kiss his hair.

Tobias clears his throat, and I turn my head back in his direction. "Apologies, Alpha. I needed to calm a royally pissed-off mate first."

He nods his head with a small smile and gestures for me to begin.

As I begin to explain everything, I feel the muscles in Kai's shoulders tighten again, so while gently rubbing soothing circles down his back, I finish my story.

"I tried to talk him out of whatever his plan was, but when I saw his eyes flick over towards Quilla, I knew he was going to attack. And I just reacted. I knew something was wrong when his teeth sank into my shoulder, but I would have never thought it was silver." I say, shaking my head, "Call me naïve, but that just didn't cross my mind until I was brought here and Kai said it was silver."

"You are not naïve in the least, Dakota. If anything, I failed you as an alpha for not teaching you the smell and effects of silver." Tobias says as he shakes his head. "I will say though, I have not been around pure, handmade silver like that in a long time." He adds while opening and closing his right hand. For the first time tonight, I noticed that his skin tone is a little lighter than its normal hue.

"Handmade silver?" Dad says in disbelief. "That is the most dangerous form of silver for us."

When I hear Dad say this, I glance over to Kai's arm where it's still looking like a second-degree burn even with Quilla's herbal tea in his system, and I can tell that his skin is still so much paler than mine and his father's.

"Kai, you went near it, didn't you?" Dad snaps as he notices where my gaze is focused.

He doesn't answer, but Tobias does for him. "Easy, Beta." He warns. "Yes, I admit he did get close to the silver, which, I have to be honest, was incredibly *stupid* on his part."

I feel Kai begin to lift his head from my shoulder in protest, but his father holds up a hand to silence him.

"However, I do understand his thought process." Tobias says as he looks at my father, "Tell me, Nathan, if it was Lori who was hurt with silver, would you not be by her side no matter the threat to your life?"

Dad looks from the alpha to Kai, then to me, and finally looks back at Mom, and he tilts his head back with a defeated sigh.

"I thought so." Tobias answers with a grin.

"Why don't the two of you go and rest for a while?" Quilla urges.

I look down at Kai, and I notice he looks just as worn out as I am.

"Quilla's right. Let's go get some rest, Babe." I tell him, and he silently nods his head. "But first let me talk to my parents for a bit."

I slowly get up from the loveseat and I follow my parents to the door of the guest room near the kitchen. Mom pulls me in for a hug, and while it's firm, it's gentle all the same.

"You scared me today."

"I'm sorry I scared you. But I am not sorry for protecting a pack member and longtime friend." I say with stubbornness.

"I'm glad you're alright now, Dakota." Dad says, "And I hope you don't think I was out of line with what I said to Kai."

"No. It's alright."

Dad nods as he enters the room, leaving me and Mom alone in the hallway.

"Thank you for helping Quilla today, Mom. You have no idea how much I appreciate what you did."

"I'd do anything for my baby girl." Mom says as she caresses my head, running her hand over my still-tangled hair. "You were so strong today. Some packs think that half-Were's are weaker because of the human blood that flows through their veins. *But,* your father told me that in certain situations he's seen over the years, half-Were's can be stronger than their full-blood counterparts. Because what can injure and even kill a full-blood doesn't do as much to half-bloods. So, keep that thought in mind if you ever doubt yourself." She says as she smiles at me and kisses me on the cheek. "Now go on to bed. I'm sure Kai will want to keep you close."

After she enters the bedroom with my father, I walk back out into the living room where I find Kai leaning against the wall that leads to the stairwell. His left leg is straight out while his right leg is tucked at a slight angle, and his arms are crossed over his broad chest. Most people would see it as a casual stance, but I know him well enough now to see the slight tremble in his left knee that's supporting his weight.

"Let's go to bed, Mate." I say as I look into his tired hazel eyes. I hate that look on his face, so I try to get them to light up if only a little bit. "But I think a shower is in order first."

I have to hold back a grin as his eyes light up with my suggestion. He takes the bait like a trout to a lure. "I'm talking about *separate* showers, wolf-boy." I chuckle as I playfully bat at his shoulder.

"You're such a tease, Love." Kai croons in my head.

I smile at him again, and I take his hand in my own, tugging him up the stairs. As I stop in front of the main bathroom, Kai tightens his hand on mine. A silent plea not to let go. I lift my other hand to caress his face, and he instantly leans into my touch.

"I am fine now, Kai. I can feel myself healing and getting stronger."

I lean in to kiss him to prove that point, but he only counters what I give him. I know this is not *my* Kai. So, I slip my left hand under his shirt, letting my fingers graze and caress the line of muscle on his stomach, and at my touch, something snaps in him. Because the next thing I know, he's pinning me to the wall.

His tall, muscular body dwarfing my own, his hips pressing into mine to keep me right where he wants me. With his right hand, he keeps mine against his stomach while his left hand pins my right arm above my head all the while still being mindful of my bandages.

Neither of us say anything. We don't need to when only our desire-driven breath fills the sliver of space between us. He leans in and presses a light kiss to my lips while I feel his apprehension leak through our bond.

Am I healed enough to take his show of love for me?

I hate that seed of doubt filling his mind, so I roll my hips into him without another thought. I feel his instant reaction to me grow through his jeans, and I can't help the moan that pours from my mouth at the feeling of his hardened length against my hot center.

"If I can get you to moan like this with clothes still on, I can't wait until our bonding ceremony, Love." Kai growls.

"I blame it on the silver making me so sensitive to everything." I croon seductively.

He deepens the kiss, and I allow his tongue into my mouth to taste me, explore me, and devour me. He backs away enough to take my bottom lip between his teeth, pulling another moan from my chest, and then his lips slowly travel down to my jaw. I want to run my fingers through his hair, but when I go to move my hand from his stomach, he tightens his grip slightly. A warning not to move.

"You are *mine* to touch, to love, and to care for. Anyone who dares to threaten you will be dealt with. And it will be a slow and painful process, I promise you that, Mate." Kai whispers darkly, and even through my desire-filled mind I can hear the growl of K come through in Kai's voice too.

"I believe you." I pant.

Kai finally pulls back, and in his brightly glowing hazel eyes, I can see his strength is returning. He releases me from the wall, and I feel the cool air fill the space where his body just was.

"Go on and get your shower, Dakota. I'll be waiting for you." He says as he slips into another room down the hall.

CHAPTER FORTY

DAKOTA

Once I get my legs working again, I step into the hall bathroom, and I gingerly tug my shirt over my head while I push my shorts down to my ankles and stare at my naked body. I look at the stark white bandages against my sun-tanned skin, and I take a breath before I lift my right arm to peel the bandage away to see how I am healing. I imagine that with pure silver I should still have red marks dotting my shoulder. But when I remove the bandage, I am shocked at what I reveal.

I am completely healed other than a few pink marks where *his* canines punctured my skin over my collarbone. I bend the three-piece mirror in a way so I can see how my back is healing, and when I see what's staring back at me, I feel nauseous.

No wonder Kai didn't want to leave me. If he did, he was going to go on a murderous rampage.

I see that my mate marking was almost defiled by that mangy mutt, and what was nausea rolling in my gut quickly turns to anger. I then turn my attention to my forearm, and when I unwrap it, I see the same thing. I am healed other than a few marks where the longest pieces of silver were embedded in my skin. I poke at the pink circles and I find I'm not even tender near them.

"Well, if I had any doubts that I'm no longer a normal human, they just went completely out the window." I mumble to myself.

"You seriously still had that doubt, Dakota?" I hear Kota chuckle in my mind like she can't believe I was still thinking I was normal.

"Well, you have yet to make an appearance, so." I tease while looking in the mirror, and I see my eyes glow in response as I feel Kota come to the front of my mind.

"Remind me to bite you the next time you come in the forest with me."

I laugh at her while I feel her retreat deeper into her forest again. I shake my head as I finish my much-needed hot shower.

After my shower, I remember I didn't grab any clothes from Kai's room. So, I wrap the beige towel around my damp frame and make my way across the hall to Kai's bedroom, hoping that maybe I finished my shower before he did. I come to a dead stop in the doorway to his room when I see him sitting on the side of his bed wearing only a pair of black shorts. His broad shoulders and defined chest and abs are still damp from his own shower. He shockingly doesn't notice me in the doorway, and I can see in his face that he's back to thinking about my injuries today. I softly pad into his room with a sly smile on my face before placing my right hand into his. When his eyes start to travel the length of my arm, goosebumps flare on my skin as his eyes widen when he takes everything in about me. My healing skin, my towel-clad body.

"You've healed already." Kai mumbles deeply.

"Yeah, I did. I was kinda shocked about it too." I say coolly, like standing with nothing more than a towel between us is the most normal thing in the world.

When he stands to his full six-foot-two height, his eyes hungrily roam my body, and I have to resist the urge to squeeze my thighs together to ease the tension I feel building in my core.

"This is the only time that you being in front of me with nothing but a towel around that beautiful body of yours gets away from me so easily." He growls possessively.

I let out a breathless, shocked chuckle as Kai takes my right arm and slowly, lovingly, and tenderly trails his fingers over my skin. Starting from my knuckles, he traces invisible lines up my arm, and when he gets to the first still-fading pink circle, he traces his index finger around that spot and then continues to the other area. Like he's playing connect the dots against each mark. He turns my arm over to look at the underside and traces each defect like he's committing them to memory. He then trails his fingers up my bicep and, as he hits the top of my shoulder, he begins to walk around me. I can't help it when my eyes close as I feel his strong fingers caress the top of my shoulder. He pauses at the back of my neck and leans in closer, his breath caressing the shell of my ear.

"You are so lucky I have restraint, Love. I can smell how much you want me." He whispers as he presses his hips into my ass, and I can feel just how hard he is for me. "You can grind those pretty thighs together all you want, but I am going to be the only one who can ease that ache between your legs."

He then trails soft kisses down my left shoulder, again taking the time to place a few more tender kisses over each spot where Caleb's long, canine teeth hurt me. I swear I could fall over that blissful edge just from

Kai touching me like this, and he knows it too. I can tell from the dark, possessiveness in his eyes, from the lazy way he's touching me, giving me just enough to get me hot, but not enough to push me over that sweet, ledge that I want him to shove me over.

"Kai." I pant.

He chuckles against my skin as he completes his circle around me and stands in front of me with my left hand in his right. His eyes hungrily dragging down my body and back up to my face again, and I can't stop my fucking legs from rubbing together with his eyes devouring me like this. He chuckles again as he steps away from me, and I almost want to whine at the distance between us. He walks over to his dresser and pulls out a burgundy shirt before making his way back over to me.

"Here, put this on." He smiles coyly at me, and I take the shirt from his outstretched hand.

My mind finally snaps back in place, and I give him a sexy smirk. "Turn around, wolf-boy, you don't get to see the full package just yet."

He lets out a bright laugh as he dips his head and turns around to give me a bit of privacy so I can pull his large shirt over my head. As the fabric comes to the middle of my thigh, I am enveloped by Kai's pine needle and cool mint scent that warms me to the tips of my toes. Before I tell him he can turn around, I rush back into the bathroom and grab the shorts I was wearing earlier. I hate to reuse them, but I figured it's better than being bare under his shirt and teasing him more than I need to. We are already walking a *very* thin line, and that would just be cruel right now.

I enter the room again, and he's still facing the wall, hands tucked into the pockets of his shorts. I see the defined muscles of his back ripple slightly as he sways lazily from one foot to the other.

"You can turn around now." I tell him, my voice lower than I intended it to be.

He turns, and his eyes darken again as he takes in my form, now dwarfed in his shirt.

"Fuck," He growls. "I thought this would be better than the towel, but I think this is worse."

"Well, I like it. I think I'm gonna raid your closet before I leave and keep some of your shirts at my place." I tease.

Kai closes the distance between us, wrapping his arms around the base of my spine, and pulls me into his body. As I look into his desire-filled eyes, my heart aches as I watch the emotion morph into fear. I see it as well as feel it coming from him through our bond. I lift my hands and rest them on his chest, gently swirling the middle finger of my right hand over his marking.

"Hey, what's that look for? Talk to me." I urge.

He drags his right hand up my back to tenderly caress my own marking and gently presses a kiss to the top of my shoulder. "I was terrified today." Kai whispers, "I was terrified of losing you. I was terrified of what the silver would do to you. What it would do to me. I wanted so badly to take your pain away, but it took all my strength to just hold your hand."

I feel something drip onto my shoulder, and when I look over at Kai, I see the silent tears rolling from his eyes.

"I feel like I failed you, and I couldn't help you the way a mate should."

I pull back from him and place my hands on either side of his face to make him look at me. Using my thumbs, I dry the tears from his face and then continue to motion for a calming effect.

"Now you listen well, mate of mine." I say as I hold his stare, "You could never fail me. Get on my nerves, maybe." I say, and that brings out a slight smile on his lips. "But fail me? Never in a million years could you do that, Kai Huntington. You showed me just how *strong* you are today. Even before I knew the purity of the silver, I knew it was making you sick. I could see it and feel it from you. But you risked your life to be by my side. Even after you were burned."

I glance down at his still red and inflamed arm and side. The healing has slowed down again, and I feel his pain like it's my own. When I go to touch the burn on his side, the muscles flutter at my light touch, and Kai closes his eyes in a grimace.

"You forced yourself to stay by my side even after you were hurt." I lift my eyes back to his, and I see relief flood his face when I pull my hand back from his side. "I wouldn't have cared if you just held my pant leg with your pinky finger; that touch meant the world to me, Kai. It was the selfless action of a mate that made me strong enough to endure what I did today. So, I will forever be grateful to you, Kai. Please, Babe, don't be so hard on yourself."

"This is exactly why us males need strong mates around. You bring calm to our chaos. Faith to our doubt. Understanding to our questions. And lightness to counter the darkness that happens when a wolf goes too long without a mate. So thank *you*, Dakota, for being what I needed right now."

When he leans in to kiss me again, it's to show his love, support, and appreciation for me, and I return it move for move. He begins to pull me to the bed, but I stop him for a moment.

"Hey, let me see if I can get you another cup of herbal tea to help with your burns. The healing slowed, and I want to try to get it working again for you." I say as I begin to walk toward the door.

"I thought I was the one to take care of you?" Kai asks with a sly smile.

"We take care of each other, Wolf-man. I'll be right back." I leave with his chuckle echoing behind me.

As I make my way downstairs, the dark and quiet living room greets me, and I quietly walk into the kitchen, flipping on a small light that's over the sink. When I look at the stove, I see it's just the empty ceramic glass top, so I reach out to Quilla to see if she's awake to ask her if she left any tea here for us.

Quilla

After Dakota and Kai went upstairs, I made sure to leave some herbal tea in one of Coraline's large pitchers and left it in the fridge in case either of them needed to drink more, then left soon after. I still had the pieces of silver that Mrs. Shade and I extracted from Dakota's wounds in the house, so I wanted to get them out of there before either Alpha or Mr. Shade got near it. So here I am, sitting in my bedroom cleaning the blood off of the pieces of pure silver at ten o'clock at night.

I still haven't told my parents about what I am or what Dakota has turned out to be. I don't really know how to broach the subject. I mean, do they even know anything about Werewolves or who I would have inherited my gifts from? And with Dakota still dealing with learning her new roles and with Jeffrey and Caleb's non-stop attacks, it just doesn't feel fair to have her help me with my issues. As I clean the cones of silver, I feel that something is still off about them. And I think back to how Kai reacted. How he was so weak and sickly looking, and how Caleb was able to still fight with his strength filling his limbs. I begin to inspect the inside of the cones that seemed to surround each tooth when I get a Zoom notice on my tablet, and I smile at who the request is from.

Atticus

I finally walk into my chambers after a busy but successful day. Alton, the patrolman who was hurt from the leg trap a week ago, is finally back on his feet and ready to go back on duty tomorrow morning. There were also a few broken bones I had to set for another patient, and one of the elderly pack members seems to have come down with the flu. But every member I was able to take care of and give them what they needed to get well again.

As I walk into my bathroom, I tug my t-shirt over my head to toss it into the hamper that I have nestled in the corner of the room. I have to say, the fashion of this century is growing on me. I am used to the billowy sleeves and ruffles of the eighteen hundreds, so the casual plain t-shirt works well for me now. I always hated the way the bloody damn frill would get in the way of everyday life, so to put that part of the past behind me is a blessing.

I hop in the shower, letting the hot water beat against my shoulders to lessen the stress of the day, and when the water begins to cool, I quickly cleanse my body, rinse and dry off. Once dried, I wrap the towel around my hips and I stare at myself in the mirror. At my wavy red hair that I inherited from my mother, and the emerald green eyes from my father. In the dark recesses of my mind, I hear my wolf, Atti, let out a frustrated growl as I feel his darkness begin to fill my mind. I close my eyes in an attempt to focus on him and I am taken to a gloomy forest where most of the vegetation and trees are withered, but if I look around into the deeper parts of the forest, I can still find a bit of his once lush green foliage. I always try to take him to those parts of the forest when I come here to look in on him to help keep us sane.

"Easy, wolf. What is ailing you?" I ask my wolf. His normally lighter red coat almost looks blood red now from the overcast gray sky. Only the star-like tuft on his chest keeps its bright white color.

"I can feel myself getting restless again, Atticus. I want to run. I want to, no, I need to search for a mate. I know you feel ourselves spiraling without the alpha near us to keep us in line." Atti growls in a borderline feral tone.

"Yes, I can feel it again too. When Alton was injured the other day, this darkness got in the way of our work. Made us second guess ourselves." I say.

"Aye. That is until you spoke with the new Tamer the Alpha found."

At the mention of Quilla, Atti lets out a contented huff through his snout, and I hear a few sweet notes of a bird's song nearby. Like just the thought of her brings us just a moment of peace.

"Aye, Quilla is a talented Tamer, even with her being new to her position." I say with a smile. *"Come, let us get some sleep. Perhaps that will make us feel better."* I tell him as I will myself out of his forest.

When I open my eyes, I find myself looking in the mirror again, at the spot where I would have a mate marking. Where I *should* have a mate marking by now.

"Ahh, stop it, you bloody asshole. Tobias didn't find his mate until he was a little over five hundred. You're only four hundred and twenty-five. You've got time." I try to give myself a pep talk in the mirror, but it does fuck all.

"Tobias was more dominant than I. That's what aided him in lasting so long without a mate. Plus, he fought in several wars. He countered his darkness with blood. We are not able to do that. We chose to follow the path of a doctor, a healer, which I agree with you on. But we do not hurt unless provoked, or it's for sustenance." Atti chimes in.

"Aye. Aye. I know."

I shake my head as I walk into my main chambers and over to the dark cherry dresser that sits against the wall, and I pull out a pair of gray sweatpants to sleep in. Kai insisted I get a pair a few years ago; he said that the ladies love the gray sweatpants on a male form. Call me naïve to this century, I don't care, I just don't understand the appeal. But I wear them anyway because they are comfortable, and it's better than the black pants that I've had most of my long life.

After I run the towel over my hair to get it mostly dry, I toss the towel into the hamper with the other dirty clothes and I grab my hairbrush so I can tame this unruly hair of mine that comes to the middle of my neck when it's down. When I go to the large oval mirror in the corner of my room, the wooden frame and legs are scuffed from years of use and movement, my eyes snag on the iPad on my dresser and I get the sudden urge to Zoom Quilla. Without overthinking it, I cross the space between me and the dresser, enter her email address, and send the request. I just hope she's still up at this time.

As the request pings to her, I head back to the mirror to continue brushing my damp hair and pull it up into a bun in the middle of my head. When I hear her answer the call, I turn to greet her, and her face goes from a friendly smile to her lips parting in a small O while a beautiful red tint colors her cheeks as she takes in my appearance. Her eyes immediately flick to my lower half then back up to my face a few heartbeats later. But that quick look is enough for that part of my body to react in a way I have not experienced in a long time.

Okay, now I understand the pups' insistence on certain women liking these gray pants. Because Quilla is the first one to notice and to have that gorgeous blush fill her cheeks.

"Hi Atticus." Her voice squeaks.

I find myself wanting to smirk at her voice, but I don't want to lead her on. She's a human, and she must have a betrothed with her beauty. A male would be insane to not want to claim this woman as theirs.

"If not, I will claim her." Atti growls, and I feel his darkening need cloud my thoughts.

"Easy, friend."

"Hello, Quilla. I hope I didn't wake you." I say as I go to pick up the tablet and carry it over to my king-sized bed that holds my six-foot-five frame.

"Oh no, you didn't wake me. I'm actually in my room cleaning pieces of silver I removed from Dakota today."

"Come again?" I ask with fear in my voice with what she just told me.

"Oh, you didn't hear?" Quilla asks as she cocks her head to the side.

"Nay. What happened?" I press.

"Dakota and I were having a girl's day, and we were attacked by the wolf that's been causing issues for Kai and Dakota. He's from the same pack that drugged Kai with that Wolfsbane."

Upon hearing this, all the blood in my body rushes to my ears, and I just keep hearing her say that she was attacked by another wolf. I hear Atti snarl viscously in my mind, and I can feel him trying to push himself to the front. To make us phase and find who would dare cause her harm.

"Atticus? Atticus?"

Her voice finally breaks through the fog in my mind, I shake my head as I say, "Oh, I'm sorry, Rosie. It's been a long day. I guess I'm more tired than I thought." I lie.

I hate the taste of it on my tongue, but I cannot let her know what is slowly happening to me. I can't scare her away like that.

"I don't believe that for one second, but I'm not gonna ask what's going on. Instead, I'm gonna ask you if there is a way for a wolf to have pure, handmade silver in his mouth and not succumb to the effects."

I chuckle at her firm tone and calling me out on my bullshit. I haven't met this woman in the flesh, and she already seems to know me. But the humor fades when she says the silver in her hands is pure and handmade.

I sit up straighter in bed and lean back against the headboard. "You said pure handmade silver? And it was in Dakota? How is she? How is the pack?" I ask question after question.

"Yes. She's fine now, resting with Kai. And yes, everyone is fine. I isolated Dakota while her mother and I extracted the silver from her bite wounds."

Quilla describes what happened this afternoon, and I go from feeling fear for her and Dakota's safety to relief that she was able to save her friend.

"I'm glad everyone is well. Thank you for keeping everyone safe, Rosie."

I look down at the silver in her hands, then back into her olive-green eyes, then to her smile. My heart seems to stop in my chest at the sight. I clear my throat and ask, "So why are you cleaning the silver? Are you planning on making a knife to stab the poor bastard when you see him again?"

"Actually, that's not a bad idea. I need to find a blacksmith, I guess."

My booming laugh fills my bed chambers, and the apple of her cheeks show a hint of pink again as she looks away for a moment.

"I know a good human blacksmith that I'm sure would help you, Rosie. But why are you really looking at the silver?" I ask, my tone going serious near the end.

"I don't know. I just kept thinking about how Caleb did it. How he had silver in his mouth and was able to fight the way he did, because when Kai was around it he looked like he was going to black out, and when Dakota's blood touched him, he got what looked like third-degree burns as a result."

I groan when I hear that Kai was around pure silver and I run my left hand through my hair, pulling a few strands free where they fall into my eyes. Quilla tracks the movement, and I can't help the satisfaction that blooms in my chest at her noticing me. I close my eyes so I can keep my train of thought before I lose it like a concupiscent teenager. And I am *way* too old to be acting like that.

"He could have used a dental form made of silicone. That is the one material that seems to lessen or eradicate the effect of silver for a time. But once silver hits the skin or bloodstream, it's bad news."

I open my eyes at her silence and I notice that Quilla's gaze is zoned in on my chest.

"So, that's what that was. That tattoo is very intricate."

I barely hear her whisper through the speakers, but I think she was talking to herself and didn't mean for me to hear it. As I look at my picture in the left corner of the screen, my throat tightens and becomes as dry as the Sahara Desert.

There on the left side of my chest is a light gray, very detailed depiction of a tree. Roots spreading out across my pectoral, the trunk of the tree continuing up my chest, and on my neck are branches with little leaves here and there filling where the canopy would be. I try to swallow around the knot in my throat at the meaning of this.

I have a mate. But I haven't a clue who she is or where I have met her.

Quilla

I finally got to see his tattoo in its entirety. I noticed it after I practically had to drag my eyes away from the low-hanging, gray sweatpants that he was very proudly filling out. I seriously have to get out more, or else I'm gonna be an easy meal for his mate once she finds out I've been staring at the most *private*- pun intended- parts.

When I mentally comment on the marking, I notice his eyes go wide with shock for a moment before he schools his features. I don't know if it's okay to see a male's mate marking or not. I know it's not a good thing for females to go around showing theirs off, but I don't know if the same rules apply to men.

"Thank you for the info on the silver. At least now I know that Caleb didn't do something shady to make him immune or something." I pause as my eyes land on his damn chest again. His muscular chest with just a little tuft of red and white hair down the center. I shake my head again to clear my mind. "I should go. It's late." I look at the clock, and it's not a lie. It is eleven-fifteen.

Atticus pauses for a moment, then nods. "Aye. You should get some sleep. It seems like you had a busy day today. Sleep well, Rosie." He says as he promptly closes the Zoom meeting, leaving me alone in my room, even though he wasn't really here in person with me. But deep in my soul, it felt like he was here all the same.

Atticus

I throw the tablet on the bedside table as I rush to the bathroom, flicking the light on while staring at my chest in the mirror.

At the bloody fucking mate marking that was not there fifteen minutes ago.

I continue to stare at the image of this tree on my chest, and it begins to fade before my eyes, the roots slowly pulling back into the trunk. As I watch this happen, red begins to bloom like blood at the corner of my vision.

Can she be? How?

I hope I am wrong about the thought that pops into my head. I close my eyes to try my bloody best to control myself.

But I can't.

"Did you mark her?" I demand as I enter Atti's forest. I notice it's a bit lighter, but with the anger I feel burning in my chest, the wind starts to howl in the bare tree branches around us when I arrive.

"Are ye fucking dense? I couldn't without scenting her first. You know that." Atti growls, lowering his head to me in a warning not to come closer.

I let out an aggravated growl as I rip my mind from his forest, and when I settle into my body again, I notice that the marking is completely gone. I can't stop the surge of anger at the now blank skin as I rear my arm back, fist colliding with the bathroom mirror, making it shatter into a million sparking pieces.

My knuckles only bleed for a few moments before I heal, but the pain I feel is enough to get my mind out of the dark spiral I just went down.

I just hope that whoever the woman is that The Great Luna chose to be my mate comes soon before it's too late.

CHAPTER FORTY-ONE

DAKOTA

"*H*ey, *Quilla,*" I say when I feel she is still awake on her end of the bond, but I feel that she's almost lonely, and I find that to be a weird emotion to feel from her. "*You okay?*"

"*Hey, Dakota. Yeah, yeah, I'm fine.*" She replies, and I can almost see her shake her head to clear her thoughts and put on a smile. "*How are you doing? And Kai? Is he okay?*"

I don't call her out on the feelings I'm getting from her, or about the images that are flashing through her head of a red-headed dude and a tree. So, I just focus on the main reason I was coming to her. I'll wait and see if she wants to talk about other things that seem to be plaguing her.

"*I wanted to know if you left any more of your Wolfsbane tea here at Kai's place. The burns on his arm and side aren't healing like they were, so I thought that would help him again.*" I say.

"*Oh yeah. I left a pitcher in the fridge. All you need to do is warm it, or you can even put it on ice if Kai would prefer.*"

"*Okay. Thank you.*" I pause, and I know she should know this, but I say it anyway. "*You know you can talk to me about anything, right?*"

"Yeah, of course I know that. Why did you think any different?" She asks, and even her voice in my mind cracks a bit.

"Because I can tell you're bent out of shape about something, and it's not about what all happened today."

"I don't know." She sighs in my mind after a moment. *"I think I need to stop talking to Atticus. Or through Zoom at least."*

"Atticus, oh, you mean the doctor? Why?"

"Have you seen the man? He's totally hot," Quilla exclaims.

"No, but I can see him in your mind, and yeah, he's not bad-looking. So, what's stopping you?"

"You can see him in my mind?" Quilla asks while ignoring my question.

"Yeah, you're not blocking me all the way, and I can see some of his features. His red hair for one." I tell her, *"But why do you need to stop talking to him on the computer?"* I ask again.

"He's got a mate, Dakota! I can't be ogling another woman's man. Especially one that could eat me!"

"What makes you think he has a mate?" I ask, chuckling at her little breakdown. Like I'd let anyone eat my friend.

"He's got this incredibly intricate marking of a tree on his chest. So that's got to be his mate marking, isn't it?" Quilla asks, and I can feel the panic in her voice.

"Maybe it's just a regular tattoo, Quilla. Maybe he doesn't have a mate yet." I say as I try to help ease her panic.

"I don't know. I just feel that something is weird between us, and I think it would be best to distance myself from him. I mean, what if his mate is close and I'm keeping him from her?"

"Oh, Quilla. I don't think it would be like that at all. So I wouldn't worry about that too much."

"Dakota. You want to know how bad it is?" Quilla says frankly. *"He was wearing gray sweatpants."* Quilla deadpans. *"And filling them out very nicely, might I add."*

"And that's bad, how?" I get out before she continues.

"All I was thinking was what it would feel like to ride him."

I am quiet for a moment. I mean, yeah, Quilla and I talked about boys, and we would joke about how we thought they would be in bed, but this, the way she said it, and maybe since I can feel her emotions, it's different. But we are both different now, aren't we?

"Okay. Now I understand why you would think if he had a mate she would eat you. But Quilla, I wouldn't change anything until you know more. Maybe I can ask Kai or Tobias—"

"No!" She cuts me off.

"Okay. I'm gonna be dumb and ask this, why?" I ask as I pull the pitcher of tea out of the fridge and I quietly search around the kitchen until I find a pan to boil a cup in.

"I don't know, Dakota. Everything is so confusing lately. I don't want anyone to know what I feel or think about Atticus. It was hard telling you, and you're my best friend, but I also don't want to hurt him. To keep him from finding the one that will make him happy and to keep that darkness out of his mind." Quilla sobs.

"Darkness?"

"I felt it again from him tonight. When I told him about what happened to you, and how I was the target for the attack to begin with, it was like he wanted to track Caleb down and... I don't even know what he would do, but it's not good."

I nod even though she can't see me, so I say, *"And that's why you think you may be keeping him from finding his mate. You think he may be getting your Tamer ability confused with the calmness that only a mate can bring? Because even I know you don't have to be in the same room for that power to work."*

"Yeah." She sobs.

"Okay. So yeah, maybe stay away from him for a while. But I will say this, listen to your own heart, Quilla. I don't know how it works for humans since y'all obviously don't have a wolf to claim the other, but you have a heart, and it knows what the brain tries to talk itself out of."

"Alright."

"I'm gonna let you get some rest too. Take some time, Quilla, but don't let a good thing pass you by," I say as I pull back from her mind to take the bubbling tea off the burner and fill up the mug for Kai.

'

When I carefully make my way back upstairs, I find Kai still lying in bed with his back against the headboard.

"Here's your tea, Babe." I say brightly.

He smiles at me as I cross his bedroom floor and I return the gesture before my eyes snag on his side, which is still an angry red color and severely inflamed. My smile falters a bit as I carefully hand him the mug, and he takes a long sip while humming at the taste.

"Thank you. Dakota. I appreciate you doing that for me."

"You're welcome." I say as I walk around the bed to get in on my side.

I try to be mindful of his arm, but he still wraps it around my shoul-ders, pulling me closer to his chest. We stay there for a few minutes as he drinks his tea and we relax into each other, and I listen to the rhythmic sound of his breathing against my ear.

After Kai finishes his tea, I already see some of the swelling start to go down, and that brings a small smile to the corner of my lips. Kai then pulls his sheet and gray comforter over us as he slides deeper into the bed, pulling me with him to get settled more onto the mattress. I trail my index finger over his light gray mating mark, and I start to think about the silver that was in my body and how I felt compared to what I could pick up from Kai and his reactions. I try to keep my walls up from Kai, so he doesn't feel what I am thinking about, and I think I succeeded when he starts to tenderly run his hand up and down my back a few times, but then he suddenly pinches my side and I let out a little yelp at the sudden sensation.

"What's going through your mind, Dakota?"

Damn.

"I was just thinking about the silver that was in me."

"What about it, Babe? Talk to me." Kai gently presses.

I take a breath and I lean up on my elbow to look him in the eye. "Would that have been enough to kill me if I was a normal, full-blooded Werewolf?"

"Yes." Kai sighs. "If that pure silver stayed in a Full Werewolf's body, yes, it would have been enough to kill in about five to ten minutes based on the type of injuries you had today. But it would've been instant if it would have been driven through a vital organ."

I begin to shake my head in disbelief when he continues, "If it were me in your shoes today, I would have been unconscious and spiked a fever two minutes after the attack. And even after the silver was extracted and wounds flushed, I mean, you see what just blood laced with silver did to me." He says as he points to his side. "And I still probably wouldn't wake up for several more hours and still would be slowly healing."

I look into his tired eyes, and I know he's seeing the fear and sorrow that is flooding my face and soul.

"I'm so sorry, Love," Kai whispers as he caresses my face, his thumb stroking my cheekbone. "But that is the truth. I hate that it hurts you to hear that, but I am not going to keep the harsh reality of my world from you."

"I know." I say as my bottom lip wobbles a bit from the image of him being hurt like that, "But I appreciate you being honest with me. I mean, how can I one day become a powerful alpha at your side if I run from everything that scares me? But just please still remember, I have been a normal human longer than I have been a half-were, so I still let that fear bubble to the surface before I can stop it."

"Fear is not just a human emotion, Love. It's a living emotion. Anything that has a soul feels fear." He pulls me back down to his chest and places a loving kiss on the crown of my head. "But I will do everything I can to keep you safe and protect you from that fear."

"I know you will." I say as I kiss his mate marking on his chest and snuggle deeper into his side. He tightens his arm around my waist, and we both let our different levels of exhaustion claim us for the night.

CHAPTER FORTY-TWO

KAI

Monday morning comes all too quickly, and I can tell by the way that Dakota is stiffly walking around my room and not talking much to anyone at the breakfast table this morning, that she's anxious about seeing the *fleabag* duo as she and Quilla call them. I get split-second images of her going after them, human teeth and her naturally long nails biting and clawing down their faces.

As we are about to walk out the front door, I grab her and pin her against the wall to get her out of her mind for a minute. When I see her eyes go wide with shock, I give her a crooked smile.

"Kai, what are you–?"

"I know what you're thinking, Love. And if you need me to hold you back from the fleabags, then I'll bring the leash that you used with me."

"Oh, bite me, wolf-boy. You're never gonna let me live that down, are you? Just a reminder for you, that was *your* father's idea, not mine."

"Yeah, I know. Now come on, let's go and show those assholes that again they didn't get one over on us." I say with a smirk.

When we arrive at the university, I walk Dakota to the door, but before we part ways, I pull her close and give her a quick kiss on the lips.

"Behave, my little alpha, I forgot the leash." I tell her through the bond.

She gives me a pointed glare, and I just flash her a bright smile as Quilla joins us in the hallway with a small smile on her own face as well.

"Good morning, you two. I'm glad to see you're healed, Kai," Quilla says while looking at my arm.

"Yup. All healed now." I agree while pulling my shirt up a bit to show her my side. "Thank you for figuring out that Wolfsbane tea, Quilla. It's a lifesaver."

She blushes at my praise, and I can't help the chuckle that bubbles in my chest.

"You're going to be a great Tamer as you get more experience, Quilla. I just know it. And I hope that if you ever find a mate, he will be smart enough to tell you that every single day."

I notice her face gets a shade redder, and she glances over at Dakota for a moment before nodding at me. "Thank you, Kai. That means a lot coming from you."

I give her a quick nod, and as I turn around to walk toward my class, I reach out for Dakota's side of the bond for a second.

"That glance Quilla just gave you, do I want to know what that's all about?"

"Nope."

She backs out of my mind, and I can't help the grin that blooms on my face. My mate is fiercely loyal to all around her, and I love her more for that.

As I continue to walk to my first class of the morning, I start to pick up on the odor of Jeffrey filling the hallway. I turn the corner and I'm hit with his full scent, but who I see before me is not Jeffrey in the least. It's a shorter girl, about five foot-three, with wavy blonde hair and navy blue eyes. She's trying to look into my eyes, but she can't bring hers up past my nose. She then flicks them back down to her hands, and I see that she's wringing them nervously back and forth in front of her.

As I take in her mannerisms, I slowly begin to pick up the scent of fear. But I get the feeling it's not the fear of me; it's fear for herself, for her safety. At that realization, my heart breaks for this girl in front of me.

"What's wrong? Please, tell me." I gently prod and I let a pulse of my alpha power flow over her. Not to demand that she tell me, but to let her know that she's safe to be around me and tell me what her problems are. "What's your name?"

"It's Emma, Alpha, sir." She says, her bottom lip trembles as she speaks. "Emma Hughes" She glances over her shoulder, then turns her attention back to me, but still keeping her eyes off my face.

I get the feeling that she would be more comfortable talking somewhere private. So, I look to my left and I notice there is an empty classroom, and I tilt my head toward the door.

"You want to talk privately?"

She nods, and I take a step to open the door, looking around to make sure no one is in there, and signal her to follow me in. Once she walks into the room, I notice a small, thankful smile tug at the corner of her mouth before she leans against one of the desks in the front row. I close the large faux wood door behind me and lean my back against it. One to act as a barricade to anyone wanting to look in, and two to just keep my back covered from any attacks. I doubt she could honestly do much damage, but my father has always told me that the one you least expect can deal the worst damage.

"Okay, Emma. We can speak freely. Please tell me; what has you so terrified?"

Emma takes a deep breath as if steeling herself before she forces her eyes up, focusing on my left ear.

"You have to stop Jeffrey and Caleb, and do it soon." She pauses for a second, then her eyes drop again to stare at the floor before she continues, "I know what happened to Miss Dakota, your rightful mate. Caleb made my dad craft the silver that was used to harm her." Emma's voice wavers as she seems to be recalling a memory.

As I process that information, K pushes forward, and before I know it, he's making me stride across the room while a burst of my alpha power fills the space. My right arm snaps out to grab Emma's shoulder. Not enough to leave bruises or anything, but enough to let her know not to fuck with us. I pick up on what K is doing, and I take control along with him, making our eyes glow and a low growl rumble in my throat.

"Do you speak the truth or lies?" I demand.

"No! I speak the truth!" Emma's navy eyes brighten to a cool blue, and I can smell her wolf come to the front, but under the stench of Jeffrey's scent, I pick up on something else. Something familiar.

"You're a half-blood?" I ask as I let her go and pull my alpha power back in.

Emma nods as she recovers from being under my power. I take a breath and I back away further, again bracing myself against the door while running my hand through my blonde hair.

"I'm sorry, Emma. But my wolf and I just needed to make sure you were not lying. I mean, apparently you know how deranged Jeffrey is." I say, waving my hand in the air. "Your father, he is human?"

"Yes. He and my mother have been secretly mated for about fifteen years before they had me, twenty years ago."

"Sounds like that bond is not celebrated like it should be, and I am sorry about that."

She shakes her head again as she says, "Caleb threatened both my safety as well as my mother's if he didn't make the silver tooth mold that was to be used to hurt your mate." She looks back up at me, this time her eyes finally meeting mine, and I see tears ripple against her cornflower blue irises.

"Please, Alpha Kai, stop Jeffrey's reign. Those of us who are far less dominant than he and Caleb are terrified."

I walk back over to her, and I place my hand on her right shoulder, and she flinches under my touch. My heart breaks for this girl in front of me. Her fear and discomfort calls to the alpha in my blood. Calling for me to protect those weaker than I am from any harm. What a true alpha should be and not rule with the survival of the fittest mentality.

"Emma Hughes, please listen well. I, Kai Huntington, next in line to be alpha, will put an end to Jeffrey Carmichael's tyrannical reign when the time is right. Please understand that I have to first take care of what he is trying to do to my rightful mate. However, once that plan is set into motion, I will take care of all issues that plague the lower, fearful members of his pack."

"Thank you, sir." Emma says and as she picks at her finger, she adds, "I overheard Caleb bragging about what he did to Miss Dakota. He figured she would be dead with the purity of the silver that my father was made to create. I mean, even with the silicone dental guard Caleb had in his mouth, he bled and was sick for a day and a half. So, when I heard how proud he was of hurting her, I had to risk coming to talk to you. I'm scared they are going to go after my dad soon too. He was so angry when he heard what his creation did, and you know well enough that any wolf would snap him like a twig."

"I fully understand your concern, Emma. I promise you I will put an end to them soon." I say. "Now, please go to class. And if you have perfume or a different set of clothes, please do what you can to mask my scent. We don't need either of them smelling me on you."

"Yes, sir. Thank you for just hearing me out. We never get this kind of treatment from Jeffrey."

"You're welcome."

I watch her leave the classroom, and I lean against one of the desks and replay her words in my mind, while my heart breaks for her all over again.

Dakota

Quilla and I walk into our first class of the morning, and as we take our seats, I notice my skin starts to itch, and I pick up on what I now know to be the metallic smell of silver. I look to my right, to the student sitting at the desk next to me, and I notice a silver bracelet on her left wrist. I try to back away from it as much as my desk will allow.

Quilla looks at me with confusion furrowing her brow, and I reach out to her through the bond.

"That girl has a silver bracelet on, and it's making my skin itch."

"Oh. Do you want to leave?" Quilla asks.

"No. As long as she stays in her seat, I think I'll be good."

As the class continues, from the first hour, going into the second, I notice that the itchiness on my skin lessens the longer I am around the silver, and when class ends on the third hour, I am completely free of the annoying itch. At this revelation, I have a thought cross my mind. Once we all pack up to leave, I walk with the crowd and casually brush my wrist against the bracelet to see what happens. I feel Quilla at my back watching the whole thing, and when we enter the hallway, she pulls me into the library, that is shockingly deserted right now. When the door closes behind us, she whips around to look at me.

"Are you freaking crazy? You could have been–"

Her rant is cut short when she looks at my wrist.

My flawless wrist. Not a burn, tint of redness or swelling on my skin.

"What the hell?" Quilla whispers as she inspects my arm, turning it over and back again to make sure she's not missing a millimeter of flesh.

"I know this is just a first-time thing, but the longer I was around that silver bracelet, the less it affected me. And look, I brushed right up against it and it didn't do anything to me." I say, pointing to my wrist again.

"It could have been a fluke, Dakota!" Quilla shouts. "Maybe it was plated silver or something, so it wasn't as strong."

"Maybe," I say, but then something that Mom told me flashes in my mind.

Your father told me that in certain situations he's seen over the years, half-Were's can be stronger than their full-blood counterparts. Because what can injure and even kill a full-blood doesn't do as much to half-bloods.

"Okay, hear me out. Can you do some research on silver and half-Were's? I think I might be able to either handle more than full-blooded Were's or maybe even become immune to it."

"Are you crazy, Dakota?" Quilla echoes again. "You're asking me to do the unthinkable! You do remember what happened to you, don't you?"

I let a pulse of my alpha power fill the space around us, and I know my eyes are glowing brightly. "Yes Quilla. I remember exactly the pain I went through. But you didn't see the look on Kai's face that night. He felt he failed me because he couldn't be there to help me the way he should have, and it took everything in him to just be in the same room to comfort me the way he did. And he got hurt while trying to be there for me. I cannot bear to see Kai put himself through that and risk his own life like that again. You are the only one I trust to research this, Quilla. Please help me see if I can become immune so I can give my mate one less thing to worry about."

Quilla looks at me in shock and then sorrow floods her face. "I'm sorry; I didn't realize how Kai felt." She thinks for a minute before taking a deep breath. "Alright. I'll figure out a way to talk to Tobias about this. I mean, he had a huge library in his den at the house, so he has to have something on that or know someone who does, like–" She pauses for a moment. "Maybe Tobias can help me in the research." She smiles, but I pick up on the small waver on her bottom lip.

I suddenly remember her declaration about staying away from Atticus, and here I am forcing her into the possibility of talking to him again if Tobias can't help her.

"If Tobias isn't able to help you and he says you need to talk to Atticus to get the answers, then you don't have to go any further. I didn't think that you may have to interact with him to get information. So, I just want to put that out there."

"No, it's okay. I do, somehow oddly enough, understand where you are coming from." She chuckles. "Besides, it shouldn't be too hard if I talk to him over the phone." Quilla shrugs her shoulders. "So, give me a week to see if I can come up with anything, and we'll go from there."

I pull her in for a hug, and as I release her I say, "Thank you, Quilla. You are the absolute best." Then I think about if she actually finds out that I can either become immune or have a very high tolerance, I think about Kai and his reaction.

"Let's keep this between us and whoever else needs to know. I don't want to worry Kai with this until we know what we can find out."

"What about Tobias?" Quilla asks.

"I doubt a bear can shit in the woods without him knowing about it. So, I just wouldn't tell him the full reason why you want to research the effects of silver on half-Where's unless he specifically asks."

We are just about to leave the library to go to our next class when we hear the door open and close behind us, and the person filling the door is the one that I want to rip apart the most right now.

Caleb.

The look of utter shock that fills his face before he can set his normal douchebag expression makes satisfaction bloom in my chest at the non-verbal 'fuck you' that I am once again standing after yet another failed attempt to separate me and Kai. I watch as Caleb's eyes drift between me and Quilla. When his eyes land on her, I see his pupils widen at the sight of her, and this sets my blood on fire in my veins.

"Please leave, Quilla." I say sternly, more for Caleb's ears than Quilla's.

"No way! I'm not leaving you with him."

"I can handle him, Quilla. It'll be fine."

She gives me a quick glance before she steps away from me, making sure to give Caleb a wide berth, but his eyes track her the entire time. Just as she's about to pass him, he takes one small step towards her, and I am instantly in front of Quilla. I know my eyes glow a bright glacier blue as a loud warning growl rips from my throat, reverberating around us for a few heartbeats before it dies down.

"Touch her, and I will kill you right where you stand." I growl, and I can even hear Kota's voice mingling with my own.

With my threat as a distraction for Caleb, Quilla takes off for the door, and she makes it safely on the other side. Caleb's humorless laugh echoes against the many books in the room and grates against my ears.

"You are so predictable, *Dakota*." He says as he spits my name like he's done so many times before. "Protecting that little human without a second thought. So very *noble* of you." He says mockingly.

"You wouldn't know noble if it bit you in the ass, Caleb."

He slowly starts to circle me, starting on my left side. His eyes linger on the exposed skin thanks to my tank top, and I silently thank the Great Luna that it covers my mating mark with the high back, but the thin straps in the front still show the skin where he knows his teeth marred me a few days ago. He continues to circle me, and as much as I hate to have him at my back, I can't let him know that it affects me.

When he gets to my right side, he begins to trail his index finger from the top of my shoulder, down my upper arm, and past my elbow. As he gets closer to where his teeth pierced my skin, I snap. I grab his wrist, and with the strength that I can only assume comes from Kota, I twist his wrist to the breaking point and I shove him onto the circular oak-stained table behind him.

"You seem shocked I actually survived your little attack." I grin. "Like I said, *Caleb,* whatever you or your so-called alpha throws at me or my chosen mate, we will overcome it. Every. Single. Fucking. Time." I bend his wrist back again, and he squirms under my hand. "So, back the hell off if you know what's good for you."

I push off him and I leave him splayed out on the table, shock, anger, and a bit of fear lingering on his face, and I take pride in knowing I caused that. When I open the door of the library to find Quilla, I run right into Jeffrey's chest. I quickly back away from him before he can get his hands on me, but I can see the look of shock on his rough features before I brush past him with a look of indifference on my face like he's the lowest threat I could imagine.

Jeffrey

After Dakota backs away from my grasp, I mentally kick myself for not being quicker to pull her into my chest and keep her there. I lost my first real chance just now to easily take her from that fucking pup. But then I remember the last mission I sent Caleb on and red flashes at the corner of my vision. I glance over and I still see my worthless Beta, who is still sprawled backwards over a table with anger and fear in his face. I realize that the fear written on his face actually came from *her* and not from me since his eyes have not locked onto my form yet.

Oh, I will remedy that real damn quick.

I let my darkening, alpha power rip through the room so violently that paper sitting on the welcome desk flies off the hard surface as the invisible tendrils of my power flow through the air. When Caleb finally meets my brightly glowing eyes, real, bone-rattling fear fills his entire body, and I fucking revel in it.

I march over to him, my footfalls angrily stomping into the wooden floorboards of this stupid library. I grab Caleb by the throat, effortlessly picking him up like a rag doll. His fingers scrape and claw at my hand uselessly as I pin him roughly against the wall, the plaster cracking from the force of my actions.

"WHY THE FUCK IS SHE STILL ALIVE?" I bellow in his face, spittle spraying on his pale cheeks. "You told me that the pure silver that miserable human made would be enough to KILL HER! So why the fuck is she still WALKING?!"

I peel him from the wall, and I throw him across the room and into a nearby bookshelf. The shelf and all the books it contained topple on top of him. I wait for a minute as he pulls himself from the smattering of books, and I grab him again by the back of the neck like the useless mutt he is.

"I'm still waiting on an answer, Caleb."

"I'm sorry, Alpha. I guess she's more resilient than I gave her credit for." His voice wavers, and it makes me sick to my stomach. If I had any stronger wolf in my pack to be my Beta, I'd fucking kill him right here, right now.

"You have failed me for the last time, Caleb. I guess I have to take things into my own hands now." I growl as I let go of his neck, and he crumbles into a wasteful heap on the floor.

I vibrate with the taste for blood, and one man's face flashes in my mind. His blonde hair dripping crimson, hazel eyes lifeless as he takes his final breaths beneath my fangs. Oh, how joyous that feeling will be once he's dead and gone and Dakota will finally be mine for the rest of her life.

Quilla

Rushing out of the library door was both the hardest thing I could do and the smartest thing to do at the same time. Deep down I know I wouldn't be able to do anything for Dakota in a real fight, but it still hurts to leave her in possible danger. I walk into the main building that houses the cafeteria, and I run smack into Kai's chest.

"Woah, Quilla. You okay?" He asks and looks around for his mate. "Where's Dakota?"

At first, I want to tell him that she's just in the bathroom, but I get the feeling that he will smell the lie for what it is, so I decide to tell him the truth.

"She's dealing with Caleb. We ran into him in the library, and she held him off so I could get away from him."

Kai starts making his way toward the door, but I am able to grab his arm to keep him by my side.

"Kai, hear me out. I don't think he will attack her outright here on campus. Plus, she said she can handle him, and I believe her." I say with a shrug of my left shoulder.

Kai takes a deep breath and then he turns back to look at me, like he can hear the truth in my words, and he relaxes a bit.

"You're right." He sighs. "Come on, let's get something to eat while we wait on Dakota."

He leads me deeper into the cafeteria, and we fill our trays then find a table in the corner of the room where Kai can have his back covered and watch for any and all threats.

Dakota

I follow the scent of Quilla and I find myself walking into the cafeteria. I spot my best friend and mate sitting at a table in the corner near the back door. As I approach the table, neither of them look up to greet me. They are so lost in poking at the food lining their trays to even notice my approach. Not even Kai picks up on my scent.

I lean my hands on the table's surface and say, "You two that lost in thought about me?"

Kai and Quilla quickly look up at my voice, and I see the surprise coloring of both of their faces. Quilla jumps up to give me a quick hug and pushes me back at arm's length to look over me.

"I'm fine. He didn't hurt me."

Kai then tugs me into his chest, but with one small inhale I hear a low growl bubble in his throat. And without even tapping into the bond, I know he's smelling Caleb's scent on me.

"It's okay. He didn't hurt me. He just tried to get under my skin."

I show him what Caleb did to me, but I make sure to show him every single moment of what I did to that little asshole.

"You are so much stronger than I am, Babe. I think I would have killed him right then and there."

"Well, he would have been asking for it. He took a step towards Quilla, so I cut him off before he could do anything stupid." I say flatly.

"Oh yeah. You were totally brave and scary, might I add," Quilla says.

"I was terrified after you left. But I knew one thing at that moment, and that was no one was going to try to hurt my Tamer again if I had anything to say about it."

Kai chuckles and gives me a quick kiss. "That's my girl. Fearless when it comes to her pack. I love you, Babe."

I settle into Kai's side, letting him cover Caleb's scent with his own. The familiar pine needles and cool mint feels one hundred percent right compared to the smoke and leather of Caleb, that makes my skin prickle. I hold on to the hope that one day soon, I will be able to keep Kai's scent on me all the time and not only when he touches me. One day all wolves will know that I am his and his alone.

CHAPTER FORTY-THREE
QUILLA

I needed to make sure that Kai was at school with Dakota the next morning so he couldn't overhear me talking to his father. So, here I am, skipping my classes for the first time in my life to knock on Tobias' door at 7:30 in the morning. I have been mentally preparing how I can word my request so that he will still pick up the truth, even if it's only the partial truth.

I'm about to knock again when Tobias opens the door with an easy grin on his face. "Good morning, Quilla. Please, come in." He says as he steps aside to allow me in the house.

"Good morning." I say as I walk in through the foyer and stand in the middle of the living room waiting for him to shut and lock the door behind me.

"To what do I owe this early morning arrival?" He says over his shoulder.

I take a breath and I just get to the point of my visit. "I have the feeling that I need to research any correlation between silver and half-bloods. Do you have any research on that here?"

Tobias turns to face me and strokes his chin thoughtfully as he ponders my request. I do my best to keep my face neutral as I wait for him to reply.

"Perhaps. Come with me into my den."

He leads me back into his office, and when I step inside the room, I can't stop my eyes from darting to his white HP desktop computer while the memory of meeting Atticus for the first time flashes in my mind. Clearing my throat, I push the memory away and I follow Tobias over to a line of books near the long back wall. He looks at me out of the corner of his eye, and I know that he saw me looking at his PC, and I feel my cheeks heat at being caught.

"Atticus didn't do anything unsavory to you, did he?" Tobias questions. "I get the feeling that you two aren't talking as much as you have been."

Damn, this dude is good at reading people.

"He's been a complete gentleman." I assure him with a slight shake of my head. "I just don't want to distract him from his work, that's all." I say, but I hear my own voice crack at the lie.

Tobias smiles at me as he runs his fingers over the spines of the hundreds of books that line the shelves in front of him while humming thoughtfully to himself.

"Why don't you go to my pack library in Montana for a few days?" Tobias turns around to face me, and I see a slight glimmer in his brown eyes for a moment before they harden in his next breath. "Besides, I think it would be for the best that a Tamer is on the grounds for a while. Help ease some of the wolves. That is if you don't mind."

Did I mention this dude is good? I can tell that he knows all too well about that strange darkness that's in Atticus. And it is getting worse. Tobias knows I can't stay away from a wolf that needs my help.

"Alright. Yeah. I can do that. Kill two birds with one stone, right? Get my research done and keep the pack in good spirits."

"Yes. I can have my private plane pick you up whenever you are ready to leave."

"You have a private plane?" I ask, shock coloring my tone.

Tobias chuckles and places a gentle hand on my shoulder. "Again, to be a powerful leader, you make sure you have some of the necessities. Like a plane. You never know if I have to fly across the country or the globe for a last-minute meeting."

"Oh, yeah. I guess that does make sense." I say shyly. "I can be ready to leave no later than the day after tomorrow. I just need to tell my parents that I'm going on a trip."

"I understand. I'll call my pilot and have them make the necessary arrangements."

"Thank you, Tobias. I appreciate this." I say, giving him a small smile.

He walks me out to my car and makes sure I get in safely before retreating into his house.

As I drive home to pack, I internally groan. "I didn't want to *actually* be around Atticus. God, this is going to be terrible. How am I supposed to do this and not want to climb that gorgeous man like a damn tree?"

I then think about the tree-shaped marking on his chest and neck, and that kills my hormonal thoughts instantly. "Oh, yeah. He has a mate. Whether or not they are bonded yet, but he still has one. Yeah... that thought is a death blow to my libido." I grumble.

Later that night at dinner, while my parents and I are gathered at the pine-colored, square dining table that fills the little dinette that is just off to the left of the kitchen, I gently broach the subject of my quick departure over our meal.

"Hey, Mom, Dad. I wanted to let you know that I need to make a last-minute trip for school. I need to go to Montana for some research on a project."

"What is this project about?" Dad asks, his copper hair catching the light from the chandelier that hangs over the table, highlighting some of the strands that are starting to gray near his temples.

"I need to look into minerals that are only present in that area. If I would have known this was part of the curriculum, I wouldn't have signed up for it. At least I won't be alone though." I add. "I know of a few people that will be going on the trip with me." I say again, twisting the truth in with the lie to make it more believable.

I will my parents to be okay with this trip. To somehow understand that this is important to me on a bigger level than I'm willing to tell them right now.

"Who all is going with you?" Mom asks as she flicks her eyes toward my father.

I freeze. And I could mentally smack myself for the names that fly out of my mouth. "Atticus, Tobias, and Coraline."

"Well, at least it's not an all-boy group with my little girl." Dad says.

If only he knew these males are far from being boys. God, how old is Atticus? I didn't even think about that.

"Okay. When will you be back?" Mom asks as she tucks a strand of her golden brown hair behind her ear.

"Friday, maybe Saturday at the latest." I tell them. "Or maybe sooner if I can get packed soon enough."

"Well, why don't you leave in the morning?" Mom suggests, "That way you can get back quicker."

"Okay. I'll message the group I'm going with and see if they can meet me at the airport sooner." I say, shocked that this is going easier than I expected. "Thank you both for being so understanding."

"We want you to do the best you can, Honey," Dad says while locking eyes with Mom again.

"Thank you." I say as I feel like at least one boulder has been lifted off my shoulders.

When I finish dinner, I rush to my room and I send a quick text to Tobias to let him know my change of plans.

Me:

Hi Tobias. I'm good to leave sooner than planned. Can your pilot be ready to pick me up in the morning?

Tobias

Good evening Quilla. Yes, I will make sure to have my pilot ready the plane tonight and I will pick you up at 7:30 in the morning and take you to the airport myself.

Me:

Thank you Tobias. That sounds good.

I grab my pink suitcase from the closet and begin to pack at least a week's worth of capris, tanks, t-shirts all of varying colors, and two dresses. I keep my shoes simple, from my lightweight sneakers to a pair of flat, white sandals. After I pack my toiletry bag of makeup, hair ties, and toothbrush, I set my bags by the door and try to get some sleep, because I know I probably won't be getting much once I get to Montana when I'm secretly pining for someone I can't have.

The next day, Dad helps me with my suitcase, setting it on the porch while I wait for Tobias to pull up. I have this nervous anticipation writhing in my belly, and I know it's because of *who* I'm going to see and not *what* I'm about to do.

You can do this. It's for Dakota. Now suck it up and deal.

Tobias arrives right at 7:30 on the dot in his black GMC Yukon.

"There's Tobias." I shout to my parents.

They give me a quick hug full of well wishes, and I dart out the door. Tobias is on the porch grabbing my suitcase while helping me down the few steps onto the sidewalk and opens the passenger door for me once we reach his SUV. He then tosses my luggage into the hatch and hops in the driver's seat to take me to the airport.

Once there, he flashes some kind of card; I guess to show he has a private hangar here, and the guard opens the gate to the terminal. Once inside, Tobias parks in front of a medium-sized, solid black jet with the initials T.H. in gold lettering on the tailfin.

"Nice plane." I chuckle nervously.

"Thanks." He says, giving me a small grin

I go to grab the door handle, but he places a gentle hand on my shoulder to get my attention.

"I just wanted to remind you to trust your Tamer instincts. They will never lead you astray."

"Thank you, Tobias. I'll keep that in mind." I say when I step out of his SUV to board the plane.

While in the air, I do my best to prepare myself for the task at hand and to hopefully ignore any feelings that I fear are going to rear their ugly head at seeing *him* in the flesh.

Atticus

The mansion is all a bustle this morning with a last-minute visitor that Tobias told me and the staff about last night. I'm curious who it will be while I'm helping to set up the chambers that are across the hall from my own. I make sure to place a soothing bundle of lavender on the pillow; that way, whoever will be occupying this space will have an easy time resting tonight after the flight.

"Oh, Atticus!" Marisol sings as she pops her head into the room.

Her brown hair is styled in a ballerina bun on the crown of her head, and she has a bright smile on her face. I notice a young gray wolf pup nipping at her heels, and she playfully bats at the little one's ear in an effort to get him to stop.

"Atticus, they're here! The town car is pulling up now." Her smile falters for a moment. "I wish Tobias came back with them though."

"Aye, but he is still helping Kai with his mate. I'm sure they will be home soon enough, though." I tell her. "Come, let's go greet the newcomer."

I put my hand on the upper part of her back as I guide her and the pup around her feet to the front yard. I see the black town car parked in front of the mansion in the long circular driveway, the one-way in, one-way out design that arches through the middle of the lush, green grass.

Alphonse, the male who is acting as alpha since Tobias is away, walks up to my side and gives me and Marisol a kind smile before he goes to open the rear passenger door. I watch as a white sandaled foot gracefully slides out of the car, and I am in no way prepared for who I see getting out.

Quilla.

I thought she was beautiful over the Zoom meetings, but her being here in the flesh? She is radiant. The cream-colored, gently flared skirt hugs her body in all the right places, and that damn brown lacy bow makes my eyes land right on her hips. Her hips sway with such grace that it makes my pants tighten at the sight. I'm just glad I'm in black slacks and not those gray sweatpants I wore the other night. As I will myself to calm down, I take in the rest of the dress. The little yellow roses that dot the fabric and call back to the nickname I inadvertently gave her.

Rosie.

And I can't help the small smile that tugs at my mouth when her eyes meet mine, and they brighten at the sight of meeting me in person. Her eyes flick down past my chin for a moment, then over to Marisol, and finally landing on the now young boy who is standing near her hips. The redheaded, green-eyed boy looking back at her and then up to Marisol for comfort from the stranger in front of him. Quilla smiles over at us, but for some reason, the smile doesn't reach her eyes.

Quilla

I pull up to the massive creme-colored stone mansion. I know this place has to have at least fifteen bedrooms in it, and I don't even want to know how many other rooms like living rooms, offices, and maybe even a kitchen or two. But all that fades after my door opens,and I am greeted by a large man. His close-shaven black hair gives him a military look, but he has kind blue eyes and a warm smile.

"Welcome to our home, Miss Rose. My name is Alphonse, stand in Alpha while Tobias is away."

"Thank you. It's nice to meet you."

He helps me out of the car, shutting the door behind me, and I suddenly get the feeling that someone is staring at me. When I look up, I see the familiar emerald green eyes and the controlled chaos of the coppery red locks of Atticus. At first, butterflies flutter to life in my stomach at the sight of him. He's taller than I thought he was. I would probably come up to the middle of his chest. The perfect spot for him to hold me close and tight against him. I smile at the thought, but then my eyes drift toward his neck, and I see those gray branches crawling up his skin, and my smile falters for a moment. I then take in the woman next to him. Her brown hair is up in a tight bun, and I see a little boy clutching her hips while trying to figure out if I am a threat or not.

Then the scene hits me like a freight train, and I try my damndest to keep my face neutral when all I want to do is dart back in this car and go back home with tears in my eyes.

I knew it. He has a mate. And *they have a kid together. Oh, fuck me. This is gonna be way harder than I thought.*

"Miss Rose, I hear you know Atticus." Alphonse begins while waving his hand toward the doctor. "Please meet Marisol and Bryce."

"Hi." I squeak, and Bryce hides further behind his mother, and I kinda feel like hiding behind Alphonse too. This woman before me doesn't look like she can hurt a fly, but I know better. I've seen what Kai, Nathan, and Tobias can do in their wolf forms.

"Please come inside. You must be famished after the flight." Alphonse says. "Then you can tell us why you're here. Tobias only said that a new Tamer was coming to us, but he didn't explain further."

"Uh, yeah. Sure. I didn't get a chance to eat on the plane, so breakfast sounds great." I force out while still refusing to look at Atticus or his mate and son.

We walk inside, and Alphonse leads us into a massive dining hall that could easily fit thirty people and even more if the chairs were pushed in closer to each other. As I approach the table, I hear a chair being pulled out for me. I turn, expecting to see Alphonse, but I see Atticus doing it instead. I feel my eyes widen at his gesture and glance over to his mate, whose eyes are darting back and forth between me and him.

"Please sit, Quilla." Atticus says, his voice tight with something I can't seem to place.

So, I just nod my head and I sit down as he pushes my chair into the table.

"Bryce, honey, why don't you go and find the other pups to play with for a while," Marisol says as her eyes flick between me and Atticus again.

I feel my cheeks flush with anticipation of being torn apart from this female.

Here it comes. She just didn't want her son to see me be fileted on the table.

"My apologies, Miss Rose. Bryce doesn't like to be around strangers much." Marisol says.

It takes me a moment to process her words. To see if I pick up on any hidden meaning...but I don't.

"It's okay." I give her a shaky smile. "I don't like strangers all that much either."

After a moment passes, large double doors open at the other end of the room, and two metallic carts that are carrying two covered dishes apiece are pushed up to the dining table by servants in white cooks' clothing. The chrome domes that cover the food are removed, and I see steaming piles of scrambled eggs, bacon, toast, sausage patties, and links, as well as pancakes with syrup and butter all laid out before us.

"Oh, just look at this feast, Atticus! It looks delicious!" Marisol declares with delight as she grips his bicep in an effort to keep herself seated.

I try not to let seeing her touch him get to me, but for some damn reason, it does.

God, I must really be a complete nutcase. I'm still fucking jealous of him while his mate is in the same damn room. Is this like a side effect of being a Tamer? You want men who are completely unavailable?

"Miss Rose...you want his...sausage... in your eggs?"

My head whips around, and I notice that the chair beside me, where Atticus was sitting, is now occupied by Marisol, and she's looking at me expectantly. And the question that I think she just asked me has my mind in the gutter.

I can't since you're his mate!

Chapter Forty-Four

QUILLA

"I'm sorry?" I choke on the words.

I grab the glass of water that somehow appeared on the table before me, and take a slow drink.

"Do you want Atticus to pour sausage gravy on your eggs?" Marisol asks again, a bit slower this time.

"Oh." Is all I manage to say, as my brain totally put that innocent sentence so far into the gutter it's not even funny. "Oh yeah. Sorry, kinda spaced out there a bit." I nervously chuckle.

"He is something to space out about, isn't he?" Marisol croons as Atticus sets two plates filled with various breakfast foods before us at the same time.

"I'm sorry?" I repeat and I instantly take a bite of egg to busy my mouth with something other than saying *I'm sorry* like a damn fool.

"I'm talking about Atticus, my dear. Isn't he just so easy to look at?"

I look at her like she's grown a second head. *Aren't mates supposed to be protective of each other? Like you touch him/her and I'll bite your fingers off? I mean, Dakota is like that with Kai, but yet she's also like that with me. Well, that just confused the hell outta me.*

"Marisol," Atticus grumbles. "Give her a day to get used to being around other Were's before you go and brag to her about me or anyone else."

"Oh, you're no fun, Atticus. How else is she to meet the other males here if I can't give her insight into their best qualities?" Marisol replies flirtatiously.

The sound of silverware clattering on the cart fills the room, and I glance over to see Atticus staring down his mate like she said something wrong, but I don't understand what it was. So, I just continue to shovel the fluffy eggs, lightly toasted bread, and a few pieces of sausage in my mouth in an effort to keep it shut.

Atticus

I have half a mind to strangle Marisol right now, but I know deep down that she doesn't realize the dangerous game she's playing at the moment. The thought of another male talking to Quilla and laughing with her makes my chest tighten to the point of pain.

Why did Tobias have to send her here? Does he feel the darkness getting worse, and he sent her here to try to calm my wolf in his absence? And this damn t-shirt collar feels too tight and itchy.

I pull at the collar of my green shirt, and I see Marisol clock the movement, then her eyes widen before she looks back down to her plate. I try to ignore the itching, but it's driving me nuts, and with Marisol's provoking, I'm in a bit of a sour mood. I stiffly turn and begin walking toward the main door of the dining hall so I can escape to the bathroom for a moment.

I just need one moment of mental and physical silence to collect myself before I go off completely. And some privacy where I can take my increasingly uncomfortable shirt off and not be a distraction or a tease for the women in the room.

"I'll be right back." I announce before I open the door.

After I walk into the hall bath, which is the only one on this side of the mansion that is a private bathroom, I peel my shirt off. The itching instantly subsides, and I see my flawless skin other than the little bit of pink at my neck where the shirt was making me itch and I was scratching as a result. It heals before my eyes, and I let a calming sigh escape my lips.

I start to think about Quilla being in the dining room with Alphonse, and it gets under my skin that she's in the room with another male. Even if he is acting as alpha, he's still unbonded himself.

"Oh, this is gonna be bloody impossible to keep my professional tone around her. What is wrong with me? She's got a mate, lover, whatever she wants to call him back in her hometown, I'm sure of it. I mean she's got to with her looks. She's gotta have males lining up and praying to be the lucky one to have her hand."

At that thought, I hear Atti snarl, and I agree with him. The thought of another male's hand on her makes me see nothing but red.

"Gahhh. Stop it you bloody asshole. She's not yours to claim."

I splash cold water on my face, tug my shirt back on, and master a look of indifference before I walk back into the dining room to find out why Quilla is here, and why Tobias thought it would be a good idea to send her.

Quilla

When Atticus leaves, part of me wants to go with him. I can tell something is off about him. That he's angry about something. But that thought fades as the large, dark wooden doors shut behind him. Before I can take another bite of my breakfast, two more males enter from a set of glass doors off on my right that comes in from a back patio.

"Oh, the food smells amazing! Alphonse, why didn't you call everyone for breakfast?" The male with brown hair and blue eyes asks as he makes his way over to the carts.

"Because this was a private breakfast, Teddy," Alphonse grumbles.

Teddy's eyes lock on mine, and he gives me a wide smile before looking at the other male that is now behind me.

"Oh look, Carlton, we have a new packmate to show around."

I look at the blonde male with brown eyes, and he is looking nervously at Alphonse, who is still staring daggers at Teddy.

"Maybe later?" Carlton asks me.

"Uh, sure." I reply.

Teddy saunters over to me, all proud male ego, and tosses his left arm over my shoulder.

"I'll be glad to show you around, doll. Just holler, *Teddy* and I'll be happy to show you around."

"I think it's best for you boys to leave and let our guest settle in first. She is here for a job too, you know, not just sightseeing." Marisol quips, saving me from mainly Teddy. Poor Carlton is just tagging along for the ride.

"Oh right, of course, Marisol. Take care, everyone!" Teddy laughs as he swipes a few sausage links from the cart and walks back out the patio doors.

Marisol leans in close to my side while placing an arm on my shoulder, and I jump at her sudden proximity. Thinking she's using the distraction to now pay me back for looking at her mate.

"Oh, I'm sorry. I didn't mean to scare you. I just wanted to tell you that their bark is much worse than their bite. They are still young men and are trying out different tactics to get females to notice them. We keep saying that their eager, proud flaunting is doing nothing but getting them ignored, but you know men, they just don't listen." She pats my shoulder, where Teddy's hand just was, and she sits back in her seat.

I breathe a sigh of relief when I'm not screaming in pain from an attack, and I smile at her. She seems to be actually looking out for me.

"Thank you. I appreciate that. And I think one day they may grow up and realize they need to change how they court a woman. I mean, they have plenty of distinguished men here to talk to. Atticus, for one." I say while looking at Marisol.

She glances from me to Alphonse then over his shoulder when the door opens and Atticus walks back in with a solemn look on his face.

"Oh, speak of the devil." I smile.

Atticus looks at me, and before I can tell him what happened with the two males, Alphonse interrupts.

"So, Miss Rose–"

"Please, call me Quilla. I insist." I cut him off, saying the same thing I did to Atticus.

Marisol then moves back to her original seat and motions for Atticus to sit in between her and me. He hesitates for a moment like he wants to tell her no, but I give him a small smile and motion with my own hand for him to just take the seat. He nods and sits without a word.

"Yes, so Quilla, what brings you here to Montana?" Alphonse asks.

"I, uh, I had the desire to research the effects of silver and what all it can do to half-bloods. I don't know if you heard, but my friend, Dakota, was hurt, but I have a feeling that there is something more to learn from her injuries."

"Ah, aye. We all heard of Dakota's injuries last night." Atticus offers. "And it made quite a few of us very angry, didn't it Alphonse?"

"Yes. I am very pleased that you were able to save our future alpha, Quilla." Alphonse says.

"Oh, I know! Atticus would be the best person to help you with your research, Quilla!" Marisol says merrily.

"No!" Atticus and I both say in unison.

"I mean, I don't want to bother Atticus and take him away from anyone who needs his help." I say while taking another long sip of my water.

God, is it hot in here, or is it me?

"I don't want to distract you from your research if you already know what you are looking for." Atticus says.

His words hit me like a punch in the chest. *He doesn't want to be around me. Of course, he doesn't. He doesn't want his mate, hello, I keep missing that part, to think that something is going on.*

"Oh, nonsense!"

Marisol gets up from the table and steps in behind me and Atticus while throwing both of her arms around our shoulders to push us together. Cheek to cheek. And I feel heat bloom deep in my belly at his skin touching mine.

"You two need to work together! What better team than a doctor and a Tamer?!" She backs away and saunters over to Alphonse, who is now giving her a look that is borderline amusement and chiding.

"I'm not going to say it with as much gusto as Marisol here, but I do think it would benefit from you two working together."

And just like that, I am walking from the dining room and into a huge library with the one wolf who I want so damn badly, but I can't have.

After the initial shock of being forced to work with Atticus, we are left alone in this huge library.

And I mean, this is freaking huge.

The room is spacious with all four walls lined with dark cherry wooden shelves that span from the floor to the ceiling, complete with little golden ladders on a roller system to get to the higher books. As I look to my left, there is a spiral black metal staircase that connects to a second level with even more books up there. This is every book girl's dream room.

I see a solid dark oak desk planted in the middle of the room and a line of shelves that are so similar to the ones back in Tobias' office in North Dakota that it feels like this space was just copied and pasted into the other home.

"Welcome to the pack library." Atticus says, breaking me out of my silent perusal of the room.

"It's huge. I have never seen something this big before." I say breathlessly.

"Tobias doesn't do anything small. He makes sure to always have whatever he may need to help his pack thrive."

"Well, in this case, it may be a good thing." I tell him.

My eyes lock onto his, and he gives me a small smile before I force myself to look away. He then leans against the desk, propping a hip on the corner and crossing his arms over his broad chest. He gives me a look like he knows there is something I am not telling him about my true reason for being here.

"Tobias just told me to help you in any way I can." He taps the side of his head, letting me know he just *literally* spoke to the alpha. "I get the feeling that there is something bigger than just looking up how silver affects half-bloods." Atticus says as he scrubs his face in agitation.

"There is. But you can't tell anyone unless specifically asked. I promised Dakota I would try to keep as many people from knowing what happened."

"Okay, you have my attention. What is it, Quilla?"

"I need to see if there is any research about a half-Were becoming immune to silver."

Atticus

This woman has had my attention from the moment I met her, and she will forever keep it until my dying breath. But what she's asking me to help her lookup? It makes the breath seize in my chest.

"What makes you think a wolf can become immune to silver? I don't think I've heard of anything like that."

"Well, we think it might actually be a thing. See, Dakota the other day was around a silver bracelet, and the longer she was exposed to it, the less she felt the effects. She even brushed up against the damn thing and it didn't burn her."

I begin to think of all the half-Were's that I have known over the years and the stories I've been told, and I get the feeling there may be something here. And for this woman, I'd tear this whole place apart to find it for her.

"Okay." I say simply.

"Okay? You're not gonna tell me that I'm crazy for looking into this, or that it's going to be nothing but a dead end?"

"No. Because research is research, regardless if you find the answers you were looking for or if it brings questions you never even thought to ask. So, we will look into this and see what we can find." I say as I nod my head for her to follow me. "Come on. I know of a good spot to start looking for some books on silver in general, and we can go from there."

As we are looking for the books, Quilla gets close to me at times, and I can just barely pick up on the scent of Teddy, one of the younger beta wolves, who thinks he's a catch for every female he sees. I also pick up on Marisol's scent too. So, Teddy must have hugged Quilla in greeting, and then Marisol, like usual, gets in on the hugging too. But any thought of that other male dissipates as Quilla goes to reach for a book on a higher shelf. Her calves straining while she gets on her tip-toes to extend her reach. The hem of her dress inching up to expose more of her thigh. My body reacts to the sight of her, and I have to fight to control the bulge growing in my pants as I reach over her shoulder to grab the book she was aiming for.

"Here you go, Quilla. You know there are plenty of ladders here, right?" I ask, and I can't help the smirk that plays on the corner of my lips.

"Why do I need a ladder when I have a tall library partner to get them for me?" She teases, and I groan internally before she quickly looks away, like she realized what she just said. But she doesn't look away quick enough to keep me from seeing the adorable pink flush to her cheeks.

After about an hour and a half of silently looking around for books, we finally found enough to get us started.

"Why don't we go out to the patio and start there?" I offer as I wave my hand toward the open door of Tobias' office.

Besides, I know it would benefit the both of us to have the pack's eyes on me so I don't go and do something stupid, like pushing Quilla up against one of these shelves and showing her just how wild that dress is making me.

Quilla

Why the hell did I just flirt with this man? I mentally smack myself at the teasing remark I said earlier. *But didn't he flirt with me too? Or did I misread that? I had to misread that.*

"This is a good spot to sit here, Quilla." Atticus says, pulling me out of my racing thoughts.

I see a lovely black metal patio table with matching chairs. The plush cushions are a steel gray color with a matching umbrella that is currently standing closed in the middle of the table. Atticus sets the armful of books down on the table and grabs the handle of the umbrella to unfold it so we can have some shade while we read through the books. I have to peel my eyes away from the way his green shirt rides up his back a little bit, showing off his tanned skin and rippling muscles.

Get a damn grip, Quilla. I mentally scold myself.

"There," Atticus says as he scrubs his hands together before pulling out a chair for me and gestures for me to take the seat. "Now the sun won't be in our eyes."

"Yeah. And it will keep us cooler too." I say, suddenly my throat is so dry it's hard to speak.

As if he's in tune with my body, he catches the eye of a lithe woman with blonde hair and he waves her down.

"Jess, would you kindly get Quilla some lemonade?"

"And please bring enough for both of us." I add before she turns around.

"Of course. I'll be right back." Jess says and nods her head at our request.

Atticus smiles at me as he pulls his chair out to sit down next to me. I turn to open my first book while he does the same, and when Jess brings out our drinks, we quietly get to work on my research project.

CHAPTER FORTY-FIVE
QUILLA

Atticus and I spend all day reading different books and making notes. By the time dinner rolls around, the only pieces of information we find are things we already know. How silver reacts to wolves in different stages consisting of fevers, falling unconscious, intense pain, and how different formulations can make those stages worse but most result in death if not remedied soon enough.

After dinner, which consists of meeting again in the dining room with Alphonse at the head of the table, Atticus to his right, and me to the right of Atticus with Marisol next to me. I see other wolves fill the room this time and take what I assume are their respective seats. Teddy and Carlton enter last and take their seat at the end of the table. Teddy flashes me a smile, and I return a small one in his direction before I turn my attention back to my plate and eat among the idle chatter around me.

Atticus

I see the way Teddy is smiling at Quilla, and it gets on my last fucking nerve. I feel Atti come forward before I can even call him to the front of my mind. Even though I chose the path of a doctor and therefore refusing any hierarchy in the pack, which was looked down on from my father's point of view, I can still feel the level of Beta in my blood, which is why I can doctor wolves and keep them in line.

And we choose now to tap into that power and send it down the table toward Teddy, so I can wipe that fucking bloody smirk off his face.

And it works.

As soon as he feels my power flow over his body, his face pales and his grin evaporates instantly, eyes dropping down to his food. I hear Alphonse's low growl next to me, and I break the flow of power over the younger wolf while flicking my eyes over to the stand-in-alpha's. His subtle nod lets me know that he respects me listening to him, and the feast continues with no other issues.

As I bring Quilla to her room later that evening, she pauses before entering. She turns to look at me while her hands fiddle with the brown lacy bow stitched to her hip. I make myself glue my eyes to her face so I don't look at her full waist and nimble hands.

"Thank you again for helping me today. Do you think you can meet me tomorrow in the library?"

"Aye. I will. Let's say about nine o'clock? I have a patient I need to look in on beforehand."

"Yeah, sure." She thinks for a moment before she tilts her head to the side a bit and asks, "Do you need help with your patient?"

I smile and shake my head. "No. It's just a follow-up from the flu. I will probably be there for no more than five minutes. So, please don't worry yourself. I'll meet you tomorrow."

I back away from her, placing a hand on the doorknob of my room in an effort to keep my hands off her. I see her eyes widen at where I am turning in for the night.

"Marisol thought it would be best for you to be roomed close to a wolf that you knew." I shake my head at what she thought was a good intention, but it's actually a form of torture for me.

"Oh, that was nice of her. I'll have to tell her that tomorrow." Quilla says as she opens her door, dashing in and swiftly shutting it behind her.

My brows furrow on her odd behavior, but I shrug my shoulder as I walk into my empty room and take a long, hot shower. Images of her in that dress floods my mind and heats my blood again, but when I think of her taking her own bath, my blood begins to boil at the images my brain creates of her.

The water barely covering her naked body while soaking in the tub. The way the warm water, I'm sure, makes her skin flush with red, and how I suddenly wish I was the cause instead.

As the water from my showerhead beats down on my shoulders, I take a breath and for the first time in my four hundred years on this planet, I wrap my hand around my raging hard-on and relieve the mounting pressure I've been fighting within myself all day with the thought of Quilla in my mind and how it would feel if it was any part of her instead of my own hand as I come undone.

Quilla

I rush inside my room at the mention of Marisol on his lips. I just do not want to see her waiting for him in his bed. I cannot take that sight right now.

I shut the door behind me, and I take in my room for the first time. The large bay window overlooks a beautiful garden full of roses in different colors of red, yellow, white, and pink, complete with well-manicured shrubs and flowering trees to complete the landscaping. I turn to my right and I see a large attached bathroom with a cream-colored marble sink, a tiled shower, and a pure white, claw-footed bathtub with golden feet and faucet.

I see my suitcase is set up on the bed. The supple, baby pink comforter dipping in under the weight of the luggage. As I walk closer to the bed, I notice a stem of lavender resting on the pillow, and I pick it up, taking a gentle inhale of its delicate scent, and it relaxes my racing heart and the tense muscles in my shoulders.

Grabbing my pajamas out of my suitcase, I head to the bathroom to draw a bath. I've never been in a claw tub before, so I want to splurge a bit. I set the lavender stem on the side of the tub and turn on the water so it can heat up before I lean down to close off the drain.

As the tub fills, I see some lavender-scented bubble bath, and I pour some of that into the water to match the flower that is still resting on the porcelain surface of the tub. I quickly undress, taking care to fold my dress and place it into the hamper that's settled in the corner of the room, before slipping under the warm water. I grab the stem of lavender, taking another whiff of its calming scent, before placing it in my hair next to my right ear. I will myself to enjoy the bath and try not to think about what Atticus may be doing next door. Trying not to imagine what his hands could be doing to my body right now.

Using my own hands, I imagine his are gripping my breasts, teasing my peaked nipples with a thumb. Then he traces an index finger down the middle of my belly, and my breath kicks up at his touch. Just as he's about to dip between my legs, I hear a door slam from somewhere in the hallway and brings me back to the present. My aggravated groan fills the air of the bathroom at both being interrupted and for even letting myself go down that rabbit hole to begin with.

The next morning, I get up and make my way to the library. When I open the door, much to my surprise, there is a chrome-covered platter waiting for me on Tobias' desk with a small bundle of yellow roses next to it. I lift the lid, and there is a stack of pancakes waiting for me, complete with syrup and sausage gravy on the side for my choice of topping. I glance over and I see a little handwritten note nestled in the leaves of the roses. The slanting, harsh marks of what can only be Atticus' handwriting.

I didn't know if you'd like syrup or gravy, so I told the kitchen to make you both. I'll see you at 9, Rosie.
Sincerely yours,
Atticus

I smile at the note while picking a rose out of the vase to tuck behind my right ear.

Today, I'm in a simple pair of black capris and a pink tank top. It was hot yesterday, and I looked at the weather this morning while I was taking a quick shower, and it's supposed to be fairly warm again today. So, I settled for comfort instead of fashion, plus I noticed the way Atticus was looking at me yesterday, and I do not want to be the reason that he and Marisol have a fight.

Filling my plate with two fluffy pancakes, topping one with standard syrup and the other with gravy, I go back to the section of the library where we stopped yesterday to look for more books. That way, by the time Atticus gets here, I will have at least something to swap the books from yesterday out with.

At nine on the dot, Atticus comes in with his arms full of the books we were looking at yesterday and he promptly stores them back on the correct shelves before taking my new pile, while adding a few of his own, into his arms and again leading me back out on the patio.

"How was breakfast?" Atticus asks as he places the assortment of books on the patio table.

"It was good. I never had gravy on my pancakes before."

He grins at me, but then it morphs into a bright smile as he notices the yellow rose in my hair. He goes to lift his hand like he wants to touch the flower, but he stops himself and clears his throat.

"Good. Glad I was able to expand your palate."

I feel him shut down. His professionalism settling in between us. I quickly pick up one of the books and begin to peruse the pages so I can keep my mind from wondering about his change of demeanor.

Atticus

This is only day two and I already want to touch her. I thought that leaving her roses was a good idea, but I didn't expect to see her with the flower in her hair.

Oh, I am just digging myself further and further into a hole.

I begin to see more and more people start to filter through the grounds, and in turn, Atti gets more and more agitated that so many people are near Quilla.

"Stop pacing, you bloody fool. She's safe here, you know that." I scold him.

"I can't help it. Too many unbonded around, and I want to claim her."

"Atti." I warn. *"She is* not *ours to claim. So get that out of your mind, wolf."* I hear him growl at me in response, but I try to ignore him. *Try* being the operative word.

About three hours later, I notice that our drinks are empty, so I reach for both glasses, placing them on the tray along with the pitcher.

"I'll be right back, Quilla. I'm going to refill our drinks. Anything you want me to bring back?" I ask as I stand with the tray in my hand.

"Oh no. I think I may be onto something though, so hurry back." Quilla responds as she takes notes from the passage she's reading.

I walk briskly to the kitchen to refill the pitcher with sweet tea and top off the metal bucket with ice cubes. I notice that there are some fresh baked desserts on the table, so I bring out a few pastries and cookies with me for a snack. As I enter the patio, what I see before me makes me freeze mid-stride.

Teddy is sitting in *my* chair, and he's pulled it so close to Quilla's that he's able to stroke her back and her hair. His knuckles brush the yellow petals of the rose tucked behind her right ear with ease. He then leans in close to her ear to whisper something in it, and my vision flares blood red at the sight.

And the next thing I know…. I'm fucking going off the handle.

Quilla

As Atticus leaves, I finish the note I was making on the first entry of half-bloods and how silver seems to react differently, but there's only one mention of it in this book, so it may be a fluke, but at least it's something.

A few minutes later, I feel someone sit down next to me, and thinking it's Atticus, I glance up to show him the passage, but who I see instead makes me pause.

Teddy.

In Atticus' chair, pulling it closer to me. And it just seems *wrong*.

"Hi, Teddy." I say, my voice wobbling with my surprise.

"Hello, Quilla." He croons, and I shiver under his touch as he runs his hand over my back. It again feels so *wrong*.,

"I'm kinda busy, and I think I'm making headway here." I say, hoping he will get the hint and buzz off.

He doesn't.

Noticing the rose in my hair, he reaches out to touch the petals, then drags his hand down my hair, and the chill that slides down my back like oil at his touch makes my stomach turn.

"Teddy, please. I need to get back to work." I say, a little bit sharper this time.

He leans in closer with a smirk on his face. "Oh, come now—"

He begins before he's violently pulled from the chair by the back of his shirt and a vicious snarl rips through the air. I stand from my chair when Teddy is thrown across the lawn like he weighs nothing and when I see who is attacking him, my heart jumps in my throat. Because who I see and what I feel are two different people.

It's Atticus' body, but that darkness I felt from him not too long ago over the Zoom meeting is flowing so strongly from him that it makes my knees want to give out. But it's not from fear of him, it's fear *for* him.

I watch helplessly as he continues to tear into Teddy. Granted, the asshole deserves to have his ass handed to him, but this... I feel that Atticus is out for blood. I then see Alphonse and two other wolves rush up to Atticus, and the stand-in alpha's voice booms over the chaos.

"Halt, Atti!"

Atticus goes still, his body shaking to fight against the command, but he stays there, frozen like a statue. I feel another body come up beside me, and I flinch before I take in Marisol's form; her face is so full of sorrow that it breaks my heart in a different way.

Pack mate hurting for pack mate.

"It's best if you look away, Hun."

I stare at her as I hear the metallic clanking of what I can only assume are chains, and I try to fight the image that wants to plant itself in my mind. I fail miserably.

Atticus being shackled by the wrists, ankles, and maybe even by the throat. Thrashing at anyone who gets near him.

I shake my head to clear the images and look back to Marisol. "What's going to happen to him?" I force out, my throat tight and burning with tears.

"He's going to be put into isolation for a bit," Marisol explains. "Just until he and Atti calm down."

I nod numbly, and I feel Alphonse come up to me next and he places a gentle hand on my shoulder.

"Are you hurt, Quilla?"

I shake my head, not trusting myself to speak anymore.

"Good. And while Teddy got his due punishment, I will be sure he knows not to pull this kind of stunt again. I sincerely apologize that he spoke to you and touched you that way."

"Will he be okay?" I ask, suddenly wanting to know his health even with what he did to me.

"He will be. It will be a few days for him to heal, but I think that may be best for him." Alphonse replies.

Later that night as I enter my room, I see a yellow rose on my pillow, and I instantly think about the same rose still nestled behind my ear. I look around to find my room is straightened and cleaned along with my dress, which has been laundered and is now hanging on the armoire in the corner of the room.

"Atticus knows how to make up a room, doesn't he?"

I spin around, and I see Marisol leaning in my doorway. "He what?" I ask dumbly.

"Atticus always knows how to make up a room." She repeats. "He goes through and makes the beds of those that get up the earliest, usually for the patrolmen. It's his way of saying thank you for what they do for the pack. And for the ladies, he leaves their favorite flower on their pillows. He must have done that this morning before he met you in the library."

"Oh, you're lucky to have him then." I say as I twirl the stem, which has been stripped of thorns, between my fingers.

"Yes, we are. But you are too, Quilla. And you may be the luckiest of us all." She says as she backs away, closing my door behind her.

I try my best to sleep, but I do nothing but toss and turn in the bed. Just knowing that Atticus is not in the room across the hall from me unsettles me. I turn one final time, putting my back to the door, and face the large window where the moon, which is a partial crescent in the sky, is shining through the glass. Something deep down in me suddenly wants to look for him. It's like a pulling sensation deep within my chest, begging me to follow it, to see where it goes.

I do my best to ignore the feeling, but Tobias' words from the airport replay in my mind; *Trust your Tamer instincts. They will never lead you astray.*

So, I turn on my other side, staring at the bedroom door for a moment, and I follow the invisible tether in my chest.

Chapter Forty-Six

QUILLA

I quietly open the door of my room and I'm met with the low-lit hallway of the mansion. It feels so different in the middle of the night. Like a slumbering beast, just waiting for something to wake it so it can wreak havoc. The pulling sensation in my chest tightens, tugging me to the left, away from mine and Atticus' bedrooms. So, I slip into my white slippers and continue down the hall. I pass the dining room and the front door of the mansion, and I'm shocked to see where I end up.

At Tobias' office/library.

"Why would I be pulled here?" I wonder aloud.

I go for the doorknob, but I find the door slightly ajar. I pause, thinking it could be a trap or something, but the invisible string that continues to pull me forward only gets stronger the closer I get to the room. So, I take a breath before I open the door fully, the hinge creaking quietly in the moonlight, and I brace myself for what I'm about to see.

Which is nothing.

I don't know what I expected. Maybe a cage with a riled wolf inside, or soldiers posted up with swords to Atticus' throat.

God, I read too many fantasy novels. Get a grip, Quilla.

I begin to move deeper into the library, and I find myself pulled to the long wall that is the backdrop for Tobias' desk. I gently trace my fingers along the shelves, and when I find a small flaw on the shelf that is about my eye level, I press my finger harder against the knot in the wood.

And it gives.

I step back with a squeak as the entire shelving unit opens up to reveal a hidden door. I look over my shoulder to make sure no one is in the main doorway; I don't want to be caught this close to the end of this invisible string and be told to go back to my room.

Once I see the coast is clear, I grab onto the dark cherry-stained shelf in front of me and I give it a tug, opening the doorway enough for me to slip in. As I peer around it, I see a white-painted spiral staircase leading up to the second floor. Lifting my right slipper-clad foot, I silently climb the stairs, the tugging in my chest leading the way in the low lighting of the stairwell. I barely allow myself to breathe until I get to the top step, and what I see gives me relief, and breaks my soul at the same time.

I found Atticus. But at the same time, I didn't.

Because the man before me is a shell of who he was yesterday, or hell, even this morning.

My eyes first land on his hands, which are chained above his head, stretched apart on either side of his body. I somehow notice the red welts on the skin of his wrists, and I swear I can almost feel his pain. From the books I've been reading, I come to the conclusion that the chains are made of silver. They are slowly burning his skin each time he moves.

I shudder as I make myself continue to take him in. My eyes take in his red hair next, which is now a darker shade from sweat dampening the strands, and it is completely pulled from the man-bun he usually wears, hanging loosely around his face. His eyes are closed, but I can tell he is aware of his surroundings by the way his eyelids flutter as the globe of his eye darts from side to side.

I am downwind enough that I don't think he will pick up on my scent, and by the absence of reaction to my arrival, I would say my assumption is correct. When my eyes finally land on his neck, I notice that his green shirt is torn to shreds, and blood coats it in various areas and even on the skin of his exposed chest and abdomen. I have no idea if it was his blood or Teddy's, but it hurts me just the same to see him with any blood on his clothes and body. I then see that gray tree tattoo staring back at me again in its full glory, from the base of his pec to the middle of his neck, just begging for me to touch it.

His mate should be here, not me.

At that thought, I turn to leave, but I don't pay attention to where I'm going. I run right into a heavy cardboard box, and it topples over with a loud clatter. Chains rattle to life behind me at the noise I caused, and a snarl rips from Atticus' throat.

Atticus

I try to concentrate on Atti while in his forest. Will him to release my body so we can co-exist again, but he's not letting up.

"Come on, wolf. You have to let me in. The silver will only get worse the longer you fight it."

The silver in the chains is something I came up with long ago. The more someone fights against it, the more it activates an electronic setup

I constructed. It sends little electrical shocks through the chains to alter the properties, making the silver stronger with each movement.

"I need to know she's safe, and away from that mongrel that touched her." Atti snarls.

"And then what? Get us back to the same red haze when another male touches her? Atti, you have got to get her out of your head. Again, she is not ours to claim!" I shout.

"But she is, Atticus! I feel it in my bones. She is ours. You two just don't realize it yet. You won't realize it until she can understand what she is to us. Not just a Tamer, but Mate."

I still at his words. Mate. Great Luna above, I would love that more than life itself. But that is a tall order for someone just getting into the Werewolf world, and being new to the Tamer life too. I don't get the chance to think too much about what Atti told me before I hear a loud clattering of boxes being knocked down. I open my eyes and let a vicious snarl rip from my throat, but who I see staring back at me with a spark of fear in her eyes, makes my heart feel like it was ripped from my chest.

The burns from the silver chains, even now being heightened from all the movement, don't hold a candle to the pain I feel when Quilla looks at me that way.

"Just look at her; how can we be mates when she looks at us like that?" I scoff at my wolf.

"Quilla, please go. You shouldn't be here." I growl, and I don't hold back. I need her to see how terrifying I am. Need her to run so she can be safe from me.

"I'm sorry. I'll... I'll go get Marisol."

I reel my head back at her mention of the pack babysitter, and for some reason, I can't hold back my question.

"Why would you get Marisol?"

She turns back around, and her olive green eyes look at me with such shock and confusion that it almost makes her look cute. She thinks that her words should make the utmost sense in the world, but I haven't the slightest idea.

She shakes her hand as if she's explaining to a complete buffoon as she says, "Marisol is your mate; she should be able to help calm you down."

I look at her, eyes wide and my body going as stiff as a board. But then something breaks in me, and I can't help but laugh at her. A body shaking, head tilting back against the curve of my spine, window-rattling laugh.

Quilla

This is why I don't tell jokes at parties. I always feel like I miss the punchline of my own joke. I have to admit though, seeing Atticus laugh after what all happened, is nice. But I just hope it's not from him losing what marbles he had left.

"I'll be back." I tell him over his still booming laughter.

I take no more than three steps before his laughter dies and his voice fills the room around us with the words that I so desperately wanted to hear, but at the same time, I'm terrified of.

"She's not my mate, Quilla."

I turn back around, and I look at him. His bright emerald eyes beaming with color, life, and happiness.

"What?" I can't help but ask.

"Marisol is not my mate. Never will be."

"But what about Bryce?" I ask, thinking back to the redheaded boy who was stuck to Marisol that day.

"What was going through your mind, Quilla?" Atticus asks, his voice low, but gentle.

I lay it all out in a rush, simply because he asked.

"That Marisol was your mate, and Bryce was your son. And I thought Marisol was going to eat me alive for flirting with you. I had to force myself to stay away because I didn't want to give into the temptation to see what it would feel like to have you touch me like I thought you were doing with her."

Atticus laughs again, but it's not as hysterical as it was. "No, Rosie. Marisol is not my mate. She is the pack babysitter, and Bryce is the son of a wolf from one of our patrol groups."

"But what about that marking?" I ask as I take a step closer to him, itching to touch that sprawling tree that crawls up his chest and neck.

"You see it?" Atticus asks with shock.

"Well, yeah. I mean, why wouldn't I?" I ask.

"Bloody hell." Atticus swears. "Okay, Atti, you were right." Atticus chuckles.

I swear I almost hear the equivalent of a wolf's laugh whispering in the air around me.

"Right about what?" I ask.

Atticus

I can just *feel* Atti prancing around like a love-sick puppy. But it makes me so happy to feel that from him. To feel the darkness that has been hanging over his forest for four long centuries, begin to lighten. Even if she says no, just knowing that we had a mate will take our darkness and push it to the far edges of our minds. I look down to Quilla, to her outstretched left hand, and I can see something flare on her skin, and I almost choke out a sob.

"Atti was right—" I begin, but then I think, how can I tell her. I don't want to just drop this on her. "Tell me what you feel when you look at me. Like right now, what do you feel? What are you thinking?" I ask instead.

"The main thing is that I don't like you being strung up like a piece of meat left to cure." She replies without a thought.

I give her a sly smile before pointing my chin to a switch that's hidden in the wall. "Give that book a tug and you can release me."

She makes her way over to a small bookshelf and pulls on the book that activates the pulley system, and it eases the tension on my arms, the manacles automatically unlocking themselves. I let out a hiss of pain as the burns from the silver finally get the air it needs to heal, and Quilla is right there, taking my hands in her own.

"I hate that you had silver against your skin. I hate that you were without a mate for so long that the darkness was threatening to take over. I liked the way that you protected me from Teddy, but I hate that you hurt your own pack mate." Quilla says as she keeps ticking off the emotions she's feeling.

I try not to growl at the mention of *him* on her lips, and it's like she feels my thoughts because she steps in closer to me, and I place a gentle kiss on the crown of her head.

"But most of all, I want to know what I am to you. How can I be what I think I might be to you when I have no wolf to bond with yours," She whispers.

"Rosie, sweetheart. You know what you are to me. It's the same thing when a human is *this* to a wolf. There is something deep down in you that will claim us. But it's different for Tamers. Where, when you claim the wolf, the marking appears for all to see. So there is no doubt to whom you belong." I tell her as I slowly kiss down the length of her hand and arm and there on her flawless skin, a vine of light gray leaves and flowers flare to life. And if she were to put her hand on my neck, over the canopy that I know to be on my skin now, it would fill any gaps that appear.

"Now tell us, Quilla, if you will accept us as such, what are you to me and my wolf?"

CHAPTER FORTY-SEVEN

QUILLA

The tender way he is holding my hands, and the way he's kissing my arm, I can feel his...love for me. My mind reels at the thought. Something so important between two people, and I can feel it blooming to life deep in my heart. And it feels right. With Atticus, anything and everything about him feels like... home.

I close my eyes, and some part of me reaches out for him, and in my mind's eye, I see Atticus in a slowly blooming forest. I watch as the once-dead and dry trees bloom to life. Like at my entrance, I am the life water they have been so desperately waiting on. I then feel something walk up beside me, a cold nose pressing into my left hand, where I notice gray vines and flowers scrolling down my arm and onto the joint of my thumb. I look past my hand, and I see a red wolf with a white patch of fur on his chest, and the mirror image of Atticus' emerald green eyes staring up at me.

"Hello." I smile, and I rest my hand on his head, and the wolf before me sighs with relief.

"Hello, My Light."

I hear his gravelly voice in my mind, and I look to Atticus for his input. I mean I've had Dakota and Kai in my mind, but this is different. And I realize it's because of the mate bond. This must be the thing I feel blooming in my chest, just like the flowers and trees all around me.

"This is what you do to us, Rosie. You give us life and beauty again." Atticus says as he waves his arms around the scenery.

I look around the still blooming forest, and I begin to hear birds chirping their merry melodies, and I know that while I feel he's right for me, I know in that moment that I am right for him as well.

"I'm glad to be that for you, Atticus. For both of you." I add while looking at his wolf. "So, you must be Atti, the brains of this operation, I guess." I chuckle.

The wolf snorts and pads over to Atticus, and it's like looking in a funhouse mirror. I can see the similarities in each form, but they are each their own being.

"I'm not going to say this will be easy for me. I mean, I'm still getting used to figuring out what it means to be a Tamer. But feeling what I do in my chest when I look at you, Atticus, I know I can't stay away."

I walk over to them, and they each touch me in their own way. Atti nuzzles his nose into my right hand, and Atticus pulls me close to his chest, where I can feel his solid body pressed tightly against mine. I lift my left hand and I finally touch that elusive marking on his skin. His low growl fills the air around us as I trace my finger along the roots, the trunk on his chest, finally ending at his neck where the vines on my hand fill any gaps in the canopy of branches. The same way I fill the dark pockets of his soul and I realize that he does the same thing for me. I never knew I was missing something until I met him.

I pull back enough to look up at him, and he gently pushes a lock of hair behind my ear while giving me a small smile.

"I'll ask again, Quilla Rose, what are you to us?"

"I am your Mate." I say with conviction.

At my words, Atticus dips his head into the curve of my neck and holds me tight to his chest, and I embrace him just as tightly.

With the side of my face still buried into his chest, I know my muffled words will still reach his ears, still reach his heart, as I say, "I want to try to be the mate that you need. To help keep that darkness and decay as far away from you both as I can. That is if you two will take me as your mate and help me learn."

Atti begins to howl a moment later, and I can somehow hear the acceptance in his song. When I look up at Atticus, I see that we are back in the attic of the mansion and his arms are tightly wrapped around my lower back.

"You will always be exactly what we need, Rosie," Atticus says as he interlocks his right hand with my left, again tenderly kissing the marking on my skin. "My mate. God, I love you so much already."

I notice the still-raw skin on his wrists and I begin to tug him towards the stairwell. "Come on, I need to tend to your burns."

"I shouldn't leave yet. At least not until the alpha tells me I can." Atticus says, standing still as a statue.

"Well, that was before you actually had a mate." I tease. "I think he will forgive you for your lapse of judgment when your mate is asking for you to go with her."

"How can I argue with that logic?" Atticus replies, his voice dipping low.

I lead him back down the stairs and through the still-silent halls. When we make it back to the doors to our respective rooms, Atticus pulls me into his without a second thought. He gently shuts the door behind him, and I pad into his room, taking in the atmosphere of what is Atticus. A clean, orderly room. His huge bed is neatly made with the blue comforter pulled back to the middle of the bed, and the gray sheets are flawlessly made without a wrinkle in the fabric. I notice the long oval mirror that I remember from the Zoom meeting where he had on the–

Nope, not going there, or should I?

"Do you have any medical supplies in here?" I ask, trying to keep my mind from venturing to *those* pants.

He flashes me a grin and shakes his head. "What kind of doctor would I be if I didn't have my own stash of supplies?"

"Okay, hotshot. You lead the way."

He leads me into a bathroom that is similar to mine, but he has muted grays and blues mixed in the marble countertops of the dual sinks and there is a gray claw tub in the corner with a walk-in shower on the back wall of his bathroom. He opens a door under the sink to pull out a hefty wad of gauze and a bottle of liquid that has familiar purple flowers floating around in it.

"You made your own version of the healing Wolfsbane?"

"Aye, I did. Your recipe was very well thought out, so I was sure to copy it down, and I made a few different variants." Atticus smiles.

"I'm glad it could help you and the others while I wasn't even here."

I grab at the gauze and tip some of the liquid onto the fibers to apply it to his inflamed flesh. He sucks in a breath, but he keeps himself still while I begin to clean the slowly healing burns on his skin. As I finish his right wrist and start on his left, I hear him chuckle under his breath.

"What's so funny?"

"I just can't believe you thought Marisol and I were mates."

"I mean, it's not all that far-fetched, Atticus. Look at it from my side; you were awfully close to her, and Bryce looks almost like you."

"What was going through your mind when you thought about her being around me, being able to *touch* me?"

His eyes flash a lighter shade of green, and I know his wolf is close to the front of his mind.

"You really want to know?" I squeak as heat rises up my neck and blooms in my cheeks. I look back down to tend to his wrist in an effort to cover my reaction to his words.

"If I didn't, I wouldn't have asked."

I sigh and I try to explain as I keep working on the injury. "Well, I was thinking—"

He cuts me off as he hooks his index finger under my chin, making me look him in his eyes.

"I want you to look at me as you tell me your thoughts. And don't hold anything back, Quilla."

I swallow hard at the heat in his eyes.

"At the time, I was thinking she was the luckiest woman in the world to be able to be around you. To be the one to run her fingers through your hair, and to touch, trace and kiss that marking of yours."

Heat flares in my face, chest, and even down to my core. I have half a thought to squeeze my thighs together, but I know that won't do me any good.

"Oh, Quilla. No woman has touched me in four hundred years. I only had one lover, and that is when I was young and entirely dumb at twenty-five." He lifts his hand, cupping the back of my neck as he says,

"Darlin' I want to be the only one on the receiving end of your kisses, your touch, and your love."

He leans in to kiss me, and I don't even hesitate. I allow our lips to meet, and at first, he's gentle. Taking his time to taste and feel me, but then something snaps and he's pushing me against the wall of the bathroom while hungrily devouring me. His tongue darts in my mouth while his hands trail up the sides of my body, tracing every inch and curve, his hips pinning me against the wall to keep me from moving.

He pulls back enough to whisper in my ear, "I loved that dress on you yesterday, by the way. Oh, if you could have been in my mind then, Quilla. For me to let you feel just what you do to me."

"Oh, I can feel that now, Atticus." I say breathlessly as I roll my hips into his. The hard, proud length of him rubbing against my center.

"Oh, Rosie." He growls. "You better stop that before I say to bloody fucking hell with the rules and take you against this wall."

"We have rules too?" I ask innocently.

I love this version of unhinged Atticus. It makes my blood heat, and I know that *I* control the outcome.

"Not as strict as Kai and Dakota have, but we can bend them more than they can since another wolf isn't stupid enough to try and claim you." Atticus grumbles as he continues to trail his lips down my neck. "Do you want me to ease some of the tension, Rosie?"

I almost want to come right there at his words, but I pull him closer to me, running my hands over his sculpted chest, and a thought hits me, and I can't help the sly smile that blooms on my face.

"Can a four hundred and twenty-five-year-old Were actually satisfy a woman of only twenty-two?" I tease, suddenly knowing full well what will set him off.

He growls as he takes the bait, and I feel his hand dip into my pajama pants, teasing my clit with expert precision with his thumb.

"Does this feel like I don't know how to make my mate climax?"

I bite my lip to try to keep my mouth shut, but Atticus only smiles as he slips two fingers inside me, slow and deep, and I can't keep the cry inside anymore.

"Oh, Atticus!" I moan.

"That's right, Darlin'. Keep screaming my name. Let every fucking wolf here know whose mate you are." Atticus growls possessively.

I didn't think that words would make me fall over that edge, but damn if his words don't do it for me. I take a nosedive over that cliff as he continues his glorious tempo with his long, deft digits and I match his pace as I start rolling my hips into his hand, driving him deeper to hit that spot that makes me see stars behind my half-lidded eyes, his thumb still pressing into the swollen bud at the apex of my core, sending me over that blissful edge once more before he withdraws his hand.

He then quickly turns and grabs a washcloth out of a nearby drawer in the vanity. I hear the faucet turn on to dampen the cloth with warm water before he turns back to me.

He tugs my pajama pants down to my ankles and presses the warm washcloth to my well-loved center. "Who's mate are you, Quilla?" Atticus asks as he cleans me.

"Yours." I respond breathlessly and without thought.

Because with him and I, there isn't a thought. I am his, just as much as he is mine.

CHAPTER FORTY-EIGHT
ATTICUS

I still feel like this is a dream. This woman, who I only met over a bloody Zoom meeting, has been the center of my every thought, and now that I have her in my arms, I never want to let her go. I never want to stop hearing her scream my name and beg me for more.

"Atticus?" Quilla asks, her voice still light and breathless.

"Yes, Rosie?"

Her eyelids flutter open, and her light grass-green eyes stare back at me, and I see a slight grin begin to tug at her lush, kiss-swollen mouth.

"Now I want to know, who's my mate?" She growls. Actually bloody growls, and I feel Atti howl in response in my mind.

"Me." I answer with my own growl. "And not another man, human or wolf, will touch you unless you or I will it."

I know she's going be a Tamer and therefore will have other men touch her, but that is the extent it will go. Because if another touches what is *mine* nothing will be able to repair the body that I will rip apart.

"Good, just wanted to make sure we were on the same wavelength." She grins.

"Rosie." I sing darkly.

"Go get a shower. You still have blood on you, and you stink."

I want to argue with her, but I take a step back to look in the mirror, and like she said, I still have Teddy's blood on me, and I still smell like a feral wolf. I groan at the sight and scent of his blood on me, and I scrub my hand over my face.

"Oh, I'm gonna have to apologize to that asshole."

"Yes, you do. But not tonight." Quilla says as she comes up behind me and traces her fingers over my arm. "For tonight, clean yourself up and just be with me. Allow me to continue to help center you, and then we will tackle tomorrow's issues in the morning."

"Aye, Rosie. That sounds like a solid plan."

She backs away from me and begins to walk out of the bathroom, and the sudden thought of her leaving makes my hand shoot out towards her before I can comprehend what I am doing.

"Where are you going?"

"I have to get another set of clothes too." She says shyly.

I look at her, and she has a few specks of blood on her pajama top that must not have been dried all the way.

"I'll be back, Atticus. I'm not going anywhere now."

"I know." I whisper.

As she steps to the door again, she looks back over her shoulder at me before she leaves with a mischievous smile lighting up her face. "One day maybe we'll shower together, but not now." She winks and then darts across the hall to her own bedroom.

When I take off the remaining tatters of my shirt and toss it in the wastebasket with a slight chuckle at my mate's teasing, I notice the marking is still on my chest. It's still gray in color, but it continues to live on my skin.

"So my guess was right then?"

I spin around ready to fight the person who just entered my room if it was not for the power flowing from him that makes my attack halt in its tracks.

"Tobias, you bloody asshole! You nearly gave me a heart attack!" I yell, then I pause as his words finally hit me. "What do you mean *your guess was right?* Are you playing matchmaker again?"

Tobias smiles at me like the cunning wolf that he is, then walks over to me, grabbing me by the shoulder. "This time I did play matchmaker with you and Quilla since you two are special. You are so lucky to have her, and I know with you being by her side, she will grow into, I think, one of the best Tamers we've had in a while."

"Aye. She's already so proficient in what she does." I say, then I suddenly remember what she said she found before I went all—as the people of this century say—ape shit crazy. I also remember who is in front of me and Quilla's plea for me to keep this from Tobias as much as possible.

"Keep her safe, Atticus," Tobias says as he starts to walk out of the bathroom. "And remember, there are rules even for you two. No *other* business until you bond." He leaves with a smirk and closes my bedroom door behind me.

I stare in shock, a bit of embarrassment but mostly pride that my mate's arousal still lingers even after she's long gone, and I was the one to cause that.

I can't help but mentally reach out to my alpha, and I immediately feel his amusement from his side of our bond. *"Keep your nose out of my mate's scent."*

"Just keep it in closed quarters, Atticus."

I finish my shower, and as I'm pulling on my gray sweats, I feel Quilla enter my room again, and even though I was calm before she entered, just feeling her presence around me sets me further at ease. I toss the towel in the hamper and I walk out to greet her, and as she takes in my form, her cheeks go three shades of red.

"Oh, that's right, you like these, don't you, Rosie?" I croon.

Her face goes from shy to sultry as she walks up to me and unabashedly crushes a kiss to my damp lips. On instinct, I pick her up by her thighs, and she immediately wraps her legs around my waist as I deepen the kiss, darting my tongue in her glorious mouth to taste her. I walk over to my king-sized bed and I gently set her down on the mattress near the headboard. I slowly climb in with her, trailing kisses down the column of her throat, and she runs her slender fingers through my air-dried hair.

"How is it that it feels like a new experience every time you kiss me or touch me?" Quilla asks breathlessly.

"I don't know, Rosie. But I feel the same way. I will never get enough of you, no matter how many more centuries I live."

I slide up higher beside her, pulling her to my chest, and she settles into the curve of my body like a perfect match, and we just exist for a few moments. Neither of us saying a word.

"Oh!" I begin after a bit of silence. "You said you were on to something before–" I trail off, still ashamed we acted the way that we did.

"Oh yes! I did find something. I took the books back to the library after… you know." Her voice quietly trails off, and my heart breaks in my chest when her body tenses up at the memory.

"I'm sorry, Quilla." I pull her tighter against my chest. "I wish I could take that memory and lock it away somewhere deep and dark."

"I don't."

"What?" I ask in disbelief.

She sits up, and she rests her left hand on my chest, right over our unique mate markings.

"I don't want you to take that memory away." She begins. "Yes, it was terrifying to see you, the quiet, calm, professional doctor that I met, fly off the handle like that, but at the same time, deep down I knew you did it for *me*. To protect what Atti had already claimed. It was the thought of you not being in your room, and being held in isolation somewhere that made our bond flare to life, and it brought me to you."

She lightly kisses me again before straddling me, but not with an ounce of desire in her movements, just the fact that she wants to be as close to me as she can, and for me to feel her weight on my body in an effort to keep us both grounded.

"I understand, Rosie. Words will never show you just how much I appreciate you taking the chance to look for me and bring me back from the brink of my own insanity." I say as I rub her back soothingly.

"I think this goes without saying, but just love me. Love all my flaws, build me up when I doubt myself, and celebrate with me in my accomplishments, because I know I'm going to do the exact same thing with you."

"You will never go a moment without love from me, Darling. You will always feel it. As you sleep, as you are a thousand miles away from me, you will feel it."

"I'm gonna hold you to it, Atticus." She smirks. "And you too, Atti. I know you can hear me too, I can feel it."

I laugh, and when I look back at my mate, I feel my wolf right there with me, staring at the amazing, beautiful, fearless, and loving woman in front of us. We kiss once more before we settle in for the night, and as I pull the covers up over our bodies, we stare at one another in the large, oval mirror in the corner of the room. I take her left hand and bring it up to my lips to give her knuckles a tender kiss, but before my mouth can caress her skin, our eyes widen at what we see reflecting back at us in the mirror.

Quilla

Last night was the best night's sleep I have ever gotten in my life. I guess that's what happens when you feel entirely safe in your mate's arms.

As I turn over in Atticus' bed to say good morning to him, I find that he's not beside me. He left me a note on his pillow saying that he went to get us breakfast. While he's gone, I find myself looking at my mating mark, and I get the feeling to research the bond between a Tamer and a Werewolf. So, I dash over to my room to grab a tank and a pair of shorts before heading to the library and easily finding the book I need. I take it back to Atticus' room to read, and when I finish the small tome, I find myself smiling down at my precious mark, and I'm eager to share my newfound information with my mate.

After Atticus brings our breakfast in, we go to the medical unit of the mansion so he can apologize to Teddy for beating the ever-loving shit out of him. I do make a point to tell Teddy that he needs to stop that kind of courting shit before he does really get hurt. I have no doubt that Atticus would have killed him if Alphonse didn't step in.

Atticus and I also take up our research again. Going from the patio to the library, to his bedroom, and maybe some extracurricular activities on the side when one of us gets stressed from the many books we read and the notes we take, but we finally made headway in finding out what I was hoping for.

"Looks like this Tamer, Frances Rose, had the same idea you had, Quilla. Does that name sound familiar to you?" Atticus asks.

"No, it doesn't, and Dad's pretty big on family history, so I think I would've heard that name at least in passing one time or another. How long ago was he alive?" I ask while looking over his shoulder at the passage in the book.

"About two hundred and fifteen years ago. He lived to be a hundred, it says here."

"So is that how long this area has been without a Tamer? Two hundred and fifteen years?" I ask.

"Aye. It's been a long time."

"I agree. So it's a good thing I'm here then, huh?" I say as we continue to make notes on Frances' research.

I don't like Atticus being near me when I start making the different variations of silver, but he stays far enough away that they don't affect him all that much.

When we are not testing the different levels of silver, Atticus takes me to see some of his patients, which I love seeing him help other people in need, and he introduces me as the pack Tamer and his mate which we both receive well wishes and praises to the Great Luna on our new found bond.

On my last night at the mansion, Atticus brings me to a private area of his medical wing where he teaches me how to start an IV line on his own arm so I can administer the various injections of liquid silver into Dakota's system in the hopes of giving her the immunity she's looking for.

By Saturday morning, I am packing up my suitcase and Marisol is making arrangements for the town car to pick me up. Atticus said he spoke to Tobias, and he has the pilot ready to greet me at the airport. After I set my suitcase out in the hallway, I dash into the bathroom to put on my rose dress again since I know Atticus went nuts for it. At least now, I can get his full reaction.

Right as I pull the zipper up my hip, I turn around to see Atticus leaning against my bathroom door jamb with his arms crossed over his chest. His red hair is tied in his usual man-bun and the first few buttons of his shirt are undone, showing off his marking.

"I loved that dress the first time I saw it, and now I love it even more now that I can show you exactly what it does to me."

His deep, Irish voice sends chills down my spine while my breath quickens as he walks towards me. He gently grabs my left hand, his thumb tenderly stroking the vines that climb up my skin, which makes the tingling sensation bloom through my whole body as he tugs me into my bedroom.

He pushes me to the edge of the bed where the crease of my knees is against the mattress, but he doesn't make any other movements. So, like any normal, sane person, I poke the bear, or in this case the wolf.

"So, what, this dress only makes you want to move me from room to room?"

He smirks, and when he looks at me, his emerald eyes are shining bright, and I know that he and Atti are here, and I am ready for them.

I find that bond between us and I tell them, *"Show me just how* wild *this dress makes you."*

He takes a step towards me, and I collapse onto my bed, and with slow, measured movements he kneels between my legs, hooking my calves over his shoulders. He folds my dress once, twice, three times, so he has my thighs uncovered, and the deep growl that fills my ears makes my core heat with desire.

"You really want to give this old heart a run for its money, don't you?"

"Awe, the big bad Werewolf can't take the desire of his young female?" I croon as his eyes continue to devour my bare center.

"Wrong words, Mate."

He straightens his back, effortlessly lifting my hips as I feel his hot breath on my sensitive core. His teeth nip at my clit, and I desperately try to hold my screams of ecstasy back by covering my mouth with my hand.

"Oh no, Rosie. This is the last day I get to see you in person for a while. I want these halls to echo with your screams for me." Atticus growls as he easily slides two digits inside me, slowly curling right where he knows I like it.

I try to hold back my moans, just to prove to him that I can, but damn, when he brings his thumb in the mix, he sends me down that glorious spiral, and I scream his name.

"Atticus!"

The vibration of his approving growl sends my sensitive center into overdrive. I almost whimper when I'm just about to climax again and he pulls his fingers away, only to be set right back on that roller coaster when he drives his tongue slowly and deeply into my heat, teasing the one spot that makes my toes curl, his teeth scraping over my highly sensitive clit. I fall over again, and again.

"That's it, my beautiful mate, keep screaming my name." He pulls back to praise me before diving back in, like a man starving for life-giving water.

And I do. I scream his name until I'm hoarse.

Once he wrings the final orgasm out of me, he gently lifts my legs off his shoulders and walks into the bathroom without another word. A moment later he comes back out with a washcloth then, kneels back down between my legs and proceeds to clean up the mess he made of me. I lean up on my elbows and I give him a contented smile.

"I love how you take care of me." I sigh.

"Always, Rosie."

After he cleans and dries me, he pulls my dress back down just as the town car is pulling up. Atticus then takes my hand in his right while he tugs my suitcase with his left and walks me to the front of the mansion. I am greeted by Alphonse, Marisol, and a few other members of the pack in a farewell gathering.

"It's been a pleasure meeting you, Quilla. I hope to see you again soon." Alphonse says while nodding in my direction.

"Oh Quilla! I'm gonna miss you!" Marisol sobs. She brings me in for a tight hug and then she whispers in my ear, "I'm glad the right gal got that handsome doctor. I never had a chance with him."

I pull back in shock, but she gives me a wink as she releases me from her embrace to stand beside the stand-in alpha. Atticus then walks me to the car and opens the backdoor, but he stops me before I can get in.

"I'll miss you, Rosie. But remember, I am but a thought away." He caresses the back of my neck and places a tender kiss on my mouth and I can't help it when my left hand traces the tree branches on his neck, and I hear him say in my mind, *But I am just a plane ride away if you need more.*

I laugh and rest my head on his chest. "Noted, Babe. Duly noted."

I slide in the back seat of the car, and Atticus shuts the door a moment later. As the car lurches forward, I watch as the man, the mate I found, get smaller from my sight, but his presence in my mind becomes bigger and bigger the further away I get from him.

"Just a thought away, right, Atticus?" I say through the bond.

"Just a thought away, Rosie."

CHAPTER FORTY-NINE
DAKOTA

I wake up in Kai's arms early Monday morning, my back pressed tightly against his chest, and I stare into the darkness while listening to him sleep behind me. Today is the day I will know if Quilla was able to figure anything out about the silver immunity.

The past few days have been nerve-racking. Just waiting to hear something. Trying to stay out of Quilla's mind. And now that I am awake, I finally feel my friend's presence tickling in the back of my mind.

"Good morning, Dakota."

"Morning." I say with anticipation.

"I figured some things out. A lot of things, actually." I can feel her grin from her side of the bond, and it makes me happy, yet, I question what she found to make her this excited about the immunity.

"I'm not going to be at school again today. So that way you'd have an excuse to come over to finally check on me and bring me any homework I missed."

"Okay. Yeah, I've been telling Kai that you've been talking to me and telling me that you're fine, just sick."

"Okay. Do you think he knows anything?"

"If he does, he's keeping it from me. But no, I don't think so." I tell her while looking back at my still sleeping mate. *"I'll be over later this afternoon."*

"Good. And bring a change of clothes with you, too." Quilla says.

She withdraws from my mind just as the alarm starts to scream at me, telling me it's six o'clock and time to get up. Kai's arms tighten around me, and he tenderly kisses my shoulder, right where my mate marking hides under my pajama top, and it sends pleasurable chills down my spine.

"Good morning, Love."

"Morning."

He continues to trail kisses up my neck, traveling to my jaw before I turn on my back to give him access to my mouth. I run my hands up his defined arms and broad shoulders, then finally threading my fingers through his blonde hair when his lips meet mine. We share a few moments just loving one another this way until the alarm screams at us again, telling us it's 6:10 a.m.

"Come on, let's get moving before I just stay in bed with you all day." I chuckle.

"I could be okay with that." Kai grins.

"One day, wolf-man, but not now. Come on, get up."

With a mocking groan, Kai and I get up to go to school. While Kai is in the shower, I make sure to stash a pair of shorts and a gray t-shirt in my backpack at Quilla's request, and I quickly take my own shower and get ready for the day.

As I am sitting in the passenger side of my car watching Kai drive, I broach the subject of going over to see Quilla.

"Quilla isn't going to be at school again today, and I'm worried about her now. I'm gonna go over after school and see her."

"She has been sick for a few days. I hope she starts to feel better soon. Should I tell my father to have Atticus call her to see if he can help?" Kai asks.

"No. Not yet, at least. Let me see her first." I tell him.

As the school day ends, I make sure to pick up any homework that Quilla may have missed and stash it in my backpack before meeting Kai at my car. When we get home and Kai parks in the driveway, he leaves the car idling for a moment before he glances over at me and gives me a small smile.

"I think while you are going to check on Quilla, I am going to go ahead and talk to my father about the next steps I should take in confronting Jeffrey once and for all."

My head snaps over to him as his words hit my ears, and I can't help the flare of fear that grips my heart.

"You are?" I whisper.

"Yes. Dakota, I have to stop Jeffrey for more than just him wanting to claim you as his mate. He is making the lower members of his pack live in absolute fear." Kai says sternly, but it's not directed at me for my questions, it's just at the situation in general.

I suddenly remember what Caleb said about me protecting a *human*, someone weaker than me.

"It's both Jeffrey and Caleb. They think that those weaker than them don't deserve protection. He said I was *noble* for protecting Quilla."

"And that is why I need to talk to my father about how I can challenge him for you *and* for his pack."

I take a deep, calming breath. This is all starting to come at me too quickly, and I don't want to think about Kai having to fight this asshole. Not yet, at least.

"Okay. You take care of what you need to." I lean over the console, and I caress his neck, rubbing my thumb just under his jaw. "Remember, *you* are my strong, loyal, and *noble* mate, and you are *mine*. I love you, Kai."

"The words *I love you* are so inadequate for the way I feel about you."

He wraps his hand around the back of my neck, threading his fingers through my hair at the base of my skull, and curls his hand into a gentle fist. He tugs enough to pull my head to the side where he leans in to press a loving kiss to my lips. When I moan at his touch, he deepens the kiss, parting my lips with his tongue as a growl bubbles from his chest. He then pulls back enough to trail his lips lightly down my cheek, my chin, my neck, and when he gets to the curve of my shoulder, his teeth graze my skin and that finally brings fire blazing in my veins and explodes in my core.

"Kai!" I gasp.

At my plea, Kai then brings his other hand up to cup my breast, his thumb flicking over my hardened nipple that is poking through the fabric of my shirt, and it sends pleasure shooting through me and I can feel that I am about to fall over that glorious edge. Then, as if sensing what is about to happen, Kai pulls his hand and lips away from me. Leaving me heaving and unsatisfied, and the smirk that is tugging at his lips makes me want to both smack him and tackle him in his seat.

"Go see Quilla, Love." Kai says, then he adds, his gravelly voice sending shivers down my spine. "But hurry back to me."

I can feel his desire to love me in a more private and comfortable area fill my mind, and the way his eyes flash a lighter shade of greenish brown tells me that K is just under the surface too, and I almost second guess going over to Quilla's. But just like Kai has his own battle to fight, so do I, and Quilla holds the answers to my fight.

So just to mess with him, I give him a playful wink and shove his shoulder, pushing him closer to the driver's door before I say, "Now out with you! I need to go see my friend and nurse her back to health."

As I pull up to Quilla's house, I see her sitting by the window in the living room waiting on me. Once I shut my car door, Quilla already has the front door open for me, and I walk right in, immediately embracing my friend.

"I missed you, Chica." I say close to her ear.

I notice she has on a long-sleeve shirt, and she's got holes cut in the wrists so her thumbs can poke through the fabric. I don't think too much of it, other than it's a little too warm to have that long of a shirt on, but hey, whatever floats her boat. We then enter the living room, and I am greeted by her mother, who is watching a reality TV show with a bowl of trail mix on the couch beside her.

"Hey, Mom, Dakota and I are going to go downstairs in the basement to hang out for a bit."

"Yeah. Hangout." I say to her through our bond.

Quilla doesn't look at me as she leads the way to the basement. Once she hits the bottom step, she turns on a light, and I see there is a chair and table set up with a dark, metal box sitting on top. Along with the box, I see a steaming kettle of what I know to be the Wolfsbane herbal tea sitting on a potholder on the end of the table.

"Okay. So, I figured out how to make the different variations of silver to supposedly help you achieve immunity. I had Atticus help me with the research." Quilla says as she pulls the long-sleeved shirt off, revealing a tank underneath. But what I see crawling down her arm makes me look at her with shock.

"What the hell, Quilla? When did you get a tattoo?!"

The black and dark gray vines and leaves that travel from mid-forearm down to the middle of her thumb stare back at me.

"Oh, this?" She says like it's not the biggest thing in the world, if anything, she *blushes*.

"Yes, that! You got a tattoo and didn't tell me?"

"Well, it's not just an ordinary tattoo, Dakota."

"Is it like a Tamer thing? Come on, Chica, you gotta tell me more than that."

"Later. Right now we have bigger fish to fry at the moment." Quilla says as she points to the chair for me to sit down.

"You're lucky that you have a point. But you are going to tell me soon."

Quilla again blushes, and I roll my eyes as I sit down and wait for her to explain what is going to happen.

"Okay, so this box is made of lead. Atticus said in his notes that I need to keep it in here so it doesn't hurt any other Were's, and once we are done with each trial, you should drink the tea to help your body heal regardless if you can handle the silver or not." She reads through a set of little index cards that I now notice is sitting beside the lead box.

"Okay. So where do we start?" I ask.

Quilla opens the box and takes out a syringe filled with silver liquid. As I stare at the needle, I suddenly think to reach out to my wolf before doing this.

"Kota, you okay with this? I'm sorry, I should have asked you sooner."

"Don't be, Dakota. I understand your thoughts on this, and I absolutely agree. If we can protect Quilla, our mate, and eventually our pack better with an immunity to silver, then let's do it. If I ever think something is not a good idea, I will let you know. But thank you for asking all the same."

"You ready?" Quilla asks as she holds the syringe up, making sure no bubbles are in the tube.

I take a breath and, with determination in my soul, I nod. "Let's do this."

Quilla then grabs a rubber tourniquet to tie off my arm so she can find my vein and easily slips in an IV catheter.

"Where did you learn to do that?" I ask in shock.

"Atticus taught me. I poked the poor guy so much before I finally got the hang of it. Thank goodness he heals quickly." She chuckles.

"Hold up. You *met him*?" I shout. "So is that where you've been this whole time? With Atticus?"

"Yeah. I asked Tobias, like I planned to, about the research, and he thought it would be best to have me and Atticus team up on this. So Tobias sent me on a private plane to Montana to meet him." Quilla smiles softly as she traces a finger over that tattoo on her arm.

I clock her movement, and how she looks at the marking. Like she's in love. Then it hits me.

"Quilla," I say gently. "He's your mate, isn't he?"

She looks at me with happy tears in her eyes and nods her head. "Yeah, he is. This is the marking that matches his."

"Oh, Chica. I am so happy for you." I say while pulling her in for a hug.

I look back to her marking and I again notice how dark it is compared to my own light gray coloring. Then I think about Mom's and Dad's, and Tobias' markings, and how dark they are.

"Wait, a fucking minute!" I exclaim. "How are you both bonded?!"

"We aren't bonded in the sense like normal Were's or those with human mates. I mean we haven't had actual sex yet to consummate anything. But I think it happened the same night we figured out what we were for each other. We just kinda accepted the other and before we turned in for the night, we noticed our markings darkening in his mirror. From what I read, it's *because* I am a Tamer that the bond is able to snap into place once the *mates* accept each other. Normal mates are usually able to hide out or keep others from touching them and therefore have a bit more time to have the Alpha complete the official bond. But, since Tamer's are around other wolves and are constantly being touched, the bond has to be set into place as soon as we understand what we are to each other." Quilla explains. "So, that's why I still have gray areas in my marking, because it hasn't been blessed by an alpha, but it still feels like the real thing for me and Atticus."

I feel tears prick the corners of my eyes. I am so happy for my best friend that words can't begin to explain the feeling.

"Congratulations. Quilla. See, I told you everything would work out in the end."

"Yeah, you did. I miss him something terrible, but I always feel him in the back of my mind, and it makes the distance tolerable."

"Well, let's get this trial over with so you can make trips back to see him." I say as I extend my arm across the table, a silent invitation to get this session started.

Quilla nods as she attaches the silver-filled syringe to the IV catheter and pushes the liquid into my vein

CHAPTER FIFTY

DAKOTA

Aften Quilla pushes the dose of silver into my IV, we wait. And Wait. I close my eyes, and I can almost feel something flood my veins, but nothing really happens. Quilla picks up a notebook, and I hear her pen scratching against the paper as she makes notes on my body's reaction.

"Should I be feeling anything?" I ask.

"No, you shouldn't have. We wanted a control silver to see how you would react to any type of silver being in your system. Liquid silver is a little more potent than when compared to the solid form. This was basically the level of plated silver that is similar to jewelry."

Quilla then grabs a saline tube to rinse the IV out, and she grabs another silver-filled syringe from the lead box to bring over. I can already feel my skin start to crawl in proximity to it.

"Oh boy. This one is gonna be fun." I sigh.

"Yeah, this one's a bit stronger. You ready?"

"Hit me."

She twists the cannula onto the syringe and injects the liquid into my veins. After a heartbeat, heat spreads down to my hand, into each finger, and then I feel it travel up my arm and over my shoulder. Once it hits my heart, the heat explodes over my entire body in an instant. Sweat starts to bead on my forehead, and my breath quickens a bit to cope with the warmth. As Quilla once again picks up her notebook to document what is going on, I start to feel my entire body tingle. Like every nerve ending is asleep.

"Are you feeling anything else besides being hot?" Quilla asks as she points her pen toward the sweat on my brow.

"I'm tingling all over like my whole body fell asleep." I grit out.

"Okay, do you want to drink some tea to make it stop sooner?" Quilla offers.

"No. I can handle it."

It takes an hour for the tingling sensation and the heat to leave my body, but when it does I finally relax a bit.

"Oh, thank God that's over." I pant. "That was intense."

"But you did great for the first trial, Dakota. I will warn you though, with each injection, the pain will get worse as we go higher up the purity chain. The kind of pain you had in your shoulder will be all throughout your body. So, I just want you to mentally prepare for that."

At hearing her words, for an instant I second guess myself, but then as soon as that thought hits me, I hear Kota growl in the back of my mind.

"Don't you dare second guess yourself, Dakota. We are doing the right thing, and we will get through this."

I can feel Kota's determination flow through me, and I take a breath as I look at Quilla, and I give her a stiff nod.

"I can do this. I have to."

"Good. Now go get a shower and drink a cup of tea so you can go home to Kai."

Kai

I walk into my house after Dakota leaves to visit Quilla, and Mom comes out from the kitchen and gives me a gentle hug as a way of saying hello.

"Where is Dad? I need to talk to him about something."

"He's in his office." Mom says. "Is everything okay?"

"Yes, Mother. Everything's fine." I smile.

I walk to my father's office and I knock on the door before entering. I see my father sitting in his overly sized computer chair and the dark cherry desk that is an exact replica of the one back home sitting in the middle of the room.

"Kai, hello."

"Hi, Dad. Can I talk to you for a moment?"

"Yes, please sit, son."

I sit in the soft leather chair in front of the desk, and I take a breath before getting into the nitty gritty of it.

"Dad, I need your advice on the best way to challenge Jeffrey for both Dakota and his pack."

Dad's eyes widen at my words, and he shakes his head before asking, "Why his pack? Do you want to lead on your own all of a sudden?"

"Not exactly, that is, if you don't mind taking them in. But I know I can't leave his pack members in the hands of Caleb or anyone else there."

"Why? What has changed?"

"I was approached by this girl, Emma Hughes. And she said that the lower members of the pack are terrified. They live by survival of the fittest there. Caleb forced her father to make the silver that wounded my mate. So I told her I would see what I could do if anything."

Dad goes silent at my explanation. Resting his elbows on the arms of his chair, fingers steepled and resting against his bottom lip while deep in thought.

"So you want to challenge Jeffrey for Dakota and his pack over the information from *one* girl?" Dad asks slowly.

"Yes. I know I should get more intel, but even Dakota said that Caleb mocked her for protecting Quilla, a human, who is weaker than her. And I know what Emma said was the truth. I made sure she wasn't another trap." I pause. "So what is the best way to go about this? Should I publicly challenge him?"

"I have a thought in mind, but for right now keep your head low, and see if Jeffrey makes another move. I will say though, trust in yourself and K if Jeffrey would make a move before I figure out a plan." Dad says.

"Yes, Alpha. Thank you for hearing me out."

"Anytime, son."

I walk out of my father's office and I see Dakota's car pull in across the street, so I make my way towards the front door with a smile on my face.

"Did you have an informative conversation, Kai?" My mother asks me as she again meets me in the junction between the kitchen and the foyer.

"Yes, I did.

"I am so glad that you have found a mate, and she makes you so happy." Mom says after noticing my smile and the direction of my stare.

"So am I, Mom. Every time I turn around, she has learned something else about herself that makes her an even stronger alpha and a stronger mate."

"I can tell. You have the same love and admiration that your father had on his face when I chose him as my mate." Mom tells me with a smile. "Go on over. I'm sure she wants to see you too, Kai."

I give my mother a kiss on the cheeks and I walk out the door while reaching out for my girl.

"Hey Babe."

"Oh hi. The door is open, come on in."

Dakota

Just as I flop down on the couch, Kai comes in the front door, and I pat the cushion beside me, telling him to sit with me. When he does, he puts his left arm around my shoulder, pulling me closer to his side, and for an instant, I wonder if he will be able to pick up on any of the silver lingering in my blood. Every now and then I still pick up a whiff of the metallic scent, so I hold my breath for a few heartbeats. When I am satisfied that he's not having a reaction, I relax further into his side, suddenly feeling exhausted.

"How's Quilla?"

"She's a little better, but still not feeling all that well." I say, giving her an out if she wants to run more trials tomorrow.

"You seem tired too, are you okay?" Kai asks as he rubs my back soothingly.

"Yeah. I guess I'm just worried about Quilla."

I hate to lie to him, but I know for a fact that if I told him what I was trying to do, he'd try to talk me out of it, and I need to do this. I need this ace up my sleeve that no one will expect.

"Okay. Come on, Love. Let's go to bed then and rest."

Kai picks me up, and carries me up the steps and into my room. He gives me a long and loving kiss as he sets me down on the bed and crawls in with me, and as we settle into one another's arms, we let sleep take us both into its blissful darkness.

Chapter Fifty-One
DAKOTA

The next morning when I get out of bed to head over to the bathroom I reach out to Quilla before I hop in the shower.

"Hey, are you coming to school or do you want to run another round tonight?"

"We can do another round if you want. Or if you want to skip classes too, we can try to run a few." Quilla replies.

"Okay. Let me tell Kai and I will be over soon."

I go back to my room after I finish my shower to find him sitting on the side of my bed tying his shoes.

"Hey Babe. Quilla's still sick, so I'm going to spend the day with her to make sure she's okay."

"Okay, Love," Kai says with a smile.

"I love you." I tell him and, to remind myself, this is why I am doing what I am doing. It's because I love him so much that I want to give him one less thing to worry about. Especially if he's going to challenge Jeffrey for me and his pack.

"Love you too, Dakota."

He stands to give me a quick kiss on the lips, and when he leaves for class, I again grab another change of clothes and go over to Quilla's.

I pull into Quilla's driveway fifteen minutes later, and my friend greets me in the doorway as I walk up her steps.

"Morning. My parents are already gone for work, so we have the house to ourselves." Quilla says by way of greeting.

"Cool. That's less eyes and ears to worry about overhearing us."

We head down to her basement again and, like the last time, I see the table and chair set up in the middle of the room. There is another, smaller table that is set against the opposite wall, and resting in the center is the lead-lined box with another steaming pot of herbal tea next to it.

"Okay, so we're going to start with the second tube first. We need to get you used to that one before we move up." Quilla explains.

"Alright. You know best. Let's do this." I say as I take a seat and extend my arm for her.

Quilla again inserts the IV catheter in my vein and tapes the tube to my skin. I watch her pull the half-empty syringe from the box, and as she brings it closer to me, I realize that while I do still feel like my skin is crawling, it's not as bad as yesterday. When she pushes the rest of the liquid silver in my veins, I brace myself for the heat and tingling that I felt before, but it doesn't come. The only thing I feel is a calm warmth flooding my body. Like when you drink a nice, hot bowl of soup and it just warms your belly. This lasts for about ten minutes before the sensation fades from my body, and I breathe out a sigh of relief that it seems to be working. I may be able to *actually* become immune to silver.

"You okay, Dakota?" Quilla asks as she makes notes in the notebook she's holding again.

"Yeah, I'm fine. This might actually work, Quilla. I didn't feel as much this time."

"You mean you doubted me this whole time?" She says while placing her hand on her chest in mock offense.

"No." I chuckle at her antics. "I did not doubt you one bit. I doubted myself. If my body could handle what we were about to put it through."

"Well, you're doing amazing." Quilla says as she hands me a cup of herbal tea. "Let's take a break so you can heal a bit. Then we can start on the next one."

I nod as I take a long sip of the tea, and I can feel it healing what parts of my body, were somewhat damaged from the liquid silver. Quilla and I head back upstairs to sit on her couch for about an hour while the drink works its magic. Just as we sit down, I see Quilla try to hide her grin behind her hand, but the blush that colors her cheeks and neck I can see plain as day.

I give her a sultry smile as I ask, "Is that the good doctor you're talking to?" Her eyes widen, and I just chuckle in response. "Your blush gave you away." I tell her. "Go on and talk to him. Besides, Imma raid your fridge for a snack."

I drink the remaining liquid from my mug and bring it with me when I get up off the couch to set it on the counter beside the sink and open the refrigerator while giving Quilla some time alone to mentally talk to her mate.

After about twenty minutes, she comes into the kitchen with a smile on her face.

"You two have a good *conversation?* I say while wiggling my eyebrows.

"Oh, my God." Quilla rolls her eyes. "We did not do *that,* Dakota Shade!"

I laugh at the mortified half-smile on her face, "But you wanted to, am I right?"

"Okay! If you can joke about my love life, then you are ready to get back to work!" Quilla says while clapping her hands together.

I shake my head as I follow her back downstairs for another round. And while this one is a little stronger than the last, I can feel my body accepting it a little bit quicker, and I breathe through the heat and pain that flows through my body.

"You're doing great, Dakota." Quilla says while she makes more notes and again hands me a warm mug of tea.

"Yeah. I figured it would be worse than this, to be honest."

"Oh, we haven't gotten to the level of pure silver yet. That is going to be the real test. We still technically have like three trials before we even get to the pure silver."

"Do you think we can start on the pure silver sooner since I'm able to handle the others better than you thought?" I ask.

Before Quilla can answer me, we hear the doorbell ring from upstairs, and for an instant, I go on high alert. As far as I know, we aren't expecting anyone to come by. I begin to make my way upstairs to see who just rang the doorbell, but when I look over my shoulder to tell Quilla my plan, I see she has a wide smile on her face, and I instantly know who's knocking on my friend's door.

"Oh, my God! He's here!?" I exclaim.

Quilla rushes upstairs to greet her mate, and I decide to stay here and give them a moment to be alone together because, I know if Kai was away from me for a long time, I would want privacy too. As I wait, I go over to the table near the back wall to set my empty mug next to the pot of tea, and I side-eye the lead box for a moment.

I glance back to the stairwell and I still hear Quilla's laugh and a deep Irish lilted voice mumbling from the living room. I look back to the box and I gently lift the lid, revealing four more syringes nestled in the black foam forms. My knees begin to wobble at the proximity to the pure silver, and the familiar white-hot pain dances in the tips of my fingers. I snatch my hand back and shut the lid, and the sensation vanishes.

Oh, this is gonna be rough.

I begin to hear footsteps echo down the stairs and the voices of my friend and her mate get louder, so I make my way back to the chair on rubbery knees. I am a few steps away from my chair when Quilla and what I assume is Atticus enter the basement. I turn to see this tall, red-headed, green-eyed man before me. His hair is tied up in a man-bun at the top of his head with a few pieces hanging down near his face, and he's in a pair of blue jeans and a gray t-shirt. But before I can even say hi to him, I swear I hear a pop of a gun echo in the room, and I feel a sudden burn in my shoulder follow shortly after.

I come to the realization that my best friend's fucking mate just shot me.

After the shock of getting shot fades from my mind, pain starts to envelop my shoulder, and I feel blood start to trickle out of the wound.

"Atticus! What the hell?" I see Quilla push him hard on both shoulders, but he stands as still as a statue. His green eyes staring a hole into my own. "I trusted you! Why did you shoot my friend, you asshole?!" Quilla continues to shriek.

As I stand there holding my bleeding shoulder with my other hand, I feel something odd begin to happen, and as I pull my hand away, I see Atticus' mouth tilt into a half smile.

He grabs Quilla gently by the shoulder to turn her towards me. "Rosie, look." He says as he points to me.

We all watch in tense silence as the silver bullet that's lodged in my shoulder suddenly eases itself out of the wound, falling to the floor with a metallic tink-tink as it hits the tile. I look from the bullet, now lying on the floor, to my shoulder, which is now healing right before my eyes, and then over to Atticus, who is sporting a confident smile, while Quilla is still mortified at the situation.

"How did you know my body would react like that?" I direct the question to Atticus. "Oh, by the way, what a greeting. I hate to see how you'd say hello if I really pissed you off." I say with a mischievous grin.

"My apologies, Dakota, but I needed to catch you off guard for my test to work." Atticus says as he bends his neck to the side by way of submission. "Besides, from what Rosie has told me about your progress, I had a good feeling you'd react that way."

"Rosie, huh?" I tease Quilla, and her face turns red again as she turns from both me and her mate for a moment.

I watch Atticus then walk over to the lead box and open it for a moment to look inside. Quilla's head snaps over to her mate, a flash of fear washing over her face before it fades when he steps away a moment later. He then pulls her into, his side, and I know it's his way of telling her he's alright, and he looks over at me again with a smile on his face.

"Looks like you healed nicely." Atticus croons.

"Lucky for you. At least I won't have to kick your ass for hurting me." I smirk.

He chuckles as he looks at Quilla again. The love for her is evident in his eyes, and I find myself smiling at them.

"Darling, I think you can step up to the pure silver now."

"He calls you 'darling' too?" I say into Quilla's mind.

"Oh, shut up. I don't pick on you when Kai calls you 'Love' now do I?" She scolds while trying to hide the light shade of pink coloring her cheeks.

I just laugh in her mind as I pull away, but I can't keep the smile off my face. Atticus sees her trying to hide her face in her hands, and he tenderly grabs her chin in his fingers and makes her look at him.

"Are you embarrassed of me being here, Rosie?"

"What?! No!"

"I'm just giving her a hard time about your nicknames for her, Atticus." I say, butting in on the conversation. "See, Quilla here didn't tell me anything about you." I add, giving her the stink eye.

"I see. Well, it all happened fairly quickly." Atticus says while pulling Quilla closer to him, and he gives her a loving kiss to her forehead.

Quilla then gives him a quick peck on the lips as she brushes past him and over to the lead box to pull out the pure silver syringe. Atticus backs up a few steps as Quilla walks over to me, but I hold my hand up before she can get closer.

"Hang on, Chica." I say as I glance between her and her mate. "I'm glad you two met one another and I hope you keep falling deeper and deeper in love." I glance over to Quilla. "And I know it's scary to have a mate and constantly doubt that you are worthy of them." I tell her as I pick up on the same thoughts that enter my own mind at times. "But as you know, having a mate is amazing. They complete you in ways you never knew you were missing before they came into your life." I say while noticing the agreement shining in Quilla's eyes at my words. "But just know, Atticus, that if you hurt my girl in any way, I will take personal offense to that, and I will make your life a living hell. She isn't just my Tamer, she is my best friend, and no one hurts her and gets away with it Scott-free." I warn while letting my alpha power pulse through the room to emphasize my point.

Atticus doesn't miss a beat as he kneels before me, his head bent to the left side to bear his neck fully to me in submission.

"I understand, Miss Dakota. And as you say, so shall it be."

I lock eyes with Quilla, and I notice the tears pooling at the corners of her eyes, and I go over to hug my girl.

"Thank you, Dakota. That means so much to me."

"Anytime, Quilla." I say. *"Besides, I can tell he loves you unconditionally. But putting a little fear in his heart never hurts."* I joke as I release her from my embrace.

I walk across the room, taking a seat on the chair again, then showing her my arm with the IV line in it and give her a confident smile. "Let's finish what we started."

Quilla approaches me with the syringe, and I take a calming breath as the familiar hot poker feeling crawls up my skin, and I can't stop the shiver that runs down my spine.

"I would give her this last injection in three sessions, Rosie. Hopefully, it will get easier and easier each time it's administered." Atticus instructs.

Quilla nods as she pushes the advised amount of silver into my vein, and in the next beat of my heart, all I feel is mind-numbing pain, and I can't help the cry that erupts from my lips.

Chapter Fifty-Two
DAKOTA

It's in that instant I knew this was the part of the trial that was going to make or break me. So, I find my connection to Kai, and what I do next leaves a bad taste in my mouth, but I know I need to do it.

I grab a hold of the invisible string that connects my soul to his, and I quickly visualize a stone wall between us, effectively cutting his mind off from mine as the pure silver in my veins feels like it's melting me from the inside out.

This is so similar to what Caleb bit me with that I start to have flashes of him leaping at me, biting me all over again. Every breath burns like fire in my chest. I feel my body get heavier and heavier, and I don't realize I've fallen out of the chair until I hit the floor and pain explodes in my mind. As I writhe on the floor, I keep two thoughts in my mind. Keep my mental barrier up from Kai and breathe. Even if it's little pants, just keep breathing.

Atticus

I watch as Dakota struggles to fight against the silver in her veins, her cries and groans of pain filling the room, and I am thankful we are in an underground basement with one heavy door leading to the backyard. I look at Quilla, and I can feel my mate's agony like it's my own. She hates to see her friend like this, and I don't blame her. She takes a step forward when Dakota makes a high-pitched scream as the silver works deeper into her body, and I wrap my arm around Quilla's waist and pull her tight against my chest.

"Atticus, let me go!" She yells as she tries to pull out of my arm.

"Rosie, please stay here. You have to remember she's a Were, so she is stronger than she looks, and she may hurt you without meaning to."

We watch Dakota roll over towards the door, and she looks up for a moment, her breath coming out in pain-filled pants.

"What... the... hell?"

I glance up in time to catch a dark figure dart away from the door, but it was too quick for me to tell if it was human or animal. That doesn't stop Dakota, though. She stands on rubbery legs, and she stumbles over to the door, running into the couch and the recliner that sits in the middle of the room facing the TV that's mounted on the wall. I watch in awe as she continues to fight her way to the door.

"Stay here for now, Rosie."

I follow Dakota but keep a few paces behind her just to see what she will do. She grabs for the doorknob with trembling fingers, and she fights back another wave of pain as she turns the knob to open the door. She tries to look around for the figure, but she stumbles as her foot catches on the kick plate of the door. I rush to her side, grabbing her under the arms to steady her, and I grit my teeth as I feel the silver that flows in her veins burn into my skin.

"What did you see, Dakota?" I force myself to ask.

"A figure." She pants. "I think. Or... I could have been seeing things."

My hand continues to burn where I'm still holding her, and I realize that the silver is staying near the top of her skin, just like the books we read said it would. I am both elated that this is working, but sad that the pain is this intense for her. Even with me just meeting Dakota, I can already tell that Kai is extremely blessed to have a mate as strong as this female before me. Even with this debilitating trial, she is still the first one to push herself with everything she has to protect her pack.

"Quilla?" I say over my shoulder, and I feel my mate walk up behind me and place her hand on my shoulder. "Please take Dakota inside while I check the grounds to make sure no one is around."

"Okay. Come on Dakota. Let's rest on the couch."

"Please...make sure everything is safe." Dakota breathlessly pleads.

"Yes, I will, Dakota."

When I am satisfied that Quilla and Dakota are safe inside and on the couch, I close the door behind me and now that the silver is no longer in my nose; I take a fresh scent of the area around me, and a grin forms on my lips.

"You little nosey asshole." I chuckle. "The forest will have bloody eyes as long as you're around."

I walk back into the basement and then close the door behind me, making sure it is locked before pulling the curtain closed. I'm not going to make it bloody easy for him to eavesdrop on people. It's been a running joke we've had over the last 375 years.

"Atticus, is everything okay? Who was around here?" Quilla asks as she sees me walk over to the couch.

She closes the distance between us, and I pull her to my chest while I will my calmness to fill her mind.

"It's alright. Everything is secure, Rosie."

I look over to Dakota, and while she's still in visible pain, I can tell it's starting to lessen. I kiss Rosie on the forehead and I release her from my arms with a small smile.

"Rosie, why don't you go and get Dakota some Wolfsbane tea? That will help ease the pain some, now that the silver has run its course."

Quilla nods as she goes over to the table where she has the kettle set up, and she pours the liquid into a mug. I walk over to Dakota and kneel in front of the couch, lifting my right arm and crossing it over my chest, while placing a closed fist over my heart, and I bare my neck to the up-and-coming alpha before me.

"Miss Dakota. I wanted to let you know that you will be an amazing alpha one day."

"What makes you say that?" She asks, her voice sounding tired and raw from her screams.

"Because, even though you were in an incredible amount of pain when you felt that we were in danger, you were the first one to force yourself to that door."

"I was just thinking that I needed to protect what was mine."

"Aye. Spoken like a true alpha. I will be proud to call you my alpha one day if you so choose."

She's quiet for a moment, and when I look at her, she has tears in her eyes. I give her a kind smile while reaching into my pocket to pull out a red kerchief to wipe her eyes.

"Thank you, Atticus. That means a lot coming from someone who is already being led by a badass alpha like Tobias." She chuckles softly.

"Here you go, Dakota. Drink this for me." Quilla says, and she brings over a mug of tea.

I help Dakota sit up on the couch while Quilla takes a seat beside her. She hands Dakota the mug and helps her lift it to her mouth so she can drink and allow the liquid to heal and restore her body.

Quilla

After Dakota drinks two mugs of tea, she is feeling better to the point where she can go upstairs to get a long, hot shower and go home to rest.

"Tomorrow is our off day from school, so you can come back over any time to do another trial." I tell my friend.

"Okay. Yeah, I'll see you then. Bye Atticus. It was nice to meet you, but maybe next time, don't fucking shoot me." She grins as she walks out the front door.

Atticus watches out the dining room window to make sure Dakota gets to her car safely. It's weird seeing him in my house. It's almost like meeting him in Montana was a dream, but here in my own house, I know it's one hundred percent real. He looks over at me, like he can feel me watching him, and shoots me a bright smile before he joins me on the couch and rests his arm around my shoulders.

"You did an amazing job, you know that, Rosie?"

"No, *we* did a great job. I wouldn't have been able to help Dakota if it wasn't for you."

I lean in to kiss him, but I'm stopped short when I hear two car doors slam and I see both of my parent's cars are in the driveway. Atticus gets up to dart out the backdoor, but at that moment I know I am tired of hiding this part of me. Tired of hiding who Atticus is to me.

"Atticus, wait."

He turns to me, and I see the silent question on his face, and I don't even have to look into his mind to know what he's thinking.

"We don't have to tell them about you if you don't want to. Just that you are my boyfriend. But I don't want to hide you anymore."

He walks over to me and cups his hand behind my neck to make me look up at him, and the loving smile that blooms over his face is enough to make me melt right here in his arms.

"If I meet them, we should tell them everything, Rosie."

I hear the front door open, and I don't have time to think things over, but I trust Atticus to know the best decision. And right now with a Tamer being mated to a Werewolf, he's right, my parents need to know everything.

"Quilla, who is this?" Mom asks in shock as she takes in Atticus' hand still caressing my neck.

"Mom, Dad. I have some things to tell you."

We are all gathered around the table after Atticus insists he makes dinner for everyone. So, once he serves us the pork chops, green beans, and roasted potatoes, the questions begin flying.

"What is going on, Quilla?" Dad asks.

"Well, let us start with formal introductions." Atticus offers. "My name is Atticus Remington, and I am the doctor for a large...uh..." Atticus pauses and looks over at me. "Ah, bloody hell, I'll just say it. I am the doctor for a large Werewolf pack out in Montana, and your daughter is my mate."

"Okay... well what a way to cut to the point there, Mr. Remington." Dad says.

"Is that all?" Mom asks.

"No," I say.

I look at Atticus, and he smiles at me as he takes my hand, intertwining his fingers with mine, before lifting our hands to his lips to brush an encouraging kiss over my knuckles.

"I also found out that I am a Tamer." I say with pride. "Do you know what that is?"

"So let me guess, Atticus, you are a... Werewolf?" Dad asks.

"Aye... I mean yes, I am." Atticus says with a cringe at using old-time dialogue.

"Oh, boy." Dad scrubs at his face while looking at my mother. "Guess it's finally caught up to the Rose line again."

"What has caught up?" Atticus asks with a sharpness to his tone.

"Quilla, yes, I know what a Tamer is. Your great-great grandfather was a Tamer, and he lived in this area too. But as far as I know, it's been two hundred and fifteen years since there has been another Tamer, at least again in the Rose family line." Dad explains.

"We honestly had our suspicions when you said you needed to make a sudden trip out of state." Mom offers.

"Even though I'm not a full-fledged Tamer, I can still pick up on some *feelings* at times. And I could feel you willing us to let you go, to somehow understand that you would be safe with who you were going with," Dad explains.

"Wow. This is a shock to hear." I say. "But at least I know now where I got it from."

"Your great-great granddad was an amazing man from what I hear. I was told stories about him from my granddad, that Frances was shared between two packs. I can't remember the names of the packs off hand, but I know the one thing he was good for was something with silver."

"What?! So Frances Rose *is* my ancestor?" I shout.

"You've heard about him?" Dad asks.

"Aye. Quilla and I were just recently doing research on the correlation between silver and half-blood Were's, and we came across his name." Atticus says.

"From what we read, Frances heard about the possibility of a silver immunity, and with what research he could find at the time, he made some adjustments to it when one of the Half-Were alphas realized he may be able to become immune. But Frances' research only provided the Were with a higher tolerance." I say.

"Aye, and I think you figured out the missing component all this time, Rosie. And that was making the silver into a liquid instead of a solid like they used back then. Train the body from the inside out to handle the silver instead from the outside in." Atticus says as he pulls me to his chest in a tight and loving embrace. "Have I told you how proud I am of you lately?"

I giggle as I pull back from him. "Only every second of every day."

"I'm happy for you, Quilla." Mom says. "You seem like a nice man, Atticus."

"And I know this goes without saying, but take care of my little girl. She's the only child we had, and I know she's going to be around a lot of Were's now that she knows that she is a Tamer and that she is a mate to you."

"I'm shocked you know about us. Mr. Rose." Atticus says.

"Well, again, when you have the family history like I do, you know there are other things that go bump in the night." Dad chuckles.

"Atticus... can you?" Mom pauses, and I see a slight blush color her cheeks, and I grin at my mate.

"She wants to see your wolf, Babe." I chuckle. "Actually, I would like to see him as well. I've never met Atti here in this world."

"All you have to do is ask, Rosie."

He stands up and tugs his shirt over his head, and my eyes greedily take in my mate's strong form and his black and gray mating mark.

"Oh my, Quilla. You must have to beat the women off him." Mom giggles.

"Nah. I know he only has eyes for me. He's mine, and everyone will know it." I say as I show her my own marking on my arm.

We watch as Atticus phases before us. It looks like it would hurt like hell, but I can feel him in the back of my mind, and there is not a blip of pain from him. After a few breaths, we see a red wolf with a white tuft of fur in the middle of his chest staring back at us.

"That is amazing. I have never in my life met a real Were." Dad says.

The wolf snorts at Dad's remark as he trots over to Mom and me. He nuzzles Mom's hand and licks her fingers as his way of saying hello. As I look at the wolf before me, I can tell that Atticus is still there even though he took Atti's form.

"You are regal, Atticus. You know that?" I say in wonder.

"Thank you, Rosie. I'm glad this didn't scare you, and I'm sorry for not showing you my phasing sooner. But I'm glad I was able to show this to you in a safe environment."

"If you tearing apart another male didn't scare me, I don't think there is anything you can do that would."

He nods his big wolf head at me, then he gathers his discarded pants in his mouth and takes them into the bathroom to put them on. He comes back out a moment later, and as he's putting his hair up in his man-bun style, he grabs his shirt, but I enter his mind to stop him. He grins as he takes his seat next to me while draping the fabric over his knee. I immediately put my hand on his neck, and even though he was relaxed before, he becomes even more relaxed as I touch his marking with my own.

"Would you like to spend the night here, Atticus?" Mom offers.

"And since I'm sure you two would like to be in the same room, all I ask is that you two... you know what? Just don't let me hear you." Dad cringes.

"I understand Mr. Rose. Thank you both for opening your home up to me."

"You mean you're going to behave?" I ask incredulously.

"Oh, your father said that he better not hear you. So, you best be quiet tonight, Rosie."

My stomach drops at his teasing tone, but the fire that lights in my core makes me want to test just how much I can take before I come undone in his arms.

"Careful, Darlin'. I may just give your parents nightmares on how loud I can make you scream my name tonight."

"You wouldn't!" I say in mock horror.

I just hear him laugh in my mind, and later that night, true to his word, he allows me to enjoy some pleasure trips quietly via his deft fingers in that one place that makes me see stars.

But with his expertly placed tongue and his thumb teasing my clit, he makes me crash over that edge again where I have no choice but to scream his name not once, not twice, but three times before he finally relents for the night.

And while part of me is mortified that my parents are hearing this, the other, bigger part of me, does not care one bit. Because while in the safety of Atticus' arms tightly wrapped around me, I feel like I am impenetrable, and I hold on to that with every ounce of my being.

"I'll be sure to apologize to your parents in the morning, but I just couldn't help it, Rosie," Atticus says as he gives me a gentle kiss on the neck.

I turn to give him a loving, sound kiss on the lips, and I tuck my head against his chest, letting my cheek rest against the trunk of the tree marked into his skin, and we let blissful sleep pull us into darkness.

Chapter Fifty-Three

DAKOTA

When I leave Quilla's place, the sun is starting to set, and in the dying light of the evening, I find myself fighting to keep my eyes open as I drive home.

This part of the trial is going to kick my ass. Come on, stay awake, damn it.

"We got this, Dakota. I'm trying to help you stay awake." Kota says, as I feel her nip at my neck in an effort to help keep my eyes open.

"Thank you. How are you feeling?"

"I'm a little tired, but I'm mostly itchy. But no matter how much I roll or rub against a tree, it won't stop. So, I assume that's a side effect of the silver."

"Remind me to tell Quilla about that tomorrow."

I finally pull up to my house, and I can tell my parents have already turned in early for the night. So, I force my legs to carry me into the house, but I only get as far as the couch before I have no choice but to collapse face down onto the cushions. I already feel myself dozing off, so before I fully pass out, I open my mind to Kai and I feel his love and a bit of worry flood my mind before sleep takes it all away.

Kai

I hear a car pull up at Dakota's house, and when I look out the window, I see that it's her car in the driveway. I go to reach for her, but for some reason, I don't feel her like I usually do. I push for her again, and this time I am met with her presence in my mind, but it's exhausted. So, I make sure she feels every ounce of love I can muster through the bond, but I can't help the blip of worry that sneaks in there too.

I make my way over to her house and I find her on the couch, lying on her belly with one arm hanging off the side. When I gently shut the door behind me, I noticed that her shoes are still on too.

What the... I hope she's okay. Is Quilla that sick where it's making Dakota this tired just by taking care of her?

I walk over to the couch and I slowly take her sneakers off, then pull down the blanket from the back of the sofa and drape it over her prone body. I then take a seat on the floor in front of the couch, while running my fingers up and down her arm in a soothing motion to keep her asleep for a while.

After about an hour, she finally wakes up when I began playing with a piece of her hair.

"I'm sorry, Love. I just couldn't help it." I say with a small smile as I push the lock of hair behind her ear.

"Oh no. How long have I been here?" She asks as she rubs her face and sits up on the couch.

I move to sit beside her while pulling her to my side. "About an hour. You were already asleep when I came over." I kiss her on the crown of her head as I rub my hand down her back. "You've been awfully tired when you come back from Quilla's the last two days. Is she that bad?"

"What did you and your dad talk about?" Dakota asks while ignoring my question.

I look away from her while leaning my head against the back of the couch and let a breath out through my nose.

"See? We both have things we don't want to talk about."

At her words, I have half a mind to demand she tell me what she's doing over at Quilla's, but the exhausted look on her face makes me hold my tongue.

Dakota must see the emotion on my face because she rests her hand on my knee and says, "Please, Babe. I don't have the energy for this right now. Can we try to relax and talk about all this another day?"

"Okay, Love." I let out a defeated sigh. "You are the voice of reason."

"And don't you forget it." She gives me a playful smile, even if it only lights her face up for a heartbeat, but it's there. "Oh! And guess what?"

"What?"

"I just found out that Quilla and your pack doctor, Atticus, are to-gether."

"Seriously? Quilla and Atticus? I did not see that coming at all. But come to think of it, they would be a great pair." I smile.

"Yeah, I knew they've been talking back and forth after you were drugged with the Wolfsbane, but apparently he's been helping her more than Quilla let on. And when…she needed to do research on something, your father sent her to Montana all last week, and they met face to face."

"Damn," I shake my head in disbelief, "I never would have thought my father would be a matchmaker for anyone, let alone Atticus. But I'm happy for him. I know he was getting a little desperate for a mate, so maybe Dad thought a Tamer would be a good thing to help keep Atticus' wolf under control, and it just happened that they were fated mates."

"Oh, they are totally in love with one another. I met him today too."

"Seriously? Oh man, you should have told me. I haven't seen him for a few months. He mostly keeps to himself now that I'm older." I smile as I run my hand through my hair, and a nervous smile plays at my lips. "I was the biggest thorn in his side when I was younger. I was always getting into trouble, fighting, and doing anything risky. So I had my fair share of scrapes and broken bones that needed to be mended by him."

"Aww. Well, I'll have to see if he will stop by sometime to meet up with you again," Dakota says, but I can tell what little bit of energy she had is starting to wane again.

"Come on, Love. Let's go to bed."

I stand and place one arm behind her back and the other under her legs so I can pull her close to my chest while I carry her up the stairs and into her bedroom. I gently sit her down on her side and while I walk around the bed to get to my side, I tug off my shirt so she can be skin-to-skin with me and place gentle, loving kisses on her temple, shoulders and each finger until we both fall asleep.

Dakota

I begin to wake up when the sun starts to shine through my closed eyelids. I moan at the rude interruption to my slumber and turn over to reach for Kai, but all I find is an empty bed, the sheets cool to the touch in the absence of his body heat.

I wonder where he is?

I look at his pillow and I see a handwritten note sitting on the white cotton fabric. I smile as I read the note from him, but yet I feel a pang of guilt for how tired I was last night, and I didn't have the nerve to tell him what I'm doing.

Hey, Love.

Mom wanted me to run a few errands for her today. You were sleeping so well that I didn't want to wake you. If you need me or just miss me, reach out and I will be right there.

Love always,

Kai.

"Good morning, Babe. I got your note. You still should have woken me up. But I love the note you left though."

"I know, but with you taking care of Quilla over the last two days, you deserved to sleep in a little bit."

Again, that damn little pinprick of guilt enters my mind at his words.

Just three more sessions and I will have the immunity I've been looking for. I tell myself.

"How long do you think you'll be out for?"

"A few hours at least. Mom wanted me to take her car into the shop for some service, and then she wanted me to go to the grocery store for a few things for dinner."

"Okay, Be safe." I pause. *"And Kai?"*

"Yes, Love?"

"I love you with everything that I can give you."

"I know you do, Dakota. And I love you and always will 'til my last breath." Kai says, and I feel his love and admiration flood through his end of the bond, and I embrace it like the lifeline that it is.

He pulls back from my mind, and I just lie there for a moment, wondering if not for the first time, if I should just tell him what I'm doing. But then the thought that he didn't tell me what he and his father talked about enters my mind and, like I said last night, we both have secrets right now.

So with that, I get my shower and I head downstairs only to find the house still empty.

"Where the hell are my parents?" I ask out loud.

"Oh, I talked them into going out for a while so I could have some privacy with you, Dakota."

I whip around to the living room, and there on my couch is Tobias in a gray button-up shirt and black slacks, with his black hair gelled back into a professional style.

"Tobias! You scared the shit out of me!" I say while clutching my racing heart.

It's then that I realize he was masking his presence from me. The alpha ruling over his pack in the most stealthy of ways.

"I do apologize, Dakota." He croons as he stands up and nonchalantly walks over to me, and for some reason I am frozen in place. When he looks into my eyes, he gives me a slight smile. "So, how's the training going?"

"What?" I squeak.

"Did I catch you off guard?"

Holy shit, He's talking about silver immunity. How did he figure out it was me? Wait a minute.

"So you were the figure I saw yesterday?" I accuse.

He gives me a smirk and steps back a few paces to give me space. "You don't get to be as old as I am and have a pack as big as I do if you don't have eyes and ears everywhere. I know what all members of my pack do at all times. Just like I knew that something was going on between Atticus and Quilla before they even met one another. Why do you think I had her go and see him? I had my suspicions that they were mates, but they just needed help to meet face-to-face, and I knew that Atticus wouldn't just up and leave his patients. So, when Quilla asked me about researching silver and half-bloods, I figured that was a good segway for them to meet. Now, I will say, it was a bit of a shock when I found out the research was for you, but then I found myself understanding your thought process." Tobias says as he slowly paces back and forth across my living room floor. "What you are doing is both reckless and dangerous, but also courageous. You didn't know if this would work to your advantage or kill you with the first trial." He pins his eyes on mine as he lets out a frustrated sigh. "And as much as I hate to say this, you are also right in keeping this from my son for now. I know for a fact he would have tried to stop you. Hell, I wanted to when I put all the pieces together."

"Oh boy, I figured you would have put everything together sooner or later. But I thought you'd at least be the cool alpha and let me think I got away with getting one over on ya." I joke as I sit down on the couch to cover my face with my hands.

I lift my head to see Tobias smile as he joins me on the couch but then it fades as he says, "When I saw you try to fight through the pain when you caught me looking in Quilla's door, I knew I had to let you finish this trial. You were in so much pain, I could feel it through the bond we share, and I knew you would do anything you could to protect Quilla and Atticus from any threat. And just between me and you, sometimes I feel like you are even more strong-willed than I am."

He drops his eyes at the admission, and I know he just showed me something I'm sure only his mate sees, weakness. And I realize in my next breath that what he said is complete bullshit.

"I don't believe that for a second, Tobias Huntington. You just said it yourself. You didn't get to be as old as you are or have a pack as big as you do if you weren't a strong alpha. We *all* have strengths and *weaknesses*. I'm just trying to overcome one of mine."

He laughs after a moment and brings me in for a tight hug. When he releases me, I see his eyes are bright with life and admiration for me.

"I don't know what we did for my son to be able to have a mate as wise as you are, but I thank The Great Luna every single day for you. And when it's time for me to either step down or for Kai to have his own pack to lead, I am beyond grateful he will have a smart, cunning, and out-of-the-box thinker like you to help lead at his side." He places a hand on my shoulder and gives it a small squeeze. "Let Quilla know to come over so she can help you get one step closer to becoming immune to silver."

He smiles at me as he gets up from the couch to leave, but he pauses at the door and turns back to me. "Also, Atticus told me that he shot you to see if silver would really hurt you. Shall I punish him for such a rude introduction?"

I laugh and shake my head. "No. I do understand why he did that, and he did apologize for his actions. But I did let him know that I can mean business if I needed to." I smirk as I let my alpha power flow through the room.

"Understood. Good luck, Dakota. And if anyone can become immune to silver, it's you."

With that he walks through the door, shutting it gently behind him and leaving me alone in my house once again.

"Damn." I chuckle. "I knew I couldn't get anything past him."

Quilla arrives thirty minutes later with the lead box in one hand and a thermos in the other after I told her we were busted by mister know-it-all Tobias.

"So he actually gave you his blessing to see this to the end?" Quilla asks.

"Yup." I say, popping the p.

"I guess I shouldn't be too shocked. I mean, you knew that he would find out eventually."

"Yeah." I sigh, "Come on, let's get this next one over with. Kai is out running errands, which again, Tobias probably set up to give us some privacy." I shake my head at the realization, and I feel a smile tug at my lips.

I lead Quilla into the dining room, taking my usual seat near the window, and prop my arm on the tabletop for her. She sits the lead box in the center and takes the partially used syringe out, twisting on a new needle as she turns to me.

"What, no IV today?" I tease, buying myself a little time before the all-too-familiar pain that I know will follow once she puts the needle under my skin.

"No, not since we are on a time crunch. Besides, I was doing the IV in case I needed to get the healing Wolfsbane into your body quickly. Which now we know we don't need to do." She says with a confident smile.

"Oh," I say with shock coloring my tone.

I never once thought about that through this whole thing. The possibility that something could have gone wrong where I would have needed a last-ditch life-saving method. Then Tobias' words come back to me, that I didn't know if it would work or kill me with the very first injection.

"Thank you." I say.

"For what?" Quilla chuckles.

"For protecting me. I didn't realize just how bad it could have been if this went south. You and your new mate," I give her a smirk, "thought of anything and everything that could go wrong, and you thought of a way to counteract that. So thank you for being the amazing Tamer that I knew you would become."

"It's all in a day's work, Chica." Quilla winks, but then her lips form a tight line and she says, "But Atticus was the one to have that forethought though. He's seen enough people over the years be poisoned and drugged, and even have variations of silver in their veins. And if he was quicker in getting their blood cleared, he would have been able to save them. So, it was a hard-learned lesson that I was able to advance with the healing Wolfsbane liquid."

I nod at her, at the knowledge of her mate's insecurities that she shared with me, and I can just imagine how hard it was on him to experience that.

"Well, let's make this immunity a first victory for you and your mate. Hit me, baby." I say with confidence.

Quilla ties off my arm again to help the vein pop to the surface, and she slides the needle under my skin, I feel the bite of silver hit my blood immediately, and I hiss at the contact. I close my eyes, and while the heat that I feel erupts through my body is still boiling, it doesn't make my chest tighten to the point of pain like it did yesterday. If I take slow, measured breaths, I can stay still in the chair and only groan occasionally as I can feel the silver continue to flow deeper into my body.

"You okay?" Quilla asks after a few moments.

"Yeah. It still hurts like a bitch, but it's a little bit more manageable this time around."

I open one eye, and I see Quilla looking at the syringe. Only one session left. Tomorrow is the make it or break it dose. I find myself looking forward to seeing if it works, but what if it doesn't? What if all this pain and fear is for nothing and I am still just as vulnerable to silver as I was when I started? I hear Kota growl in the back of my mind, and I don't even have to hear her words.

Worry about tomorrow's achievements or failures tomorrow.

Nothing you do today will change the outcome of something that hasn't even happened. So that's what I do. I will body to get used to the silver in my blood, to be the stronger one, and push back against the pain and weakness that tries to take me under.

Emma

I am walking through *his* house because I heard that he wanted to speak to Caleb about something to do with Alpha Kai and Miss Dakota. So, I quietly make my way over to Jeffrey's office, where thankfully, the door is left open a crack so I can see and hear inside. He's sitting on a high-backed red leather chair in front of a solid black desk with orange trim lines. The purple drapes that are closed behind him add to the darkness in the room. There are two gray female wolves at his feet, and the way they cringe with each brush of his hands through their fur makes my stomach crawl. I know he will use the girls later for his own sick pleasures against their will, but if the alpha makes it an order, you obey it or else.

"I am finished playing with those two. Either Dakota will understand that she belongs to me, or no other male will have her. She will force my hand to kill her if she doesn't come to her senses and accept me as her mate. As for that fucking mongrel Kai, I will kill him just to show every other wolf that comes here not to just up and claim females as his own."

"What are you going to do?" Caleb sneers.

"Why the fuck would I tell you that, Caleb?!" Jeffrey shouts, and the wolves at his feet flatten their ears to their skulls while trying to back away from his outburst. "Where do you think you're going? I didn't excuse you." He grabs both wolves by the scuff and the painful yelps only make his smile darken before his gaze lifts to Caleb's. "All you need to know is that their time together is coming to an end all too soon, under the coming dark sky."

I begin to back away as I hear his threat, and I have a feeling I know when he's going to attack Kai, but when I try to run, I stupidly kick the door and it creaks open. Both of their eyes are on me in an instant and I feel Jeffrey's oily alpha power pin me to the spot. Kai's power, while it was strong, held a kindness, a fairness to it, and I rather be held under Kai's power than this.

"Oh, look at what we have here, Jeffrey." Caleb croons darkly. "A little rat."

"Bring her here." Jeffrey snaps.

Caleb roughly picks me up by my shoulder, pulls me into the chamber, and throws me down on my knees in front of Jeffrey.

"Emma." He drawls. "Are you spying on us?"

"N—"

"Be careful how you answer that mutt." Jeffrey snaps as he backhands me across the cheek.

As I go tumbling backward from his brazen reaction, I hear Caleb and Jeffrey's laughter fill the room at my weakness against them.

"Oh, we are going to have fun with you. It's been so long since we had someone new to play with." Caleb rasps.

"She'll probably break before you even get started, Caleb." Jeffrey laughs.

I feel myself start to shake, fear taking root deep in my chest, and I know I am not strong enough like Dakota is to fight back. If I had only a fraction of the strength she does, that'd make me feel better about dying at their hands; at least I would go down kicking and screaming, but now? I am forced to keep my mouth shut at the horrors that I am sure are about to come my way.

Caleb grabs me by the back of the neck and pulls me into the middle of the room. He goes to snatch my shirt, intent on ripping it over my head, when we all hear a vicious snarl explode from the doorway. I look over to see a light gray wolf, his muzzle lifted in a threatening snarl, canines glinting in the low light of the room making them look even more deadly. His tail is held high, and from the hint of white at the tip, I know who this wolf is and my heart sinks for him.

"What is this, a meeting place for half-breeds?" Caleb goes to grab for my arm, and this time the wolf leaps for the Beta, tackling him to the ground due to his hulking size.

"Run, Emma." His gravelly voice fills my mind from the familial bond we share.

I stare at my cousin for a moment before I unknowingly take a step back.

"Cyrus, they'll kill you."

"Then I'll gladly let my last act be protecting my little cousin from these fuckers. Now go!"

He snarls again, and I do the very thing he tells me to do. I run.

Chapter Fifty-Four

KAI

While I am waiting for my mother's car to finish up in the shop, I decide to walk downtown. After about three blocks, I see a little quaint jewelry store, and I smile as I walk towards it. As I get closer to the door, I notice someone familiar on the other side of the street. The blonde-haired, blue-eyed girl from the university. The very one that told me about Jeffrey and his twisted way of leading.

Emma.

And I can see the fear written on her face, and it takes everything in me to stay on this side of the sidewalk and not run to this terrified girl and protect her. So, I make myself settle for a nod as I walk into the shop.

When I walk in, I immediately feel the tingling and nausea that comes from being around silver, and I notice there is a case full of it nestled in the left corner. I make my way to the other side of the store, rolling my shoulders to work the tingles out of my muscles when I hear the door ding again and I see Emma walk in and over to me.

"Hi, Emma. What are you doing here?" I ask quietly as I look over the various rings, bracelets, and necklaces in the glass case.

"I needed to let you know that *he* is getting worse." She says, her lips trembling.

I let a pulse of my power flow over her, to let her know she is safe with me, and for some reason, I swear she leans into my power more than she did last time. This gives her the courage to speak freely around me.

"I caught him saying that he was going to give Dakota one last chance. Either take him as her mate or he said *no other male will have her*. He plans on killing her if she doesn't go with him. And he is going to kill you as an example for other wolves coming here and not to claim a mate as quickly as you did."

Red fills my vision so quickly that I have to take a breath to keep my actions in check. The fact that this bastard just threatened my mate and the fear that is just pouring off this poor girl makes me and K want to phase and rip this asshole to pieces.

"I am working on it, Emma. I promise. Just give me a little more time. But please, do not do anything to make yourself a target." I plead.

"I think that may have happened if they didn't take an eye for an eye with my cousin. He stepped in to protect me a little bit ago."

I run my hand through my hair in aggravation. "Well, do not do anything else to put yourself or your cousin at risk if he got away. I promise it won't be too much longer."

Emma wordlessly nods and rushes out of the store with her head down.

As I go to leave the store myself, something catches my eye, making me pause. Sitting in the case on a faux cream neckline is a necklace with a round opal stone fixed in the center of the chain and it immediately reminds me of a moon, with the light and dark areas that mix on the surface, but the areas of light pinks, purples, and greens makes me think of how Dakota brings color to my life. So I flag down a woman in a khaki pencil skirt and a red blouse to buy it.

Dakota

This session lasted about twenty minutes before the tingling and the heat that filled my veins faded. I am just finishing up the cup of herbal tea when I see Kai pull his mother's car into the driveway and park it in the garage.

"Damn, that wore off just in time." I say, feeling a little stronger after this session. I'm tired, but it's the same as if I did a workout; an accomplished exhaustion.

"I'll run before he comes over. Where do you want your last session to be?" Quilla asks.

"Probably your place, but I'll let you know in the morning."

"Deal. See ya later."

Quilla rushes out the door, and I run upstairs to take a quick shower to wash any remaining silver from my skin, and I make it back to the couch ten minutes before Kai comes over. As soon as he opens the door, I see him trying to hide a smile but failing miserably.

"What's your issue?" I chuckle.

"Nothing." He grins.

"Bull. Now spill it." I say as I pat the space beside me on the couch.

He sits down and pulls a medium-sized navy box that would come from a jewelry store out from behind his back.

"While I was waiting for Mom's car, I found a little jewelry store, and when I came across this, I thought of you."

I take the box from his hands and I open it. The crisp snap of the new hinge revealing a stunning opal necklace resting on a dark gray pillow.

"Oh, Kai." I gasp. "It's beautiful."

"I was just about to walk out, but when I saw this sitting in the case, I knew I couldn't walk away. You are my beautiful, strong, smart, and loyal mate, and if it were not for The Great Luna, I never would have met you. You bring color to my life that I never knew I was missing. You help make me a stronger man, a stronger wolf, to see things from different perspectives. You challenge me to be better for you, and therefore our pack one day. And that *will* happen. You will be *mine* and only mine." He pulls me into his chest while rubbing my back, his hand lingering on the mate marking on my left shoulder blade. "This necklace is a promise that we will soon be whole, infinite, and complete."

I lift my head from his chest, and I can feel his love pouring over from his side of the bond. I see it in the way his eyes linger on mine, and he shows it by the tender way he kisses me when our lips meet a moment later. I pull back after a few heartbeats, a bit breathless from our short make out session, and I turn around while pulling my hair to the side.

"Put it on for me?"

He pulls the necklace from the box and fastens the clasp at the back of my neck, letting his fingers linger on my skin for a moment before he leans in and traces light kisses from behind my ear and down the length of my neck. I can't help the breathy moan that escapes my lips at his attention. Then he tugs my shirt down to let his lips and even the tip of his tongue trace the lines and curves of my marking, and that finally breaks me.

"Oh, Kai."

"Yes, Love?"

I feel him in my mind, his desire, and I don't know if it's just from being around him more or maybe it's from the silver sessions making my emotions run high, but he has no idea how badly I want to love him. To be a complete mate to him in every single sense of the word.

"What are you thinking, Love?"

At that question, I show him. Show him images of us in bed, doesn't matter whose, just in bed, tangled in sheets. His body hovering over mine. I let him feel my perception of him sinking slowly and deeply into me, his hips rolling in rhythm to my own. Both of us loving each other in the best way we can. Becoming *of one body* as mates do. Each of us finding our own release together. I hear a possessive growl rumble from Kai, his eyes glow bright brown as he tightens his arms around my stomach, pulling my back tighter against his chest.

"You have no idea how much I want to make those images real for us." He says, and I feel him harden behind me as the images replay in his head.

"Why can't we just bond and get it over with?" I whine. "Your father knows we are true mates. Why can't that be enough?"

"Because another has tried to claim you. And even though you have made it clear that you do not claim him, he is still not letting it go, and the fact that he claims that I swooped in and stole you away is enough to keep us from being able to bond and *other* things." Kai says, his voice dipping into a deep and seductive timber near the end.

"I know. Deep down I know. But I want you. I want *all* of you."

"You will get me in due time, Mate. I promise. I do not give up what is mine so easily. I am just waiting for the right time, and this is not the week for that."

"I trust you, Kai. I trust you know the best timing to fight for me."

The next morning, Kai and I get up for classes like usual, but this time I can feel Kota pacing in her forest. She's nervous about something.

"What's wrong?"

"I don't know. Something is coming; I can feel it. We need to get this last session done before tomorrow night. I just wish I knew why I have this feeling of being the only protector tomorrow."

"Okay. Just take a breath, Kota. We got this. Maybe it's just the anticipation of getting this close to the finish line that has you so worked up." I soothe.

She growls like she wants to believe my words, but there is still something nagging at her, and I feel it too. And it's like she said, I also feel the need to be the protector for tomorrow, but I do not for the life of me understand why. So, we go through the motions of school, which goes off without a hitch. The only thing that makes me feel worse is the fact that the fleabag duo is missing in action.

"Hey, I'm gonna come by your place after school to get this finished." I tell Quilla while we are at lunch.

"Sure thing." She looks at me for a moment, and with the slight tilt to her head, I can tell she's in her Tamer mode. I feel her trying to calm Kota and me, and it helps a little.

"What's wrong with you two? You're stressed. Is it about the last session?"

"We don't know. I just know we need to get this over with tonight."

"Okay. Yeah, come over after dinner." Quilla says.

Dinner at my place goes by in a blur. I only half hear Dad talking about another new client he was able to get on board at the bank, and Mom spent the day with Coraline again, I think, but everything runs together and I can't really say what was what.

Once dinner is over, I follow Kai upstairs and I act like I am going to pull a jacket out of my closet to wear tomorrow—I realized the other day that I did leave a jacket over at Quilla's, I just didn't know this would be the excuse to go and get it.

"Hey, Babe. I'll be right back. I left my jacket over at Quilla's and I need to get it. Love you."

I give him a kiss on the cheek and dash out the bedroom door before he can say anything. I know it's a shitty excuse to leave at six o'clock in the evening for a jacket, but right now I don't care.

I arrive at Quilla's house and, like always, she's waiting for me by the door, and she quietly ushers me in.

"Go downstairs, I have some tea warming up on the stove now, and I'll be down in a minute." She whispers. "My parents are upstairs." She points above her head with her index finger.

I nod my head and quietly make my way to the basement, sitting in the familiar chair and waiting for my friend to join me.

"Okay, here we go." Quilla says as she sets the kettle on a potholder in the middle of the table.

"So have you figured out what has you and Kota in a frenzy?"

"No." I sigh.

"Well, let's finish what we can control." Quilla says with determination in her eyes.

All I do is nod at her. I watch as she, for the final time, pulls out the syringe from the lead box, the last bit of silver sloshing around in the clear tube. She attaches a new needle and ties off my arm with a rubber tourniquet, and when the needle glides under my skin I feel... warmth flow through my body, and I brace for the pain.

I wait for a moment, two, three, but...nothing comes.

I feel a slow smile begin to pull at my lips, and I watch as Quilla puts the now empty syringe back in the box, and she turns back to me with her notebook in her hand, pen poised to take notes.

"How do you feel?"

"Fine. I only feel warm inside. Just like the first injection you gave me."

I want to jump for joy, but I keep myself glued to the chair and wait a few more minutes. I find myself looking down at my arm, at the crook of my elbow where the injections took place, and I swear I see little beads of something start to flow from my pores. Upon closer inspection, I see little silver bubbles oozing out of my skin, and the more I look over my arm, the more I see.

Silver, dotting my skin in every available pore.

"Uh, Quilla? Is this supposed to happen?" I ask while waving my hand over my arms.

Quilla steps closer, and I watch her face go from calm and assessing to full-on joy.

"We did it! This means your body is officially immune to silver!"

"How do you know for sure?" I ask.

"Atticus and I did some testing, and we figured out that once the blood got used to silver it would start to push it away. But of course, our testing was on a much smaller scale, but we figured the outcome would be the same when comparing the notes on solid silver and the higher threshold limits." Quilla says.

I smile as I look down at my arm again, and I run my index finger over the silver bubble, watching it smear over my skin with satisfaction blooming in my chest.

"We did it, Dakota. We can now give Kai one less thing to worry about. We can be a stronger alpha and protect what is ours to a higher degree now." Kota says.

"Yes, we are. Thank you for supporting me through this too."

"What you do, I do. Again, if I felt that this wouldn't have had any benefit to it, I would have said so long ago."

I feel her fade back into her forest, and I look up at Quilla, who is still wearing a bright smile on her face, and I jump from the chair with a laugh, pulling her in for a celebratory hug.

"Hey...a little tight there...Chica." She mumbles.

I pull back with an apologetic wince. "Sorry! Have I told you how freaking awesome you are?"

"Only about a million times. But I'm glad to hear it. Now, go get a shower to get that silver off you and go home to your mate. When are you going to tell him what you did?"

"I don't know. Maybe sometime after tomorrow. I still feel like something is going to happen. Once I know that everything is good, then I will go from there and tell him when I feel the time is right."

I make sure to grab my jacket that is still hanging on the back of the chair, take a shower, and head home. When I open the front door, the house is again dark and quiet. I don't see anyone on the couch, and when I go to look for Tobias' presence, I find he is asleep in his house across the street. No one pulls a stunt like he did and gets by with it the next time.

I make my way upstairs, and I open my bedroom door to find Kai lying in my bed, already asleep. I silently slip into bed beside him, running my hand over the broad expanse of his shoulders.

At my touch, while still sound asleep, he turns over to pull me into his chest with his arm wrapped around my waist. I snuggle deeper into his side and I let all the stress of the past few weeks fade from my accomplishment tonight. But that nagging feeling of what tomorrow will bring still nips at my heels.

I'll deal with this feeling tomorrow. I think as I fall asleep in the safety of my mate's arms.

CHAPTER FIFTY-FIVE

DAKOTA

I wake up the next morning and as I turn over to greet Kai, his side of the bed is empty. It's still warm, so I know he hasn't been gone for long. While I snuggle up to his pillow, I reach out to his mind so I can figure out where he is, but when I do, I can't find his end of the bond.

I begin to panic.

I jolt upright and start to untangle myself from the sheets when he walks back in my room still in the same sweatpants he slept in last night. I try to reach for him again, but I still can't find him.

Jumping from the bed, I meet him in the middle of the room, my arms wrapping around his torso and my head colliding against his chest, and I hold him tight as fear begins to take hold of my heart.

"What's wrong, Love?"

"I can't feel you." I whisper. "It's like I'm trying to look through a fog. I can somewhat feel a connection, but I can't find where it ends." I tell him, now that I can understand what his side of the bond feels like.

Oh my God, what if this is an undocumented side effect of the Silver Immunity? After all, from what I heard, that half-were was not mated.

Tears begin to burn my eyes, and the back of my throat turns ashen at the thought that I won't ever be able to talk to my mate in that intimate way again.

"It's okay, Love. It's just a new moon tonight."

"I'm sorry." I whisper, not hearing his words for a moment. Then they hit me. "What?"

"It's a new moon tonight. I am pretty much a normal human right now."

"So that's why I can't feel you. Does the new moon affect me too?" I ask.

"I don't know. The only way I can explain it is, I don't feel K like I usually do. I have to look for him in his forest, and even if I do find him, it's still a struggle for us to connect to phase or for me to tap into his strengths."

Upon hearing his explanation, I close my eyes to look for Kota. When I enter her forest, I immediately find her and still feel connected to her like I did yesterday. My eyelids flutter open, and I look into Kai's hazel eyes that seem more tired than usual.

"I don't think the new moon affects me. I can still feel Kota like I did yesterday."

"That's good to hear, Babe. I'll be honest, I hate this feeling. Please don't take this wrong, but I hate feeling human. I feel so weak and vulnerable."

"It's okay. I'm used to being weak, but you've had K all your life. So, it makes sense that you would hate it with a passion." I say and I instantly know what will make him feel better. To be around his pack. "Come on, let's get dressed and spend the day with Mom and Dad."

After Kai and I grab some clean clothes, I head toward my parent's room to use their master bathroom while Kai uses the hall bath.

When I meet Kai in the hallway a few minutes later, I find him leaning against the wall, his head tilted back, looking at the ceiling. When he hears me coming down the hall, his head turns in my direction, and when he sees what shirt I'm wearing, his eyes light up with humor.

He traces his index finger over the wolf howling at the moon and chuckles, "When did you get this?"

"At the boutique downtown when Quilla and I went shopping that day." My voice falters at the end when I remember that day. But when I feel Kota's presence in my mind, she helps me remember the recent achievement that we figured out *because* of that day.

"Well, it looks amazing on you, Love," Kai says.

"Thank you." I reply with a smile as I push a piece of my hair behind my ear.

He smiles at me, and after tugging his shirt on I lead him downstairs, where I see Mom and Dad sitting on the couch

"Good morning, Honey." Dad waves at me.

"Hi, Mom. Hi, Dad."

Kai and I sit on the loveseat, and he drops his head against the back, and he lets out a heavy sigh.

"New moon blue for you too, huh?" Dad jokes, knowing exactly what my mate is feeling.

"Yup," Kai says while popping the p. "Such a great time, isn't it?"

"Oh yeah, it's amazing!" Dad laughs dryly.

After we all sit in the living room watching TV all day, the scent of beef that's wafting from the crock pot in the kitchen tells me it's almost time to finish dinner. Mom's making beef and vegetable soup, and as I get up to help her, we all hear a knock on the door.

I turn my head at the sound, and I notice Dad and Kai's shoulders tense, and the flicker of fear that flashes over both of their features breaks my heart. I realize they cannot tell by scent if the person at the door is friend or foe, and they think they won't be able to protect us like they usually can.

So, I take a slight scent of the air, and I smile at them as I walk closer to the door.

"Dakota." Dad warns.

"It's okay, Dad. It's just Tobias and Coraline."

"The new moon doesn't affect you?" Dad asks.

"Nope. Go figure right? I'm just learning all kinds of new things about me," *If you two only knew.*

I open the door to let the two alpha's in, and before I close it, I see Quilla's Sentra pull up.

"Get on in here, Chica!" I smile. I bring her in for a quick hug when she steps up on the porch. "What are you doing here?"

"Tobias called me and told me he was coming over to your place and invited me to come along. He said he wanted us to be together as much as we can tonight. I wish that Atticus could be here, but he needed to be home to care for the sick and injured patients since they will be weaker tonight." She pauses and then curls the hand that proudly shows her mate marking into a soft fist. "I miss him being in my mind." She whispers.

"I know. I feel the same way ,and mine is in the room with me." I reach out and grasp her shoulder. *"At least we can still feel one another."* I say, trying to lighten the mood. *"It terrified me this morning, though. I thought not feeling Kai was a side effect we didn't know about."*

"Oh, I bet." Her eyes widen. *"Oh my God. We didn't even think whether it would mess with the bond like that."*

"It's okay. I understand that you couldn't keep your mind focused on my problems when you had distractions *of your own."* I wiggle my eyebrows, and Quilla's face turns three shades of red.

"You girls coming or not!" Dad yells from the dining room.

"Yeah!" I call back over my shoulder. "Come on." I hold open the door for her and make sure to lock it before heading into the kitchen with Quilla on my heels, to help Mom finish dinner.

Once we place the vegetable soup on the table at five o'clock, we all eat among idle chatter; even Dad and Kai liven up a bit at the company. I guess it's the safety in numbers thing that helps them relax.

After dinner, the men go into the kitchen and help wash dishes. Dad scrubs them, Tobias dries them and Kai puts them away since he's the most familiar with the kitchen layout than his father. I watch them all work together, and if I didn't know what tonight was, I never would have thought anything was different about them. I realize then that, no matter what, having a pack around keeps the soul happy. I feel a smile pull at the edges of my mouth, but when I hear Quilla's phone beep, it widens into a full-on grin.

"Is that the good doctor?" I tease.

"Well, duh." Quilla tries to hide her lovestruck smile but fails miserably. "He said everyone is finally stable, so he's hopping on the plane now to come here. He said it would be about three hours before the plane lands."

"Hey, that's great!" I exclaim. "The whole gang will be here soon."

Once the guys finish up in the kitchen, Kai comes back into the dining room and sits down in his chair beside me while Dad and Tobias do the same with their mates.

"Hey, Honey?" Mom says while running her hand down Dad's arm. "Would you be up for a walk?"

"That actually sounds like a good plan, Lori." Coraline grins. "Come on, Tobias, let's walk under this dark sky together."

Tobias smiles at his mate before he leans in, and gives her a soft kiss. "How could I ever say no to you, Sunflower?"

I pull Kai's ear down to my mouth and whisper into it so I'm not overheard. "Sunflower? That's cute."

Kai just smiles at me and grabs my hand. "Come on, Love. Let's go for a walk."

Kai

Dad is the first one to lead Mom out the door, then I lead Dakota through with Quilla right behind us. Nathan and Lori are the last ones out of the door, making sure it's locked behind them. I know there is a little park close by, so we all walk quietly down the sidewalk and enjoy the warm nighttime air.

I still can't help but to glance over my shoulder a bit more than I usually do since I don't have K with me to help protect my back, but knowing that Nathan is behind me settles some of my worry.

When we get to the park, Quilla sits on a nearby bench while looking at her phone, and I smile after Dakota tells me Atticus is texting her on the other end.

I grab my mate's hand to walk in the opposite direction of our parents, and we end up near a small pond where little ducks and swans are swimming on the surface and softly vocalizing to one another.

"You know, this is my first new moon that I have been out of the house. I usually just stay inside until morning." I say as we sit down on the dark green metal bench.

"Oh, Babe! You should have told me. We could have stayed home."

"It's okay. Besides, I never had someone at my side to help make this night easier."

I pull her in, her hand resting against my chest, and give her a sound kiss on the lips. Without even feeling her in my mind, I can tell exactly how my kiss makes her feel.

Her hand gripping the fabric of my shirt in her fist. The little breathy moan bubbling from her throat that I greedily swallow down my own. I lean in closer so when I lift my hand up to caress her breast through her shirt, my body covers the action from anyone else.

"Kai." She breathes.

"Yes, Baby?" I tease as I flick my thumb over her pebbled nipple poking through her top.

"Kai, someone could see us."

"No one's gonna know, Love. Unless you start getting louder." I say, dropping my voice to a lower octave.

I press the pad of my thumb against the peak still showing through her shirt, and I start to knead her soft flesh with a firm yet slow movement. She drops her head against the curve of my neck while sucking her bottom lip between her teeth.

I lean in to kiss her neck, gently grazing my teeth over her slowly reddening flesh. Her thighs pulse together for a moment, and I hum possessively in her ear.

"I'm counting down the days when I can make you squirm *and* satisfy that need you feel when I touch you like this." I say as I begin to trail my hand up her jean-clad thigh and closer to what I know is her aching center.

"Kai!" She says a little louder and I can't stop the smirk on my face when an older couple passes by on the other side of the pond and turns their heads at Dakota's cry before rushing off with looks of disgust on their faces.

"You asshole." She whispers when she pulls herself together a bit.

"You like it." I croon.

I lean in to kiss her again, but a moment later we suddenly hear an ear-splitting scream. And my stomach sinks at that scream.

I know that pitch.

My blood runs cold as I jump up from the bench; the desire that was making my lower half fill my jeans immediately evaporates as that voice fills my ears.

"Kai! Wait!" Dakota calls after me.

Even with my connection to K cut off, I am still faster than she is. My longer legs carry me across the park to an open field that is half surrounded by pine trees. I skid to a stop in the middle of the clearing, and who I see standing in the middle makes the blood rush to my ears.

Jeffrey with a knife to Emma's throat.

"Let her go, you fucking bastard!" I scream, my body shaking with the need to save her.

"I knew she would lead you to me. You can't walk away from a broken wolf!" Jeffrey laughs while pushing the knife closer to Emma's throat, and I see a bead of blood begin to well against the blade.

"You're going to fucking pay for this." I growl as Dakota makes it to the clearing a few paces behind me, eyes wild and taking the scene in before her.

Dakota

"Hey Kota, remind me to start running track or something. Damn, he's fast." I say as I finally catch up to Kai after he took off.

I don't get her response because I feel her stiffen at the scene before us. A blonde-haired girl is being held with a knife to her throat by Jeffrey. And from the way that Kai is acting, he knows this girl. A gentle breeze blows towards me, and it carries with it the slight scent of silver, and my stomach drops.

"Kai. Babe, that blade is made of silver. You need to watch it."

I am met with silence, and my heart freezes in my chest. He can't hear me or smell the silver.

"Kai!" I scream, but it's too late. He's moving forward, toward the unknown danger, before I can even stop him.

Kai

I can't take looking at Emma. Her eyes are bloodshot from crying, and the fear filling them breaks my heart further for her. Gathering what strength I have in this now human body, I leap toward Jeffrey because he too is weaker tonight, and I have my natural honed strength thanks to Dad always sparing with me, especially on nights like tonight to keep my body strong even when my wolf is not with me.

I rear my right arm back, intending to punch him straight in the face, but I see a glint of silver in the lamplight over my head and then fire.

Fire burns across my exposed chest and before I can even begin to mentally scream at how stupid I was for giving him such an easy fucking target, the fire turns to white hot pain to the point where I can't take a breath without making the sensation worse.

"What did you say? That I would pay for this?" Jeffrey laughs. "Seems like *you* are paying for taking what is *mine.*"

"Fuck off." I growl with venom in my voice and I somehow leap at him once more, but instead of Emma's screams, I hear Dakota's.

Dakota

I freeze like a statue at the sight of that silver blade cutting into Kai's chest. Ripping the fabric to the point where I can see the little shards of silver splinter off from the knife and imbed themselves into his skin.

"Fuck off."

He growls through the pain, and he leaps for Jeffrey again. I watch in slow motion as the knife connects to his body for a second time, this time across the stomach.

Something in me. No. In us. Kota and I. Something deep breaks in us at the sight of our mate being so brutally attacked, and on a night like this.

A new moon.

Unfair fight.

Mate's hurt

Mate's dying. Kota chants.

What good is this silver immunity if my mate is killed? I growl.

Protect.

Get rid of the threat.

Save them. Kota growls in my head.

"Kai!" I bellow and then I start running.

Kai

I push forward again, in one last attempt to get Emma away from him, but that damn blade gets me again. This time slicing me across my stomach, from my right side and almost dissecting the first attack on my chest.

The pain builds, and my body stops listening to me, and I stumble backward, landing hard on my back, making me cry out at the movement.

I close my eyes for a moment, and I hear someone screaming my name again.

"Kai! No, Kai, please!"

It's Emma, but I can't get my throat to work. I am so heavy. It's an effort to just get my eyes open. It's at this moment that, even though I am human right now, I am still one hundred percent allergic to silver.

And I'm dying.

I feel my lifeblood pouring out of the wounds on my chest and stomach. The last sight I see isn't even going to be my mate, but instead the backs of my eyelids all because of a damn lunatic.

I feel myself slipping more, but when I hear an unfamiliar snarl erupt from over my head, K, somehow by the grace of The Great Luna, pushes forward and helps me hang on for a little bit longer.

I open my eyes, and what I see before me confuses me, but something from K lets me know the sight is a good thing, and I'm glad I got to witness it at least once.

Dakota

When I see the knife connect with Kai a second time, I break.

Anger. Red-hot anger fuels me and Kota, and we agree on one thing and one thing only.

Protect our mate.

So we do.

As I rush to close the gap between us, I focus solely on the person who harmed what is mine, and not noticing anything else around me. I reach Kai's prone, bleeding body, the irony scent filling my sensitive nose making me sick to my stomach.

I let a vicious snarl rip from my throat, directing it at Jeffrey as I stand over Kai's broken body and dig my claws into the dirt.

Chapter Fifty-Six

DAKOTA

I flatten my ears close to my skull, lifting my tail as a challenge for Jeffrey to move and lift my lips in a wide-toothed snarl. I finally phased, but I can't celebrate it like I should be able to. With my now heightened nose, I can smell the silver starting to mingle with Kai's blood the longer I stand over him.

I snarl again at Jeffrey while taking a step closer to him to keep his attention on me when Tobias and the others run into the clearing. I give my alpha a low warning growl not to come closer since I know he will not be able to smell the silver either. He seems to understand my warning, but in that moment of distraction, Jeffrey pulls something out of the back pocket of his jeans.

I hear an explosion rocket through my wolven ears as I feel something hot bite into my shoulder. I can't stop the painful yelp at the injury, but that turns into a wolfish grin as I feel the silver bullet slowly start to force its way out of my shoulder and drop into the dirt with a muffled thud.

I look back up at Jeffrey, his face pales while shock morphs his features. I think about wanting to talk to him, and I feel Kota pull back from that part of my body, changing my throat from wolven to human vocal cords.

"You seem shocked, Jeffrey." I say with a hard, cold tone. "You didn't think that yet again we would be able to beat you at your own game, did you?"

"You bitch! That miserable boy you claimed as your mate is on the ground dying, and you still have the nerve to fucking mock me!?"

He aims the gun again, but before he can get his trembling finger on the trigger, I coil my hind legs up under me and I dive for him. I snatch his wrist in my jaw, and bite down. His blood fills my mouth, and I almost whine at the taste. It's a bitter revenge for making my mate bleed. As bones begin to crack under my molars, he drops the gun into the grass and tries to take a step back, but I bite down harder to keep his wrist in my grasp.

He stumbles over a branch, landing on his back, and I go down with him, pushing my right front paw into his neck to keep him from trying to roll away.

"You hurt what is *mine!*" I snarl, showing him my razor-sharp canines, which are entirely too close to the jugular vein in his neck.

My eyes flick over to Emma. I see her show me three fingers, and I somehow know what I can do in this situation.

"So, I'll be taking the girl and her parents. An eye for an eye. Nathan! Come and get them and take them to Tobias' home."

"Don't you dare!" Jeffrey growls.

"*Shut up!*" I growl louder than he does. So loud that a few slumbering birds in the trees above us take off at my voice. "You are nothing but a fucking coward, Jeffrey. Your soul is as black as the sky tonight. Attacking another alpha when he is at his weakest because *you* can't take him at his best. You are a disgrace to all alphas." I lean in closer, my whiskers stabbing into his neck, and my teeth graze the skin where his artery is hiding underneath. "Your time's coming, Jeffrey Carmichael. You will die by either Kai's teeth or by mine. But either way, your days are numbered."

I dig my claws into his neck as a promise to make it my teeth next time, and I back away from him. He is instantly to his feet and running away like the damn coward he is. Once I don't see his figure any longer, I take a breath, and it hits me again.

Kai's blood.

And somehow I can tell he's slowly fading from me by the scent. The silver, even with the moon hidden, is slowly killing him.

I take a step toward my mate, and when feel Kota pull herself back from within my mind, I phase back into my human body. My bones and muscles shift painlessly from one form to another, and no one cares about my naked body. Not when Tobias, Coraline, and Dad are all watching as Quilla tries to apply pressure to Kai's chest and stomach but fails to slow the blood.

I kneel beside Kai's head while placing it in my lap and brushing his sweat and blood-soaked hair to the side. He's barely breathing, and I know we have just a while longer before he's gone. Tobias tries to get near his son, but again, even with the moon hiding in the sky, the alpha cannot get closer.

"We have to get him to Atticus, he—" Tobias' voice is tight with shock and fear and he stops mid-sentence as he remembers he's not in Montana and Atticus is still probably stuck on the plane at ten thousand feet in the air.

Dad then comes as close as he dares with Emma holding onto his arm. I glance at him, and he has a look of determination in his eyes. Like he knows something we all don't.

"We can call the hospital and get Doctor Peterson. She is a doctor I found here, and she knows of Werewolves and how we work."

"What?" Tobias asks.

"Talk to a check-in nurse named Lisa. Tell her we have a *special* patient, and she'll know what to do."

Tobias seems to somewhat snap out of his stupor, and his face fades from showing fear to the stoic alpha I know him to be, and he looks at me.

"Can you carry him to the SUV?" He asks as I hear the vehicle pull up with Mom in the driver's seat.

I nod and call Kota forward so I have the strength to carry our mate to the SUV. Mom opens the hatch, and I gently lay him in the open space, then climb in beside him. Before Mom can close the hatch, Quilla jumps in the back with me, and when she looks at me, her eyes are wide but focused.

"I can feel him a little bit. I have to work to find him, but I can still grab onto his lifeline. I'm *not* letting go, Dakota. I'm doing everything I can to help him hang on." She says as she holds his left hand so tight in her own that her knuckles turn white.

"Thank you." I rasp.

Once Mom finally closes the hatch, all the adrenaline leaves my body in a rush. I look down at Kai, his face still bloody, eyes still closed, lips looking paler by the minute. I'm too angry and scared to even let tears roll down my cheeks. I'm just numb. I lift a trembling hand and place it on Kai's mating mark, the only way I can feel connected to him right now. I let my head tilt back against the trim of the SUV and I try to reach out to him through the bond, even though I know I'll only find a dark abyss, I can't help but try to reach for even just a minuscule flicker.

I'm so focused on trying to find Kai's mind that I don't notice the SUV moving or Tobias making a call on his phone until someone answers on the other end.

"Hello, emergency department." A brisk female voice answers.

"Yes, I need to speak to a nurse by the name of Lisa. It's important." Tobias says.

He's trying to keep his voice strong, and to those who don't know him, he's cool and collected, but to me, I can tell he's forcing it. And the grip on the phone tells me he's hanging on by a thread.

"This is Lisa. What can I do for you?"

"I have a *special* patient. My son. And I was told to ask for you and Doctor Peterson."

"Oh, shit." She whispers quickly. "How far are you out?"

Tobias looks at Mom, and she replies, "About ten minutes."

"Alright. What are the injuries?" Lisa asks, and I can tell she is moving through the hospital by the rustling of what sounds like a chair being rolled and a door opening and slamming shut a moment later.

"Silver knife wounds." Tobias pauses, collecting himself. "Across the chest and the abdomen."

"Damn, and it's a new moon tonight for you all, isn't it?" Lisa asks.

"Yes."

"That may be the very thing that's saving your son's life right now."

"Tobias, tell her the knife splintered." I whisper.

He turns to look at me, and the flash of pure agony on his face makes my chest hurt, but he needed to know.

"What was that?" Lisa demands.

"The knife was designed to splinter on contact." He growls.

"Shit. Alright. I'll let Doctor Peterson know. You all out front yet?"

"Pulling up now." Mom answers for her.

I see out the side window, a woman in her mid-forties with her light brown hair up in a tight bun on the top of her head walk out in a pair of pink scrubs while wheeling a gurney out a side door. My fingers tighten on Kai's slowly cooling hand.

"I will go with him, Dakota." Quilla says while squeezing my hand. "You get yourself cleaned up for now."

"Okay." I say, and now that I know I only have a few more moments left with my mate in my arms, I finally break down. I look to my Tamer with hot tears streaming down my face. "Please bring him back to me. Don't let him die, Quilla."

As the hatch opens up, I see Lisa take one look at Kai, and her face goes from friendly to serious in a second. "Come on, let's get him inside."

"I'm coming with him." Quilla says and Lisa gives her a once over, then nods without another word.

They pull Kai from my side and lift him on the gurney, his right arm falling limply off the bed. I watch a drop of blood drip off his middle finger before Quilla picks his arm up, placing it at his side, and she quickly lifts the railing to keep it there.

With him not being near me, without my hand touching his, I can't talk myself into believing he's alive. I want to hold him, and deep down I know I have to let him go for now. But it still hurts like hell to let him leave my side. I'd rather be shot with a silver bullet all day than go through this feeling of not having my injured mate in my arms.

As the two women, one a complete stranger and the other my best friend and Tamer take my mate's bloody and broken body further and further away from me, I keep my eyes locked on them until they walk through a metal door on the side of the building where I have no choice but to avert my gaze. When they disappear through the door, I don't realize I've moved until I hear Mom and Dad approach the back of the SUV. Mom has a damp washcloth she must have gotten from the ER, and Dad has a change of clothes for me. Mom helps me sit on the edge of the hatch while she wipes Kai's blood off my arms, face, torso, and legs. Then, Dad hands her a set of blue leggings and a black top for me to slip into.

"Come. Let's go inside." Tobias announces once I'm fully clothed. "Lisa has a private waiting room set up for us."

We all make our way into the private ER waiting room and take seats in different areas of the room. Tobias and Coraline are closest to the door that leads to the OR, and I am in the seat across from them. Mom and Dad sit a few chairs away so Dad can be near the door we entered and make sure no one else comes in unannounced.

And we just wait.

After thirty minutes pass, I feel Mom looking at me. My eyes flick over to her, and her face goes from a forced, wobbly smile to confusion.

"Dakota, wasn't that bullet silver too? How were you able to stand being around it? And how did that bullet get out of you?"

I stare at my mother for a moment and then my gaze slides over to my father before finally landing on Tobias. He gives me a small nod, telling me it's time to let the cat out of the bag.

I lean forward, resting my elbows on my knees, and stare at the shiny tiled floor of the hospital.

"Silver can't hurt me anymore." I say, my voice rough from screaming and crying. "I made myself immune to it."

I hear three collective vocalizations of shock at this, of course, Tobias is the only one who isn't surprised.

"How on earth did you do that, Dakota?" Dad asks.

I pick at my fingernail as I say, "After I was attacked by Caleb and when the pure silver didn't kill me, I thought that maybe it was just a lucky break. But when I was exposed to a silver bracelet, and the longer I was near it the less I felt the effects, I had Quilla look into it. Then, she and Atticus started to research the possible immunity, and they came up with a plan." I sit up straighter in my chair while looking over to my parents and glancing over to Coraline. "So over the last week, I've been getting silver injections from Quilla, and they worked. Silver cannot stay in my body anymore. Just like that bullet, my body forces it out now."

After a few minutes of silence as everyone takes in what I just told them, Dad is the first one to react. He walks over to sit next to me and takes my hand in his own.

"That was very brave of you, Dakota. And I want to let you know I'm proud of you." Dad gives me a soft smile and pulls me into his chest to hug me.

"Thank you, Dad." I say into his shirt.

He kisses me on the top of my head and then walks back over to where Mom is still seated near the main door, and we all settle back into worried silence as we wait to hear any news about how the surgery is going.

As the hours tick by, 11:30, 12:30, 1:30 in the morning, I keep trying to reach out to Kai. Hoping that as the hours get closer to sunrise, I will be able to find a little piece of him. But, I'm still met with the absence of him in my mind. And I find that the more I am met with that darkness, the more I feel Kota get antsy, and with us finally phasing, I can feel her constantly lurking under my skin, just waiting to come out again. I feel her pacing around in her forest, and I try to keep my own legs still, but I find myself crossing one leg over the other, then tucking them up under me, and finally setting them back on the floor.

I scrub my hands over my face as the sudden need to barge into that operating room and demand they allow me to watch over Kai fills me. I feel eyes on my back, and I look over to find Dad watching me again. I usually hold his gaze until he is the first to look away; that's just the alpha in me, but this time I am the first to look away from him, and I wrap my hands around the back of my neck.

I hear Dad get out of his chair, and he kneels down in front of me, placing his hand on my shoulder. "Hey. Talk to me. What are you think-ing?" He asks gently.

"What am I thinking?" I scoff, tears burning the back of my throat. "I'm sad. I'm sad that it took Kai getting stabbed for me to finally phase. I can't allow myself to celebrate it because my mate is fighting for his life right now. I'm mad that I can't be there for Kai. I'm his mate, and I should be the one holding his hand. It's taking everything I have in me to stay in this chair. I feel Kota pacing back and forth in her forest, and it makes me want to do the same here." I pause, and a thought hits my mind, and I can't help the sob that rips from my throat. "I can't feel him through the bond, and I keep thinking that if he's going to die, it should be in my arms and not on a fucking metal operating table!"

I break down, and I barely feel Dad pull me into his chest and gently rub soothing circles down my back for a few minutes.

"Shhhh, Sweetheart."

He pulls back and gently grips my face in his hands while running his thumbs over my tear-soaked cheeks in a way that reminds me so much of Kai that it makes fresh tears fall.

"Listen to me." Dad says this time, using his whole palm to dry my face. "Trust in your Tamer. I know that Quilla may still be new to her abilities, but from what I have seen and heard of her doing, she's already so well-versed in what she does. So, believe that she will be strong enough to help your mate pull through this. And I know Doctor Peterson is a very intelligent woman too. I trust her wholeheartedly."

I nod at my father's words, and I pull back from him while using the inside of my shirt to dry my face more. Then after a moment, I'm back to wanting to walk in that OR. I know I need a distraction, and an idea pops into my head.

"Hey, Dad? Can you tell the story of when you and Mom met? I need a distraction if I'm going to be able to stay in this chair."

Dad looks at Mom, and she gives him a small smile and walks over to sit in the chair next to mine.

"You know, Dakota, that's not a half bad idea. Besides, I would like to relive that time, Honey." Mom says.

Dad lets out a sigh as he stands up and takes the seat across from me. Mom once again goes to sit by her mate, and he wraps his arm around her waist while smiling up at her. She runs her hand through Dad's hair then trails it down the side of his neck until it comes to rest on his chest where we all know his mate marking hides under his black shirt.

"Okay. I'll tell you all the story of how I met my beautiful and rare mate."

Chapter Fifty-Seven

NATHAN

The early morning sun beats down on my dark gray coat as I trot through the forest to do my normal perimeter sweep of the pack grounds. I make sure no lone wolves are lurking around, and no traps are set by hunters or other wolves alike to harm our pack members. As Beta to the South Dakota pack, it's my job to protect the pack just as much as it is Alpha Baldric's.

I get to the edge of the forest, and I'm glad to find that there are no threats. I huff out a snort of satisfaction as I turn to head back to the pack house, but as I begin my trek through the forest, I pick up on the scent of a lavender field not far from me, and just as I get ready to leap over a fallen tree trunk, something else tickles my nose.

Peaches.

I turn back in the direction of the lavender field to see what is causing that scent, because I haven't noticed any peach trees growing anywhere near here and we are too far away from town to pick up on scents from the farmers market. When I clear the line of trees and the lavender field comes into view, I drop low to my belly and flatten my ears to my head at what I see before me.

A woman.

A human woman, to be exact. She's on her knees picking some flowers and putting them into a small basket that hangs on her arm. She tucks a piece of her medium brown hair behind her ear, and with the sun shining down on her head, it makes the strands almost look golden in places. The breeze picks up again, and I realize the smell of peaches is coming from her.

"What is a human doing this far in the forest?" I ask.

"I don't know, but I feel like she could be special." Nate responds.

"Don't tell me you're thinking, mate? Come on, Nate. She's human; how is that possible?"

"My nose has never led us wrong before with tracking, so this to me is no different. Let's get closer to her and get to know her."

"No. Not like this." I say glancing down at my paw. *"Maybe we can find her in town or something."*

I turn to leave, but I fail to watch where I step. My left paw steps down on a dry rotting branch, and it snaps under my weight, making the woman's head snap up at the sound. I sharply turn my head and we lock eyes for a moment, my breath catching in my chest. I am staring into the most beautiful eyes I have ever seen. It's like looking into an endless ocean, and I would gladly drown in those waters for her.

"Oh yeah. Absolutely picking up on mate vibes here, Nathan." My wolf croons.

At his words, I turn and bound through the forest, leaving the woman behind me, and I hope she gets out of the forest as safely as she entered. When I get back to the house, I go into a little wooden shed that a few of us with carpentry skills built so we can phase and get dressed before we walk into the pack house. With so many females here, and most being bonded, it's best to keep as many naked males from running around the grounds as possible out of respect for the mated pairs.

I find my container with my name on it, and I throw on a pair of black sweatpants and a gray t-shirt, then I head into the house. Before I make it to my room, I pass Parker, the alpha's third top wolf, in the hall. He is about an inch shorter than my six foot three height, and his black hair hangs loosely in his dark blue eyes.

"Morning, Nathan." He smiles, but then his eyes widen, and he motions for me to enter my room.

We walk inside and close the door behind me. "What's wrong?" I ask.

"What's up with you, Nathan? Did you change your cologne or something? Your scent is different."

"Told you." Nate sings.

I try to ignore my wolf, and I look back to my pack mate, who I have always felt like he was a brother to me. We got into all kinds of trouble as kids, and we even fought in a war once together before finding Alpha Baldric.

"I don't know, Parker." I answer slowly, "I think I may have just found my mate." I say as I rake my fingers through my dark brown hair, "But I'm afraid for her."

"Why?" He chuckles. "You know she will be welcomed into the pack with open arms."

"You don't understand, man. If it's true, then my mate is human."

"No way! It can't be. Maybe that human was around your Werewolf mate. Sometimes, these things can be tricky. That human could have hugged your mate or something." Parker scoffs.

I shake my head as I hear his words, and they just feel wrong. "No, I don't think it was a mistake, or my true mate's scent was on this woman. We locked eyes, Parker. She looked at me, and I knew in my soul that she was mine." I feel Nate swell with pride knowing that our mate is out there and unknowingly waiting for us.

"What are you going to do?" Parker asks, his voice dropping low. "Are you going to tell Baldric?"

"No. Not yet. I want to meet her first. I have to take this slow with her. Once she finds out that I am not human." I pause because the thought that hits my mind makes my chest hurt. "She may run from me. So I don't want the pack to celebrate only for it to blow up in my face later."

"I understand," Parker says. "I won't say anything. Your secret's safe with me."

☐Over the next few days, I take extra time on my perimeter checks to see if I can spot this woman, my mate, again. I find that she comes to the forest every three days to pick fresh flowers to place in her basket, and I just lie down on my belly and watch her with rapt fascination.

She sings to herself at times, and I love listening to her voice to the point where I even dream about her singing to me. So I continue to hide in the treeline for the next two times I see her, just watching her from afar. But on the times I see her after that, I take a step closer and closer until I end up a few feet in the middle of the lavender blooms and just silently stalk her.

Chapter Fifty-Eight

LORI

I've known for the last three times I've come to pick flowers to put on the tables of the bakery/diner where I work part time, that a wolf has been watching me. When I saw him the first two times, I was scared he was going to attack me, but these last few visits, he's just watching me, and I somehow know he won't hurt me. Call me naïve, but I think if he was going to attack me, he would have already done it. But today is the closest he's gotten, and he thinks he's hidden in the lavender blooms, but his pointed, dark gray ears are poking up over the flowers.

"I can see you, you know." I deadpan to the wolf like he can understand me.

I usually talk to animals with a baby-like voice, but with this animal, I talk to him like he's human. I try to chalk it up to him being a wild animal that can eat me and not the neighbor's Jack Russel. I look over to the wolf, and his dark chestnut brown eyes look up toward his ears, and I swear he gives his large head a firm shake, like he knows he should have hidden better than this.

As I continue to look at him, I have this sudden desire to run my hands through his rough coat. I reach a hand out toward him without thinking, but I snatch it back before I allow myself to close the distance between me and this wild animal. I notice the look of what I can only assume is fear from being near a human flash over his face, and he begins to back away from me. As he takes another step, I, for some insane reason, want to keep him from leaving my sight.

"Wait." I say. "Will I see you again?" I ask, still not understanding why I think this wolf can understand me, but I ask it anyway.

Nathan

"I can see you, you know."

I look up and notice my ears are poking out over the flowers, and I mentally smack myself for the amateur move. So, I lift my head higher and lock eyes with her again, and I can absolutely agree with Nate, this woman is our mate. I feel a pull towards her, like there is a magnet on her and it wants to draw me closer. But a little voice in the back of my mind taunts me, planting little seeds of doubt in my heart.

How can she, a human, be bonded to a full Were like me? Will she accept who I am and walk by my side, or will she reject me and run for the hills?

The sudden fear of her rejection hits me like a shot to the chest, and I find myself backing up from her.

"Wait." She pleads. "Will I see you again?"

I hear her words and I turn back around to look at her, and from her tone, I know she is beginning to feel something, but she doesn't understand why she's feeling this way towards what she thinks is a *wild animal.* In that moment, I know I can't let her down. So I nod and I playfully bark two times and paw at the ground, hoping she picks up on what I'm telling her.

She laughs a bit hysterically and shakes her head. "You want to meet here again in two days?" She guesses, and I bark once at her. "This is crazy. I'm talking to a wolf. A freaking wild animal, and the bad thing is, I think you understand me."

At hearing her actually call me a wild animal and the way she laughed at the situation like she's going nuts, I begin to think that maybe the fates did get this wrong. Maybe she won't be able to handle what I am. To know things that are told over campfires are indeed real. I can't stand the thought of her being terrified of me. So, I take one last look at her before I bound off into the forest.

Lori

I watch the wolf take off like a dart into the forest, and something deep in me wants to run after him and be near him. Especially since that look of fear flooded his face, I want to snuggle into his rough yet warm coat and stay there. I shake my head to clear my thoughts and begin my walk back to town.

"I've been in these woods too long; I'm starting to go crazy. I should be scared to death of that wolf, not trying to make fucking friends with it. He could easily attack me and use my bones as toothpicks." I think out loud, but somehow I cannot picture that wolf hurting me.

Still, I decide then and there that I am not going to come back to this forest in two days' time. I need to clear my head and get back in touch with reality.

Nathan

Two days later at the end of my normal patrol, I end up at the lavender field only to find it empty.

So I wait.

And wait.

And wait.

Three hours turn to four and then five. By then, I start looking around the rest of the lavender field, thinking that maybe she found another spot to pick flowers from. But after another two hours of looking, I don't find her, and my stomach drops like a stone. My fear has come to light, and it hurts like a silver blade to the gut.

She's terrified of me.

I slowly make my way back to the pack house, not even bothering to phase back into my human form as I enter the house and pad into my room. I jump up on the circular ledge near my window and will the rays of sun shining through the glass to warm my dark and empty soul.

Later that night, after I smell that I missed dinner, I hear a knock on my door and Parker pokes his head in with a plate of food. My stomach growls, but I don't make a move to phase so I can take it.

"What's wrong with you? Are you hurt?" Parker inquires.

"No. But being injured would be the better alternative." I tell him through the unique bond we share through the alpha.

"What happened?"

"She didn't show up."

"Oh, shit, man. I'm sorry. Maybe she got tied up with something and couldn't make it." He offers. "Maybe you can go into town and look for her."

"I wouldn't even know where to start to look for her."

"You know her scent, don't you? And you're the best tracker in the pack, so I don't think she would be an issue for you to find."

I think about his words, and I try to imagine her scent in my nose. The sweet smell of peaches with a touch of those lavender flowers. As I imagine those smells, I pick up on the undercurrents of flour, sugar, and grease.

"A diner. She works at a diner."

"There you go! If you want, I'll take your post in the morning while you go and look for her."

"Seriously?" I ask in shock.

"Yes, dude. Now stop sulking, eat, and go look for your mate in the morning." Parker smiles.

I leap off the windowsill to phase, and I slip into a pair of shorts before I take the plate from his outstretched hand.

"Thank you, brother. I appreciate it."

CHAPTER FIFTY-NINE
NATHAN

The next morning, I make sure to take a nice hot shower, pull on the best pair of dark blue jeans I have over my hips, and button up a moss green shirt over my chest before emerging from my room.

I walk out of the pack house with a renewed spring in my step as I hop into my vintage 1969 Camaro. The blue paint with a white racing stripe down the middle has faded a little bit over time, but this car is a classic and has seen me through a lot in life. As I drive into town, I roll my window down with the hand crank and let all the scents hit me until I find where the diner is. And I know I have the right one when I pick up on this woman's peachy scent with a touch of lavender underneath.

I park in front of a quaint Mom-and-Pop diner and take a slow breath before exiting the car; the door creaking a bit on the hinge when I slam it shut behind me. I open the door to the diner, and the little bells hanging above my head ring cheerfully to announce my arrival. I take a seat in the corner near the kitchen so I can look out over all the patrons sitting in different areas of the dining room and keep my back protected at the same time.

I go to pick up the menu from the table to see what I want to order when the kitchen door swishes open beside me. Someone briskly walks by with a serving tray in hand, loaded with plates of steaming hot food, and when the familiar peach and lavender scent hits me, I have to bury my face in the menu in an effort to control Nate. I feel him try to surge forward to go after her, and I know with him being so close to the front of my mind, my eyes will be glowing with his presence.

"Get back or you'll blow the whole fucking thing!" I scold.

Once I get my wolf under control, I glance up at her, and my heart skips a beat. Her medium brown hair is up in a high ponytail that drapes from the crown of her head, and it sways from side to side as she walks around to deliver the orders to the other customers in the diner. When she delivers a plate of food to a middle-aged woman, her smile is so bright and friendly that it lights up her whole face. She then goes to the check-in counter and looks at what I assume is the table roster, and when she looks in my direction, our eyes collide, making my heart lodge itself in my throat.

Will she recognize me? If she does, will she run?

I don't get much time to think about anything else before she approaches my table.

Lori

The diner is busy this morning, but I love it. It helps the day move faster, and I get a buttload of tips too. When I go over to the hostess desk to check my table roster to make sure I'm caught up on everyone, I notice that I have a new table in the corner, and when I look up, I stop for a brief second at who I see. I know my usual customers that come in from day to day, but this guy, I don't know his name at all, but I *feel* like I know him. Like I've seen him before.

But that's ridiculous.

As I approach this new customer, we lock eyes, and I can't help but become mystified by them.

Those eyes. A beautiful chocolate brown. Almost reminds me of... No! Don't go there, Lori. You're tired and just imagining things. You're just feeling a little guilty for dipping out from a wild animal. *Remember that part?*

"Hi there." I plaster on a smile as I walk over to his table. "Welcome to Pappy's Diner. My name is Lori, and I'll be your server today. What can I get started for you?" I ask as I pull out my notepad and stand with my pen poised over the paper.

"Lori."

His deep voice rumbles my name, and it makes me shiver. *Shiver.* It's like when my name falls from his lips, it touches my soul. I shift my weight on my other foot, but I can tell from the slight tick at the corner of his mouth that he's trying not to smile at how I reacted.

"That's a pretty name, Lori. My name is Nathan Shade; it's nice to meet you."

He nods his head in my direction, and I can't help the nervous laugh that bubbles from my throat. "Thank you. Um, what can I get you, Nathan?"

He looks at the menu again, but then he sits it down and looks back at me. "I've never been here, so what do you recommend?"

"Oh, um." I think for a moment. "The Pappy's special is good if you're a meat lover." I say, and this time his face does light up in a half smile like I just told a private joke that only he knows. So, I continue to explain what goes into this special. "It's chicken, bacon, and roast beef, topped with grilled onions, mayo and lettuce. All that deliciousness stacked between two slices of toasted sourdough bread. And if you want dessert, I'd say add in an apple pie too, but that's my opinion." I smile.

"That sounds great. I'll take both, please."

"Okay. And what would you like to drink with that? We have Pepsi, Dr. Pepper, Sprite, tea, coffee, and water."

"I'll take a Dr. Pepper. Thank you." He says, and I take the menu from his hand with a small smile and walk through the swinging door that leads to the kitchen to pin up his order for the cook.

After a few minutes, the cook rings the bell that Nathan's food is up, and I take it out to him with a smile. I go around to check on my other tables, and I can feel his eyes are on me, but it's not in a creepy way. It's weird, but it's like I already feel comfortable around him, and this dude is still a practical stranger. But I feel better with Nathan's eyes on me compared to the dude sitting at the counter waiting on his to-go order. I give him a look that asks *what the fuck are you looking at* and go back to bussing my tables.

As I go to fill up the coffee mug of my last customer, I feel something different in the air. I look over my shoulder and I see Nathan is just staring down into his pie like it holds all the secrets to the world in its sugary, fruit-filled crust. I take a look around to make sure I'm not needed anywhere and I make my way over to his table.

"So, how was your meal, Nathan?"

At first, he doesn't look at me, and I double-check to make sure no one is flagging me down before I pull out the chair to sit across from him.

"Hey. Is something wrong? Did you not like your food?"

Nathan

After Lori drops my food off, I casually watch her work. Her smile and laugh warms my soul, and I love how she's not afraid to stand her ground. I saw the look that she gave that dude waiting at the counter when she caught him looking at her long legs, and I know that look could have brought a Were to his knees.

For the first time in my eighty-two years on this earth, I feel like a teenager again. Giddy with anticipation, but yet terrified of what to say to her. I'm usually good with talking to people, but it's normally in casual settings and for business meetings with Alpha Baldric. But this? This is completely different. How I talk to her is what will make or break this relationship before it even starts. Like one of the bigger things, other than me being a Werewolf, is how I am eighty-two but look like I'm twenty-four. Most sane people would run from shit like that.

At those thoughts, I drop my gaze from her and poke at my apple pie, and I don't look up when I hear her approach my table.

"Hey. Is something wrong? Did you not like your food?" She asks, and I try to ignore her, but she sits across from me, and I can feel her fear rolling off her. I don't need a mate bond to feel it, I hear it in her voice and see it in the tense line of her shoulders.

"No, no. The food is great. I just have a lot of things on my mind, that's all." I say as I try to force a smile on my face.

"Is there anything I can help with?"

Oh, Sweetheart, if you only knew.

"No. Thank you though."

"Okay. Let me know if I can help you with anything." She offers, and she gets up from the table when we hear the door ding again, letting the servers know someone just came in.

After I finally finished the pie, which was amazing, I get up to pay my bill at the hostess desk, making sure to leave Lori a hefty tip. I begin to make my way toward the door when I feel Lori come up behind me, and she grabs at my sleeve, her fingers brushing against my palm, sending electricity rocketing up my nerves and right into my soul at her touch.

"Um, Nathan?" She pauses, her cheeks glowing in a gorgeous shade of pink. "Come by again tomorrow; I hear the special pie is going to be cherry if you like that."

I can't stop the huge grin that spreads across my face at her wanting me to come back here.

"I love cherry pie. I'll be sure to come back." I begin to pull away, but an idea pops in my head. "What time do you get off tomorrow?"

"I get off at five."

"Would you like to go for a walk tomorrow when you get off? That is if you're not too tired after your shift?" I ask, praying that she will agree.

"Sure. I'd like that." She smiles while tucking a loose strand of her hair behind her ear.

"I'll see you tomorrow afternoon then." I give her a wink, and I can't help the chuckle when the pink to her cheeks turns a shade redder and spreads to her ears.

I am just about to brush my thumb over her cheek when an older woman's voice rings out, making Lori jump back from me. "Miss Bradley, you have tables to tend to." She snaps.

"I'll be right there, Martha!" Lori shouts. "Sorry. I gotta go."

"It's okay. I'll be back tomorrow." I say with a grin as I force my legs to step back from her and walk out of the diner.

I walk through the main door of the pack house with a spring in my step, and when I get to my room, I again pass Parker in the hall, and I quickly invite him in.

"You look happy," Parker jokes as he playfully punches my shoulder.

"I talked to her today, man."

"I can tell that. What did she say?"

"Nothing much. But I need you to take my patrol tomorrow afternoon. I'm meeting her again tomorrow, and I'm going on a walk with her." I grin.

"Oh, Great Luna above, spare me," Parker rolls his eyes.

"Oh, you're just jealous, that's all." I half-joke. "But your mate will come one day too, Parker." I finish when he gives me a hard look.

"Yeah. I hope so." He says flatly as he walks to my door, "I'll cover your post again tomorrow." He gives me a tight smile as he shuts my door behind him.

Chapter Sixty

NATHAN

I arrive at the diner the next afternoon at four o'clock and take the same table that I did yesterday, near the kitchen against the back wall. When Lori finishes up with one of her customers, she turns to head toward the kitchen, and when she sees me, her whole face lights up and it warms my entire body.

"Hi, Nathan! What can I get you?"

"I'd love that pie you were talking about yesterday." I smile.

"Oh, right! The cherry pie. You want anything else?"

"I'll take a cup of coffee with it." I tell her. "Are you still getting off at five today?"

"Oh! Yes, I am. Sorry, it's been busy, and I completely forgot. I'm kind of a scatterbrain at times."

"It's okay. I can tell you take your job seriously. And if tonight isn't a good time—" I say, but she cuts me off.

"No, no, no. It's alright." She chuckles nervously. "I'm going to go get your pie and coffee now."

Lori brings out my order, and I watch her for the remainder of her shift. Absentmindedly taking bites of the pie and sipping the coffee that I hardly taste because my attention is on this amazing woman in front of me.

About five minutes before her shift is over, I pay before I walk outside and casually lean against the building with my hands in the pockets of my jeans to wait for her. The door dings, and I watch as she waves her goodbyes to the other servers inside before stepping out on the sidewalk to look around for me.

When her eyes land on my form, I almost don't remember to stop the growl that threatens to crawl up my throat as her eyes travel over my body, taking in my muscular form honed from years of training and fighting. I smile and fall into step beside her as we begin to walk down the sidewalk together. I take her to a little park to watch the ducks swim and to have a little privacy.

I lead her over to a weather-worn wooden bench, and I have to force myself not to drape my arm around her shoulder, even though my fingers are itching to touch her.

"So, what do you do for a living, Nathan?"

"I'm the financial advisor for my pack."

Lori's head snaps over to me, and I realize with horrifying clarity what I just said.

"Smooth move there, Fabio." Nate snorts.

"It's a special ops headquarters, filled with mostly guys. So you can imagine that things can get pretty crazy there. Like animals. So we nick-named our barracks 'the pack house.'" I say, hoping she will take the lie for what it is.

"Oh, I can just imagine what a house full of men would be like." She chuckles.

She makes a slight move like she wants to lean into me, but she stops herself. I pick up on the faint smell of her fear again, and it breaks my heart that she's scared of me. Without much thought, I slowly put my arm around her shoulders and I wait for a moment to see if she moves from me. She tenses when she feels my arm brush against her, and just when I'm about to pull away, she finally leans into me.

I sigh through my nose as relief washes over me, and I drape my arm fully around her, pulling her tighter against my side while resting my cheek on the top of her head. We sit like that for a few minutes, just watching the ducks lazily swim in the pond, neither of us saying a word.

After what feels like years just went by in the blink of an eye, I hear her chuckle lightly.

"What's so funny?" I ask.

"It's just I've never been this... comfortable with a man before."

I again, have to work to bury the wave of jealousy that another male has touched her, but I have to remind myself it happened way before we ever knew the other existed.

"Most of the guys I've dated are lucky to get a kiss on the cheek or even hold hands on the third date, and here I am snuggled up against you like I can't get enough."

"Lori." I say, my voice dropping a few octaves. She looks up at me, and I can tell she wants to get lost in my eyes, and I caress her face, rubbing my thumb against the apple of her cheek. "I feel just as comfortable with you. I feel like I am a stupid teenager again when I'm around you. Constantly thinking I'm going to say something stupid to make you run."

Lori

As I sit on the bench with Nathan, I find myself wanting to get closer to him. I feel so comfortable with him. Like he's given me back a part of myself that I never knew I was missing until I met him. And the way he slowly draped his arm around me brought all the butterflies to life in my belly. He's not the kind of guy to just make a move and expect you to take it. It's like he's silently asking without using his words, and when I do finally lean into his side, I feel that I can't get close enough. When I feel his cheek rest against the top of my head, I close my eyes and allow this man to become my whole world while I'm in his arms.

I can't help the chuckle that bubbles from my throat when I realize that many a date has been ruined because I haven't been all touchy-feely with a guy since college, and with Nathan, I've known him less than twenty-four hours and I'm already leaning into him like a lovesick puppy. After I tell him that, the way his voice drops into a sultry tone makes my core heat with desire, and this absolutely has not happened since college.

"I feel just as comfortable when I'm with you. I feel like I'm a stupid teenager again when I'm around you," Nathan tells me, and when I look into his dark brown eyes I suddenly feel that he's older than he looks. He has this old soul feel to him, and maybe that's why I feel so comfortable with him. He's not all about getting to third base like the other twenty-something guys that I meet at the diner are.

"I better get you home. It's getting late." Nathan says as the hum of a lamppost buzzes to life overhead and the sun starts to set.

He helps me to my feet, and I keep my arms wrapped around his bicep while I lead him to my apartment complex a few blocks down the road. As I pull myself from his side and I go to open the main glass door, I pause and turn around to face him again.

I shyly bite my bottom lip between my teeth when I look back at him. "Can we meet again tomorrow?"

"As much as I'd love that, Sweetheart, I can't. I have patrols tomorrow afternoon, and I already asked my pack mate to cover for me twice now. So I need to get back to my post." Nathan says with sorrow filling his voice and eyes.

"Oh, okay." I say, feeling like he just made the whole world stop spinning at his rejection of meeting me again. "Goodnight then." I say as I turn back around to enter through the door.

I take a few steps, but I pause again, and for some reason, I cannot let him leave without having some kind of plan to meet up, even if it's a few days later. Anything will do. So I spin in place and I watch his broad back slowly walk away from me and without thinking, I swing the door open and I shout at him.

"Is this something I can tag along on?"

Nathan

I hate the look of rejection on her face at telling her that I can't meet her tomorrow. I need to keep Baldric off my tail for now until I can summon up the nerve to tell her the truth about me and before she meets the rest of the pack. So that means going back on my patrols and maybe taking a few of Parker's as a repayment for helping me.

After I watch her walk into her apartment building, knowing she's safe behind the door, I turn and force myself to walk away. Just as I am about to hit the sidewalk and make a dash for the forest to phase and maybe go for a hunt to burn off some of this uneasiness that is lying in my chest, I hear the door swing open again and I hear her sweet voice call out to me.

"Is this something that I can tag along on?"

I turn and look at her, dumbfounded by her request for a moment. I never would have thought she would even ask something like that. I close the distance between us, my long legs eating up the sidewalk, and I pull her into my chest without thinking, and I feel her arms wrap around my waist.

"I'd love that, Sweetheart." I say as I nuzzle my nose into her neck, gently taking in her scent. "I'll pick you up at five tomorrow when you get off work."

"Actually, I'm off tomorrow, so I can meet you at any time."

"Okay. Meet me at the diner then at ten. My patrol runs that route, so I can meet you there."

"Okay. I'll see you then, Nathan." Lori smiles up at me while resting her hands on my chest.

"I can't wait, Sweetheart."

I kiss her on the cheek before I reluctantly let her go for a second time and watch her walk into her apartment building again, only this time I wait until I watch her walk up the stairs to get to her second-floor apartment before I walk away. I hate leaving her alone, but I make myself focus on meeting her tomorrow and sharing this part of my world with her even though she doesn't understand it yet.

Chapter Sixty-One
Nathan

I hurry to start my patrol the next morning, and even though I don't phase like I normally do when I make my perimeter run, I still make sure to be mindful and watch for any dangers that may be lurking in the woods, especially since Lori is going to be this space with me later today.

Once I'm satisfied that this part of my route is clear, I get closer to the trail that leads to town, and I walk toward the diner where I promised I would meet Lori.

At first, I think about her backing out like she did from the lavender fields, but I remind myself that was when she was agreeing to meet a *wild animal* and not the human that was living under his pelt.

Before I round the corner, all nerves evaporate when I pick up on her scent and I find myself smiling before my eyes even land on her, but when I finally see her sitting on the bench in front of the diner, everything in the world fades around me. She's dressed in a pair of skinny jeans with hiking boots and a purple t-shirt tucked into the waistband of her pants.

"Hello, Sweetheart. Nice choice of attire." I say as my eyes travel up her body, her cheeks flushing with a cute tint of pink.

"Thanks. I figured we'd be doing a lot of walking." She says as she waves her hand over her jean-clad legs.

I hold out my hand for her, and she takes it with a smile. "Yes, but it's not that hard of a walk. The ground is mostly flat here."

I check the street to make sure it's clear of cars before we cross and make our way into the forest. I keep my eyes up from Lori's gaze so that when I call on Nate again to help me check this part of my route; she doesn't see my eyes glow with his presence, but I don't let go of her hand. I interlace our fingers together, and her touch makes my heartbeat flutter in my chest. ,

Once I've looked over everything in this section, we move around a large boulder, and I pick up on another scent. I pull Lori into my side and I lift my finger to my lips, silently letting her know to keep quiet as the animal I smelled walks in front of us.

Lori

I loved how Nathan eyed my outfit, how his eyes slowly traveled down my legs in a way that made me feel he was mentally undressing me. Or that could have just been in my mind because I was certainly looking over him in that way. The way his strong, broad chest filled out his white t-shirt and his light blue jeans hugging his all too powerful legs and hips in all the right places.

When he leads me into the forest, I notice the way he walks is so confident. Like he travels this way so much that he could walk it in the dead of night with little to no light and he wouldn't trip. As we pass a large boulder, Nathan crouches down while pressing a finger to his lips to tell me to keep quiet. His actions make me wonder if he saw my wolf. Maybe I can share him with another human, and I won't feel as bad about talking to the animal, but what I see before me is just as amazing.

A doe with her fawn slowly walks out in front of us. She silently chews on a few pieces of grass while her little one nurses for a few moments. Her ears flick around as if listening for any movements around them, and I barely breathe so I don't scare them off. Nathan's arms tighten around me, and when I look up at him, I see that his eyes are a lighter shade of brown, and I can almost see them coming alive with joy at the sight before him. He must feel me looking at him because he tilts his head down, and I smile at him as he pulls me closer to his side, and we continue to watch the doe and her fawn slowly walk away from us, disappearing deeper into the forest.

"That was amazing. I've never seen a deer that close before." I say in awe.

"Yeah. I see them a lot out here. I like seeing them in their natural habitat. It reminds me that there are still innocent lives here in the forest, and it makes me want to continue to keep this area safe for them." Nathan says as his eyes scan the space around us again.

I think about the many animals out here that would mean harm to these two delicate creatures, and I wonder if my wolf has ever hunted something like that. He probably has for food, of course. I shake the gruesome image of him attacking the doe or the fawn from my mind as Nathan tugs me to my feet and continues to lead me through the forest.

When we come to the lavender field, I try to keep the panic from my face when the memory of dipping out on my wolf hits my mind. Did he come back here looking for me? I again mentally smack myself for thinking that a wild animal would be pissed about me ditching him.

I turn my attention towards Nathan as he walks through the soft purple blooms around us, his large hands, which I'm sure have seen their fair share of work over the years, are tenderly brushing each petal as if they are the most precious thing in the world to him and I find myself wishing I was on the receiving end of his touch instead. As that thought hits me, I bend down to pick a stem before he can catch me staring at him. Once I get my head out of the gutter, I look up in time to watch Nathan flop down in the middle of the field, and I hear him take a deep breath as he surrounds himself in the soft, relaxing scent.

"You like it here, don't you?" I ask, laughing.

"Yes. I do. It holds a good memory for me." Nathan replies as he sits up, and his dark chestnut eyes look over at me.

I can't help as the image again flashes between his features to those of my wolf. I don't know if it's just the guilt of not meeting him here or just oddly missing his form that keeps his memory fresh in my mind, but something about Nathan keeps bringing me back to that damned wolf. I notice how Nathan's eyes look exactly like...

No.

I take a step back from the man before me. He notices the change in my demeanor, and the way he tilts his head to the side in such a way that screams animal, I can't help the squeak that comes from my mouth.

"No. No, no, no, no. It can't be. I'm going crazy." I ramble.

"Lori. What's wrong?" Nathan says, concern filling his voice.

I shake my head as I start to back away from him, but I make it only ten steps. Almost like each one I take away from him gets harder and harder to make. It feels like I'm trying to walk through quicksand. So I just stand still, my shoulders shaking with confusion and fear, and I swear I almost feel pain flow down my spine at my actions. I hear Nathan run after me, his boot-clad feet crashing heavily on the forest floor.

"Lori, please don't go." His pleading voice makes my heart beat painfully in my chest. "Please, Sweetheart, talk to me." He whispers.

"I can't. It's impossible." I murmur.

"Sweetheart, please tell me what's going through your mind." Nathan asks, his voice tight with emotion and it's like I can almost feel his pain at me running from him, his fear that I'm going to stop seeing him like it's my own.

"What I'm thinking is too crazy. I need time to sort it out myself first."

The request that enters my mind hurts so much that I clutch my fist to my chest and I tilt my head back to the darkening sky. I feel hot tears fall from the corner of my eyes, and it feels almost like déjà vu at what I'm about to say.

"Please let me go for now. Can we meet in two days? This time no matter what, I'll be here."

I hear a movement behind me, like something hitting the ground. When I turn around, I find Nathan on his knees before me, his head hung low between his shoulders. He looks as if my words were daggers and I just plunged them hilt deep into his chest, right into his heart. Like my request to stay away from each other for two days is telling him he's not allowed to live. And to be honest, I feel the same way. As soon as the words left my lips, the breath stopped in my chest.

He lifts his gaze to mine, and his eyes look like they are almost glowing. I make myself think it's just the setting sun and tears lining his eyes that are the cause, but when I hear the light growl in his voice, I somehow *know* it's from something more.

"As you say, so shall it be," Nathan says slowly. "We will meet here in two days and hear your decision."

He hangs his head again as if in defeat, and I want nothing more than to help him to his feet. To tell him that I will be with him, but that sane part of my brain tells me I'm nuts for wanting to be with someone like him.

He's not normal.

My inner voice scoffs. I want to tell that bitch to go to hell, but she keeps my feet glued to the spot.

"Nathan, I—" I shake my head and I take a step back. "I'm sorry."

I force myself to turn around, and I run. I run out of the forest, down the street, and into my apartment building. But before the glass door shuts behind me, I hear a mournful howl fill the night sky, and it sends chills down my spine, because I know who *exactly* that howl belongs to.

I feel tears slide freely down my face as I rush into the building and up to my apartment. As I close and lock my door, I hear something in my mind, and I freeze with my hand on the lock.

"Please, come back to me, mate of mine."

The voice isn't Nathan's deep soothing tone, but I can tell it's a part of him.

"Give me time." I somehow think the words back to him, and I can almost feel him settle at my words.

Chapter Sixty-Two

LORI

The two days pass in a blur. I call out of work for fear of running into Nathan there, but at least that would have been an excuse for me to see him without actually breaking our pact. Ever since I swear I heard that voice in my mind, he's in my every thought during the day and in my dreams at night. No matter how much I try to distract myself, I always end up thinking about him. His laugh, his smile, the way his body felt next to mine. The way his head hung in sorrow when I ran from him that night. It all taunts me, and now that today is the day that I am to meet him in the forest again, I'm terrified.

"What am I going to say to him?" I think aloud. "I don't understand any of this. How is he even real? This is stuff that is told in fantasy books. It isn't supposed to be a real thing." I refuse to say aloud what I think...no, what I know he is now, because it just sounds too weird to be true.

Nathan

I have barely been able to concentrate on patrols for the last two days, and my sleep has been terrible. I feel like I am a walking zombie as I make my way around the pack house. I plaster on a fake smile when I'm around others, especially Parker. I don't want his pity right now at my mate's rejection, or else I'm going to rip him apart. Nate and I are fighting between me wanting to just hide away, mourning at the loss of her, to him wanting to hunt and spill blood in an effort to control the dark anger in him. I've let him hunt a few of the older bucks in the vicinity as both a way to ease his bloodlust and to provide food for the pack this week, but knowing that today is the day that we are to meet up with Lori, no amount of hunting can bring him comfort.

So, here I am, sitting on a rock in the lavender field, waiting for our beautiful and confused mate to come and tear our beating heart from our chest.

Lori

Heading into the forest, I make my way to the lavender field, and there on the rock I see the man that has been filling my thoughts for the last two days. I notice he looks so worn and depressed. He looks the same way I feel. The wind kicks up around me and blows toward Nathan, and I see him take a long, slow inhale and his lips turn up in a sad smile.

"Peaches and lavender." He mutters.

"What?" I ask breathlessly.

"Your scent. It's what I fell in love with first." He says no longer hiding what he is.

"Nathan, I'm scared. How are you something that is found in fictional storybooks?" I ask, "When I look at you right now, it's taking everything in me not to run to you and hold you. To tell you that everything will be alright. I want that, but I don't understand why I feel that way." I say while trying to hold back a sob.

Nathan looks at me, and the next instant he's in front of me, eyes glowing brightly at my sobs, and I take a step back in fright.

"Please, Sweetheart. Don't be afraid of me. I would never hurt you." Nathan says softly. "And it's taking everything in me not to touch you either. It's the mate bond trying to pull us together."

"The what?" I squeak.

"Let's start with this." He reaches his hand out and interlaces his fingers in my own. "We talk about what I am." He looks at our intertwined hands, his thumb tracing my knuckles for a heartbeat before looking back up to my face. "I am a Werewolf, Lori."

I look away from him as his words sink in.

He said it. The very word I have been dreading to speak or to hear. The thing in stories that should be completely fake. How can this be a real thing?

"Lori? Please tell me what you are thinking, Sweetheart." He pleads.

I look back at him, and his eyes are still glowing brightly in my direction, and I take a step back, my hand shooting up to cover my mouth to keep the yelp from erupting in the air around us.

"Your eyes."

"Yes, Sweetheart. That is my wolf coming to the surface. He feels you're scared too and wants to let you know that you are safe and you are protected, and he wants to console you."

I lower my hand from my mouth, and I feel tears prick the corners of my eyes. "I'm so scared, Nathan. I don't know what to do."

I take a step closer to him and hesitate for a moment, while Nathan just stands there, letting me decide whether I to go to him or not. After a heartbeat, I can no longer go without him holding me, touching me, or smiling at me. I throw myself into his arms, and he wraps me tightly against his chest, and it feels like something lifts between us.

"Better?" Nathan croons, and I can almost hear his smile.

"Yes," I say simply.

Nathan leads me over to a fallen tree trunk so we can sit down for a bit and hold one another for a while longer. As he begins to rub soothing circles down my back, I tighten my arms around his waist as a thought forms in my mind.

"Nathan?"

"Yeah, Sweetheart?"

"Can I see him?" I ask.

"See who?" He begins and in the next instant, he tenses when he understands who I want to see. "Oh. You mean my wolf."

I nod into his chest, not trusting myself to speak right now.

"Lori," Nathan says as he pulls me back enough to look at me, but I keep my eyes down. "Lori, please mate, look at me." He pleads while placing a finger under my chin to insist I look at him.

I see a prideful smile spread across his face as he places a gentle kiss on my forehead before standing up from the log and looking down at me.

"I would be honored to show you my wolf." He begins, "Please, stay here, and I will go into the tree line over there. I will say, watching the phase for someone new to my world can be a little disturbing. I'll be right back."

Nathan disappears into the trees, and after a few heartbeats pass, I see the wolf I met a few weeks ago emerge from the brush. His dark gray coat shimmers in the sunlight, and those familiar dark brown eyes stare back at me.

"There's my beautiful wolf." I think in his direction.

"You claim the wolf before the man." I hear a voice snort in my mind. *"You are an odd one, mate of mine."*

It's the same voice I realize from the other night when he pleaded for me to come back to him. At first, I didn't know what to call him, but since I've heard his voice twice in my mind, I somehow know his name, and as this large wolf sits in front of me, I find myself smiling at him.

"Well, Nate, you are the first one I met. So, I think it's perfectly normal to react to you more than Nathan."

Nate looks at me in shock that I knew his name. We both know that Nathan never said anything about him, and I can somehow feel his pride at me knowing his name.

"What is it you humans say? Love at first sight?"

"Yeah. I guess so."

I stare at the wolf in front of me and, just like that second time I saw him, I want to run my fingers through his rough pelt. I get up off the log to kneel in front of him, and I start to extend my hand towards him, but I pause.

"Can I touch you?" I ask, my voice barely above a whisper.

"You never have to ask that of us, Mate. I am yours to touch as you wish."

I raise my hand, and Nate pushes his cold, wet nose into my palm, and I hear a low whine bubble from his chest at my touch. I run my thumb up the length of his muzzle and in between his eyes. Then, I flatten my hand against his large head, and as I travel down the length of his thick neck, I begin to bury my fingers into his coat. The top is rough, just like I imagined it, but the closer I get to his skin, the softer it gets. I continue until my hand is in the middle of his back, my fingers flush with his skin, and I stop. Nate looks over his shoulder, and I know he sees the fresh tears that are silently falling like rivers from my eyes.

"What's wrong?"

"I don't feel worthy of you. Of either of you. I have no idea how to exist in your world. What if I fail you?" I sob.

"You could never fail us, Lori."

This time when I look at Nate, it's not his voice I hear; it's Nathan's. I can still feel Nate in my mind, but Nathan's presence is stronger this time, like he's using Nate's mind to talk to me, further enforcing that they are of one body.

"The Great Luna, the goddess that made my kind, would not allow mates to come together that didn't complement one another," Nathan says as he turns to face me and presses his cool nose against my cheek to soak up the tears. *"I do not doubt for one second that you were destined to be mine. Yes, you are human, but it's not impossible for your kind to be mated to one of us. It has been done in the past, and it continues to be done even now. And for what you don't know about us, we will teach you."*

I wrap my arms around Nate's neck, and I feel his large head curl into the curve of my shoulder. When I think about the body in front of me, I can feel only Nate, but when I close my eyes and I allow my mental walls to fall, I can feel two souls fills my mind and I cling to the larger of the two and when I do that, I know I have Nathan in my mind as well.

"I hope I can live up to your expectations." I say into Nathan's mind. It feels as simple as breathing now that I can sense both the man and the wolf and pick which direction I want my thoughts to travel.

Nathan

"Please, don't move from this spot." I tell her while pulling away from her embrace and darting back into the woods to phase. I quickly tug my jeans over my hips, foregoing the shirt, and race back over to her.

Before I can tell her that she will always live up to any expectation I can ever ask of her, she's taking in my naked torso. My washboard abs, my wide shoulders, and my defined chest. But when I see her eyes widen, I look down and I notice something new on my skin, and my heart swells with pride when Lori notices my, no, our mating mark. She reaches her hand out to brush her index finger over my chest, and I can't stop the growl that rumbles in my throat. She snaps her hand back like I bit it, and she looks sheepishly at me.

"Do you not want me to touch that?" She asks.

"Oh no, Sweetheart. I love that you noticed it and you, want to touch it." I can't help the low growl in my voice since Nate is so close to the surface again, but Lori doesn't seem that scared now.

She leans in again, and when she traces her index finger over the gray swirls and lines of the mating mark, I groan.

"Did I do something wrong?" Lori asks, but the tone in her voice is teasing, she knows it's not like that at all.

I smile when I realize if I have this marking then, "You tell me." I grin. "Turn around for me." I instruct.

She does, and she pulls her hair to the side while I gently tug the collar of her shirt down to reveal the matching mark to mine. If we were to draw them on paper, they would fit together like a puzzle piece. I trace my thumb over her marking, and the moan that escapes past her lips goes straight between my legs, making me harden painfully against my jeans.

"What is this?" Lori pants. "I feel like it's important to you, to us."

"Yes, Sweetheart. This is important to all of us." I whisper so close to her ear that I can see every single ridge of goosebumps that blooms on her skin. "This is a mating mark. And the one you have here." I place a kiss on the bare skin of her shoulder. "Matches the one on my chest perfectly. This shows to others that I am taken, and if another male were to see yours, then they would know that you belong to me." I growl possessively.

I pull her back against my chest as we both sit on the forest floor together. Marking to marking, heart to heart as I continue to trace Lori's marking with my fingers, my lips, and even my tongue once until she moans so loud that it scares off a small flock of birds above us.

"Sorry." She says to both me and the birds. She looks back over her shoulder with a sultry smile on her face. "That was... amazing."

I chuckle. "Yes, it was." I look up at the sky and I realize that it is getting closer to dusk and I don't want to keep her out here too much longer.

"I need to take you home."

She spins in my arms, and she looks at me like I told her to go live under a rock and never come back out. "I don't want to leave you. I want to stay with you."

"I want nothing more than for you to be by my side, Baby. But I would need to introduce you to the pack first, and right now if someone so much as laughs at you for being human, I'm afraid I'd kill them on the spot, and I don't want you to see that. Not yet, at least." I explain.

"How could you kill one of your pack mates? I mean, aren't wolves social creatures?"

"Yes, Sweetheart, we are. But there is a hierarchy too. Alpha's and their mate, Beta's with their mates, the alpha's third, and so on down the line." I say.

"Where do we fall in that line-up?" Lori asks.

I do not miss the full meaning of her question, and my chest fills with pride for how smart my mate is.

"We, my incredibly smart mate, fall into the Beta category. I am the alpha's next most dominant wolf. I stand in for him if he either needs to be somewhere else or if, Luna forbid, he falls ill, I step in to take his place. So, that is why again if a wolf so much as sniffs in your direction the wrong way, in my eyes he forfeits his life."

"Well, hopefully, no wolf is stupid enough to give me a sideways glance then." Lori says half joking.

"You're not scared of what I just told you?" I ask, truly shocked by her words.

"Not really. I mean, I have a picture in my mind of what it would be like if that were to happen. But I know you would do what you needed to in order to protect me, and in that, I am not scared in the least." Lori grins.

I don't even miss a beat. I take her hand in mine and I kiss her knuckles as I say, "Tomorrow. I'll come by and pick you up tomorrow to bring you in to meet the whole pack."

"The whole pack?" She squeaks. "How many are we talking about?"

"Oh. You're right. Maybe not the whole pack. You and I are still unbonded. So another stupid wolf could get it in their head that you are their mate and–" I stop mid-sentence when I hear Lori's sharp intake of breath at my words. "What's wrong?"

"It's just when you said that another wolf could try and say I'm his mate instead of you, it hurts to hear you say that." She says while searching my eyes for the reason why she's feeling the way she does.

"Oh, Sweetheart. That's perfectly normal. That just goes to prove what we have together is real. You don't want anyone else but me, and I feel the same way about you." I firmly grasp her chin in my hand to keep her gaze on me. "You are *mine,* and no one will ever take you from me. I would sooner cut off my own hand than give you up."

She leans in closer, her eyes dipping to my lips, and I have to force myself not to press my mouth to hers.

"Not yet, Lori. If I kiss you now, I am not going to be able to stop at just a kiss, Sweetheart. And we can't do more than that until we bond. It's considered bad luck for the relationship to consummate it before the bond is locked into place by the alpha. And I won't be satisfied to only use my mouth or my fingers on you. I can't entertain the idea of more because I'll be damned if I ruin a good thing before it even starts."

"Okay. I think I can understand that." She nods and pulls back from me a little bit.

"Come on, let's get you home. It's late, and I want you well rested before you meet the alpha and a few others tomorrow."

I stand to my full height, pulling her to her feet while tucking her close to my side and walking her back to her apartment. I kiss her on the cheek and watch as she walks into the building and makes her way up to the second floor, safe for one final night away from me.

After I watch the light flick off from her apartment, I enter the forest and quickly phase, taking my clothing in between my teeth, I run back to the pack house, my long stride eating up the forest floor in record time. As I hit the edge of the main grounds, I phase back and quickly dress before entering the house and making my way toward Alpha Baldric's meeting chambers to see if he is still there this late in the evening.

I approach the solid dark purple door and knock three times when I see light pouring out from under the crack between the frame and the floor.

"You may enter." A gruff voice echoes through the heavy door.

I shove open the wooden door with my shoulder, and I see standing at the liquor cart parked near a bay window, a tall, muscular, barrel-chested man with a pure white beard braided down the middle of his chest and his clean-shaven head reflecting the low lighting of the room. He pours himself a knuckle of bourbon before sitting back down at his overly large, black stone desk.

"Alpha Baldric, I'm sorry to barge in this late, but I have a request for you." I say with a smile on my face, but it fades a bit when I see that Parker is also there in the chamber.

"Is this about your so-called human mate, Nathan?" Baldric inquires.

My eyes shoot to Parker, and I can't stop the growl that I shoot at the third-rank wolf. "You told him?"

"He asked me where you were, and you didn't say to not tell him if he asked." Parker shrugs his shoulders.

I give him a pointed glare before I bring my eyes back to the alpha. "Yes sir. I would like to bring her here to meet you and yours and a few others for now. Get her used to being around other Were's before introducing her to the whole pack."

"So you told a human about us?" Baldric snaps.

"I told my mate about us." I correct. "What's wrong? I thought you would be happy for me?"

"A human has no place in the pack. Their fear of us stinks up the air."

"Well, I promise once she gets comfortable with us, she'll be fine." I say.

"We'll see about that. You're dismissed. We will, I guess, meet this *human* mate of yours tomorrow at dinner." Baldric says as he waves me off.

I walk out of the chambers, and just as I am about to close the door, I hear Baldric whisper something to Parker. I know I shouldn't eavesdrop, but I can't help it.

"Parker?"

"Yes, Alpha?" Parker responds.

"Thank you for telling me about Nathan. And I will say, I know you've been wanting to move up in the ranks of the pack for a long time. I noticed that you've been doing fairly well when you were taking over the perimeter checks so *he* could act like a damn love-sick pup. If you want your shot at becoming my Beta, this is your chance."

At hearing my alpha's words, I take a step towards the door to demand what the fuck he means by this when I feel Lori in the back of my mind. Almost like she knows I'm pissed about something, but I don't let her know what it is.

"*Why are you still up?*" I ask as I back away from the large purple door and make my way to my bedroom.

"*I was about to doze off, but something coming from you woke me.*" Lori says sleepily in my mind.

"*I'm sorry. It's just pack shit, that's all.*"

"*It feels a little more than just* pack shit. *Is everything okay?*"

"It is now. You actually stopped me from causing a fight." I sense her worry for me flow through the bond at my admission. When I push back the feeling that I am alright and I'm happy with her in my mind, and I feel her settled down again, *"I'm alright, Sweetheart. Please get some rest. I'll see you in the morning."*

"Okay. Good night."

"Good Night, Lori. I love you."

I can feel her smile at my words and then her own love for me as she says, *"I love you too, Babe."*

Chapter Sixty-Three

LORI

The sunlight shining through my window wakes me the next morning, and everything that happened last night comes rushing back to me.

Nathan, the sexy, protective, kind, funny, charming guy, is a Werewolf, and we are mates.

I sit up in bed, pulling the covers up to my neck like that will keep the insanity at bay. But as I think more about the whole situation, I know in my soul it's right. That somehow I am the only one that Nathan will ever have, and he is the only one for me too. Maybe that's the reason that I've never felt comfortable with other men. It's because they weren't made for me. And when I did go all the way with that guy in college, I felt guilty afterward. It's because deep down, my soul knew there was someone better for me.

I look out my window, and I can see the woods in the distance, and I wonder if Nathan is out there acting as Beta and keeping the grounds safe. I decide not to bother him, but I somehow keep my mind open to him in case he wanted to reach out.

After I get out of bed and take a quick shower, I stand in front of my closet and try to think of an outfit for tonight when I meet his pack members. Ever since Nathan told me I stopped him from picking a fight against one of his pack mates, I have been antsy about tonight's dinner.

What if they don't accept me?

I try to push that thought to the back of my mind as I continue to look for the appropriate attire for the evening.

After about thirty minutes of searching my closet, I pull out a dress and a pair of black slacks along with a blouse that would match nicely. Both are of similar color schemes of white, pink, and purple, and I study them as I lay them on the bed.

"What do I wear to something like this?" I groan after looking at the tie-dye flowy dress or the black slacks with the blouse of white, purple, and pink geometric shapes. "Something fashionable with heels, or dressy casual and loafers in case I need to run?"

I must let my anxiety flow over to Nathan because I am feeling him in my mind a moment later, and his presence calms me.

"Good morning, Sweetheart. How did you sleep?"

"It was alright. It would have been better if you were with me." I tease. I hear his growl in my mind, and I can't help but laugh at him.

"You think my growl is funny, Mate?" Nathan asks with a note of humor in his own voice.

"Yeah, kinda. So, what does one wear to the meeting of wolves?" I ask, trying to lighten the mood.

"As much clothing as possible." Nathan replies in a serious tone. *"Especially to cover your mating mark, please. Only mates and healers or appointed doctors are allowed to see them."*

"Noted. So the slacks, blouse, and loafers, got it."

"See, you are a quick learner, Honey," Nathan croons. *"Dinner is at five o'clock tonight, so we have a little time to kill before we meet the pack. Did you want to walk the forest with me again? And then I can walk you to the pack house from there."*

"Sure. I'll make sure to bring a few things to freshen up once we get there." I say.

About two hours later, Nathan is at my door, dressed in a crisp dark blue button-up shirt and black pants. His dark brown eyes look over my outfit, and I shiver under his intense stare.

"You look beautiful, Sweetheart," he says as he tucks a strand of my loosely curled hair behind my ear.

"You don't look half bad yourself." I tease with a wink as I look over his frame again, and my eyes may linger at a certain part below the belt for a breath longer than it should.

"You're walking a fine line, Sweetheart," Nathan growls as his hand travels to the back of my neck and gives it a firm squeeze.

I let out a breathy laugh because I want nothing more than to cross that damn line and see just how much different being with him would be compared to the others. But I remember his words about not being bonded and how it's not a good thing to cross at the moment, and I tamp the bratty desire down. For now.

Nathan removes his hand from my neck, and he offers me his arm to escort me out of my apartment. I laugh as I take his arm and close the door behind me, then walk out of the building and into the forest. I begin to think that this area is starting to become like a home to me, but I realize that it's not where I am; it's who I am with. And as long as I am connected to this man at my side, anywhere will feel like home.

We pass our lavender field, in the very spot we met just a few weeks ago, and I pause for a moment while I pick a bundle of the delicate purple flowers to slip into my hair.

"You know, that day you first saw me in my wolf form, I was drawn here by your scent," Nathan says.

"My scent?"

"Yes. Each mate has a specific scent. I don't know if you would pick up on mine or not. I don't smell my own scent, so I couldn't begin to tell you what to look for," Nathan says. "It was the scent of peaches that made me investigate because I knew there was nothing natural here that would cause that."

I smile at the thought of that fateful day as Nathan continues to lead me through the forest, and that makes me begin to wonder. Can I pick up on his scent? I mean, I smell what I assume is his body wash, like a fresh mountain stream, but I would think his *scent* would be of something a little more... intense. So I just keep close to his side and will whatever it is in me to wake up and do what it's supposed to do.

The trail that we are walking currently is a bit rougher than the other day, loose rocks and small branches that fell from the trees above crunch, and roll under my feet. Nathan comes to a sudden stop, and in front of us is a large fallen tree that blocks the entire path.

"We'll have to go back the way we came, I guess. Take the path we did the other day." I offer.

"Nonsense." Nathan smirks as he steps over the tree with ease, his long legs easily clearing the rough bark. "See, it's easy."

"Yeah, lucky for you. You have legs a mile long. I, on the other hand, am short compared to you and not that nimble."

Without another word, Nathan leans over the tree, grips the top of my hips with his large hands, and hefts me over like it was nothing. I stumble into his chest and I place a hand on his pec, right over where I know his own mating mark hides beneath his shirt. The gray swirling line peaks from his collar and crawls up his neck, stopping in the middle of his skin.

"I *am* the lucky one, Sweetheart. But in a different way than my height advantage." Nathan whispers against the shell of my ear, causing gooseflesh to ripple across my skin.

I lean into his neck, right over his marking, and I freeze.

"Fresh cut grass and leather." I whisper so low that I almost think he didn't hear me.

He pulls me back, but I keep my eyes on the ground, because the way I feel right now with his scent still fresh in my nose, I'm afraid of what I'll do when I look at him. His scent warms my heart, my soul, my blood, and my core. I want nothing more than to have his scent envelop me. Images of him kissing me, touching me, *and loving* me, flash through my mind. I have to dig my toes into the insoles of my shoes to keep my feet planted. If his scent makes me feel this way, I can just *imagine* what my scent does to his highly sensitive nose.

"What did you say?" Nathan asks me slowly.

"Nothing, I." I begin, but his finger caresses my chin and I feel something pulse from him, through the bond we share. It's a gentle nudge, but one that I can't ignore, so I look up into his glowing brown eyes and I heave a defeated sigh.

"Fresh cut grass and leather." I repeat louder this time. "That's what you smell like to me."

"And how did that make you feel?" Nathan growls.

"It warmed me, made me feel safe..." I pause. Oh, the hell with it. "I finally understand why you are so careful with how you *interact* with me." I blush.

His low grumble in his chest vibrates against my fingers that are still splayed over his chest.

"And why is that, Mate?"

I roll my eyes.

He will not let this go. I mentally whine, but I make sure to keep my internal monologue to myself. *He really wants to know? Fine.*

I give him a sultry smile, and I step closer to him, pressing my hips firmly against his, and I feel the hardening length of him proudly fill his jeans.

"When your scent hit me, I wanted to climb you like a damn tree. I wanted to be surrounded by nothing else than your arms and your scent."

I somehow think of the images and push them his way. At first, I didn't think it worked, but the way his nostrils flare, and the pulse fluttering in his neck lets me know that he got the images just fine.

"I will make that happen for you soon, Sweetheart. After we meet the pack and get the blessing of the alpha first. Then he can bond us in the coming days." Nathan promises as he caresses my neck while running a thumb under the line of my jaw. "And I will make any desire you wish come to life."

My entire body flushes at his words, and I have to force myself to step back from him, but I can't help the challenge in my voice when I say, "I'll make sure to hold you to that declaration, Mate.",

Nathan laughs with such love and admiration filling his voice as he picks me up, one arm under my legs and the other around my shoulder blades, and carries me the rest of the way through the woods until we come up to an ivy-coated, dark brown, stone mansion. All laughter fades from me when I know that more Werewolves exist through that door. Nausea flares in my stomach when Nathan sets me down on the ground, and he waits a beat before letting me out of his embrace.

"Lori, Baby. It's okay, you don't have to be nervous." Nathan says, "I'll be right there with you."

"I know, but it's almost as bad as meeting the guy's parents. Only these people can eat me." I say while trying to hide my fear behind a joke.

"Well, they'd have to get through me, and I am not a weak wolf. Plus, I've got several years on most of these wolves, other than the alpha."

"You know, I never thought to ask. How old are you?" I say while eyeing him from head to toe. "You look about twenty-four."

"You really want to know the answer to that, Sweetheart?" He raises a brow in challenge.

I don't even have to think about it. "Yes. I do." I can't keep running from things about him and his species if I am to be even a halfway decent mate.

He nods, hearing my determination in my answer. "I'm eighty-two years old."

"Oh." I respond in shock, "I figured you'd be like way over a hundred."

Nathan laughs, "No. Now Alpha Baldric is one hundred and ninety-two, but everyone else is seventy and under."

At first, the ages, or more so this alpha's age doesn't click, but when the numbers form in my mind, I can't keep the pulse of fear from my heart.

"How long does your kind live?" I ask slowly.

"Take a breath, Baby." Nathan soothes as he places his hand on my left shoulder blade, and I'm instantly set at ease from his touch. "We can live for a very long time. I have met a handful of Were's that have been here for a millennia."

"One thousand years old?" I squeak.

"Yes, Lori. There are few things to kill us, so that helps with the lifespan. Plus, the bigger the pack, the more powerful the alpha, and therefore can live longer."

Suddenly the front door opens, and Nathan is instantly in front of me to protect me from the uninvited intrusion. When Nathan sees who it is, he steps back to my side while taking my hand in his.

"I thought I heard someone out here." A man with short black hair that hangs in his blue eyes says. "Oh, is this the lucky lady, Nathan?"

This man steps towards me with an outstretched hand, but the low growl in Nathan's chest rumbles between us as a warning. "Watch it, Parker."

"Easy, man." He says while putting his hands up in surrender and bends his head to the side to show his neck to Nathan.

"He's showing his respect to his Beta and that he means you no harm. That is why he bares his neck to us." I hear Nate's gravelly voice in my mind before I even have to wonder what just happened.

"Thank you. Can you let Nathan be with us too?" I ask knowing in the short time that I've been around these two that they are both fiercely protective of me, and Nate has a shorter fuse than his human counterpart.

"Thank you, Baby. See? You know how to get us to calm down." Nathan praises.

"You're welcome."

Nathan leads me into the house when Parker backs up from the door, and I am met with four more people. I take one look at the tall, muscular man with a full white beard and a clean-shaven head that stands in the middle of the group, I know this has to be the alpha, and his presence unsettles me. It's like he's looking *through* me and not at me. I feel the dirt that's crusted on his boots gets a warmer look than I do. And it terrifies me.

I glance over and at his side is a slender woman, her silvery blonde hair pinned up in a neat updo at the top of her head, and her piercing blue eyes seem to hold years of a harsh life. The other two—a man with brown hair pulled back in a low ponytail at the nape of his neck, and another female with black hair, which is braided down her back at least give me a curt nod.

"Dinner is almost ready, Nathan. And I suggest you keep that *human's* fear under control, or I'm going to lose my appetite." The alpha snaps while looking down his nose at me.

Nathan watches in silence as the alpha and the little group around him walk into what I assume is the dining room down the hall.

"That was Alpha Baldric, if you didn't guess already." Nathan says through gritted teeth.

"I'm sorry. I'll just—" I begin to take a step back to leave, but Nathan whips his head back to me, and his glowing eyes make me stop short.

"You have nothing to be sorry for, Lori. And if you leave, then I will go with you."

"Nathan. No." I say as tears prick the corners of my eyes, "I will not allow you to choose me over your pack that you've spent so much time with."

Nathan softly grips my arms and strokes them lovingly for a moment. "You will not be making me choose, Sweetheart, they will be. No matter what species it is, Mates make one another stronger. *I* am stronger now because of you. I will not change that fact for anything in this world." He leans in and places a tender kiss on my forehead. "Now let's walk into that dining room and show them that you are not just any human. Show them that you are *my human*."

Chapter Sixty-Four

LORI

Nathan takes my hand as we make our way toward the dining room, and I walk at his side with my head held high.

"One thing though, can you let me know how you're feeling throughout this dinner? Maybe if I can see and feel how you compose yourself, I can follow you."

"Absolutely, Baby." Nathan says as he opens his mind completely to me, and I actually feel he's a little anxious too, which makes me feel just a bit better about my own nerves.

As we walk through two large metal double doors that lead to the dining room, I am met with a dark atmosphere. The walls are lined with stone gray wallpaper accented by creme-colored crown molding. A bulky black wooden table that has snarling wolf heads carved into the legs sits in the center of the room, the wrought iron, three taper chandelier hangs low from the ceiling in the center of the table, and two large, floor-to-ceiling windows with arched tops carved into the wall face the bright green living forest outside.

I see the large, rough form of Baldric at the head of the table with his still quiet mate at his side. I don't allow myself to look at the alphas, instead, I glance at the guy with the ponytail and the woman with the braid sitting on the other end of the table.

"That's Edgar and Louise. The alpha's second top wolf, who is also a doctor, and his mate." Nathan informs me as he leads me around the table where our backs are toward the large windows and we are facing the double doors that have shut since we walked inside.

Nathan pulls out a chair that is only two spaces from the alpha and helps me sit down. He must be able to pick up on my nerves at being so close to the alpha because when he pushes my chair in and before walking over to his own, his fingers trail lightly against my shirt and right over my mate marking that hides under the polyester fabric. His touch sends shockwaves through my body, and I have to fight back a shiver.

"Oh, you are horrible." I chuckle nervously.

Nathan lets out a quick laugh, and when he takes his seat next to me, we both catch the alpha eyeing Nathan's action. I can feel the growl that Nathan forces back down his throat from the alpha's side-eyed glance at me, and I pat his knee for a moment, which, thankfully, seems to help him calm down.

After a moment of silence, two servants come in from a single black door off to the left of the room, rolling in dinner carts that carry an assortment of steak, lobster, and chicken along with a variety of vegetables, potatoes, and rice to go along with the meal. The alpha wordlessly fills two plates with steak, vegetables, and rice for himself and his mate, and as Nathan goes to take the spoon from Baldric's hand, the alpha instead, tosses the spoon back in the bowl and begins to eat his meal. I can feel

Nathan's anger flare at the apparent jab, but I just push myself into his mind and try to give what I think is a soothing caress to his thoughts.

"Thank you, Mate."

"I'm guessing that's not supposed to happen?" I ask shyly.

"No. And it's pissing me off." He snaps.

I hear a touch of Nate's voice in my mind, and I place my hand on my mate's broad shoulder.

"Maybe he's got a tick up his ass or something. You know, maybe he rolled around in the dirt too much today and picked it up earlier. I hear they hurt like a bitch in certain areas."

Nathan looks at me as he drops a spoon of rice onto his plate, and then his smile blooms on his face and he shakes his head as he finishes serving himself and then serves me. Once my plate is filled, and with a pointed glare to the alpha, Nathan hands the spoon to Edgar, who follows suit with filling his own plate as well as his mates.

"Care to share what is so funny, Nathan?" Edgar inquires.

Nathan's smile fades, and he looks at the wolf across from him.

"Oh, come on, Edgar. It's probably a private conversation between mates." Louise chuckles quietly.

"Well, they seem to be on our side at least." I say.

"Yes, Louise, it—" Nathan pauses and then smiles. "You know what, she was just wondering which one of us has a tick up their ass because even she can feel the tension in the room."

I stare at Nathan in disbelief for a moment before I pinch his side and I ask in a strained voice in his mind, *"Why the fuck would you tell them that?!"*

"To show them that you can pick up on hidden jabs that would go over most human's heads."

"Well, I, for one, think that's none of her business." The blonde snaps beside Baldric. "Whether or not my mate has a parasite on his person is none of her concern. And for her to even have that kind of thought is disconcerting." She says as she looks down her nose at me.

I feel like the air has gotten ten degrees colder, and the darker look in her eyes makes me feel like prey, and I try to tamp down the beat of fear that flows in my veins. But I'm assuming I don't do a good job because Baldric's nostrils flare once and his eyes narrow on me. Nathan sees this and grabs my hand, placing it on the table between our plates as he takes a bite of his steak. I feel his strength fill me, and I give him a reassuring squeeze.

Just as I am about to take a bite of my lobster, I feel Nathan stiffen beside me and then the double doors at the other side of the room burst open and my mate is instantly to his feet, his arm shooting out in front of me as a protective barrier. I see a dozen or so people flow into the room, and they act like this is a party. Whooping and hollering like lunatics and at the center of the group is Parker with a broad and cocky smile on his face.

"Parker, what are you doing here? This is a private dinner." Nathan snaps, and I can pick up the thoughts from him of, *unmated males,* and *some of these fuckers push their luck too much by trying to claim a female they think is theirs.* And just under Nathan's thoughts, I pick up on Nate's internal mantra. The same phrase over and over again. *Protect our mate.*

I place my hand on the small of Nathan's back while my fingers tighten into a fist around the fabric, but his focus is solely on Parker, and my touch does little to break his protectiveness.

"Ah, come on, Nathan," Parker croons, "The pack just wanted to see what kind of mate The Great Luna *cursed* you with." He laughs darkly as he comes to stand between Nathan and his alpha.

His jab angers me. No, not anger; that's too easy of a word. It completely pissed me the fuck off. I am *not* a curse, and no one is going to insult me like that.

"Well, at least Nathan has a mate. Where is yours?" I ask as I narrow my eyes at him in a challenge.

His face goes from all cocky and mocking to dark and dangerous in an instant. "You fucking bitch!" He snarls at me.

Parker tries to move around Nathan's chair to wrap his hands around my throat, but Nathan's large hand wraps around his instead, and my mate slams his pack mate onto the table with a glass-rattling roar.

"Don't you *ever* speak to my mate like that again! You are so fucking lucky I don't kill you right here, right now, Parker." Nathan growls, and I can feel just how powerful my mate is.

I remember that little pulse of power from earlier in the day, when he insisted I look up at him, and that power fills the room tenfold. It's at that instant that if Nathan wanted to, he could be alpha in his own right, but somehow I know deep down he likes being a Beta instead. But even with his power flowing through the room, I can't help the worry that starts to build in my blood from all the whispers at Nathan's outburst and him screaming for all to hear that I am his mate.

"See Nathan! This is why we don't co-mingle with humans in my pack! They take your rational thinking and make you throw it out the door. Look at what you just did to my third and our dinner. I have told you over and over again; that humans make us weak!" Baldric's booming voice fills the room and makes my ears hurt.

"Yeah, how do we know they are true mates? Do they have matching markings?" A male asks with a smirk.

"You fucking mangy mutts will never see my mate's markings. I'd die fighting all of you before that happens." Nathan snarls.

Hearing him say he would gladly die fighting to protect me makes me realize just how dangerous this could become. I shoot my hand out toward him, gripping his forearm while trying to keep myself grounded but also trying to keep him at my side because all I can see right now is the plate in front of me. The tunnel vision that is gripping my head from the intense amount of fear constricting my heart is blinding.

"That's it! Get that human out of here! Her fear has sullied my mansion enough! Parker, remove her!" Baldric demands.

"Seriously, Alpha? I'm still picking your dining plates out of my back," Parker complains as he drops a bloody piece of china onto the table.

"Fine. Then I'll do it." Baldric snarls darkly.

Nathan's head snaps to his alpha, and I can feel a mix of sorrow at what I am about to see and anger at his alpha's words fill my mind. I watch as Baldric shoves out of his chair and swiftly changes into a large, dark brown wolf. His jaws open wide, showing me rows of sharp teeth and fangs. Then I watch Nathan change for the first time.

I see the muscles in his back, legs, arms, and neck spasm as his clothes are shredded, and he fades into the large gray form of Nate. He meets the alpha's attack head-on, teeth snapping together as they both go flying across the table to land in the middle of the room in a tumble of claws and teeth.

"Lori, please get out of here while I hold him off." I hear Nathan growl in my mind as he gets back to his feet first.

"I would, but I'm going to run into the others, and they look like they have no issues with grabbing me."

Nathan's large head whips around to look at the room, and I watch helplessly as Baldric gets to his feet and prepares to lunge for Nathan when he's not looking at him.

"Nathan! Don't take your eyes off him!" I shout.

In a swift, powerful motion, Baldric launches into the air, barreling toward Nathan. Before he can even think about dodging, the alpha's teeth sink deeply into my mate's shoulder. I scream as I watch Nate's form being thrown like he was nothing more than a toy, across the room and he lands into what I now see is a hearth, since the group of Were's parted like the red sea when my mates wolven body was thrown in their direction.

I wait with bated breath until Nate appears again, and when I do, I see that his dark gray coat is darker. For a moment I think it's soot from the hearth, but I can see something dripping down his left shoulder, landing on the dark wood floor, turning the spot crimson.

My mate is bleeding. Because of me.

I scramble over the table, knocking over what food was left to reach my mate now that there is room for me on the floor as more and more Were's back up against the walls to give the fighting wolves space.

"Nathan! Nate!" I call to them.

"I'm alright, Sweetheart." I hear Nathan in my mind, but his voice is tight from pain.

"No, you're not! You're hurt because of me!" I sob as I reach his side.

"She's right, Nathan. Normally, I know you would never take your eyes off an attacker. This is what I've been telling you. Humans make you *weak*." Baldric yells from the other side of the room while still in his wolf form, his long teeth making some of his words slur.

Right then, watching my mate face off against his pack, the ones that I can tell he's held in such high regard over the years, ostracize him because he met me, a human, makes me sick to my stomach and I can't stop the angry words that fly out of my mouth.

"You know what? You need to shut the hell up."

I hear a collective breath fill the room around me, but the sound that I only care about is the one that comes from my mate. His snort of shock and approval for standing up for myself.

"Can you still fight if you need to? I don't want to poke the wolf if you can't back me up."

"Poke away, mate of mine. Show me what you got," Nathan croons with a wolfish smile.

"What did you just tell *me* to do, you measly human?!" Baldric roars while showing me his sharp teeth dripping with saliva.

"I told you to shut the hell up. I thought you Werewolves had better hearing than us *humans* do." I ask simply. "You know nothing about me and Nathan, about how our bond started. Yes, I am terrified, but you know what, that is what makes me *stronger*. Knowing that there are things out there that can kill me makes me more vigilant. And from what Nathan told me about mates, and how precious they are, I thought you would be ecstatic he has one."

"You are not his mate! A wolf of his caliber cannot be mated to a weak human!" Baldric shrieks as he lunges for me again, but a blur of dark gray shoots across the floor.

Nathan again meets his alpha's attack mid-air and this time he deals a similar blow to the wolf, taking a large bite out of the alpha's shoulder, but as Nathan tries to pin him to the ground, Baldric's jaw clamps around Nathan's right front leg. His pain-filled howl rips through my heart, and I feel hot tears rolling down my cheeks at the sound. When Nathan finally frees himself, he backs away from the alpha, slowly limping back over to my side.

"Let's go, Lori. We need to get out of here. I don't have a good leg to stand on in this form." Nathan says as he shifts his weight back and forth to give each injury a moment of relief.

I look over my shoulder and, thankfully, the wolves are smart enough to back away from us so we can retreat out of the dining room. Once Nathan and I are in the middle of the hallway, I glance over my shoulder and I spot the front door only a few more feet away.

"We are almost to the door. Just a little bit more walking, Babe." I urge.

"Good. Please, Sweetheart, go in that door to your right. That was my room. Please get a few outfits so I can phase and be at least modest in front of you." Nathan says.

"After all this, and you're still concerned with modesty? You amaze me, Nathan."

I enter his room, grabbing his blue duffle bag while stuffing it full of jeans, sweatpants, t-shirts, underwear, and socks along with a few other things I think he may need, and join my mate again in the hall. As I watch him stare down at what I can already feel is his former pack, I notice he's beginning to tire. He's switching his weight between his injured legs quicker to give the other a moment's rest.

"Nate, Nathan, please mate, come with me." I say, sounding so formal. I don't know where this comes from, but it feels right.

"Nathan, who do you choose? Your pack that you have been with since you've been a pup? Or a human that you have only known for what, all of three weeks?" Baldric asks venomously.

Nathan changes whatever he needs to about himself to be able to speak to everyone in this mansion so his words are not missed by a single ear. "If I have to choose one over the other, I will always choose my mate."

"Then as Alpha of the South Dakota Pack, I hereby strip you, Nathan Shade, of your Beta status, and banish you from my pack." Baldric decrees.

At those words, the only way I can explain the pain that is pouring from Nathan at that moment is like his soul was just ripped from his body. Pain that is even worse than the bite wounds that marred his shoulder and leg are secondary to the white-hot sensation that is flowing through his entire body now. And the howl that follows is so full of agony that it hurts every facet of my being.

My mate then goes from standing strong against the pack to collapsing on his side, pawing at the wooden floor like he wants to dig a hole to bury himself in. I wordlessly rush to his side and place a hand on his head. He opens one eye, and the whine that escapes through his nose is like a knife to my already broken heart. And in that moment, I'm *done* with these assholes and their narrow-minded ways.

"You all are pathetic. You are not a superior species in the least. You are just like normal humans. You judge what does not fit into your perfect little world." I say with calm anger.

"Please, Lori, don't provoke them. I have nothing left to protect you with."

I hear Nate's gravelly, mournful voice whisper in my mind. The defeated timber, bringing more tears to my eyes for him and everything he's lost this night, all because he chose me.

"Don't talk to me any further, human." Baldric sneers. "Take your broken wolf and leave my grounds."

I help my mate to his feet while supporting him on the way to the door. I grab the handle and swing the door open, but I pause for a moment. I have the feeling that words mean a lot to this world, and I look over my shoulder at the pack behind me.

"You are no alpha if you cannot support one of your own with something as precious as a mate, no matter what species they are. You lead with a vicious tongue and actions, and I am glad that you will not be my alpha. This *broken* wolf is more of an alpha than you will ever hope to be. I chose Nathan as *my* alpha and will follow him for the rest of my life because The Great Luna thought I would be a *blessing* to him." I say as I shoot a venomous glare at Parker. "I hope that when you meet your mate, you won't be forced to choose between her and the pack, Parker. Because she's going to get the short end of the stick with your attitude on the matter." I glance back to the alpha still in his wolven form. "May The Great Luna deal with you and yours as she sees fit because I know me and mine will live a happy life for years to come."

I help Nathan limp out the door and into the darkening forest around us to begin our life anew. Whatever that may be now.

CHAPTER SIXTY-FIVE

NATHAN

Lori helps me walk through the forest, and we end up at a little stream near our lavender field.

"Let's get you cleaned up." She mutters softly as she strokes my wolven head tenderly.

As she starts to soak some washcloths that she must have gotten from my old room, I slowly phase, and when I do, I try to block my mind from Lori as pain consumes me.

Pain from the wounds reopening as my body pulls from one form to another, and they bleed afresh. Pain of my beta status being ripped from me. And the pain of being a lone wolf now.

So, I sit in front of Lori, a broken, bleeding, naked man, and I keep my head down because I can't bear to look at her right now. I have failed her in so many ways I can't begin to count.

"I'm sorry." I mutter.

"No," She says sharply while pointing a wet finger at me. "None of that shit. I can tell you're trying to block me out. You're trying to save me from the pain you're feeling, but, Nathan, Baby, we are in this together. I am *not* going anywhere. Please, let me be what you need most right now. Let me be both mate and pack for you."

As I hear her words, I can feel the sincerity in her voice, and I can no more stop the tears that flow from my eyes than I can hold my breath. I let the walls that I built around me crumble to mental dust, and I let her feel every ounce of my anguish. She pulls me into her chest without a second thought. Not bothered one bit about my bloody, naked body. She only cares about me and my well-being. We stay locked in each other's arms for a while, and I will Nate to see the effort she's putting into us, and while he appreciates it, this is something that he will have to work through on his own, as will I.

Lori pulls back eventually and shows me a sorrowful smile. "Let's get you cleaned up." She repeats, but this time she gets to work on me.

She wets the washcloth again and tenderly begins with my forearm first, wiping away the blood that began to clot from the puncture wounds. She stares at my arm as the injury heals before her eyes, and she looks back up at me again with a light smirk.

"That's a neat trick." She says while trying to lighten the mood.

I try to return her smile, but I know it doesn't reach my eyes. "Yeah." I whisper.

She then cleans off my shoulder, and after that heals, I slip into a pair of black sweats and a black t-shirt to match. I will my legs to hold my body, and we slowly make our way back to her apartment where we collapse on the couch and sit in the darkness with only a sliver of the moon filling the room with its milky white light through the window.

"So what do we do now?" Lori asks softly while tracing her finger down my arm.

I gather her closer to my chest and I take a deep, shaky breath of her scent, willing it to fill the voids in my soul.

"We start living our lives, I guess. How do you feel about moving to North Dakota?"

"I will go wherever you go, Nathan. Wherever we are is home to me."

Two weeks later, Lori finds the perfect house for us, and with the money I have in my personal savings account that I acquired over the years, I buy the house for her, and we move in to start our new life. But no matter how much I want to celebrate having Lori at my side, I cannot bring myself to be the man she fell in love with. At night when Lori is asleep, I go into Nate's forest to check on him, and his sky is bleak. The trees and grass are slowly dying, and I keep hearing the thoughts of *'lone wolf'* slip from him. I try to keep this from Lori; I don't want to bring her any more grief, but the way she looks at me at times, I know she can feel it too. I almost want to tell her I wouldn't blame her if she left me, but I know deep in my soul that she would go down burning with me if it came to it.

A few nights later, after we moved in the last of the boxes and got all of the furniture from her apartment set up, we silently lay in bed. Normally while around Lori, I wear sweats and a t-shirt to bed, but after some insisting on her part that she wants to sleep skin to skin, we settle on me only wearing sweats.

Tonight Lori is snuggled up next to me in a purple silky pajama tank and shorts to match with her head resting on my chest. I can tell she has something on her mind from the way she's tracing my gray mating mark with a thoughtful index finger. It still feels like she's touching a part of my soul, but it's muted and not as electrifying as before, but I hold on to that familiar feeling like a vice.

"Something has been bothering me, Nathan." She begins, and I tense under her hand, waiting for her rejection. "No, Honey. It's nothing bad, I promise." She lifts her head from my chest and props herself up with her elbow digging into the mattress at my side. "It's just, aren't we still unbonded?"

Her question ignites a wave of pain through me, and I lift my hand to caress her cheek. "How can you still want to be bonded to someone like me? I have no pack. And just because we are mates, I don't want to make you bond with a lone wolf." I whisper.

"Are you hearing yourself?" Lori asks gently. "You were exiled from your pack because of your love for me, for your mate. How can I turn away from that? I want you, Nathan Shade. I want all of you. I want to be bonded to you, as your mate, as the other half of your soul."

"We don't have an alpha to bond us, Sweetheart." My voice cracks.

"Well, like I said three weeks ago, I consider you my alpha." Lori says and then, with a gleam in her eye, she adds, "So, bond us."

At her demand, something changes in me. Acceptance blooms in my chest, and she's given me a role again. As this feeling flows through me, I feel Nate perk up, and he's suddenly clawing at my mind to get to the surface.

"Let's bond to our mate, Nathan. It won't be as strong as an appointed alpha bonding us, but it will be enough to show other males that she is ours and ours alone." Nate growls.

I take a breath and let Nate come forward since bonding is done by the wolf and human sides being of one mind. As Nate and I merge, I feel that my power is stronger and, like her words demanded, I am *her* alpha. And I intend to rise to that role with a grace I haven't felt in almost three weeks.

Lori

Nathan takes a deep breath, and when he opens his eyes, I see that they are glowing brighter than I have ever seen them, and I know that Nate is just under the surface.

"I, Nate, wolf to Nathan Shade, ask that Lori Bradley accept us as her mate. So that we may be the ones to protect you, love you, make you whole, and be the other half of your soul. In accepting us, you will complete the mate bond that we as your personal alpha can accomplish." Nathan says in a deep, growling voice that only his wolf can give him.

"I, Lori Bradley, take you, Nate, wolf to Nathan and Nathan Shade, the man, as my mate. So that both of you can protect me, love me, and be the other half of my soul. But I promise to love you, and protect you as much as my human body will allow, and be the other half of your soul. I accept you both and therefore complete the mate bond." I reply, somehow knowing what I need to say at this moment.

I feel something snap between us. Almost electrical. It warms me from the roots of my hair to the ends of my toes. Filling every single cell of my body, making sure no space inside me is left untouched. I thought I felt Nathan and Nate before, but now, it's like I can feel every breath they take, every beat of their heart like it's my own. I find myself gripping Nathan's arm, my nails leaving half crescents in his skin and my breath panting like I've run a marathon.

"Oh wow. That was... intense." I breathe shakily.

I look up into my mate's eyes, and while they are still glowing brightly, I can tell that Nathan is with me and not his wolf counterpart.

"Are you okay?" I ask.

I feel pure happiness flow from him like water over a dam. I smile and scoot in closer to him, wanting to be surrounded by the lighthearted feeling that I am *finally* getting from him. My eyes flick down to his chest for a moment, and I feel that something has changed.

At first, I don't realize what it is, but when I see his marking, a desire so primitive blooms in me that I even find myself wanting to growl possessively at what stares back at me.

The pitch black swirling and curving mate marking grabs my eyes.

I run a delicate finger over the lines starting from the strong curve of his pec and following up over the curve of his collarbone and up the expanse of his neck, which has risen to just shy of his jaw.

Nathan closes his eyes as a pleasure-filled groan fills the room and vibrates through my fingers, and I can't help the chuckle that erupts from my throat.

"I am *more* than okay, Mate," Nathan says while trying to catch his breath.

He forces his eyes to open again, and he smiles at me, and for the first time, after all that shit went down, it finally reaches his eyes.

"Thank you, Lori. You knew exactly what my wolf, and I needed to feel whole again." His gaze burns into my face, into my soul, and I shiver under his stare.

"That's good." I reply with a quiver in my voice, but then something deep in me knows he loves a challenge, and that same part loves to throw those said challenges right in his face.

So with a smirk playing at my lips, I move to straddle his stomach and I slowly lift the hem of my shirt up, up, and up over my head, tossing it on the floor in a whisper of fabric against the wooden planks. I then lift my arms to the nape of my neck, making my breasts perk to attention, as I gather my hair in a messy and loose updo and ask, "Now, what are you going to do now that you're whole again?"

Nathan studies me for a moment; he's either shell-shocked at seeing my naked body for the first time or confused by my question. But that only passes for a moment before I see the cocky smirk that I fell in love with grace his handsome features.

"I have an idea." He growls.

Nathan grips my waist, sitting up in bed, and pulls me close to him. Skin to skin. My heavy and needy breasts pressed firmly against his chest. His hand travels up the center of my back and comes to rest at the nape of my neck, holding my head right where he wants it. He leans in, so slowly, and I want to pull his mouth to mine. To finally taste him, but he's got me pressed so tightly against him and my head held firmly in his grasp that I can't move. And while normally I would bristle at a man acting that way, I relish it while in Nathan's arms.

I close my eyes when he leans in closer, to where he's just a breath away, and I prepare for his lips to collide with mine. I wait a moment, and when I realize he's left me hanging, I can't help the groan that bubbles from my throat as I feel his lips instead gently trail over my jaw, and down my neck.

"You think I'd give you what you want so easily? I've been waiting my whole life for you, Sweetheart. I'm going to take my time with you for a while," Nathan croons as his lips dip below my collarbone and gets dangerously close to the curve of my right breast.

"Nathan, please. I want you." I pant.

"You shall get me in time, Mate."

He takes my hardened nipple in his mouth, closes his lips around the sensitive bud and slowly sucks. This elicits a moan out of me so loud that I think the people in the house across the street may hear it. He growls against my soft flesh, and I can already feel my climax building, brick by loving brick.

Nathan then turns us and gently lays me back on the bed, his lips never leaving my body, until I am settled into the mattress. He then lifts his mouth from my breast and again slowly trails his lips up my neck and he *finally* finds my mouth. His tongue swiping over my lips to beg for entry, and I gladly open for him. My hands shoot to his hair and I pull him closer, but still, that's not enough. I want him to be under my skin just as much as I want to be under his.

"Nathan." I moan.

Without taking his mouth from mine, his hand travels down my body; his touch is so feather-light across my belly that gooseflesh ignites across my skin before his hand dips into my pajama shorts. I arch my back into him as a finger eases into me. I gasp when he adds another and teases the glorious spot that makes stars begin to form in the corner of my mind, but Nathan keeps them just out of reach from me.

"I need more." I plead breathlessly.

He growls into my mouth, and the next thing I know there is only air between us, and I feel the proud hardness of him press against my hot core.

"Is this what you need, Mate?" He asks as he brushes the tip against me.

"Yes!" I plead.

As his lips take mine again, he fills me inch by glorious inch. His body shakes with the need to sink into me with one thrust, but he's being mindful of our first time together and making sure I am able to adjust to his size before going further. I claw at his neck, his back, and shoulders while rolling my hips to help seat him fully inside of me.

"Oh, Nathan!" I moan loudly once he's filled me to the hilt.

"That's right, Mate. Scream my name. Let me hear you."

Nathan pulls out of me to the tip and then slams into me over and over and over. Loving me like no other has before with each thrust of his hips and each time his mouth devours mine. And I know, in this moment, that once we somehow untangle ourselves from one another, there will be no morning-after guilt like I've felt in the past. Only contentment with the one that was made for me.

At that thought, Nathan drives in once more, hitting that spot that makes the stars that were dancing just out of reach, come crashing down and I explode. Screaming his name as loud as my throat can muster, and he follows right behind me. Both of us falling over that blissful edge as one, and I wouldn't have it any other way.

Chapter Sixty-Six

Nathan

Six months later

Today when I walk in the door to the home that Lori and I have built together, I have a smile on my face for more than one reason these past few months. I have news to tell my mate.

"Sweetheart! Where are you? I have news I want to share!" I shout as I shut the front door behind me and walk into the kitchen, where I see Lori making lunch for herself.

"What is it, Nathan?" She asks as she takes a bite of her sandwich.

"I found a job at the bank as their accountant for major business accounts. I showed them how I worked." I pause, pushing the memory behind me. "With several accounts for a private employer, and they hired me on the spot."

"Oh, that's amazing, Baby! I am so proud of you." Lori beams as she wraps her arms around my neck, and I pull her against me while I spin her around in the air.

"Thank you. Sweetheart."

I nuzzle into her neck, and I take in her peach and lavender scent into my nose. But before I set her down, I pick up on something else. Something softer.

I push her back at arm's length and look at her in the eyes. "Did you change your perfume?"

"No, why?"

I think about the scent again, and then a slow smile forms on my lips as I finally remember where this soft, new scent comes from.

"I think I know what's different, Lori." I say, my voice a low rumble.

"Why are you looking at me like that, Nathan?" Lori asks, and I don't have to look at the reflection of me in her eyes to know mine are glowing. It's the little intake of breath that is a dead giveaway every time.

"I am looking at you this way, because." I begin as I pull her back against my chest, marking to marking, while my hands rest on her flat belly. "You, my beautiful, smart and strong mate, are pregnant."

"I'm what?!" She exclaims as she spins in my arms to look up at me. "How can you tell?"

"I can't exactly say what it smells like, but under your normal scent, there is something different. Something soft and new, and I've been around one pregnant Were before and she had this same smell."

"Really? I'm pregnant?" Lori asks again, and I nod.

She then bursts into part laughing, part crying as she again wraps her arms around my neck. But just as suddenly as she does this, she's backing away again with a spark of fear in her eyes.

"Nathan? How do Were pregnancies work? Are they longer or shorter than humans? Are there different risks? What about new and full moons?"

She shoots off question after question, and I grab her wrists to pin her hands against my chest.

"Sweetheart. Take a breath for me." I say, and she does. "I am going to do some research on this. Like I said, I was only around one pregnancy, but it was only in passing. I will find out how they work." I promise, and I give her a sound kiss on the lips.

After two months of trying to get into any database, I can remember hearing about while in *that* pack, I am hit with nothing but dead ends. Apparently, all the passwords that I knew have been changed. Deep down I knew that would happen, but it still pisses me off.

I finally drag myself out of my office, and I make my way upstairs to our bedroom. I find Lori on her side of the bed, and she's caressing her slowly growing belly, which is now about nine weeks along.

"You are so beautiful." I whisper as I tug my shirt off and slide in next to her.

"You're not half bad looking either for ninety." Lori grins.

"I'm eighty-three, mate." I growl at her teasing tone.

"Well, you're getting closer to ninety than you are to eighty."

"I can still love you like a twenty-year-old." I say as I lift her nightgown over her head and remind her just how *young* I still am for her in all the ways I know she loves.

As we come down off our love high, I pull my mate into my chest and I finally tell her about my failed research.

"I'm sorry, Lori, but I wasn't able to find anything on what to expect for a Were pregnancy. I've been locked out of any databases I knew of."

"It's okay. We'll just have to play it by ear. Or in your case, by nose." She playfully taps my nose with her index finger, and I snap my teeth in the air towards her finger in a playful bite, and I am rewarded with a laugh that warms my soul.

"Hey, Nathan. Can I ask something?"

"Anything, Sweetheart." I croon.

"I know is stupid, but can we go back to the lavender field? I want to bring a flower back and dry it." She asks sheepishly.

"That is in no way stupid, Lori." I say as I kiss her on the forehead. "Besides, that field is huge. We don't even have to go near my old patrol grounds."

The following week, we travel back to South Dakota. We first stop in at Paddy's diner to get a bite to eat, which consists of the Paddy's Special for me, a cheeseburger for Lori, and apple pie for the both of us. Then we walk hand in hand down the sidewalk and we enter the forest about half a mile away from the border of Baldric's territory, where it's considered no-man's land.

At first, I feel a pang of longing to be back with the pack that I knew for so long, but images of that night fill my mind, and I abruptly shut and lock that door. Because now I have something so much better happening around me that I would have missed out on if I had chosen the pack instead of my mate. I lead Lori to the lavender field, where she picks a few flowers and places them into little plastic containers to keep the petals from being crushed when she puts them in her purse.

We spend a bit of time in the field, sitting on a fallen tree and just taking in the subtle lavender scent around us while we both let images of that fateful day we first met filter through our minds.

The girl with golden brown hair in the sun and the wolf with a man hiding under his pelt.

As dusk begins to settle in the air around us, I walk Lori back through the forest and to our car so we can make the long drive back home. As we hit the sidewalk, I can't stop the low growl that bubbles in my throat as a familiar scent hits my nose. Lori's hand tightens around my arm in an effort to help ground me when she picks up that I am smelling someone from my old pack.

There, sitting on a bench, is Edgar with a long, dark brown trench coat and a heather gray newsboy hat on his graying head. It's the doctor as well as the alpha's second, or I assume he's still the second since I was exiled. Edgar looks over his shoulder at us and he stands, taking off his hat and bares his neck to me and Lori as he stands before us.

"Hello, Beta. It's good to see you again and that your new life is treating you well."

"I am no longer your Beta, doctor, I reply tersely.

"I do remember that, Nathan. But I do not agree with how Baldric treated you. Which is why I resigned as part of his top wolves and became the full-time doctor for him. But to me, you will always be my Beta." Edgar says.

"Well, thank you. I'm sorry that you had to make that decision, though."

"I'm not. And like you, I'd do it again if I needed to. I had my mate's full support on the matter as well. I know I made the best decision for the both of us." Edgar then smiles as he takes in Lori at my side. "I see congratulations are in order for you and yours."

Lori stands closer to me, and I wrap my arm protectively around her.

"He means well, Lori." I tell her when I smell the doctor is truthfully happy for us.

"Thank you, Edgar. We are about nine weeks into the pregnancy." I tell him.

"That is amazing news, Nathan! You and yours are in North Dakota, are you not?"

At my shocked expression, Edgar chuckles. "Sorry, but I can smell the countryside on you both."

I nod at him, and he smiles as he looks over at Lori.

"Let me guess, you two have questions about the little one, don't you?"

"Can you tell us anything, Edgar?" Lori asks with a touch of hope in her tone.

"I unfortunately, cannot. But I do know of a doctor in North Dakota. She and I keep in touch once in a while. I met her when I went back to medical school a few years back to help get me up to speed on today's procedures. She is very aware of things around her, and she knew I was different from the first time I sat beside her in class. So, she is very well versed in Werewolf physiology and how Were pregnancies work." Edgar pulls out a piece of paper from a small notebook, and I watch as he writes down Dr. Madison Peterson and her phone number.

"Contact her and tell her that Edgar Keys recommended you."

Present day

I look down at my daughter and I wipe the tears that have finally slowed a bit at my story, from her cheeks.

"So after your mother and I got home, I called Doctor Peterson, and she was amazing with your mother, and she was able to answer all of our questions without much thought. When it was time for you to be born, I wasn't as scared as I thought I would be. Not with Madison around. And with you being in our life, in my life, I finally felt like I had a pack again between you and Lori."

I kiss the top of Dakota's head, and I glance over to my mate, who has tears in her eyes at all the memories I re-lived for both of us. I then look over to the alpha's and I knew that Tobias had notions of what could have happened, but in his somber expression now, I can tell that he's hurting in a different way. Hurting because of the choice I was forced to make and I know he's thinking about what he would have done in that moment. We both know without a doubt what would have happened.

I turn my attention back to my beautiful daughter and, with the strength that Lori was able to give to me twenty-two years ago, I let my own diluted alpha power flow over Dakota and let it fill the room.

"So when I tell you that Kai is in the best hands possible, I mean it. I trusted Doctor Peterson with you, and I trust her with Kai. And you have Quilla in there with him too." I say, glancing at Tobias, and will him to believe my words too.

"Thank you, Nathan."

I nod at his response as I continue to hold Dakota tightly against my chest, and I feel her relax a bit in my power.

549

CHAPTER SIXTY-SEVEN
DAKOTA

ad's story distracted us for four hours. It's 4:30 in the morning, and I jump in my chair when I feel a familiar presence enter my mind. Everyone looks at me, and I give them a wobbly smile.

"It's Quilla."

I sit up in my chair, leaning forward with my elbows on my knees and my hands angled to cover my lips. I feel Dad and Tobias place a hand on each shoulder as if to connect to me so they can hear Quilla too.

"Quilla?" I hear the fear coloring my voice even in my mind. She is about to tell me the fate of my mate and I am terrified.

"Hey, Dakota. So far, everything is going well. Kai is stable, and we just cleaned out the wound to his abdomen. It was deep, and the shards of silver seemed to be never-ending, but we finally got them all. I'm working on his chest wound now while Doctor Peterson stitches his stomach closed. We are trying to get the silver out before the sun comes up. Before he becomes a full Were again."

I can tell my friend is tired but determined to finish this. *"Please continue to take care of him for me, Quilla. I trust you. Thank you so much."* I say with hot tears streaming down my face at her update.

We all look at the clock and know that sunrise is in an hour, and we wait with bated breath for any further updates.

Fifty-eight minutes later, Quilla and Dr. Peterson walk out of the O.R. in blue scrubs and still wearing their surgical caps with equally exhausted looks on their faces.

"Are you Kai's father?" Dr. Peterson asks Tobias.

"Yes, I am. And this is his mate, Dakota." Tobias says while pulling me to his side to show our united front.

Dr. Peterson nods, "As I am sure you are aware, the operation was long and complicated." She begins, and my stomach drops at her tone.

Short, cold, and professional. I can't tell if this is going to be good news or bad. I glance over at Quilla, and she gives me a small smile.

"With the assistance of Miss Rose, we were able to remove all the shards of silver from Kai's wounds. We are currently running his blood through a dialysis machine to see if we can filter any remaining silver out of his bloodstream, and we are waiting to see how that will fair right now."

"Oh, thank God." I sob.

"Thank The Great Luna for you both," Tobias says.

"I'm just hoping the dialysis machine will work the way we think." Quilla says while rubbing the back of her neck with her hand.

"I know of a way to make the machine work more in our favor."

I know that voice.

When the Irish lilt to his words fill the room, I see Quilla's face light up.

"Atticus!" Quilla says brightly despite her exhaustion.

"Hello, Rosie." He then looks at Dr. Peterson with a smile. "Hello, my name is Atticus Remington, Tobias' pack doctor. May I assist you and my mate in making sure we can isolate any remaining silver from Kai's blood?"

Dr. Peterson nods, and they begin to walk through the O.R. doors, but my words stop them in their tracks.

"Can we see him?" I plead.

Quilla glances at the doctor and gives her a serious look. "Actually, having his mate at his side will help him heal."

Dr. Peterson nods again, and she leads us through the hospital and to the ICU floor. She takes us to a private suite, but stops before she opens the door.

"I need whoever the alpha is here to make the order that if I say I need everyone out, that you will go. You all are a lot stronger than my staff and I can't have anyone hurt on my watch."

"As you say, so shall it be," Tobias says formally. "The only ones that will stay in the room will be myself and his mate. And I will make sure she stays by my side." Tobias adds.

When the doctor is satisfied with the decree, she opens the sliding door to Kai's room where I see Quilla and Atticus already working diligently on the dialysis machine.

Dr. Peterson turns to us before we enter the room. "I will warn you, Kai has a lot of medical equipment on him. I'm shocked that I didn't have to run a trach for him to breathe while he healed. His left lung collapsed, and fluid was filling the right one. He is extremely lucky to be alive."

"Please, let us see him." Coraline asks, pure worry filling her blue eyes.

The door finally opens and Tobias, much to Coraline's reluctance, lets me enter the room first. Dr. Peterson was right, Kai's body is covered in so much equipment I only see bits and parts of his skin. Full oxygen mask on his face. IV tubing running from both arms. One is a drip for medications and the other for the dialysis machine.

The white bandages that cover his chest and stomach are dotted red in areas where he must still be bleeding past the stitches. Next, I see lead wires crawl across his torso that must connect to a heart monitor. When I look at the screen, I can only assume that the slow-beating lines should be stronger. But I'm happy that they are just beating at all.

As I approach his bedside, I notice that his skin is no longer the bright and healthy hue I've gotten used to; it's so pale that it's almost grey. When I take his fingers in my right hand, I can feel just how cold he is. After I finish looking over his still-broken body, I press my warm lips to his cold knuckles, and it's like the sensation breaks my last thread of composure. My knees no longer have the strength to hold me, and I crumble onto the floor, head resting beside Kai's cool body while I let my emotions flow silently down my face.

I hear Atticus pick up a file from the end of the bed, and I force my eyes to look up at him. Waiting for him to tell me what's going on.

"He's lost a lot of blood. His blood counts are all over the place." He looks to Dr. Peterson. "Did you give him any blood, Dr. Peterson?"

"No. I knew with him being a Were, that human blood may make him worse than he is now."

"Okay. We can help with that now. I can take blood from Tobias since he is both his father and alpha."

Tobias is already nodding his agreement to give whatever his son needs.

Quilla then walks over to her mate and takes his hand. "And you can take blood from me too. Tamer's blood can help just as well."

"Darling, you are already so tired. Are you sure?" Atticus asks, leaving it up to her for a final say.

"Yes. If this will help Kai like I feel it will, then I want to do it." She says with determination.

"In that room over there." Dr. Peterson points over her shoulder. "Is all the equipment you will need to draw blood. I estimate he needs about three full bags to even begin to get back to normal counts."

Atticus nods, and I watch as he leads Quilla into the room with Tobias on their heels.

While I am waiting for them to get back with the blood, I force myself to stand to my feet, and I gently rest my palm against Kai's cool cheek, right under the oxygen mask that rests on his mouth. I run my thumb over his temple and then through his hair before I lean my forehead against his, trying to reach out for his mind since the new moon is out of the sky.

And a fresh new wave of tears hit me as I am still met with darkness from his end. I press my nose against his skin and I inhale deeply. I can still pick up the scent of pine needles and cool mint over the tangy, coppery smell of his fresh blood and the antiseptic scent of the hospital around me.

"Please, Kai." I whisper into his ear. "Please, come back to me, my mate, my alpha. I need you by my side. I am nothing without you."

I hear Atticus come back to his bedside once he is finished setting up Tobias and Quilla for the blood donation, but I don't move from Kai's side. I need to feel him against me. To keep my hand against his skin, to just remind myself that he's still alive. I watch as Atticus walks over to the dialysis machine and takes a sniff at it, then after a moment he gives a satisfied nod and turns to me.

"What did you do to the machine?"

"I added an herbal Wolfsbane filter of sorts to it. With the healing properties of the dried flowers, I made a filter out of cheesecloth so it would be small enough to catch any slivers of silver and heal the blood before it goes back into him. Then once I can replenish the blood he lost, he should start to heal on his own. Granted, it's still going to be slow, but it will be a vast improvement to what's going on now." Atticus says.

This is a different side to him than I've seen before. Instead of the lightness and smile lines like the first time I met him, there is a hardness to his eyes. Calm and calculated. And instead of smile lines around his eyes, there is firm determination between his brows. Looking at him now, I know this is the doctor's side of Atticus, and he will figure out the best treatment to get my mate back to full health along with my Tamer.

About twenty minutes later, Tobias leads Quilla out of the little side room and helps her into a recliner that's sitting near the window. Once she's settled into the beige, faux leather, Atticus takes his place by her side, instantly doing what he feels she needs to make her comfortable. Covering her with a white blanket and propping her feet up.

Tobias walks over to me and gives me a tight smile. I notice his skin is a touch lighter than it was, but I know better than to comment on it. He looks at his son and he allows a look of pure pain and fear at Kai's slumbering form to cross his face for a heartbeat, two, three. But then his alpha mask is back on, and he turns around to face Atticus, who is perched on the arm of the recliner and making sure his mate is eating a high protein and carb-heavy snack.

"Atticus. I know things can change in an instant, but do you foresee anything happening to my son as of right now?"

"I think he is stable enough for you to leave for a while. I hear you have some new members to welcome into the pack." Atticus says with a tight smile.

I wonder who Atticus is talking about, and then I remember the girl I claimed from Jeffrey. The same one that Kai knew and was used as a setup for this attack.

"Who is she, Tobias? Why was she coming to Kai?"

"From what Kai told me, she was coming to him and was begging him to take care of Jeffrey. He and Caleb run their pack as a survival of the fittest, as you well know. If you're weak, you're dead. And Jeffrey made her father craft the silver that hurt you. If the man didn't comply, Jeffrey would have tortured the man's wife and Emma."

"Thank you for sharing that and for accepting them into your pack."

Tobias nods his head at me, and as he's leaving the ICU room, he gives his mate a kiss on the cheek and looks at my father, apparently an alpha/beta thing being exchanged, and then he's out the door.

A few hours after I pull up a chair and take my spot next to Kai's bed, his first blood transfusion is complete. Atticus runs more tests and finds that while whatever numbers he's looking at are beginning to go up, he says they are not at the normal levels. So, he trades the empty blood bag for the second one, and then we wait some more.

I lean back in my chair, still keeping my hand interlaced with my mates while I watch Atticus and Quilla. How Atticus instantly goes back over to her once his job is done for the moment, and it turns into a waiting game. She stands and insists he rest in the recliner while she sits in his lap. Her legs are tossed over the arm of the recliner, and his large hand supports her back while idly twirling her coppery hair around his fingers as it cascades softly down her back. I find myself clinging to their happiness and praying to God, to the Great Luna, that they can bring my mate back to me. That I can once again smile when Kai looks at me, touches me, kisses me, and be the light and strength for me when I feel like crumbling in on myself.

Twelve hours after surgery, Atticus is finally satisfied with Kai's blood-work and says his levels are where they should be for a Were.

"Rosie, would you help me change his bandages, please?" Atticus asks while unpacking fresh bandages, tape, and mounds of gauze.

"Sure," Quilla says simply as she takes out a large baggie of what I assume is dried Wolfsbane.

Atticus looks at her with a quizzical expression, and she smiles. "I figured it wouldn't hurt to add them to the bandages."

"You amaze me more and more every day, Darling." Atticus croons with a kiss to her temple.

As they remove the bandages from Kai's chest and stomach, I have to hold back the sob that wants to tear from my throat. Both wounds are an angry red with tiny lines of pink branching off from the slash marks in something similar to a root system in a tree. Blood still oozes from between the pitch-black stitches in his skin. I have to force myself to watch as his wounds are tended to, even though my stomach twists nauseously from the sight.

After Atticus and Quilla finish tending to Kai's injuries, I hear the ICU doors swish open behind me and I pick up on a new, yet familiar scent. I turn and I see Emma standing in the doorway.

"Hello, Emma. How are you doing?" I ask gently as I wave at her to come in.

Emma stays in the doorway at first, but when I give her a small smile, she rushes over to me and wraps her arms around my waist. I can then feel the girl's fear for Kai through the bond that I can only assume came from Tobias making her pack.

"Hey. It's okay. He's still healing." I whisper into her hair, but it's also a reminder for me to believe it too.

"Thank you, Miss Dakota. For getting me away from *him* and that pack," Emma says while sobbing into my shirt.

I pull her back to look me in the eye, and with determination I haven't felt in my voice since Kai got hurt ,I say. "That is what a *true alpha* does. They protect their pack no matter the cost. You and yours are in one of the best packs in the U.S. now. So, take solace in that. You do not live in fear any longer." I say while pushing my own alpha power toward Emma to show her that she is safe.

Emma nods and stays with me for a while, telling me stories of what happened leading up to her eventual play in Kai's attack. At hearing her tell the tale, I want nothing more than to finally bring these assholes down.

CHAPTER SIXTY-EIGHT
DAKOTA

Later that evening, after Emma has gone to her new home for the night, Atticus insists I eat the tray of food he brought up from the cafeteria before we all turn in to try and get some sleep. I stay in the recliner by Kai's bed while everyone else sleeps in the private waiting room across the hall.

Just as I am about to let sleep pull me under, I begin to pick up a faint scent filling the air. It almost smells sickly and with a tinge of sweat. I sit up to look at Kai and notice his skin has a slight sheen to it and when I wrap my fingers around his arm, his skin is warm. No, it's hot, burning hot. And the sheen I see on his skin is sweat. His breathing, I notice is quicker, and that is when I finally put it all together that he's running a fever. I know I need to get Atticus, but there is no way in hell that I am leaving my mate's side now. So, I reach out to the doctor through the bond we all share through Tobias.

"Atticus." I find his slumbering mind, but he doesn't stir at first. So I push harder. *"Atticus!"*

"Yes, Dakota?" Atticus answers, albeit groggily, but with a quick alertness that follows.

"I need you now. Kai's running a fever."

"I will be right there."

I look back at Kai's feverish body, and I can't just stand here looking at him like an idiot. I need to do something. I rush into the bathroom and run the coldest water I can get out of the faucet while I look for washcloths or hand towels, anything to be able to soak the fabric and put on his body. After I find a few washcloths, I see a pale pink basin under the cabinet. I fill it with cold water and gingerly walk it to Kai's bedside while pulling his bed table over to me with my foot. I dip the rag into the water, wring it out, and place the cloth on the base of his neck while being mindful not to get his bandages wet.

"I'm here, Baby. I'm going to try to help you with this fever. Please don't give up on me, Kai." I plead.

I wring out two more compresses and I place them low on his stomach, again avoiding the white bandages with more red splotches dotting the fabric where he bled through again. Five agonizingly long minutes pass, and Atticus and Quilla finally walk in the door and rushes over to me.

"Do you know what his fever spiked to?" Atticus asks briskly.

"No. I didn't even think to take it. My only thought was trying to work on getting the fever down." I say as I shake my head. "What kind of mate am I? I didn't even think to take his temperature." I sob angrily at my failure to do one simple thing.

"Hey, it's okay, Dakota. You were right to think about getting it down first until we got here. You are not at any fault here." Quilla says as she lays a hand on my shoulder, and I feel my frayed nerves calm a little.

I watch as Atticus briskly walks over to the little closet that is nestled around the TV on the long wall opposite the bed and pulls out two dark glass dropper-style bottles from a duffle bag he stashed in the cabinet. He looks over the bottles to make sure he has what he needs before walking back over to Kai's side. I look over at Quilla, wondering if she knows what he's going to do.

"It's okay, Dakota. They will help with the fever. It is echinacea and white willow bark." Quilla says with a smile as she looks at her mate.

"That's exactly right, Darling," Atticus says with a brief glimpse of pride in his voice before turning his attention back to Kai and administering the medications under the tongue.

After about ten minutes, Atticus takes his temperature, and it's still 104.5 degrees. Worry and helplessness fill his eyes as they bounce from Kai's prone form to the IV tubing protruding out of the crook of his arm, and finally landing on the dialysis machine that is sitting idle in the corner of the room.

"What are you thinking, Atticus?" I ask, but at the same time, I'm terrified of his answer.

He scrubs his hand over his face and lets loose a heavy sigh. "I'm thinking we may have to start that dialysis machine again. A fever like this in a Were usually means there's still silver somewhere in his system. But I have smelled his blood, and I don't pick it up from that. And he's healing at a normal rate for an injury this grave, so I don't think it's an infection somewhere. I honestly have no idea where this fever came from." He says, defeated.

I can hear the worry in his tone at failing Kai, and from the way that Quilla stiffens at my side, I know she can feel it through their bond. She gives me a small smile as she makes her way over to her mate, placing her small hand on his broad shoulder, and she gives him a warm kiss on the cheek.

"We will figure this out. And we will *not* fail, do you hear me, Atticus Remington? Now what would you do if you were back home in Montana?" She challenges.

His lip tilts up on one side at her words, and he looks back to Kai for a moment, his eyes more focused than before.

"Let's start the machine again. Would you help me, Rosie? And Dakota, please keep those cool compresses going on his torso also."

At his orders, we begin our respective jobs, and then it's a waiting game.

An hour goes by since we started our treatment, and Kai's fever is still not below 103.2.

"Damn it. It's got to be a piece of silver, but where is the bloody thing?" Atticus growls as he begins to remove the bandages and sniffs at Kai's injuries.

As I watch him do that, a thought hits me. "Do you think I can try smelling for it?"

Atticus looks at me and then he slowly nods. "Yes. And maybe since you are now immune to silver, you may be able to pick up on it easier than I can." Atticus backs away from the bed and waves a hand to invite me into his place. "Go for it, if you think you can."

"Okay, but I think I can find it better if I phase. Let Kota's nose work in our favor." I say as I feel my wolven counterpart begin to rise to the aid of her mate.

I feel the phase roll over my body for the second time for the need to save my mate, only this time without the adrenaline filling my mind, I have to swallow the scream as the phase takes over. I feel every muscle rip and tear, every bone bend and pop and break into the new form. I finally settle into my wolven body, shaking out the blondish-brown coat as my claws click on the tiled floor.

I look over at Atticus and Quilla, and I can see the slight smiles on their lips at my phasing, but again we cannot celebrate it until my mate comes back to me. I gracefully leap onto Kai's bed while being mindful of where I place my paws so I don't move him. My eyes focus on his wounds, and I fight the urge to lick them as Kota's thoughts go to trying to help her mate.

"We are helping him by finding this piece of silver." I tell her.

I begin scenting his body, starting at the wound on his stomach. I drag my nose over the injury while keeping just a breath of air between us, so my cold nose doesn't touch him. After I make two passes over the long slashing wound, I don't smell any silver. I turn my head away, and I let out a quick snort to clear my nose of the coppery scent of blood. I begin my search again, this time starting higher on his body so I can scent the wound on his chest, but something makes me stop. I turn to clear my nose again, and I smell the area in between the wounds, his unmarred skin that separates the island of injuries.

"Atticus. Here. It's under his skin. We have been so focused on the wounds that we didn't look at the skin around them."

I tap my nose against Kai's still-too-hot skin so Atticus knows exactly where the shard is, and I quickly scent the rest of my mate's torso to make sure this is the only one hidden under his skin. Once I'm satisfied that I don't find any more, I jump down from the bed and watch Atticus get to work with Quilla at his side.

She opens a scalpel from its protective wrapping, handle side up as Atticus slips into a pair of gloves. He takes the offered instrument and then turns to Kai. He finds my nose print, and he deftly makes an incision in the middle of the site as Quilla then hands him a pair of tweezers. I watch helplessly as Atticus searches in the open incision and then, a heartbeat later, he pulls out a shard of silver no bigger than a grain of rice. Quilla then grabs a metal bowl, and I listen to the tink, tink of the silver piece clatter against the metal. She immediately takes off into the bathroom, and I hear the toilet flush a moment later.

I quickly grab my clothes from the floor, and head into the bathroom so I can phase. When I come back thirty seconds later, I can already see a vast improvement in Kai. His breathing has slowed to a slumbering rhythm. His skin has already cooled immensely, even if it still has a slight sheen to it from his sweat.

"A shard of silver that small caused all this?" I ask in disbelief.

"Yes. When I said that silver is deadly to Were's, I meant it. If we wouldn't have found that in the next hour or so, he would have been too far gone to save," Atticus says as he walks over to the couch and collapses into it with a heavy sigh.

Quilla immediately joins him, falling into his side and resting her head on the right side of his chest, while tracing his mating mark that climbs up his neck. I look back at Kai and find myself doing the same thing, brushing my index finger over our own marking that travels down his skin.

I pull a chair closer to his bedside a moment later, and as I continue my gentle caress of his neck, his body moves for the first time since the attack. With tears in my eyes, I watch as his head slowly rolls over to the side, as if at my touch, his slumbering body finally knows where I am.

The hours continue to tick by, and it's been four days since the attack, and Kai has still not woken up, but he's getting better every hour. Both Atticus and Dr. Peterson have been in agreement on his treatment, and Kai's oxygen mask has been replaced with a nosepiece, and IV bags have been removed, but they left the IV tubing in his arm as a precaution for now. The only things that remain are the heart monitor leads and the bandages, of course, but I've noticed that less and less blood seeps through the fabric each time they are changed, which I have helped with thanks to Quilla's guidance.

After tending to my mate for the morning, I lean back in my recliner with my feet propped up on the footrest, and I drape the white hospital blanket over my body so I can try to rest for a while. As I look at Kai's still sleeping form, I let sleep take me into its heavy darkness as well with one phrase in my mind.

Heal and come back to me, mate of mine

Chapter Sixty-Nine

KAI

After what seems like an endless night, I begin to feel something against my skin. A breeze and I barely hear what sounds like birds chirping in the distance, but they are so muted I almost don't believe I'm hearing them. I try to open my eyes, but I can't. I can't move any part of my body, and it takes everything in me to even take a breath.

Why is my body so heavy?

Then, as the breeze starts to kick up around me, I feel my body is finally coming alive, and I feel pain. But I can't pinpoint where it's coming from. It's an all-consuming pain, and I wish for the blissful darkness of slumber again just to avoid it. But something catches my attention over it all. It's so light that I almost missed it, but I feel a featherlight touch on my neck, right over where I know my mate marking is, and immediately think of her.

Of Dakota.

At that thought, I fight past the pain, past the heaviness of my limbs, and I make my eyes open. I'm lying on my back, and at first, my sight is nothing but a big blur. All I see is gray, what I can only assume is the sky, and muted greenish brown of the trees around me with bits of black and silver smoke skittering near their branches.

Through my sluggish thoughts, I put together that I am in K's forest. I hear a pain-filled whine next to me, and when I roll my head to the left, I feel it at the same time I see K's body. Pain blooms across my chest and stomach, and I know it's from the same angry red wounds that mar K's body.

I look at his lackluster brownish-blonde marble coat, and I see the tiredness and pain in his eyes.

"Kai. Please friend." He moans in my mind, *"Touch me. Let's finally connect after the new moon and begin the healing process."* K begs as a tendril of that black, silvery smoke slowly inches closer to him.

I fight to get my arm to move, as images of that night flash brokenly in my mind. I have a feeling that this is the last shot I have at getting back to my mate. That solid black and bright silver smoke barrels towards us, and when it touches my skin, I can feel it trying to take me into its ominous embrace and never letting us go.

"I'm not leaving her." I growl as I lift a trembling hand toward my wolf, and he stretches his neck to help me close the distance between us as the darkness quickly begins to cloud my vision like a vicious black tidal wave. The last thing I see is my hand lightly touching K's wet nose.

Antiseptic, sickness, blood, and fear forces the darkness from my mind. A soft flow of air enters my nose, and I try to breathe it in deeper, but I am rewarded with a flash of white-hot pain from my chest expanding to take in more air. I try to groan at the sensation, but my throat is so dry and irritated that nothing will come out.

After I work through the pain, I slowly begin to take stock of what else I feel. A soft bed under me. What I can now understand is a cannula sitting on my face giving me oxygen, the gentle flow of air going into my nose, and I hear someone sleeping next to me. The slow inhale and exhale of breath coming from my left side. My eyelids flutter open, and it takes a moment for the black dots on the ceiling to stop spinning before my vision settles.

I roll my head to the left, and I am terrified at how much that simple movement sends waves of exhaustion through my body. I almost let my eyes fall closed again, but I see something next to the bed. A recliner. At first, I'm confused by the form curled up under the white blanket, but when I see the long, light brown hair and notice her hand is next to mine, I realize it's Dakota. I try to lift my arm to rest my hand on hers, but that simple movement makes the pain explode anew through my body, and this time the moan escapes my lips, and memories of what happened to me come flooding back in a dizzying rush. Dakota's head snaps up at my voice, and I don't have time to work through the pain before she can see it.

"Kai?" She asks, and the break in her voice hurts my heart to the same degree of pain as the rest of my body.

I try to talk again, but my throat is still so dry and raw that words are impossible. So, I reach out to her through our bond, and the pure relief that floods her mind when I enter somewhat confuses me, but I press on into her mind.

"Yes, Love."

Tears begin to fall at my voice in her head, and I itch to wipe them away with my thumb, but my body won't move.

"Please, Love. Don't cry. I can't wipe away your tears yet."

Dakota gently lifts my arm, and with her moving me, I feel no pain. She places my hand against her cheek, and I slowly move my thumb back and forth to wipe her tears.

"Better?" She asks, her lips wobbling as she speaks.

"Yes, " I say simply.

"I want to hold you so badly right now, but I don't want to hurt you." She sobs while running her hand through my hair.

I try to tell her that she could never hurt me, but my voice still won't work.

"Can I have a drink? My throat is like sandpaper."

"Oh! Of course." She gently lays my arm by my side, and she jumps up from the chair to grab a bottle of water and a straw before making her way back over to me.

"Just take slow sips. We don't need you coughing." She instructs.

"Yeah. Just trying to move my arm feels like I'm being cut all over again."

After I take a few careful sips, I finally feel like the desert my throat has become is quenched enough for me to talk. I look around the room as different scents of who has been here begin to hit me, but I only see Dakota in the room.

"Where is everyone?" I ask hoarsely.

"Atticus took everyone down to the cafeteria to get some lunch. I wanted to stay here and watch you." Dakota tells me while fiddling with my fingers.

"Have you been eating?" I ask.

She laughs at my question like it's the funniest thing in the world, and the best I can do is arch an eyebrow at her. I hear what I assume is a door swish open behind Dakota. She misses the sound over her laughter, but I smell who is coming in, so I don't bother to warn her.

"What's so funny, Chica?" I hear Quilla ask.

"Just Kai asking if I've been eating."

Quilla, Atticus, and both of our parents come rushing to my bed, and they go from looking like Dakota lost her mind to pure, undiluted relief at seeing me awake.

"Oh, thank goodness you're awake, Kai." Quilla beams.

Everyone showers me with the barest of touches, to not jostle my body, and well wishes and praises to The Great Luna at my recovery, but I only have eyes for my mate right now.

"You still haven't answered my question, Dakota Shade." My voice rasps with a lazy grin that I know she loves.

"Yes, Kai Huntington." She laughs while matching my full name with hers. "I have been eating."

Atticus comes over to my bedside with a clipboard in hand and a slight smile turning up one side of his mouth, but his eyes are set in hard focus. I know this from growing up with him, and I have Dr. Remington here with me.

"How's your pain, Kai?"

"As long as I don't move, it's bearable." I reply, my voice still no higher than a whisper.

"But the slightest movement will cause a ten on the pain scale?" Atticus asks.

I nod, and just this movement sends a hot wave of pain through me, and I suck in a breath through my teeth. Dakota is at my side in an instant, taking my hand to cradle it close to her chest.

"Alright. I've brought some of my homemade pain medicine from Montana," Atticus says while going over to a closet near the TV, pulling out his duffle bag to find what he's looking for.

He brings over a dropper-type bottle, and he drips a few drops of the tasteless liquid under my tongue, and almost instantly I feel the pain lessen to where it's a dull stab instead of hot pokers. I look over to Dakota as Atticus makes notes in the chart of what he just administered and give her hand a slight squeeze to get her attention.

"I'm still trying to remember...What all happened? How long has it been since the attack?" I ask, my voice finally feeling a bit stronger.

"It was six days ago." Dakota says while looking from me to the group around us.

My parents, Nathan, Lori, Quilla, and Atticus. Our little pack stuck together while they were hoping for the best but expecting the worst with me. I then get a memory of a blondish-brown wolf in my mind, and I look to my mate again.

"Am I remembering this right?" I ask while furrowing my eyebrows. "Did you phase, Dakota?" I hold my mate's blue eyes, and they begin to well with tears.

"Yes. I did." Her voice breaks. "The catalyst I needed to force the phase was you being hurt. I hate that it came to that. I'm sorry." She says as she looks away from me on the last word.

"Don't you dare *be sorry,"* I say through the bond so I can use my full voice.

Her gaze snaps back to mine, and I know she feels the full weight of my words.

"You wanted to protect what was yours. To protect your mate. You and Kota agreed on that simple thought, and you were able to break through that wall that kept you two from becoming one."

"Thank you. Baby," Dakota says as she gently strokes my hair.

"Can I see?" I ask aloud.

Dakota smiles and nods her head as she steps a few paces away from my bed to stand in the middle of the room where I will have a perfect view of her. She closes her eyes, and even through our bond, I can feel Kota even more than I used to, and in that moment I know my mate's wolf will come to her in an instant.

Dakota gracefully lets the phase take her. Slowly allowing her muscles, ligaments, and bones to flow into the form of her blondish-brown wolf with a bushy tail. As the wolf matches the one that stood over my freshly broken body, I feel tears begin to form in my eyes for my mate's accomplishment. She takes a gentle leap into my bed, sits in between my legs, and lets me just look at her in all her regal, wolven glory.

"My God, you are beautiful." I say in awe.

"You think so?" Dakota asks with a snort.

"Oh, Love, I know so. I want to phase, and run off with you right now." I tell her.

I see her eyes go wide, and I can feel her fear as my words flow into her mind, but I close my eyes once and give her the barest of shake of my head.

"Don't worry, Love. I know phasing would make things worse again for me. But I still can't help but think about what it would be like." I say, giving her a smile.

She gives me her own wolfish grin, and she slowly moves closer to me, being mindful of her steps so she doesn't move my body, and rests her head on my thigh. My right hand is close enough to caress her ear, so I begin to massage her soft fur between my thumb and index finger.

"That feels so good." Dakota moans. *"Is this how you felt when you were in your wolf form and I was rubbing you?"*

"Yes. I absolutely loved it. I'm sorry I can only get to your ear."

"Don't be sorry, Babe. I'm content as long as you're touching me." She pauses and then says, her voice tight with tears even in my mind, *"As long as you're touching me, I know you're alive."*

She lifts her left paw and drapes it over my leg to hold me as much as she can in this form. I continue to lazily stroke her ear, and I can feel both of us begin to doze off. She slips from my mind and I do the same from hers, but knowing we are in each other's embrace, the darkness doesn't seem so all-consuming.

Chapter Seventy

KAI

A few hours later, I wake up and find my father sitting in the recliner that Dakota had occupied earlier today.

"How are you feeling, son?"

I hesitate for a moment. I want to tell him I'm fine, but even I can smell the lie for what it's worth on the tip of my tongue. From the slowly healing tissue of my chest and stomach that hides under the bandages, the lingering smell of the apparent fever I had, and the saltiness of the sweat that still coats my skin, all remind me that I am still far from being 'fine'.

I close my eyes, and as I try to lift my hand to press my fingers into my eyes in aggravation, I am rewarded with a wave of pain, just by trying to coax the muscles into that simple movement of my arm.

"I wish I could say I was fine, but I'm still far from that." I groan.

"I am just so relieved that you are finally awake. Healing from a silver wound takes time, son. You are extremely lucky to be alive. The knife Jeffrey used was designed to splinter upon impact. The wound on our stomach, the first point of contact, had the most shards embedded in the skin, muscle, and arteries and it took Dr. Peterson and Quilla three hours just to tend to that, let alone an hour for your chest." Dad explains.

As I hear his words, I look down at my body, and with the information Dad just told me, I now fully understand why I'm still in so much pain. I close my eyes to come to terms with this when another image flashes in my mind. Emma with a knife to her throat, tears streaming down her face.

My eyes snap open, and I look over at my father. "Emma? What happened to Emma? Please tell me she is safe."

Dad smiles and nods. "She is safe. Emma and her parents are members of my pack now."

"How is that? I didn't challenge Jeffrey for her." I ask in shock.

Dad laughs slightly and looks at Dakota's still sleeping wolf form between my legs. "Your mate did. When she phased, she attacked Jeffrey. And let me tell you, even after being shot with a silver bullet, your mate is a force to be reckoned with.

"Wait. Hold up. Dakota was what?"

Dakota

I begin to wake up in the middle of Kai and Tobias talking about what happened and just when I was about to let them know I was awake I freeze when I hear Tobias say I was shot with a silver bullet and hear Kai's reaction to that. I knew I was going to have to tell Kai about my immunity soon, but I was hoping to wait until he was healed and released from the hospital. That way I could do it in the safety of our home, in each other's arms. But now, I'm gonna have to have that conversation sooner than I wanted to.

"That is something you and your mate will need to talk about. But back to your main question concerning Emma." I hear Tobias begin, "Dakota told Jeffrey that since he hurt what was hers, she took what was his. So, I took Emma and her parents and made them pack so they would be safe from Jeffrey and Caleb."

"Thank you, Dad."

With those simple three words, I can feel the weight behind them. He is able to now lie in this bed a bit easier knowing that his injuries and the fact that he was so close to dying, wasn't for nothing. That the girl who came to him for help is now finally safe and away from the tyrannical rule of the so-called alpha and his beta.

The door to the ICU room swishes open a moment later, and I smell Atticus and Quilla walk in. I decide this is the best time to *wake up* and turn over on my other side where I am able to look at my mate head-on. I cross my front paws at the ankle and I idly flick my tail a few times.

"You look so regal, Love," Kai croons in my mind as I see his eyes rove over my form.

"I love being in this form. Kota helps make things seem so simple. Like now, all I know is you are our mate, we love you, and I want to be protected by you, but also be there to protect you as well. But right at this moment, we have the thought to tend to your wounds and help you get better."

"Thank you, Baby. K and I feel the same way. I hate that my body is not strong enough to protect you or love you the way a mate should. I feel like I'm failing you, and I'm sorry."

"Didn't we have this conversation a few weeks back?" I tease. *"You are in that bed because you were protecting me and Emma. And on the most*

dangerous night to boot. You will never fail me and never fail our pack. So stop beating yourself up, Kai."

Atticus clears his throat to get Kai's attention, and my mate breaks eye contact with me to look at the pack doctor.

"Everything is finally getting back to normal for you, Kai. You gave us quite the scare, I will say that." Atticus says as he unloads fresh gauze, tape, and dried Wolfsbane on the bedside table. "We still need to keep those wounds clean. Would you like for me to change the bandages, or would you like Dakota to change them for you?" Atticus says while looking at me with a smirk, like he knows what our answers will be.

"You still want to tend to my wounds, Love?" Kai teases.

"Yes, I feel like I haven't done enough for you since the attack. I will be right back." I leap down off the bed, take my discarded clothing from a nearby chair and head into the bathroom with Atticus' chuckle echoing behind me.

After I change and come back out, Atticus shows me the dressings and reminds me of the steps I need to take after I remove the old bandages.

"Thank you, Atticus. I got this." I say with a smile.

"Okay. We will be back in an hour." Atticus says.

"Make that two hours. I believe they have some things to talk about," Tobias says as he stands from the recliner and gives me a knowing look.

When everyone leaves, I feel awkward for the first time in a long time with Kai, and deep down I know why. I just hope he can understand my thought process with what I did.

I walk closer to his bed, and I interlace my right hand with his left, and I gently sit beside him while I run the fingers of my free hand through his blonde hair. He leans into my touch and closes his eyes for a moment before looking back into mine with such love that I can feel it clean down to my toes.

"You ready for me to start?" I ask as I glance down at his bare torso.

"Yeah." He whispers.

I stand and I place my hands against his chest to begin to pull the tape off, but I feel him try to pull back from my touch. I have to remind myself that it's not *my* touch he's pulling away from; it's how tender his body must be.

"I'm sorry, I'm going to hurt you."

"It's alright, Love. Do what you have to."

I begin to pull at the tape on his chest again, and I feel him trying not to tense against me and his eyes close tightly to fight against the pain and to keep still. I finally get the tape off, but I know for a fact that since the wound on his stomach is larger, it's going to be more sensitive.

"I have an idea. Hang on."

"What are you doing?" Kai asks a bit breathlessly.

I go into the bathroom, and I bring out the rubbing alcohol and a white washcloth. "I'm going to get the bandages damp before I take them off. Loosen the adhesive first." I beam.

Kai smiles as I get to work on him, and I can remove the bandage on his stomach with ease.

"You are so resourceful, Love," Kai says.

I blush at his praise, and after I wipe down his injuries with the extra washcloth that Atticus left me, I know I need to wait for the skin to dry before applying any more. So, I just take a moment to look at my mate. Look at the life slowly coming back into his still tired hazel eyes, but they are getting brighter and brighter each day. His smile is becoming more genuine and less pained. I notice that Kai looks at the space between us and he slowly raises his left arm with a grimace to make more room for me.

"Kai, please don't move."

"It's okay. Please lie next to me, Mate."

I slowly ease down next to him, resting my head on his shoulder and being careful not to touch his drying wounds. Out of habit, I begin to lightly trace his gray mate marking, and a flare of anger courses through me when I finally notice just how close that damned knife came to marring that precious marking. Kai must feel my anger because he slowly rubs up and down my back to soothe me.

After a few minutes, Kai is the first to break the silence between us. "Dad said you were shot with a silver bullet." Kai pauses like he's trying to figure out what to say next.

So, I sit up to look down at him, and he keeps my hand on his chest while his own stays on my back. Over both markings. Keeping us connected on a much deeper level.

"But I feel that you and Dad know more than you are letting on. Did that bullet hurt you, Love?" Kai asks as his eyes search mine.

I take a deep breath, and I can see in his face; the question and worry about my well-being, and a little bit of hurt flashes in his hazel eyes that I would keep something like this from him. For a moment I feel guilt trying to settle in the pit of my stomach, but then I remember Tobias saying I was right in keeping this from his son, for now. He would have fought tooth and nail about my trial, and if I had listened, Jeffrey may have been able to kill us all that night. With that thought, I shove that feeling of guilt away like a seed in a downpour.

"Yes, Kai. Jeffrey did shoot me with a silver bullet." I tell him with my head held high.

His eyes rove over my form, down my neck, and over both shoulders looking for any imperfection on my skin. I tug the collar of my shirt down over the shoulder that was shot to show him the healed and flawless skin.

"There's more, isn't there? What's going on, Dakota?" Kai asks, his voice becoming a touch demanding.

I take a breath and just rip the metaphorical band-aid off. "Silver can't hurt me anymore. I— "

"That's impossible. No one can have a silver immunity." Kai says, cutting me off with a scoff.

"Kai, nothing is impossible. I asked Quilla to do some research, and she found one wolf in particular that was a half-blood like me, and he was the first brave enough to try it. He was the first that was able to achieve a higher tolerance. Quilla just took that research and perfected it for total immunity."

"So you mean to tell me that you and Quilla tried this based on the writings of *one* werewolf!" Kai raises his voice. "Do you have any idea how dangerous that was?" He chastises.

"Put yourself in my shoes, Kai! I was terrified the day Caleb bit me. I was scared for myself and what would happen with pure silver in my veins. But once I found that I healed quicker than I should have and when I was around silver for a second time, I found that the more I was around it, it didn't affect me at all. So I got to thinking, maybe I could become immune. It was Quilla *and* Atticus who did the research and made sure the reward outweighed the risks. I wanted to be able to protect *you.* To have this ace up my sleeve to protect my pack in the way no one else could." I seethe.

"Protecting the pack is *my* responsibility. And for Atticus to be involved and to go along with this, I'm going to kill him." Kai says threateningly.

"You will do no such thing, Kai Huntington!" I say as I send a pulse of my power over him to make my point clearer. "I know you're mad that I–"

"I am furious!" Kai yells, and he clutches his chest as the pain starts to break through his anger-fueled rage.

"Kai, stop. You're going to hurt yourself." I say, trying to de-escalate the situation.

"My mate, Tamer and Doctor went behind my back to make you a guinea pig on something they didn't even know would work!" Kai pants, then his voice builds near the end again.

"Kai, you need to calm down." I plead again.

"I thought we were a team. That we had no secrets." Kai says between breaths.

"Oh, like you don't have secrets?" I say, jumping off the bed and to my feet. "You kept Emma from me. I could have helped you with her. And I get the feeling that you were going to challenge Jeffrey without me even knowing. How is *that* any different from what I did?" I snap. "If I didn't make myself immune to silver, we all would be fucking dead right now, including Emma." I chuckle darkly as I say, "Your dad was right in agreeing not to tell you."

"What did you say?" Kai asks slowly.

"Your dad knew what I was doing. And while he, like you, didn't agree with it, he *trusted* me. Trusted Quilla and Atticus with the task. We were not going into this blindly, Kai. We *knew* this was dangerous! And I was able to exploit one of my weaknesses and become a better alpha because of it!" I shout. "I was the *only* one that could go against Jeffrey that night because of it. The only one that had the strength to fight back." I say, my voice tight with unshed tears.

As my final words echo out of the room, we stare one another down, both panting for different reasons. Mine from shouting, but Kai's I can feel is a mix of his shouts but trying to cope with the pain he caused himself too. I begin to roll my eyes at his stubbornness, but he closes his eyes and at first I think it's because he's trying to compose himself, but when I feel darkness flow from his side of the bond, it takes all I have in me to keep my knees from buckling, but the tears are the one thing I can't hold back. As I feel him block off his connection to me, I feel like a knife was plunged into my heart.

"Kai. Please. Don't block me." I plead, my voice breaking with each word. "I can handle the silent treatment, but please don't block me. I can't handle not feeling you all over again."

Then, a moment later, our heads whip to the door as we feel Tobias' power roll into the room in full force. It's so powerful that I can barely keep my knees locked even though the power is not forced solely on me.

"We can hear you two yelling from the waiting room." Tobias says coolly. "Dakota, why don't we switch places? Apparently, I need some time to talk with my son," He says flatly.

At first, I want to argue. Part of me doesn't want to leave because I can't feel Kai again and the trauma of that night comes flashing back in a dizzying rush. I need to have my eyes on my mate; that is the only way I can tell he's alive. But from the power rolling off Tobias, even I know that the order that was worded as a request is futile to fight against.

I take one last look at my mate, who I realize is not even looking at me. His gaze is fixed on the window, watching the rain that began when we started arguing roll down the glass. The sky matches my heart without his presence in my mind. Grey, rain-filled, and sorrowful.

I make myself take the first step, and I see Quilla gracefully walk up to the door, always being there for me when I am at my breaking point. I rush into her arms, both of us pulling the other in for a bone-crushing embrace, and I cry into her shoulder as she leads me away from my mate's room. Or, hopefully, he's still my mate after all this.

Kai

As I see the reflection of Dakota in the window disappear from my sight, I hear K snarl at me for hurting her, but I even try to block him too.

"How can you do that to her? Hasn't she suffered enough?" Dad asks briskly. "Is this really because you think she put herself in danger over something she didn't know would work, or could even kill her? Or is it because she didn't include you? Because you would be the overbearing mate and keep her from making herself better and maybe even, if I dare say, a stronger alpha than you?" Dad challenges.

"I don't want to hear this. Get out." I snap as I push my power over my father to get him to listen.

Dad bursts out laughing. Booming laughter, with his head tilting back as his body shakes with the sound when he feels my power slide over his skin.

"I'm going to let that attempt slide because you are obviously not thinking with your whole head here, Kai."

Dad pauses for a moment while leaning in closer to me. His smile fades in an instant, and he unleashes his full power on me. I feel like I am being shoved deeper into the bed, and it almost hurts to breathe, and it's not from the wounds that marr my body.

"Now, you listen to me, son. And I suggest you listen well. Maybe Dakota should have told you. But that is neither here nor there now. Who are you to try and stop her from becoming stronger? If I knew I could do what she did, I would. But Dakota had the uniqueness of her half-blood heritage on her side. She had pure silver in her veins once, and she *lived*. You had a haggard mixture of silver slice into you and look at what almost happened. I know you can feel just how close you were to dying, Kai. Hell, I can still feel it through my bond with you. Your *mate* was in no way blinded when she approached Quilla about this. And Quilla was smart enough to enlist a *doctor's* help. Quilla and Atticus spent days in my library back in Montana researching the side effects and anything at all they could find on half Were's becoming immune and then running those experiments. So, for you to have the *gull* to question any of *my* pack members like that truly hurts, Kai. And for you to question your own mate, I am ashamed right now that she is mated to you. Your mother has done some things that yes, I have thought were reckless over the many years we have been together, but I never allowed her to leave the room until we were on the same page, and if we couldn't at that time, I may have blocked her, but she still felt me there in the back of her mind."

As I hear Dad talk, I feel K claw his way back into my mind, and I feel how proud he is that his mate was able to achieve so much, but I am still pissed at what all Dakota did behind my back.

"And trust me," Dad says as he backs away and goes to stand at the foot of my bed. "I thought about telling her she was foolish for even entertaining this idea. But Kai, I couldn't do it. I went by Quilla's house on probably about day five of the trials. They were starting on the pure silver, and Kai, your mate, was amazing. Yes, she was in pain, but she sensed me by the door, and she pushed herself up off the floor because the alpha in her wanted to protect Atticus and Quilla. After I witnessed that, I couldn't tell her to stop. But I did talk to her the next day, and the determination in her eyes told me she wasn't going to back down. She was going to see this through. And like I heard her say, she was the only one who could fight back against Jeffrey, and she could do that because of her immunity that she fought tooth and nail to achieve. So, I think instead of bashing her and making her feel that she lost her mate all over again, you should praise her and acknowledge the sacrifice and risk she took so that she could one day protect what is hers."

Dad then walks over to my left side and with a sly smile he adds, "Now I wasn't going to do this, but I am going to try to heal you as much as I can right now with the power I can pull from the pack because you will need to be able to get on your knees to beg for your mate's forgiveness. Plus, I'm going to force you to see just how strong she is."

Chapter Seventy-One
DAKOTA

After Quilla leads me into the small waiting room and I take the first chair that I come to near the door, she takes the seat next to mine without a word while still rubbing soothing circles down my back. As we wait for Tobias to finish with his son, I tell my parents, Quilla and Atticus, what we were arguing about while my sobs grow heavier as I get closer to the end of my explanation.

"He's so mad at me." I cry. "He blocked me, and it's like the night he was stabbed all over again. His mind is dark, and I don't know if he's alive or not."

Dad slides into the empty chair next to me, and he pulls me into his chest with a gentle but firm embrace. "Kai will come around. Tobias will talk some sense into him." He says while kissing the top of my head.

"What if he doesn't, Dad? I can't take losing Kai for real this time." I hiccup as more tears flow from my cheeks. "Maybe I was wrong in keeping the immunity from him." I whisper.

"No," Quilla pipes up from my other side. "We were right in that. Tobias even said it himself. We did the right thing, Dakota. Don't let anyone tell you any different."

"I agree with Quilla." Atticus chimes in next. "And I'm honestly hurt that he didn't trust me enough to know that I had your best interest at heart. If I thought for one moment that the probability of you being hurt outweighed the benefits, I would have told you and wouldn't have let you move forward."

I nod, and we all feel Tobias' power roll into the room before he walks through the door.

"Dakota." He says my name briskly, but I know his tone is not intended for me.

I look to Quilla then, my dad, and nod at them to let me go. I walk toward the alpha while being mindful to keep my eyes averted.

"Yes, Alpha?" I ask with the slightest bend to my neck to let him know that I mean him no challenge. I have never felt him this riled before, and it was all because of what I can only assume was a one-sided, harsh discussion with his son.

"Please come with me." Tobias requests, and I follow without a thought.

We walk down the hall towards Kai's room, but he pauses just before the door. I can feel there's something different, but I don't understand what it is, and I look back at Tobias with confusion on my face.

"Kai is fine, if that's what you're worried about. Or should I say, he's still alive." Tobias says matter-of-factly. I tilt my head and wait for him to elaborate on what he means by this. "I stripped him of his alpha status."

"You what?!" I ask sharply.

"Calm yourself, Dakota. I did this temporarily. My son is, unfortunately, like me, and he has to be shown the hard way sometimes." Tobias sighs while pinching the bridge of his nose.

"The way you make it sound is like you had your fair share of fighting with your father." I say as a mild joke.

"No. Not with my father. He and my mother both died when I was very young. But it was against the wolf who took my father's place. His Beta. You see, I never wanted to become an alpha. I was led to believe that I would not be a worthy leader, and back in that time, there were many wars going on and I didn't want to lead my men, my pack, into battle and lead them astray. I felt that because of the sins my father committed, I would be forced to follow in his footsteps. And because of that thought, it almost cost me finding my mate." Tobias smiles at the apparent memory the story brings up, but then he shakes his head, clearing his thoughts. "But that's a story for another time. Right now, Kai is a regular member of the pack, but he still knows what it's like to be alpha. I did this so he can see, like I can, just how powerful you have become in your short time after finding your inner wolf. It will take only a simple phrase from you, 'Come stand by my side, my alpha,' to release my command from him."

"How will I know when to say that?" I ask.

"If I have to tell you that, Darling, then you are in the same boat as my son. And I know you are smarter than that. I have seen it so many times now. Trust your instincts, and you will never go wrong." Tobias says as he pulls me in for a gentle kiss on the cheek and he walks away, leaving me alone at the door to my mate's room.

I take a breath before I open the door, and when I walk in, I notice the bed is empty. My stomach drops at the sight, and I rush further into the room, and I find Kai sitting in the recliner next to the rain-slicked window, his head still turned, looking out into the parking lot. As I walk closer to him, I notice something is indeed different. I can still somewhat feel his alpha power, but it's diluted, almost caged, and I know I'm the only one who has the key to release him again. Kota tickles the back of my mind, and I welcome what insight she may have.

"You know what we can't do right now, don't you?"

"Yeah." I sigh. *"We can't be at the same level as he is, and we can't touch him, right?"*

"I think we can touch, but yes, we do have to keep our heads above his. We must show him that we are the alpha and not him." Kota informs me.

As much as I hate to hear her say that, I know she is right. And I know why Tobias did this. To show Kai that I am not this weak half-breed that always needs to be protected. We should be viewed as equals, and in order for a hard-headed alpha to see what is right under his nose, you take what he values most. Power. I find that alpha power flowing in me like second nature, and I take a seat on the windowsill with my head held high.

Kai

I watch as Dakota comes in and sits on the windowsill without a word to me. Before I can even wonder what she's doing, I instantly understand my father's words.

I'm going to force you to see what I do within your mate. But I am going to go a step further and take your arrogance and status from you, for now. And if she deems you a suitable mate, then she will be the one to release you.

I'm the level of a normal pack member. Not a beta, not even part of the seconds and thirds of the pack. I am the lowest of the low right now. I begin to think of what all Dad told me Dakota was able to accomplish, and I can't make myself look in her direction as my words to her come flooding back to me.

I then feel K's presence bleed into my mind as he says, *"You should be ashamed of how you treated her."* He snarls. *"I can feel just how powerful she's become; why are you so blind to it?"*

"I guess I was just so focused on protecting her from Jeffrey and Caleb that I didn't realize she wasn't as fragile as I thought."

"No, she is not. She may still be new to this world, but she is a quick learner, and you better understand that before you royally fuck this relationship up."

I sigh as I try to look Dakota in the eye to get her attention, but I can't, and no matter how hard I try, I can't make my eyes go higher than her collarbone. I lean my head back against the headrest of the recliner, blowing out a ragged breath. Dakota's head tilts in my direction, but she doesn't say anything.

I shake my head, and I close my eyes in frustration. "Da—" I try to say, but my father's command is so strong that I cannot speak her given name. She is only Alpha to me. Strictly formal.

Dakota must figure this out because she waves a hand at me and says, "You may say my name."

"Dakota." I pause, feeling weird for being able to say her name, but I push forward to finish my sentence.

"Dakota, I am truly sorry. I was acting like the biggest jerk to you."

"Acting like? Oh, Honey, you *were* the biggest jerk." She snaps.

"Can I finish?" I toss back in aggravation at her jab.

"Excuse me?" Dakota says as her head snaps in my direction and my stomach drops like a stone.

She stands from her perch and slowly walks over to me and, for the second time in my life, I feel like prey and for some insane reason; I close my eyes. Like I don't want to see her land what my human brain perceives as the killing blow. But instead of pain, I slowly start to feel her alpha power fill the room, and it's...strong, powerful.

My eyes snap open, and I stare at the shiny tiled floor under my slipper-clad feet. I can feel just how strong of an alpha my mate—no, I can't even call her that right now. I can feel how strong of an alpha Dakota has become in the short time she's been aware of Kota. Dad's right. She's amazing and resourceful, and I am not worthy of her right now.

I remember what it's like to be alpha. For people to look to me for protection and guidance, and Dakota could easily overpower me and I realize I would be proud of that. Again, Dad is right on another thing; I need to be shown some things the hard way to see what is right under my nose.

I glance in her direction and instead of being afraid of the power rolling off her; I want to be comforted by that power and know that I am protected just as much as she can inflict pain if she deems fit.

"May I ask that you sit on the arm of the recliner? I would like to be near your power and take comfort in it." I ask, and I don't even try to hide the weakness in my voice.

"I can do that." Dakota says simply as she perches on the arm of the recliner. She still doesn't touch me, but I am enveloped by her power, and I release a contented sigh as it settles over my skin.

Dakota

As I sit on the arm of the recliner, I notice Kai settling deeper into the chair, relaxation evident in his limbs. I also note that his light blue hospital robe hangs open. His exposed torso shows me that Tobias finished re-bandaging his injuries. A wave of anguish floods my chest knowing that I was not able to care for him, but at the same time, I am glad that he was tended to at least.

"I understand now why you kept this from me," Kai whispers, but he shakes his head, and I somehow pick up that he can't freely say what he wants to. "Dakota, may I speak freely? I need to say some things that you may think are 'talking back' to an Alpha, but I need to say them to get you to understand my thought process."

I think for a moment, letting him wonder if I will indeed grant his request. I watch him fiddle with the belt of his robe for a heartbeat before I finally nod my head. "You may speak freely, as pack to alpha."

"Thank you." Kai nods, and he continues explaining himself to me. "Like I said, I do understand now why you kept this from me. I can't lie and say that I am not still angry, but it's not at you all the way. It is mainly at me and my single focus. I always think that I need to be the protector, that I need to be the strong and unbreakable one. But that's not right. Mates are meant to be there for one another, and who am I to stop you from making yourself better? I am proud that you took the chance to make yourself stronger, to give yourself an ace in the hole to overcome us all." Kai pauses, and he closes his eyes as he bends his head to be closer to me without touching, and he lets a small smile tilt the side of his mouth up in pure content. "I can feel just how strong you have become in the short time you have been aware of Kota. I was blinded to it before, but now that I am 'no longer an alpha'." He says using air quotes. "I can feel your power."

As his words fill my ears, I begin to feel his walls crumble around us. I almost break down at his familiar presence flooding my mind again, but I know I can't. Not yet, at least. As his mind fills mine, I pick up on his thoughts and know he wants to touch me. To just be around his alpha and to feel safe. So, I take his right hand in my left, and I feel his happiness flow merrily down the bond.

"I sincerely apologize for yelling at you. For making you feel that protecting your pack wasn't your place. Dad told me that Quilla and Atticus were working together on this for days before you ever started. He also told me that even though you were in pain with one of the trials, you still forced yourself up to your feet to protect Quilla and Atticus when he snuck up on you all."

I scoot in closer from my position on the arm of the recliner, and I gently place my hands on either side of his head, bringing it into my lap and tenderly run my fingers through Kai's blonde hair.

"Thank you for the sacrifice you made. You didn't know if this would work, but you trusted in your Tamer and the pack doctor to help you achieve your goal." Kai says as he caresses my thigh and gently strokes the curve of my knee with his thumb. "I am so thankful that The Great Luna gifted me with such a determined, loving, smart, beautiful, and resourceful mate that right now, I don't feel like I'm good enough to be *your* mate. And I wouldn't blame you if you... rejected me."

Kai whispers the last part so low that if it wasn't for my heightened hearing, I would have missed it. Hearing him just voicing those words makes me feel like he just plunged a knife into my heart. How could I ever think about rejecting him?

Yes, he was out of line. Yes, he was all *I am alpha, hear me roar,* and *I'll protect my mate no matter what,* but to even think about ever rejecting him. No way. I lean in and I place a soft kiss to the top of his head while breathing in his pine needle and mint scent. That only scent that can put me at ease, the only one that ever will.

"Kai." I begin, but he cuts me off.

"One more thing. I'm sorry for blocking my mind from you, but can I ask why that hurt you so much? I would like to understand that more." Kai asks while bearing his neck to me since he's asking someone higher up to answer a direct question.

I sigh, and I gently push him off me, and I allow him to look me in the eye when I explain it to him. His hazel eyes are so full of inquiry and yet joy at being able to look his alpha in the face.

"It hurt because after I was able to get Jeffrey to leave and I finally got the full view of how hurt you were, I still couldn't find you through the bond because of the new moon blocking you from K. I was able to convince myself that you were at least breathing because I had you in my arms, but when you were taken in for surgery, I didn't know anything. I didn't know if you were alive or dead for hours while you were back in the operating room. I remember telling Dad that if you were to die, it should be in the arms of your mate and not on a fucking metal table." I wipe away a stray tear at the memory. "And when you blocked me for a second time, it brought that night back full force."

My voice finally breaks as I can't keep the tears back any longer, but I notice that Kai too has his own falling down his handsome face. He stands up to get closer to me, but he stumbles, still not being strong enough to walk on his own. I rush to his side where we both settle on the floor, and I pull his head into my chest while he brings his arms up and around my back to pull us even closer.

"I am so sorry. I am so incredibly sorry, my alpha." Kai whispers into my shirt.

"What happened to calling me your mate and Love, huh?" I joke, my voice still watery.

Kai pulls back, and I allow him to look into my face, and he gives me his trademark smirk that I love so much.

"I am sorry, my alpha, my mate, my Love." Kai says.

We just stay on the floor holding one another, consoling the other as alpha to pack, as mate to mate.

"Are you okay?" I ask, and I let him feel the loaded question for what it is. For his injuries, for his ego that just got a rude reality check.

"I'm better. I still have a long way to go, but I know I will get there when the time comes. I know that what I see in front of me is the best thing I could ever hope for, and I will stand by your side no matter what."

"Are you ready to tackle this world as equals? No secrets *at all*. And no matter what, we talk about what the other wants to do and look at it objectively, and by no means do we block the other out completely. I do understand there are times that I may not have full access to your mind, but keep that thread alive between us."

"As you say, so shall it be," Kai says formally. Then he lifts his hand to wrap it around the back of my neck. "May I kiss you?" Kai whispers.

"Oh, I don't know," I say teasingly. "Fraternizing with the alpha may not look good on a lower member like yourself."

"I'll take my chances." Kai says with a smirk.

"I hear there may be promotions coming up." I say. "You think you have a shot at moving up in rank?"

"I hear the alpha is smart, and she'll make the best decision for her pack, and I am in full support of it."

His thumb strokes my jawline as he pulls me closer to him, and when his lips brush against mine, they are tender and loving. They don't ask for anything more than what I'm willing to give. I smile against his mouth and I pull back a bit, taking his bottom lip between my teeth, and I hear him growl in response. I move back in towards him, tracing my tongue over the seam of his lips and he opens up for me, matching each stroke that I give him, again showing me that I am still in control of this situation and he's following me with ease. I pull back one final time and rest my forehead against his, both of us panting from our exploration of the other.

"Come stand by my side, *my* alpha." I say the words that will allow Kai to come back into his power, and I feel it rush over me.

I watch as he lets out a breath like a boulder was just lifted from his shoulders, and I was the one to do that for him.

"There you are, my love." I smile.

I place a hand on his chest, right over his mate marking, and I again remember just how close I was to losing him. As the thought hits me, I know I don't block it from Kai soon enough because his hand shoots up and cups my chin to make me look at him.

"Hey, I'm here now. I am alive, on the mend still, of course, but I am alive, Love."

We help each other to our feet, and he sits in the recliner, but this time he pulls me into his lap. I am mindful to keep my distance from his injuries, but he pulls me closer to him all the same. I lean my head against his shoulder while Kai runs his hands up and down my back, occasionally tracing my mate marking through my shirt, and I shiver under his touch, which he rewards me with a light chuckle.

I can feel exhaustion filling both of our bodies, so I pull down the blanket that is resting on the back of the recliner and I drape it over both of us. I lift my head from Kai's shoulder in time to watch his eyes slowly grow heavier to where he can no longer fight to keep them open, and he finally falls asleep with a smile on his face. I gently kiss his cheek, and I rest my head once again in the curve of his shoulder, and I gladly let sleep take me as well.

Chapter Seventy-Two

Atticus

I check the time on my watch, and it's been a little over three hours since we all walked out of Kai's hospital room. Thankfully, there has been no more yelling, but I need to make sure that the idiot didn't hurt himself more after Tobias tended to his wounds.

"Rosie, come with me, mate. Let's check to see what's going on with the temporary alpha and her pack member."

Quilla looks up at me, and I watch as worry and anger flash over her features. My little rose has a bit of a mean streak, and I don't blame her for it.

We walk hand in hand to Kai's room, and when I pull open the sliding door, we are met with low growls from both Dakota and Kai, who were asleep in the recliner. I hear them both laugh softly at their reactions, and I know they must have repaired their relationship. Plus, I can feel Kai's power mingling with Dakota's through the air. I know what Tobias did to his son, and I'm glad the alpha handled it the way he did.

"Look who's on the mend in both ways, Babe," Quilla says while looking back at me, then she directs her next statement to Dakota.

"Please tell me you made him grovel? That seems suitable for what he put you through, Dakota."

Kai's head snaps in her direction, and Dakota looks like she's on the verge of laughing, so I give them something to laugh at. I scoop Quilla up and toss her over my shoulder while I stride over to the couch in the corner of the room before I spin Quilla where she is sitting sideways in my lap while I press my back as close to the corner as I can.

"Did you just put the two of you in the corner, Atticus?" Dakota asks after a moment.

"Aye, I did. I need to show my mate not to poke a wolf like that." I say while giving Quilla a pointed look.

"Oh, like this?" She teases while poking me in the chest over and over.

I just roll my eyes while laughter fills the room, but I let Quilla feel and see the humor in my eyes at her antics, letting her know that this was my plan to somewhat break the ice that has formed between me and Kai.

"Babe, can you get up please?" Kai asks Dakota.

"Oh! I'm sorry, was I hurting you?"

"No, Love. But I have more *groveling* to do." Kai says while giving Quilla a pointed smirk.

Dakota helps Kai to his feet, and he slowly makes his way over to my mate and me. I immediately notice Kai's trembling legs and him grinding teeth together to hide the pain he's in from moving, and I know if I see it, so does Quilla. I tighten my arm around her just as she begins to move from my lap.

"No, Darling. Stay here. Trust me, this is an alpha thing right now."

"But, you're not an..... oh, an alpha thing for Kai. Sorry," Quilla says.

"You really know how to remind a wolf of his place in the pack, Rosie." I say with a teasing note in my voice.

"Hey! I said I was sorry. I didn't mean anything by it, Atticus, and you know that," Quilla squeaks.

"I know, I just love seeing you go red." I say as I trace her cheek with my thumb.

"I am not red." Quilla huffs even though she knows it's a lie.

I chuckle out loud at my mate, and this earns me a quizzical look from Kai.

I shake my head as I say. "It's just my mate here doesn't seem to know her colors."

Quilla huffs out a shocked sound that I would tell another about our conversation, and she smacks me on the chest in mock aggravation before she hides her face in the curve of my neck.

Kai smiles, but I watch his face turn serious in the next breath. "While I love seeing the banter between mates, may I have both of your attentions?"

Quilla lifts her head from my neck at Kai's words. She looks from me to him, and I pull her closer to my side in a silent request to let him say his peace.

"Atticus, Quilla, I owe you both an apology. I doubted you when Dakota was looking into and attempting her silver immunity. I didn't realize the careful and well-thought-out planning you all did. I should have known that the man who helped raise me and tended to the many injuries I got over the years would put my mate's health above all. And I should have known that the rare Tamer that our pack has been blessed with and the long-time friend of my mate would have been just as invested in her wellbeing too." Kai then kneels on one knee and bares his neck to me and Quilla. "I hope you accept my humble apologies." He adds through gritted teeth.

"Kai, please get up off the floor before you make my job more difficult." I say with a light, teasing tone.

Kai nods as Dakota helps him to his feet, and as she leads him across the room, I stand from the couch with Quilla in my arms. I gently set my mate down and look back over to Kai with a prideful smile as he settles back into the safety of his bed.

"I accept your apology, Kai. Just don't make the mistake of questioning my research again." I warn.

"Of course." Kai says with a sharp nod.

I walk over to the bed with Quilla on my heels and check over Kai to make sure he hasn't pulled any stitches. Once I'm satisfied with that, I lock eyes with Dakota, and then my mate and I take a note from her book. Let's poke the wolf and see just how forgiving he is.

"Say, Dakota. Why don't you tell Kai how you and I first met?" I challenge.

I immediately see her eyes go wide and then a knowing smile graces her face.

"Oh, well my dear Atticus, how can I tell a wolf, who cannot kick your ass just yet, that you shot his mate with a silver bullet to test her immunity at that point?"

At first, Kai is just staring blankly between us, eyes pinballing trying to figure out if we are toying with him. When his eyes land on Dakota's, she gives him a nod, and he immediately looks over at me.

"You did what?" He demands.

I give him a flat look that says, *yes I did, and I would do it all over again.*

"I should still kick your ass for having that smug look on your face, but did someone at least get a picture of Dakota? I'm sure her face was priceless." Kai chuckles.

"Bite me, wolf-man." Dakota laughs.

I find myself chuckling along with them, and I feel Quilla's eyes on me. When I look at her, I see pure love on her face.

"What, Rosie?"

"Nothing, I just know how mad you were at Kai. Hell, I was too, but seeing you forgive him makes me happy that we can overcome this together as a pack and family."

"We will always overcome whatever trials life throws at us, Rosie. I believe that nothing will ever break apart true love and family bonds."

CHAPTER SEVENTY-THREE
DAKOTA

After some convincing from Kai the next morning, I am sitting in the cafeteria of the hospital with Mom, Quilla, Atticus, and both alphas at a table situated in the corner of the room.

As I sit in the booth poking at my breakfast, I can feel Kai in the back of my mind fighting sleep. I know he doesn't like how much he's been sleeping and how quickly he succumbs to it over and over, but I tell him it's his body's way of healing.

"Sleep mate. You need it. Stop being stubborn." I gently scold him.

"Since you asked so nicely." He teases, but I can already tell he's slipping into his healing slumber, and I find myself smiling as I feel his phantom touch caress my face and he finally submits to the demands of his body.

"What are you smiling about?" Quilla jests.

"It's just Kai. He doesn't like how much he needs to sleep."

Quilla nods her head in understanding and gives me a shoulder bump. "He'll be home and back to normal soon enough. Right, Atticus?"

The doctor tilts his head toward Quilla, who was in the middle of a discussion with Coraline and my mother.

"Yes, Rosie. I was telling Alpha Coraline that Kai should be ready to go home tomorrow. He's finally healing nicely now that his bond is repaired with the pack. Granted, he still needs to take it easy for the next two to three days, but he can rest further at home," Atticus says while looking around to everyone at the table, but giving Quilla a wink when his eyes meet hers.

"Since he should be coming home soon, Coraline, do you need any help getting his room cleaned up? Maybe fresh bed sheets and a good dusting?" Mom asks.

"Oh, Lori, that is a wonderful idea. I'd be grateful for your help." Coraline replies with a smile.

As the two women leave, Atticus decides to meet up with Dr. Peterson to have a meeting about how she can further assist other Were's who may come into her ER, and of course Quilla tags along. So, I decide to go back up to Kai's room.

He's been moved out of the ICU finally and is in his own private room on the main floor of the hospital. I slowly open the door and, after scanning the room, I find him asleep in the recliner by the window. He's wearing a forest green houserobe that his mother brought from his closet along with a pair of scrubs, and I shake my head at his sleeping form.

"Didn't even take a blanket." I scold, my voice barely a whisper so I don't disturb him.

I grab the white knitted blanket from the bed and drape it over his body. I wait for a moment to see if he stirs as the fabric settles over him, but he's out like a light. I quietly make my way over to the neighboring recliner and slowly pull up the footrest to get comfortable and just watch him sleep, the steady rhythm of his breathing the only thing filling the room.

Kai

I notice something warm covering my body, and the scent of honeysuckle and strawberries fills my nose. I open my eyes and notice the white blanket from the bed is draped over me, and when I look over in the recliner on my right, I see Dakota leaning back, her head tilted toward my chair, and she's sound asleep.

I chuckle silently to myself as I gingerly sit up in the chair, only a slight twinge of pain pulling at the wound on my stomach as I rise to my feet. I take the blanket and drape it over Dakota's sleeping form, then lean down to lovingly kiss her forehead before I make my way over to the windowsill.

I rub at the still-healing wound on my stomach to help ease the ache. I still have a light bandage on to keep the fabric of my shirt from irritating the skin, but the wound on my chest is healed to a barely visible line now. The only reminder that I was ever injured there. I look back to Dakota's sleeping form and smile at her knowing that I can tackle anything life throws at me as long as she's at my side.

Dakota

I open my eyes and notice that Kai is not in his recliner, but I have the same blanket that I covered him with now on me. I sit up and notice a shadow by the window, and I find my mate sitting on the windowsill just watching me sleep. I shake my head as I lower the footrest and sit on the edge of the recliner.

"You amaze me, you know that?"

"How is that, Love?" Kai asks.

I stand to my feet, wrapping the blanket around my shoulders as I make my way over to him. He stays where he is on the windowsill, so I wrap my arms around his shoulders, resting my chest against his back and draping my arms down the front of him, bringing him into the blanket with me.

"You always find ways to still care for me even though you are still healing." I say as I lean closer, pressing my lips to his cheek.

"All this because I put a blanket over you? Wow. I can't wait to see what happens when I step it up a notch." Kai says playfully.

"You are horrible, you know that?" I scold playfully while giving him a light smack on the shoulder and backing away from him.

"Oh, come on, I know you like it." He croons while rising from his perch to follow me.

I look at him, and for the first time since he's woken up, his eyes are glowing brightly, showing more shades of green than I have ever seen in his hazel eyes, and it sends chills up my spine. I try but fail to keep the smile off my lips.

"Down, Fido." I say, lifting a palm between us. "You haven't been cleared for... strenuous activities yet." I say coyly.

"Then, being in the same room with you shouldn't be allowed. Bad for the blood pressure and all."

Kai's eyes rove my body, and a shot of heat blooms in my blood. It's at that moment, I know him to be almost back to normal, not quite one hundred percent, but a lot closer than he was a few days ago; than he was a week ago before he woke up.

"Just one little kiss?"

I laugh at him and shake my head. "There is no such thing as a *little kiss* between us, Kai." I stare at my mate, and I want nothing more than to be in his arms again, him kissing me like we did before all this went to hell. "*But* I'd like to see you try." I challenge.

Kai growls in response, and somehow he's backed me against the wall without me even knowing. His body is so close to mine, but not touching. His sock-clad feet flush against my own. He leans into my neck, his nose barely skimming against my skin, but I know he's slowly taking in my scent, just like I am doing with his. He slowly presses his body against mine, his hands pinning my arms to my sides, and he leans in, taking my lips with his in a slow, tender caress. He tilts his head to deepen the kiss, but this is not the type of kiss where anything more is needed. No tongues, no teeth scraping over lips, or desire fills growls or moans. The only thing we need is to relish in the other. The way we taste, the feel of our body heat merging with one another, the soft sounds of us taking a breath when we break apart for a heartbeat before going back for more. This is nothing but a slow dance without the music.

Kai finally relents, and with his forehead pressed against mine, he whispers, "How's that for a *little kiss*?"

I pull my bottom lip between my teeth and act like I'm contemplating what just happened when in reality, I'm trying to get my brain to form words. Kai's predatory gaze tracks the movement, his brightly glowing stare bouncing from my eyes to my lips and back again while patiently waiting for my response.

"Huh, so Kai Huntington can do a little kiss." I say nonchalantly.

Kai laughs, but the movement makes him press a hand to his midsection. "Don't make me laugh like this, Babe."

After gently pushing him away from me so I can peel myself from the wall, Kai laces our fingers together as I lead him back to bed. But instead of lying down like I planned, he pulls me down next to him where we sit side by side on the mattress.

"I can't wait for you to come home so we can get back to our lives and put the last few days behind us." I say while toying with his index finger.

"I know." Kai whispers. He pulls me close to his side, rubbing his hand up and down my arm. "But you know there will be at least one more encounter with him, right?" He asks gently.

"Yeah." I sigh, "But this time it won't be under a new moon and you'll be able to smell the dangers and I'll be able to talk to you."

"You're right about it not being under a new moon. And this is not going to be on his terms only. Since it's a challenge, there are certain rules that both of us need to follow. But I am going to make sure it's under the next full moon, so we have some time to spare before this fight happens." Kai declares.

Later that night, Dad and Tobias decide to go to a local restaurant, and they bring back a hearty feast for everyone. Take-out containers filled with steak, shrimp, and a variety of sides to go with each fill the second bedside table Tobias rolled in a moment ago. Mom and Coraline walk in a few minutes later, after I assume they finished getting Kai's room ready for his release tomorrow, followed by Atticus and Quilla.

"What is all this about, Tobias?" Coraline asks with a chuckle to her mate.

"A celebration, my dear. We first celebrate Kai's recovery, thank The Great Luna for that, and." He pauses while looking at me with a genuine smile. "We have Dakota's achievement to celebrate. She's finally become one with her wolf and is able to phase alongside us."

I begin to feel my cheeks flush a light pink at the alpha's praise, but then Kai speaks up and the pink shade fades and I feel pure love and honor at my mate takes its place.

"It's her *achievements,* Father. Both her phasing and her silver immunity. We celebrate both of those accomplishments tonight."

"Right you are, my boy!" Tobias shouts his agreement.

Atticus and Dad have been going around filling plastic cups with everyone's drink of choice, and we all raise a cup at Tobias' shout.

"Here, here!" We all echo as one.

"Thank you, Kai."

"What, for telling the truth?" He lifts an amused eyebrow, but then I see his eyes turn serious. *"You're very welcome, Mate. You deserve much more than a simple meal."*

"Well, I hear our kind lives for a long time, so you have plenty of opportunities to show me just how much I deserve your praise."

Kai shakes his head as he unboxes the food that was set before us on his bedside table, and as a pack of eight, we dine together. I can feel our powers intertwine with each other to help Kai finish healing on his last night at the hospital.

Chapter Seventy-Four

KAI

The next morning, as Dad, Mom, Atticus, and Dr. Peterson are going over my discharge papers, I am in the bathroom getting my first good shower since the attack and I'm able to put on actual clothes rather than wearing hospital gowns or scrubs. Since we had dinner last night, I felt the power combine from our pack to heal me completely. I don't even have any scarring thanks to Quilla's power.

I step out of the bathroom just as Atticus stashes the discharge papers back into the folder at the foot of the bed and Dr. Peterson is shaking my father's hand as a sign of farewell.

"Dr. Peterson, I know you're busy, but I'd like a moment of your time, please." I say as she takes a step back from my father to leave. She nods briskly, but a friendly smile pulls at her lips.

"I want to sincerely thank you for saving my life. And for that, I will be forever grateful." I say, bending my head down in a show of respect.

"You're welcome, Kai. I will say, you gave me a run for my money, but you also helped me learn a lot about your people. I am glad that I was able to help bring you back to your family." She says as she walks out the door, then she pauses to look over her shoulder at me, "But, I don't want to see you come back in through my ER anytime soon." She adds in a playful tone.

"Yes, ma'am. I'll do my best." I grin as we all walk out of the hospital with our heads held high.

After the eight of us take a few hours to relax in the living room, we let ourselves slowly get back into the normal rhythm of life while the smells of cooking meat and vegetables float through the air from the kitchen. When it's almost time to pull dinner from the oven, Mom and Mrs. Shade make their way into the kitchen to make the side dishes to complete the meal.

Since it's going to be a few more minutes before we eat and now that there is more room on the couch, I lean back against the armrest and pull Dakota against my chest. She no longer settles against my body before I hear a small knock on the door, and I growl at the sound.

Everyone I know is here in the house, so who is it? I look over to Dad, and his face lights up with a knowing smile. My mate sees this too and, of course, immediately calls him out on it.

"What's the smile for, Tobias?"

"Oh, I'm having someone special drop by." Dad grins as he opens the door.

I look past him, and who I see in the doorway makes my heart swell with happiness.

"Emma,, I whisper.

I stand up from the couch and I get no further than the edge of the living room when she spots me, pushes past Dad to run over to me and I pull her into my chest as she begins to cry into my neck.

"I'm so sorry you got hurt because of me." Emma sobs.

I pull her back to look into her tear-filled blue eyes, and I give her a small smile.

"You have nothing to be sorry about, Emma. This is what a true Alpha does. He or she—" I say while looking over Emma's shoulder at my mate, and she gives me a playful wink. "He or she protects their pack, and sometimes it puts their life on the line. I am so happy that you are part of this pack. You and yours will *never* live in fear ever again." I promise.

"My parents and I have been living in a house in Montana because Alpha Tobias thought it would be wise for us to be away from this area for a while, and I can tell you we have never felt safer in a strange territory." Emma says with a wobbly grin.

"Come on, dry those eyes, Emma. Dinner should be ready soon, and I would love it if you join us. Plus, I want you to also hear the plan I'm going to discuss tonight." I say as I quickly dry her eyes and lead her as well as Dakota into the dining room just as Mom brings out the food.

As the three of us, along with Dad, Nathan, Atticus, Quilla, and finally Mom and Mrs. Shade, gather around the table, Dad lifts his wineglass in a toast before we eat.

"I want to say a few things here that I am thankful for, but first, welcome home son." Dad says while tipping his glass in my direction, "You have overcome a very dangerous journey and I am so grateful to all my pack members and those outside of the pack that played a part in bringing my son back from the brink of death. And I am also thankful to have added three new pack members to the ranks. I am glad that the

Hughes' no longer live in fear, and they have everything they will ever need now to be safe and well cared for. Here is to a growing pack and to our health!" Dad lifts his glass and we all follow suit, clinking our glasses with our neighbors and taking a sip. Dad looks at me and he nods once. "Did you have anything you wanted to say or announce, Kai?"

"Actually, yes." I reply as I rise to my feet. I don't have a glass in my hand, but I can tell that everyone is just as invested in what I have to say. "I wanted to talk to my pack mates and my family about my decision. In three days' time, I am going to publicly challenge Jeffrey for Dakota as my rightful mate and for his pack members, unless they have a better leader in mind. It will be under the next full moon, which will be four days later, and I was thinking about having it take place in the very park that he tried to kill me in."

"Oh. I like the little slap in the face at the location, Babe," Dakota croons from my side with a devilish grin.

"If you want Kai, I can walk the grounds with you to help find any potential footing issues so you're not taken off guard during the fight." Nathan offers.

"I appreciate that, Nathan. Thank you."

"I like that idea, Nathan. I knew I made a smart move in making you my beta." Dad grins.

"Well, that was one of the many things that I was in charge of at my old pack. Making sure the grounds were safe, so it's no different now." Nathan says while taking a bite of his food to hide the slight nervous twitch of his mouth.

With that decided, we all finish dinner among idle chatter just like any other normal evening.

Dakota and I turn in for the night, and when I walk into my bedroom, I pull her into my chest and over to my bed, where we both sink into the soft mattress. She pulls the covers over us, but we do nothing more than hold one another. After a few moments, I find it odd that with what I just discussed at dinner for my mate to be as silent as she is.

"You're awfully calm for what I just laid before the family."

"I know. It's just, I don't know, I can't really explain it. One part of me is scared about the fight, but I refuse to think about any other outcome other than you winning." She sits up to look at me, her eyes pinging back and forth between my own. "Promise me you won't lose. Promise me that you and you alone will claim me as your mate."

I sit up and I gently wrap my hand around the base of her neck while pulling her close to me, almost nose to nose as she rests her hands on my chest.

"Jeffrey got his chance to get one over on me, and he will never get another. This ends with *him dying* and *me* claiming you as my mate. That is the only outcome that I will allow. You have my word, my mate, my Love," I declare as I send a wave of my alpha power over her to make my words clear.

"Yes, my mate, my alpha." Dakota says with a slight nod, but then a smirk graces her lips as she says, "I'm going to make sure that you know something too, Mate. Maybe I can give you some extra incentive to fight for."

"And what could you possibly give me?" I tease.

She leans in, softly pressing her lips to mine, and I hungrily meet her stroke for stroke. Without breaking contact, she pushes me onto my back while tossing a leg over my hips, straddling my torso. After a moment, she pulls her lips away from my mouth, and she stares down at me with a lazy, kiss-high smile.

"Oh, what can I give you?" She asks mockingly as she glides her hand down my chest, stomach, and lower. My breath hitches as she caresses me through my sweatpants.

"Dakota." I pant.

"This is what I'm going to give you. I want you to remember the feel of my hand against you, around you, and I want you to imagine that once you win in the fight against that weak, insufferable alpha," She makes a point to grind her hand into my hardening length making my head tilt back into my pillow with a groan, "The next time I do this, it will be without any barriers."

"I will make sure that happens, Love," I growl with possessiveness, and I buck my hips against her where I am the one on top now. "And the next time I do this." I tease as I knead her breast with my fingers, my thumb flicking the hardened, peaked nipple through her t-shirt, and I am rewarded with a moan pouring from her throat. "You will be *my mate,* and I will love you in all the ways I have been imagining. That is my promise to you, Dakota Shade. You are *mine,* and no one takes what is mine."

CHAPTER SEVENTY-FIVE

KAI

The next morning as Dakota and I walk downstairs, we find Mom and Dad sitting at the island eating breakfast.

"Good morning, son. Dakota." Dad nods. "Did you sleep well?"

"We did." I answer for the both of us as I help Dakota into a chair next to my father.

We eat in silence, but I can tell from how Dakota is picking at her plate that she has something on her mind.

"Hey Babe, what's wrong?"

"I hate to ask this first thing this morning, but it's been bugging me since I woke up."

"Don't feel bad, Love. What is it?" I ask as I rub my hand down her back in encouragement.

"Where do you plan on telling Jeffrey about the challenge? If it's at the college, don't you think you should tell Dean Coleman first?"

"You know, your mate has a point, Kai." Mom grins.

"I agree. You can't challenge Jeffrey if the dean isn't aware. You don't know how many humans attend the school that unknowingly walk among Werewolves." Dad says.

"I didn't even think about that." I look over to my father. "Dad, can we call Dean Coleman and have him meet us here to discuss the plan?" I ask.

"Absolutely, son. I can talk to him for you, but we meet at a different location. Remember, Kai, you never bring an outsider into your personal space. You don't know yet if he sides with or against Jeffrey," Dad informs.

"Right, thank you, Alpha. That was my lack of forethought. I know better than to bring a possible enemy into my personal space." I scold myself with a shake of my head.

"It's alright, Kai. That is what I am here for. To teach you the correct ways of the alpha. I didn't learn all of what I know in one night, son." Dad smiles.

"Where do you think is the best place to meet him?" I ask, "What about meeting him at the university since that is the place where I plan to initiate the challenge?"

"I think that's a good idea." Dakota agrees.

"Yes, so do I," Dad says. "I will go call Dean Coleman now and get this set up right away." He adds as he stands and walks into his office, shutting the door behind him.

Mom gives me a determined smile as she rises from the table to clean up the kitchen. I offer to help her, but she insists Dakota and I go into the living room and wait for Dad to come back out. So that's what we do. I lie back on the couch while Dakota rests her head against my chest, and I play with her hair while we watch a comedy show on TV.

Dakota

As Kai and I begin to relax on the couch, we hear a knock on the door. Before I can even think of moving, Coraline gracefully strolls past us to let my dad and mom in.

"Hey Mom, Dad. What are you two doing over here?" I ask with a smile.

"Hi, Sweetheart. Tobias said to come over to discuss important pack matters with you two," Dad explains as he goes over to the loveseat with Mom on his heels.

When Tobias enters the living room and stands by his mate a moment later, Kai and I sit upright on the couch to hear what the alpha has to say.

"I spoke with Dean Coleman, and after some vague explaining of what has been happening between you four, I honestly think he's on our side. He's had suspicions that Jeffrey has been up to no good, but he's never had proof before. So, he's agreed to meet with me, Kai, Dakota, and Nathan tomorrow morning at 6:00 am, before any staff or students arrive."

"Thank you, Alpha. I appreciate what you have done." Kai says formally with a slight nod to his head.

Tobias walks over to his son and places a hand on his shoulder. "This is what a good alpha and a tight-knit pack does, Kai. We help one another."

I watch my father nod in agreement, and I can tell he will gladly attend this meeting with us without a second thought. I am so happy to see him be so involved and falling into his beta role with such honor.

Later that evening, after we finished eating dinner, which Dad and Tobias made for a change, I settle back onto the couch with Kai lounging next to me. I listen to our fathers put away any leftovers and clean the dishes, working together like a well-oiled machine, but my eyes keep drifting past them. To the sliding patio door where I can see the line of pine trees that tower over the house in the backyard.

"Run. I want to run with the pack." Kota whispers in the back of my mind.

At her words, I get up off the couch to walk over to the door and stare out at the vast expanse of forest before me. I glance over my shoulder at Kai and wonder if he's able to phase yet. His eyes meet mine, and I see the flash of confusion at my sudden change of demeanor, but it's Dad's voice in my mind instead of my mates.

"You want to run, don't you?"

I look at Dad, and his brown eyes are glowing brightly, and I know Nate is just under the surface.

"Yes, but—" I begin.

"What are you afraid of, Honey?" Dad asks.

"I'm worried about Kai. I want to run, but what if he's not ready, or he pushes himself too soon? And I don't know if I should ask him, or just wait."

"That is something you and Kai need to talk about, Honey. Only he can answer what his body is capable of."

"Do we need to leave these two alone, Nathan?" Tobias asks knowingly.

"Yes, we do." Dad says, giving me an understanding smile as he pulls Mom into his side and heads into the backyard with both alpha's on their heels, softly closing the door behind them.

Once we are alone, Kai turns to me with a look of concern on his face. "Please, tell me what's wrong?"

He pulls my back to his chest, marking to marking, and he rests his head on the curve of my shoulder while we both look through the glass.

"I want to run, Kai. I want to phase and run under the night sky with my pack, but—"

"You're afraid of asking me if I think I'm ready to phase. You think I may push myself too soon just to run with you."

He hits fear for fear like a hammer to a nail, and I just nod my head.

"I am fine, Love. Yes, I will need to take the first phase slowly after healing, but I can phase, Dakota. So, if you want to run, then let's run for your first time; as a pack." Kai says while letting a wave of his alpha power flow over me to show me just how ready he is to phase and run with me.

"Okay." I smile. "But promise me that if you get tired or start to hurt—" I begin but Kai cuts me off again.

"I promise I will keep you informed on *all* my feelings."

He purposely leaves it open for interpretation, and I can't help the rush of heat that travels up my neck and into my cheeks.

"You two ready?" Tobias asks as he pokes his head around the back-door.

"Yes, Dad. We are." Kai answers as he leads me outback where the rest of our family is waiting on the deck.

As we step out on the back patio, I remember the last time I was out here during the full moon when I first tried to phase and failed even when

Tobias tried to force the phase out of me. I gently shake my head to clear the images because now, I know I will be able to phase my own terms, and I hear Kota growl her agreement in my mind.

"Come! Let us run as one tonight." Tobias croons as he walks to the center of the yard, and he flawlessly phases into the solid black fur of his wolven form.

Coraline is the next in line, and her white coat gracefully flows over her body and she stands by her ebony-colored mate. Dad phases next, his dark gray pelt blending into the distant treeline almost perfectly. After a few moments, the three wolves look toward me and Kai expectantly, and I nod my head in acknowledgement.

"Let's go, Babe. Let's run with our pack." I give Kai a wink, and I take a few steps and allow the phase to take my body, and when I meet up with my father and the alpha's I have settled into Kota's blondish brown form.

Kai

I find myself smiling at how seamlessly my mate has phased. Pride and love builds in my chest for the woman, for the wolf in front of me who is being greeted by my parents and her father.

I make sure to push those feelings towards her through our bond because I promised her I'd let her know what I was feeling, but it's also to somewhat hide the anticipation of phasing for the first time. I know I am fully healed and it shouldn't be an issue, but it's almost like using muscles, ligaments, and bones after being in a cast for six weeks, it's ingrained into my human blood to be apprehensive of the first step.

I feel K pushing against my mind, and I can feel he is strong; he's not afraid to take over my body, so I trust in my wolf and I close my eyes, letting him take over. Granted, it's not as fluid as it normally is, and I feel the muscles in my chest and stomach painfully stretch for a moment, but before I can even process the pain, it's over and my paws sink into the lush grass of the backyard. I open my eyes when I feel a body snuggle up beside me, and I take in Dakota's lithe form next to mine.

"Are you okay?"

"Yes, Love. I feel amazing." I say.

I lick her nose and take a bounding leap away from her while letting out a playful bark. *"Let's run!"* I exclaimed to everyone through our branching bonds.

Dakota

Kai darts out of the backyard, and Tobias takes off after him with Dad chasing right behind them. Glancing at Coraline, her bright blue eyes encased in a glowing white coat, nods once and she takes off after her mate, son, and beta. I look over my shoulder at Mom, and she shoos me away with a tear in her eye.

"I love you, Dakota. Have a good time, Sweetheart."

I bound after my pack mates and find them playfully chasing, nipping, and growling at one another, and I happily join in the fray as we leave the neighborhood. Kai singles me out and chases me up onto a hill ,where we have a beautiful sight of the cityscape below us.

The last bit of orange mixing, with the deep blues and purples of the nighttime sky with stars dotting the horizon above us, and below the lights in the different buildings, homes, and cars shining a soft amber.

Kai steps up next to me, tongue lolling out of the side of his mouth while panting to catch his breath. He looks so happy, and I feel the same way. Kai catches me staring at him and angles his body to press his forehead against mine.

"This is amazing, Kai. I love that I can share this with you." I tell him.

"I love it too. This is everything that I dreamed of and more."

Tobias, Coraline, and Dad finally reach us, and we all take a moment to look out over the horizon as one. Five overly sized wolves standing on a hilltop with our coats in varying colors. I'm sure it would make for a great photo-op if we thought of bringing something along to be able to take pictures.

We continue to run together for a while. Our paws light on the ground, chasing one another like ghosts in the brush, barely leaving a disturbed path in our wake. Kai shows me how to track the footprints of deer, rabbits, and mice that live in the forest while Dad shows me how to look over the grounds to make sure they are safe for us to travel. I make sure they both feel how much I appreciate their lessons through the bonds between us.

This is the one thing that I love while being in my wolven form; we don't require words to let the other know what we need to do or how we feel. Actions, gestures, and feelings are the only forms of communication we need.

As the waning moon rises higher in the sky, letting us know it's getting later in the evening, we make our way back to Kai's house and reluctantly phase and turn in for the night. Because tomorrow is when the real games begin.

CHAPTER SEVENTY-SIX

KAI

As I'm lying in bed at four o'clock the next morning, I find myself staring up at my ceiling with my mate snuggled tightly into my side, her head leaning on my chest while sleeping peacefully beside me. I allow myself to feel content in that moment. Almost let myself believe that this fateful meeting isn't in two hours. But I know that after this conversation, it will be nothing but careful planning and staying focused until the fight with Jeffrey is over. This makes me even more grateful that Dakota suggested we run last night together.

One night of happiness for us to desperately cling to will help us get through these next few days.

Dakota begins to stir next to me, and I gently place a kiss on her head as she drags a finger lazily down the center of my chest, sending shivers of pleasure down my spine.

"Good morning, Love."

"Morning." Dakota replies, and she sits up enough to look into my face, and I know she can already see the gears turning in my head.

"You're already thinking about what's coming, aren't you?" She asks.

"You know me too well already, Baby. Yeah," I sigh. "But, I was also still thinking about running with you, your dad, and my parents. I loved it; thank you again for suggesting it." I say while trying to lighten the mood.

"Anything to make you and my pack happy. I do aim to please, Kai." She says as she gives me a playful wink.

"That you do, mate of mine." I smirk as I swiftly pin her to the bed, my body hovering over her own.

Dakota smiles at me and places her left hand against the mate marking on my chest. I know from her little intake of breath that my eyes are glowing brightly, and I growl at her reaction. She lifts her head, pressing her lips lightly against mine, and when she pulls away, I follow her down, giving her my own kiss.

At first, it's light like hers was, but when I skim my tongue across the seam of her lips, they part and I greedily deepen the kiss. When her arms wrap around my neck, pulling me even closer, I give into her. Our chests and our stomachs line up like puzzle pieces, but when our hips align next, I can't help but roll my hardened length into her hot core. I can feel her heat against me through our clothes, begging me to make her mine in every single sense of the word. She moans when the friction hits that aching spot at the apex of her thighs, and as I flex my hips once more, my bedroom door suddenly opens.

"Kai, Dakota are you two up?"

I growl at Dad's voice while Dakota hides her face into the curve of my neck trying to get her panting breath under control.

"Ah, yes, I see you both are up. Now please untangle yourselves, and perhaps take a cold shower, then get dressed and meet us in the dining room." Dad replies with a knowing smirk.

After Dad leaves, I look back at my mate, who is trying and failing miserably to hide her laughter behind her hand.

I rest my forehead against hers. "I think if it was your dad who caught us instead of mine, I would be picking myself up out of the street." I chuckle.

"Probably," Dakota replies while laughing along.

We do as Dad suggested and untangle ourselves from my bed, get our showers, unfortunately in separate bathrooms, and get dressed before we make our way into the dining room. When we walk in, Mom smiles at us as she brings in the carafe of freshly brewed coffee and sits it in the middle of the table along with two coffee mugs before sitting down next to my father. I pull out Dakota's chair for her to sit down, and when I take my respective chair, I meet my father's gaze, and I can't miss the mischievous gleam he has in his eye. I am just about to reach out to him through the bond to tell him to stuff that look up his ass when Dakota gives my mother an angelic smile, and I know my crafty mate is about to stir the pot.

"Good morning, Coraline. I hope you and yours slept well because Kai and I were so rudely woken up this morning." Dakota says, giving Dad a glare.

"Oh, Great Luna, help me." I cringe with a smile.

"Do I want to know what your mate is talking about, Kai?" Mom asks.

"No, not really, Mother." I say.

Dad's laughter fills the air as he pulls two coffee cups close to him, pouring the dark brown liquid into the empty vessel. "I walked in on our son and his mate this morning, Sunflower."

"Kai Huntington!" Mom scolds me while smacking me on the shoulder.

"What? It's not like we did anything!" I defend while rubbing my shoulder.

"Oh, I don't know about that one, Kai. It was pretty intense." Dakota teases, and Dad actually high-fives my mate at her jab.

"You are so not helping, Dakota." I warn as heat travels up my neck at my father outing us to my mother and my mate of all people, playing along.

"Tell that to the redness in your cheeks, mate." Dakota taunts.

"You want me to show them just what we were doing?" I shoot back. *"I have always been told to finish my meal while at the table, and you, my dear, could easily be my main course."*

Her eyes widen as the mental image of her laid out on this table, my head between her legs while her body shivers with pleasure, plays out between us. Her eyes dart away from mine, looking anywhere but at the table, and I smile wickedly at her.

"Okay. Point taken."

"Okay, so on to more serious things," Dad says, pulling me back to reality. "When we meet with Dean Coleman, and if we feel he's on our side, we are going to tell him everything." Dad says.

I nod, and we all go over the proper ways to begin this conversation. As we talk, I feel the desire that was flooding my veins a moment ago fade and transition into a calm focus.

Dakota

An hour late,r Dad, Tobias, Kai and I walk into the main hall of the university to meet up with Dean Coleman.

"Good morning, everyone." The dean greets us while firmly shaking the hands of the men around me and gently caressing my own. "Please follow me."

He leads us into his office down the hall, and after we all walk in, he closes and locks the door behind us while pulling the blinds down as well. I notice that Dad nonchalantly leans against the wall next to the door, crossing his arms over his chest while Kai, Tobias, and I move closer to the large gray and cream-colored metal desk.

"Please sit, if you wish," Dean Coleman says as he waves a hand over the three worn burgundy fabric chairs set up in front of his desk. "And please call me Mr. Coleman or Sam, whichever you prefer. Dean is a little too formal for what I think we are about to discuss."

"Thank you again for meeting with us, Mr. Coleman." Tobias begins, keeping to formalities and exuding professionalism.

"Of course. You said in our phone conversation that your son and his girlfriend are being violently attacked by someone in my student body and that something deeper is going on that I may not fully understand." Mr. Coleman looks between me and Kai and I can tell that he suspects something; he just doesn't know what.

"That is correct, Mr. Coleman. We come here today to discuss a solution that will help my son and his girlfriend, but that solution will also include every single student here at this school." Tobias says.

"How so?" Mr. Coleman cocks his head to the side while staring the alpha down.

"Tell me this. What is your stance on Jeffrey?"

"Jeffrey Carmichael? I honestly don't understand how he makes it in his classes. He's hardly ever present, and he is known for occasionally having outbursts during lectures, especially in the last ten months. And to be honest, Caleb isn't much better." Mr. Coleman pinches the bridge of his nose and looks at all of us in turn. "Why do I get the feeling you all know exactly what's going on here?"

Tobias nods to my mate, and he sits forward in his chair to look the dean in the eye. "Because we do know, Mr. Coleman." Kai says. "There is no easy way to say this, so I am just going to throw it out here. We are Werewolves, Mr. Coleman. And you have many more here in your university, including Jeffrey and Caleb."

Mr. Coleman leans back in his chair as Kai's words sink in. His eyes scan over us and his skin pales a bit. "Seriously?" Is all he can manage to say at first. "For the last six years I've been here, I've had Werewolves as students and didn't know about it?"

"We are normally very private creatures unless our mate is in danger or we have been so long without one that it makes us go crazy." Kai offers.

"I know it's a lot to take in, but things are quickly spiraling out of control, and,my son is the only one that can stop it." Tobias says.

At the dean's confused look, we give him the abridged version of what has been happening between Kai, Jeffrey, Caleb, and me.

"Well, I'm glad to hear that you are alive and well, Kai," Mr. Coleman says after a few moments.

"Yes, unfortunately for Jeffrey and Caleb, I live to fight another day." Kai replies.

"Okay, while I still don't really understand everything, I get the gist of it. So please explain what will happen. I need exact details, mainly will any of my human students be in danger?" Mr. Coleman asks, his voice becoming firmer and more focused after the initial shock wears off.

"Tobias and myself will be crowd control." Dad begins from his perch against the wall. "If Jeffrey or Caleb makes a move tomorrow, then they forfeit the challenge and they can be killed by either Kai, Tobias, or even myself. Challenges are very straightforward. We cannot immediately go into a fight as soon as the challenge is discussed. They are designed to be planned for a certain place and time."

"Especially since the challenge is a fight to the death, they get very gruesome and violent. So they need to take place in a private area." Kai says.

"So believe me when I say, no one will be harmed tomorrow. The humans will probably be shocked to find out that they have been going to school among Werewolves, but other than that, nothing else will happen. I will make sure to keep to my word." Tobias says.

"Thank you, Mr. Huntington, I appreciate that. So, yes, Kai, in the morning may openly challenge Jeffrey." Mr. Coleman agrees.

"Thank you, Mr. Coleman. I appreciate your understanding on this matter and being open to this drastic change that is about to happen." Kai says. "Because when I verbalize the challenge for Jeffrey, the other wolves will have no choice but to react to my declaration. So, just be prepared that you will see many pairs of glowing eyes."

"What? Glowing eyes?" Mr. Coleman says, showing fear for the first time.

At this, I can't help but speak up for the first time. "After all of what you've been told, the glowing eyes are what throws you for a loop?"

"Well, I didn't know that you all had an actual outward sign other than becoming a wolf." Mr. Coleman says nervously.

My nose begins to tickle with a smell that I haven't experienced yet, and Kai picks up on my confusion through the bond.

"He is curious, Love. I think he wants to see our eyes, but he's apprehensive in asking that question." Kai says.

I look back at the dean,, and I give him a confident smile. "Do you want to see a demo before the big event, Mr. Coleman?"

"You can show me now, Dakota?" Mr. Coleman asks.

"Sure," I say. *"You all want to show him at the same time?"* I ask down our respective bonds and I feel their agreement flow back in response.

We all close our eyes and let our wolves come to the surface, and when we open them again, I hear Mr. Coleman's audible gasp at the sight.

"That is freaky, but amazing at the same time. They glow the same color as your eyes." He says in awe. "I figured they would be yellow or amber."

Tobias laughs out loud and relaxes a bit in his chair, his long legs straightening while he crosses them at the ankle. "You, sir, have been watching too many bad Hollywood movies." After a moment, Tobias looks between me, Kai, and Dad as he says, "You know what, which one of you want to fully phase and show him exactly what we can do?"

"Dakota, why don't you show him? I think your wolf is the most beautiful to showcase what we are." Kai says with a genuine smile.

"Oh, so I'm the poster girl of all Were's huh? Gee, thanks, Kai." I roll my eyes, but I can't keep the smirk off my face. "I'd be honored. Prepare to be amazed, Mr. Coleman!"

I go to the middle of the room, and I slowly let Kota take over so I don't tear my clothes. I keep my eyes locked with the dean as I feel my body pop and contort into my wolven form.

"That... is amazing." Mr. Coleman whispers, completely shell-shocked.

As I shake out my coat, I notice that Mr. Coleman's eyes are still locked onto mine when he begins to get out of his chair, but at Kai's low growl and brightly glowing eyes, the dean freezes in his tracks.

"I would recommend not trying to touch her, Mr. Coleman." Dad warns. "Again, this is Kai's mate, and he does not like another male touching her, especially since you are not pack."

"That would be a good way to lose a finger, huh?" Mr. Coleman says.

"That and more, Mr. Coleman." Tobias replies solemnly.

At Tobias' warning, Mr. Coleman backs away from me, Kai instantly relaxes, and his eyes stop glowing as brightly.

"I'm sorry, Mr. Coleman, it's just again, mates are very precious to us and we strive to protect them in any way we can." Kai explains.

"No need to apologize, Kai. If anything, I'm sorry. I didn't understand how you all felt about your...mates." Mr. Coleman waves an apologetic hand in my direction.

"I think that is about all we need to discuss this morning, Mr. Coleman. If you like, we can talk more tomorrow before Kai makes his move." Tobias says.

"No, unless you think I need to know something else, then you have my blessing. Just again, please do not let any harm come to the human students tomorrow." Mr. Coleman pleads.

Dad opens the door for us as Kai picks up my discarded clothing and follows me into the bathroom so I can get dressed.

"Well, that went off without a hitch, didn't it?" I ask as I walk out of the stall in my human form a minute later.

"Yeah. Actually, that went better than I thought it would. Now, let's just hope that everything will go as smoothly tomorrow, and all hell doesn't break loose." Kai says.

"Hey, I trust you, your dad, and mine to keep the peace. Everything will be fine, Kai."

Kai gathers me into his chest and looks at the reflection of us in the mirror. "Please continue to keep me grounded, Babe. That will give me the clear head I need to get through the next few days." Kai says.

"As you say, so it shall be, Alpha mine." I smile.

We walk out of the bathroom to meet up with our father's out in the parking lot and try to take it hour by hour as the countdown to when this challenge will be initiated is set into motion.

Chapter Seventy-Seven

DAKOTA

The next morning comes all too soon, and I roll over in Kai's bed to just hold him for a moment, but his side of the bed is empty. I open my eyes and find that the room is still dark with just the barest hint of purple seeping through the window from the slowly rising sun.

I sit up in bed and notice my mate standing in front of the window, still in his sweat shorts from last night. The softly glowing light cascades down his bare chest and arms. Slipping out of bed, I slowly make my way over to him, pressing my cheek against his bare back while I wrap my arms around his waist.

"Morning, Babe." I whisper.

Kai takes a cleansing breath and turns in my arms to face me. He lifts my chin with his index finger, his eyes bouncing back and forth between my own, and it's almost like he's trying to get lost in my light blue eyes. He leans into my neck and slowly takes in my scent while letting his breath tickle against my skin, and I know he just put his scent on me. I tighten my grip on his forearms, and I release my own breath against his chest.

"Morning, Love." Kai rasps.

I can feel the apprehension leaking from his side of the bond, even though he's trying to block it from me, so I do what I do best.

"You ready to tackle this day, Babe? I can't wait to see the look of utter shock on those assholes' faces when they see you."

He finally smiles, pulling me closer to him while pressing a quick kiss to my lips. "I'm ready to tackle anything as long as I have you by my side, Love. Let's get dressed and talk to our dads about how to approach this."

True to his words, I feel Dad's presence as well as my mother's filling the air along with Tobias and Coraline in the living room below us.

"Good morning, Kai. Dakota." Tobias says when we enter the living room five minutes later.

"Good morning." I nod to the alphas, who are sitting on the loveseat, while my parents are taking up the couch. "Morning, Dad, Mom."

"Morning, Sweetie." Dad smiles as he moves from his place beside Mom and perches on the arm of the couch to make room for me and Kai.

As we take our seats, my mate gets right to asking how he is to proceed with today's meeting.

"Father? What do you think is the best way to approach this meeting?"

"I think we should arrive before everyone else and confront Jeffrey as soon as we see him. What do you think, Nathan?" Tobias asks.

"I agree. That way we can see who all comes in too." Dad replies.

While I listen to them talk, something isn't sitting right with me. It feels wrong to go about it this way. I look at my father and Tobias, then to Kai, and I touch my mate's hand. "May I say something?"

"Yeah, of course, Love. What's on your mind?" Kai asks, looking at me earnestly.

"Forgive me if this sounds stupid, but I feel like it would be almost like an ambush if we arrived first. I want to show Jeffrey and Caleb that Kai is just as strong as he was before the attack, and he can walk in under his own power. So, I think we should wait until everyone is in the cafeteria and then walk in."

As my words fade, no one speaks for a few long moments, and I begin to shake my head with humiliation. "I'm sorry; that was a stupid thought. Just ignore me."

"No, Dakota." Tobias and Kai say in unison.

"I like that plan, Babe." Kai says with an approving smile

"That is a brilliant plan, Dakota." Tobias says. "Spoken like a true alpha. I will call Mr. Coleman and tell him to gather everyone for a meeting in the cafeteria."

Tobias gets up from his chair and pulls his cell phone out to make the call while Kai, Coraline, Mom, and Dad all smile at me.

After a few minutes, Tobias comes back into the living room with a determined gleam in his eyes. "Alright, Mr. Coleman will have the cafeteria filled by the time we get there. Nathan, you and I will be crowd control while Kai and Dakota approach Jeffrey."

"Now, that one I have an issue with." Kai says while lifting a finger, "Should Dakota get that close to him? I mean I am challenging him for her."

"Don't worry, Kai." I say while placing my hand on his knee, "I planned on standing off to the side a little, anyway. And in case he does go off, I would be able to get out of the way and help lead people out with our dads."

Kai nods, and he stands from the couch and extended, his hand towards me. "Let's go." He says as he gives me a smile, but it doesn't reach his eyes.

As I reach for his hand, I can feel his nervousness through our bond, so I push a wave of calmness and strength toward him as I gently squeeze his fingers.

"Thank you, Dakota."

At those simple words, I can feel the weight of them and how much my presence at his side means to him right now.

"Anytime, Babe."

As we pull up to the university and Tobias finds a parking spot, we all unload from his SUV and walk toward the solid metal door that leads to the cafeteria. I hear Kai take a breath as we hear Mr. Coleman say that a student has an important announcement to make and waits for everyone to quiet down.

"Are we ready?" Tobias looks back at me and Kai, his eyes already a lighter shade of brown but not fully glowing.

"Yes," Kai says, and I watch him set his shoulders back and hold his chin high, as confidence fills his hazel eyes when he winks at me.

Just as Kai places his hand on the door handle, we hear two car doors slam. I turn to see Quilla and Atticus rushing up to us, and my friend wraps her arms around my neck.

"Sorry I'm late, Chica. I couldn't let you all do this without your Tamer here, but Atticus wanted to be with me, so I had to wait for him to get back from checking on a patient."

"Better late than never, Quilla. Thank you for wanting to be here. You are the best." I tell her while hugging her tightly.

Kai

I watch Dakota and Quilla have their moment as I hear the questions begin to roll from the other side of the door. When I pick up on the faint scent of Jeffrey and Caleb, I fall into alpha mode.

Calm, collected, and determined to get this challenge active.

"I'm ready. Let's get this started."

I feel my own power fill the air around us along with my father's, Dakota's, and Nathan's. Each invisible tendril mingles together to give us the fuel to walk through these doors. I push down on the handle and I shove the door open so hard that the metallic sound of the door hitting brick rings out, making the entire student body whip their head in our direction.

Dakota was right; making an entrance this way is so much more satisfying than I thought, as the vicious, angry growl that echoes over the harsh whispers makes my blood sing with the anticipation of the fight.

"Kai!" Emma shouts as she rushes over to me from the crowd. "I'm so glad you're back."

I pull her into my chest for a quick hug and whisper into her ear, "Go stand by my father; he will make sure you are safe. This is the beginning of the end for *him.*"

She takes her spot next to my father, who, as we planned, stays by the metal doors, leaving them open for a quick corral if needed for an escape.

I continue to walk into the middle of the cafeteria, where Mr. Coleman is still standing with a forced friendly smile on his face. Dakota stops walking by my side and stands a few feet away, but close enough where I know she's safe, then Atticus and Quilla stand at my back against the wall. Atticus makes sure to keep Quilla behind him but also keeps his stance closer to Dakota in case he needs to get to her as well. And finally, Nathan takes his place near the kitchen where he knows there is another back entrance to either guard or escort people to safety.

As I look out to the student body before me, I see the confused looks of the humans and the knowing glances of the Were's staring back at me.

I turn to shake Mr. Coleman's hand, and he gives me a nervous smile. "Thank you, Dean Coleman, for allowing me to do this on *your* territory."

"Of course." He says as he makes his way over to my dad and awaits the outcome of what I am about to do.

I lift my head and look over the student body again as I say, "Good morning, fellow students. I'm just going to cut to the main matter of this impromptu meeting. I, Kai Huntington, am a Werewolf. An up-and-coming alpha. And Dakota Shade here is my rightful mate. However, Jeffrey Carmichael has unsuccessfully tried to either take her from me or tried to kill me, on a new moon mind you, to try and take me out of the picture." I explain, and the collective gasp from the wolves after hearing about the brazen attack of an alpha on the new moon erupts through the room.

"YOU WERE SUPPOSED TO DIE, YOU PIECE OF SHIT!" Jeffrey bellows angrily. "You came into *my* territory and stole Dakota away from *me*."

His words set Dakota off, and she interrupts him. "I have never been your mate, and I never will be, Jeffrey Carmichael," Dakota says, pushing her alpha power towards him.

"Please, Dakota, stand back. I understand your thoughts on this and need to confront him again, but we are trying not to poke the wolf here."

She steps back and allows me to control the floor again.

"Father, Nathan, please be prepared to hold Dakota back in any way you see necessary. I think you both know what Jeffrey may end up declaring to put me on edge and run the risk of me automatically losing." I tell my father and beta and I feel a spark of acknowledgment in their bonds.

"And you think that by attacking me during a new moon with a silver blade was the best way to go about this?" I challenge him. "Attacking me and trying to kill me when I am at my weakest?" This time I hear a collective breath from everyone, even the humans, at my words.

After a moment, I hear screams and growls begin to fill the room around me, and I see my mate has phased and is standing closer to her father, teeth bared in warning toward Jeffrey. I notice the slight shift in his stance, and I know we all missed the subtle signs that he was about to run past Nathan and out the back door like the damn coward he is.

Dakota phases enough so everyone is able to hear what she has to say to the miserable male in front of her.

"I told you before, Jeffrey, your days are numbered, and this cowardly alpha stunt will stop. I will not allow you to run any longer."

"Or if you want me to kill you now, Jeffrey, then keep running." I warn, "I have a lot of pent-up frustration for what you have done to me and mine so a chase will be just what the doctor ordered for K and I." I add on letting my full power fill the room and every single wolf here has no choice but to bare their necks to me. Even the humans avert their eyes, which makes Jeffrey's shine with terror.

"Alright, fine. Name your terms, Huntington, alpha of no pack." Jeffrey spits.

"That was cute." I chuckle darkly. " I, Kai Huntington, *future* Alpha of Montana, challenge you, Jeffrey Carmichae,l for the right to call Dakota Shade, the female in question, my mate. This, mind you, is a fight to the death. The losing male must not live, for he will always pine after her. However, I also challenge you for your pack. I know how you rule over them, and it's not right. Alpha's are to be protectors and educators for the pack, not be ruled as only the strong survive. The location of the battle will take place in," I say, pausing for a moment, letting a sly smile play on my lips. "In the very park that you tried and *failed* to kill me in just a week and a half ago."

Jeffrey still has the gall to laugh in my face, but I don't let it get to me. It's his way of trying to control the situation. "Oh, I guess that's where you really want your grave to be, huh, you wannabe alpha?"

"Nope, that's going to be your grave, you pathetic bastard. Care to guess when this little battle will take place?" I grin wickedly.

At first, Jeffrey has no clue what I mean, but then understanding and fear flicker across his features, and I can't help but laugh.

"Ah, yes. You know, good. At least I know you're not completely stupid. It will take place on the full moon, which is four days from today.

We fight when we both are at our strongest." I declare, "Do you agree to the terms of the fight?"

"I get to make one request as well, you inexperienced mutt." Jeffrey snaps.

I growl at his insult, but I make myself hold my ground as he speaks his own terms to the challenge.

"You are correct. I know you get to make one request, now, what is it?" I ask, fearing what crazy thing this bastard will make me agree to.

"Since you are so dead set on Dakota being your mate, you are not allowed to touch her or even be around her until we fight." Jeffrey says, his tone deathly venomous. "And *if* you win, then you can put your paws all over her as you wish."

At his words, Dakota, who has phased back into her human form and got dressed at some point, tries to lunge toward Jeffrey. I feel Dad's power snap out and mentally chain her to the spot, but she tries to break even his command.

"How dare you request that?" She shouts.

"Baby, please calm down. This is what he wants, to make this hard on both of us. But I have plans, Love."

"He wants to try to leave me unprotected. To show that you cannot save your own mate." Dakota sobs.

"You are never unprotected, Love. Just let me take care of things. Please, calm yourself for me." I say gently, and I feel her relax against my father's mental hold on her.

"I guess that seems fair. However, that goes for you as well. You and any other member of your pack cannot touch her or plan an attack on her. If you do, you forfeit your life to me." I say with just as much venom in my voice as he did with me. "Are we clear on the rules?"

"Crystal clear." Jeffrey snarls, "In four days time we will meet in the park at moonrise. Until then, neither of us will have any contact with Dakota ,and no harm will come to her by me or mine."

We all feel a crack of electricity fill the room as the challenge is set into place and the rules bind themselves deep within our bodies. Jeffrey and his beta are the first to leave as the voices of the student body, of Were's and humans alike, begin to understand what just happened and start to voice their anger in hushed whispers and cold, hard stares. As Jeffrey rushes past my father, he gives him the cold shoulder, but my alpha doesn't let the brash gesture set him off like I feel I would have.

I turn to my mate next as I feel her poking around in my mind like she's making sure that our connection is still there. I give her a soft smile, and I will my phantom touch to caress the back of her neck and let the feeling of my lips pressing against her fill her senses.

"I told you I had plans." I croon in her mind.

Her eyes snap to mine from across the cafeteria floor. *"I'm sorry I doubted you."* She whispers.

"You have nothing to be sorry for, Baby Girl. I know this was stressful for you. Everything will be alright." I promise.

Just as I am about to leave, I hear my name being called. I look back to the bleachers and see that everyone is standing, bearing their necks to me other than the tall, dark-haired male that stands in the middle of the crowd.

"My name is Ethan White and on behalf of everyone here, I pray The Great Luna gives you the strength to put that piece of shit down like the mutt he is for what he did to you and yours. If you need help with anything, please let us know." He looks down at a blonde girl on his right, a human I realize, and she lovingly nods to him. "My mate and I are more than happy to lend a hand in any way we can."

At Ethan's words, the cafeteria erupts in a chorus of well-wishes and more declarations of assistance if needed. I offer my appreciation to the group as we finally walk out of the cafeteria, but this time, we go home in separate vehicles. I'm riding with Dad and Nathan while Dakota rides with Quilla and Atticus.

This is just the first of many days without Dakota at my side, and I make myself hold on to the light at the end of the tunnel. To when I can wrap my arms around her again. Until then, it's a battle of willpower to keep myself in check.

Chapter Seventy-Eight
DAKOTA

Something wakes me in the middle of the night, and when I roll over to grab onto Kai so I can go back to sleep, I remember that he is over at his house. In his bed, alone, just like I am. Sadness and anger fills my chest in the same breath. The memory of that asshole alpha telling me that Kai and I can't touch, can't be with one another, burns in my brain.

I look over in the corner of the room, at the cot that Quilla set up to stay with me until all this is over. My friend is still sound asleep, so I decide to tiptoe down into the kitchen for a cold glass of water to try and calm myself enough so I can go back to sleep.

After I grab a cold bottle out of the fridge, I then grab a glass from the cabinet as I make my way to the Island. I pull out the barstool and plop down onto the seat while pouring the liquid into the glass, and I take a deep swig. I set the glass down as I run my hands through my hair, letting out a sigh and fighting the urge to rush over to Kai's bedroom to be with him, to hold him.

"I thought I heard someone down here."

I turn and find Dad standing in the doorway to the kitchen with a small smile on his face.

"I'm sorry, Dad, I didn't mean to wake you. I just couldn't sleep anymore."

"It's okay, Honey. You want to talk about it?" Dad asks as he sits beside me, leaning his forearms on the island.

"You know how hard it is to be away from your mate." I begin, and my voice cracks when I say, "I can't imagine what it will be like being in the same room as him and not being able to touch him."

Dad pulls me into his chest and pushes his power over me for a calming effect, and it helps set me at ease a little bit. "I know it will be hard. But know this, and please don't think I've ever doubted Kai's strength, but him not being near you will make him fight even harder to see that he is the winner." Dad takes my hand in his and gives it a loving squeeze. "Your mate actually anticipated Jeffrey making this kind of move as well."

"So, again, he kept something from me." I say in annoyance.

"Yes," Dad says slowly, "But, think Dakota. You are smart, Honey. Think of why your mate needed a genuine reaction out of you."

I think about it and it takes all but a moment before it hits me like a freight train. Not touching one another was nothing compared to what Jeffrey could have requested. Being unable to use the bond would have driven the both of us crazy, and Kai needed my reaction to be real to make Jeffrey think he got one over on us yet again.

"Thank you, Dad. Thank you for opening my eyes to what could have happened."

"You're welcome, Sweetie. The bond is better than nothing. It might not be the real touch, but it's enough to keep you both sane until this is all said and done."

"Yeah, it is." I close my eyes, and I can feel that Kai is still awake. "I'm going to go back up to my room. I can feel Kai is still up, so I'm going to talk to him for a while."

Dad gives me a kiss on the cheek, and we walk upstairs and into our respective rooms. As I slide into bed, I close my eyes to enter Kota's forest. I find her next to a large, glistening lake, and the moon in her realm shines just as bright and high as in my own world.

"Hello, Dakota."

"Hey. How are you holding up?" I ask as I sit by my wolf and place a hand on her head.

"Not well. I want to be near our mate. This upcoming battle has me on edge, and I want to comfort K and remind him that he is the stronger alpha. I can feel that he is just as restless as Kai is."

"I'm the same way." I look up into the sky as I lean back on my hands. "Isn't there a way we can go to them, go to their forest?"

Kota snorts; like my question is the funniest thing she's heard.

"What?" I ask.

"I was thinking the same thing. I remember back when we first met K and Kai, I was actually able to see K in his forest and that's how I brought you and Kai together. But I figured it was a onetime thing to bond us."

"Do you think you can do it again?"

"I don't know. I mean, we were in the same room when I did it the first time. I don't know if I can do it again, let alone with this distance between us."

"Well, I say we give it a shot. What's the worst that will happen? We will only end up back here, and we will have to handle the phantom touches we can get."

Kota nods her head, and I lean in closer to my wolf as we both close our eyes and think of our respective mates, the man and the wolf we so desperately want to be near.

After a few moments pass, nothing seemed to happen, and I let go of Kota's coat, letting an aggravated sigh roll from my chest.

"Gahh, it's not working! I guess it was a onetime thing, Kota. But at least we tried."

"Dakota."

At the sound of Kota's voice, the slight lilt of awe in her tone, my eyes fly open and something so achingly familiar hits my nose that I almost break down in tears.

Pine needles and cool mint fills my nose and envelopes my entire body.

"We did it, Kota." I say slowly at first, and then I look at my wolf, and I see a lupine smile grace her long muzzle. "We did it!"

"We did! Now let's go and find our mates." Kota takes a scent of the air, and she takes a step to the right in the direction of where Kai and K are. *"There, over that way. We are upwind, so they will not smell us coming."*

"Well, let's go say hello all stealthy like." I jest.

As we get closer to our mates, we find them in a clearing, both lying on the soft, lush green grass. Kai is on his back looking up at the sky, and K's head is on his chest. As I hear Kai talking to his wolf, Kota allows me to hear what K says in response.

"I knew this would be hard on us not to be able to touch Dakota, and I thought I could force my way through this until the fight is over, but K, just touching her through the bond isn't enough." Kai says, still staring up at the sky.

"I know. I can tell you want Dakota as a physical being, and I am just barely content with touching Kota through our bond. Yes, I would love to be

able to feel her next to me again, but I know that patience is key right now. We cannot let our drive for our mates cloud our judgment."

"I know you're right, K, but the human part of me actually is afraid I'm going to break and say the hell with it and go over to Dakota's place. Then Jeffrey will have a reason to kill me, and I would not be allowed to fight back. That is the only thought that is stopping me from acting on that desire. I cannot lose to him, K. I was so close to losing to that bastard once; I refuse to let that happen again. I can't hurt Dakota like that." Kai says angrily.

K nods his head against Kai's chest, knowing that even Kota has images from that night still fresh in her mind as well.

"I still pick up on the images from Dakota when she sleeps, and what I looked like from her point of view. I would do anything to be able to wipe those images from her mind." Kai whispers.

I find myself silently crying at hearing our mates talk like this. It's weird to see them both in the same place talking about me and my own wolf. I look at Kota and I feel her own sorrow that matches the feeling that is blooming in my chest.

"Let's go to them. But no scares, no funny stuff. Let's go and comfort our mates." I tell Kota through our bond.

"I agree. This is way too serious of a conversation to make a mockery of."

I step out of the tree line and I see a small branch in front of me. I make a point to step on it, and two heads whip in our direction.

"One way you can help me with those nightmares is to replace them with memories of us being happy."

"How did? When did?"

"Wow, I actually managed to render you speechless, Kai." I tease.

Kota and K instantly go to one another, rubbing their muzzles and wrapping their tails together as they walk over to the tree line, but being sure to keep us in their line of sight. I look back to Kai and I take a step towards him, but he retreats a step and I know I can't stop the flash of hurt at his rejection of my approach.

He falls to his knees when he sees the pain on my face, and he hangs his head in agony. "Please mate. I am not rejecting you, but, Babe, we can't touch. I cannot break the agreement."

"I know you can't touch me in the real world, but ,Kai, we are not really in the same space. This is just like the phantom touches through the bond, but this has a more realistic effect." I say softly.

He looks up at me, and, just like me, he feels the truth in my words. At that realization, I rush over to him, and he wraps his arms around me, spinning me around and around until we collapse into the grass. I land on my back with a soft thud while Kai lands on top of me. I grab him by the back of the head and pull him closer to me, crushing our lips together, and just like he usually does, he devours my mouth in a clash of tongues and teeth. Our breath comes out in haggard pants as we show one another just how much we've been missed in the last twelve hours.

Kai pulls back just a fraction of an inch, his lips still so close they brush my own when he speaks. "How did you do this? I thought this was impossible."

"I don't know, Kai. All I know is that I knew I wanted to be with you again so badly, and Kota felt the same way. She thought about the first time we met, and how she was able to start our bond, so we ran with it, and here we are."

"I'm so glad you figured it out, Baby." Kai leans in and kisses me a few more times.

After we have our fill of loving each other, we settle into one another's arms and just stare up into the night sky, taking comfort in the other's presence.

"Kai?" I begin.

"Yes, Love. What is it?" Kai asks as he brushes a piece of my hair behind my ear.

"First of all, I know that you anticipated Jeffrey making this request of us not touching until the fight. I was peeved that you didn't tell me, but I understand that you needed my genuine reaction at the school." I trace a line down his arm, and I watch gooseflesh bloom in my wake, and I find myself smiling at what my touch does to him. "I also know it could have been so much worse than what it is. Not being able to use the bond to talk to you or feel you would have killed me, Kai."

"I know, and I'm sorry I didn't tell you, but like you said, I needed your honest reaction to distract *him* from knowing how far he could have gone. I know that not being able to talk to you, to feel you through the bond by *his* request, would have driven me mad. I would have been a danger to anyone who tried to stop me from getting to Jeffrey, even my own father."

I shiver at the images of Kai fighting everyone who would have tried to stop him. My father, Atticus, and even his own father would have been ripped apart in Kai's crazed bloodlust for the one who ripped me from his mind.

"I'm so glad you had the forethought to plan for that."

"I try, Babe, I really do." Kai quips trying to lighten the mood. He then looks to the right, and I see the sun slowly beginning to rise above the horizon, and Kai turns back to me with a sorrowful look. "We need to go back to the real world now."

"Can't we stay here?" I whine even though I know he's right.

"I wish we could, Love, but I still need to talk to my dad about a few things and then meet with your dad about something too."

He stands up, and he helps me to my feet, but before he lets me go, he gives me one final longing kiss and then reluctantly steps back.

"I love you, Dakota Shade, and this will not last forever. I will be back in your arms for real before you know it."

"I love you too, Kai Huntington. I do not for one instant doubt your strength, Babe."

With that, Kota and K trot over to us, and we both take one last look at our mate as we allow our eyes to close.

When I open my eyes again, I am in my room with Kai's pine needle and cool mint scent only a memory in my mind.

Chapter Seventy-Nine
DAKOTA

The next seventy-two hours pass by in a blur. It consists of me and Kai meeting in his forest by night and by morning, Kai talks with his father about what he needs to do for the battle.

When I go downstairs the following morning, I notice Coraline sitting in the living room with my mother. Both women drinking a cup of coffee and quietly talking together.

"Good morning, Mom. Coraline." I say as I sit down by Mom on the loveseat.

"Good morning, Dakota. Did you sleep well?" Mom asks.

"Yeah. I did." I smile as I think about being in Kai's forest last night.

"Dakota, I apologize for coming over so early, but I must tell you something about the upcoming battle." Coraline says as she sits her cup down on the coffee table in front of her.

"Okay. What else do I need to know?"

"I hope that Kai has told you that this will get gruesome, and there will be bloodshed."

"He has, yes."

"Good. But no matter how bad things get, no matter how hurt your mate is, you cannot interfere, Dakota." Coraline says gently but sternly.

I hear her words, and images of Kai getting hurt again at the jaws of Jeffrey fills my mind and makes my stomach ache. Deep down I know this has to happen, and this is something I can't help him with. He needs to prove that he is the stronger wolf and, in turn, I will show that I am the stronger mate and let things happen as they should.

"I understand, Coraline. I hate it, but I understand."

"The only loophole that will allow you to interfere is if Jeffrey has outside help. Then that will allow you to help the one that you have chosen as your own," Coraline says.

"That is a good thing to keep in mind because we all know that Jeffrey will not play fair." I scoff.

"And that's what I'm most afraid of," Mom says.

I glance over at Coraline, noticing the tense lines of her shoulders that she's desperately trying to conceal, but I know her well enough to see her subtle change. I get up from the loveseat, taking the empty spot next to the alpha on the couch, and I set my hand on top of hers while giving her a small smile.

"I know this will also be hard on you too, Coraline." I begin, and her eyes snap up to mine. I can see the tears threatening the fall over and spill down her cheeks. "Kai is your only son, and you have to watch him fight for his life so he can have his mate. I'm sorry that it has come to this. I feel like it's my fault. Maybe I didn't make it clear enough to Jeffrey before that I wanted nothing to do with him, but when I do think of that, I know that is not the case. Jeffrey still would have gone off his rocker no matter what."

"Please do not ever think this is your fault, Dakota. This falls completely on Jeffrey and his blind desire for a mate, no matter who she is. I know that my son is strong and he will win, but it's a mother's instinct to worry, just as it's the same for an alpha's instinct to worry about her pack."

"I just can't believe that the battle will take place tomorrow. I'm just glad that my daughter has two strong alphas to help her through this. And I'm glad that your father is going to be there for you too, Dakota." Mom says as she comes over to sit next to me on the couch and places a hand on my shoulder.

"And where do you think you're going to be?" I chuckle. "There is no way I am going to watch this battle without my mother by my side. Just because you're not a Were doesn't mean this doesn't concern you as well, Mom. I mean I can protect you, and I'm sure Coraline will too."

It takes a moment for Mom to comprehend my words before surprise is evident in every line of her body when she hears that I actually want her there. I understand why she's feeling the need to stay away. She's worried about her presence, her fear, being a possible catalyst that will make Jeffrey even more feral.

I turn to my mother and take her hand in my own. "Listen to me, Mom, I want you there with me. Please don't think that your fear will make things worse. We all are going to be scared when this starts. Besides, like you said before, fear helps you remember there are things out there that can kill you and makes you more vigilant."

"Oh, thank you, Honey. You can count on me to be there for you. I promise," Mom says with a wobbly smile.

"Lori, Dakota? What do you both think about fixing a big dinner for everyone? Make it a sort of good luck dinner and I am going to say

Dakota's night as a 'free' woman, because Kai I'm sure will ask you to bond as soon as the fight is over." Coraline says. "They are out currently looking over the battlegrounds now, so we have time to fix a nice dinner."

"Do you think you can handle being in the same room with Kai and not touch him?" Mom asks.

"Yeah, I think so. It will be hard, I'm not gonna lie, but I can manage." I say as we all walk over to the alpha's house to prepare dinner for tonight.

Kai

Dad, Nathan, and I are all gathered at the park where the battle will take place in twenty-eight hours. Nathan looks over the grounds with me but keeps any questions or tips to himself until we walk the entire space. Once we make a complete circle and end back up in front of Dad, Nathan stands tall with his arms crossed over his chest and stares me down like every bit the Beta he is.

"Tell me what you found, Kai. What potential footing issues do you see?"

"I know that I want to stay away from the tree line to the east. The roots are starting to break the ground there, and my claws could get stuck in the wood. Now, it would be a good place to corner Jeffrey, but I still need to be careful in case he can dodge my attack."

"Right. That's good." Nathan nods.

"I noticed that on the western side of the park, there are loose rocks that could cause a slipping hazard." I tell him as I walk over in that direction to get another look at that area again.

As I look over the loose rocks again, I notice that Nathan is examining an obvious defect in the ground that would even break a wolf's leg if it was stepped into the wrong way, but his gaze keeps glancing in my direction like he's trying to build up the nerve to tell me something.

"Nathan, is there something you want to talk to me about?" I ask pointedly.

The Beta takes a deep breath as he stands to his full height and looks me over like he's assessing me, and I can feel his anticipation flow from him like it's a tangible thing.

"You may speak freely, Nathan. Please tell me what is on your mind." I urge.

"Kai, please don't take this as me giving up on you, but I know that you are worried about Dakota and what could happen if things...go badly." Nathan pauses.

"You're right. I have been thinking about that. Believe me, I don't want to go down that route, but I cannot ignore that possibility either." I say, and the words leave a bad taste in my mouth.

"Just know that I will protect her, and not just because I am her father. I'm a Beta again, and my place in her life has changed. I will protect her with everything I have, Kai. No matter what happens, Jeffrey will not get her." Nathan says with conviction in his voice.

"Thank you, Nathan, and know that your words mean a lot to me. I'm sure this is hard for you to go through with your daughter, but at the end of all this, she will have a mate that will complete her. That thought alone is what is making me fight harder. But I do have to say though, your daughter is very talented." I say with a sly smile.

"In what way?" Nathan asks with a growl in his voice, thinking the worst at my words.

"Oh my God!" I say in exasperation while throwing my hands up in the air. "I have done nothing to her virtue. Damn, even my own mother thought that. I do know better." I say with a sharp tone. "Especially since Jeffrey is trying to claim her. No, I was talking about how resourceful Dakota is. She's figured out a way into K's forest."

"She what? I didn't think that was possible."

"We'll, she and Kota figured it out. So that's how we have been handling being apart for so long, and I'm not ready to go on a rampage." I matter-of-factly.

"I thought you were handling this awfully well, so now I know why." Nathan says with a smile, and I can see just how proud he is of Dakota shining in his eyes.

"Gentlemen, how is it going?" Dad asks as he walks over to us with his hands behind his back.

"It's going well, Father. I know all the potential footing issues and how I could use them to my advantage.

"Good, Now, let's go home. Your mother just told me that they are fixing a good luck dinner and a celebration on Dakota being, as your mother called it, a 'free woman' for one more night." Dad says while making air quotes around *free woman.*

I find myself grinning at Mom's term because she already knows that, as long as my injuries are minimal, I want to bond with Dakota as soon as I can.

Dakota

Mom, Coraline, and I just finished preparing dinner when I hear Dad's car pull up in the alpha's driveway, and I instantly feel Kai on the other side of the door. As I feel him get closer to the house, I have to remind myself that I cannot touch him.

Oh boy, this is gonna be harder than I thought.

Coraline gives me a look as she comes back into the kitchen to grab the pitcher of tea I made, and she gives me a determined look that says she will make sure Kai and I do not break the order set on both of us. I give her a quick nod of appreciation before I grab the plates and begin setting the table.

I hear Dad walk in the house first, and I watch as he gives Mom a welcoming and loving embrace, and I see something similar play out between the alphas. I make myself set the last plate down when I see Kai step in through the door and shut it behind him. Our eyes meet, and before I know it, I have taken a small step in his direction, but a low warning growl from Kota makes me stop in my tracks.

"Kinda sucks being the fifth and sixth wheel huh?" Kai jokes through the bond.

"Yeah, it does." I laugh. *"So, how did inspecting the grounds go?"*

"It went well. Your dad is very thorough. I appreciate that a lot."

After everyone sits down to eat, again making sure that Kai and I are far enough apart where we don't even have the possibility to touch shoes under the table, we have a nice meal, chatting like we don't have a care in the world.

I can feel that Tobias and Dad are proud of me and Kai. Of how we have been able to compose ourselves tonight, and while granted we have been passing phantom touches back and forth knowing that we can do more when we turn in for the night, makes things a little bit easier to handle.

I look over Kai's shoulder at the clock mounted on the wall, showing the time to be 10:30 in the evening, and I look at him with a small smile.

"It's getting late, Kai. You need to rest as much as you can."

"Alright." Kai nods. "And know this, Baby Girl," Kai says with all the power and love he can pour over me through the bond, "Tonight is the last night that I am kept from you. This time tomorrow evening, you will be in my arms for real, and I am never letting you go."

"Yeah, and neither will I." I whisper, trying to keep my emotions in check.

Mom, Dad, and I get up from the table to go home, and I have to force my feet to keep moving away from Kai. I remind myself that we will meet in his forest in just fifteen minutes, and that thought helps me reach the porch. As I make my way down the steps and Tobias begins to shut the door behind us, the sharp pain that blooms across my temple makes me stop dead in my tracks, and I can't stop the yelp that rips from my throat.

"Dakota!"

I hear Kai scream my name followed by a strong wave of power from Tobias that makes Kai stay in the house. From the painful throb in my head, all I see are flashes of dark figures, rough hands, and pain. All-consuming pain fills my body as if it's my own.

"Dakota? What's wrong?"

I feel Dad's hand on my shoulder, and when I lift my head to look at him, the real world comes into focus around me, and I go from utterly confused, to wholly furious, to terrified all in a heartbeat. My eyes snap to Tobias as I say the words that burn like acid in my veins.

"It's Quilla. Get a hold of Atticus, now. Something's happened to her."

CHAPTER EIGHTY

DAKOTA

"What about Quilla? What's wrong?" Tobias asks, and I pick up on the note of fear in his voice.

"All I could see were dark figures taking her from her room. I could feel her terror and then pain. I don't know if she blocked me at that point, or they knocked her out." I growl. "How far away is Atticus, or is he back in Montana?"

"He was earlier, but he's flying in tonight to be here for the fight tomorrow." Tobias says but then pauses, his eyes going distant for a moment. "He just said that her parents called him and told him she's missing."

"Dakota, can you give Atticus the location of where Quilla was taken to based on what you saw from her?" Dad asks.

"Oh, I'll do more than that." I scoff.

"Atticus will be here in twenty minutes." Tobias announces.

"What do you think you're going to do, Dakota?" Kai asks sharply as he steps onto the porch, but his mother keeps him pinned in the corner against the house. "You can't be thinking about going to rescue her?"

"Why not, Kai?" I snap. "She's *my* Tamer. You can't go and save her because if Jeffrey sees you, he'll think he can have free dibs on you, and I'm not going to let that fucking happen. If I go, he can't touch me. So, I'm going to use that to my advantage. I am going with Atticus to get Quilla and bring her home where she's safe." I declare.

I turn to Dad, and I know he's the next best wolf to help me. I can't have Tobias involved because of Kai, and it could make things worse for my mate.

"Dad, can you come with me, at least until Atticus can meet us at Quilla's place?" I ask, "I think that's going to be the best place to start tracking her."

"You don't even have to ask. I will help you in any way I can, Dakota." Dad replies.

"Be careful, you two," Mom says as she gives us both a quick hug.

"We will." I say.

I look over my shoulder into Kai's glowing hazel eyes, and I notice the slight tremble in his shoulders telling me he's fighting against himself to stay glued to the wall of the house.

"Be smart out there, Dakota, please." Kai says, using the bond to caress my cheek.

"I will and we will be back before you know it, with everyone safe and sound." I promise.

I quickly descend the stairs with Dad on my heels and as my feet hit the ground, I say over my shoulder, "Let's phase so we can get to Quilla's house faster, and Tobias, please make sure that Atticus knows we're coming to help."

"Already done, Dakota." Tobias says.

Kai

I watch as my mate and her father slowly phase out in the front yard, not caring at the moment if someone sees them. They are two wolves on a mission, and nothing will stop them, and it's in that moment, even with the fear filling my blood, I feel pride swell in my chest for how brave my girl is.

"She will be an amazing alpha for you one day, Kai," Dad says somberly. "She didn't hesitate on figuring out what to do and how to go about doing it."

I watch my mate and her father grab their discarded clothing into their mouths and take off across the street, disappearing into the tree line to cut across town quicker and to get away from any more prying eyes.

"Yeah. She has a habit of doing that." I say, and my lip twitches at the corner, "But that's what I love about her. She is always thinking about her pack and the bigger picture and how to protect them."

"Come on, everyone. Let's go back inside and await their return." Dad says as he ushers me, Mom, and Lori back into the safety of our home.

Dakota

"Do you have a plan on what you're going to do once we get to Quilla's house?" Dad asks.

"Not really. I just need to get into her room and pick up their scent and confirm who I think took her. The only thing is, I don't know if Quilla ever told her parents about me or what she is. So, that's the only part I'm gonna have to wing it on."

We arrive at Quilla's place about ten minutes later, and I already see the twinkling bits of glass strewn about on the lawn, like little stars that have fallen from the sky, and they are slowly dying out. With a growl at the sight, Dad and I dart into a large bush to phase and get dressed. I walk up to the front porch, and I knock twice on the front door, and I hear Quilla's dad mumble something from the other side before he opens it a crack. Once he sees it's me, he opens the door fully to let me and Dad in.

"Oh, Dakota, thank God you're here." Mr. Rose says as he closes the door behind us.

I notice Mrs. Rose is sitting at the dining table with several pictures of Quilla laid out before her. Her tear-stained face looks between them and her husband to see if he agrees with the picture she's selected. I then notice a metal baseball bat in Mr. Rose's hand, and I instantly know that will do nothing to a Were, and my chest constricts at the thought.

"I still think we should call the cops, Michael," Mrs. Rose sobs.

Michael walks over to his wife and gently takes her hand in his own while pushing the pictures of his daughter away from her. "Carla, we can't. Atticus already said we shouldn't. I mean, you remember what he is." Michael says hurriedly.

"I know Michael, but I can't sit here and do nothing!"

"Do you all know something about Atticus?" I ask as I look over my shoulder at Dad, who is now leaning against the door, acting like a living barricade, and I give him a quick nod of appreciation.

"Atticus is...special, Dakota. And we know he will be the best person to be able to save our daughter. That's all you need to know," Carla says while wiping her tearful cheeks. "I just wish he would get here already. He said he'd be here by now."

"Oh well, that makes things easier for us too then." I say. "Atticus is not the only Werewolf here. I'm one too, and so is Dad," I say while jerking my thumb over my shoulder, and Dad gives the Rose's a small wave.

"Are you serious? Have you always been one?" Michael asks me.

"No. I came into my wolf a month ago." I say as I wave him off from asking any questions. "Right now I need to go to Quilla's room and look around. I can track who took her and I can help Atticus bring her back." I then turn my attention to Dad. "I know I don't have to tell you, but please only let Atticus in when he gets here."

"I will." Dad responds.

Michael nods, and he leads me upstairs to Quilla's room, and before I even open the door, the scent of her fear fills my nose, and I have to bury the growl that threatens to pour from my throat. I try to brace myself for the destruction I may find her bedroom in, but no amount of preparation can lessen the fury in my blood.

Her room is a wreck. Bedsheets ripped and thrown about the room. The vanity set that Quilla would sit at to put her makeup on is turned over; the cosmetics littering the floor, and some containers are open, the beige liquid staining the carpet. When I reach the window, I see her sheer purple curtains are shredded puddles on the floor. And the glass. It's broken into jagged pieces, and blood coats several of them. When I look at one that is at my eye level, my reflection shows my angry, red face, and my eyes are glowing the brightest blue yet because of whose scent I pick up lingering with Quilla's fear.

"I am going to fucking kill Caleb," I snarl.

I then see a car pull up, and I somehow know it's Atticus. It's like what Tobias said one time, he knows where all members of his pack are, and right now, so do I.

I break the remaining glass out of the window and, with a muttered curse from Michael filling my ears a moment before I leap from the second-story window, I land hard in the grass below. Atticus meets me in the center of the lawn while Dad opens the front door to stand on the porch and await my next request. As both men look at me, they immediately bend their necks and kneel before me. Their actions break through the red haze that filled my vision, and I realize my alpha power is flowing from me at an all-time high.

"I'm sorry. Get up." I say gruffly as I try to calm my power a bit. I then direct my next words to my father. "Caleb took her. Tell me, if I kill that bastard now, will that mess up Kai's fight with Jeffrey?"

"It could ,yes. Especially since Caleb is Jeffrey's beta. Jeffrey could lie and say you retaliated and attacked Caleb when Quilla went with them willingly." Dad says.

Both Atticus and I growl at Dad's words, and I can tell the doctor is hanging on by a thread.

"We are going to get her. Without *me* killing anyone. Dad, please stay here and protect Quilla's parents. Atticus, you and I are going to get her."

"No disrespect, Dakota, but what about the challenge?" Atticus asks.

"What about it? I already thought about it, and if Jeffrey or Caleb lay one finger on me, then Kai will know, and all bets are off." I say darkly.

"My apologies, Alpha," Atticus says while baring his neck again to me.

"I'm sorry." I say while pinching the bridge of my nose. "It's just smelling Caleb set me off. I appreciate your concern about the challenge, Atticus, I really do. But like I said, Kai and I talked about that, and we are using the fact that neither of them can touch me to my advantage."

"You two get going then," Dad says. "I will stay here as you requested and protect the Rose's. Atticus, please leave me your keys in case I need to move them."

Atticus hands over the keys to his car, and he silently looks to me for my next move

"Thanks, Dad. Atticus, we phase and track Quilla. I can pick up on *his* scent, and I know we can follow it to where they have her."

The doctor nods at me and, in one swift movement, he goes from man to wolf in the blink of an eye. His red fur covers his large, muscular body, and I notice he has a white marking on his chest that travels up to the middle of his neck. His green eyes look over his shoulder at me, urging me to lead him to his mate. I nod and I phase along with him, then pick up my clothing to hold them between my teeth. I take a few samples of the warm air around us, picking up on the scents I need, and I bound off into the night after them with Atticus hot on my tail.

CHAPTER EIGHTY-ONE
DAKOTA

After running nonstop for fifteen miles, we finally find a worn-down factory where Quilla's scent stops. Atticus and I slip into an area of high grass as we drop low to our bellies and quietly survey the area for a few moments.

"I see one entrance in the front. No windows on the first floor, and I don't smell anyone else around." I tell Atticus.

"I'm going to go around back and see if I can find another entrance." Atticus tells me before silently making his way through the grass and around the building.

While he does his search, I keep an eye on the front to make sure no one comes in or leaves through the door. After what seems like a lifetime, I feel Atticus enter my mind.

"I found a back door." His voice in my mind is quick and short.

I wait for more information from him, but what makes me move is when I feel his anguish fill my mind like it's my own. And I fear he's found the worst. I race toward the back, darting through the partially open door, and when I round the first corner I see my friend in the arms of her mate.

My broken, bloodied, and unconscious friend.

At her condition, a new wave of anger fills every cell in my body, and I instantly phase and tug my clothes on while making my way over to Quilla and Atticus.

"Quilla? Can you hear me, Chica?" I say while I gently take her hand in mine.

She doesn't stir, and Atticus pulls her closer to his chest while stroking her hair. "Please, Rosie. Please come back to me." His shaking voice whispers.

At the sound of her mate's voice, Quilla slowly opens her eyes. She blinks a few times to focus in on Atticus and her eyes go from confusion to sorrow, but I know it's from her mate being sad and not her own injuries for just a moment until her brain catches up to what was done to her body, and a groan escapes her lips.

"Quilla. Tell me what hurts, Darling?" Atticus pleads.

"You came for me." Quilla answers instead. Her voice sounds so small and weak.

"Of course, Rosie. I will always come for you." He declares as he gently kisses her forehead.

"Quilla?" I say as I touch her hand again to get her attention.

She looks over at me, and regret fills her face before she can look away.

"What happened, Quilla?" I ask.

"I'm sorry, Dakota." Quilla says, her voice barely audible even to my ears.

"Hey." I say, pulling her face back to look at me. "You have absolutely nothing to be sorry for. You—" I begin, but then a thought hits me, and

I stumble back a step in shock. And that thought explains why Quilla will not look at me. "No. No. No, no, no. Those fuckers did not."

I run my hands through my hair in an effort to keep from punching something and giving into the want, the deep-seated need to make them pay. To bleed for what they did.

"Can one of you tell me what happened?" Atticus asks.

"Oh, please. If you have to ask that, then you take after your so-called alpha and choose any woman that you want as well."

We all freeze at the sound of a new voice. The one that I know so well. I can't stop the snarl that rips from my throat, echoing off the walls and rattling the windows at the sound of Caleb's voice grating my ears.

"How dare you take what is *mine!*"

"Consider that payback for taking Emma from us," Caleb says. "One weakling for another. But I have to say, that girl is good at what she does. I haven't felt this close to my wolf in *years*. And Jeffrey feels even better, and you know how long he and his wolf have been at odds." Caleb taunts.

It's taking all I have in me not to say to hell with everything and attack this piece of shit before me. But that is his plan. To get me so utterly pissed that I make a move and ruin the challenge for Kai. To make things easier for Jeffrey to win. And I refuse to let that happen. I feel Quilla's fear begin to build and the hint of wondering why I'm not doing anything about all this.

"Quilla, please know that it is taking everything I have to just stand here. I want to rip Caleb limb from limb, but please understand that I can't jeopardize the fight for Kai."

"I know, I understand," Quilla says, sounding so tired in my mind.

I give Caleb a growl, and I take a step back, signaling for Atticus to get up and get Quilla out of here.

"Ah, Dakota. I see you have stumbled upon my pre-fight power-up." Jeffrey gloats as he walks in behind his Beta, and Atticus growls from behind me at Jeffrey's tone. "I haven't had a Tamer in so long. I've forgotten how good they were at taming the darkness in our wolves."

"Jeffrey, I don't give a fuck what kind of power-up you think you got, *my mate* will still be the victor of this fight." I snap.

I try to put on a brave face. Not to let them feel just how utterly terrified I am at the power that is now flowing from Caleb and Jeffrey. It's so much stronger than before, and I realize that they could even go toe to toe with Tobias, and even he would have an issue fighting against them. It's in that moment that I know I need to get Atticus out of here. Now. Hell I may not even be able to hold them back, but I know for a fact that the doctor himself is not dominant enough to fight them. The only thing I have on my side is the rule of the challenge.

"Atticus, I am going to try to keep their attention on me. Please get Quilla out of here. I'm sure you can feel it, but these two are a lot stronger than before."

"You know, why is it always the crazy people that think they can just take and take from others and no one will come after them? Again, Jeffrey, this just goes to show how low of an alpha you really are." I say.

I know it's not a good thing to poke the wolf right now, but I have no choice. I need his attention on me while Atticus is slowly making his way toward the back door. Jeffrey laughs at me. His voice is so loud and booming it rattles in my head, distracting me for a heartbeat while he pulls his gun out to aim it at my chest. His laughter dies while his face morphs into pure fury.

"You think I care if you come after me?! I feel amazing after I beat it out of your little Tamer. I feel like I can take on the world, baby! You are the stupid one in not joining me, but that will be remedied soon enough." He smiles darkly.

Out of the corner of my eye, I see Atticus slowly open the door wide enough for him to fit through it with Quilla in his arms, but he knocks something over in the process and Jeffrey's eyes leave mine and locks onto my friend and her mate. I quickly look to my left and I see a dust-covered tarp lying on a table. As I go to grab it, I hear the gun Jeffrey had in his hand go off as the tarp covers his face. I dart toward the back door before he can get off another shot, and I see Atticus has already phased and is running across the field with Quilla on his back.

I quickly follow suit and catch up to him, but when I do, I notice there are blotches of blood dotting the grass. At first, I think it's from Quilla, but when I match Atticus' speed, I see his side has bright red blood matting the fur, and what shocks me more is the scent of silver coming from the wound.

"Atticus! You're hurt. We need to stop so I can try to get the silver out of the wound."

"No. We need to get Quilla as far away from them as possible." Atticus says, voice tight with pain, but filled with determination. *"I'll be fine."* He tells me, but he stumbles a few steps before he can right himself with an angry huff.

"You sure you don't want to stop?" I ask again.

"I can't until I know she's safe under Tobias." A deeper voice echoes in my mind, and I know this is his wolf and not the man talking right now.

"Then, let's move." I reply, pushing him forward and through the late-night streets.

Chapter Eighty-Two
DAKOTA

As we get further away from the factory and make sure we aren't followed, I reach out to Dad as we run.

"Dad. We got Quilla back, but Jeffrey and Caleb are pissed. Please move Quilla's parents somewhere safe."

"Understood. How is Quilla?" Dad asks.

"She's hurt, but alive. And please let Tobias know that Atticus was shot with a silver bullet. I don't know the extent of his injuries yet."

"I'll let him know. You concentrate on getting everyone home safely." Dad says firmly.

Atticus

I push my body to its limit, and the only thing that is keeping my feet pounding against the dirt, the grass, and the pavement, is the broken woman on my back. I can tell she's trying to block me, but she's not able to completely, and the sliver of her mind that is open allows me to feel her pain on top of my own. I almost whine when I see Tobias' house come into view, and the alpha rushes outside to greet the three of us. Dakota phases as soon as she hits the porch and begins to bark orders to Tobias.

"Tobias, please take Quilla inside and begin tending to her injuries; I need to take care of Atticus first."

During this time, I have slowly phased, grinding my teeth against the pain in my side at the bullet wound reopening with my shifting shape, but my mind is on my mate. Her unconscious body, bloody, and bruised. I will my arms to let her go when Dakota lifts her and hands her over to Tobias.

As the alpha walks through the door with Quilla in his arms, Dakota kneels down to look at my bloody, injured torso, neither of us being bothered by our naked bodies, especially with her back turned away from me where I don't see her own personal mate marking.

"Dakota." I grind out, "Please go and take care of my mate."

"I will as soon as I help you. No one else can do this, and you know that." She says as she helps me to my feet and leads me into the laundry room on rubbery legs.

"What I want to know is how you are still walking?" She pauses for a moment. "How did you become immune to silver?"

"I am not immune, Dakota." I hiss as she helps me sit down on the metal table that stands over a drain in the center of the room. "I can handle a bit more silver than most Were's from being a doctor over the years, but I do have my limits."

"Okay. Let's get you fixed up so you can be with Quilla," Dakota says with a smile.

She dashes out of the room to get whatever supplies she can find, and I gingerly inspect the angry red bullet hole marring the side of my stomach. It's trying to heal, but every move makes it reopen and bleed again. Dakota comes back a few moments later with a metal bowl of Wolfsbane water, a sharp blade, and syringes along with some gauze and tape. I feel the room begin to spin around me as the silver finally starts to affect my system, and Dakota helps me lie on my side so she will have easier access to me and I will be less of a fall risk.

She then takes the syringe and fills it with the herbal water, and it's like an ice cube to the white-hot pain filling my mind. Almost numbing to a point.

"I'm sorry, I'm going to have to open the wound more to get the bullet." Dakota says as she drags the blade across my sensitive skin, and it takes everything in me not to grab this metal table and bend in my hands. Quilla's face enters my mind, and I cling to her image to help me cope with the pain.

"Have you ever thought about being a doctor?" I rasp while trying to make small talk and keep my mind off the new wave of pain.

"And take your thunder, Atticus? Nah, I couldn't do that." Dakota smiles while poking around the wound and finally grabbing onto the bullet.

I fight to keep my mouth closed as the scream threatens to rip from my chest, but in a few heartbeats the pain is gone, and I slowly feel my body begin to heal around the injury, but I know it will be a good forty-eight hours before I am completely healed.

Dakota sets the bullet into another bowl. The metal upon metal clinking together with a muffled clatter. I gingerly sit up, testing my side, and I can at least move as long as I do it slowly. I look at Dakota, and I bare my neck to her.

"Thank you, Dakota. I appreciate your care."

"You're welcome, Atticus. But no need to be all formal. Just a simple thank you is good enough."

"Thank you." I say again while lifting my head, "For more than just tending to my wound. You helped me get my mate back. For that, I will be forever grateful."

"It's what pack does, Atticus. They help one another." Dakota says as she hands me a set of clothes that I didn't realize she brought in the room with her.

I nod at her and once I am dressed, Quilla begins to fill my mind, letting me know she's awake.

"Can you assist me once more? Quilla is awake, and I need to go to her." I ask.

"Absolutely, Dakota says as she helps me off the table and takes me to the guest room.

As we get to the door, I look over at Dakota before she can knock, "I know you want to see her, but can I have a few minutes alone with her?"

Dakota nods and backs up a few steps. "Yes, I understand, Atticus. Just please let me know when I can see her too."

"Aye. I will call for you when it's time."

When she walks away, I open the door and slowly walk inside. Quilla is set up on the right side of the queen sized mattress, and I gently sit on the side of the bed, because one, I don't want to jostle her too much, and two, I have to be mindful of my injury.

I slowly take in my mate's appearance. The bruises on her arms from rough hands pulling her around, the bruise on her cheek and split lip from most likely being backhanded. I can tell from the way she's breathing that she may even have a few broken ribs too. The more I look at her, the more I want to rip both of them apart, and if it wasn't for the bloody challenge, I'd take my sweet fucking time tearing them apart for every ounce of fear and pain they put my mate through. I run my hand roughly through my hair, pulling it from the hair tie and letting it cascade down my neck. This movement must wake Quilla because I hear a small whimper escape her lips.

"Rosie? I'm here, Darling." I croon as I ever so gently caress her face.

"Oh, Atticus, it was horrible."

Her sobs break my heart, and I quickly but gently get into bed beside her and pull her to my chest. "Shhhh, Rosie. Don't cry. Everything will be alright now. You're safe." I whisper into her hair.

"How can you say that?" She asks, "I just made the enemy stronger, Atticus! How can you even be here with me?"

"Hey, now." I say while hooking my finger under her chin, but she keeps her eyes averted from mine. "Rosie, look at me."

At my words, her eyes flick u,p and I see tears roll down her cheeks, and I use the pad of my thumb to wipe them away.

"Let me ask you this. Did you willingly go to them? Did you intend to calm their wolves?" She shakes her head. "From looking at you and feeling your pain through the bond, I'd say you put up a helluva fight, Rosie, before that even happened. You are in no way at fault, Baby."

At that, she breaks down in my arms and she throws herself into my chest, both of us wincing at the pain it causes.

"You're hurt." Quilla says as she caresses my side like she knows where I'm hurting.

"It's already healing, Darling," I tell her.

She looks into my eyes with tears still fresh in her own. "It was horrible, Atticus. I tried to be strong. Tried to fight back, but they were just too powerful, and I couldn't focus on Dakota to tell her what was going on fully. I think I only got bits and pieces to her."

"Rosie. It's okay. You're safe, and I'm here to protect you now. And I'm not letting you out of my sight."

Dakota

As I let Atticus and Quilla have their time together, I go into the living room with the others. I sit next to my father in the wingback chair, feeling tired all of a sudden, and when I glance at the clock on the TV stand, I see it's two o'clock in the morning. I realize I have been in non-stop alpha mode for the last three and a half hours. I then look over to Kai and I realize what's going to happen in the next seventeen hours.

"Babe, it's late, please go and rest for a while."

"I'm fine, Dakota." Kai responds roughly, but I know it's not directed at me; it's the situation.

"Kai, please get some sleep. You need to be at your absolute best tonight. You didn't feel what I did from them. He has gotten so much stronger, Kai. I don't even know if Tobias could easily win in a fight against him right now. I think the only thing that would help your father is how big of a pack he has behind him. Jeffrey is that in tune with his wolf right now."

After a moment, Kai finally relents. "Okay. I'll go rest for a while, *but* wake me if anything happens." Then he adds through the bond, *"If you can sleep or at least rest, please come to my forest. I need to touch you to make sure you're alright."*

I nod as I watch him walk upstairs, and I keep quiet until I hear his bedroom door close. Once I do, I whip around to Tobias, already thinking about the next step.

"So what do we do now? Go on with the fight like nothing happened, or do we add to the challenge? Jeffrey and Caleb need to pay for what they did to Quilla." I growl.

"Additional items can be added to the challenge, but that goes for both parties. So, where you can add the wrong they did to Quilla, they can turn around and fight you for the rights to her." Tobias says.

"Damn it." I growl as I slam my hand against the arm of my chair, "Tobias, is there anything I can do? They hurt what was mine, again. I need blood this time." I say, and I know my eyes are glowing because Tobias' flicker in response from one alpha to another.

"Believe me, I understand your drive to do something. The alpha in you wants to show that there will be repercussions for those who hurt what is yours, but again we have to tread carefully here too. No matter what, and it even pains me to say this, but since it is the same person that did you wrong again, Kai's need to claim you as his mate is first on the agenda. And since this is already a fight to the death, in my eyes it will be killing two birds with one stone. Again, I know that doesn't sit well with you; hell it doesn't sit well with me, but that is the way it must be." Tobias says.

Deep down I know that Tobias is right. Kai's need to claim me has to take priority over all other things, and I can't allow anything to come between that for us. Just the thought of losing both Kai and Quilla makes my stomach turn and my blood run cold.

"I understand, Alpha." I say formally.

Mom, Dad, and I decide to sleep in Tobias' apartment-style room in the basement so we all can be safe under one roof. Just before I let myself fully slip into what I'm sure will be a restless slumber, I find my way into Kai's forest. With Kota again leading the way, we find our mates lying in the grass-covered clearing; Kai's head is on K's side, using his wolf like a pillow, and they both are asleep.

As I snuggle into Kai's side, I know I need to talk to Dad about something in the morning, and I know he's not going to like it, but it's something I need to do all the same.

CHAPTER EIGHTY-THREE
DAKOTA

The next morning I wake up, and I can feel the pull of the full moon already, and it's stronger than last time now that I am connected to Kota. I get out of bed and I find a set of clothes sitting on the nightstand and a note from Dad saying that he went over to our place to get them.

I quickly dress and I find him in the little kitchenette that is built into the corner of the basement, fixing breakfast just like he would at home. Mom is already at the little bar, poking her toast into a sunny-side-up egg with a few links of sausage on the side.

"Good morning, Dakota." Dad says as he sets a plate down for me.

I eat only because I know I need to, but I don't feel like eating at all. My stomach is in knots about what's to happen tonight and what I'm going to witness. But that thought is also what gives me the fuel to ask one more thing from my father.

"Dad, will you be willing to teach me to fight in my wolf form?"

Dad looks at me, his mouth agape and his brown eyes shining brightly. "Why do you want to know how to fight, Dakota?" Dad asks after a moment. "You can't interfere with Kai's fight."

"I know that. But I don't trust Jeffrey or Caleb. And I have to be able to fight alongside Kai if Caleb gets involved." I say with conviction.

Dad takes a breath while running his hand through his hair, and I know he can feel just how determined I am to see this through.

"Alright. I'll teach you some maneuvers."

"Thank you, Dad. I know I'm asking a lot of you, but I know everyone will feel better if I go into this prepared."

We head over into our backyard so Kai doesn't see what we are doing and also because I don't want to interfere with the utter, deathly calmness that I feel coming from his side of the bond. I close the connection between us enough that he knows I'm giving him the privacy he needs but keep it open where all he needs to do is push against that wall and it will crumble down in an instant.

Dad stands in front of me with his hands on his hips, and I can tell he's trying to find the best words to explain what I need to do.

"In all honesty, you just need to trust in Kota. She has enough primal instincts to do what needs to be done in a fight. But it does help to go into it with a plan."

"Alright." I nod.

Dad tugs his shirt off, phases out of his pants, and shakes out his dark gray coat once he settles into his wolven form. I follow suit and meet him in the middle of the yard. He shows me ways to go for the throat or side of an opponent and to go for the back legs in this form. If I can take out a back leg, that almost eliminates any leaping attacks and lessens the ability for an opponent to dodge one of my own, especially if I go at them from the opposite side of the injury.

I slowly move through the motions of attacking Dad in the ways he showed me. Then, once I get the hang of it, he changes tactics, and he is the one to try to attack me so I can learn how to protect my vulnerable spots and look for any good openings he may give me to strike back. But it's all controlled and to a point where I have a moment to think about what I am going to do before I do it.

"Good job; now let's run them for real."

"What? No, Dad, I might hurt you. What you have shown me is good enough." I say.

"What's going on here?"

Our heads whip around, and we find Tobias standing on our deck with his arms behind his back.

"I was showing Dakota some offensive and defensive tactics in case she may need them." Dad tells the alpha while letting me in on the conversation.

"Good idea. Dakota, go ahead and show me what you can do. Don't worry, I won't let you hurt the other too badly, and I'll be able to heal you both as well." Tobias says.

I look from Tobias to my father, waiting to see what either of them will do. My father then gives me a wolfish grin and lopes to the far side of the yard without another word. Just as I am about to make my way over to the opposing side, Dad darts back around and lunges for me. I am caught off guard for a heartbeat, and I feel his canines barely graze my ear before I can dodge out of the way. When he lunges for me again, this time I am prepared for it, and when I dodge I take a small bite out of his hip area before I dart out of his reach.

Dad growls at the wound I inflicted and I can't tell if the growl is a good thing or a bad thing right now, and for the first time since Kota and I have been connected, I feel weak and scared at the snarling wolf before me.

"Hey, stop that. We are strong and smart. If we are scared in a mock fight against our father, how can we hope to help Kai and K if they need us?" Kota says. *"I can tell that Nate is the one we are actually fighting here and not really your father. Do you trust me to take over?"*

"Kota, you never have to ask. Just give me a little nudge and take over. We are one now, and you are better at some things than I am."

As I say this, I feel Kota take over, and I find my human body is in her forest. I look into the little lake beside me, and I can see what is going on in the real world as if I am looking through a window. When I put my hand into the water, Kota and I become one, either one of us could control our wolven body at a moment's notice.

Kota lunges to her right and Nate follows, but then at the last second changes direction and takes a bite out of his right shoulder and uses her back legs to push off him, effectively sending him flying across the yard, which earns him a few more cuts from the branches littered on the ground. Right then and there I know I never would have been able to do that to my dad. Kota is able to separate personal feelings better than I can.

Nate gets back to his feet, and he lunges for our throat, but Kota ducks at the last second, and she grabs onto his hind leg at the ankle, teeth sinking deeply into the skin, but not enough to break bone. While Kota was focused on his leg, I can somehow see Nate's head turn and his jaws open wide before he clamps down on our hips. Kota lets out a strangled yelp as Nate throws us across the backyard, and we end up rolling a few times before we slam against the weathered doghouse.

"Kota, get up." I plead.

She lifts her head, and we see Nate stalking us. Head hung low, slowly panting as he limps towards us. Even with all the gusto that Kota had at the beginning of this fight, I can feel she's losing it. I mean, Nate is something of nightmares right now. His dark fur matted with blood from the bite wounds and cuts we inflicted on him. His eyes, while they still look like the honey brown eyes of my father, they hold a bit more primal, animalistic spirit to them. His long, white canine teeth gleaming with saliva.

We watch as Nate picks his injured leg up to rush us, and even as a tripod, he's fast. I plunge my hand into Kota's lake and I push into her wolven body.

"MOVE, KOTA!"

I make our body move out of the way as Nate leaps at us. I notice that, true to what Dad said before, his strength is greatly reduced due to him having only one spring in the back. So, using that to our advantage, I jump a bit higher than he did and I level my body in a way where I can sink our teeth into his neck, right behind his ears. Our sharp canines just barely piercing the skin.

Nate tumbles onto the ground, and we roll once, twice, before my legs splay out to stop us, and Nate whines through his nose. Pleading for me not to bite down.

"Enough!"

At Tobias' command, I remove my teeth and take a step back from Nate. I swallow hard when my eyes lock onto the damp fur of Nate's neck again. The indents left behind from *my* teeth that sunk so deep that I can see the pale skin behind his ears. When I look in his face, I can still see the lingering fear in his eyes for a moment before pride fills them.

"That was a good fight, you two," Tobias says as he meets us in the middle of the lawn with a firm nod.

"*I could have killed him.*" I whisper to both Dad and Tobias, my voice void of any emotion.

"*I know it's difficult to think of what you did as a good thing, Dakota.*" Dad tells me as he finally gets to his feet and shakes out his fur. "*But that was the instinct I was talking about. Letting you and your wolf become one where you have the plan and your wolf has the instincts to act on your plan.*"

"You did well today, Dakota. Don't let the human part of your mind tell you any different. This was an animal fight, and you did what was needed. And you will do what is needed again if forced." Tobias says as he sets a hand on my wolven head.

I let a sigh roll out of my nose as I feel his alpha power pulse over me. I look at Dad, who is already healing, as he comes up to me and rubs his head against my own, and licks my nose playfully.

"*You could give your old man a run for his money, Sweetheart. Good job.*"

This breaks through my fear-induced shock, and I give him a playful bite in the air near his muzzle. I was going to give him a dig about being old, but I stop short. Instead I say, "*Thank you for helping me with this, Dad. I know this is probably the last thing you wanted to show me, but I needed to be prepared before tonight.*"

"It's alright, Honey. I probably would have eventually taught you how to fight, but you just sped up the task."

Tobias then walks up to the porch and opens the door for Dad and I to walk inside so we can get cleaned up.

After I get cleaned up and dressed, it's around three o'clock in the afternoon, so I decide to go over and see how Quilla is doing along with Atticus. Tobias leads me over while he sends Dad to make one final check of the battlegrounds to make sure nothing has changed since the last time they were there. When I enter the alpha's house, I can feel that Kai is still in his room, mind still deathly silent and somewhat closed off, but still lingering in the back of my mind.

As the alpha takes his spot next to his mate on the couch, I make my way back to the guest room where Quilla is.

"Quilla, it's me. Can I come in?" I ask while knocking on the door.

"Oh! Ye–Yeah. Come in." She quips nervously through the door, and I can't help but smile at her tone of voice.

"I won't be long. I just wanted to see who—I mean how you were doing?" I smile fiendishly.

"Oh my God, Dakota." Quilla moans while hiding her face in Atticus' bare chest, his tree marking on full display for me to see again.

"Sorry, Chica. I had to." I laugh. "But seriously, how are you doing? Both of you?" I ask while sliding my gaze to Atticus.

"I'm still a bit sore, but Atticus and the alphas have been making sure I get some of my herbal tea, and it's been helping a lot."

"I'm glad you're getting better, Quilla." I say as I take a seat on the side of the bed to give my best friend a hug.

"Thank you for saving me, Dakota. And for helping Atticus as well." She says as she looks back at her mate.

"It's nothing, Quilla. You thanking me for saving you is like thanking me for breathing. It was a no-brainer. I will *always* save you. You're my sister from another mister, woman! And I protect my family." I say with a smile.

"I love you, Dakota."

"Love you, too." I give her a kiss on the cheek and smile at Atticus before leaving the room so Quilla can continue to heal.

I make my way into the dining room and I sit in one of the middle chairs while placing my elbows on the faux wood surface. I need to talk to Kai. I can't stand the silence from his mind anymore. Especially since it's four o'clock now and only five hours until the battle. So, I close my eyes while gently tapping on Kai's mental walls. After a few moments, I can feel a little peephole open up from his end.

"Hi. Can I see you in your forest for a few minutes?" I ask gently.

"Alright."

His voice is so quiet and his tone so hard in my mind that if it wasn't for the bond, I would swear it's a different man in my mind. I feel Kota reach out for K and in a blink of an eye I am in their forest, but the atmosphere is different. It's a bit darker, and overcast. The usual sound of birds and running water is gone, and in its place, is the silence you hear before a storm rips from the sky.

Kota and I look for our mate, and after a little bit of searching, we find Kai sitting on a boulder near a small, flowing brook. His head bent down, and he just watches the water flow past him. Kota's head then snaps to the left, seeing her counterpart in the tree line, and she darts after him.

I take slow, quiet steps toward Kai and I wrap my arms around his neck from behind, resting my head on the curve of his shoulder. At my touch, I feel the tension leave his muscles while his hand comes up to rest against mine at the base of his neck.

"Thank you, Love," Kai rasps.

"Anytime Babe. All you have to do is ask for me, and I will be there for you." I say as I plant a gentle kiss behind his ear.

"I didn't want you to see the things that I've been thinking about," Kai admits.

"Kai, I am not this fragile little girl anymore. I'm not saying that I will like what you are thinking, but, Babe, I know you need to think of those things. Please let me in and share this burden with you." I plead as I move around him and press my forehead to his.

He closes his eyes, and I slowly feel the wall between us crumble, and I get the images of what Kai thinks Jeffrey may do.

Blood coating two wolves in several places. Both panting heavily and Jeffrey is;

Going for his legs,

For his soft belly.

His back.

Shoulder.

Neck.

But my mate has a counter move for everything, and no matter what, he comes out the victor. Suddenly, I feel Kai's thumb on my cheek and I don't even realize that I'm silently crying.

"I'm sorry that I am the reason for your tears again, Dakota." Kai whispers while he kisses away their salty tracks.

"Please don't be sorry. I'm crying for both of us." I sniffle.

Kai sighs as he bends his head back for a moment to look up at the darkened sky above him. "Only with you can I be this brutally honest." He looks at me again, and I see his hazel eyes shine with tears of his own, with his fear. "I am scared, Dakota. I have gone through every. Single. Scenario. In my mind, I come out the victor every time. But what if I falter? What if I somehow royally fuck up somewhere and he kills me and takes you?"

I pull Kai into my chest, and I run my hands through his hair while pouring every ounce of power I can over him. I then push him away enough where I can look directly into his eyes for a moment.

"Listen to me, Kai Huntington. You *will not* fail me tonight. You and K are strong, and you will defeat Jeffrey and make me your mate by the end of the night." I lean in to kiss him soundly on the lips, and when I pull away, I try to plant a smile on my face that is genuine. "Sorry, Babe, but you're stuck with me for the rest of your life, and from what I hear it can be for a *very, long* time."

Kai finally gives me his true smile. The lazy grin that lifts a corner of his mouth. "Dakota, you are my rock to stand against when I feel like I'm falling, my light when all I can see is darkness. I want to thank you from the deepest part of my soul for all you do for me, for us."

"I will always be there to give you strength, to pull you back from your darkness and despair." I say.

"I will come back to you, Dakota Shade, that is my promise to you, Kai says as he stands before me, gently grabbing my arms while stroking my skin with his thumbs. "Just a few more hours and I will make you mine in every sense of the word."

He turns me around and pushes me back against the rock before he kisses me deeply and wholly. His tongue parting my lips to taste me in a way that feels like he will never get enough, and neither will I.

I wrap my hand around the back of his neck to pull him closer, and our hips crash into one another. I feel the hardness of him grinding against my hot and sensitive center.

"I am going to have you soon," Kai rasps in my ear, and he cups my breast in his hand and squeezes roughly.

I send him images of where I want, where I need that hand of his to be, right between my legs. The sensation feels so real that my knees want to buckle under my weight.

"Oh, Luna above, if you feel this good in here, you're gonna be the death of me in the real world." Kai growls as his finger flexes against me, and I scream out.

His hand is finally where I need it. Buried in the waistband of my pants, and deep inside me. His thumb then moves sideways against my clit as he adds in another finger, and I fall over that blissful edge so quick and hard that I am ripped from his forest, and I am left panting and fighting off the orgasm alone in the dining room.

"You left before I could hear you scream my name, Dakota."

CHAPTER EIGHTY-FOUR
DAKOTA

I compose myself just in time when Dad gets back from checking the battlegrounds so he can take me home where I can get dressed for the fight

"I know you didn't physically touch him, Dakota–." Dad begins.

"I didn't, I swear!" I snap before he finishes his sentence, and he looks at me in confusion. "Sorry. I'm just a nervous wreck." I say, trying to explain my reaction.

"But since you were in his house, it would be best to take another bath to get all scents off you," Dad explains as he walks me across the street. "It will be less of a trigger for both wolves.

I nod as we enter the house, and I take another bath, reluctantly washing any lingering scent of Kai from my nose and body. But nothing can take away the feeling of his hands on me, and I cling to that memory like a lifeboat.

After I dress in a pair of yoga pants and loose fitting t-shirt, that I make sure is high enough in the back to cover my marking, I meet up with

Mom and Dad in the living room before heading out the door a moment later.

Once we are all gathered in Dad's car, we back out of the driveway at the same time that Tobias, Coraline, and Kai get into the alpha's SUV. Kai gives me a two-finger salute, and my cheeks get hot all over again. I see him smile like he knows exactly what his gesture did to me before he enters the backseat of the vehicle.

Right before we pass our houses, I see Atticus lead Quilla down the steps and into his car.

"Hey, shouldn't you be resting still?" I immediately reach out to my friend to ask.

"I am better, Dakota. And I am going to be there for you and Kai. I'm not getting out of the car; that was the only way that Atticus would let me come along. But I am a Tamer, and the only wolves I calm are those in my pack, which, the two main members aside from my mate, are you and Kai."

"You are going to give me a nervous breakdown, you know that?" I tease.

"Yeah, Atticus said the same thing. But the one I'm worried about is you." Quilla says.

"I am not going to do anything unless provoked." I promise.

We arrive at the park, the seemingly innocent and beautiful park that will soon become a bloody battleground, before I know it. To the same place where I almost lost Kai a few weeks ago. Dusk has fully settled in and the full moon is hanging high in the sky.

Yet another full moon where I cannot bask in its milky white light with my mate. To run with the pack as wolves and enjoy the night like we're meant to. I hold on to the fact that this will be the last night we lose a glorious full moon experience.

Mom, Dad, and I all quietly exit the car, and we walk to the edge of the clearing just as Tobias parks his SUV on the opposite side.

"You two stay together, please." Dad instructs me and Mom. "I have to go over to Tobias and Kai."

I nod and square my shoulders. "Okay. Go and do what you need to do, Dad. I know you have Beta business to attend to. Mom and I will be fine." I tell him as I wrap my arm around Mom's waist, pulling her closer to me.

Dad nods before he walks over to the alphas, bares his neck to them in submission, and then stands tall beside them, waiting on Tobias' next order.

"You doing okay?" Mom asks while her eyes search my face.

I watch Kai step into the middle of the clearing, waiting for his opponent to arrive. "I don't know. Ask me again when this starts." I say truthfully.

Jeffrey and Caleb saunter into the clearing a few minutes later. Their cocky bravado bleeds out of them, and they act like they've already won the war. Jeffrey glances at me, and the evil smirk that spreads across his face makes my skin crawl. I force the growl that threatens to come out at the sight of them back down my throat because I have the feeling if I make any sound, it would set off either wolf.

Dad then walks into the clearing and stands between my mate and the psycho wolf that wants to take me from him as Tobias and Coraline walk over to Mom and me.

"Dakota, I know you will not like this, but this is coming from your mate as well as your father. They want me to command you to stay here and not to interfere. I tried to tell them to give you the benefit of the doubt, but they insisted I speak with you. So, what do you think I should do?"

I don't even think about my answer as I say, "Don't give me the command, but if I make a single move toward Kai, then put it on me. But I will ask that you remove it if I feel something is off. I do not trust either of them, and if they fight dirty, then so will I."

"Agreed. Coraline, please stay here and protect Lori."

"Yes, Alpha." Coraline answers as she takes her place in between me and Mom.

"Thank you, Alpha. I appreciate you listening to me." I say.

Tobias nods as he walks across the clearing to stand by my father while casting his gaze over the two men before him.

"Alright, gentlemen." Tobias begins, voice firm and monotone. "You both should know the rules to this fight, but I will remind you of them all the same. This battle under the full moon tonight is to decide who will take Dakota Shade as their rightful mate as well as who will lead the pack of this area. This battle, of course, is a fight to the death. Any questions, gentlemen?"

"No, Alpha," Kai says while staring daggers in Jeffrey's direction

"Nah. Let's get this over with so I can forget the lot of you and move on with making Dakota *mine* and have her begin rebuilding my pack." Jeffrey sneers.

Growls fill the air all around us from Tobias, Dad, Coraline, and thankfully Kai's is the loudest of them all to cover my own snarl at

Jeffrey's callous words. I'd rather jump off a damn cliff than have his spawn growing inside me.

"I'm going to take my fucking time ripping you apart," Kai snarls deeply.

"I'd like to see you try, pup." Jeffrey grins darkly.

Tobias and Dad slowly back away and once they are on the other side of the clearing, a moment passes before Kai and Jeffrey instantly phase, their snarls and sharp barks fill the air around us. I stare at Kai's brown coat with his beautiful blonde marbling as it shifts with each step he takes around his opponent's form. Jeffrey's black coat with splotches of gray makes him look ratty and disheveled, and not at all regal like my mate.

As each wolf takes a moment to size the other up, to look for any weak points, Jeffrey is the one who makes his first move. He dives low, trying to grab at Kai's right front leg, but my mate easily dodges the attack and he's close enough to a nearby tree that he jumps off of it and uses it to propel himself up and over Jeffrey's shoulder.

Kai is able to inflict the first wound on his opponent, his teeth sinking deep into Jeffrey's muscle before Kai pulls away a heartbeat later. Dark red blood trails in a grotesque arc from his bright white canines as the liquid runs down Jeffrey's shoulder. I clamp my hand over my mouth to keep my excited cheer buried in my chest, and I have to make sure to keep my mental walls up so I don't distract Kai with my emotions.

They begin to circle each other again, but this time Kai goes in for his own frontal attack toward Jeffrey's throat, but his teeth only meet empty air as the other wolf dodges out of the way at the last second.

Kai

"Damn it." I swear.

As I whip around to get Jeffrey back in my line of sight, he's already coming after me again. The claws of his back legs dig into the dirt to shove him forward, and I don't have time to dodge out of the way before he clamps down on my foreleg. His teeth pierce flesh and muscle, but his position puts the delicate area at the back of his head right in line with my own jaw. I open wide and I bite down.

"Just a little more, Kai and we can end this!" K shouts as we try to blend together and make the killing blow.

I hear a crunch of bone, and for a moment I think it's Jeffrey's skull cracking under my teeth, but when pain fills my mind, I realize he bit down on my leg, shattering the bone in one swift move. I try to hold on to the back of his head, but K's pain-filled yelp makes us release the alpha, and he darts away.

"Fuck! We were so close!" I curse as the throbbing pain in our leg sends stars floating at the edge of our vision.

"Well, the dumbass should have gone for our back legs." K pants in my mind.

"We go for his then. You ready?"

"Let's go." K growls darkly.

Dakota

It all happens in slow motion. Jeffrey grabbing Kai's leg, Kai's jaws latching onto Jeffrey's neck, and then bones being snapped by powerful jaws, the painful yelp of my mate, him panting as he stares Jeffrey down, then leaping after him again to go for the next attack.

I don't realize I've taken a small step forward until I feel Tobias' power snap over me like mental chains around my feet and legs.

"You cannot interfere, Dakota." Tobias orders, and I feel the command settle into my limbs. *"Kai has to make the right decision at the right time to end this, but it will only get worse until that time comes."* His anguished tone makes my heart hurt as Kai takes another bite out of Jeffrey's side, but also receives two bites himself on his shoulder and hip and I watch helplessly as my mate's blood drip, drip, drips onto the grass under his paws.

Kai

Dakota's right; since this bastard forced Quilla to tame his wolf, he's stronger than I gave him credit for. But what he has in brute strength, I make up for in having a powerful alpha, a plan of attack patterns, and youth on my side.

I keep taking bites out of him to weaken him, but after the third attack he's picked up on my tactic, and each time I get one good bite in, he counters with one or two of his own.

I know I have to get away from him for a few moments before this backfires on me, so on my final attack I act like I'm going to leap in the air and when he stands to counter my attack, I use the blood that coats the grass to slide underneath him and I sink my teeth into his mid-thigh.

The crunching of bone fills my ears as I pull my teeth from his flesh and dart away from him on my three good legs before he can get to me.

Jeffrey's anger-filled snarl echoes through the air, and as I turn to see what he's doing, he's somehow closed the distance between us even with his injured leg, and he's in front of me. I try to back away but realize with blood-chilling terror that I've ended up in the area with the loose pebbles and I can't get the traction I need to get away.

Jeffrey takes his paw, claws stretched out, and rakes it up my side. I feel and hear the sound of ripping flesh, and I yelp and howl in pain. K pushes to the front of my mind and angrily snaps at Jeffrey's throat, forcing him back a few paces, giving us the room we need to get out of the rocks and back on firmer ground again.

I stand there for a moment, my head low, ears pinned back, my good legs braced wide for balance, panting just as heavily as he is. Blood flows freely from my side, and I stare him down, daring him to make his next move. I'm getting tired of this. Tired mentally of this pecking game, and tired physically. With this last attack, I can feel I'm losing too much blood, and it's getting harder for my body to heal quickly.

I need to end this now before it's too late.

Dakota

It's taking everything in me not to scream, to beg someone to stop this. Kai's fur is more crimson than brown, and I can tell he's starting to slow down. His breath is becoming more and more labored while Jeffrey's getting more crazed with each mouthful of blood he takes. I grab onto

Coraline's hand so tightly I feel a bone pop in her hand, but either she doesn't notice it or she doesn't care.

I suddenly feel Kota perk up in my mind, and I feel her looking around in a panic.

"*What's wrong?*" I ask.

"*I don't see him.*"

"*Who?*"

Just as I ask that question, I see a pair of brown eyes glowing in the forest, staring at my bloody and weakening mate.

CHAPTER EIGHTY-FIVE
DAKOTA

"Tobias, let me go. Release the command."

"No, Dakota. I can't," Tobias responds briskly.

"You don't understand; it's Caleb." I say with fear bleeding into my voice.

I watch as Caleb gathers his legs underneath him, waiting for the right time to pounce. I know Kai doesn't see him, and even if he did, I doubt he'd be able to get away from an uninjured wolf.

"Tobias!" I scream at the alpha.

Caleb lifts one paw, and I know in the next breath he's about to leap.

Kota and I instantly agree on one thing; as soon as his paws leave the ground, we are breaking our alpha's command.

Caleb jumps a moment later.

I grab onto the mental chains holding us back, and as I snap them, Kota takes over my body. We dart across the blood-stained grass and we leap into the air, my mouth wide open, ready to bite into Caleb. As my teeth sink into his shoulder, pushing him away from his intended target, we tumble onto the grass a few feet away. When I think that I am going to land on top of Caleb, he turns and pins me to the ground while trying to latch onto my throat. I lift my front paws, pressing one into his chest to keep his jaws from my neck while using the other to protect my throat just in case he somehow gets past my guard.

"His belly! Back legs to his belly!" I hear Dad scream in my mind.

I curl my hind legs under Caleb as he continues trying to snap at my neck, and I buck with my back legs, landing a solid hit to his soft stomach.

I hear the fur and skin tear above me a moment later. His yelp of pain makes him back away from me, and I take that moment to get to my feet, but I don't stop. I dart after him and I bite into his other shoulder. While I'm this close, I take my front paw and sink my claws into his back while dragging it down his side. He yelps again, and I use that moment to rush away from him.

As I stand there panting, I take in his bloody body, and for an instant, I'm shocked that I did that to Caleb, but that quickly fades when I remember what all he did to me and my pack, and this is nothing compared to all the pain and torment he's caused.

After I am satisfied that he's paid for trying to ambush my mate, I turn to the two wolves behind me and phase my throat enough so I can speak to Jeffrey.

"I knew you wouldn't make this a fair fight, Jeffrey!" I snarl.

I feel everyone's eyes on me. I can feel hot anger from Tobias on me breaking his command. I feel Kai's fear for me being out on his field, but relief and appreciation for me saving him.

"And you just lost the war, Jeffrey. Since you had outside help, that means I can get involved in this fight now too. I fight alongside the one that *I* choose as my mate."

Tobias enters the field, and his gaze slides over all of us. "She is correct, Jeffrey. Dakota is now free to assist the one she has declared as her mate since you broke the rule of no outside help."

I go over to Kai and I lick the wound on his side enough that the blood finally begins to clot. I just hope that little bit of healing will help him gain some much-needed strength back.

"Thank you, Love." Kai whispers, voice thick with pain.

"You're welcome, Kai."

"You ready to finish this, Kai?" I ask out loud.

"Yes, I am." Kai growls.

"I want Jeffrey for now. I have some bones to pick with him." I say, lifting my lip in a snarl.

"By all means, pick away. I have the same for Caleb as well." Kai growls.

Kai and I step up to our respective opponents, and we push them back where our fights won't interfere with the others.

I begin to circle Jeffrey in the same way Kai did, and the so-called alpha tries to keep me in his sight, but he stumbles every few steps as he tries to use his broken back leg and fails every time.

"Jeffrey, you have hurt me and my pack for the last time. I want you to pay for almost killing Kai in this very park. And for the most recent offense, taking *my* Tamer and beating her to the point where she had no choice but to calm your wolves. No one, and I mean *no one,* hurts my pack mates and gets by with it." I say as my voice mixes with Kota's, much like that first time we used our power against him.

I let Kota take over as she relentlessly takes bite after bite with her sharp canines and swipe after swipe with her claws against Jeffrey's brutalized body. I thought the metallic taste of blood would make me queasy, but I find that as much as Kota relishes in the taste, I do as well to a point. It's the fact that we are righting so many wrongs and it satisfies the need for justice that thrums in my veins.

Kai

I face off against Caleb, and I'm thankful that my mate tore into him like she did. I know with what strength I have left, I would not have been able to fight him if he was in full health. As soon as I look into his bloodshot brown eyes, anger fills my limbs, and I take vicious strikes against him as I list every single thing he's done to my mate, to me, and to Emma.

"Because of you biting my mate with pure silver, she did the unthinkable and made herself immune to silver. She could have died if she wasn't able to accomplish that."

I bite his hip.

"Because of you drugging me with Wolfsbane, I almost killed my mate and everyone around me."

I bite his foreleg.

"Because of how you treated Emma, she came to me for help, and you knew that. You took advantage of her and used her to get to me seventeen days ago and tried to kill me, all because you and your so-called alpha are weak."

I bite into the same shoulder as Dakota, driving my fangs deeper into the injured flesh.

"Dakota, I'm done with him. You want to switch to finish this?" I ask all the while turning Caleb little by little so he and Jeffrey are essentially back to back.

"Yes, I am finished with Jeffrey as well."

I circle Caleb as Dakota does the same with Jeffrey, and we end up with our final opponents of the night, and I am eager to end this here and now.

Dakota

I let Kota to the front of my mind because I know she has the instincts to do what needs to be done quickly and efficiently. As she takes over our body, she lets out a howl that I'm sure vibrates through everyone in this clearing. A pre-victory howl before her death blow.

She then zigzags in front of Caleb, trying to make him figure out where she will be coming from. She jumps to the right, and he follows with what he thinks will be an easy bite to the side, but at the last possible second, Kota whips her head around and goes for Caleb's utterly exposed neck and bites down, *hard*.

I hear muscles and arteries severing easily beneath her teeth.

We feel Caleb's blood fill her mouth, and Kota almost whines at the metallic taste, knowing that he will no longer be a danger to our pack, our family, and ourselves. Once we feel his body go limp against our mouth, and once Kota is satisfied that Caleb is indeed dead, she retreats deep enough into my mind so that I am in control again and I can watch as Kai finishes off Jeffrey once and for all.

Kai

I continue to take bites out of Jeffrey to weaken him further, and when he looks over to see that Dakota has finished off Caleb, I decide it's time for me to do the same while his head is turned.

I leap right for his throat, for the quick kill, but in my haste, I step down on my injured front leg and it gives under my weight. And I miss that small opening I had.

Jeffrey takes advantage of this mistake, and his teeth sink into the scruff at my shoulders. He turns his whole body, throwing me across the field like I'm nothing but a chew toy. My back slams hard against a thick oak tree, and I feel several bones pop in my spine as a result, but no sound escapes my body as the wind is knocked out of us.

I try to stand, but my body won't listen to me. My legs won't hold my weight. I look up at Jeffrey's large wolven form, his fur matted with blood, and he's slowly limping in my direction. My vision goes blurry from getting knocked against the tree and from the blood loss finally catching up to me. I try to blink the haze away, but nothing helps.

I paw at my eyes for a moment, and when I look back, I notice the outline of Jeffrey's shape has changed. It's at that moment I feel K surge to the front of my mind, helping my vision to clear, and I see Jeffrey's human form grab at his discarded clothing, pulling something from the heap of cotton and jeans.

I blink again, and before I can coax my eyes open once more, I hear a gunshot rip through the night sky, following a pain-filled yelp ripping through my ears.

Chapter Eighty-Six

Kai

"**D**AKOTA!"

I scream her name, and I don't even realize I've phased until I try to place a hand on the blood-soaked fur of her chest. The burn of the silver bullet that pierced the skin is tertiary to the pain in my heart and body from phasing.

I can tell she's still alive, but fading from the damage caused by the bullet, and this snaps something deep inside K and me. I whip my head around, and I let an anguished-filled snarl rip from my throat as K and I become one body, become one mind in our wolven pelt.

Jeffrey phases back in an attempt to meet my assault, but before he can even make a single move, K's jaws clamp tightly around his throat, but not a crushing blow yet. He gives me time to use our back legs and push them into the softness of his belly, to dig in our claws with such power that I easily disembowel him with one swipe.

"Finish it." I growl at K.

He instantly snaps his powerful jaws, breaking bone, tearing ligament and muscle with his razor-sharp teeth, and tearing out the throat of the wolf beneath his jaws. We watch as he collapses lifelessly into the crimson-stained grass while his blood pools under his broken body.

We step back, and K throws our head back, letting a victory howl echo into the night for a moment before looking back towards our mate. Our girl, who is still lying deathly still on her side where we last left her. I phase, slowly this time, and my body is on fire on the inside from the injuries being torn anew at my shifting shape, but I force myself to walk over to her. As we get closer, K makes me stay back as the scent of silver hits us again.

"I'm sorry, but we can't get near her again. We were lucky the first time after she got shot that it didn't kill us then, but now with no fight left in our body, I fear it will."

I hate hearing K's words, but deep down I know he's right. I collapse to my knees at that thought, and I just stare at Dakota's brownish-blonde fur matted with both dried and fresh blood. I try to reach for her through the bond, to at least let her feel my phantom touch, and it's at that moment I finally understand what she experienced when I got hurt.

Her side of the bond is dark, and if it wasn't for the ever-so-slight rise and fall of her chest, I would think she was dead.

"Dakota." I whisper, unshed tears making my voice crack and wobble.

"Kai?"

I hear a voice, but it's off to my right. I look to find Quilla there, holding a heavy gray blanket, and over the scent of iron still filling my nose, I smell herbs coming from the fibers. Wolfsbane herbs.

"Wrap this around her so you can carry her to your dad's SUV and take her to the hospital." Quilla says.

"But the silver."

"Kai, it's okay. Just carry *your* mate," Quilla says quietly.

As I wrap the blanket around Dakota's wolven form, I feel K's power bleed into my arms and legs to help me pick her up. I gently lift her and walk the few steps over to Dad's black GMC Denali and place her in the hatch. Nathan is at my side in an instant, helping me into the back so I can slowly dress in the extra pair of sweat shorts and t-shirt I brought with me.

"Nathan, you drive my vehicle and get to the hospital. I'll stay here and clean up." Dad announces as his eyes lock on mine. "Atticus, you and Quilla need to go as well so you can assist in the surgery." Dad adds while looking at the doctor.

"Yes, Alpha," Nathan and Atticus say in unison.

When we arrive at the hospital, I barely hear Nathan on the phone with Lisa to let her know of our situation. I'm still staring down at Dakota, willing her mind to open back up to me, but I only get little blips of her here and there before it goes dark again.

The hatch to the SUV opens up, and Lisa greets me with a string of curses under her breath.

"We need to have her in her human form for Dr. Peterson to do the surgery." Lisa says, "Do you know what's the best way to get her to change?"

Nathan and Atticus are quiet for a moment, but I look from Dakota to the nurse as I allow them to take her broken body from me.

"Let me force her change." I rasp. "She's an alpha, so she needs another alpha to make the command."

I slowly emerge from the SUV, and pain threatens to take my breath as I move. When my feet hit the pavement, I have to lean against the cool metal of the SUV to let my body recover from moving around.

"Can you walk?" Lisa asks.

I nod and force myself to walk with Lisa, Quilla, and Atticus, who sticks to my side in case I need a hand. We walk through a metal door on the side of the hospital; the smell of antiseptic and death fills my nose in an instant. I push the latter aside as I follow our little group into the O.R. where I see Dr. Peterson already in her surgical attire, hands up so she doesn't contaminate her gloves.

"Kai, you need to make her phase and do it quickly, so I can get the necessary images I need." She says quickly.

I nod as I step over to Dakota's prone form on the metal surgical table and I rest my forehead against the soft fur of her cheek, "Love, you need to phase so the doctors can help you and bring you back to me."

I dig deep in her mind to find any spark of her, and when I finally do, I send a wave of my power over her to force the change. I watch helplessly as Dakota phases and even while unconscious, she cries out in pain as her wound opens again and pulls in new ways around her human body.

As her screams continue to echo in my ears, I want to stay with her, I can't make myself let go of her hand. Nathan tries to pull me away, and I somehow find the strength to try and fight against his grasp. I almost succeed, until I feel Nathan's hand clamp around the back of my neck and I feel a pulse of power flow over me, making me stop my fight against his hold.

"You need to leave with me, Kai, and let everyone do their job." Nathan says in my ear.

I take one last look at Dakota's prone form before Atticus, Quilla and Dr. Peterson block my view of her and Nathan pulls me away from the O.R.

Nathan and I walk to a private waiting room where I see Lori sitting in one of the chairs. She jumps up at our entry, fear evident on her face.

"Do they know anything yet?" Lori asks.

"No, Kai just got her to phase. So now, we wait." Nathan says, voice hard and devoid of emotion.

"Um, Mr. Shade?" A petite brunette nurse says from the doorway.

Nathan turns, and he takes the small box of medical supplies along with a set of green scrubs from her with a tight smile.

"Dr. Peterson said to give this to you."

"Thank you." Nathan says as she walks away with a firm nod.

I walk to the chair next to the one Lori was sitting in and I fall into it, no longer able to stand with my slowly healing body. I let my head fall back against the chair and look up at the tiled ceiling, just staring at the little black dots that decorate the plaster.

"Hey, are you okay?" Lori asks gently.

"I failed her." I whisper.

"How is that?"

"I couldn't protect her from Jeffrey again. He still got one last attempt on her life before I could end his."

"Kai, this is not your fault. You were injured, and Dakota need-ed...wanted to help you. I know if the roles were reversed, you would have done the same thing." Lori says, then she gently takes my hand in hers with a small smile. "Right now what you can do for her is go with Nathan and let him treat your injuries so you can be there for my daughter when she's out of surgery."

I hear the truth in her words as a trickle of blood runs down my back and chest from underneath my shirt. I nod and Nathan helps me to my feet while leading me into a private room so he can treat my injuries.

About thirty minutes later, Nathan and I emerge from the private room, and I'm covered practically everywhere in bandages. My neck, my arm where the bone was snapped in half, my shoulders where I was bitten, my right side where claws tore flesh, my hips, and even my leg all have the white gauze taped to my skin. Since the blood is now able to clot, I can already feel my body beginning to heal, and strength slowly returns to my limbs as I wait for Dakota to come out of surgery.

After an hour goes by, I'm starting to get anxious, and so is K. I feel him pacing back and forth in my mind and I take a deep breath to try and calm him as well as myself as we wait for someone to come out and tell us what is going on with Dakota.

Just as I rest my head against the back of the chair, the O.R. door opens and I am on my feet in an instant, the healing wounds pulling, but they don't reopen. Quilla walks past the metallic double doors while she takes off her surgical cap. Her eyes meet mine first, and her gaze makes my heart freeze mid-beat in my chest.

She gives me a smile after a moment and then says, "She's going to be alright, Kai. Dakota got through surgery just fine."

"When can we see her?" I want to say *when can I* see her, but I know her parents have just as much right to see her as I do.

"I can take you to her now. Atticus and Dr. Peterson are just getting her set up in her room." Quilla then looks over her shoulder at me as we walk down the halls. "Your mate is already awake and asking for you, Kai."

As we approach the door where I can already pick up on Dakota's scent, Quilla's words finally click in my head.

Mate.

Dakota is now one hundred percent *my mate*. There is no one else to claim her but me.

I open the door and I see Atticus making notes on a chart he has splayed across the bedside table and Dr. Peterson adjusting the IV drip over Dakota's right shoulder.

"Ah, Kai. Hello there." Atticus says with a smile as he tucks the paperwork into the folder and slides the hook over the footboard of the bed.

"Mr. Huntington, I guess I should have made it clear that I didn't want to see *anyone* from your pack in my ER again." Dr. Peterson says with a grin. "Are you alright though? Do you need me to look over your injuries?"

"No. I'm fine. Thank you for helping Dakota. I appreciate it more than you know."

"We'll leave you two alone now." Dr. Peterson says as she looks to Atticus, who is already at the door with Quilla tucked up under his arm.

As the door clicks shut, I look at Dakota, and while her smile isn't as bright as it usually is, she's smiling at me all the same.

"Hey." She whispers.

"Hey."

I walk over to her and gently take her hand in my own, her eyes immediately locking on the bandage that supports the healing bone underneath.

"I'm fine, Dakota. I'm worried about you more."

"There's nothing to worry about now." She says quietly. "Hey look, we're touching in the real world now." She grins.

I look at our hands. The feel of her cool skin against the heat of mine. I think back to the first moment I touched her after I killed Jeffrey and all the times after that, and not once did it occur to me that I was touching her.

Touching my mate. I laugh humorlessly, pressing my free hand to my face.

"What's so funny?" Dakota asks.

"After all this time, I just realized that I am finally touching you. That I can finally call you my mate, and it didn't cross my mind at all until Quilla and now you pointed it out."

"That only shows that your victory meant nothing to you as long as I was in danger. You wanted to make sure I was alright before you went all 'she's my mate, hear me roar'." Dakota smiles, and my heart melts at her smiling at me.

I gently slide into bed with her, partly because I want her near me, but the other part is I can feel myself tiring from standing by her bed. She takes a sharp breath through her teeth when I jostle her a bit, but she nods, telling me to get comfortable.

Once I do, she rests her head on my shoulder, and I pull her as close as I dare to my side. I lean into her hair and, over the lingering scent of iron, I pick up her honeysuckle and strawberry aroma that sends me into a tailspin every time. The fact that I was so close to losing that again makes me hold her just a fraction tighter.

Dakota

"I was so scared, Dakota." Kai whispers into my hair.

I pick up on the images of what I looked like from his viewpoint, and I understand completely where he is coming from. I grab onto his hand, being mindful of the healing bone, and I interlace our fingers together.

"I'm sorry I put you through that. It's just when I saw the gun, I knew what was in it and I had to do something."

"It's alright now, Love. We are finally able to be together, and we will be bonded soon. I promise." Kai says as he kisses the top of my head.

"Good. Now, how about you let the rest of our pack in? I'm sure they all want to see us and congratulate you on your victory." I smile.

Kai growls, and I see his trademark lazy smile playing on his lips. I untangle our fingers and I wrap my left hand around his neck, pulling him down so I can kiss him. We both take it slow, savoring the other. Allowing our tongues to dance across teeth and lip. He pulls away, taking my bottom lip between his teeth as he does, bringing a moan out of me that sets his glowing hazel eyes ablaze with desire.

I smirk up at him. "Down, wolf-boy. You'll get me in good time." I run my finger down the middle of his scrub-clad chest. "Now be a good mate and let our pack in to join us."

Kai chuckles as he gets off the bed. "You always know how to make me laugh, Love." Kai winks at me as he opens the door and walks down the hall to gather our pack mates.

When Kai comes back with Mom, Dad, Quilla, Atticus, and the alphas, they all shower us with congratulations and well wishes. And with this pack, this family around me, and my mate holding my hand while he sits on the side of the bed, I already feel strength returning to my body, already feel the bullet wound in my side healing.

"Dakota." Tobias says, getting my attention, "While I am still a little... peeved as you kids call it, about breaking a formal command from an Alpha." Kai's attention turns to me at his father's words and before he even moves, I know Kai is about to get between me and his father. I put a hand on his shoulder to stop him, and Tobias continues a moment later, "I am grateful that you noticed the ambush before it happened."

"You're welcome, Alpha. I apologize that I broke your command, but I had no choice. And I would do it all over again if it meant keeping my mate alive."

"I wouldn't have it any other way, Dakota." Tobias smiles.

Chapter Eighty-Seven
DAKOTA

That night after Kai has healed enough to venture out of the hospital, I talk him into helping our dads get dinner for all of us. Mainly so I can have some alone time with Quilla, Mom, and Coraline.

After the men leave, I turn my attention to the ladies around me. "What happens now?" I ask.

"About what, Dakota?" Quilla asks.

I instead watch Coraline and Mom exchange looks, and Mom smiles at me.

"The bonding ceremony." Mom answers for me.

"Oh, yeah!" Quilla exclaims. "What does one do to prepare for something like this?"

"I don't really know. Nathan and I did it in our bedroom at the house, so I'm not the best person to ask," Mom says.

"Oh my God, Mom. That sounded so gross" I still have to hold my side when I laugh, but it feels good to do all the same.

"Oh, get your mind out of the gutter, Dakota Shade," Mom scolds me with a smile.

Coraline then walks over to me and sits on the side of the bed while placing a hand on my shoulder. "The ceremony, my dear, is grand. It's somewhat the equivalent of your human marriage, but it's more personal. Kai will show you that he can care for you and therefore, for the pack." Coraline explains.

"But hasn't he already showed me that?"

"Yes, but this is still different. What the ceremony requires is for Kai to wash your back. To show that he can take care of the most basic needs of his mate." Coraline begins, but my shocked expression makes her pause.

"My back?" I ask. "I don't like that. I mean, I know you all are family, but I still don't want anyone seeing our markings."

"Oh, not to worry. You will be facing us, and Kai will be the only one to see your markings. And don't feel bad for thinking that way. I was appalled when Tobias told me that he would be washing my back in front of the whole pack." Coraline chuckles, and her words comfort my racing thoughts.

"Okay good. At least I'm not crazy for thinking that." I say with a relieved sigh, "Now what do I do for Kai, or do I even do anything?"

"Oh yes. You will then open his shirt and wash his chest." Coraline continues explaining.

Quilla chimes in and says, "Oh, I see. They wash the location of their markings."

"Right." Coraline nods. "That little act means that you both care for what the markings mean to one another and that you will do the simplest thing to make your mate content. Then, Tobias will have you both repeat the vows that will bind you two as one. Now you can of course make your own vows, as long as they have certain words in them."

"What are the words that need to be said?" I ask.

A moment later, Mom's voice fills the room with the vows I remember hearing when Dad told the story of when they met.

"I, Lori Bradley, take you, Nate, wolf to Nathan and Nathan Shade the man, as my mate, so that the both of you can protect me, to love me, and to be the other half of my soul. But I promise to love you, and protect you as much as my human body will allow, and to be the other half of your soul as well. I accept you and therefore complete the mate bond." Mom wipes at a single tear that rolls from her cheek. "I can't wait to hear you say something similar to Kai, Sweetheart"

"Thank you, Mom." I motion her in for a hug, and when she pulls away, my eyes lock with Quilla. "Oh, what kind of dress do I wear? Is there something special? Quilla, we need to go dress shopping when I get out of here."

Coraline laughs, and she pats me on the shoulder. "You don't need anything special. I think humans call them a ballgown or a prom dress will work just fine." She looks out the window for a moment, like she's remembering something, and I notice a small smile form on her lips. "I wore a fine green silk gown with gold piping running down the seams. I had the idea of embroidering our initials on the sleeve. T.H. and C.H."

"Coraline, that sounds beautiful." I say.

"Can bonding dresses be passed down the family line?" Quilla asks.

Coraline's eyes shine with happiness, and she looks at me. "If the mates chose to, yes."

I lower my head to the alpha as I ask, "Coraline, may I have the honor of wearing your dress and having mine and Kai's initials added to the fabric?"

"I am the one that would be honored to pass it along to you, Dakota. I'm sure your mom will help me with the stitching and if any alterations are needed."

"Absolutely." Mom smiles.

After Mom and Coraline make the plan to meet at the alpha's house to make any necessary changes to the gown, the guys come back with dinner. We all eat in my room together and say our farewells about two hours later.

When Kai and I are the only ones left in the room, we snuggle together in the bed and let the much-needed sleep take over and get us one day closer to being bonded.

The next morning I wake up to Kai's fingers gently brushing my hair behind my ear. I smile up at him and snuggle deeper into his chest, just content to let him touch me all he wants. I almost let sleep take me once more if it wasn't for a slight knock on the door and an unfamiliar male voice filtering into the room.

"Just here to remove your bandages, Miss Dakota."

I lift my head in time to see Kai's nostrils flare as he picks up on a scent, and before I know what's happening, he's jumped up from bed and dashes across the room, pinning the guy to the floor by the neck.

"How dare you say you'll touch my mate with the stench of Jeffrey on you?" Kai growls darkly. "Do you still side with him even after his death?"

"Kai!" I shout.

"No Alpha! I despised his reign."

I hear the man say with a slight shake in his voice, but I pick up on something else about him. He's a half-breed like me, and he could have the status of a beta if given the chance. I pick up on another movement by the door and see Emma standing there with her mouth wide open in shock and eyes brimming with tears.

"Emma?" I ask.

At my voice, Kai and this other wolf look up toward the door, and Emma's tears finally flow down her cheeks.

"Cyrus? Oh, Cyrus, you're alive."

"You know him?" Kai asks as he backs away from the wolf on the floor.

"Yes, he's my cousin. He saved me from Jeffrey after he suspected that I was talking to you. Cyrus fought him to give me an opportunity to get away."

"After that night, I was exiled for protecting you. To *them* I was stronger than you, so I should have turned a blind eye. So after I left, I found a job at a doctor's office for a while and ended up here just this week." Cyrus explains.

"Oh! Kai, Dakota, make him part of your pack, or have Alpha Tobias take him in." Emma pleads.

"Emma, no. I'm fine on my own." Cyrus says.

"Nonsense." I say.

I don't know what it is about this man, but I have a feeling he's going to be a good beta for Kai.

"I know Tobias will be happy to add you to the ranks. As you know, I'm Dakota. And the attack first, as questions later guy is my mate, Kai Huntington."

"My name is Cyrus Brooks. It's nice to meet both of you, even if your mate wanted to beat me to a pulp." Cyrus smiles as he bends his neck in submission.

"I apologize for attacking you the way I did, Cyrus," Kai says as he helps the male off the floor.

"All is forgiven, Alpha Kai," Cyrus says as he walks out with Emma at his side after she comes in to give me a hug and wishes me well..

Atticus then comes in a few minutes later, pulling my chart from the foot of the bed to check on my latest blood work that he did while Quilla removes my bandages since they obviously weren't done. I can tell she wants to ask, but I give her a stiff shake of my head, and she gives me a small knowing smile.

"You are healing very nicely, Dakota. Are you ready to get out of here?" Atticus asks with a small grin.

"Beyond ready." I smile.

"I'll get the paperwork together for you." He says as he walks out of the room.

Kai takes me to his home thirty minutes later, and I immediately go into the bathroom and get a well-deserved bath. As I finish up, I put on a pair of shorts and a t-shirt that I keep in Kai's drawer and meet him in the living room, where I find him sitting on the couch waiting for me.

Just before I sit down, I have a thought pop in my head. "Babe, I'll be right there; I want to talk to your dad about something." I ask as I feel Tobias' presence in the house.

Kai nods as I make my way down the hallway, and I knock on the door to the alpha's office.

"Tobias, may I talk to you for a moment?" I ask through the door.

"You may."

I take in his extravagant office, and I let out a slow whistle. "Nice office."

"Thank you, but I know you didn't come here to talk about the decor." Tobias grins.

I smile back at him and eagerly tell him about the idea I have.

After my discussion with Tobias, we venture out of his office and, when we walk back into the living room, he claps his hand on his son's shoulder. "Kai, my boy, it's time to get you ready for the ceremony, and it is best that you and your mate say goodbye for now. Until later tonight, that is. Let's say seven o'clock?"

"Sounds good, Tobias. I will see you later, Babe." I say as I give Kai a kiss on the cheek.

"Yes, you will, Love. I can't wait to make you *mine* in every way I can."

Heat rises in my cheeks at his words, and I dash out the door before I can pick up on the images that I am sure are going through his mind.

When I walk into my house, I am greeted by Quilla, and she leads me into my bedroom, where Mom and Coraline have set up a modest makeup and hair station on my dresser. I look over to my right and see a dress bag hanging from my closet.

"As promised, Dakota, here is your bonding dress." Coraline says as she unzips the bag.

The dress is even more beautiful than I imagined. It will come mid-knee, and the neckline is high in the back, and a little lower in the front, but still enough to be modest. The gold piping running down every seam will complement my curves, while the green silk will caress them.

"Oh, Coraline, it's even more beautiful than I imagined." I say.

"And look at this," Mom says while pulling the left sleeve up and showing it to me.

I see at first the golden lettering of T.H. and C.H. in an elegant cursive script, but then below that, I see K.H. and D.H. added in to match.

"Thank you, Mom." I say. "I love this." I add to Coraline.

"Let's get the woman of the hour ready, then we'll get dressed next." Quilla exclaims.

The women all do my hair and just enough makeup to accentuate my natural beauty. A little bit of blush on my cheeks, a little mascara and matching green eyeshadow, and a nude lipstick.

For my hair, Mom lets it fall down my back in soft curls to help make sure my markings stay covered, and then I put my feet into gold ballerina flats to complete my look.

I am taken into our living room where I am told to wait until it's time to leave. Another hour passes before Coraline, Quilla, and Mom enter the living room again, and they are all in their dresses for the evening.

Coraline in a simple royal blue gown with white at the ends of the sleeves and around the collar. Quilla comes out next with a yellow dress that has little red roses stitched into the bodice, and finally, Mom has on a lavender-colored dress complete with a little stem of the plant attached to the middle of her modest neckline.

"You ladies look beautiful." I say.

"Thank you, Tobias picked out the dresses honestly. I tell, you that man had good taste when I first met him, and he still has good taste now, even after all these years." Coraline says. "He says he picks color with meaning. My dress, for example, is the first time we met. It was snowing and cold, and it was during a hard and depressing time in his life, and I am the one that gave him purpose to move forward." She says as she touches the white parts of her dress.

"So then my dress has to be from the first time I met Atticus. When Tobias put me on the plane to meet him in Montana, I was wearing a yellow sundress with roses on it." Quilla says.

"Then you all know what my dress is then." Lori says. "It's the first time I met Nathan, in the lavender field." Lori says.

"I wonder what has gotten into my mate all of a sudden. I mean, he's usually good with this kind of thing with me. But for your two as well? Makes me think he's up to something," Coraline says.

Kai

After I get dressed in a pair of black dress slacks and a deep green button-up shirt, I meet my father under the weeping willow tree in the backyard. It's enough coverage to be a private ceremony, but there is enough space in the branches to let the remaining light filter through. Dad even made sure that Emma and her parents, along with Cyrus, who

Dad made part of the pack upon Emma's insistence, were here along with us. Dad is wearing something similar to me, but his shirt is a deep blue color. Atticus and Nathan are the next ones to arrive, and they too are in black pants paired with a yellow and lavender shirt.

"They are here." Dad announces. "Everyone in their places."

I take a breath and stand by Dad, and off to the side are two chairs. One facing backward to the audience and the other facing toward them, each has a copper basin of warm water and a green washcloth next to it. I hear the back door open, and I see Mom, Lori, and Quilla all walk in, and I notice that their beautiful dresses match the dress shirts of their mates perfectly.

I smile at my dad's unique touch, but when I see my mate walk out into the backyard, my heart freezes for a beat in my chest. I know the dress she is wearing is my mother's, and my mate looks radiant in it. I glance over at my mother and I catch her wiping at a tear.

"Thank you, Mother. My mate looks just as beautiful as I'm sure you did when you wore that dress." I tell her, and she nods as Dakota stands before me.

"You look absolutely radiant, Dakota." I say as I allow my eyes to rove over my mate's form.

"You look very handsome as well too. I don't think I've ever seen you in something so fancy. I like it." She teases.

Dad clears his throat to get everyone's attention before I can say any more to the beautiful woman in front of me.

"Today is a glorious occasion. Today is the bonding between two souls that will complete one another the ways no one else can. And I am beyond grateful to the Great Luna that those before me are my own son and his amazing mate. While they have had their fair share of tests to prove how strong their bond is, they have overcome all obstacles and proudly stand before us today. I understand that you both have written your own vows to one another?" Tobias asks.

"Yes, Alpha." We say in unison.

"Kai, you may go first, then Dakota, then we will finish with the washing of the mating marks." Dad says.

I take a breath while taking her left hand in my own and look into her beautiful blue eyes as I tell her my vows.

"Dakota, you have made me the happiest man alive. You have made me see what a mate means to us, and before I met you, I never understood what I was missing in my life. I love you, Dakota Marie Shade. You make me whole and fill the darkness with your light. You keep me in line when I push the boundaries, and no other can do that." I say while showing her the image of Cyrus and me in the hospital. "I am so humbled that the Great Luna has blessed me with such an amazing mate, and I can't wait to spend the rest of my life with you."

Dakota beams up at me, and she recites her vows with happy tears dancing in her eyes, "Kai, you have brought out the best in me. Before I met you, I didn't even know what I was or what was right under my nose." Dakota begins while looking at her father. "I was so afraid that I would never be good enough for you, but you showed me time and time again just how perfect I am for you and helped me believe in myself and my inner wolf. That is what a mate does; they build one another up and give them the boost they need to make themselves better. We complete one another in ways no other can. I can't wait to see what we can accomplish through life, and I know we can do anything, as long as I have you by my side."

As we complete our personal vows, Dad steps aside, and I lead Dakota over to the chair. She sits down and rests her arms on the back as I tenderly brush her hair to the side. I have to hold back my smirk when I notice her skin pebbles with goosebumps at my loving touch.

"Now, Kai, you will wash your mate's marking, and with this simple task, you will show that you understand how precious these markings are to us. Then you and your inner wolf will say the words that will complete the bond."

I feel K come to the front of my mind and we become one body again, and when we speak, our voices meld together as animal and human. We pick up the green washcloth, dip it into the water and when we wring it out to place it against Dakota's skin, we say our vows.

"I, K the inner wolf to Kai, and I Kai Hunting, the human counterpart of K, ask that Kota and Dakota Shade accept us as their mate. So that we may be the ones to protect you, to love you, to make you whole, and to be the other half of your soul. In accepting us, you will complete the mate bond that our Alpha can bestow upon us."

After I wash and dry her back, I pull her dress back up on her shoulders before setting her hair in place and helping her to her feet.

"Now, Dakota, it is your turn. Please take Kai over to the other chair." Dad instructs.

Dakota

I have to force my mind to clear to be able to focus on Tobias' words. I thought that Kai touching my marking before was pleasurable, but it took everything in me not to bend my head back at his touch. It was like he was touching every single cell in my body, not just my soul like before.

I take a breath and lead him to his chair and sit him down. As I begin to unbutton his shirt, I see his breathing kick up a notch in anticipation, and I know I'm not the only one to have this reaction at least. I undo the last button and soak the washcloth in the basin to my left. When I begin to wash the marking on his chest, I watch in pure awe as he lets his head tip back against the chair, letting everyone know what my touch does to him.

I feel Kota come to my mind in that instant, and we finally say our vows.

"I Kota, inner wolf of Dakota, and I Dakota Shade the human counterpart of Kota take K the wolf and Kai Huntington the man as my mate so the both of you can protect us, to love us, and to be the other half of our soul, just as we promise to love and protect the both of you and to be the other half of your souls. We accept both of you and therefore complete the mate bond."

As I drag the green cloth over his marking once more, he lifts his head, and we both watch as his gray marking turns solid black before our eyes. Something snaps in place between us, and I relish in the feeling. I feel everything there is about Kai even more than I did before. I can almost feel his heart beating as fast as mine, I can feel his happiness as if it was my own.

"And with that, I Tobias Huntington, Alpha of Montana and now of North Dakota packs hereby pronounce Kai Huntington and Dakota Shade-Huntington, bonded mates under the blessing of the Great Luna!" He shouts with gusto and everyone in our little pack cheers and whistles at our bonding.

Kai then stands up, shirt still wide open, and extends his hand to his father. "Thank you, Alpha, for blessing us with such a beautiful ceremony."

"You're welcome. I am glad to be here to witness my son find his mate at such a young age and to see that mate grow into the amazing leader that will one day stand in our place." Tobias says. "Now, my fearless young daughter-in-law, you want to get your parents up here?"

CHAPTER EIGHTY-EIGHT
NATHAN

"Excuse me?" I can't help but ask.

"I know you two didn't have a formal bonding, so I asked Tobias if he could do yours today too." Dakota quips from beside her mate.

"Oh, Honey." Lori says with tears in her eyes.

"Dakota, I don't want to take from your day, Sweety," I tell her.

"Nope, I don't want to hear that, Dad. You sacrificed everything you had to make a life for you and Mom and eventually for me. You all deserve it just as much as Kai and I do." Dakota says.

"And I don't mind sharing this day with you all. In fact, I love the idea." Kai chimes in with a wide grin.

"So what do you say, Nathan?" Tobias asks with a raised eyebrow.

I look from the Alpha to my daughter, who is snuggled under the arm of her mate, then behind me to the little pack that has formed since we met the Huntington's, then my eyes finally land on those of my mate. The tearful, yet hopeful look in her eyes makes me weak in the knees, and I know I can never say no to her.

"Let's do it. Let's renew our bond, and this time, the right way." I say. "*You thought our bond was good before, just you wait, Sweetheart.*" I croon through our bond.

"*As long as you are by my side, I would go anywhere with you, Nathan.*" Lori says.

We take our places in front of the pack while Atticus and Quilla replenish the copper bowls with fresh water and fresh lavender washcloths.

"You may say any personal vows if you wish," Tobias says.

"I'll admit since my lovely daughter and Alpha brought this out of the blue, I am completely speaking from the heart here." I begin. "I knew from the moment I saw you in the lavender field twenty-one years ago that you were meant to be mine, but I was afraid that once you found out what I was you would always just be out of reach from me and I would forever be running after you. Lurking in the shadows just to keep from going mad. But you accepted me and my inner wolf with open arms once you understood that we were real. You have made up for what I lost that night; you gave me the confidence to become your own personal alpha, and with that love, you gave me a daughter who grew up to be beautiful and strong just like you. Lori Bradley-Shade, you and you alone gave a lone, broken wolf the world and made me whole again. And I want to continue to love and care for you for the rest of our days."

Lori takes my hand in hers and she speaks from the heart with a bright smile on her face, "When I met Nate in the lavender field all those years ago, I never would have imagined that he hid a human under his fur, but I somehow knew deep down that he wasn't a normal wolf. Once everything came out and I understood what you two were, I knew then that I could never leave you. And you were patient with me and told me everything I wanted to know about your world and what I meant to you. And you were so brave in standing up for me that night, risking everything you built just for this little human. I knew in my soul that I had to take this lone wolf and make his broken soul whole again. And in that love, we made our beautiful daughter and made our own little pack again, which I knew completed another little part of you. I will continue to love you and be the mate that you need because as the new Beta to this pack, I need to be there for you now more than ever."

We then go over to the chairs and, much like my daughter, I wash Lori's back as I say the correct bonding vows.

"I, Nate, wolf to Nathan Shade, ask that Lori Bradley-Shade accept us as her mate so that we may be the ones to protect you, to love you, to make you whole, and be the other half of your soul. In accepting us again, you will complete the mate bond that our Alpha can bestow upon us."

I dry her back, and she then leads me over to the second chair, sits me down, and unbuttons my shirt, exposing my chest.

While she soaks her own washcloth, she repeats her own vows, "I Lori Bradley-Shade, take you Nate, wolf to Nathan and Nathan Shade the man, as my mate, so that the both of you can protect me, to love me, and to be the other half of my soul. But I promise to love you, and protect you as much as my human body will allow, and to be the other half of your soul as well. I accept you both again, and therefore, completing the mate bond."

"And with that, I Tobias Huntington, Alpha of Montana and now of North Dakota packs, hereby pronounce Nathan Shade and Lori Shade fully bonded mates under the blessing of the Great Luna!"

Cheering erupts for us just as loud as it was for Dakota and Kai, and I wrap my arms around my mate and give her a quick kiss as I feel the bond snap into place even stronger than it was before. I then open one arm for my amazing daughter, and she peels herself from her mate and joins her mother and me in a family embrace.

"Thank you so much, Dakota. You have no idea how much you asking about this means to me." I say.

"It felt right, Dad. So I went with my gut feeling." Dakota smiles.

"Come, it's time to celebrate!" Tobias announces. "Let's all run as one. As pack both old and new." He adds as he looks at Cyrus with a smile.

I turn to my mate, and she backs away a step. "You have fun with your run, Nathan. I'll be at home waiting."

"No, Sweetheart you're not. You will be with me. You may not be able to phase, but I am not going to leave you out anymore. I will carry you on my back, Sweetheart. No more missing out on pack runs. No more full moons missed. You will be with me in every way you can."

She nods, and we watch as the alphas, Kai and Dakota, Emma, Cyrus, and Atticus all phase. The only ones who decide to stay behind of their own choice are Emma's parents. We watch as Quilla takes her spot on Atticus' back, and she smiles at Lori. My mate laughs and gives me a playful shove.

"Then let's run, mate. Show me what all the fuss is about."

Dakota

I can feel the pure happiness flowing from my parents so much they are almost glowing with it. We all run with Tobias and Coraline leading the charge. Kai is behind his father, and I am on his left while Cyrus is already on his right.

The alpha leads us up to the top of the hill that overlooks the city again, and we all look over the cityscape, each pair enjoying the sight in their own way. Eight wolves and two humans standing proudly on the hillside as one. Thankfully, this time I had the forethought to have Tobias set up a motion activated camera so we can have a picture of this moment to keep forever and pass our story along to anyone who will listen.

I look to my mate, at the pure love in his eyes for me, and I give him a quick lick on the muzzle before leading the group in a howl of celebration.

CHAPTER EIGHTY-NINE
DAKOTA

After we all make our way back to the alpha's house, Tobias now has a surprise for me and Kai.

"Since you are now bonded, your mother and I thought you would like your own space." Tobias says with a hidden smile. He hands us a set of house keys, and Kai takes them from his father.

"It's just down the street from both of our houses, so that way neither of you are never far from us or Nathan and Lori," Coraline says.

"Thank you, Dad, Mom," Kai says as he embraces his mother and shakes his father's hand.

Kai then turns to me, and I see his eyes are already glowing. His gaze burning into mine and it sets my blood on fire.

"Please, mate, don't make me wait any longer." Kai pleads in my mind.

I smile as I place my hand in his and he leads me away from his father's house, away from living with others to living with each other for the first night of the rest of our lives.

Kai

It's all I can do not to lift Dakota over my shoulder and haul her into the house. Into our new house.

It looks like it's a nicely decorated home, but I only care about finding the bedroom at this second.

After being told over and over again that I cannot touch my mate, I am thrumming with need. My pants are starting to get too tight from the thickening bulge pressing against the zipper.

When I finally find the master bedroom, I lead us through the threshold and shut the door behind me as Dakota walks about the room. The only thought I have right now is being mindful of taking that dress off her, because I know if I tore that dress like I want to, Dakota will rip me a new one.

"Dakota, I want you out of that dress. Now." I growl.

"Oh, you do, huh?" She teases as she wiggles her hips at me.

"Dakota." I warn.

She slowly unzips the back and lets the fabric fall down her body, and I see the pure white bra and sexy panties left behind.

"Don't move." I say.

I walk over to her and slowly circle her, taking in every curve of skin that I can see. I then trail my finger over her shoulders, making sure to kiss that gorgeous blacked mate marking on my pass behind her. I continue to touch and kiss her skin in every spot I can see. She begins to squirm under my touch, and when I see she's rubbing her thighs together, I let a desire-filled growl bubble from my throat.

"Dakota, I am going to take my time with you, Baby Girl. I have so much pent-up need for you that I don't think one night will satisfy me." I tell her as I unclasp her bra, letting it fall to the floor.

"You are so perfect." I groan as I take in her naked, supple breasts for the first time.

"Kai, please." She moans as I just stare at her.

"Please what, Mate?" I ask as I step in closer, and I bend my head down to take her right nipple between my teeth, and she shoots her hands into my hair.

"Kai!"

I back her to the bed and without breaking my connection to her skin, I lay her down on the mattress.

"You are mine, Dakota. I am going to love putting my scent on you, in you, just as I am going to love having your scent on and in me."

I trail my lips in tender kisses down her neck, and her belly, and when I get to her lacy panties, I tug them off with a finger, baring her completely before me.

"I want you Kai; I want all of you. Please." Dakota moans.

"Then all of me you shall have."

Dakota

He first gives me his finger, just one for a few minutes. Curling and teasing me, and just when I'm about to explode, he pulls back, and I almost groan at the loss of his touch. But then fills me with two digits, just like he did in his forest. Only this time, it's in no way a phantom touch. He is real. This is real between us, and after what felt like a lifetime of longing looks and teasing touches, we are finally able to give the other what we want. And with that thought, Kai leads me over that blissful edge for the first time tonight.

He then pulls his fingers away before dipping his head between my legs and takes his time devouring me. Tongue sinking deep and right where I need him, teeth grazing my clit sending me over that edge with such ease this time that I am thankful we are alone in our own house now because I moan and scream his name until the windows rattle with my voice.

Kai hums his approval against my core, and the sound feels like it rattles my bones, and I almost come again just from that alone.

"My beautiful, amazing, smart, and strong mate." He croons as the sound of him unzipping his pants fills my ears, and I watch the proud length of him jut from his hips. "Are you ready for this final piece of me, Love."

"Stop talking and love me, Kai. We both have been waiting long enough." I say as I sit up enough to wrap my hand around his neck, pulling him fully on top of me.

I feel his hardness brush against my sensitive core, and I arch my hips into him, silently begging him to fill me, to make all those images I sent him become real.

"You tell me if I hurt you." Kai slowly inches into my core, and my head tilts back into the pillow with my loudest moan of his name yet.

"Oh, Kai! Oh, Luna, yes!"

I barely comprehend when he's fully seated in me until he pulls back and thrusts in again, and again, and again. His growls and grunts mingle with my own moans and screams, and with each movement, my orgasm builds deeper and deeper in my belly, but Kai keeps me on that cusp until his own climax is on the precipice of falling over.

"Come for me, Love. Let's fall together." He commands as he pulls back to the tip and fills me with one quick movement and we both instantly fall over that edge at the same time that I dig my fingers into his back in an effort to hold on, to keep myself grounded as I feel his own release fill me to the brim.

Kai pulls away and rolls over on his back, trying to catch his breath. I lean into his chest while I drape a leg over his thigh.

"Are you okay?" He asks.

"Yes Kai. I am perfect. That was perfect."

"Good. Because it was absolutely amazing to me. But anything you do to me is amazing, so I just wanted to make sure that I wasn't just a biased party."

I laugh at him, and he pulls me closer to his side while giving me a loving, slow kiss.

"I love you, Dakota *Huntington,* and I can't wait to see what this life brings us," Kai says.

"I love you too, Kai, and I love how your last name sounds with mine. I also know." I begin as I trail my finger down the middle of his chest. "That my fantasies of how I wanted you to love me surpassed my expectations."

"Oh, they did, huh?" Kai says as he pulls me on top of him, my hips straddling just above his erection. "Let's then get into some of my fantasies. This time though, we won't be interrupted." He says darkly.

I grin at him as I slide down his body, hovering right over where he wants me, taunting him with my body. Instead of sitting down like he wants, I lean forward, slipping my hand between us, my fingers wrapping around his proud length, and I whisper in his ear, "I don't care who sees us now. You're *mine,* and I want the whole damn world to know it." I growl as I begin to pull, rub, and tug at him until I can tell he's about to explode.

"Dakota." Kai moans breathlessly.

"Remember when I told you the next time I touched you, there would be nothing between us? I keep my promises, Baby."

Before he can even form a coherent thought, I seat myself on him. His head tips back into the pillow, and he is the one growling and groaning my name until his own release fills me again and I helplessly fall right behind him.

We take turns loving each other through the night until we are both thoroughly satisfied and we have no other choice but to sleep.

As days turn into weeks and weeks into months, Kai and I learn all we can about leading a pack so when we decide to make our own, the transition will be seamless. But as of now, we are content with where we are.

Just living in the moment, and spending much-needed time together, because I can tell something is coming and we need to trust our instincts and each other to face whatever may be in our future.

EPILOGUE

DAKOTA

I am standing in Tobias' house waiting for Coraline to finish dinner during our normal meeting of the Full Moon Feast. I find myself looking at the picture of our small pack from the hillside after the bonding ceremonies hanging in a black frame on the wall. I smile at the memory of that night, and just as I am about to walk toward the dining table, I notice another picture on the wall.

I step closer to the golden frame and I see a younger Tobias and Coraline with two other males and a female. The smiles on their faces are bright, and they all have their arms linked together at the elbow. The man next to Tobias has dark brown hair and matching eyes with what looks like bluish-white lightning bolt tattoos snaking up his arms. The woman on his arm has red curly hair with bright green eyes, and she has a delicate, bright red tattoo that looks like a fire licking up both of her forearms.

Then my eyes land on the last man. His blonde hair and green eyes stare back at me, and I realize that his skin is empty of any markings. As I stare at this picture, into this strange man's eyes, I feel that they are important somehow and maybe one day I will know the names of the people in this picture. But it's not tonight.

"Dinner is ready, everyone! Let's eat." Coraline calls from the kitchen.

As I take my place by Kai at the table, I look over our group. Look over Mom, Dad, Tobias, Coraline, Atticus, Quilla, and Cyrus and I find myself smiling over our pack. There is one thing that I have realized after all that Kai and I have gone through over these past few months, is that as long as we have each other, we can face anything as a team and come out the victor or we all go down trying.

And with that thought, we eat and finally enjoy this full moon as a pack, without any fear. Without any outside forces telling us we can't.

ACKNOWLEDGEMENTS

I would like to thank my mom for her support while I continue to work toward my dream of becoming a writer. You have always told me that if I want something bad enough to go for it, and I am so glad that I had you with me to share this experience with.

I also want to give a shout-out to all my beta readers on this project. Natascha, Sara, Kaiidth, and Kristy. I appreciate each and every one of you for taking the time to read through this story and for giving me your honest feedback. You all were able to give me tips and ideas so I could polish this story and make it even better than before.

Also, I want to give a BIG thank you to my cover artist, Chastity. You took my vision, and you made it BETTER than I could have ever hoped for! Thank you so much for all the hard work you put into making this cover art for me!

I bid you all farewell until the next book!

THANK YOU & OTHER WORKS

Dear Reader,

Thank you so much for taking the time to read Dakota's and Kai's story!

If you enjoyed *The Wolf Within* as much as I loved writing it, I would love to hear from you!

Please consider leaving your review on Good Reads and/or the location where you purchased this book

Also, don't forget to check out my debut novel,
Everyone Has Secrets.

Available now on Amazon and Barnes & Nobel in both paperback and E-book.

Eighteen-year-old Taylor Sparks grew up in a small and seemingly perfect town. Until a year and a half ago when her carefree life was turned upside down on one dangerous night. As she strives to put the past behind her and finish her last year of high school, her life is again thrown into a spiral when a new student, Bryan Evans, arrives.

Relationships are tested, insecurities are brought to light, and long-buried truths are slowly unveiled. In this gripping tale of deception, betrayal, and redemption, lives will be forever changed as the consequence of keeping secrets becomes all too real. Everyone has secrets – but can they withstand the devastating power of the truth?